TRACIE PETERSON
AND
JUDITH MILLER

THE PATTERN OF HER HEART

BETHANY HOUSE
PUBLISHERS
MINNEAPOLIS, MINNESOTA

Published by Bethany House Publishers
11400 Hampshire Avenue South
Bloomington, Minnesota 55438

Bethany House Publishers is a division of
Baker Publishing Group, Grand Rapids, Michigan.

Printed in the United States of America

ISBN 0-7642-2896-X (Paperback)
ISBN 0-7642-0118-2 (Large Print)

Library of Congress Cataloging-in-Publication Data

Peterson, Tracie.
    The pattern of her heart / Tracie Peterson and Judith Miller.
        p. cm. —(Lights of Lowell ; bk. 3)
    Summary: "When tragedy strikes, Jasmine Houston must uproot her family from the Northern mill town of Lowell and take over her family's Southern plantation. Tensions are high, and the lives of the slaves they've promised to protect hang in the balance"—Provided by publisher.
    ISBN 0-7642-2896-X (pbk.) — ISBN 0-7642-0118-2 (lg. print :pbk.) 1. Women plantation owners—Fiction. 2. Southern States—Fiction. 3. Plantation life—Fiction. 4. Slavery—Fiction. I. McCoy-Miller, Judith. II. Title III. Series: Peterson, Tracie. Lights of Lowell ; bk. 3.

    PS3566.E7717P38 2005
    813'.54—dc22

                                                  2005018442

Dedicated to Lana Nicol
A friend who brings joy to my heart.

Special thanks to
Martha Mayo
University of Massachusetts Lowell
Center for Lowell History

TRACIE PETERSON is a popular speaker and bestselling author who has written over fifty books, both historical and contemporary fiction. Tracie and her family make their home in Montana.

Visit Tracie's Web site at: *www.traciepeterson.com.*

JUDITH MILLER is an award-winning author whose avid research and love for history are reflected in her novels, many of which have appeared on the CBA bestseller lists. Judy and her husband make their home in Topeka, Kansas.

Visit Judy's Web site at: *www.judithmccoymiller.com.*

CHAPTER · 1

Mid-August 1857

THE PRIMROSE-YELLOW skirt of Jasmine Houston's gown fluttered in the early afternoon breeze, the satin-banded hem settling like a field of daisies across the thick green grass as she stooped in front of her five-year-old daughter. Gently cupping the child's small dimpled chin in her palm, she issued a silent prayer of thanksgiving for Alice Ann's return to health before making eye contact with the child. "We must go upstairs and prepare for your birthday celebration before our guests arrive."

The little girl hopped from foot to foot while pointing at one of the distant barns, where the Houstons stabled their ever-increasing herd of Arabian horses. Her cornflower-blue eyes glimmered with anticipation as she turned back to her mother. "Am I going to get my pony today?" she quizzed.

Jasmine nibbled at her lower lip, for she didn't want to shed tears. This was, after all, a day for rejoicing, not a time of despair. The entire family had been waiting for over three months to celebrate Alice Ann's birthday, waiting and praying the child would live through the debilitating illness that had ravaged her frail body. *Scarlatina maligna*, Dr. Hartzfeld had told them—a fancy name for a highly dangerous form of scarlet fever. A disease that could leave Alice Ann with lifelong medical problems . . . if she lived. The doctor had whispered his final assessment, fearing the pronouncement of a death sentence upon the child would send Jasmine into a depression.

Instead, his words had propelled her into bustling activity. With a mother's fear and determination, she enlisted the aid of attendants to assist with Alice Ann's care. Hopeful the disease would not spread to other members of their family or the community, Jasmine had immediately quarantined the household and ordered small doses of belladonna for all who came in contact with the child. She had diligently researched every piece of medical advice that came her way, and most importantly, she had requested that every person in the community pray for Alice Ann.

Now, looking into her daughter's bright blue eyes, she knew all those months of diligent care had been worth it. Dr. Hartzfeld's predictions had been wrong. Alice Ann's health had been restored, and she was now the same precocious little girl she'd always been. Amazingly, there was no evidence she'd ever suffered the debilitating illness. However, healthy or not, Jasmine believed the child still too young for her own pony.

So how could she best answer the child's question? "We never promised you a pony as a birthday present. What about the toys we looked at in Whidden's Mercantile?" Jasmine inquired as she took hold of Alice's hand and led her into the house.

"The doll was pretty, but I want my very own pony. Spencer has *his* own horse," she said, her pink lips forming a tiny pout.

"But you must remember that horses require a great deal of work. They aren't like a toy that you can play with for a short time and then put aside. They must be cared for every day."

"Spencer could take me with him when he goes to take care of Lockspur."

Jasmine smiled at the child's pronunciation. "*Lark*spur," she gently corrected. "And though it's true you could go with your brother to the barns, he might not enjoy having you in tow all the time. He and Moses like to spend time with the horses by themselves. They might feel as if you're intruding. Besides, Spencer didn't receive his pony until he was seven years old."

"But I can ride better than Spencer," she argued, her pout once again returning.

"What's this I hear? Our birthday girl isn't unhappy, is she?" Nolan called out as mother and daughter walked down the hallway, approaching his library door.

Jasmine stopped and met her husband's warm gaze. "We're discussing birthday gifts."

Nolan balanced his chin between his thumb and index finger and looked down at his daughter. "This sounds like a particularly interesting topic. Did you make a special request for your birthday?"

Alice tilted her head and looked up to meet her father's sparkling eyes. "You *know* I want a pony, but Mama said Spencer was seven when he got his pony. I'm a much better rider than Spencer was when he turned five, don't you think? And I'm almost five and a half," she hastened to add.

Jasmine wondered if the girl's remark was meant to evoke sympathy from him. After all, it was Nolan who had promised Alice Ann that she would have a superb birthday party once her health permitted the celebration. He had spent hours going over the details with her, planning a picnic on the back lawn, where everyone would come to celebrate the fact that she was now a big girl—a whole five years old. At the time, Alice had been too sick to care about any of it, but as her health began to return, she'd joined in with her father, planning the grandest of all birthday parties. Jasmine credited Nolan with giving Alice Ann a reason to fight the illness.

Nolan smiled adoringly at the child. "It's true that you're well on the way to six years of age, and you're certainly much more grown up than Spencer was at your age. I believe he was still playing with his toy soldiers and riding a pretend stick horse when he was five."

Jasmine gave her husband a warning look.

"The fact remains, however, that you're still very young. It seems that being around Spencer and Moses has caused you to believe you're able to do everything they can do. However, you must remember they are nearly ten years old, and that makes them a good deal older than you. They are also young men, and as such they may play in a much rougher fashion."

"But I'm a good rider, aren't I, Poppa?"

"Indeed you are. But your mother is correct; five is *very* young for a horse of your own. Come sit down with me for just a minute."

Alice Ann wriggled into place on the divan and then looked expectantly at her father.

"I want to tell you a story about a little prince who lived in a faraway land. His father, the king, loved his little boy very much and wanted his child to be happy. So every time the prince mentioned there was something he desired, the king gave him the item. The little prince quickly learned that all he needed to do was state his desire and the king would hasten to purchase it. So the little prince continued this ritual, making more and more lavish requests of his father. Each day the gifts would arrive and be given to the little prince."

Alice Ann's eyes danced with delight, her soft brown

curls bobbing up and down as she nodded her acceptance of the little prince's good fortune. "And did he want a pony?"

"Oh, that was one of his very first requests," Nolan replied. "But the prince received so many gifts that he didn't appreciate or take care of any of them. He soon grew bored and nothing made him happy."

Alice Ann gave her father a questioning look. "But his pony made him happy, didn't it." Her words were stated with absolute authority.

He shook his head. "Only for a very brief time. As I said, the prince quickly tired of each gift he received. But then one day the prince was at the market with a servant, and he saw a man with the most wonderful puppy he had ever seen. It was a happy little pup with a wagging tail and lots of soft fur. He told the servant to get him the dog, but the owner refused. The puppy was not for sale." Nolan glanced at Jasmine.

"And *then* what happened?" Alice Ann asked.

Nolan settled back against the arm of the divan and rubbed his chin. "Well, the king sent word to the man and told him to bring his puppy and come to the castle. The king offered to purchase the puppy with several gold pieces, but the man still wouldn't give him the puppy. And no matter how many gold pieces the king offered, the man continued to refuse. Finally, the king asked what he needed to do in order to buy the puppy for his son."

Alice Ann straightened and gave her father her undivided attention. "What did the man say?"

"He said the prince would need to prove himself."

With her chin resting in one hand and her eyes shining with wonder, she asked, "How was the prince supposed to do that?"

"He would be required to care for the animal. So, in order to test the prince, the puppy remained at the castle.

Each day the man checked to make sure the prince had fed and played with the dog. Within only a few days, the prince thought the man should be willing to give him the puppy, but the man still said no. Each week the prince asked for the puppy, and each week the man said no. So the prince continued caring for the puppy, and the man kept coming to the castle to ensure that the puppy was cared for. At the end of the year, the prince asked if he could have the puppy."

"And what did the man say?" Alice Ann asked in a hushed tone.

"The man said to the prince, 'The puppy is already yours. Because you have cared for him and loved him, you've made him your own. Through your actions, you've shown the puppy he can trust you and you are his master.'"

Jasmine gave Nolan a warm smile and then patted her daughter's plump hand. "Come along, Alice Ann, we must go upstairs and get ready now."

The child grasped her mother's hand tightly. "Thank you for the story, Poppa. I've already picked out a name for my pony."

"Did you *listen* to the story?" he called after his daughter as she bounded down the hallway.

"Yes. And it was very good," she responded emphatically.

Jasmine glanced back at Nolan and shrugged as their daughter ran up the steps. "I'm not sure she completely understood. Unfortunately, I fear she's going to be terribly disappointed when she opens her package."

"We'll see," he replied absently.

Jasmine climbed the stairs and met Martha in the upper hallway. "I'll see to Miss Alice Ann if you have other matters that need your attention," the maid offered as she stacked sheets in the linen chest. "Being around Miss Alice Ann reminds me of being with your grandmother. This child was certainly named after the proper person—she's got the same bubbly enthusiasm."

Jasmine smiled at the comparison as Alice Ann scampered into her bedroom. Jasmine knew her grandmother's former maid missed the old woman very much. The two had been more than employee and employer; they had been the best of friends. "She reminds me of Grandmother in many ways also. I truly wish Grandmother had lived long enough to actually hold Alice Ann in her arms."

"But she died knowing that if you gave birth to a little girl, her name would be Alice. I know the thought that she would have a namesake made her very happy. And Alice Ann flits about this house with the same authority as her great-grandmother—just like she's in charge of the whole wide world."

"You're right on that account, Martha," Jasmine replied with a laugh. "If you're positive you don't mind helping Alice Ann dress, it would be truly helpful. I can fix her hair once she's dressed. I'd like to check on Spencer and then see to baby Clara. You can send Alice Ann to the baby's room when you've finished."

Martha nodded and whispered, "Alice Ann doesn't suspect she's getting a new doll, does she?"

"No, although I fear she may be disappointed. She's talked of nothing but a pony lately, and I believe she's positive her father won't fail her."

"Don't you worry. She's just like her great-grandmother Wainwright. She'll be happy as can be with whatever she receives."

"I hope you're correct." Jasmine was not nearly so confident of her daughter's reaction to the gift.

"You can always tell her that if she isn't pleased with the doll, you know several little girls who would be delighted to have it. She'll soon change her mind," the older woman said with a wink. "'Course, we can't go giving it away—I spent too many hours on that dress and cape for her dolly," she added with a chuckle.

When Jasmine brought the doll home from Whidden's several weeks ago, she had drawn Martha into her confidence and shown her the gift. It had taken only a moment for Martha to decide the doll needed additional clothes and that she would immediately begin the task. It would be her birthday gift to Alice Ann, she'd insisted. During the past weeks, Martha had used her free time to stitch a cream wool doll's dress and matching hooded cloak. With loving care, the older woman had embroidered tiny pink and blue flowers and green leaves around the hem of the dress and then attached a small pink tassel to the hooded cape.

"The dress and cape are beautiful, Martha. If Alice Ann isn't overly disappointed with the doll, I know she'll be delighted with the clothes you made."

"Mama, are you coming?" Alice Ann called from her bedroom.

The two women exchanged a knowing look and rushed down the hallway in opposite directions. If they didn't soon get the children dressed, their guests would arrive with no one at the door to properly greet them.

"Elinor!" Jasmine greeted. "I am so pleased you've come."

"I wouldn't have missed it," Elinor said, extending a package.

"You didn't need to bring a present. Having you join us is gift enough," Jasmine admonished as she took the ribbon-bedecked offering.

"I hope Alice Ann will like it. I saw Martha in Whidden's two weeks ago, and she mentioned the doll you had purchased. Mrs. Whidden gave me the doll's measurements. I fashioned a matching bonnet for Alice and her doll, but you must set it aside until after she has opened *your* present, or she'll wonder why I've chosen to make her such a gift."

"What a wonderful idea, Elinor. She will absolutely love it."

"I trust her health has continued to improve."

"Indeed! You would think she'd never suffered a sick day in her life. When I watch her running about, I'm truly amazed by her recovery. Now, do come out to the rose garden with me. I believe most of the guests have arrived, and we've gathered on the lawn to visit and allow the children to play some games before we have our refreshments. How have you been?"

"I've been just fine. It's so good to see you."

"Since you began attending church on Kirk Street, I don't see you often enough. It's been at least several weeks since we've seen one another, and Martha didn't mention seeing you at Whidden's. I was beginning to worry *you'd* taken ill," Jasmine said as she looped arms with Elinor and walked her to the backyard.

"It's difficult to get away from the boardinghouse. As you know, mill work is hard and the girls put in long hours. And of course they expect to find hot meals and a clean house upon their return. When I do have free time, it seems it's filled by attending one meeting or another and helping with various church functions. There's precious little time left to go calling, but be assured that I've missed our visits also."

"Speaking of helping with church functions, I met your new pastor and his daughter two weeks ago. In fact, Spencer insisted we invite them to the party today. He and Moses have become fast friends with young Reggie."

Elinor grinned. "I don't doubt that statement for a minute.

I believe Reggie is quite the tomboy, but she seems a very sweet girl."

"She can straddle and ride a horse better than both of the boys, though I doubt her father realizes she does so," Jasmine confided.

"I imagine someone will be quick to advise him. The ladies of the church are keeping both Pastor Chamberlain *and* Reggie in their sights."

"No doubt! After all, the women do outnumber the men in Lowell. I do believe every single woman in town views Justin Chamberlain as an excellent prospect."

"Not *every* single woman," Elinor said. "The last thing *I* want is another husband."

Jasmine tilted her head and arched her perfectly shaped eyebrows. "I stand corrected—*almost* every woman." Elinor had been widowed twice and was not yet thirty and three years of age. Jasmine eyed her friend cautiously. "Still, it always seems to be those who protest something that end up wading deep in its cause."

"I've seen the time when I was forced to wade deep in horse droppings," Elinor protested, "but it didn't mean I desired to be there."

The two women laughed and waved in return as Alice Ann and several young friends sprinted past them, waving wildly.

"It certainly does appear she has returned to full health. I understand there was a case of scarlatina maligna in Billerica, and the child now has dropsy. A terribly sad consequence," Elinor stated.

"I, too, heard that distressing news. Dr. Hartzfeld warned us early on to be very careful during Alice Ann's period of convalescence. It seems to be a surprisingly dangerous time."

"How so?"

"If the patient chills or takes a cold, the entire system can be affected, leaving the person with a chronic illness, such as dropsy or even permanent deafness," Jasmine explained.

An involuntary shudder seized her after she uttered the words, and Elinor patted her arm. "I know you've been through a horrible ordeal, but the child is living evidence of answered prayers. I believe a good number of Lowell's residents were on their knees for Alice Ann. And it looks as though you've invited most of them today," Elinor said with a smile as she looked about at the crowd gathered for the party.

Jasmine laughed and shook her head back and forth. "Not quite. However, Alice Ann would have been delighted had we extended an invitation to the *entire* community. Do come and greet Nolan before Taylor and Bella whisk you off to themselves. Bella frequently tells me they don't see you often enough."

"If my brother and his wife had their way, I'd quit my position as a keeper at the boardinghouse and move in with them. I know it would help them if I would do so. With that houseful of children, Bella needs all the assistance she can receive. However, I don't think such a move would be to my liking. I much prefer my life at the boardinghouse. Even with my long hours, I have more freedom than would ever be possible as a live-in nanny."

"I believe you're correct—but I do understand that both Bella and Taylor would love to have you with them," she said as they approached Nolan, who was standing among a group of men, holding their younger daughter on his hip.

"I'll take Clara," Jasmine said as she lightly touched her husband's arm. She took the child in her arms, but Clara wanted no part of it. She struggled until Jasmine relented and put her on the ground, then immediately grabbed her father's leg.

"Sorsey," she demanded.

Jasmine laughed. "Seems everyone wants a horse." She met Nolan's twinkling eyes and got the feeling she was missing something as he laughed. "Look who's come to Alice Ann's party," she said as she turned to Elinor.

"Elinor! We'd given up on you when you didn't arrive with Bella and Taylor," he said.

"I've taken to going places on my own rather than relying upon Taylor and Bella as escorts," she quietly replied as she bent to brush a curl from Clara's forehead. "I can't believe how big she's grown."

"Nor I—she turned two last month, and it seems she was born only yesterday."

Nolan grunted softly as a small towheaded child plunged against him and captured the leg not yet possessed by Clara. "And this is Zachary—McKinley and Violet's little boy, who will be four years old next month. It seems we're celebrating birthdays all the time," he said, tousling Zachary's hair.

"You said we could see the horses," Zachary demanded.

"Indeed I did, nephew. Why don't you wait for me by the stable door."

Zachary eyed him for a moment. "You won't forget?"

"I promise to be there straightaway." The boy hurried to the stables as if racing some imaginary friend.

Nolan turned back to Elinor while Clara gave up her hold and toddled toward a crowd of well-wishers. "We are delighted you've seen fit to join us for Alice Ann's joyous gathering. Perhaps you could convince my wife that it's high time we were favored with some refreshments. How much longer must we wait, my dear? We're all nearly famished. Isn't that correct, gentlemen?" he asked, raising his voice loud enough to be heard by the nearby collection of men.

The group nodded in unison, reminding Jasmine of little boys playing follow-the-leader. "I'm certain none of you would tell a fib since you're in the company of Pastor Chamberlain," she said, casting the pastor a glance. He was tall and well muscled, built more like her stable hands than a man of the cloth. At least he didn't look like any man of the cloth she'd ever met.

The preacher scrutinized the group with a stern look upon his face. "Please speak up immediately if you told an untruth by saying you're hungry. Believe me when I say that the rest of us are hoping there are several of you, because we'd feel it was our duty to eat your portion—and we'd do so with great delight."

The men broke into laughter at the preacher's remark, but none admitted he was willing to give up his portion of food.

"Well, it appears we had best serve our picnic, and Alice Ann can open her gifts afterward. We'll have cake and lemonade after she's finished with her presents. How does that sound, gentlemen?"

"Tell me where the line will form and you'll not hear another word out of me," Matthew Cheever replied. "My biggest fear is that some tragic event will strike one of the mills and they will call me away."

"That is what you get for being so important to the mills and the Boston Associates," Jasmine teased.

"Just follow me," Nolan said, waving the men forward. "I'll see to it that they never find you, Matthew."

Jasmine raised her eyebrows as she watched the men march off. "They do act like young boys at times, don't they?"

"Indeed. I'd say you'd best give the order to laden the tables with food," Elinor said with a giggle.

"If you'll excuse me, I'll see to matters in the kitchen and put Clara down for her nap," Jasmine said. "Promise you'll stay long enough that we can have a good visit before you leave."

"I promise. Now don't let me keep you from your responsibilities."

———

Elinor filled her plate and surveyed the small groups gathered at the tables arranged on the lawn. There wasn't a place for her at the long table where Bella and Taylor were seated with their children. Several other families had joined the Mannings, and it appeared as if two or three other individuals were still vying to find a seat. Accordingly, Elinor turned and headed off in the other direction, finally detecting a pair of available chairs.

"May I join you?" she asked.

Three youthful faces peered up at her. "If you don't mind listening to talk of horses and fishing," Spencer Houston replied with a wide grin. Moses and Reggie Chamberlain nodded.

"I enjoy both of those topics and many others," Elinor said while juggling her plate and attempting to be seated.

Moses jumped to his feet and hurried around the table. "Let me help you, Miz Brighton," he offered while pulling the chair out for her.

"Thank you, Moses. You'd think I could manage on my own, wouldn't you?"

"These chairs don' move very easy on da grass," he said. " 'Sides, it's proper manners for men to help ladies be seated."

"Men? You and Spencer aren't men—you're just little boys," Reggie teased.

"Big enough to know more than little *girls,*" Spencer retorted.

"Perhaps I should look for another seat. It appears I've already started an argument," Elinor said.

"Nah, we's jest playing," Moses said. "We tease each other all da time."

"Right—it's 'cause Moses and me, we like each other," Spencer agreed, leaving Reggie out of the thought altogether.

Elinor took a sip of water, pondering the boy's statement. Spencer indeed saw himself and Moses as equal in every way; the only problem was, the rest of the world definitely didn't see it that way. Moses was part Negro, and in the eyes of the world he was not at all like Spencer Houston. It seemed a pity that such beliefs kept people from the kind of friendship enjoyed by Spencer and Moses. Seeing that the children had stopped to watch her, she leaned forward as though ready to plot a scheme. "If that is what teasing is all about, then I hope you'll soon be teasing me. Elsewise, I'll think you don't like me," she said with a grin.

The trio giggled with a hearty enthusiasm that drew the attention of guests at nearby tables, and Elinor placed a finger to her lips. "Shh—they'll all want to join us since we're having such fun."

"Do you like to fish, Mrs. Brighton?" Reggie inquired.

"Indeed. You know, portions of my early years were spent in Portsmouth, England, and Portsmouth is on the ocean's edge. Later I lived in London, and we had a marvelous river, the Thames. I've always loved the water, although I confess I'm not always a successful fisherman. Perhaps one day before school begins you'll invite me along on one of your fishing expeditions."

"Reggie always catches the mos' fish, but we all pretty good," Moses said.

"And I'd much rather go fishing than attend school. Let's don't even talk about that," Reggie hastened to add.

Elinor took a bite of fresh fruit salad before turning her attention back to the group. "*None* of you like school?"

"I do," Moses quickly replied, bobbing his head up and down.

"I'd rather ride horses, but I suppose school's all right," Spencer agreed.

"Not me—I don't like it. Not now and not ever," Reggie stated with an emphatic nod.

"Is that because you're going to be attending a new school, Reggie?" Elinor asked.

She shrugged her shoulders. "That too, but school is the same everywhere. It's tiresome."

A long shadow fell across the table as the girl spoke. Elinor looked up to see Justin Chamberlain standing nearby and nodded in recognition. She doubted, however, that the pastor would remember her name. Even though Elinor was a member of his church and attended services every Sunday, she had chosen to remain somewhat anonymous. After all, Pastor Chamberlain was new to Lowell and there were many names and faces to learn—especially those of the church ladies determined to seek his undivided attention.

Elinor turned her attention back to Reggie. "But you *are* going to give school your very best effort this year, aren't you?"

The girl squirmed in her chair for a moment before answering. "I suppose," she replied with lackluster enthusiasm.

Justin settled his plate and cup on the table and seated himself between Reggie and Elinor. "You must remember that doing the things you enjoy will be directly related to how well you perform in school," her father said before taking a bite of fried chicken.

"Well, I personally believe it is much too pretty a day to be worried about the next school term," Elinor said. "What have you found enjoyable here in Lowell that you've not found elsewhere?"

"Two friends who like to do the same things I like," Reggie answered quickly.

Moses giggled, his eyes wide with delight. "She's da first girl I ever knew who'd put a worm on her fishing hook."

"I'm awed by your fearless nature, Reggie," Elinor said, placing one hand upon her ruffled bodice. "No doubt one day you are going to lead an adventuresome life, and your father will be very proud of you."

Elinor could feel Justin Chamberlain's gaze upon her, but she refused to look up. Her words were meant to encourage Reggie, and she feared the pastor might not take kindly to them. Possibly he would think she was encouraging the child's daring behavior.

———————

Nolan watched closely as Alice Ann opened her gifts, pleased by the child's enthusiastic thanks as she untied the beribboned presents and tore open the paper. Jasmine grasped his hand as Alice lifted the lid from the box containing her doll. With a squeal of delight, the child pulled the doll from the paper-lined box.

Nolan leaned down and whispered into Jasmine's ear, "You see? I told you there was no need to worry."

She nodded, her eyes fixed upon Alice Ann as the child hugged the doll tightly to her chest.

"She's pretty, isn't she?" Alice Ann asked, looking directly at her parents.

"Not as pretty as you, but she is a lovely doll," her father replied.

The clothing Martha had sewn and the ribbon-festooned hat Elinor had made both met with hearty approval from the guest of honor, who immediately began the process of changing the doll's clothing.

"Why don't you wait awhile longer before you begin

changing the doll's clothes and come along with me?" Nolan suggested, extending his hand. "There's something I want to show you while your guests are waiting for their lemonade and cake."

She carefully tucked the doll back inside the box, taking pains to place it atop one of the tables—out of reach of the younger children.

"Where are we going?" she asked as she took her father's hand.

"It's a surprise," he said while leading her across the lawn and toward the distant barns.

They trod along silently until Nolan stopped and waved his arm high in the air. At his signal, Paddy rode out of the fenced corral. He was sitting tall and proud atop one of the Arabians and leading a black, white-stockinged pony along-side. Nolan watched Alice's reaction as Paddy approached.

She looked up and met his intense gaze. "Is the pony mine?" Her voice was no more than a whisper and difficult to hear above the thumping hooves.

Nolan knelt on one knee and wrapped an arm around his daughter's waist. "Do you remember the story I told you earlier today?"

"Yes, about the prince wanting a puppy."

"And do you remember the rest?"

She gave several quick nods. "The prince took care of the puppy and became his master."

"But not right away," Nolan added.

"After a year."

"Yes. And a year is a long time to take care of an animal. So I think we should give you a year and see how well you're able to take care of this pony. What do you think, Allie?" he asked, using the pet name he'd dubbed her with shortly after birth.

"I think that's fair. But only if someone will lift me up

when I need to reach things," she added thoughtfully.

Nolan tilted his head and laughed at her serious reply. "I would agree. Why don't you say hello to the pony, and then we must return."

She gave him an impish grin. "Can I ride her for a short time?"

"In your party dress? Your mother wouldn't soon forgive me for such an offense. I think we had best wait until tomorrow for a ride."

Paddy jumped down from the giant Arabian and walked the pony closer. "I do na think anyone would be carin' if ya gave the pony a wee pat on the nose," he said with a wink. "And I promise to have 'er ready for a ride on the morrow."

"Thank you," she said.

"So what is it ya'll be callin' the animal?" Paddy asked as the two men watched Alice Ann stroke the animal.

"Winnie," she stated quickly. "All my life I've wanted to name a horse Winnie."

"All your life? Well, that's an extremely long time," Nolan said with a laugh. "Winnie it is." Then noting her serious expression, he said, "And a mighty fine name, I might add."

"I best be takin' Winnie back to the barn now," Paddy said, "but she'll be there waitin' for ya tomorrow."

Alice Ann fixed a childishly admiring gaze upon Paddy. "You're coming back for cake and lemonade, aren't you?"

"I would na miss it. Be sure and tell Kiara to save me a piece of cake," he said. "After all, it's na every day a lass turns five years old."

"I'm almost six. And today isn't really my birthday," she corrected in a hushed tone as though entrusting him with a weighty secret.

"Aye—right ya are, lassie. I'd nearly forgotten."

"Thank you for going to pick up the pony," Nolan said

while taking hold of Alice Ann's hand.

"Fer sure an' it was my pleasure," he said while swinging upward and settling into the saddle on the larger horse. He tipped his hat and rode off, the pony dwarfed in the shadow of the huge white Arabian.

"I like Winnie, and I'm going to take very good care of her," Alice Ann announced as they began to walk back to the house. "Can I go and tell Spencer?"

"Exactly what do you plan to tell him?" Nolan inquired, his curiosity piqued.

She stopped and stared up at him. "That I have a year to take care of Winnie and make her mine."

"Close enough. Yes, you can go and tell Spencer. But walk—don't run," he hastily added. He knew Jasmine wouldn't be pleased if Alice Ann appeared back at the party with grass stains on her new dress.

Nolan strolled across the open field, enjoying the unexpected respite from the earlier heat of the day. A cool breeze ruffled the tall grass that covered the acreage beyond the house, and he glanced at the sky. In the west, a narrow bank of gray clouds was beginning to form. A thunderstorm might be heading in their direction. They needed rain, but he selfishly hoped any impending downpour would wait until after his daughter's birthday festivities. Attempting to accommodate all of their guests inside the house could prove a challenge to even the best hostess. Entertaining the children alone would be a brutal test of skill.

Jasmine was hurrying toward Nolan as he drew nearer. He smiled broadly and waved, surprised by her frantic gesture for him to hurry.

"Are you ready to serve the cake?" he asked, panting to catch his breath.

Her face was ashen. "No, not now. I've received a telegraph. I must talk to you—*alone,*" she said, her voice choked with emotion.

Leaning against his side, Jasmine allowed Nolan's strong arm to uphold her as they walked into the library. "Read this." She handed him the message.

"After you sit down," he said, leading her to a chair. She acquiesced and then waited in silence as he read the telegraph.

"Something terrible has happened," she whispered. "I can feel it in my bones."

Sitting down opposite her, Nolan enveloped Jasmine's hands in his own. "Jarrod is likely traveling to simply attend to some business matters," Nolan said.

"Jarrod Forbes is my father's lawyer, Nolan. I can't believe he would journey to Massachusetts unless he's come to convey bad news. I wonder if he's telegraphed McKinley. Surely McKinley would have said something when he and Violet arrived at the party. His telegraph will likely be waiting for him when he arrives home. Do you think we should tell him?"

"Yes, of course. But let's not assume the worst."

Jasmine grasped his hands tightly. "Nolan, he says he will be arriving in a few days with news from The Willows! If the news were good, Father would have written or telegraphed himself. Something has happened to Father."

"Your brother David and his wife are with your father. If he had taken ill, they would have immediately notified you."

She clutched the bodice of her dress, her eyes frantic. "Nolan, I can't explain it, but I can't help but fear that something is terribly wrong. Please . . . go and tell McKinley that we must talk with him."

CHAPTER · 2

JUSTIN CHAMBERLAIN seated himself and smoothed a sheet of paper in front of him. Sunday was quickly approaching, but he'd not yet prepared his sermon. If nothing else, he wanted to begin his ministry by challenging his parishioners to use their imaginations and reach out to others. Not that Lowell wasn't one of the most forward-thinking communities in the nation—but even Lowell could do better. He was testing the waters with his new congregation and evaluating their response. He dipped the nib of his pen into the glass bottle of ink and had barely touched pen to paper when Reggie raced through the front door and slammed it with a mighty thrust.

Startled, Justin jerked his arm and grimaced as a blob of ink dropped from the tip of his pen and spattered upon the pristine sheet of paper. "Regina! Why are you running, and why did you bang the front door as though Satan himself were on your heels?" he called out before turning in her direction.

"Maybe not Satan, but close enough!" she panted while hurrying to his side.

Her hair was a shambles, with the braid that had been so neat that morning now flying wildly in every direction. A smudge of dirt covered her right cheek, and she was wearing a pair of trousers! He'd learned long ago that he ought not be surprised by his daughter's behavior, but *trousers*. He'd not overlook this particular offense.

"What are you doing in that unspeakable attire?" Thoughts for his Sunday sermon were evaporating as quickly as the ink on the nib of his pen.

"They're coming!" she said, pointing frantically at the front door. "Hide—unless you want to consume your afternoon entertaining them."

"Explain yourself, Regina. Who are *they*?"

"Church ladies—*hundreds* of them," she hissed through her teeth while still pointing at the door.

"Hundreds? I don't think we have that many church members. Even if every member were a woman, we wouldn't number in the hundreds."

"This is no time to discuss the number of church members, Father. They're coming down the street with cakes and pies and wearing their fancy feathered hats. I'm going upstairs to hide, and you should do the same. There will be no ridding them from the house once they get inside," she cautioned, running out of the parlor and upstairs to the attic bedroom, which she had claimed as her own the day they moved into the house.

Justin knew Reggie was correct. He'd not be successful in holding a large number of intrepid women at arm's length. Since the day of their arrival in Lowell, the good ladies of St. Paul's had been anxious to ingrain themselves into every aspect of his home life. Thus far, he'd been partially successful in holding them at bay, yet he doubted whether he could mollify a large group. He walked to the large front window and stood to one side before carefully moving the drape with one finger—just far enough to see the front street. Five women were marching toward the house with an undisputable determination.

"There aren't hundreds—only five," he called up the stairway.

"Five will seem like hundreds once they get inside the house!" she shouted. "Don't open the door!"

A sharp rap brought an immediate halt to their conversation, and Justin heard the creak of rusty hinges as Reggie closed the door of her attic bedroom. Rocking back and forth on the balls of his feet, he contemplated his decision. He needed to work on his sermon, yet he couldn't ignore the kindness these women were attempting to bestow upon his household. Perhaps if he explained his plight, they would understand and hasten off to help some soul truly in need of their assistance.

Another sharp knock brought him to action. He hastened to the hallway and opened the front door—but only wide enough to accommodate his slim body. "Good day, ladies."

"Good day, Pastor Chamberlain," Martha Emory greeted. "We've come bearing gifts," she said, motioning toward two other women carrying desserts.

"And daughters," he said under his breath.

"Excuse me?" Mrs. Emory said.

"And how very kind you are to do so," Justin said with a feeble smile. "I'll take them to the kitchen."

"No need. We can do that." Mrs. Emory gave the door a hefty shove that nearly landed Justin on his backside.

In the blink of an eye, they were inside, soaring about the house like a swarm of bees to honey.

"What have I done?" he muttered. Of course, no one heard or answered his question. The women were much too busy hurrying from room to room, taking inventory of his household. He stood transfixed as the women surveyed the rooms, discussing his lack of furnishings and how best to arrange what little had been left in the house.

"Ladies, please!" he said, raising his voice to be heard above their chatter. "I do not want any assistance. I have household goods I'll be bringing at a later date, and there's certainly no need to worry about the few items that are here. Besides, I must attend to my sermon. So if you'll excuse me," he said while walking toward the hallway. He earnestly hoped they would follow so that he could escort them out the front door without further discussion.

"You go along and write your sermon, Pastor. The others can unpack, and Caroline and I will rearrange the furniture in the parlor. You *have* met my daughter, Caroline, haven't you?" Mrs. Emory inquired, pulling her daughter forward.

"Yes, of course. We met on Sunday."

"And *my* daughters, Rachel and Sarah," Mrs. Sanders said, clutching her daughters to her side. "Rachel has a vast knowledge of the Scriptures, and Sarah is an excellent cook. Just wait until you taste the cake she baked for you."

"Thank you, Sarah," he said, giving the gangly girl a forced smile.

"Caroline baked the apple pie," Mrs. Emory hastened to add. "I doubt whether you'll taste any better."

"I don't doubt your word," Justin said. "Truly, ladies, I do not wish to have any assistance with the household, but I thank you very much for the pies and cakes. Right now what I need is peace and quiet in order to prepare my sermon."

"We'll be quiet as church mice," Mrs. Emory said with a loud chortle, obviously finding her play on words humorous. The fact that no one else was laughing didn't seem to bother her in the least.

Justin stood holding the doorknob of the open front door. "Ladies?" he encouraged, his eyes moving between the group of women and the door.

"I'll not leave until I've accomplished what I set out to do, so you might as well get busy on your sermon, Pastor. I'm going to clean this house. I can't imagine why it wasn't completed before your arrival," Martha Emory said, yanking a crocheted table runner off an old table and giving it a robust shake.

Reggie had been correct—it did seem as though a hundred women now inhabited their home. With a disgusted grunt, he gathered up his paper, pen, ink, and Bible and hurried off to retrieve a chair from the kitchen before heading to his bedroom. Once inside, he quickly arranged a make-shift desk by using one of the trunks for his writing area. There was little doubt he'd be suffering with an aching back come morning.

"I told you! You shouldn't have let them in."

"Reggie! How did you get in here?"

His daughter wriggled out from beneath his bed in the same unladylike attire she'd been wearing earlier. "There's a hole in the floor of the upstairs closet. I tied a rope and dropped down through it—I found the opening the day we moved in," she explained.

"An opening in the floor? And where did you land?"

"In the pantry. And I didn't knock over any of the food or utensils," she said smugly. "When the ladies weren't looking, I tiptoed out of the pantry and into your room."

"I think you would have been more satisfied upstairs. After all, there's nothing for you to do here in my bedroom. I'm going to be writing my sermon, and you'll need to sit and be quiet."

"As soon as they're all in the parlor, I'm going to sneak

out the back door and go play. We're taking Mrs. Brighton fishing today," she added.

"Who is 'we'?" Justin inquired.

Reggie heaved a sigh and furrowed her eyebrows. "Me, Spencer, and Moses. I told you after Alice Ann's birthday party that we were going to teach Mrs. Brighton how to fish," she explained.

She *had* told him, but he'd immediately dismissed the remark without giving it further thought. "And where do you plan to go fishing?"

"At the river. We found a nice spot, and Mrs. Brighton said she'd bring a picnic. It's going to be great fun. Did you know Mrs. Brighton is from England? She grew up in Portsmouth and London. I think I'd like to visit London one day. Mrs. Brighton said some of the people speak with an odd accent, but she talks just fine, don't you think?"

What would Louise think of their child, he contemplated. She'd likely be appalled at the girl's behavior. Or perhaps she would find Reggie's tomboyish antics acceptable. He wondered, yet he would never know.

How he had missed Louise throughout these past ten years as he'd struggled to rear Reggie. Managing a daughter had been more of a challenge than he'd ever imagined. Although Louise's parents had offered to raise Reggie as their own, Justin had refused. Reggie deserved better than losing both of her parents at birth, and truth be told, he needed Regina. Having the child all these years had given him a purpose—and kept a little piece of Louise alive too.

Reggie jostled his arm. "Don't you think, Father?"

"What? Oh, yes, I think Mrs. Brighton speaks quite eloquently."

He tapped his index finger against his pursed lips and waited for a moment. "It's very quiet out there," he whispered. "Do you suppose they've gone?"

"Take a peek and see," she suggested. "But open the door just a crack," she cautioned.

He nodded his head and tiptoed to the door, carefully turning the knob in a clockwise direction before slowly opening the door. After listening for a moment, he whispered, "I don't hear anything."

Reggie removed her shoes and walked over to him, her bare feet silently gliding across the wooden floor until she reached his side. "You go first, just in case. I don't want them to see me if they're still somewhere in the house."

Justin opened the door a bit farther, but still it remained silent. Careful to close the bedroom door after himself, he ventured onward, into the kitchen, his library, and then the parlor. With the exception of his bedroom, the sparse furnishings had been rearranged throughout the house, and the ladies had departed.

"They're gone! They've left their pies and cakes and rearranged the few sticks of furniture, but at least I can complete my sermon."

"And I can go fishing," Reggie said with a delighted smile.

"So long as you're home in time for supper."

"We're having a picnic, remember?"

He hesitated and gave it some thought. "I'm sorry—you *did* mention a picnic. Then please be home shortly thereafter. And, by all means, don't forget your fishing pole."

———

Elinor finished packing the picnic basket and then carefully tucked a checkered cloth atop the contents. "That should be enough food for *several* days," she muttered as she lifted the container from the table.

Careful to watch her step while approaching the Merrimack River, she failed to see Reggie near the water's edge until the child called out to her.

"Hello, Reggie. Have you been here long?"

The girl positioned her fishing pole on the grassy bank and came running toward Elinor. "No. I thought I would be the last one to arrive, but I'm first," she said. "There's a verse like that in the Bible, I think." She furrowed her brows for a moment.

"I believe you're talking about the verse where Jesus says that many who are first will be last, and many who are last will be first."

"Yes, that's it. I guess it has nothing to do with fishing, though," Reggie said with a cheerful giggle. "I told my father you're from Portsmouth and London and that we're going to teach you how to fish. I thought I would never get out of the house, though; that's why I'm surprised I'm the first one here. Another group of proper church ladies—that's what my father calls them—came to visit. They keep coming to our house bringing cakes and pies and more cakes and more pies," she said, waving her arms like an exasperated old woman.

It was impossible not to smile. The child was so expressive that she used her whole body to tell a story. "I would think you and your father would be pleased to have the pies and cakes," Elinor said.

"Not *that* many—there are only two of us," she said. "Oh, look! Here come Spencer and Moses. Come on, you two, before we've caught all the fish," she called.

The boys rushed down the bank and plopped down alongside Reggie and Elinor, each one holding a fishing pole.

"You find us some worms or grubs?" Spencer asked.

"Nope, you go find your own. I got enough for me and Mrs. Brighton to get started."

The boys appeared surprised when Elinor took a worm

and threaded it onto her hook, but Reggie withheld any reaction.

"She sure doesn't act like my mama." Spencer whispered, staring at Elinor in awe. "She'd *never* put a worm on a hook."

"You did a real fine job—now let me see you get a fish," Reggie said, obviously not so easily impressed.

Elinor adjusted her straw bonnet, then tossed her line into the river. "I'll do my best, but don't go too far away. I may need your help."

"I'll do my best," Reggie said, giggling as she repeated Elinor's words.

Moses and Spencer rushed off to find some bait and were soon back and settled on the bank beside Reggie and Elinor, all of them determined to catch the first fish of the day. Had any passersby come upon them, Elinor was certain they would consider their little group quite a sight: Spencer in his crisp, clean clothing and his hair freshly combed; Moses in his neat yet less expensive breeches, his complexion nearly as white as Spencer's; Elinor in her pale green day dress and straw bonnet. And then there was Reggie. Obviously, the girl was determined she'd rather dress and act the part of a boy, which was exactly the same way Elinor had felt at Reggie's young age.

"You understand this isn't the best time of day to fish," Reggie said with the authority of an expert fisherman.

"Ever'one knows dat, Reggie," Moses said, leaning forward to give her a disgusted look.

"Does not!" Reggie shouted

"Do too!" Spencer argued.

"Did *you* know it, Mrs. Brighton?" Reggie asked.

Elinor was unsure what to say, but she didn't want the children's arguing to continue. "I believe I may have heard something to that effect, but had you asked me when to schedule the best time to come fishing, I would certainly have been at a loss."

Spencer and Reggie looked at each other, obviously unclear about who had gained Elinor's agreement. Spencer shrugged his shoulders and turned his attention back to his fishing line. Her words had deflated their argument—at least for now.

"How come you and Moses were late?" Reggie asked as she wiggled to find a more comfortable position.

"My mama's been *disturbed* ever since Alice Ann's birthday party—at least that's what my father calls it—disturbed."

Reggie's interest was piqued, and she once again changed her position in order to gain a better view of Spencer. "How come? I thought the party was very nice—except that I had to wear a dress. And I really liked Alice Ann's pony. Were you jealous she got a pony, Spencer?"

"Naw. Besides, it's not really hers yet. She has to prove she can take care of it, and I'm thinking she'll lose interest in a few weeks. Alice Ann's not like us—she doesn't know what's important and what's not. She'll be off playing with her dolly and forget about Winnie. *Winnie!* Did you ever hear such a silly name for a horse?"

"Winnie," Moses mimicked in a girlish voice.

The two boys began giggling and didn't stop until tears rolled down their cheeks.

Reggie waited until they quieted and then said quite demurely, "I think Winnie is a perfectly suitable name for a horse. It's every bit as good a name as Larkspur. And you still haven't told me why your mother is disturbed," she added, suddenly sounding quite grown up.

Spencer peeked around Moses with a startled look etched upon his young face—almost as though he expected to see someone other than Reggie sitting on the riverbank. "She's disturbed because she got a telegram from Grandpa

Wainwright's lawyer down in Mississippi. He's coming to see Mama and Uncle McKinley. Papa says he should arrive later today or tomorrow. Mama thinks something bad has happened to Grandpa."

Reggie's eyes opened wide, and her eyebrows shot up like two miniature mountain peaks. "Like he's *dead* or something?"

"Reggie!" Elinor cautioned.

Spencer's head bobbed up and down in agreement. "Yep! That's what she thinks and so does my uncle McKinley—but not me. Me and Poppa think Grandpa's probably just sending the lawyer to take care of business for him."

"You're likely correct, Spencer," Elinor hastened to agree, not wanting Reggie to question the boy any further. "What do you think about eating our picnic lunch since the fish don't seem to be biting?" she suggested.

A chorus of agreement sounded and the children immediately jumped up and began to help. They spread the lunch of fried chicken, pickled beets, hard-boiled eggs, watermelon pickles, and thick slices of buttered bread on the checkered cotton cloth and then filled their plates, again and again and again—particularly Reggie, who couldn't seem to eat enough to fill her stomach.

"And I thought I had packed enough food to last us several days," Elinor told the children as she began repacking the basket. "There's one last piece of chicken if anyone wants it," she said while holding the drumstick between her fingers.

"I'll take it," Reggie said, quickly relieving Elinor of the crispy chicken leg and taking a bite. "This is gooood chicken," she complimented, waving the drumstick like a fat wand.

"Thank you, Reggie."

"Me and Moses can't stay much longer," Spencer said as

he once again dipped his line into the water.

"How come? You were late and now you're gonna leave early?"

"Don't get all mad at us, Reggie. We don't want to, but it was the only way I could even get permission to come at all. Mama wants us at home when that lawyer comes. She says she doesn't want to be worrying about where I am when she has to be focused on other important matters."

The response didn't assuage Reggie's irritation. "Didn't you tell her you'd be at our usual fishing spot?"

"*Yes*. But it didn't matter what I said. She told me I had to promise to be home early."

Elinor patted Reggie's arm. "It is obviously very important to Mrs. Houston that Spencer return home on time. We can stay for a while longer if you like, but I think Spencer and Moses should do as they've been instructed."

"I know. I guess we might as well all leave," Reggie replied dejectedly. "Want to walk me home?" she asked, her features beginning to brighten a bit.

"Of course. I'd be pleased to walk with you," Elinor said.

A short time later, Elinor and Reggie bid the boys farewell and headed for the parsonage.

"Don't forget to tell me what happens with the lawyer," Reggie shouted to Spencer as he and Moses climbed the bank and walked toward the bridge.

"I will."

Both boys waved, and Elinor noted the forlorn look on Reggie's face as the boys sauntered out of sight. "Do you wish you had a brother or sister—someone to keep you company, like Spencer and Moses?"

"They aren't brothers; they're friends."

"Yes, I know. But they live nearby one another, and they can be together almost as if they were brothers. I merely wondered if you would like that same companionship," Elinor said.

"I guess I'd like a friend that lived close by—but not a brother or sister. That would mean having a baby around, and babies aren't any fun. I want someone my own age."

"I see. Well it appears you've made two good friends even if they don't live in town where you can see them every day."

"Uh-huh. But it's not good to get too close to friends," Reggie said as she skipped along beside Elinor.

"Why is that?"

"Because every time I make a friend, we move to another town, and then I have to start all over again. Boys are easier to make friends with, though. Girls act snooty, don't you think?"

Elinor laughed. "Sometimes they do. But there are girls who are welcoming and kind too. Perhaps you've not tried as hard because you prefer doing the things boys like rather than girls' activities."

"Maybe. But you'd think more girls would like to fish and ride horses, wouldn't you?"

"You'd think," Elinor agreed. "I thought it was difficult growing up without having my mother around when I was a little girl."

Reggie swung around to face Elinor and began walking backwards. "Did she die like my mama?"

"She died when I was born, so I never knew her."

"Just like me," Reggie said.

"But I had brothers and sisters. We remained in Portsmouth for a short time, but then my father located a position in London and we all moved there and our grandmother lived with us. She helped raise me," Elinor explained.

"Father said my grandmother offered to take me too, but

he said no. He wanted to keep me with him. That was good, don't you think?"

"Absolutely! You're a very fortunate girl to have a father willing to rear a little girl all by himself."

"We've managed pretty well—except for the moving around. I don't like that part, but Father says maybe we'll be able to stay in Lowell until I'm all grown. Wouldn't that be wonderful?"

"Indeed, it would. We'll have to begin praying that God keeps your father as pastor at St. Paul's for a very long time," Elinor said as they approached the parsonage. "Thank you for the fine day, Reggie. I had a very nice time."

"Please come in and see my room," she pleaded while tugging on Elinor's hand. "It's in the attic, and I've found a secret hole in the floor."

"Yes, do come in," Justin Chamberlain offered as he stood up and stepped from behind a rose-covered trellis on the front porch. "I finally completed my sermon notes and came outdoors for a breath of fresh air."

"I really must be getting back to the boardinghouse," Elinor replied. She wasn't sure why, but the pastor's offer suddenly made her feel self-conscious.

"Pleeeease," Reggie begged. "I do want you to see my room."

"I'll come in, but only long enough to see your room. Then I must be on my way."

Justin reached for the picnic basket. "I doubt you'll want to carry this upstairs for your grand tour."

"Thank you," Elinor said and followed along behind Reggie, viewing the large attic room where the side walls sloped at a severe angle, making the room somewhat difficult to navigate without bending over. "You may need to do a bit of furniture rearranging as you grow taller. If not, you're apt to bump your head at night should you sit up too quickly," Elinor said with a grin.

"Father said the very same thing. Come see my special trapdoor."

Elinor viewed the opening that dropped into the kitchen pantry. "I wonder who made this opening. I bet there are lots of stories we could tell about why and who crawled down through that hole," she said in a hushed voice.

Reggie's delight was obvious. "It *is* exciting, isn't it?"

"Yes. In fact, it almost makes me long to be a little girl again," Elinor said as the two of them walked down the stairs.

"I didn't notice you two carrying any fish," Justin noted as they reached the bottom step.

"Actually, I did manage to hook one, but it was so tiny we let it go," Elinor said. "The children tell me that mid-afternoon is not a good time of day for catching fish, so I felt fortunate I caught even the little one."

"And she put her own worm on the hook and even took the fish off," Reggie informed her father.

"It appears my daughter is impressed with your abilities even if you didn't catch a lot of fish. And compliments from my daughter are not easy to come by," he added.

"Then I'll consider myself fortunate," Elinor said.

"Please stay and have a piece of pie or cake with us," Pastor Chamberlain offered.

Elinor glanced at Reggie, and the two of them giggled. "I'm sorry. I shouldn't laugh at your kind offer. However, Reggie confided that the good ladies of St. Paul's brought several cakes and pies earlier today."

He gave a firm nod. "Earlier today, later today, yesterday, and the day before that—and not merely the ladies from St. Paul's, but from all around town. I have more cakes and pies than we can ever hope to eat. I'd need to purchase a new preaching suit if I ate all of those sweets," he said with a grin.

"I don't think the ladies realize that man does not live by sweets alone. Come and see."

Elinor's eyes widened at the spectacle. All horizontal space in the kitchen and dining room, with the exception of Pastor Chamberlain's writing desk, had been covered by every imaginable dessert. The sight took her breath away. "Oh my! This is astonishing. You must begin turning them away."

"I have attempted to do so from the very beginning. None will take no for an answer. Even when they see the laden tables, they refuse to take their offerings home."

"Perhaps Reggie should begin selling some of these delicacies," Elinor teased.

Moments later Elinor left for home, completely unaware of the inspiration she had planted in a young girl's heart.

CHAPTER · 3

JASMINE HEARD the sounds of an approaching horse and buggy from her upstairs room and quickly walked to the window overlooking the small circular driveway that fronted their home. Jarrod Forbes stepped down from the carriage, and she watched as he slowly surveyed his surroundings. Mr. Forbes had aged since she'd last seen him and now wore spectacles and carried a silver-tipped walking cane. His hair appeared more gray than black, and there was a surprising stoop to his shoulders. The lawyer had always held his head high and his shoulders squared. At least that's what her father had said about him. Jasmine had long thought Jarrod Forbes aloof and proud, though she didn't get that impression at the current time.

She heard the front door open and then Nolan's and McKinley's voices as they greeted their guest. Mr. Forbes had sent word of his arrival at the Merrimack House yesterday and asked to meet with them this morning. She knew McKinley would prefer the early morning meeting—he disliked being pulled away from his work at the Corporation during business hours.

Bracing herself for what she was convinced would be bad news, Jasmine took a deep breath, pursed her lips, and slowly exhaled before descending the staircase. "Mr. Forbes," she greeted as she joined the gentlemen in Nolan's library. "I trust you had a pleasant journey."

She feared the lawyer's inability to meet her eyes didn't bode well for the discussion that would later ensue.

"My voyage was uneventful, thank you."

"Has my husband offered you refreshments?" she inquired.

Nolan nodded. "Yes. Martha will bring a tray shortly."

"Then I suppose we should all be seated," she said, suddenly feeling ill at ease standing in front of Nolan's oversized mahogany desk.

Mr. Forbes tugged on the hem of his vest and sat down opposite McKinley, his focus upon the wool carpet. He cleared his throat several times and repositioned his cane in varying stances until Jasmine finally jumped to her feet and removed it from his hand.

"I'll place this in the umbrella stand so you won't have to worry with it," she said without giving him opportunity to protest. "Now, why don't you tell us what brings you to Massachusetts."

Apparently her tone bore enough impatience to prod the man into action, since he immediately reached into his small leather case and withdrew a sheaf of papers.

"Perhaps I should sit near the desk so that I may arrange these documents," he said, finally looking at Jasmine.

"Of course. Let me assist you," she offered graciously.

Once the official-looking paper work was spread out on Nolan's desk, Forbes pulled a handkerchief from his pocket and wiped his perspiring forehead. "Your father entrusted me with the task of personally coming to meet with you. Unfortunately, I must begin by advising you that your father and my beloved friend went to be with the Lord on the six-teenth of June."

A loud roar filled Jasmine's ears, and she heard a scream. Was it her voice or had someone else shrieked? The room swirled. Nolan's face was above her, fading in and out, his voice calling her name. She willed her lips to move, yet they failed her.

Her eyelids fluttered open, and she could feel the damp-ness of a cool compress upon her forehead. She forced herself to focus upon Nolan's face.

"My dear! You gave me a fright," Nolan said as he con-tinued to dab her forehead with the moist cloth.

"I do apologize, Mrs. Houston," Mr. Forbes said. "For-give me for my lack of sensitivity. I should have better prepared you for the news."

The lawyer's words brought his earlier announcement rushing back to mind. Her father, dead for more than two months—and she hadn't even known. All that time she had overlooked his lack of communication by thinking him busy with the plantation.

Nolan assisted her as she struggled to sit up on the floor and then move slowly to a chair.

"What happened to my father?" she asked.

The lawyer looked at Nolan, obviously seeking affirma-tion that he should speak. "You must tell her," Nolan said.

"Yellow fever."

Jasmine gripped the chair arm. "Did he suffer terribly?"

"No more than the others," Forbes hedged.

"*Others?* Then there's been an epidemic?"

Nolan furrowed his brow and took her hand in his own. "There's no need to hear all the details at once, my dear. You're already in a weakened state of mind."

"I'm not in a weakened state of mind, Nolan. I'm sad

and frightened, and I need to know what has happened at The Willows."

"My wife has returned to her full capacity, Mr. Forbes. You may speak freely."

"Are you certain?" he inquired in a quivering voice.

"Yes!" Jasmine sat up straight to emphasize her forceful reply.

"The illness struck with a vengeance. It wasn't widespread, but where it did hit, the misery was tragic. Unfortunately, the area around your home was struck particularly hard."

Jasmine's eyes widened with sudden realization. "Our brother David and his wife?"

The old lawyer slowly moved his head back and forth. "Gone. Your brother Samuel as well."

"No!" she screamed. "Not our entire family."

Distress lined Mr. Forbes's face as he retrieved his handkerchief from his jacket pocket and began to once again daub his forehead. "I fear the news only gets more dreadful."

"I shall do my utmost to remain calm," Jasmine said.

"Your uncles and cousins . . . there are few remaining and—"

She motioned for him to halt while she grappled for the fan she'd placed on a nearby table. Snapping open the hand-painted object, she began to wave it back and forth with a fervor that stirred the air for all of them. "Continue," she said, as though her behavior were quite normal.

"None of them survived, except for your distant cousin Levi Wainwright," he said in a nearly inaudible voice. "Oh yes, and Lydia, Franklin's daughter."

"That few? How could that be?" This time it was McKinley who interrupted.

"The plague hit hard in the area. How a small number can endure while others perish is a mystery to all of us—

always is. I believe a few others survived—relatives by marriage. Lydia's husband, Rupert, and one or two others. Rupert advised me Lydia is traveling abroad and not yet expected home. Of course, your distant cousin Levi always was a strange individual—never did live on the plantation with his family. Had aspirations of becoming an artist and still travels a great deal—usually only comes back south during the winter months. As I said, the area was hit particularly hard, and with most of the family congregated on adjoining plantations . . ." His voice trailed off as though he'd lost the energy to continue.

Jasmine laid the fan on a marble-topped table and turned her full attention upon the lawyer. "I don't mean to appear unappreciative, especially since you've traveled all this distance, but why didn't you immediately send word back when we could have been of assistance to our father?"

"I was following his direction, Mrs. Houston. He forbade me from notifying either you or your brother. He feared you would contract the fever if you came to The Willows. He watched both Samuel and David die and said he wouldn't lose another child.

"He required me to give my word that I would not notify you until the outbreak had ended. In any event, you could not have come, for the entire area was under quarantine. I set sail as soon as I was notified that the quarantine would be lifted. Your father wanted me to personally deliver these papers and go over the details with you and McKinley."

McKinley pulled his chair closer to the desk. He seemed unnaturally calm. "What are these papers?"

"Your father's last will and testament and handwritten letters to each of you. Obviously, you must make decisions regarding the plantation and your slaves."

"*Our* slaves? Neither of us believes in slavery, Mr. Forbes.

You may turn the survivors free as far as I'm concerned," Jasmine said.

"Don't speak so hastily, Mrs. Houston. There are many considerations that must be addressed before you determine exactly what is to be done with them."

"Go on, Mr. Forbes," McKinley said. "We're listening."

"There's a cotton crop that must be harvested. Someone needs to go to The Willows and take charge—get the crop in first and then decide if you'll move back and take over the plantation." His final words were a near whisper.

McKinley appeared more stunned by Mr. Forbes's announcement about the crops than the death of their family members. "You want one of us to return and oversee the harvest? Why, that's preposterous! I can't leave Lowell or my position with the Corporation. My wife is due to have a child in a few months, and we're in the process of building a new home. Besides, I know nothing of harvesting a crop. Can't the overseer tend to the cotton?"

Mr. Forbes leaned back in his chair, the import of his task obviously weighing heavily upon him. He rubbed his temples and gazed at McKinley as though he were a child with an inadequate ability to understand the profundity of their circumstance.

"The overseer?" Jasmine inquired. But Mr. Forbes didn't need to answer. His expression revealed the answer.

"The overseer and two-thirds of the slaves are dead. I hired a man to act as overseer, but he can't possibly handle this situation. The plantation requires immediate attention by someone with more authority than a newly hired over-seer. Under normal circumstances, that would be you, McKinley. However, your father drew his will giving his property to you and Jasmine in equal shares. He states in article three of his will that the two of you must come to an agreement as to how the plantation will be managed."

McKinley reached for the document. "Does he prohibit the sale?"

"No, there's no such prohibition. Upon the deaths of David and Samuel, your father rewrote his will. He knew neither of you would have any desire to operate the plantation, nor did he wish to force you into such a situation. However, in his letter he does ask that the crop be harvested if at all possible. Surely you must admit that permitting the crop to sit in the fields and rot would be improvident. Your father would abhor such inaction. On his behalf, I would plead for one of you to come back to The Willows and attend to matters immediately. The cotton will not wait indefinitely."

Nolan brushed a lock of hair off his forehead and shook his head. "There is no easy answer to this dilemma. Even if Jasmine or McKinley agreed to go and oversee the harvest, how could it be accomplished with so few workers?"

Jasmine gave him a tender smile. *Workers.* He couldn't even bring himself to say they'd be using slaves if they brought in the crop.

"Unaffected plantations in Louisiana are willing to hire out some of their slaves, and several plantations are planning to take advantage of the offer. The plantations nearby that suffered a large number of deaths have discussed the possibility of sharing their slaves. They would work one week at one plantation and the next week at another. Of course, you have to hope you don't get the week when it rains," he said with a halfhearted smile.

Jasmine fidgeted with her hands, overwhelmed by all she'd been told. It was impossible to imagine that most of her family had perished. But it was equally hard to make a choice about what should be done. "It's obvious we can't come to an immediate decision, Mr. Forbes. We need time to discuss the matter more fully before coming to a conclusion."

"Of course, of course. I didn't expect you to give me your answer today. I know there is much to digest, but you must remember the crop will be ready for harvest by the time you make the journey. You dare not tarry for too long."

"I presume arrangements were made . . . properly made . . . for my family," Jasmine said, suddenly changing the subject.

"Of course. Your father saw to those who went before him and left instructions with me for the remaining deaths, including his."

"That sounds very much like Father." Jasmine knew her father would have thought of everyone else, even if it took his last ounce of strength.

I'll leave these papers with you to peruse, and if you have questions, you know where to reach me. Otherwise, I'll await your decision." Mr. Forbes used the arms of the chair to steady himself as he began to stand.

"A moment, Mr. Forbes," McKinley said, waving for the man to remain seated. "Has any of this information been reported to the Boston Associates? Undoubtedly they need to know the state of affairs among those men with whom they have contracts. The mills are dependent upon receiving the anticipated cotton shipments."

Forbes nodded in agreement. "I understand. I talked with no one prior to coming here. My first obligation was to your father and the promise I made him. However, I am prepared to speak with the Associates prior to my departure, or you may report on my behalf if you desire."

"I believe they would appreciate hearing from you directly," McKinley replied. "I'll talk with Matthew Cheever, and we'll arrange a meeting as quickly as possible."

"Since I plan to depart for Boston once you've made a

decision regarding The Willows, could we possibly meet in Boston? My ship sails for Mississippi in ten days and I had planned to spend the remainder of my time in the city. I promised to bring my wife some finery, and it may take me a few days to complete my shopping," he added with an exhausted smile.

"I'm confident we can accommodate you. We can send a telegraph, and once we receive word regarding the time and date, I'll notify you."

"Good enough," Mr. Forbes said, once again struggling to stand.

"Let me retrieve your cane, Mr. Forbes, and I'll see you to the door," Jasmine offered.

"No. You remain seated, Mrs. Houston. You've had more to contend with this day than I."

"Indeed, my dear. You remain seated," Nolan said as he took the older man by one arm. "I'll accompany Mr. Forbes."

Mr. Forbes leaned heavily upon his cane as Nolan escorted him across the thick wool carpet. Jasmine waited until she heard the tapping of his cane upon the wooden floor in the hallway before turning her attention to McKinley.

"Do you want to return home and discuss this matter with Violet—or perhaps fetch her and we can all take our noonday meal together?" Jasmine asked.

He shook his head. "No. I can tell you, sister, that I'll not even entertain the notion of returning to The Willows and bringing in a cotton crop. If you want to do so, then that is all well and good, but I say we should immediately sell the place."

"That may prove more difficult than you think," Nolan said as he strode back into the room.

"How so? The Willows turns a handsome profit. There

ought to be any number of investors willing to purchase such a plantation."

"That's not what Forbes tells me. He just said there are two plantations that have been on the market for over a year now and still have no buyers. Additionally, he tells me that because the fever devastated the area around Lorman, it will prove more difficult to find a purchaser until the fear of a repeat epidemic dies down."

McKinley stood up and began pacing back and forth between the settee and Nolan's oversized desk, his shuffling feet brushing the carpet nap first in one direction and then the other. "This is indeed a fine predicament," he said while raking his fingers through his thick hair. "We can't even properly mourn the loss of our family because of a cotton crop. I say we let it rot in the fields. What difference does harvesting the cotton make if we're going to sell the plantation anyway?"

"Not a very fitting tribute to our father or our brothers, do you think? We should at least honor Father's final request, McKinley."

"Surely he realized what he was asking would be impossible for either of us to accomplish," her brother argued.

Leaning slightly forward, Jasmine watched as her brother paced in front of her. McKinley had always been the sensitive male member in their family, yet suddenly he appeared cold and indifferent. She'd never seen him so detached and aloof. His behavior was as disturbing as the decision they must make. Surely he didn't truly believe they should sit back and permit the crop to lay waste.

"Nothing is impossible if we trust in the Lord and maintain a proper perspective. Perhaps Violet would be willing to remain in Lowell with her parents while you traveled with Nolan and me to The Willows. With three of us, we could conduct the necessary business more rapidly. You or Nolan could oversee the crop, and I could attend to putting the house in order to place it for sale and help with the book-work," she suggested hopefully.

"Did you not hear me? There is no way I can travel to Mississippi. I'll not leave Violet with her parents when our child is due to be born in December. You know she's frightened something will go wrong again."

Jasmine nodded. Violet had suffered the loss of a stillborn child early in her marriage, and it had nearly incapacitated her throughout this pregnancy. Even though she'd subsequently given birth to one healthy child, the thought of another stillborn baby loomed in her mind, and she was convinced she would have difficulty once again.

"I thought Violet appeared happy and relaxed at Alice Ann's party. Only two months ago, she wouldn't have considered such an outing. You could at least ask her, McKinley. She likely relies upon her mother more than you for consolation at this juncture, don't you think?"

"How would you feel if Nolan left you in such a circumstance, Jasmine? Would *you* think it his duty to hurry off to harvest a cotton crop, or would you believe he should remain at home with you? I'd venture to say you would not bid him farewell without an argument. Violet's condition aside, I must see to my position with the Corporation. I cannot merely walk in and say I'll be back once I've harvested the cotton and sold my father's plantation. No, Jasmine. If one of us is to go to the South, it will be you, for I'll not be bullied or shamed into going."

"Is that what you think? That I'm trying to bully or shame you? Go home to your wife and your position at the Corporation, McKinley. Your primary concern appears to rest with the Corporation rather than the plantation," she said in a soft yet resigned voice. "I'll manage things in Mississippi without your assistance. However, I'll not seek your permission for the decisions I make. If you plan to wash your hands of this matter, then I expect you to sign over your right of authority so I may transact business without your signature. Otherwise, I'll be hampered at every turn as I wait upon the paper work being shuffled back and forth between Mississippi and Massachusetts."

McKinley leaned against Nolan's desk in a half sitting, half standing position. "You want me to sign over my portion of the inheritance? Is that what you're asking? Because I won't do that—I won't."

Her eyes filled with sadness as she met his piercing eyes. "I don't want your inheritance, McKinley—I want your help. But please understand that although you've refused your assistance, I would never consider taking your inheritance. Father intended it for you, and you shall have half of whatever remains when all is said and done. All I've asked is that you sign over your authority so that I can conduct business without the necessity of your signature."

"I'll ask Mr. Forbes to draw up a paper in the morning." His voice was cold.

"Until today, I hadn't realized how much you've changed, McKinley. I fear your position with the Corporation has begun to harden you. Please don't lose your kind heart and generous spirit. We've lost the rest of our family—we mustn't lose each other."

"You're right, of course." His voice cracked with emotion as she embraced him. "I'm sorry, but I just cannot accompany you. Please forgive me."

"There's nothing to forgive," she whispered.

———

Later that night Jasmine sat alone brushing out her long brown hair. She looked at herself in the mirror with each stroke. She couldn't comprehend that her father had died.

She couldn't make it real in her mind.

"I suppose I won't fully believe it until I see The Willows and his grave," she murmured.

"Did you say something?" Nolan asked as he came into the room.

She sighed and put down the brush. "I can't believe they are gone."

He came to her and put his hands upon her shoulders. Bending low, he kissed her cheek. "I cannot imagine a more difficult day for you, and yet you bore it with such grace. It is hard to even imagine one's entire family wiped out in a matter of weeks."

"I've seen epidemics like that before. There was one when I was a little girl," Jasmine remembered. "I think I was nearly six. I remember many of the older people dying, yet no one on our plantation seemed to get sick. At least I don't remember there being sickness." She turned and stood. "There is always something to worry about. I think of how close we came to losing Alice Ann. I worry every time one of the children starts sniffling."

"But you cannot live in fear."

Tears welled in her eyes. "No. I know the truth of that. Still . . . I'm afraid."

He pulled her into his arms. "Cast your cares upon the Lord."

"I'm trying to," she whispered, allowing his embrace to reassure and comfort her. "I'm trying."

———————

Reverend Chamberlain snapped open his pocket watch and glanced down at the time. The Ladies' Aid Society would be in the midst of their meeting, but if he entered the church quietly, he could be in and out without being observed. At least that was his plan. He silently chastised himself for leaving his sermon notes at the church when he'd attended last night's meeting. If he hadn't had to go searching for Reggie at the last minute, he wouldn't have laid them down.

No sense blaming the child for her inquisitive nature, he decided. At her age, he, too, would have been off exploring the nooks and crannies of the church. However, he had become concerned when, after a good ten minutes of searching, he'd not located his daughter and been required to enlist the aid of several church members. After another period of searching, Mr. Emory had located Reggie in a narrow crawl space off one end of the sanctuary. Of course, Reggie hadn't understood all the excitement. After all, she had followed her father's instructions and had remained inside the church. On their way home, Justin attempted to explain his concerns but had finally given up.

Reggie was correct; she hadn't disobeyed. Next time he would have to issue more explicit instructions, he decided as he carefully opened the church door and tiptoed across the wooden floor of the vestibule.

He could hear the muffled voices of the women drifting from inside the sanctuary. From the sound of the animated voices, he doubted their meeting would soon be over, and he exhaled a sigh of relief. He took another step toward his small office but stopped short. Had he heard someone utter his daughter's name?

As surreptitiously as a cat stalking its prey, Justin padded back to the sanctuary doors and placed one ear against the cool, hard wood.

"Well, I can't tell you the depth of my irritation when Rachel came home from town and told me she'd seen the preacher's daughter going door to door selling cakes and pies," Nancy Sanders proclaimed.

"*Our* cakes and pies?" another woman asked in a sharp voice.

"Well, of course, *our* cakes and pies. Do you think the preacher or that wretched child can bake?"

"She's not *wretched,* Nancy. Unkempt, perhaps, but I believe she's surely a sweet little girl underneath it all. You need to remember that she hasn't had the advantages of your Rachel. Growing up without a mother's influence and training has surely been difficult for the girl—and her father."

Justin couldn't determine who made the comment, but his lips curved slightly upward. At least not all of them considered Reggie to be wretched.

"Well, he certainly doesn't appear interested in doing anything to help the girl. He brushes off every attempt that Rachel and I, as well as these other ladies, have made to assist him," Mrs. Sanders responded. "And now he's permitting the child to venture about town selling the pastries we baked for them."

"She even attempted to sell some of them to Mrs. Whidden at the mercantile. When Mrs. Whidden questioned her, the child stated Elinor Brighton had made the suggestion."

"Do you suppose she's set her cap for the preacher and fears that her baked goods can't compare to ours?" Nancy Sanders inquired.

"Elinor? She's no more interested in finding a husband than I am," another woman replied.

"You're already married, Nettie," someone said.

"Exactly my point. I'm not looking for a husband, and neither is Elinor Brighton. She's been twice widowed and has hardened her heart against such matters."

"I say the entire situation is pitiable and a poor reflection upon the church," one of the women commented.

"Indeed! My husband tells me they had to drag the girl

out of a crawl space she was hiding in last night during the deacons' meeting."

Was that Martha Emory speaking? It sounded like her shrill voice, and Harry Emory had been the one to locate Reggie the preceding night.

"There's little doubt the child needs a woman's hand. She has come to a point in her life when she needs to be turned down the proper path. I'm sure she has no idea how to properly fashion her hair or put needle to cloth. What's to become of her when the time comes for her to find a suitable spouse? There isn't a man alive who desires a wife who can't keep a proper house."

"Absolutely! Can you imagine a girl such as Reggie attempting to act as hostess for her father a few years from now? Why, the girl will have absolutely no idea how to handle herself in proper society. Watching her these past few weeks has been a painful experience," another woman commented.

Justin's jaw tightened as he listened to the women discussing his only child—the daughter he dearly loved and cherished beyond his wildest expectations. Their words cut like a knife, and a part of him longed to rush through the doors and tell them all that he cared little what they thought—that their scathing words were of no consequence to him or his daughter. Perhaps a good sermon on gossip and maligning others would be in order.

Yet, as Justin crept back to his office, he knew at least a portion of what he'd heard was correct. Reggie *did* need a woman's guidance in her life. He should have realized his failure to provide someone to teach Reggie social graces would lead to disastrous results. Without a sound, he closed the door behind him and settled into the oak spindle-backed chair.

"What do I do, Lord? I don't want a wife, but the child

needs a woman's hand in her life. Who among these women could help my Reggie?" he whispered into the silent room.

He stared out the office window at the grassy side yard, where the parishioners occasionally gathered for summertime picnics and festivities, and hoped he'd be given a divine answer to his query. This was one problem Justin didn't want to solve on his own, for if he knew nothing else, he knew his daughter. She *would* resist.

The sound of clattering footsteps and Reggie's voice startled Justin from his silent reverie.

"Guess what happened!" she shouted, her arms flapping up and down like an agitated chicken as she skidded to a halt in front of his desk.

Justin surveyed his young daughter. Her hair was unkempt, her clothing was soiled, and dirt smudged her forehead and both cheeks. He assessed the child as though she were a stranger and knew he needed an answer to his prayer—immediately.

"Did you hear me, Father? Guess what happened?"

"What?" he asked, forcing himself back to the present.

Reggie plopped down in the one remaining chair and folded her arms across her chest. "Spencer is leaving. His grandpa and uncles died, and now his family has to go somewhere down south to pick and hoe cotton. Isn't that terrible? I wouldn't want to hoe cotton. Do you think Spencer could come and live with us? I don't want him to leave. He and Moses are the only friends I have in Lowell." She sat up straighter. "I told him we'd come and talk to his mother and see if she'd let him stay with us. What do you think? He wouldn't eat too much, and he doesn't get into trouble very often. Do you think we could?" she asked, her questions tumbling out in rapid succession.

"No, Reggie, we couldn't do such a thing. First of all, Spencer's parents are not going to leave him in Lowell if they're moving down south; second, I don't think Spencer or any other member of their family will be hoeing cotton; and third, we aren't going to go and talk to Mr. and Mrs. Houston. I am truly sorry your friend must leave, but this is none of our business."

"But, Father, I promised."

"You should have come and talked to me prior to making such promises," he admonished quietly.

She tucked one leg beneath her and wrinkled her nose. "Won't you at least talk to his mother?"

"Put your leg down, Reggie. That's a very unladylike position," he instructed. "If Mrs. Houston wishes to discuss Spencer's future with me, I'm quite sure she'll stop by the house."

"Why does it matter if I sit like a lady? You never cared before."

"Well, I should have. I've gone far too long without correcting your behavior."

She frowned and jumped up from the chair. "I'm going home," she announced, darting from the room and headlong into Mrs. Sanders, who was standing directly outside Justin's office with the other members of the Ladies' Aid Society.

"Why, Regina, how pleasant to see you. Have you been enjoying the cake Rachel baked for you and your father?"

Reggie hesitated for only a moment. "We didn't eat it. I sold it instead."

Mrs. Sanders gasped, obviously taken aback by the girl's forthright reply.

"I got twenty-five cents," she proudly announced. "Mr. Parker was going to give me only ten cents until I told him it was for the church benevolence fund, so he decided to give me an extra fifteen cents."

"You *lied* to him?" Mrs. Sanders directed a condemnatory glare into the preacher's office.

"No, Mrs. Sanders, she did not lie. She has donated all of the money toward the benevolence fund. Quite frankly, I thought it a better idea than letting the desserts go uneaten," Justin said. "After all, we are only two people and you all had been so very generous with your gifts."

With a downward glance, Mrs. Sanders sputtered an apology to the preacher and then busied herself searching her reticule for some unknown object.

"I thank you for your words of regret, Mrs. Sanders, but I believe it's Regina, not I, that you've affronted," Justin said as he took hold of his daughter and gently moved her until she was standing directly in front of him. With his hands resting upon Reggie's shoulders, Justin met Mrs. Sanders's embarrassed gaze. "I'm certain you'd like to offer Reggie your apology."

CHAPTER · 4

MCKINLEY WAINWRIGHT paced back and forth in front of the Lowell railroad depot, straining to his full height as he peered down Merrimack Street before turning his attention to Dutton Street.

His lips curved into an unconvincing smile as he stopped beside Mr. Forbes. "Mr. Cheever should be arriving at any moment."

Jarrod Forbes removed his spectacles and wiped them with his handkerchief. "So you've told me—twice now. The sun is much too bright for my liking. I'll wait for you and Mr. Cheever inside the depot," he said before glancing toward the sound of a shrill whistle in the distance. "Sounds as though the train should be arriving soon also."

Mr. Forbes leaned heavily upon his cane and hobbled off to the doorway of the depot. Matthew was seldom late, and McKinley began to worry that an emergency had occurred at one of the mills. He hesitated, attempting to decide if he should send one of the boys running to the mills. The train shrieked an earsplitting whistle, and McKinley motioned to a young lad. He'd just completed his instructions to the boy when he saw Matthew's carriage round the corner.

"I won't need your assistance after all. Mr. Cheever is approaching," he said, tossing the boy a coin.

"Thank you, sir," the boy said as he caught the coin and then tucked it into his pocket.

"I was growing concerned," McKinley said as his father-in-law stepped down from the carriage with his case in hand.

Matthew waved his driver on and then strode alongside McKinley. "I thought I had all of the contracts assembled, but after reviewing them this morning, I realized several were missing. I was required to stop at the mill on my way. Finding the remaining documents proved more time-consuming than I had anticipated. Where's Forbes?"

"He's waiting inside the depot. He was determined to be on the train, even if neither of us accompanied him," McKinley replied.

Matthew laughed. "Likely he's concerned about all that shopping he must accomplish in Boston before his departure."

"How wonderful it must be to have nothing more pressing than the purchase of a few trinkets weighing upon one's mind," McKinley said as they entered the depot.

"Pleased to see you made it in time for our departure," Mr. Forbes said as Matthew stepped forward and grasped the older man's hand. "I began to fear you wouldn't make it."

"I wouldn't miss an important meeting with the Association. As I told McKinley, I was delayed by a few misplaced contracts but have managed to set everything right."

"Then let us board," Forbes declared, suddenly seeming to have gained new momentum.

The three men boarded the train and settled into their seats. The train had barely pulled away from the station when Jarrod Forbes nodded off to sleep.

"Doesn't appear as though we'll be having much discussion with Mr. Forbes on the way to Boston," Matthew commented while giving the older man a sidelong glance.

McKinley grinned and nodded in agreement.

"How has my daughter reacted to all this news regarding the plantation?" Matthew asked. "Her mother tells me Violet appeared somewhat withdrawn when they visited yesterday. Yet when Lilly questioned her, she wasn't forthcoming."

"She's distraught. I've attempted to reassure Violet that I will not go to Mississippi, but I think she fears I'll relent if Jasmine becomes more forceful."

Matthew leaned back against the seat and closed his eyes for a moment. "Quite frankly, I don't believe this entire ordeal should rest upon Jasmine's shoulders, especially if you want to share in the proceeds of your father's estate," he said rather sternly.

"What? You think I should leave Violet—in her condition and after her difficulty? I question whether your daughter would ever fully recover if she lost another child. And there's my position with the Corporation to consider. Besides, I know nothing about harvesting a cotton crop."

Matthew rubbed his fingertips across the deep creases that lined his forehead. "It's entirely your decision. I'm pleased that you've put your love for Violet and the unborn child first. However, Violet mentioned the fact that you expect to receive your full share from your father's estate. Jasmine and Nolan have much at stake in this matter also, and I'm surprised they would agree to take on full responsibility. Leaving their horses and business to the care of others could prove very risky for them—and you can be sure they question their own ability to harvest a crop."

"Then you think I should go?"

"I find more fault with your ultimatum regarding the inheritance than in your decision to remain in Lowell. You might find spending some time in prayer to be beneficial . . . and you might want to say a word of thanks for your sister while you're at it."

McKinley stared out the train window and contemplated Matthew's words. Perhaps his decision had been hastily made. Yet the thought of going to Mississippi was out of the question. Instead, he would offer to assist Paddy and the other folks whom Nolan would leave in charge of his holdings. To make this issue a matter of prayer, however, would be impossible. Though he knew his stance regarding the inheritance was selfish, he would not accept less than the share allotted him in the terms of his father's will. After all, as the only remaining son, he could have contested Jasmine's inheritance. Besides, he *needed* the additional funds! The downward turn in the economy during the past few years had taken a heavy toll on his investments, which was a fact he did not wish to discuss with his father-in-law.

McKinley tried not to linger long on the topic. Thinking about the plantation made him remember his father and the conflicts they'd had over his own decision to remain in the North. He knew his father never fully agreed with his decision. Nor could Malcolm Wainwright ever fully understand McKinley's hatred of slavery. He could almost hear his father's protests, even now.

"But you benefited every day of your life from the work of our slaves," his father had once argued. *"How can you turn away from all that I offer? How can you turn away from your home?"*

And indeed McKinley had struggled at times with that decision. There were moments when he remembered the sweet smell of honeysuckle as it drifted on the evening air. He remembered the parties and family gatherings. He had, when young, imagined himself quite happily settled with his own plantation and slaves.

I'm sorry, Father. How could I explain to you what I never quite fully understood myself?

The train came to a jerking halt at the Boston railroad station and ended his musings, at least for the moment. Nathan Appleton's carriage awaited them outside the depot, and within a short time, the three men were delivered to the front door of the Appleton home, where Nathan personally greeted them.

"A pleasure to meet you, Mr. Forbes. I do wish it were under different circumstances," Nathan said as he led them into his library. "Many of the Associates are traveling abroad for the summer, but most of them will return to America in the next two weeks. Let me introduce you to the members who are able to be in attendance."

Nathan quickly made the introductions and invited the men to be seated. "I trust you've heard the latest financial news," he said with a worried look in his eyes.

"I've heard nothing of interest. Is something amiss with the Corporation?" Matthew inquired.

"We received word yesterday that the New York branch of the Ohio Life Insurance and Trust Company has failed. It appears the insolvency was caused by a massive embezzlement of railroad bonds, which will, of course, leave enormous debts," Nathan explained.

Wilson Harper mopped the perspiration from his forehead. "New York bankers restricted all routine transactions immediately. We've heard that investors who held stock and commercial paper immediately rushed to make deals with their brokers. The telegraph we received this morning says that stocks fell ten percent in one day. Fortunes are being lost overnight. Terrible! Terrible!" Harper said, shaking his head back and forth.

"The banks wouldn't honor routine transactions? Why?" McKinley asked, his fear mounting at this turn of events.

"All their depositors wanted payment in gold; however, the bankers knew they couldn't meet the demand until the expected gold shipment arrived from San Francisco. They announced their gold shipment is due by mid-September. I believe they gave the anticipated date in order to allay the fears of their depositors, but I'm not certain it's been successful. I'm hoping panic doesn't spread to Boston, yet we likely need to withdraw some of the Corporation's funds in the event there's a nationwide collapse."

"I doubt that's going to occur. This country is economically sound, don't you think?" McKinley inquired in a hopeful voice.

Josiah Baines glanced around the room. "You were but a child when the economic crisis hit in 1839, but those of us who struggled through that time haven't forgotten. I learned many a lesson then, which is the *only* good thing I can say about that period in my life."

"True! I think the most important thing I discovered was to diversify my holdings and always retain a fair sum of gold," Thomas Clayborn commented.

"So long as you don't put your gold in the bank," Wilson said with a hearty laugh.

Josiah and the other men nodded in agreement before Nathan once again took control of the group. "Mr. Forbes, why don't you tell us some *good* news? I think we would all appreciate an encouraging word."

Jarrod Forbes glanced toward McKinley and Matthew before addressing the men. "I doubt you'll consider what I have to say good news. However, it could be much worse," he began.

The Associates listened attentively. However, McKinley noted that each of them had paled a bit by the time Mr. Forbes finished his report.

"We are truly sorry for your loss, McKinley. I know this

must be a terrible blow for you," Nathan said. "Please be assured that if you are needed in Mississippi, we will make every attempt to accommodate you. We would be willing to secure your position on an unpaid basis for as long as necessary to close the estate."

"Thank you, but arrangements have already been made. My sister and her husband will soon depart in order to oversee the cotton harvest and sell the plantation," McKinley replied, careful to avoid eye contact with his father-in-law.

"I don't want to appear insensitive to your loss, McKinley, but I'm wondering if the plantation can be sold with an assignation of the contract we had with Malcolm?" Wilson Harper inquired.

Jarrod Forbes cleared his throat. "I believe I can answer that question. Malcolm placed a proviso in his will that if his heirs made a decision to sell the plantation—and he was confident they would—they were instructed to use due diligence in seeking a buyer who would enthusiastically embrace the fulfillment of his contractual obligation with the Boston Associates."

"I might add that any buyer would be foolish to look elsewhere," McKinley said. "The Associates have always been generous in dealing with the cotton growers."

Wilson nodded. "However, some may view the purchase as an opportunity to renegotiate. Such a possibility could eventually lead to a breakdown with the other growers. I'm not attempting to create problems, merely hoping we won't be blindsided by a sale."

"Of course, you understand that Mr. and Mrs. Houston are going to The Willows at great hardship to themselves and their young family," Matthew Cheever said. "I don't think anyone can expect them to be overly concerned about the ongoing contracts. They are, after all, in the horse business. The sale of cotton to the Associates in no way affects their future, and I don't believe we can have any expectation in that regard."

"Yes, of course," Josiah agreed. "However, if Malcolm made mention in his will, I believe his daughter will want to respect her father's dying wishes. Coupled with the news regarding the embezzlement scandal, this turn of events comes as a double blow. Do we know how many of our contracts were affected by the epidemic?"

Jarrod Forbes raised his eyebrows. "To some extent, all of them. However, the Louisiana plantations didn't suffer much damage. Most of them lost only a few slaves or possibly a family member, while the Mississippi plantations lost entire families and large numbers of their slaves." He leaned forward. "As you know, the cotton harvest will soon begin in earnest. Once I return home, I'll be able to supply you with a better estimate of what you may expect."

"In the meantime, since we already have a meeting scheduled for the third week in September, I believe there's little we can accomplish at the moment," Nathan said. "Matthew, if you would spend some time reviewing the contracts and prepare a report as to the amount of cotton we have on hand, I believe it would be helpful. And Mr. Forbes, once you return home, any additional information you can supply will be appreciated. Please assure the plantation owners we are aware of their circumstances and will make adjustments as necessary. We can always look to foreign markets if necessary."

"Please don't move in that direction too quickly," Forbes said. "After all, with the news I've heard today, it appears that if we're to keep this country from another depression, we must conduct business within our own borders."

Nathan shifted in his chair. "I agree—whenever possible."

"And profitable," Wilson muttered.

McKinley watched Jarrod Forbes for a reaction. It didn't appear as if he'd heard Wilson Harper's rejoinder, yet McKinley knew that the remark was the mantra of the Associates. As long as the ledger was showing a marked profit, they would continue doing business with the Southern growers. But if the foreign markets could compete by producing cotton at a lower price and of equal quality, the Associates would have no loyalty to their Southern brothers. And that argument would be McKinley's defense should his father-in-law attempt to convince him he should go to the South to assist in protecting the cotton contract with the sale of The Willows.

———————

Jasmine opened the top center drawer of Nolan's desk and retrieved the letter Jarrod Forbes had given her on the day of his arrival in Lowell. The edging of her lilac print day dress caught on the drawer and snagged a small hole in the fine lace. She would mend it this evening. But for now she wanted once again to read the missive. Although she had already examined the contents of the letter many times, reading her father's message soothed her. The neatly scripted words connected her to those last days before his death, providing her with a window into his final thoughts and concerns.

After carefully unfolding the letter and pressing the creases flat, Jasmine permitted herself to focus upon the final words from her father.

My dear daughter Jasmine,
It is with a sad heart that I commit to paper my final thoughts. You have been my heart's delight—a daughter any man would be proud to call his own. I don't discount that we've had our disagreements from time to time, but such is to be expected in the course of rearing a child.

Now my life on this earth is drawing to an end, and I find it difficult to say the many things I wish I had said to you throughout the years. Please know that I am proud of the woman you have become and the strength you have exhibited in difficult times. It grieves me that I must now place yet another burden upon you, but you will have Nolan and McKinley at your side as you accomplish the task of settling my estate.

I trust you will be judicious in handling the bequest you will receive upon my death. It has taken our family a lifetime to amass these holdings. Therefore, I pray you and your brother will be good stewards of this bounty. Obviously, it will be imperative that you and McKinley come to The Willows and oversee the final harvest. I am not disillusioned by any thoughts that you or McKinley will return and make your home within these walls, but I trust you will both make every effort to secure a good price for the cotton and exercise due diligence in locating a purchaser who will cherish this land as I have.

Jasmine refolded the page. There was no need to read further—she'd nearly committed the letter to memory. Had her father truly believed McKinley would leave his position with the Corporation and travel to The Willows?

"So here you are, my dear," Nolan said as he took three giant strides across the expanse from the doorway to her chair and kissed the top of her head. "I thought perhaps you'd gone off to town without telling anyone."

She laughed at his comment. "I think Alice Ann or Clara would fuss loudly enough to alert the entire household if I attempted to leave."

He glanced at the folded letter. "Rereading your father's missive again?"

She nodded and gave him a feeble smile. "I read his words and feel compelled to do as he's requested, yet my anger toward McKinley won't subside. I understand his concerns over Violet and his position at the Corporation, but he acts as though none of this poses any imposition upon our family."

Nolan sat down, giving her his undivided attention. "Your brother may project that attitude, but he knows how difficult leaving Lowell will be for us. He realizes the responsibilities we have."

"If so, he hasn't indicated as much to me."

"I imagine he's dealing with a hefty portion of guilt. After all, I'm certain your father's words to McKinley were very explicit—just as they were to you. We must accept his choice."

"I've accepted his decision, but I don't respect it."

Nolan reached forward and with one finger tipped Jasmine's chin upward until he was looking into her eyes. "As long as you continue to respect your brother, you need not like his decision. Don't judge him too harshly, my love, for if I were forced to decide between my wife and my father's estate, I'd most definitely choose you. Remember, I did not always have anything to do with my family business. I disappointed my father at every turn. My brother was the one he depended on."

"And Bradley could see nothing but business," she murmured. "There ought to be a balance. Must a man choose only one or the other?"

Before he could respond, Spencer walked into the room. His lips were tightened into an angry pout, and there was a stubborn look in his eyes. "What if I live with Reggie and her father?" he asked.

A moment passed before Jasmine could completely digest what her son was requesting. "You want your father and me to leave you in the care of Pastor Chamberlain while we travel to Mississippi?"

Apparently Spencer interpreted her calm response to

mean she might actually acquiesce, for the sullen look in his eyes was now replaced by a hopeful glimmer.

"Your father and I could list a host of reasons why such an idea is completely out of the question. However, suffice it to say that you may not remain in the care of Pastor Chamberlain. You, Alice Ann, and Clara will accompany us to The Willows."

The sparkle disappeared from his eyes. "If I can't stay with them, then let me stay here at the house. The servants can look after me," he countered.

"I've already told you we will not leave you here. Besides, the only servants who don't go to their own homes every night are Martha and Henrietta, and they'll be traveling with us. Please don't make any other suggestions, Spencer—you'll only be further disappointed by our answer."

"Poppa," he said, turning his pleading face to his father.

Jasmine could see the wavering look in Nolan's eyes. They had discussed this matter at length. She knew Nolan wanted to concede—tell the boy he could remain in Simon and Maisie's care, where he and Moses could begin the school year as scheduled. But he had finally agreed they ought not divide their family. Spencer belonged with them. If need be, she argued, they could hire a tutor or Spencer could attend school in Lorman. They both knew he'd be unhappy, but they were family and Jasmine was determined they remain together.

"I'm afraid we can't grant your request this time, son," Nolan said. "Try to view this as a grand adventure. You'll have opportunities to see new things and meet new people. Moreover, this may be the final time you'll have an opportunity to visit The Willows."

Spencer turned and marched from the room without another word.

"You see!" she said, jumping up from her chair and slapping the letter onto her husband's desk. "This situation is going to destroy our family while McKinley will continue with life as usual. Yesterday Spencer hid in the woods behind the barns and sent Moses to tell me he'd run away; today he's plotting to live with Pastor Chamberlain and his daughter at the Congregational parsonage! Who can guess what tomorrow will bring."

Nolan raked his fingers through his thick hair. "I believe if we're to survive this, it's going to take a lot of prayer and a sense of humor. I'm planning to spend time with Paddy regarding the contracts that must be fulfilled while we're gone."

Jasmine sighed. "We have much to lose if anything goes amiss with our West Point contracts."

"And the new ones with the Virginia Institute. I'm thankful I insisted Paddy be involved throughout the negotiations with both schools. He knows many of the details, and although he's young, he's become an astute businessman. I don't believe anyone will take advantage of him," he added before moving to the far side of his desk.

"You remain convinced that we must travel by train?" she inquired while watching her husband unlock the bottom drawer of his desk.

Nolan pulled a thick folder from the drawer and dropped it with a gentle thud. "If we're going to arrive in time to oversee the harvest, traveling by train will be the most expeditious. Of course, we'll be required to travel the portion into Lorman by boat," he explained.

"I was thinking it would be much more comfortable for the children if we traveled by ship rather than train, but you're correct—time must control our decisions."

Nolan's fingers rippled through the pages, his attention on the folder of papers, and Jasmine knew his thoughts were now fixed upon the vital contracts they must fulfill during the next year.

———————

Paddy ran his skilled hands down the leg of one of the Houston farm's finest Arabians. The animal was one of their best, and Paddy thought he had noticed a faint limp as one of the stable hands had led the animal to the barn a short time ago. The last thing they wanted was one of their top studs developing any problems. The horse farm prided itself upon the stellar care and the resulting excellent stock bred and raised on their premises. And even though large fees had been offered from time to time, Nolan refused to have their horses used for breeding purposes at any other farm.

"I'll not have others diminish the value or beauty of our horses by breeding them with animals of a lesser quality. The money offered pales in comparison to the damage that would result from poor breeding," Nolan had maintained when Paddy had asked why he would turn down such a large amount of money.

Paddy's respect for his employer had continued to grow through the years. His childhood of hardship and suffering in Ireland seemed to diminish a little more every day. Sometimes when he talked with his sister, Kiara, he would remember bits and pieces of the past, but for the most part, he kept those thoughts tucked away where they couldn't hurt him. Life was good here in America. Paddy knew that. He heard the stories of oppression that came with each new Irishman to Lowell. Times hadn't changed in his homeland. The famine might have passed, but landlords were still cruel and the government was neglectful. Paddy wondered in all honesty if anything good could ever come to Ireland.

He shook off the thought. His life was in America—not Ireland. With the passing of time, Nolan had increased

Paddy's duties and drawn him into every aspect of the business. Nolan had given Paddy opportunities to observe negotiations and discussions to purchase and sell the horses, acquire ancillary land, and help plan the new facilities being constructed for the additional horses. Yes, Nolan Houston was a man of honor and intelligence, and Paddy counted himself fortunate to be in his employ.

"Is there a problem with Glory's Pride?"

Paddy started at the sound of Nolan's voice. "I did na hear you come in the barn, Mr. Houston. I thought I saw him limpin' a wee bit this mornin', but it appears my worries are unfounded."

Nolan frowned and moved into the stall. "I'm not doubting your assessment, but let's move him out of the stall and take a look."

"Right ya are," Paddy said as he led the horse out of the enclosure and walked him out the barn doors.

Nolan remained at a distance, watching the horse as Paddy led him in a wide circle. "I can saddle and mount him if ya like," Paddy called.

"No. I believe he looks fine. Probably only a rock in his shoe that's worked itself loose, but you might keep an eye on him. If you notice he's having problems after we're gone, have the blacksmith take a look at him."

"Don't ya be worryin'. I'll take good care of this big boy," Paddy said proudly as he patted the horse.

Nolan nodded. "If it weren't for you, I'd be hard-pressed to leave the farm, but I put great faith in you and your ability, Paddy. I'm leaving you with a great deal of responsibility, but you know we'll see that you're properly rewarded."

"Go on with ya, Mr. Houston. You and the missus already pay me more than a fair wage. Truth is, I should be paying *you* for the privilege of workin' with these fine animals."

"You'll be required to do even more while we're gone, Paddy, and if you have some time, I'd like to go over these contracts with you. Once we've discussed all of your additional duties, I doubt you'll turn down the additional wages."

"I'll be with ya as soon as I get Glory's Pride back in his stall," Paddy said as he led the horse back into the barn.

The day was warm, and the smells of hay and silage mixed with the pungent odor of the celebrated Arabians stabled inside the barn. In early spring, the farmhands had erected a crude table from old boards and sawhorses and placed it under a large elm not far from the barn. Then on days when the weather permitted, they would join together for their noonday meal around the table, sharing stories and laughing as they ate their thick slices of soda or rye bread with cheese and drank cool water from the nearby spring.

Nolan had settled himself on one of the makeshift benches and was spreading out papers across the table as Paddy drew near.

"Ya best be hopin' a breeze does na come whistlin' through the trees and send those papers flyin' about the countryside," he said with a twinkle in his dark brown eyes.

Nolan laughed but heeded the remark, placing a smooth gray rock atop one stack of papers and his hand upon the other. "I've arranged the paper work into what I hope is an intelligible order. The contracts and other documents regarding the horses that are being sold to both West Point and the Virginia Institute are in this group. I've also included the authentication papers for each of the horses. Everything is set up exactly as I've handled it in the past, so there should be no problem. You will receive a bank draft from each of the institutions as set out in their individual contracts—I've prepared a separate sheet in the ledger for you to make the accounting, and I've talked with Mr. Cameron at the bank."

Paddy ran a finger down the list of instructions and

pulled the ledger book closer. "I understand. And all I need ta do is give the draft to Mr. Cameron? Will he na be givin' me a statement of receipt for the funds?"

"Indeed he will," Nolan said, pleased by Paddy's astute question.

"And what do the gentlemen sign showing they've received their horses?"

Nolan shuffled through the papers. "This paper is what they're to sign. And if you feel uncomfortable for any reason, you can ask the men to accompany you to the bank, and Mr. Cameron will assist you in completing the paper work. In fact, if you have any financial needs, you can rely upon Albert Cameron. However, I have great faith in you, Paddy, and don't think you'll have any problem at all. I'll leave these papers in the bottom drawer of my desk, and before we depart, I'll give you the key."

Paddy pushed the dark mass of curls off his forehead and stared at Nolan. Had the man gone completely daft?

"Ya're gonna give *me* the key to your desk?"

Nolan laughed and pushed away from the wobbly table. "I trust you with the horseflesh in that barn. Those Arabian Shagyas are far more valuable than anything in my desk, Paddy. There are other matters we'll need to discuss before my departure, and you'll likely think of additional questions for me, but I wanted you to know that I have every confidence that you can handle the business in my absence."

"Thank ya, Mr. Houston. I'm honored to be helpin' ya."

Paddy swiped his hand down the leg of his breeches before shaking hands with his employer, then hastened into the barn as Nolan strode off toward the house. Grabbing a brush, he walked into a stall and began grooming Fiona's Fancy, an exceptional sorrel Shagya that he'd always considered one of their finest animals. With a smile on his face, he ran the brush through the horse's thick coat and began singing the old Irish lullaby Kiara had sung to him when he was a young ailing boy back in Ireland. It was the one piece of Ireland he couldn't seem to shake.

Kiara stood with her hands on her hips in a mock display of anger. "Will ya look who's finally able to darken me doorway? I do ya the honor of offering ya a good home-cooked meal, and ya can na even show up on time," she scolded.

Rogan pointed a thumb at his wife while directing his attention at his brother-in-law. "I think yar sister is a wee bit upset with ya," Rogan said with a wide grin.

"It's been quite the day, what with the Houstons planning to depart within the week. I had to have me a chat with Mr. Houston, and then I got busy with the horses," Paddy explained.

"Don't be tryin' to soften me up with yar excuses, Paddy O'Neill. Sit yarself down while I tell Nevan and Katherine to wash up for supper. We're nearly starvin' to death waitin' on ya," Kiara said as she removed her apron.

Paddy embraced his sister and laughed. "Ya do na look to me like ya're starving to death."

Kiara laughed and slapped his arm with the apron. "Do na forget, I'm eating for two." She pulled loose and marched out of the room.

"Do ya think she's truly upset that I'm late?" Paddy asked as he and Rogan sat down at the table.

Rogan shook his head back and forth. "She's thinkin' Bridgett will be comin' and she won't have the dishes washed before she arrives. I told her to quit her frettin', that she could have little Katherine or Nevan wash the dishes. Somehow she did na think havin' our four-year-old daughter or seven-year-old son washin' her best dishes was a good idea."

"Then it may be up to me since I'm the one who was late. Of course, I do na think she'll entrust her dishes to me either," Paddy said with a laugh.

"Oh, but I will," Kiara said as she walked into the room. "Ya best be hopin' Bridgett is tardy also!"

"Uncle Paddy!" the children hollered in unison.

Paddy stood to hug his niece and nephew and then quickly directed them to their chairs. "We must eat with the greatest of speed tonight," he told them. "Perhaps we should have a contest to see who can eat the fastest."

"Stop that nonsense or they'll be choking down their food, thinkin' it's the proper thing to do," Kiara warned. "Just remember, ya're still my *little* brother—I'm sure I can find a proper punishment if ya're gonna misbehave."

Nevan and Katherine peeked at him from beneath their thick dark lashes, a smile dancing upon Nevan's lips.

"Ya're pleased it's me instead of yarself that yar mother's givin' a tongue lashin', aren't ya?" Paddy asked with an exaggerated wink.

"Aye and ya best be careful or she'll yank yar ear if ya do not mind yar manners," Nevan replied. Although he spoke with the same Irish brogue of his ancestors, Nevan's American birth toned the drawl down quite a bit. Paddy thought he almost sounded comical, but would never have told the boy such a thing.

Katherine bobbed her head. "And Nevan should know best about that. Ma says he has the manners of the pigs sloppin' at the trough."

Paddy's and Rogan's merry laughs and the smell of Kiara's tantalizing meat pie filled the room. "I fixed the special butter sauce ya like on yar meat pie," Kiara said to Paddy.

His nose tilted heavenward, and he inhaled deeply like a dog sniffing its prey. "And is that yar special sweet peas with mint?" He eyed the covered serving dish as she placed it in front of him.

"Aye—and mushrooms in cream sauce," she added, nodding toward another bowl.

He rubbed his hands together. "I can hardly wait to begin."

"Not until we give thanks," Kiara warned as she sat down.

The five of them joined hands and Rogan led them in prayer—less eloquent and briefer than Kiara would probably have liked but nonetheless duly thankful for the food that God had provided and Kiara had superbly prepared. Paddy added a hasty amen to the prayer and immediately spooned a generous serving of mushrooms onto his plate.

"So when do ya think the Houstons will be returnin'?" Rogan inquired.

"Hard tellin'," Paddy replied after swallowing a forkful of the meat pie. "This is mighty good," he said, using his fork to point at the dish.

Kiara smiled and nodded. "So Mr. Houston's plannin' to leave you in charge of the horses while he's gone?"

Paddy's chest swelled with pride. "Aye. And he told Mr. Cameron at the bank that he's to deal directly with me. And he gave me the key to his desk."

"It's proud I am of ya, Paddy," she said. "But I'm *still* not excusin' ya for being late to supper."

The children giggled at their mother's retort, and Paddy winked at them. The two of them were a delight—with dark lashes that matched their tawny brown curls and eyes the soft brown shade of a hazelnut. Katherine possessed her mother's lovely face and kind disposition, while Nevan was brave and puckish like his father.

Katherine leaned close to Paddy, her chubby cheeks made even fuller by her wide smile. "We're havin' nut cake for dessert," she whispered to her uncle with a gleam in her eyes.

"And were ya thinkin' ya might want to have yar uncle Paddy eat yar piece?" Paddy asked in a hushed voice.

Katherine rubbed her tummy while wagging her head back and forth. "I have enough room for me cake."

Rogan laughed and ruffled Katherine's hair. "Ya'll have yar share of trouble gettin' sweets away from this one, Paddy."

They finished their supper, and while Kiara cleared and washed the dishes, the men settled on the front porch and watched as Nevan and Katherine attempted to capture fireflies in the front yard.

"Looks like that's me cousin Bridgett headin' this direction," Rogan said, using his pipe as a pointer, a curl of smoke rising from it.

"And who's that with her?" Paddy asked.

Rogan shook his head and squinted. "I do na think I know the lass," he replied as Kiara stepped out the door and joined them on the porch.

"Bridgett said she might be bringin' along one of the girls from work," Kiara informed her husband and brother.

"Does she attend St. Patrick's?" Rogan asked.

"I do na know. She's new to Lowell and to the mills. I think Bridgett has taken a likin' to her."

Paddy watched from the porch as the twosome drew closer. Bridgett was gesturing wildly, and her lips were moving as rapidly as water pouring over the falls. Except for aging a bit, Bridgett hadn't changed much since Paddy and Kiara had first met her aboard the ship on their voyage to America. Bridgett, with her auburn hair and fiery temper, had been delighted when she learned Paddy and Kiara were traveling to the same town in Massachusetts. The three of them had been shipmates and then journeyed on to Lowell, where Bridgett moved into the Acre with Rogan and her granna Murphy, and Kiara and Paddy headed off in another direction to become indentured servants.

"It seems a lifetime ago since we first met Bridgett . . . and yet only yesterday," Paddy said to his sister.

"Aye, yet I'm happy to be livin' in the present and not the past."

Paddy nodded knowingly. "I hear Bridgett has finally got herself engaged."

"I'm makin' her weddin' veil and the lace for her gown," Kiara said. "She's wantin' to take a wee look at what I've got finished."

"A wee look? The last time me cousin came for a wee look, she was here for three hours," Rogan said with a hearty laugh. "So if there's any talkin' ya're wantin' to do with yar sister, ya best be speakin' up in a hurry."

Bridgett waved as she and her friend turned onto the flower-lined path leading to the front steps. "Sounds as though ya're havin' a merry time. We could hear ya laughin' a half-mile away."

"Do na be telling a fib afore ya ever reach the front door, Bridgett Farrell," Rogan called out to his cousin.

"'Tis the truth I'm speakin' and ya know it fer certain," Bridgett said as she reached the front porch. "This is me friend, Mary Margaret O'Flannery. She's na yet been given her own looms, but she's training with me at the mill. Mr. Dempsey's been watchin' her, and he said she'd likely be on her own in another week," Bridgett announced, beaming at her new friend. "Mary Margaret, this is me cousin Rogan Sheehan and his wife, Kiara. This fine-lookin' lad is Kiara's brother, Padraig O'Neill. And the two lovelies out there catchin' fireflies are Nevan and Katherine."

"Pleased to make yar acquaintance," Kiara said while the others echoed. "Perhaps we can sit out here where it's a wee bit cooler than in the house."

Paddy watched as Mary Margaret sat down beside Bridgett on the carved wooden bench. She was a pretty lass, with long, slender fingers as creamy and white as a piece of ivory and thick auburn hair that had been fashioned into a braid and coiled atop her head.

"Do ya find the mills to be to yar likin', Mary Margaret?" Rogan asked.

"Aye. 'Tis true it's hot and humid inside the mills, but the pay is good, and if I get me own looms, I won't be complainin' about conditions. Bridgett tells me ya're a stone carver."

"Aye. Liam Donohue taught me the trade, and he's a far better carver. But together we're managin' a fine business."

"I took her through the cemetery on our way here," Bridgett put in, "and showed her the headstones you and Liam have carved with the shamrocks."

Rogan laughed. "And did ya show her the ones carved by the Yankees? They tried to carve shamrocks, but their shamrocks turned out lookin' more like trees. Back then, the Yanks had na seen what a shamrock looked like—but at least they tried to engrave somethin' that resembled one."

"And what do ya think of Lowell?" Kiara inquired. "Are ya findin' it altogether fine?"

"'Tis nice enough, I suppose."

At least ten questions popped into Paddy's head that he wanted to ask Miss Mary Margaret O'Flannery, but before he'd had a chance to ask even one, Bridgett called a halt to the visiting and insisted that the ladies go inside.

"I'm thinkin' it might be cool enough to step inside for a few minutes," she said. "It's anxious I am to be seein' what ya've accomplished on my veil and the lace for my dress."

"It's anxious ya are to be *married*," Rogan retorted with a broad grin. "I think Granna Murphy was beginnin' to think she'd never see ya put yar bottom drawer of linens and finery to use."

"Stop with yar teasin'—I'm na yet thirty, and a good single man is na easy to find in these parts. And ya need na be worryin' yarself over my bottom drawer. Every last piece of my finery will be put to *good* use."

"Ya best keep that information in mind, Mary Margaret. It pays for a lass to keep a sharp eye for a good lad," Rogan said. He slapped a palm to his forehead. "In fact—ya might want to remember that Paddy is an upstanding lad who's still not found him a lass to call his own. Isn't that right, Paddy?"

Paddy felt the blood rush to his cheeks and shot a quick look at Mary Margaret, who had visibly blanched to the shade of pale parchment. Fearing the lass might faint, Paddy moved to her side and supported her with one arm.

"Ya need na pay Rogan any heed. The man enjoys causin' others discomfort. Let me help ya to a chair inside, and once ya sit down, I'll fetch ya a glass of cool water," Paddy said, leading her into the house.

Paddy glanced over his shoulder at Rogan as he escorted Mary Margaret inside. Rogan gave him an exaggerated wink. "Ya can thank me later," Rogan whispered loudly enough for all of them to hear. "If yar na havin' that weddin' too soon, Bridgett, maybe Paddy and Mary Margaret could join you and Cullen at the altar and have ya a double weddin'," he added with a loud guffaw.

Paddy gazed heavenward and wondered if the meat pie and nut cake he'd eaten only a short time ago were worth the embarrassment of the moment. And poor Mary Margaret—she'd not even had the pleasure of Kiara's cooking before being subjected to Rogan's torment!

Chapter · 5

THE WHITE COTTON curtains fluttered at the window as a breeze drifted into the kitchen of Elinor's boardinghouse. Although she'd mixed and set the bread dough to rise before the girls departed for the mills, the kitchen had already become uncomfortably warm when she finally placed the loaves in the oven. After wiping her hands on a linen towel, she removed her stained apron and tossed it atop the wooden worktable. If she hurried, she would have time to take a cool, damp cloth to her face and properly fashion her hair before the girls arrived for the noonday meal.

Unbraiding her hair as she walked down the hallway, she stopped short as a knock sounded at the door. Holding her unbridled tresses in one hand, she stared at the door. "Who could that be?" she muttered.

For a brief moment, she contemplated ignoring the unwelcome interruption but finally yielded. A new boarder might be standing on the other side of the door, and she could certainly use the additional funds. Still holding tightly to her loosened hair, she yanked the door open with her free hand. Her mouth went dry. Oh, why hadn't she ignored the knock?

Justin Chamberlain stood across the threshold, staring at her. His lips were moving, but the only sound that she heard was the roaring noise in her head. After his lips stopped moving, he smiled and waited.

Utterly embarrassed by her unkempt appearance, Elinor stood rooted to the floor, unable to speak. After all, what respectable woman would answer the door in such disarray? It wasn't until the pastor had turned and stepped down off the small stoop that she finally found her voice.

"Please! Wait! I apologize. I didn't expect to see you when I opened the door. I thought perhaps it was a boarder that had come looking for a room. I was going to my rooms to brush my hair. I don't usually wait until so late in the morning to prepare myself for the day," she hastily explained.

Her words flowed forth like a babbling brook, and Justin grinned as he returned. "I'm the one who should apologize. It was rude of me to appear on your doorstep without first inquiring when it would be convenient to come calling. However, I find myself in a dilemma. I've been praying for an answer to my problem and you came to mind. Not that you should . . . well, that is . . . consider yourself a-a . . . divine answer to my prayer and feel . . . well . . . compelled to fulfill my request," he hastened to add.

He was stammering and tripping over his words, and now Elinor smiled at him. "Come in, Pastor Chamberlain." She stepped back to allow him entry. "I promise I won't feel duty bound to carry out your request if you'll promise to overlook my untidy appearance,"

"You don't look untidy in the least."

The pastor was stretching the truth with his kind remark, but at least his words helped ease her self-consciousness. She directed him to the parlor and then said, "If you'll excuse me for one moment, I'll find a ribbon to tie back my hair; then I'll join you. Do be seated."

Moments later, Elinor rejoined the pastor, who, instead of sitting, was pacing back and forth in front of the faded settee. "You could quickly wear out a carpet with your pacing," she said lightheartedly. "How may I help you?"

Justin immediately ceased his pacing and sat down opposite her, hunching forward and resting his arms atop his thighs. Beads of perspiration dotted his forehead. The poor man appeared to be at a complete loss as to how he should begin speaking to her.

"Is there a committee at the church you need me to assist with?" she asked, hoping to aid him.

"No. In truth, this has nothing to do with the church. Things are going as well as can be expected. It's generally difficult when a congregation must adjust to a new preacher—and his daughter," he added.

"And even more difficult for the preacher and his daughter to adjust to a new community, I would guess."

"Not so difficult for me. I was ready for a change. But the move has been more challenging for Reggie."

"Most people say that children easily adapt to change, and I suppose to some extent that is true. But for some it proves a difficult task. Reggie is a charming young lady, and eventually she will find her niche here in Lowell. You must give her time."

Justin appeared to relax and settled his weight against the back of the cushioned chair. "Reggie is the reason I've come to speak with you." His voice cracked.

"There is some problem? Has she taken ill?"

"No, nothing so easily solved as a visit to the doctor," he replied. "This matter is a bit more complex. When you visited the parsonage with Reggie, you may have noticed the house was rather sparsely furnished."

"Well, yes, but Reggie told me the remainder of your household goods were in Maine and that you would be going back to retrieve them before summer's end."

"Exactly—and therein lies my problem. I should have returned to Maine before now, but the timing never seemed proper. And now school will soon begin. I must go after our belongings before winter sets in, yet I don't want Reggie to miss school, especially the beginning of the school year. I fear that being gone when school begins will only make her adjustment more difficult."

Elinor tucked an errant strand of hair behind one ear. "I agree."

They stared at each other for a moment, and Elinor suddenly realized the preacher's dilemma. "You want Reggie to live here at the boardinghouse while you go to Maine?"

"I know it's a great deal to ask, what with all your other responsibilities here at the boardinghouse and throughout the community. Preparing a little girl for school each morning when you're already busy cooking three substantial meals for your boarders and . . ." His voice trailed off.

She tapped her finger across her lips and thought for a moment. "Do you think it might be more suitable to have Reggie live with someone who has children—perhaps a girl her own age?"

"I truly understand your reluctance to take on such a responsibility," he said.

"I'm not averse to the arrangement; I was merely wondering if your daughter would be happier and adjust more easily if she were with other children."

Justin folded his hands and met her gaze. "You went fishing with Reggie, and she tells me she's stopped by on a couple of occasions to visit you."

Elinor nodded.

"Then I'm certain you realize Reggie is not a child who

makes friends with other young ladies—she's not a girl who fancies learning how to set a proper table or dress in the latest fashions. She likely would choose to stay with the Houston family, but they've already departed Lowell. Besides, I probably would not have made such a request of folks who aren't members of the church. To do such a thing would surely have caused tongues to wag," he said with a weary expression.

"Having difficulty with a few of our opinionated church members, Pastor?" She smiled.

"Some of the good ladies of the church think Reggie lacks the proper social graces. And I must admit they are probably correct. I hadn't given much thought to the fact that she's growing up and some of her behavior is inappropriate for a young lady."

Elinor brushed a smudge of flour from the skirt of her utilitarian gray cotton dress. "Don't permit Martha Emory or Nancy Sanders to force their rigid standards upon you. Childhood is precious. Reggie has ample time to learn the etiquette of a proper young lady. She'll develop an interest when the time is right for her."

"I suppose you're correct, but Reggie can be quite a handful from time to time."

"Are you attempting to convince me I should tell you no?" she asked with a broad smile.

"No, not at all. Yet I don't want to . . . well, take ad-advantage of you, as I know you've truly m-more than enough to keep you busy," he stammered.

"'Tis true I tend to keep busy," she replied. "However, one more girl in the house ought not pose a great deal more work. I have time in the evenings when I can assist Reggie with her school lessons, and I think hearing about the mills from my boarders will interest her."

"So you're agreeable to the arrangement?"

"Only if you gain Reggie's approval. I do understand that you're faced with a difficult predicament, but if Reggie is forced to come live with me, I fear we'll both be unhappy. However, you may tell her that I would be most delighted if she would agree to come visit for the duration of your journey. In fact, if it will relieve any anxiety she may have, tell her that she is welcome to stop by and visit with me about the arrangement."

Justin beamed and exhaled a deep breath. "I'm relieved to know you are willing to entertain the possibility. And I'll pay you the rate you would receive for a boarder and an extra five cents a day for checking her schoolwork," he added hastily.

"No need to match a boarder's rate, Pastor. I'll have Reggie reside in my rooms. Otherwise, I'd be required to seek permission from the Corporation to have her stay in the house. This way, I'll neither be giving up boarding space nor be required to obtain consent from anyone."

"Yet you'll be preparing her food and seeing to her laundry and other needs. I insist."

Elinor glanced at the clock. "First we must gain Regina's approval. Then we can decide upon the remaining details. However, the girls will soon be arriving for the noonday meal, and I must see to my hair and finish preparing their food."

The words had barely been uttered when Justin jumped up from the settee as though he'd been struck by a volley of buckshot. "Forgive me. Not only have I come to your home uninvited and unannounced, but I've also detained you far beyond any reasonable expectation."

A laugh escaped Elinor's lips. "No need to rebuke yourself so harshly. I've enjoyed our visit and look forward to Reggie's answer. When would you plan to depart for Maine?" She followed him to the door.

"If at all possible, I'd like to leave immediately following church services next week. I haven't mentioned my departure to the church elders, but I've been in contact with a Congregational preacher, Arthur Conklin, who will be arriving in Lowell next Friday. He sent me a letter shortly after I arrived in Lowell and stated he's interested in spending time in our fair city. Seems he's visited England and now wants to draw some comparisons between our textile community and some of those he toured while across the sea— says he's writing an essay regarding the impact of the textile mills on homes in America and abroad."

"Doesn't sound like overly fascinating reading material," Elinor said with a giggle.

"No, I don't suppose it does. However, he's agreed to preach in my stead in exchange for use of the parsonage during my absence, and I am in hopes the elders will be agreeable to the idea. Of course, I wanted to have proper arrangements for Reggie before firming up the plans with the elders, although I've told Reverend Conklin he's welcome to come and stay at the parsonage in any event," Justin said as he opened the front door.

"That's most kind of you. I'll look forward to hearing Reggie's decision."

Elinor closed the front door and raced through her sitting room and into the bedroom, pulling the ribbon from her hair as she ran. One glance in the small mirror that hung over her dressing table gave her a start. She looked a fright. Damp strands of hair clung to her forehead, and a streak of flour lined her cheek. Too late to fret, she silently admonished herself. If she didn't hurry, her bread would be ruined and there would be no food on the table for the noonday meal.

"You seem happy," Lucinda said as she hurried into the house a short time later.

Elinor agreed. "Indeed! It's a beautiful day, and all is well with the world," she said while rushing back and forth, retrieving bowls of food from the kitchen.

Lucinda and Ardith stared at her as though she'd gone daft, but Elinor didn't care. She continued to smile and was singing when the girls left the house to return to work. Perhaps it was the thought of having Reggie come and stay with her. The child would break the monotonous routine of her life, and that prospect held great appeal.

"Please make her anxious to come and spend time with me, Lord," she uttered aloud before she continued singing the first stanza of "All Hail the Power of Jesus' Name."

Jasmine sighed as she settled into her mother's beloved rocking chair in the parlor. The journey to Mississippi had taken its toll on all of them—especially the children. They hadn't adapted to their new surroundings as smoothly as Jasmine and Nolan had hoped. Many tears had been shed since departing Massachusetts, but Jasmine continued to believe they would soon adjust.

Shadows were growing long across the willow-lined driveway leading to the Wainwright mansion when a knock sounded at the front door. Jasmine placed her mending in the basket beside her chair and hurried to the door.

She squinted in the early evening dimness. "Rupert Hesston? Is that you?"

"Has it been so long you've forgotten what I look like?"

She laughed and stepped back to permit him entry. "It *has* been a long time, but you haven't changed so much that I wouldn't recognize you. The lighting is inadequate," she added.

"Well, I must say that *you* have changed dramatically. The years have been very good to you, Jasmine. But you always were a beauty. Did you know that when I was around eighteen years old, I attempted to convince our mothers we weren't truly related so that I could call on you?"

"No, Mother never mentioned such a thing."

For some reason, Rupert's remark made her feel uncomfortable. Perhaps because Nolan had gone to visit with their overseer, Mr. Draper, and hadn't yet returned. Silly! Rupert was, after all, a distant cousin on her mother's side and McKinley's closest friend during their childhood years. In fact, he was now related to her on both sides of the family, for he had married Lydia Wainwright, one of Uncle Franklin's daughters and Jasmine's full cousin.

"Come join me in the parlor. Nolan and I were going to visit you once we were a bit more settled here at The Willows. I apologize for my tardiness. There's no excuse for not immediately calling upon you to express my condolences. Please forgive me."

"No need for an apology. I can only imagine the difficulty of having to return under these circumstances. The harshness of this epidemic has been dramatic among our families and friends. Thankfully, Lydia was in Europe and escaped the illness, and I suppose I'm just too ornery to die."

"Are there any other family members who survived?"

"Lydia is your uncle Franklin's only survivor, though one of your uncle Harry's grandchildren lived. I believe the boy has gone to make his home with a relative in Tennessee. Lydia might have been delighted to rear the child had she been here to make her wishes known. I truly despair over the thought of delivering so much bad news."

"She doesn't know?"

"She sailed for Europe in early June. She had no set itinerary, and although she has written to me, it's impossible to send word back. There is nothing she could have done, and had she returned home earlier, she might have contracted the fever herself. Like you, she'll have to deal with the shock, yet she won't be forced to feel helpless and watch as her family dies."

His words were a painful reminder of the horror Jasmine had been attempting to set aside ever since she'd arrived at The Willows. "I'll look forward to seeing Lydia upon her return. Please tell her to call on me or send word if there is anything she needs," Jasmine offered.

"That's very kind of you. And what of my good friend and cousin McKinley? Did he return to Mississippi with you?"

"No. Like you, I had hoped he would accompany us. However, he found it impossible to do so at this time. His position and family . . ." Her words trailed off into silence.

Rupert stared at her as though he expected her to say more, but when she remained silent, he said, "I recall your father telling me McKinley had married into the textile industry."

Jasmine was taken aback by the comment. "Married into the textile industry? I find it hard to believe my father would make such a comment."

He brushed the end of his dark brown mustache with his fingers. "Not exactly his words, I suppose, but I do recall Malcolm mentioning the fact that McKinley's father-in-law held a lofty standing within the textile industry and that McKinley had accepted a position with the mills. Hard to believe."

Had she detected a note of disdain in his voice? Rupert had always been judgmental and derisive, even as a young boy.

"How so?" she inquired. "Do you think McKinley ill-equipped for such responsibility?"

"Not at all. He is bright—there was never a question of his intelligence. In fact, he made the rest of us look like dolts.

What surprises me is his ability to embrace Northern ideals and attitudes. Of course, he had the influence of both you and his grandmother Wainwright. And I suppose when he fell in love with a Northern girl, it became easier to turn against his Southern heritage. He's probably embarrassed to return."

Jasmine narrowed her eyes as she attempted to keep her anger in check. "Neither McKinley nor I have turned against our Southern heritage. There are aspects of Southern life we do not embrace. However, we are not embarrassed by our beliefs. Rather, we are proud of them, Rupert."

The sound of the children clattering down the stairs caused Jasmine to turn her attention away from her guest. The diversion gave her a moment to calm herself. She needed to control her temper. Nolan had cautioned her they would be better served by remaining friendly with their Southern neighbors and divulging as little information as possible regarding their future plans.

"Come here, children. I'd like you to meet one of our relatives," she said as the three children were escorted into the parlor by Martha and Henrietta.

"Rupert, these are our children, Spencer, Alice Ann, and Clara. This is my cousin Rupert Hesston," she told the children.

Rupert smiled at the girls and shook Spencer's hand as though he were a grown man. Spencer's chest swelled beneath his cotton nightshirt.

"We're off to the kitchen for some milk," Martha said.

"And cookies," Alice Ann added with a broad smile that dimpled her cheeks.

"Lovely family," Rupert said as he watched the children leave with the two women. "Only whites working in the house now? What's happened to your father's house slaves?"

Jasmine dug the tips of her fingernails deep into her

palms and forced a demure expression. "Many of the house slaves died during the epidemic. Martha and Henrietta accompanied us from our home in Lowell. They have been in our employ for many years, and our children are comfortable in their care."

"But what of the others? I know there were some who survived, for I visited The Willows both while your father was ill and after his death. Did you relegate them to the slave quarters?"

Before she could answer, Nolan bounded through the front door and strode into the parlor. "I saw the horse out front and wondered who had come calling," he said, looking first at Rupert and then at his wife.

"Nolan," she sighed, relieved to have an ally. "I don't believe you've ever met Rupert Hesston, a distant cousin and Lydia's husband."

Nolan stepped forward and shook hands with their guest. "No, I don't believe I've had the pleasure. Although I do recall hearing your name mentioned. You and McKinley were friends as young boys, weren't you?"

"Indeed! We were inseparable, though different as night and day. I was in town earlier today and one of the locals mentioned some of the family had returned from up North. I hurried over, hoping that McKinley had returned. Of course, I'm pleased to see Jasmine also," he hastily added.

Nolan gave a hearty laugh. "I understand completely. I know McKinley would be pleased to see you also, but circumstances prevented him from being here. And how is Lydia faring?"

"I was telling your wife a bit earlier that Lydia will be returning from Europe in the very near future. I know she'll be pleased to see Jasmine, as they were dear friends during their younger years. How are you managing with your crop? Any problems getting the slaves to work for Mr. Draper?

Always difficult when you have to put a new overseer in place, especially during a crisis," he said.

"Things are going as well as can be expected under the circumstances. Mr. Draper is trying his best to meet my expectations."

Rupert nodded and stood up. "I didn't plan to stay long this evening but wanted to come by and see if there was anything I could do to help."

"That's kind of you. I'll be certain to send word if we need assistance," Nolan said as he grasped Jasmine by the arm and walked to the foyer.

"Thank you for calling on us, and please tell Lydia to send word when she arrives home," Jasmine said as they bid her cousin good-bye.

The twosome remained on the front porch until Rupert was well out of sight and they could no longer hear the sound of galloping hooves.

"There's something about him," Jasmine told her husband. "Something that sets my teeth on edge."

"Are you sure it's not the setting you've been forced to deal with?" he questioned sympathetically.

She shook her head, her focus still fixed to the road. "No, it's not just that. Rupert embodies an attitude that we shall be forced to face head-on before long. Once the community gives us time to settle in and mourn, they will descend upon us with their comments and reprimands," she said sadly. She drew a deep breath and blew it out again. "Mark my words. We shall soon reap their judgment."

Jasmine leaned down and pulled several weeds from the mound of dry dirt covering her father's grave before she placed a bouquet of wild flowers near the joint headstone. The marker had been carved and set in place at the time of her mother's death and forced her to accept the reality that both of her parents were now gone from this world.

"We'll need to have the engraver carve the date of death," Jasmine told her family in a trembling voice as she wiped a tear from her cheek.

"Why are you crying, Mama?" Alice Ann's lips quivered as she asked the question.

"I'm sad because your grandpa Wainwright died and I won't see him again," she said, feeling the sting of her words.

"But we'll see him in heaven, won't we?"

"Yes, dear. My sadness is that I must wait until then to see him again."

"But you always tell me that I'll be more grateful when I must wait for something."

Nolan and Jasmine exchanged a smile. "You are exactly right," Jasmine said. "Enough of this sadness. Let's go back to the house."

"Can I go fishing?" Spencer asked.

The journey to Mississippi had been exhausting, and Spencer's attitude since their arrival had improved little. He refused to be happy, except when he was at the small pond with his fishing pole. Thus far, school in Lorman was a fiasco. The school term had started nearly two weeks earlier than it would in Lowell. As if to punctuate his unhappiness, Spencer had become a constant source of trouble for the schoolmaster, and Jasmine and Nolan were daily receiving reports of his mischievous behavior.

"Be sure you return in time to wash up for supper," Jasmine instructed, thankful it was Saturday and she wasn't forced to deny his request.

He ran off without a reply, his feet pounding through the grassy meadow that surrounded the family cemetery. Jasmine took Alice Ann's hand and strode alongside her husband, who had hoisted Clara into his arms.

"I'm concerned about Spencer," she said to her husband. "He seems to be intent upon remaining unhappy."

"And making the rest of us unhappy in the process," Nolan agreed. "Yet I must admit, with all of the problems we've encountered here at the plantation, I've had little time to listen to his woes, which I fear only adds to his anger. It seems the little time I have with him is spent chastising him about his unpleasant behavior and poor performance in school."

"I'm hoping that once we've finalized arrangements for the additional workers and actually begun the harvest, things will slow down somewhat."

Nolan gave her a feeble smile and nodded. "I've asked the overseer to assemble the slaves Monday morning to tell them of our decision. I think it would be good if you were with me so they know that we are in agreement."

"Yes, of course. Martha can look after Alice Ann and Clara, and I'll have Henrietta make sure Spencer gets off to school on time. Have you advised Mr. Draper of our plans?"

Clara struggled to free herself from Nolan's arms and he soon stooped down and set her on her feet. She toddled alongside him while holding tightly to his finger. "No. I haven't decided if I can trust him to keep a confidence, and it's best the slaves hear the plans from us first."

"No doubt Mr. Draper will be as surprised as the slaves."

"Probably more so," Nolan said. "While Mr. Draper realizes we don't believe in slavery, I'm sure he has no idea we would actually free all of them."

"I only hope they'll agree to what we're offering. Otherwise, there's no way we'll be able to get the cotton harvested."

Clara released her father's finger, plopped down on the grass, and then raised her outstretched arms. "Tired of walking, are you?" he asked, lifting her high in the air and circling around until she giggled before setting her back on the grass. Nolan turned toward Jasmine, his countenance now more serious. "And what is the worst thing that could happen if we failed to bring in the crop?"

"I'd feel as though I'd failed to carry out my father's last wish," she ruefully admitted.

Nolan wrapped her in an embrace. "I don't believe your father would be supportive of our plans to free the slaves, so it's time you ceased being so hard on yourself. Nothing in our lives is dependent upon this crop."

Jasmine leaned back and looked into her husband's eyes. "Perhaps not, but if we are to carry out our plan and give the slaves their freedom, they'll need the money to establish themselves up north. Giving them freedom without any means to support themselves as they attempt to begin a new life is tantamount to setting them up for failure. Wouldn't you agree?"

"Of course. However, worrying is not going to change one thing. I believe the slaves will quickly realize that they are actually working as freed men to bring in this crop. I don't think there will be many who will choose to immediately leave the plantation. If they do, we can point out the difficulties they'll face and wish them well. And there may even be some who will be afraid to leave, especially the house servants."

She knew her husband was correct. Worry would serve no purpose but to render her useless. They were, after all, doing the proper thing by freeing their slaves. Surely God would see them through any difficulties that might lie ahead.

Alice Ann skipped off toward the house, and her younger sister raced on her chubby legs to catch up.

"After the announcement is made tomorrow, I'll talk to Prissy," Jasmine said as the two followed their children. "Since the day we arrived in Mississippi, she's talked openly with me. Perhaps she'll be willing to tell me what the reaction is in the slave quarters—especially if there's any backlash from the other plantations. By the way, did I tell you she and Toby plan to marry?"

"No. Somehow, it doesn't seem possible Toby should be old enough to wed."

"He was small for his age when he was young," she said, "but he's come into his own as a young man. He's eighteen now."

"Interestingly, Toby made a deep impression upon me when I visited Mississippi for the very first time. More than anyone other than you, I remember the first time I saw Toby here at The Willows."

"Truly? Tell me," Jasmine said.

"At supper the evening my brother and I arrived at the plantation, Toby was—"

"On the swing above the table stirring a breeze and fanning away the flies."

"Exactly. And I recall how he waved to you and flashed his big toothy grin from his perch."

"And how he'd fall asleep on that swing. Yet I recall only one time when he dropped his fan. Thinking back on his young life saddens me. How irresponsible and unfeeling to have a young child performing such a task. Can you imagine one of our children relegated to such a duty?"

"I truly cannot. However, we can't change what's happened in the past. All we can do is hope to change the future. It pleases me to know Toby has found someone to love, and Prissy seems a fine choice. If our decision to free the slaves should cause problems among the slaves on other plantations, I believe we can rely upon both Toby and Prissy to advise us."

———

As they rode side-by-side to the slave quarters on Monday morning, Nolan gave his wife a sidelong glance. She rode with a beauty and grace that made any horse appear stately.

"Not quite like riding one of our own horses," he said, hoping she would relax if he talked about horses rather than the announcement they would shortly make to the slaves.

"No, but she's a good animal with fine lines," Jasmine replied. "Father always bought good horseflesh—not Arabians like ours, but good stock all the same."

They rode on in silence until they reached the overseer's home, where the slaves stood congregated in one giant huddle. Most—especially the women—appeared frightened. A few angry faces peered at them as they dismounted, and the remainder seemed completely indifferent.

Nolan and Jasmine walked up the steps of the overseer's house and stood on the porch in order to be more easily seen and heard.

"Are you certain you want me to speak?" Nolan asked as they moved to the railing along the porch.

"Yes. If I speak, they'll still wonder if you are truly in agreement with my decision. There would be fear you might convince me to change my mind."

"Then stand beside me as I speak so they know we are united," Nolan said before turning to look into the sea of dark faces. "Thank you for coming out here this morning."

The overseer leaned toward Nolan. "They wasn't given no choice 'bout where they'd be this morning or any other morning," he said before spitting a stream of tobacco juice over the railing.

Nolan ignored the remark. "We asked Mr. Draper to have you assemble here this morning because we have an announcement to make. We know you've been concerned about what will happen to The Willows and to you and your families since Mr. Wainwright's death."

He scanned the assembled group but saw nothing except wary eyes staring back in return. No one said a word—they simply watched him and waited.

"As you may or may not know, neither Mrs. Houston nor I believe in slavery. In addition, her brother, McKinley Wainwright, who is the joint heir to The Willows, does not believe in owning slaves either. It's for that reason we've asked you to assemble here today. First, we want you to know that we are going to sign your papers, and all of you will become freed men, women, and children."

There was a gasp and a low rumbling among the group, but when Nolan motioned with one hand, the group again fell silent.

"You also realize there is a cotton crop that needs to be harvested. This leaves us in something of a dilemma, but we hope we've found a solution that will be acceptable to you. Each person who chooses to remain at The Willows and help pick the cotton will receive payment for his work so that when you leave here, you can travel north and have enough money to sustain you until you find some form of employment. Please understand that you are not required to remain. You will be freed whether you choose to stay or leave, but we hope you will see it is in your best interest to remain until the crop is harvested. Do you have any questions?"

No one spoke.

"Surely you must have some questions. Please don't be afraid to ask—there will be no more whips or dogs on this plantation. You have the right to inquire about your future."

"If we don' wanna stay and help with da cotton, when you gonna give us dis here freedom?" one of the men shouted from among the crowd.

"Miss Jasmine has already signed your papers. We will be

giving them to you before you walk away from this gathering. What you decide to do about your future is then in your own hands," Nolan replied.

Jasmine motioned for the overseer to move a wooden table off the porch. Nolan carried a bench, and Jasmine followed the two men as they situated the table in front of the crowd. Nolan pulled a sheaf of papers from his satchel and handed them to his wife.

"As I call your name," she told them, "please come forward and I'll hand you your papers. I apologize if I call the names of the deceased, but I do not have a list of those who were struck by the epidemic. However, a family member is entitled to the papers of any deceased relative."

"John Marcus," she called.

A muscular broad-shouldered slave stepped forward and neared the table.

"I need you to place your mark on this ledger page, which shows I have released you. That way we both have a record that you once were a slave at The Willows but are now free," Jasmine explained.

Nolan watched as the slave leaned over the table and made his mark. John's eyes were filled with disbelief and anticipation as Jasmine handed him a paper stating he was now a freed man.

"I's mighty thankful, Missus," he said, clasping the paper to his powerful chest. He held the paper high in the air and the crowd roared their approval. "I be stayin' to help with dat cotton," he said with a wide grin.

One by one, the slaves stepped forward, received their papers, and returned to the crowd as freed men and women—no longer subject to the whims of a white master. When the last paper had been signed, Nolan asked for a show of hands of those who planned to immediately leave. There were only two—a young man and woman who said they'd take their chances without the additional money.

"You can either begin work today or wait until tomorrow morning. It's your choice," Nolan said.

"Is you gonna keep count on how much we pick an' pay us accordin' to our work?" one of the men inquired.

"Yes. Since Mr. Draper won't be needed to oversee you in the fields, he'll weigh what you pick and keep a ledger account of it—and please don't put any rocks in your bags," Nolan said. "It won't be me but your fellow workers who will find your actions unfair. You'll be cheating them by receiving more than your share of the money."

"I's goin' out there and get started right now," John Marcus announced.

They watched the crowd disassemble, most of them hurrying off to retrieve their canvas picking bags.

Wendell Draper carried the table and chair back up the steps to the porch. "May I speak freely, Mr. Houston?"

"Of course."

"Old Mr. Wainwright was a good man. He treated his slaves better than most. Personally, I think you're making a mistake by setting these slaves free. Ain't my decision, of course, but they're better off right here than they'll be trying to make it on their own up north. That problem aside, you're going to be in mighty deep water when word spreads of what you're doing here."

"You planning to start the trouble?" Nolan inquired.

The overseer slowly shook his head. "I wouldn't do such a thing, Mr. Houston. You're misunderstanding my concern. I have no intention of saying anything to anybody, but slaves talk among themselves, just like you and I."

Nolan shrugged. "I don't expect them to keep their freedom a secret. It would be too much to ask."

"You could have waited until the crop was in to tell them."

"I won't use slave labor to bring in a crop. And why should I care if the slaves talk among themselves? It's human nature to discuss and make plans with your fellow man."

Draper leaned against the porch railing. "No offense, Mr. Houston, but you're a Northerner. I'm talking about word spreading to the other plantations. Our slaves—"

"Freed men," Nolan corrected.

"Our *freed men* are going to go over to those other plantations and tell the slaves you've given them their freedom. Believe me, it won't take long till word gets to the big house, and once word reaches the big house, the master knows. I'm afraid you're going to be in for more trouble than you bargained for."

"And I think you're borrowing trouble," Nolan replied.

CHAPTER · 6

September 1857

WITH MUCH LESS grace and decorum than her father who was following behind her, Reggie Chamberlain bounded up the two steps of Elinor Brighton's boardinghouse carrying a satchel stuffed with clothing and other miscellaneous belongings she believed to be the necessities of life.

"I thought perhaps you'd decided not to come and stay with me," Elinor said from the open doorway.

"Why would you think that? I told you I wanted to come," the girl casually replied.

Justin shrugged his shoulders and flashed an apologetic expression in Elinor's direction. "I told her you were going to be anxious. Especially since I advised you we'd be arriving as soon as Reggie tossed a few belongings in her bag."

"I did think you would arrive in time to join us for dinner. Have you eaten?"

"No, but Reggie had enough breakfast to hold her until supper, didn't you, Reggie?"

The girl wagged her head back and forth. "No. I told you I was hungry when we left the house."

Justin shifted his gaze back and forth between his daughter and Elinor. "It appears I'm incorrect. We'll go to the Merrimack House and have a meal together. Then I'll return with Reggie and be on my way."

"There's more than enough food left from dinner to feed both of you—if you have sufficient time, that is," she offered. "You can put your satchel in the bedroom," she said to the child.

Justin glanced at the clock. "I'm already getting a late start. I'd best be on my way. You can have Reggie eat an extra helping for me."

"Give me a moment," Elinor said, hurrying down the hall before he could object.

Her efficiency in the kitchen proved helpful. Within only a few minutes she had placed a loaf of bread, a hunk of cheese, two pieces of fried chicken, and a piece of cake in an old metal pail. She hurried back to the door and handed the tin to the pastor.

"I wouldn't want you leaving town on an empty stomach. You can eat this along the way."

"It's little wonder Reggie is so fond of you," he said.

She didn't know exactly why, but it pleased Elinor to know Reggie had spoken kindly of her.

"I put my satchel under your bed," Reggie announced as she skipped back into the hallway.

"And where did you place all your belongings?"

Reggie gave her a confused look. "They're in the satchel."

Elinor and Justin laughed aloud, but Reggie appeared vexed. "I don't know what's so funny."

"I'll explain later. Why don't you walk your father out to the wagon and bid him good-bye. I'll wait for you here."

Elinor watched from the doorway as Justin leaned down and embraced his daughter. He kissed her; then they appeared to exchange a few words. Soon Reggie was running back to the house. She stopped outside the door and waved until her father was out of sight.

"Come right this way and we'll find you something to eat," Elinor suggested as Reggie walked back inside the house.

"Chicken would be good."

"Then you're in luck—because chicken is what I served for dinner today."

Reggie giggled. "I know—my father told me."

While the child ate her dinner, Elinor took up her needlework and began stitching.

"What are you making?"

"A sampler," Elinor replied.

"What's a sampler?"

"It's a piece of needlework that is made using a variety of stitches—some difficult and some simple," she explained. "Many times young girls make them when they first begin to sew. My first sampler is hanging in the bedroom. My grandmother taught me the stitches."

"How come you're making another if you already have one?"

Elinor laughed. "I think there's plenty of space in a house for more than one sampler. However, I'm making this one for a raffle the Ladies' Aid Society will be hosting next month—if I complete it in time."

Reggie peered across the table. "Looks like you're about finished. Think we could go fishing?" she asked.

"Well, I don't know why not. It seems a perfect day, and we've several hours of daylight left. Did you bring your fishing pole?"

The girl bobbed her head up and down. "I put it out behind the house by your shed. I'll go and get it," she said, obviously delighted.

"I'll meet you in front of the house." Elinor tucked her stitching into a small basket, deciding to carry it along with her to the river.

"Do your boarders know I'm going to live with you?" Reggie asked as they neared the Merrimack River.

Elinor straightened the folds of her blue-and-cream-striped day dress, then settled on the grass a short distance from the water's edge. "I believe I've told all of them. Why do you ask?" she inquired as she pulled her needlework from the basket.

Reggie glanced over her shoulder and met Elinor's inquiring gaze. "Were they angry?"

"No, of course not. Besides, except for breakfast and dinner, they're gone from early in the morning until supper-time. In the evening some of them go to town or to the library, and there might be one or two who visit in the parlor with their friends. I think you'll find most of them nice enough."

"Do any of them fish?" Reggie inquired as she tossed her line into the water.

"I don't believe I've heard any of them mention fishing, so it appears you may be stuck with me—and perhaps Moses. Have you talked to Moses since Spencer's departure?"

"Only once. He said since Spencer's gone, his mama doesn't let him come down to the river."

"Then where did you see him?"

"At the river, but don't tell," Reggie said.

"I promise."

"Spencer was mighty unhappy about going to Missis-sippi. We promised to write to each other."

"And have you?" Elinor asked.

"Not yet—but he hasn't written to me either."

"Perhaps that's something you can do tonight while I'm working in the kitchen. Then I can post the letter for you tomorrow. What do you think?"

"I like that idea. I wish he were here so we could go to school together."

"What about Moses? I'm certain he's lonely without Spencer also. Maybe the two of you can begin walking to school together. We could go and talk to his parents and see if that would work."

"Sure would be better than having to walk into that school all by myself every day. I never saw a school quite so big as that one. I'm always scared I'll get lost just trying to find my way around."

Elinor laughed. "It's not all that big, Reggie. But it is a very nice school."

"Did you know Moses is colored?" she inquired absently.

"Yes, as a matter of fact, I did know that."

"He doesn't look colored. He looks white. But he says he's truly colored, so I believe him. Even Spencer says it's the truth. At my school in Maine, they don't let the Negroes go to school with the whites. We had a colored family in our town," she said in a whisper, as though it were a secret, "and Father said they should let the children go to school with us, but they wouldn't."

"That's true in many places here in the North, Reggie. Even though most Northerners oppose slavery, they still want to keep people divided."

"Seems silly, doesn't it? Moses is just a boy. He's no different than me."

"Indeed it is silly," Elinor replied with a warm smile. "And just as you said, Moses is a boy. But you, Miss Reggie, are not."

Reggie frowned. "Well, I know that. But . . . well . . . you know what I mean."

She nodded in complete understanding. "Of course I do."

The men's voices were escalating out of control in their upstairs meeting room at the National Building. McKinley realized that if Nathan or Matthew didn't soon bring the group to order, pandemonium would rule.

"Gentlemen! Gentlemen!" Nathan shouted while rapping a wooden gavel on a podium at the front of the room.

But they paid him no heed. McKinley was certain that few could hear him above the clamoring din that now filled the room. Matthew motioned to McKinley. "Nathan tells me there is a bell tower above this room. The stairway is out that door," he said while pointing toward the rear of the room. "Do you think you could make your way up there and ring the bell? It's the only way we're going to settle this group."

McKinley nodded before wending his way through the crowd. The stairway proved dark and dusty, and he wondered how many years had passed since the bell had been used. He carefully made his way across the platform and unwound the rope. With a mighty heave, he pulled the rope and then spun backward and fell to the platform as the frayed rope broke off in his hand. The bell swung, and the heavy clapper fell against the iron with a mighty gong that shook the platform. Even with his ears covered, McKinley flinched at the reverberation. He edged his way back to the stairs as the momentum caused the bell to swing back and sound once again.

Silence prevailed when he reentered the meeting room with the rope still hanging from one hand.

"Thank you, McKinley," Nathan said. "And now that I've been able to gain your attention and bring this meeting to some semblance of order, I would request your cooperation in maintaining this order until the meeting is adjourned.

I understand emotion runs high at this moment, and I am prepared for discussion regarding the tragic sinking of the SS *Central America*. However, chaos serves no purpose in this meeting."

McKinley had anticipated heightened emotions this evening, but he had expected the same decorum he'd always observed among the Associates in the past. Although Nathan Appleton appeared calm, McKinley realized the scene he had observed in this room was a true gauge of the catastrophe that would challenge the entire country. He wanted to remain calm, yet he knew that the hurricane that had sent a million dollars in commercial gold to the ocean floor would cause financial repercussions throughout the country.

Josiah Baines waved his hand in the air and then stood. "Is there any additional word on the ship or its contents? I've heard the entire fifteen tons of federal gold intended for our eastern banks was on that ship."

"Unfortunately, I'm told that is true," Nathan said. "As most of you know, the *Central America* sailed directly into the path of a severe hurricane off the coast of South Carolina. The passengers made a valiant effort for four days, bailing water and carrying coal to keep the iron boilers lit. Distress rockets attracted a small Boston brig, and the women and children were transferred and saved. A few men were later rescued after the ship went down, but over four hundred perished—a much greater loss than fifteen tons of gold."

"I doubt the banks or our creditors will think so," one of the men called out.

"I realize there are widespread reports of financial instability being carried between cities by telegraph message, but we must not let emotion rule our decisions, gentlemen. When a small group of us met several weeks ago, we were distressed by news of embezzlement in the New York branch of the Ohio Life Insurance and Trust Company. We did take it upon ourselves to protect as much of the corporate funds as possible. You must remember, however, that there was a rush on the banks and we were able to withdraw only a third of our corporate investment."

McKinley knew the men should offer up a prayer of thanksgiving that Nathan and the others had shared their insight and taken immediate action. If it had not been for political friends directing them to bankers sympathetic to future and continued industrial growth, the Associates would have lost much more. For in less than one month's time, the financial backbone of the country had been affected in a monumental way.

"We're thankful for what you accomplished," Thomas Clayborn commented. "Josiah tells me there are problems with the Southern cotton growers to add to our list of concerns. Can you give us the details?"

For the next half hour, Nathan outlined the epidemic that had plagued the South, along with the remaining details gathered by Matthew over the past several weeks.

"We expect a further report from Jarrod Forbes by the end of the month advising of any shortfall in the crop," Matthew added. "However, given the recent turn of events, we may see a marked decrease in sales. If that's the case, we'll need to decrease production and may not need the volume of cotton we had previously contracted to purchase. With luck and proper oversight, this may work out in the end."

"Are you anticipating layoffs?" Wilson inquired.

Matthew hiked his shoulders in an exaggerated shrug. "Who can say for certain. If we decrease production, you can be sure there will be layoffs. In fact, we may be forced to temporarily close several of the mills. Time will tell. I will keep you informed, and any of you are more than welcome to visit my offices and go over the ledgers and reports whenever you are in Lowell. I will, of course, continue sending written reports on a regular basis."

"I know all of you concur that Matthew can be counted upon to maintain our best interests as he makes his decisions in Lowell," Nathan said. "This is going to prove to be a trying time, gentlemen. I trust you have all invested wisely."

———

"Will ya soon be ready, lass?" Rogan called to his wife. "We need to be gettin' loaded into the buggy if we're to make it to the church before the weddin' begins. I do na think Bridgett is gonna be happy if ya do na have her veil there by the time she's due to walk down the aisle."

"See to Nevan and Katherine. They're dressed and ya can load them into the buggy. There's plenty of time. Bridgett told me the bishop insisted on the Mass commemorating Michaelmas before the weddin'. Them that's invited to the weddin' can remain in the church whilst the others go on about their celebratin'."

"I do na think Bishop Fenwick will look kindly upon our strollin' into the church in the middle of Mass," Rogan called up the stairs. "Why the lass decided to have her weddin' today is beyond my understandin'. If it's good luck she's lookin' fer, then she should be havin' the weddin' on St. Patrick's Day or Shrove Tuesday, not September twenty-ninth."

With expert ease, Kiara adjusted her cluster of dark auburn curls and then added the gem-studded comb Jasmine Houston had given her as a gift on her own wedding day. She gave herself one final look in the mirror before descending the stairs in a pale blue wool gown that highlighted her creamy complexion.

"She chose the day because it's a Saturday and most of their friends do na work so late on Saturday. Also, she knew Bishop Fenwick would be in Lowell, and she's considerin' it an honor to be married by the bishop—as would most," she added.

"Ya look as lovely as the day I married ya, lass," Rogan said with a twinkle in his eye. He leaned down and brushed her lips with a fleeting kiss.

With his blarney and warm kisses, the man could still cause her heart to flutter. "Go on with ya, Rogan Sheehan, or we'll be late to the church for sure."

"Is that a fact?" he asked as they stepped out onto the porch. With a hearty laugh, Rogan pulled her into a tight embrace and kissed her soundly while the children watched from the buggy.

"Da!" Nevan hollered, then covered his face with both hands.

"Am I causin' ya a bit of embarrassment, lad?" Rogan asked with another laugh before assisting Kiara into the buggy.

"Is Paddy comin' with us?" Kiara asked.

"He left more than an hour ago. I had him take Bridgett's veil with him," he said with a broad grin.

"Ya were rushin' me when me brother's already delivered Bridgett's veil?" She gave him a playful slap on the arm.

"Aye, and ya should be thankin' me instead of abusin' me," he replied while vigorously rubbing his arm.

Kiara laughed at his antics and settled beside her husband for the short ride to the church. She was pleased for the diversion Bridgett and Cullen's wedding would provide. What with the wedding and the private Michaelmas celebrations, the Irish citizens of Lowell would be celebrating until the wee hours of the night, though many would likely suffer the consequences come morning.

"Can ya tell me why Bridgett decided to be married at St. Peter's instead of St. Patrick's, where she's been attendin' church since she set foot in this country?" Rogan asked. "I do na think she made a wise decision. St. Patrick's was good enough for our weddin'."

"The bishop agreed to officiate if they held the weddin' as soon as he completed the Mass for Michaelmas. And ya can na deny that St. Peter's is much bigger and much prettier than St. Patrick's. Now ya need to quit finding fault with Bridgett's decisions."

"'Tis a sad day when a man's forced to give up a supper of goose with sage and onion stuffing. Especially when he's been looking forward to such a meal since last Michaelmas Day." He hesitated for a moment, his brows knit in a frown. "I do na recall any problem fittin' our guests into the pews at St. Patrick's on our weddin' day."

"Ya need to be rememberin' that when we took our vows, I did na have any relatives except for Paddy, and very few friends either. Bridgett and Cullen both have many friends from church and the Acre, as well as the people they work with. I'm thinkin' that will make for a mighty large group of guests—more than ya could comfortably seat at St. Patrick's.

"And if it's yar stomach ya're worried about," Kiara continued, "ya can be sure there will be plenty of food. Granna Murphy's been cookin' for days, and if I know yar granna, there will be a fat goose with sage stuffin' and plum sauce waitin' fer ya."

"And I'm hopin' she'll add some apples to the stuffin', too," he said with a lopsided grin as he pulled back on the reins and the horses came to a halt near the corner of Gorham and Appleton streets, where the wedding guests had begun to congregate.

"Paddy!" Rogan called as he waved his young brother-in-law forward. "Did ya deliver the lace?" he whispered. "Yar sister will na be forgivin' me if the delivery went amiss."

"Aye, that I did. And glad Bridgett was to get it too. I think Granna Murphy was as worried as Bridgett. The two of them could na get the veil out of me hands and shoo me out of the house fast enough."

Rogan laughed as he gave Paddy an enthusiastic slap on the back. "I'm thinkin' Granna was breathin' a sigh of relief when she saw ya with that veil. She was likely worried she would na get Bridgett married off as planned."

"Come on with ya," Kiara said as she took hold of Rogan's arm. "We need to be getting inside or Bridgett will think ya've forgotten ya're to walk her down the aisle."

"How could I be forgettin' such a thing when I've my wife to remind me?" he asked with a wink.

A short time later, Rogan walked down the aisle with Bridgett tightly clasping his arm. The bodice and sleeves of her flounced heather gown were edged with the intricate lace Kiara had created to perfectly match the lace adorning her veil.

"She looks quite beautiful," Kiara said once Rogan sat down beside her.

"Aye, but shaking like a leaf, she was. Likely worried about what's to come on her weddin' night."

A quick jab of Kiara's elbow wiped the smile from his face. "Careful, lass, or ya're gonna be causing me permanent injury."

"I doubt that. Now hush before the bishop throws ya out on yar ear," she whispered.

After leading the couple in the recitation of their vows, Bishop Fenwick peered over his expansive girth, read a prayer from his missal, and pronounced Cullen and Bridgett McLaughlin husband and wife.

Fiddle and accordion music wafted through the cool September air, and the wedding guests soon began to wander from Granna Murphy's congested house and out into the streets of the Acre. Paddy walked alongside a small group as they meandered down the street and then stopped for a moment to watch the cheerful crowd. He breathed deeply. It had been far too long since he'd had time to actually enjoy himself. Nolan Houston's departure for Mississippi had resulted in little time for Paddy to socialize, and he hadn't realized until this evening how much he missed being among his friends.

He slowly downed a cup of wedding punch and leaned against the clapboard wall of Kevin McCurty's pub as couples paired off and began to dance.

Liam and Daughtie Donohue laughed and bowed to each other as they finished their dance. "Good to see ya, Paddy," Liam said as he and Daughtie drew near. "I've been wonderin' how ya're managin' at the farm without Mr. Houston."

"I find I do na have much time to relax anymore, so I was mighty pleased to have an excuse fer a night to enjoy myself."

Liam patted him on the back. "Ya can be mighty proud of yarself, Paddy, to have Mr. Houston trust ya running his stables at yar young age—and Irish to boot. Not many could boast of such an accomplishment."

"Thank ya, Liam. I must admit there are times when all the responsibility is worrisome. Right now, I've got me a beauty of a horse—not a Shagya, but still a fine animal we acquired specially for an instructor at the Virginia Institute. Training the mare was going very well until I attempted to get her to lead off with the right foot." He raked one hand through his curly hair. "Now she's proving to be the most stubborn animal I've ever encountered."

Liam shook his head. "Then let her lead off with the left. What difference does it make to ya, lad?"

"The Institute wants all of their horses to lead off with the right foot so when they march in a line, they're synchronized. I've had everyone at the farm attempting to work with her, but no one's been able to succeed."

"Ya should be tryin' Baucher's method."

The three of them turned to see who was speaking.

"Well, if it isn't Mary Margaret O'Flannery," Paddy said. "Have ya met Mary Margaret?" he asked, turning toward Liam and Daughtie.

"I don't believe we've had the pleasure," Daughtie replied. "Are you new to Lowell?"

"Yes. I work with Bridgett over at number five—at the Boott mills," she added.

"How is it that we haven't met you before now?" Daughtie asked.

"I have na been here but a short time, and I do na know many folks yet. But I attend St. Peter's every Sunday. Bridgett says once I become more accustomed to the work hours, I'll have more energy and want to become more involved in activities. Right now I'm content to do my work and little more," she commented.

"Bridgett is correct. It takes time to adjust. Even though it's been many years since I worked in the mills, I well remember the weariness of those first months. Ah, Liam, there's Kiara and Rogan. I haven't had an opportunity to speak to them this evening. It was a pleasure to meet you, Mary Margaret—and good luck with that horse," Daughtie added.

Liam grinned at Mary Margaret. "I believe you were going to tell Paddy how to correct that problem with his horse, weren't you?"

"Aye—that I was," she responded sweetly. "'Twas a

lovely weddin', don't ya think?" she asked, turning her attention back to Paddy.

"Aye. Bridgett's a lovely lass, and Cullen's a lucky man to be havin' her as his wife. Did Bridgett happen to tell ya that she sailed to America on the same ship as Kiara and me?"

Mary Margaret tilted her head, and he noticed a sparkle in her bright blue eyes. "She told me Rogan saved his money to pay her passage and that Lowell has been the only place she's lived since comin' to America, but she did na tell me about the voyage."

"Then sit yarself down, lass, and I'll tell ya what Bridgett was like when she was a very young lass."

Liam stepped away from the couple to greet some friends with a slap on the back.

For a brief time, as Paddy regaled Mary Margaret with stories of life aboard the ship with Bridgett and Kiara, he was transported back to his youth. Back to a time he'd not thought about for many years—a time when death had crept into their home and snuffed out the lives of his ma and da, and then hovered nearby, eager to claim his life also. Those were days filled with despair. Paddy knew that had it not been for Kiara, he would have perished on the Emerald Isle. He always dreaded such memories, but somehow sharing them with Mary Margaret made them seem less worrisome.

"So ya see, 'twas Bridgett who made the match between Kiara and Rogan," Paddy explained.

"What's that I hear ya tellin' the lass? That yar hopin' I'll find ya a match?" Rogan teased as he approached the couple.

Paddy's cheeks flushed at the comment. Once again, Rogan had embarrassed him in front of Mary Margaret.

"When the time comes that I'm lookin' for a match, I do na think I'll be needin' someone to help me," Paddy retorted.

Rogan emitted a loud guffaw and slapped his thigh,

obviously enjoying Paddy's discomfort. Mary Margaret remained silent, her gaze fixed upon Paddy. Had the lass not been within hearing distance, Paddy would have given Rogan Sheehan an earful.

"If ya act as though his teasin' does na bother ya," Mary Margaret whispered, "he's more apt to stop. Next time, just give him a smile and tell him ya'll be sure to let him know when ya're ready."

"Should there be a next time, I may be forced to give him a taste of his own medicine!"

"Do ya na realize that's exactly what he wants? To get ya all riled up?"

Rogan ceased his laughter and turned his attention back to the young couple. "Liam tells me the lass appears to know all about trainin' horses and is willin' to give ya some lessons."

Before Paddy could reply, Mary Margaret jumped to her feet. "Now ya would na be exaggeratin' a wee bit, would ya?"

"Ah, lass, so ya're catchin' on to me tricks, are ya? Though I may have overstated the facts a bit, 'tis the truth that Liam said ya're talkin' like a lass who knows her way around horses," Rogan countered.

"Me master in Boston owned horses—I cared for his children except when their tutor had them for lessons. Ornery lot of youngsters, they was. Their ma died, and instead of spendin' time with his children, their father bought them gifts. They all had horses, and it's many an hour I spent waitin' at the stables while they was riding or taking their lessons."

"So are ya then considerin' yarself an expert? Because, if it's an expert ya are, I'm thinkin' Paddy could put ya to work at the Houston stables," Rogan prodded while directing an exaggerated wink at Paddy.

Mary Margaret shook her head, causing her soft curls to swing to and fro. "I'm na an expert, but I do know Baucher's method works, for I've watched it used on horses meself."

"And what *is* this Baucher's method?" Paddy asked.

"'Tis a whole system of trainin' a horse. But for gettin' the horse to lead off with his right foot like ya were mentionin' earlier, ya must first get the animal well in hand, with his head in an easy position. Then ya need to make certain his hind legs are well under his body. Once ya have done that, ya bear yar hand to the left and give an increased pressure to the animal's right leg."

Paddy scratched his head as he attempted to process the method Mary Margaret had just explained. He gave a gentle shrug of his shoulders. "'Twould be worth a try since nothin' else has worked."

"And would ya na be willin' to try it otherwise?" she asked.

He detected a flash of anger in her blue eyes. "I do na know. I'm na a man to change my way of doing things if they're workin'. Does na make any sense."

"Have ya never considered there might be an easier or better way to perform a task? Is that na reason enough to change?"

"I suppose 'twould be cause enough," he agreed. "But if ya're sayin' ya think I should be shiftin' the entire way we train our horses to this Baucher method ya're talkin' about, I do na think that will happen. We pride ourselves on selling the finest, best-trained horses in the country."

"Aye," Liam said as he rejoined the conversation. "Even West Point and the Virginia Institute buy Arabians from the Houston Stables."

"The Shagyas?" Mary Margaret asked, recognition shining in her eyes.

Paddy squared his shoulders and his chest swelled. "Ya know of our horses?"

"I heard me master speak of them at the time he was buying another horse. He said he had seen the Shagyas, and though they were beautiful animals, he found them to be far too costly."

"Ha! The man is a fool. Ya need to come to the stables and have a look fer yarself," Paddy said.

Liam waved at Rogan as he and Kiara approached. "Our young Paddy has invited Miss O'Flannery fer an outin'," he told them. "Say, Paddy, when was it ya were gonna be comin' to escort Mary Margaret to the farm?"

Paddy glanced at Mary Margaret, uncertain what he should do. If he set a time, the lass might tell him she had no interest in keeping company with the likes of him. And if he said Liam had twisted his words, Mary Margaret might be insulted and think he didn't find her attractive. Of course, it would be altogether impossible to find the lass undesirable, with her piercing blue eyes and hair the shade of gingered carrots.

"I'm thinkin' we can arrange the time fer ourselves. Would ya like to dance, Mary Margaret?" Paddy asked, anxious to escape Liam and Rogan's antics.

"Aye, that I would," she replied.

Before there was opportunity for further discussion, Paddy led the slender beauty off toward the assembled dancers.

"Have ya found a good Irish family to live with here in the Acre?" Paddy asked as he put his arm on her waist.

"The Corporation put me in one of the boardinghouses," she explained.

His eyebrows raised to resemble twin peaks. "In one of the boardinghouses?"

The flounce of her deep green dress shimmered as they

twirled in time to the spirited music. "Aye. And why is that surprisin' ya?"

"I would think ya would prefer livin' among yar own people," he said. "Na many of the Irish lasses live in the boardinghouses, and them that do say they're treated poorly. I'll talk to Bridgett. I'm sure ya could live with Granna Murphy, who's a fine cook."

Mary Margaret's dancing came to an abrupt halt. "And why would ya be thinkin' to take it upon yarself to talk to Granna Murphy? I've got a perfectly good voice, and if I want to move to the Acre, I'm more than capable of doing so without yar help. And I have na been treated poorly at the boardinghouse. Mrs. Brighton keeps a good house and will na tolerate foolishness," she retorted.

"Are ya feelin' a wee bit too good to live with yar own people?" Paddy asked.

Mary Margaret's eyes flashed with anger. "Who do ya think ya are to be sittin' in judgment of me and where I choose to live?"

"Ya have more than yar share of a temper, Mary Margaret O'Flannery."

"So I've been told!" She gave a small stomp of her foot for emphasis.

Paddy narrowed his eyes as he glanced at her foot and then met her angry gaze. "Ya should na take offense so quickly."

She put her hands on her hips, her elbows pointed outward like two triangular blockades. "And you should na be attemptin' to pass yarself off as a horse trainer when ya do na even know anything of Baucher's method!"

She marched away, her hair flying as she threaded her way through the crowd. The lass had a sharp tongue and more than her share of pride! Who did she think she was, questioning his ability to train a horse? He crossed his arms and leaned against the wall, continuing to track her every move. She had stopped to talk to someone. He elevated himself to full height and strained to see above the crowd. Timothy Rourke! Why would she want to speak with *him*? Everyone in the Acre knew Timothy traded one lass for another at the drop of a hat. Yet even the brokenhearted continued to tag after him, seeking attention. What special charm did Timothy Rourke possess?

Paddy ignored Rogan, who was pointing his thumb in Mary Margaret's direction as he approached. "Why did ya let that bonny lass escape? Can ya not see she's talking to Timothy? Get yarself over there before he offers to walk her home."

"If it's the likes of Timothy Rourke that interests her, then she's na the lass for me," Paddy said while still keeping Mary Margaret in his sights.

"Then why are ya still staring after her like a lovesick pup?" Rogan asked. "If it's fear that's holdin' ya back, I'll go and fetch her back here for ya."

"I do na need yar help," he said, breaking loose of the firm clasp Rogan held on his arm and striding off.

He could hear Rogan's deep belly laugh as he approached Mary Margaret. He gave momentary thought to walking past her and pretending he didn't see her standing with Timothy Rourke. But if he did such a thing, Rogan would find some other way to embarrass him.

He approached the lass feeling a combination of fear, hope, and discomfiture. "I was wonderin' if I might escort ya home this evening," Paddy inquired.

"She already has an escort home," Timothy said.

" 'Twas Mary Margaret I was askin'."

She met his expectant gaze. "And why would ya want to escort the likes of me? A lass with a dreadful temper?" she inquired sweetly.

"I'll explain while I'm seeing ya home," he replied, now feeling somewhat more confident.

"If ya want to wait until I'm ready to go home, then ya may escort me. But I do na have to be in the boardinghouse until ten o'clock, so until then, I believe I'll accept Timothy's offer to dance."

Tim Rourke grasped Mary Margaret around the waist. As he began to lead her off, he whispered to Paddy, "No need to wait—I'll see the lass to her boardinghouse."

Paddy scowled at his rival. "I'll na be leaving without her. It's *me* that'll be seein' her home."

Filled with envy, Paddy watched Mary Margaret and Timothy. The man would not turn her loose for even a moment.

"He hangs on her arm as though he's afraid I'll steal her away," Paddy muttered aloud, angry he hadn't insisted upon dancing with Mary Margaret himself. Instead, he stood idly by while Timothy held her and danced another eight-handed reel.

"Come join us for a game of kick the turnip," Johnny Kelly urged as he tugged on Paddy's sleeve.

"I do na want to play games," Paddy retorted. There was more irritation in his voice than he'd intended, and Johnny's smile quickly changed to a frown. "I'm sorry if I hurt yar feelings," Paddy called out as the boy hurried away without another word.

It seemed as though hours had passed before the musicians finally set their instruments down and cited the need for something cool to drink. Paddy quickly stepped forward to claim Mary Margaret. "If ya're to be home by ten o'clock, we best be leaving," he said.

Her face was flushed from the dancing, and damp curls clung to her forehead, forming an auburn frame around her creamy complexion. "I'm having such fun I now am wishin'

I would have asked Mrs. Brighton for special permission to return later than ten o'clock," she said.

He raised an eyebrow. "So ya find Timothy Rourke pleasant company?"

"He's a lively sort of fella and can dance better than most. He did na miss a step on the jigs nor the hornpipe, though I do na think he can step dance as well as I. He said I should wait until the fiddlers returned and give him a chance to outshine me," she said with a cheery smile.

"I do na doubt he's tryin' to talk ya into staying a wee bit longer. If the fiddlers hadn't stopped for a drink, he'd still be fightin' to keep ya by his side. And then what would Mrs. Brighton say when ya returned home late?"

Mary Margaret's laughter filled the air like the soothing sound of a rippling brook. "I do na know, but I'd like to think she'd be understandin'."

"My buggy is at the end of the street," he said, leading her through the crowd.

"Timothy said there would be some strawboys comin' to call at Granna Murphy's later this evenin'. I do wish I could stay and see that bit of fun," Mary Margaret said as they reached the buggy.

"I do na know who told him there would be strawboys, but I've heard nothin' of it. The custom of going strawing is not often practiced in the Acre."

Mary Margaret's eyes shone with excitement. "I've never seen strawboys, and I'm thinkin' it would be amusing to see the young men dressed in their straw costumes while performing a jig or singing a song. Of course, I would na be able to guess their identity, but all the same, 'twould be fun trying."

"Aye. 'Tis true that the performance of a group of strawboys can add much to the weddin' festivities, but I think Timothy Rourke was speaking out of turn. I do na think ya'll be seeing any special performances this evenin'. Timothy would say whatever words he thought might entice ya to remain in his company a little longer."

"Ya seem mighty anxious to discredit him."

"I'm only speakin' the truth. Ya can ask any of the lasses he's trifled with," Paddy said as he helped her into the buggy.

"So ya think I'm a lass whose head is easily turned by the smooth talk of an Irishman?"

He thought for a moment as he pulled on the reins to direct the horses into a right turn down John Street. "I canna say for certain, but it appears ya might be."

Her lips tightened and her eyes narrowed. "Ya are an incorrigible man, Padraig O'Neill. Since the first time I set eyes upon ya, ya've done nothing but find fault with me."

"I'm merely attemptin' to direct ya down the right path," he explained.

She bristled at his reply, and her eyes darkened with anger. "When I need help making my decisions, I'll ask. Until then, I'll thank ya to keep yar opinions to yarself."

They rode in silence, Paddy's gaze firmly fixed upon the horses and Mary Margaret's back to him and her arms crossed tightly across her chest. Once again he'd managed to alienate the lass. Why couldn't she see that he was merely attempting to look out for her best interests?

"Like I told ya earlier, if ya ever plan to wed, ya're going to have to learn to control yar temper," Paddy finally said as he pulled back on the reins and they came to a stop in front of her boardinghouse.

Her lips puckered into a tight knot as she turned to face him. "Plan to wed? Is *that* what ya think? That the only thing I have to look forward to in my entire life is finding a man to marry? Ya flatter yarself, Padraig O'Neill!"

Before he could make his way around the buggy, Mary Margaret had jumped down and rushed toward the boardinghouse. She vanished behind the front door before he could say another word.

CHAPTER · 7

October 1857

NOLAN LEANED back in his chair and rubbed his weary eyes. He'd been staring at the ledgers, bills, and records of the plantation all morning. Fortunately, Malcolm Wainwright had been a meticulous man when it came to his holdings. Any information Nolan needed was at his fingertips— including papers of ownership for every slave now living at The Willows, along with a ledger listing personal facts about each one. The slave's name was followed by notations for medical treatment, type of clothing supplied, Christmas gifts, and a listing of special abilities and characteristics. A carefully inscribed date of entry preceded each detailed fact.

The swishing sound of Jasmine's skirt caused him to turn as she entered the library. "You look particularly lovely today," he said, enjoying the sight of her even more than he had years ago when they'd first wed.

"You are becoming quite the Southern charmer, Mr. Houston," she said with an exaggerated drawl.

"What I say is entirely true—I've always said you look stunning in yellow. You're like a ray of sunshine on a dreary day."

Jasmine laughed as she drew closer. "I believe the South has also rekindled your desire to write poetry. What have you been doing in here all morning? The children were hoping you might join us outdoors for a noonday picnic under the trees."

"Going through this paper work."

"I told you I would take care of the ledgers, my dear. I don't expect you to assist Mr. Draper and do the bookwork as well."

"Wendell doesn't need my assistance at this point. Besides, your father's slaves are now freed men. They can come and go, work or not—it's their own choice. Mr. Draper no longer makes their decisions; he merely directs those wanting to work to the tasks that must be accomplished."

"Miz Jasmine?" Prissy stood in the library doorway, twisting her hands.

"Yes, Prissy? Is something wrong?"

"Massa Wade from Bedford Plantation has come calling. I had him wait in da parlor. He says he has business wib Massa Nolan. Should I show him in?" The girl's voice quivered as she spoke.

"Did he say something to frighten you, Prissy?" Jasmine inquired.

"No, ma'am. But yo' daddy bought some slaves from Massa Wade one time. He treats his people real bad—likes to use da whip."

"There's no need to worry, Prissy. We'll not let anything happen to you or any of the others. You go back to what you were doing, and I'll see to Mr. Wade."

The girl's even ivory teeth shone like a string of fine pearls as she beamed at Jasmine. "Thank you, Missus," she said before hurrying off toward the back of the house.

Nolan arched his eyebrows. "I assume you know Mr. Wade?"

"The Bedford Plantation has been in Harold Wade's family for years. None of the Wainwrights have had a close association with the Wade family, however, because Father didn't particularly like Harold. I can't imagine why he's come. Do you want to see him here in the library, or do you prefer to entertain him in the parlor?"

Nolan stood and walked around the desk. "Why don't *we* entertain him in the parlor. Perhaps he won't stay long, and we'll be able to join the children for their picnic."

She clasped his arm and gave him a winsome smile. "And here I thought you'd completely forgotten the picnic."

Harold Wade stood with his elbow perched on the fireplace and his gaze fixed upon the foyer. Except for turning toward the young couple as they entered the room, he remained motionless.

"Mr. Wade. It has been some time since I've seen you," Jasmine said. "I don't believe you've met my husband, Nolan Houston."

Mr. Wade gave a slight nod of his head and finally stepped away from the fireplace to shake hands with Nolan. "My pleasure, Mr. Houston. Sorry about your family, Jasmine. We were never close, but I always respected your father."

"Thank you, Mr. Wade," she said. "Won't you be seated?"

"I prefer to stand—problems with my back. Besides, my business shouldn't take long. I've come to make a proposition, Mr. Houston."

Nolan sat beside Jasmine on the brocade-upholstered settee. "What kind of proposition might that be?"

"Like most everyone in these parts, I lost slaves to the fever. From what I'm told, I lost more than the rest of you. Then, to make matters worse, a lot of my field slaves aren't recovering as quickly as I had hoped. I thought it was probably their usual laziness, but the doctor tells me they need more time to fully recover. Says I'll never get another good day's work out of any of them if they go back to the fields before they're back to full strength," he complained.

"Perhaps if your slaves had been healthy and well fed before the fever hit, they would have fared better throughout the epidemic," Jasmine said.

Mr. Wade ignored her remark and turned his attention to Nolan. "I'm wondering if you'd consider striking up a bargain with me whereby we would share the use of our slaves until the cotton crop has been harvested. Some of the other owners have worked out such an arrangement, and I thought you might be interested in doing the same. Or have you already made such an arrangement with others?"

"No, I haven't entered into an agreement with any of the other owners. I understand your dilemma, Mr. Wade, but I doubt we'd be interested in doing such a thing for the entire harvest. If you're in dire straits at the present time, I can ask our folks if they'd be willing to go and help out for a short time."

Mr. Wade looked at Nolan as though he'd taken leave of his senses. "Ask your folks if they'd be willing?" he asked before emitting a harsh laugh. "Those *folks,* as you call them, are *slaves.* And they've got no say in whether they'd be willing or not. They do *what* they're told, *when* they're told, and *how* they're told. Now, I realize you live up north, and likely you don't hold with the idea of slavery, but you need to readjust your thinking while you're in Mississippi."

"Thank you for your suggestion, Mr. Wade, but we appear to be doing just fine with our own method. If you'd care to ride out to the fields with me, we can inquire about your proposition. However, I don't anticipate a large number will agree."

Harold Wade looked at Jasmine as though he expected

her to explain Nolan's behavior, but she merely smiled and nodded at him.

"We shan't be long, my dear. Please tell the children that if they are willing to wait a little longer, I'll join you for that picnic you mentioned."

Nolan realized their visitor thought he was completely daft. Men such as Harold Wade didn't stop to have picnics with their wives and children during the harvest, and they certainly didn't inquire whether their slaves were willing to work. But Harold didn't realize the men, women, and children harvesting the crop at The Willows were no longer slaves. And this was a fact Nolan didn't wish to divulge at this juncture.

"I got about ten healthy men and maybe five women that I could trade off with you," Mr. Wade said. "They're all good pickers. Overseer might have to take a whip to one or two to keep them moving, but otherwise they're well trained. You think you could spare that many of your *folks*?" he asked as they rode to the cotton fields.

Nolan gave the man a sidelong glance. "I can spare as many as are willing to go," he said while waving at Mr. Draper.

"Something wrong?" Wendell Draper asked as he pulled on his reins and brought his horse alongside Nolan.

"Would you gather together everyone working in the fields so we can talk to them for a few minutes?"

Mr. Draper tipped his hat and then bounced his heels into the horse's shanks, signaling his animal into a gallop. When Nolan and Harold Wade reached the south cotton field, all of the hands were awaiting them, their heavy canvas bags bulging with the morning's pickings.

"I apologize for taking you away from your work," Nolan started, "but Mr. Wade from over at Bedford Plantation is wondering if any of you would be interested in helping him bring in his crop. He wants to trade off workers. I told him I didn't think any of you would be interested, but it's up to you."

Mr. Wade rolled his eyes heavenward and shook his head. "Craziest thing I've ever seen in my life. One of these mornings you're going to come down here and every one of these darkies is going to be gone."

Nolan shrugged. "Guess that could happen." The two men watched as the workers gathered into small groups to discuss the proposal.

"Massa Nolan," one of the men said as he approached.

"Yes, Henry?"

"There's twenty of us men who's willin' to go over an' work at the Bedford place, but how's that gonna work when you do the weighin' here at The Willows?"

"You won't get anything on the days you're at Mr. Wade's, but I'll give you double what you pick on the days when Mr. Wade's men are here. Does that sound reasonable?"

Henry nodded. "Can we stop going over there any time we decide we'd rather stay here and work?"

"Absolutely. You can go for half a day, every other day, or however you decide, and you can quit whenever you decide."

Mr. Wade motioned to Nolan. "You can't do it that way—you'll need an overseer to bring them back and forth. They need to be on a schedule."

"For their own protection, I'll write out a pass for each of them to travel back and forth, and I'll furnish a wagon for those who want to travel to your place as a group. If they decide to leave without the group, they can walk back on their own. It won't take any additional overseer. I wouldn't say anything to discourage them, or they may decide not to help at all."

"If it's not overstepping my bounds, Henry, can you tell me when you think you and the others will come to the Bedford?" Mr. Wade asked between clenched teeth.

"We's thinkin' on comin' tomorrow mornin', unless it's rainin'. Iffen it's rainin', we be stayin' here."

"Absolutely! After all, I wouldn't want any of you to get wet," Wade retorted sourly before turning his attention back to Nolan. "I keep thinking this entire ordeal must be a bad dream and that any moment, I'm going to awaken."

"Bad dream? You should ask these people about bad dreams, Mr. Wade. They've been living a nightmare for years!" Nolan considered something for a moment, then added, "One more thing: you may not lay the whip to any of these men nor discipline them in any fashion."

Wade pulled his hat low on his forehead. "Very well. I'll plan on seeing your folks in the morning—if it doesn't rain, and if it isn't too hot, and they don't decide they'd rather sleep," he replied dryly before riding off.

Nolan took the plate of food Alice Ann offered and sat down on one of the quilts Jasmine and Prissy had spread on the neatly manicured lawn. He wrapped a piece of thick ham in a slice of crusty bread that had been slathered with fresh churned butter and helped himself to a cup of lemonade.

"Are you going to come sit with me, Allie?" he asked.

"Me and Clara want to sit with Prissy. Mama can sit beside you," she said.

Nolan laughed. "What if Mama wants to sit beside Prissy?" he teased.

"Mama always sits with *you*," Alice Ann said matter-of-factly.

Jasmine and Spencer sat down on either side of Nolan. "I received a brief letter from McKinley," Jasmine said. "He says Violet continues to do well. The baby is still expected in early December, though he says Violet is hoping for late November. If it's a girl, they've decided to name her Madelaine Rose."

"A girl?" Spencer shook his head. "I'm hoping the baby will be a boy."

"I know you are, dear," his mother replied. "You are rather surrounded by girls. However, if it's a girl, it appears they've decided to name the child after my mother, although McKinley did say they plan to actually call the child Mattie Rose. I've never quite understood why you would christen a child with one name and then use another," she said to Nolan. "If they don't want to refer to the baby as Madelaine, why not simply name her Mattie?"

"But what if it's a boy?" Spencer insisted.

"They've decided upon Samuel Malcolm Wainwright should they have a boy."

Spencer nodded his agreement. "Sam. I like that much better than Mattie."

Jasmine smiled at her son. "I'm certain you do." She handed her husband a glass of lemonade. "I suppose this is McKinley and Violet's way of paying respect to the family, though I would have viewed his help here at The Willows as a greater tribute. I even thought to write and tell him so but knew it would only serve to further anger him."

"I'm pleased you restrained yourself," Nolan said. "Your brother is acutely aware you're unhappy he didn't come along to assist us—no need to cause a breach you would later regret. Any other news from Lowell?" he inquired before taking a bite of the thick ham sandwich.

"No. His letter was brief—merely an update of Violet's condition and the names they had chosen for the child." Jasmine took a drink of the cool lemonade. "I'm interested in hearing how things ended with Mr. Wade."

"Surprisingly, a number of the field hands agreed to go to Bedford and help with his crop. I truly didn't expect any of them to entertain his request," he replied. "For the life of me, I still cannot understand why they're willing to go over there. Surely they realize Wade will treat them no better than his own slaves."

"I thought they'd prefer to be here where they would earn their picking money. How are you going to handle the situation when Mr. Wade's slaves are here?"

"I'm going to pay double on those days. I doubt whether any of Wade's slaves are as motivated to pick as our field hands, so I offered to weigh out and pay double to our men."

"That was kind of you, yet it doesn't seem like enough of an incentive to make them want to go. I am truly baffled," she said. "What do you think, Prissy? Why would they want to go to Bedford?"

The girl shuddered at the question. "Um, I don' know, Miz Jasmine, 'cause that's one of dem places I'd never even want to visit. That massa Wade is a bad one. But iffen you wanna know, me and Toby can ask around and find out what dem men down in the quarter is thinkin'."

"Just so long as they don't feel obligated to go over there because of us. We don't want any of them feeling they must help Mr. Wade," Jasmine said.

"Never know what some people is thinkin'," Prissy said as she lifted a cup of milk to Clara's lips and helped the child with her drink.

By week's end, all of the men who had volunteered to assist at the Bedford Plantation stated they had erred and no longer wished to continue the trade. Nolan did not question their decision but was content to have the arrangement cease. He didn't like dealing with Harold Wade or the man's overseer and was pleased when their final labor exchange had been completed.

Accordingly, he was surprised to see Harold Wade and John Woodson, the owner of Rosewood, approaching the mansion on a cool evening some ten days later. He sat on the upper veranda and watched as plumes of dust kicked up around the horses' hooves.

"Gentlemen," Nolan greeted as he stood between two of the large columns forming the decorative colonnade that fronted the house.

"May we join you?" John Woodson inquired.

"Of course," Nolan replied. He waited at the top of the outer stairway that led directly to the veranda. "What brings you to The Willows?" he asked as they reached the gallery.

"Distressing news," Wade said.

Nolan noted the warning look Woodson directed at his companion.

"Why don't we sit down?" Mr. Woodson inquired in his thick, syrupy drawl.

"Something I can help with?" Nolan asked when the men had finally made themselves comfortable.

"I'm certain that you can, Mr. Houston. I told Harold on the way over here that I've heard you're a man of reason, and I know you're going to make a sound decision," Woodson said.

"Decision about what?"

"Seems the reason your *folks* were so willing to come over to my place and work is because they wanted to tell my slaves about what's going on over here. They've created chaos for me and many other owners," Harold said, his face now contorted in anger.

"Now, Harold, don't get all riled up. We've come to talk like gentlemen," John said. "You see, Mr. Houston, while you find nothing wrong in what you're doing, your actions have caused unrest among our slaves. Coupled with the difficulties caused by the epidemic, this unwitting action on your part has changed a problematic situation into something much more complex."

"I truly don't understand why you are placing blame upon me. I sent no one to Mr. Wade's plantation except at his express request. And I might add that he received more than he gave in the bargain. I did not complain, nor did the field hands. Mr. Wade was aware my hands were working without supervision and as freed men."

"No! I did *not* know you considered them freed men. You told me they did not need supervision as you let them work whatever hours they desired. Now they've told our slaves that they're going to receive money for their pickings and that you're going to set all of them free once you bring in your crop."

"It seems they secretly made their way onto other plantations while they were out with the passes you gave them and have now spread word throughout southern Mississippi and Louisiana," Mr. Woodson added.

"I imagine this is somewhat exaggerated, gentlemen, but I'll not deny what you've heard is true. My wife and I do not believe in slavery, and I'll not apologize for our beliefs or what we're doing. We're bringing in the crop only because it was one of Malcolm's final requests. Jasmine wanted to honor his wish, and we saw it as a way to provide funds for the freed slaves to begin their new lives."

"New lives!" Wade spat as he shot to his feet. "I *told* you he's crazed and that we'd get nowhere attempting to talk to him."

"Sit down, Harold," Mr. Woodson ordered. "Surely you can understand our concern, Mr. Houston. We not only fear unrest among our slaves but also believe they will begin to run away. And where do you think they are going to run to?"

"I have no idea," Nolan replied.

"Why, they're going to come *here,* where they believe they will receive safe haven. They think that if they can make it as far as The Willows, you'll protect them and grant them the same freedom and funds as you've promised your own slaves."

Nolan leaned back in his chair and folded his fingers to form a tent. "Though I would like nothing better, I cannot grant freedom if I don't hold their papers. You need only explain that fact to them."

"Do you think we are so naïve that we believe you? Papers mean little to those of you who are intent on giving the colored man his freedom," Wade snarled.

Woodson motioned for Wade to cease talking. "If you insist upon this foolishness," he asked Nolan, "would you at least consider telling your slaves you are reneging on your offer so that word will spread and we can once again control our slaves? You can later tell them the truth when you actually set them free."

"I'm sorry, but I can't do that. I believe you men are worrying needlessly, and I suggest you tell your slaves the truth: I can free only the slaves that belonged to Malcolm Wainwright."

———

Prissy waited anxiously at the end of the driveway, watching the road for any sign of Spencer Houston. He should have been home from school two hours ago, and now the missus was fretting something awful. She danced from foot to foot, uncertain if she should report back to the big house or continue watching. Surely the missus would realize she was still waiting at her assigned post. Maybe she should edge her way down the road a ways so she could see over the small rise in the roadway. Fear gripped her as she attempted to make a decision. She'd never gone off on her own. What if the missus thought she was trying to escape and run away?

A nervous giggle escaped her lips as she remembered she was now allowed to run away if she wanted. Slowly at first and then with a more determined step, she walked down the dusty road and up the small hillock. It was there she thought she saw something—or someone.

She moved more quickly and then began to run as she realized what she was seeing. "Spencer!" she screamed. "I'm coming, chile!"

Spencer was struggling to get to his feet when she reached his side. She tried to hide her horror. The boy's face was swollen and bleeding, and there were cuts and bruises on his legs and arms.

"You lay still, Spencer. I'm gonna go get your pappy so's he can carry you back home," Prissy said.

The boy nodded his agreement.

"Who did this to you?" she asked before hurrying off.

"Boys at school," he whispered. "They hate us 'cause we don't believe in slavery."

Prissy jumped to her feet. "I be right back with help." She raced down the road with white-hot fear rising inside her—a fear of what had happened to Spencer Houston and a fear of the future.

CHAPTER · 8

HUMMING UNDER her breath, Prissy worked the cloth back and forth on the mahogany table in an easy rhythm, then suddenly brought her work to a halt. Had she heard something banging on the house? She cocked her head to one side and listened. With a shrug, she returned to her polishing but then a persistent knock sounded at the front door.

"Who could that be?" she muttered while shoving the cloth into her waistband and scurrying down the hall. "Them young'uns best not be playing tricks with me."

Since Master Nolan had made his announcement to the slaves that he was giving them their freedom, not many folks had come calling at The Willows. In fact, since young Spencer's incident after school, there hadn't been *any* visitors. Of course, it didn't seem to bother Master Nolan none, 'cause he said they was all gonna leave Mississippi once the cotton crop was harvested. Prissy wasn't so sure that was going to happen. Talk of leaving frightened her. All she wanted to do was marry Toby—and the sooner the better. She didn't want no more trouble in her life, and with all this talk of freedom, there was bound to be trouble. She could feel it coming, just like a summer storm filled with jagged lightning.

Her eyes widened when she reached the front door, and she froze in place.

"Are you going to open the door, or must we do it for ourselves?" Lydia Hesston inquired irritably from across the threshold.

"Afternoon, Prissy," Rupert said. "Why don't you show us into the parlor and then tell your mistress she has company. Think you can manage to do that?" he asked with a sneer curling his lips.

Lydia pulled off her gloves as she leveled an arrogant glare in Prissy's direction. "I can find my way into the parlor. Go and tell my cousin I've come to call on her."

"Yessum." In her haste to depart the room, Prissy tripped on the edge of the patterned red and black carpet, nearly landing flat in front of Rupert.

"Clumsy girl," Lydia chided while Prissy regained her balance and rushed from sight.

"Mean-spirited woman," Prissy whispered.

Perhaps it *would* be worth leaving the South if she didn't have to put up with the likes of Mr. and Mrs. Rupert Hesston, she thought. How Miss Lydia and Miss Jasmine could be cousins—blood-related—and act so different was beyond Prissy's imagination. Both from the same family . . . one was filled with meanness and the other with love.

"Hard to unnerstand," she muttered.

"What's hard to understand?"

Prissy startled at the sound of her mistress's voice. "I thought you was outside in da garden," she replied. "You got company, Miz Jasmine. Yo' cousin Miss Lydia and her husband is come to call. They's in the parlor."

"Lydia has returned? How wonderful! Would you fix some tea and bring it to us in the parlor, Prissy?"

She hesitated. The last thing she wanted to do was go

back in the parlor and serve tea, yet she wouldn't refuse Miss Jasmine. "Yessum. I be bringing it ta you directly."

She considered asking Martha or Henrietta if they would serve tea and then offer to look after the children, but she thought better of the idea. Miss Jasmine might question why she would do such a thing. Prissy didn't want to lie to the mistress, but she could hardly tell Miss Jasmine what she thought of her relatives. Best to serve tea and remain silent, she decided.

Being careful to watch her step, Prissy carried the tray to the parlor, placed it on the walnut serving table beside Miss Jasmine, and turned to leave.

"Why don't you remain, Prissy? You know, Lydia, it's Prissy we have to thank for finding our Spencer, who was injured on his way home from school. She bravely went searching for him and then came running for help once she saw his tragic condition," Jasmine related while patting Prissy's hand.

"I's got silver that needs polishin'," Prissy said while backing toward the door.

"The silver will wait. Sit down here and have a cup of tea while I tell of your heroics," her mistress insisted.

Mrs. Hesston's mouth gaped open, and if Prissy hadn't been so frightened, she would have laughed aloud at the sight.

"Jasmine! Whatever are you thinking, inviting *her* to have tea with *us*? Have you taken leave of your senses?"

Rupert gave his wife a knowing look. "You see? I told you she's become completely irrational."

"*I'm* irrational? It's *you* people who are irrational. You won't tolerate *anyone* who doesn't believe exactly as you do. Spencer is evidence of that! Even though I disagree with slavery, I would never teach my child to hate those whose views differ. And I am not hesitant to say that evil permeates people who would teach such behavior."

Prissy shrunk back, wishing she could make herself invisible. Mrs. Hesston had pulled a handkerchief from her reticule and was dabbing her eyes as she looked to her husband for consolation.

"I cannot believe any of this," Mrs. Hesston said. "I came here seeking comfort from one I remembered fondly. Since my return from abroad, I've been surrounded by tragedy. First I discover my immediate family has perished, and now I find that one of my few living relatives has turned against me in my time of grief."

Jasmine set her cup down with an authoritative clunk. "Don't be overly dramatic, cousin. We've all suffered. I, too, lost my family members and have suffered grief. However, life goes on. We must each move forward in the way that God leads. Fortunately for me, I find that He is leading my family away from this place!"

———

It was midafternoon when Justin Chamberlain's horse-drawn wagon lumbered to a stop in front of the boarding-house on Dutton Street. He set the brake and jumped down, pleased to finally be back in Lowell. Packing the dishes and glassware had taken a fair amount of skill and patience, and then arranging all of their household goods into the wagon had proven more of a chore than he had ever imagined. He'd soon grown weary of the task. As he now surveyed the loaded wagon, he realized his lack of enthusiasm was apparent.

Louise would be appalled to see her carefully stitched quilts shoved atop the rough-edged barrels and crates—containers that would likely snag and rip her painstaking handiwork. But he had needed something to tightly pack the dishes and glassware, and the quilts were at hand. Besides,

Louise wasn't alive to see what he had done, and Reggie wouldn't care.

"Father!" Reggie squealed as she bounded out the door and threw herself into his arms. "You've finally come home!"

Justin firmly wrapped his arms around the gangly ten-year-old and kissed the top of her head. "I believe you've grown at least an inch during my absence."

"Then you should have returned more quickly," she said, tightening her chokehold.

He loosened his daughter's clenched fingers and took a step back while gently grasping her waiflike shoulders. She looked amazingly ladylike, wearing a bright blue print dress accentuated by rows of tiny pin tucks. Her soft brown hair was neatly combed and tied with a matching blue ribbon, and instead of dirt smudges, she bore a dusting of flour on one cheek.

"You look quite charming. Tell me how you've been," he said as they entered the front door.

"I've been wonderful—except for school. If I could have stayed at the boardinghouse and helped Mrs. Brighton all day, I would have been *very* happy."

"Pastor Chamberlain! When did you arrive?" Elinor inquired as she came down the hallway from the kitchen.

"Just now. I came straight to the boardinghouse. I couldn't wait any longer to see Reggie," he said, giving his daughter a bright smile.

"Do come in and sit down. I must say that I'm almost sorry that you've returned. Having Reggie with me has been most enjoyable."

Justin's eyebrows arched. "Truly?"

Reggie folded her arms across her chest and gave her father a look of mock indignation. "Why are you acting surprised?"

"Who says I'm acting?" he retorted, wrapping his arm around Reggie and drawing her closer.

"I know you're only teasing," she said. "You missed me bunches."

"You are absolutely correct on that account. And all of your friends from back home said to tell you hello. I even have some letters for you, but I promised I wouldn't turn them over until you agreed to answer each one."

Reggie's eyes sparkled with delight. "Is there one from Peter?"

"I believe there is. However, I want to hear all about your new school before I give you the letters. Otherwise, I'll not be able to pry a word from you."

"I'm doing fine in my classes. Aren't I," she said to Elinor.

"Indeed she is. I can't say that Reggie is thrilled with the school or her classmates, but she does her lessons as soon as she returns to the boardinghouse, and her teacher has written several notes praising her work. I've saved all of her papers for you to review."

"That was very thoughtful," Justin said before turning his attention back to his daughter. "And what is it you dislike about your classmates and the school, young lady?"

"The school is much larger than the ones I've attended. I like smaller schools."

"And your classmates?" he urged.

"The girls are very persnickety and the boys don't want to play with a girl, so they're mean—except for Moses. He's still nice to me."

"I see. Then it sounds as though you have your work cut out for you if you're going to make friends, and it appears you've already taken the proper steps with that new dress and ribbon in your hair."

"I didn't wear this dress to please any of those girls. One

of Mrs. Brighton's boarders gave me several dresses. She said they were more appropriate for a schoolgirl than a woman of her years."

"Yes, Ardith is nearly an old maid—she must be all of ten years older than Reggie," Elinor teased.

"Perhaps I should offer her a few coins for the dress," Justin suggested.

Elinor shook her head. "She was pleased Reggie was willing to wear the dresses. I think it would spoil her gift if you offered to pay her. Do tell us about your journey. Reggie was worried you had fallen victim to some difficulty. But I attempted to reassure her that all was well."

"There is no denying I was gone longer than I anticipated, and I do apologize for my delay. Both the packing and the journey were more difficult than I expected. There was a great deal of rain on my return, and with the weight of the wagon, I made little progress each day. Also, I stopped in Portland for a brief visit with the church leader who appointed me to the position here in Lowell. He and his wife are fine people, and since I was passing nearby, I decided to stop and see them. Rather thoughtless of me, now that I think about it," he said apologetically.

"Not at all. We've been having a grand time, haven't we, Reggie?" Elinor said enthusiastically.

"I learned how to bake bread while you were gone," Reggie proudly announced.

"Now that is truly an accomplishment," Justin replied. "And when will you be baking some of this fine bread for your father?"

"You can take a loaf home and have a taste this very evening," Elinor suggested.

Justin rubbed his hands together. "I can hardly wait to sink my teeth into it. But be prepared, young lady: I'm a harsh judge of bread, and you'll not be getting any praise unless it's justly deserved," he teased.

Reggie giggled at his remark. "I'm not worried. If the bread suits the girls who live here, I believe you'll find it passable."

"Harsh critics, are they?"

Reggie bobbed her head up and down. "Some of them like to complain about most everything. If the soup is a little too cool or a little too hot, if they hoped for white bread and Mrs. Brighton serves corn bread instead, if they have to work three looms instead of two at the mill, or if they must share their bed with two girls instead of one. Mrs. Brighton says not to pay them any mind when they're short-tempered. She says they complain because they're tired, but I think they're spoiled by Mrs. Brighton's fine food and good treatment."

Elinor blushed at Reggie's praise. "The girls receive fine treatment at all of the boardinghouses," she said with obvious embarrassment.

"I'm sure Reggie speaks with great authority regarding your abilities. I would like to remain and visit, but I believe we had best get the wagon home. I hope to unload at least a portion of the goods tonight and then finish tomorrow— especially since it will be Saturday and I'll have Reggie there to assist," he said, winking at his daughter.

"Let me get your loaf of bread. Do you want to pack your clothes tonight or come back and get them tomorrow, Reggie?" Elinor asked as she began to rise from her chair.

"I'll come back and see you tomorrow. I'll fetch the bread," she said, jumping to her feet.

"Wrap it in one of the linen cloths in the far drawer."

"I will," Reggie called over her shoulder as she raced off to the kitchen.

Justin shook his head. "I can't believe how much she's

changed. She appears much . . ." He hesitated and then shrugged his shoulders.

"Happier?" Elinor ventured.

"That too," he said. "I insist upon paying you for all you've done," he said as Reggie hurried back into the room, carrying the linen-wrapped bundle.

"We can discuss that matter at another time. And don't you forget to come back for your belongings, Reggie," she instructed as she gave the girl a hug.

"I won't. Thank you for letting me stay with you."

"You are most welcome," she said warmly.

The trio made their way out to the wagon, and Justin lifted Reggie up onto the seat. "I'll let you know what I think of Reggie's baking," he called out as he slapped the reins and flashed a smile at Elinor.

———

The sun had not yet crested the ridge of hills along the eastern fringes of the city when Justin Chamberlain forced himself from a sound sleep and settled his feet on the rough and splintered floorboards of his small bedroom.

He rubbed his eyes and raked one hand through his mop of disheveled hair in an attempt to pat down the errant strands that circled his head like ruffled chicken feathers. "Good enough," he muttered.

The previous night's work had continued until the cover of darkness made it impossible to safely continue unloading the household goods. He had secured the tarp-covered wagon in the barnlike storage shed at the rear of his house and then spent the next hour caring for his horses.

He'd gone to bed promising himself he would arise early the next day and finish unloading the wagon before Reggie awakened. That way they would have the entire day to uncrate and arrange the goods. Granted, it would take more than one day, but with an early start, he hoped to accomplish a great deal.

He was carrying the last of the crates into the front room when Reggie bounded down the stairs and met him in the parlor. She stood before him in an old cotton nightgown that had belonged to her mother. Wild wisps of hair flew in all directions as they escaped the long braid hanging down her back.

"You began without me," she accused.

"You need not worry. I haven't unpacked one thing, so there is still plenty to do. In fact, we'll be fortunate if we have everything unpacked by this time next week."

"I could remain at home all next week and help you," she volunteered.

Justin laughed aloud. "I think not, young lady. If the choice comes down to our living in chaos or your attending school, we'll live in chaos. We'll complete what we can today and work on it each evening next week."

"If you ask the teacher, I'm certain she'll send my work home."

"It's more important that you attend school than unpack boxes," he replied. "Now why don't you run upstairs and get dressed while I fix us some breakfast. Once we've finished our meal, we'll begin."

His daughter grumbled under her breath as she shuffled out of the room and up the steep flight of stairs, her feet slapping heavily on the wooden steps in a childlike display of irritation. Justin ignored the exhibition, knowing Reggie would be sorely disappointed that her actions failed to annoy him.

A hearty breakfast of eggs, bacon, and Reggie's home-made bread, along with a crock of raspberry jam supplied by Elinor, was waiting on the table when Reggie entered the kitchen in an old, faded dress that was too short.

"It appears you've grown since you last wore that dress," her father remarked as she plopped down on the wooden chair.

"The skirt may be a little too short, but it's plenty good enough to wear while I'm unpacking boxes."

"You're right about that. Incidentally, this bread is excellent." He waved the jam-laden slice he held in one hand.

Her eyes brightened at the praise. "Thank you. I'm pleased you like it. I'm going to attempt making some all by myself next Saturday. I'd like to make some on Monday, but since I must go to school . . ." Her voice trailed off as she gave her father a questioning look.

"Next Saturday it shall be. And I'll look forward to it with great anticipation," he replied. "Shall we get to those boxes?" he asked as he picked up their plates and cleared the table.

Reggie nodded. "It's nice to have all of our furniture again, isn't it?" Reggie asked as they began opening boxes.

He agreed. The furniture was scattered about the rooms in complete disarray, and yet there was comfort in being surrounded by their own belongings.

"I never saw this before. Who made it?" Reggie inquired, holding up an intricately stitched sampler.

"Your mother made it the year before we married."

"It's beautiful. May I have it?" she asked, tracing her finger over the raised stitching.

Justin was surprised by his daughter's request. "Of course. You can have anything of your mother's you desire. In fact, I know she would be delighted that you appreciate her handwork."

"Can I take it over to Mrs. Brighton's and show her?"

Justin mumbled his agreement while unwrapping the hastily packed dishes. "It appears I didn't secure these as well as I thought."

Reggie surveyed the broken plate and grinned. "So long as three of them remain unbroken, we'll do fine."

"Three?"

She gave him a look of surprise. "We'll need to invite Mrs. Brighton for supper, don't you think?"

Her father was kneeling on the floor, reaching deep into one of the crates. "Oh yes, of course."

Once again she had surprised him. Reggie, so slow to make friends, especially with adults, had apparently grown quite fond of Elinor Brighton during his absence. The thought pleased him. After the incident at the church, he was acutely aware his daughter could use the guidance of a woman.

"Were you expecting company?" Reggie inquired as a knock sounded at the door. She stood up and peeked out through a small opening in the parlor drapes.

The knocking continued and Justin sat back on his heels. "Are you going . . ."

"It's them!" Reggie hissed. She tiptoed back to her father.

"Them? Who is *them*?"

"The church ladies!" she whispered. She leaned closer to her father's ear as the knocking grew more insistent. "We need to hide."

"Pastor Chamberlain!" Winifred Mason's shrill voice called from the other side of the door. "Try the back door. I know he's in there! I'll look through the parlor windows and see if anyone's in there." She had apparently taken charge of the group.

Justin rose to his feet. "We can't hide in here, Reggie. I'll tell them we're busy and ask them to return at another time."

"On a school day," she said quickly.

He smiled and nodded while walking to the door.

"Ladies!" he greeted, positioning himself to block their entry.

"My dear husband saw your wagon in front of Mrs. Brighton's boardinghouse yesterday and told me you had returned with your furniture and household goods," Winifred said, the frightfully large feather on her hat bobbing back and forth in time with her exaggerated movements. "Believe me, it didn't take long before I spread the word to the other ladies that we must come over here today and assist you."

"You are very kind to offer, but Reggie and I have the situation under control. We've already unpacked most of the crates and boxes," he explained.

"Tut, tut, this is women's work," Martha Emory said. "You and that young child can't properly arrange a household. Come along, ladies," she commanded as she gave the door a hefty shove.

Justin flattened himself against the wall as the women stormed the house. They hesitated in the foyer for only a moment before turning their attention to the parlor. The chaos and disorder beckoned them onward like soldiers who had glimpsed the enemy. They charged into the room with fierce determination etched upon their faces. They had observed their obstacle, and they would conquer!

Martha placed her parasol in the umbrella stand with a definitive thunk. "You were gone for so long we thought perhaps you'd return with a wife. You *didn't,* did you?"

"No," Justin replied softly while watching the remaining ladies begin digging through their belongings. "As I said, Reggie and I are quite capable of completing this task without assistance," he insisted, though no one except his daughter appeared to hear him.

"You see? There's no need to worry, Caroline," Martha remarked to her very eligible daughter.

Caroline's face reddened, and she quickly turned a dagger-filled glare upon her mother.

Reggie edged close to her father's side. "Tell them to leave," she pleaded as the women began rearranging the parlor furniture.

He shrugged his shoulders. "I don't believe there's any way to get them out," he said, now resigned to his fate.

"Do *something!*" Reggie implored.

"Ladies! Please don't move the furniture. I'm quite happy with it just the way it is," he requested feebly.

Winifred looked at him as though he'd lost his mind. "You can't have the divan sitting in front of the window. The sun will fade the fabric."

"Indeed!" Caroline agreed.

"I'll close the draperies," he argued.

"You'll forget after one or two days," Martha insisted. "If there were a woman—a *wife*—to attend to such matters on a daily basis, then such an arrangement might be acceptable."

Although Justin and Reggie made several more attempts to halt the women's ministrations, their suggestions went ignored. Finally, Justin sat down and watched while Reggie paced back and forth behind him, muttering words of irritation and disgust. When the group had the parlor arranged to their satisfaction, they clumped up the stairs to accomplish their next mission.

"Who could *that* be?" Justin asked as another knock sounded at the front door.

He pulled open the door and was greeted by the unremitting chatter of another group of women from the church. The thought of slamming the door was tempting, yet he maintained his dignity.

"Ladies! I do believe I have all the assistance I can stand for one day."

"You can never have enough help when it comes to settling into a new house," Cecile Turnvall remarked as she, Abigail Mitchell, and Charlotte Brown bustled into the parlor.

There was no stopping Cecile. She and her comrades immediately set about moving all of the furniture the first group had arranged only a short time earlier. They tugged and pulled and huffed and puffed until the furniture was settled into a display that met with her satisfaction.

"That is *so* much better," she triumphantly announced. "Men have no sense of design and balance."

Justin stared into the room. This group had returned the furniture to much the way he'd arranged it earlier in the day.

"Well, I have never been so insulted!" Winifred remarked as her small group came down the stairway in time to hear Cecile's pronouncement. Winifred marched into the parlor with her mouth agape as she viewed the change that had taken place during her absence. "The furniture was perfectly arranged when we went upstairs. What have you done, Cecile?"

Cecile's eyebrows furrowed. The woman was obviously confused. "I have set things aright in this parlor," she answered calmly.

Winfred turned to her companions. "Gather your belongings, ladies. We're not wanted here, and I'll not be a part of making the pastor's home into a gaudy facsimile of how a genteel home should appear."

Justin stood helpless as Winifred, Martha, Caroline, and the other ladies who were members of the first contingency pinned their hats in place, yanked their parasols from the umbrella stand, and marched out the front door with the same vigor and determination with which they'd entered earlier.

"Now let's get started in the dining room," Cecile said to her collaborators.

Reggie tugged on her father's sleeve. "Are you going to let them continue changing things around? Soon another group will show up and then another."

Justin shrugged in confusion. "There's no way to stop them. You know I've already tried."

"Well, these ladies wouldn't get away with this in Mrs. Brighton's house. Sometimes the girls try to rearrange the furniture in the parlor or dining room, but Mrs. Brighton puts her foot down and immediately calls a halt to such activity. She would never allow such behavior in *her* house."

"It's too bad Mrs. Brighton isn't here right now," he said wearily. "Perhaps she would help us do the same. I believe I'll go make sure the door to my study is locked. I don't want them in there rearranging my books."

Justin searched for his daughter a short time later, thinking perhaps the two of them should take their fishing poles and head off to the river. If the good church ladies were determined to occupy his house, then he and Reggie might as well enjoy themselves for the remainder of the day. But Reggie was nowhere to be found. Finally he remembered the secret opening in her upstairs closet and thought maybe she'd gone to hide in her room.

"Reggie?" He knocked on the door before entering her room, but she wasn't there and the secret opening in the floor was securely covered.

He sat down on her bed but jumped to his feet when a burst of commotion erupted from downstairs. He hurried down the steps and stopped in the hallway. Elinor Brighton was standing beside Reggie, loudly clapping her hands.

"Ladies! Give me your immediate attention," she commanded in an urgent tone before once again clapping her hands together.

A distinct look of irritation crossed Cecile's face. "What is it?" she asked.

Unwavering, Elinor met Cecile's formidable gaze. "You must *all* leave—immediately."

"And might I ask just what authority you have in this matter?" Charlotte inquired.

"Exactly my question also," Cecile added.

"I have been asked to arrange the house in a manner that will be most beneficial for Reggie as she undertakes her duties in the house. With all due respect, I must request that you leave, or I'll be forced to use Pastor Chamberlain's broom and sweep you out," she said with a lopsided grin.

Elinor watched as Cecile Turnvall picked up a vase and crocheted scarf and began to arrange them on a side table. "Get the broom, Reggie!"

Cecile's mouth opened into a wide oval. "You're serious!"

"That I am," Elinor replied as Reggie reappeared with a straw turkey broom. "I know your hearts are in the proper place and that your intentions are well founded. However, the pastor has asked you to leave, but you've not done so." She waved the broom back and forth above her head. "Will you now leave peaceably, or must I put this broom to a use for which it was never intended?"

The women cast unhappy glances at Elinor, but she didn't waver. Instead, she remained in place, wearing a pleasant expression on her face while they prepared for their departure.

"How *dare* she act in such a bold manner! Why, she's simply trying to snag him for herself," Charlotte whispered to Cecile.

"We'll see about that! I know Martha Emory has plans for her Caroline and the preacher. I'm going to tell Caroline that she had best get busy, as she has some obvious competition," Cecile said loudly enough for all to hear. "Although at her age, Elinor Brighton hardly seems competition."

"She's merely using the girl in order to win him over for herself," Abigail agreed.

Elinor remained steadfast and didn't say a word until the last of the visitors exited the house. "I believe they're gone for good," she said as she closed the door. "From what they said, I imagine they'll be quick to tell the others what's occurred."

"I can't believe you actually succeeded in forcing their departure," Justin said with a hearty laugh. "And to think they actually believe you came here because you're interested in finding a husband."

"And not just any husband, but you. The very idea!" The two of them burst into gales of rippling laughter, not stopping until they were breathless.

Justin glanced at his daughter, who was staring at the two of them with a strange look in her eyes. "Good job, Reggie," he said. "Thank you for fetching Mrs. Brighton."

"You're welcome."

A strange faraway look remained in Reggie's eyes. Justin tilted his head to one side, attempting to discern just what his daughter could be thinking. Perhaps she was coming down with a cold. He shook his head and uttered a silent prayer that this would not be the case.

CHAPTER · 9

MCKINLEY FOLLOWED behind Matthew as the two entered the home of Nathan Appleton. The gathering this evening would likely reveal the same behavior that was being exhibited throughout the entire Northeast. An ominous apprehension shrouded the room like a proclamation of death. McKinley shuddered as he inhaled a deep breath. The air was thick with fear.

"They've prepared themselves for the worst, and that is good," Nathan whispered.

"For once I wish I could disappoint them," Matthew replied with a look of weariness.

Nathan nodded and moved to his desk. "Gentlemen, we'll not keep you waiting. Matthew has brought a report and his recommendations."

McKinley accompanied Matthew to the desk and began to arrange the sheaf of papers in his case while Matthew greeted the members of the Boston Associates.

"We are all acutely aware the banks have been closed since the thirteenth of October. To date, there is no indication when they may reopen. Already there is a rise in unemployment. Real estate and grain prices have begun to decrease, although there are predictions the South will not suffer as greatly as the rest of the country due to their slave economy. Personally, I fear that if some means isn't found to slow down the panic, we will find ourselves in a deep recession."

"I agree," Nathan said. "However, a financial panic can be like a malignant epidemic that kills more by terror than by real disease. Consequently we must remain level-headed."

Matthew nodded his agreement. "But we must also be prepared for a tumultuous period, especially here in the North. We must have a definitive plan of action. From the reports I've received to date, we will continue to receive the cotton shipments as contracted from all of our Southern growers. I anticipate little shortage due to the yellow fever outbreak among our largest producers. However, if we don't employ a replacement for Samuel Wainwright in the near future, we may face difficulty next year. Most of our contracts are due for renewal, and we'll need someone to negotiate with the Southerners—unless we look elsewhere," he hesitantly added.

A hush fell over the room. Even McKinley ceased shuffling through the paper work and directed his full attention to his father-in-law.

Finally breaking the silence, Thomas Clayborn rose to his feet. "Whatever do you mean by that remark, Matthew?"

"I've been contacted by an envoy representing the Russian cotton producers. They are very interested in wooing us back—their prices are certainly more competitive . . ."

"I thought we decided a number of years ago that the Russian cotton was inferior and we were not going to use substandard raw materials," Leonard Montrose said.

"It appears the quality, at least what I saw, was equal to

what we've been receiving," Matthew replied. "If the Russian prices continue to drop and the economy doesn't quickly recover, I believe this is an option we'll need to seriously consider."

"What they show you and what they actually deliver will likely be entirely different," McKinley put in. "And what of our loyalty to the growers who have so capably supplied you through the years? If the country is to survive, should we not continue doing business within our own borders when products are available?" He was unable to keep his anger in check.

"You have a valid point, my boy," Nathan said. "However, our first duty is to our investors. If the recession continues, we may want to consider the Russian cotton, but we should first give our Southern growers an opportunity to meet an equal price, don't you think?"

The men muttered among themselves as a haze of cigar smoke floated upward and layered the room.

Matthew leaned forward. "I'm more than willing to give all of our suppliers equal opportunity, but if we sign contracts with the Southern growers, we will be bound and it will matter little what price the Russians offer. How do you plan to overcome such an obstacle? As in the past, I believe the Southerners will insist upon contracts."

Nathan took a sip from his glass of port. "Once again, present them with an option. Tell them we will make every effort to purchase their cotton, but we'll not be signing contracts at this time. It will be their choice."

"You're gambling with our future, Nathan," Robert Woolsey cautioned.

"The South will likely pursue and win the English market. If the Russians don't actually come through or if their product is inferior, we could be left without any cotton whatsoever. I believe we should contract with at least half of the Southern growers in the event this plan with Russia proves foolhardy," Matthew suggested.

Nathan nodded his agreement. "All of life is a gamble, Robert. Fortunes are made and lost in the blink of an eye. Only the brave weather the storm."

"Or drown," Robert countered. "To lose my own investment is one thing—I have a vote in the matter. But we are responsible for the futures of more than ourselves. Give pause to think about the vast number of employees and suppliers who work for us and will be affected by the decisions we make this night as well as in the future."

"No need to become maudlin," Josiah Baines said. "We all realize these are weighty issues we're settling upon."

"And we do have time to wrestle with some, but Matthew cannot be expected to move forward without direction," Nathan said.

Robert Woolsey stood to be recognized. "What is the situation regarding layoffs in the mills?"

"Layoffs will begin within the next month, and I surmise several of the mills will be closed down," Matthew answered. "I truly dislike being the bearer of bad tidings, but all of you are intelligent men who understand what has happened as well as I do. The system of paper currency and bank credits in this country has caused wild speculation and gambling in stocks. Even President Buchanan has reported that the fourteen hundred banks in this country have been irresponsible and are deferring to the interests of their stockholders rather than the public welfare. Until there are restrictions forcing the banks to back their paper currency with gold and silver, these problems will continue. Let us hope Congress will finally take definitive action."

"Well said, Matthew," Nathan exclaimed. "Even those of us who own stock in many of these banks want to see matters handled in a more appropriate fashion."

McKinley surveyed the room and wondered what these men must be thinking. His investments were of a much lesser value than the holdings of these men, yet he knew he stood on the brink of financial ruin. Fear had become McKinley's constant companion, and he wondered if the calm appearance of these men was merely a façade. He longed to confide in his father-in-law, though his pride prohibited him from speaking.

Samuel had been his one confidant throughout the last several years. He had looked to his older brother as a mentor and a refuge where his secrets would be protected. Only Samuel had known McKinley's financial woes. Only Samuel had known that, in his haste to provide Violet with the same worldly possessions she'd enjoyed in her father's home, he had overextended himself—and he had continued down the same path even to this day, contracting and beginning to build an ever bigger and more lavish home for his family. He'd borrowed well beyond the worth of his investments. The only thing that could possibly pull him from his financial abyss was the sale of The Willows. He could only hope Jasmine would bargain well for its sale.

"For now, what say you in regard to new contracts, hiring a replacement for Samuel Wainwright, layoffs, and the many other issues bearing down upon us?" Matthew inquired.

"I suggest we empower you to cautiously move forward with layoffs where needed. In regard to the contracts, we have several months before we need make a final decision. Let's give that topic additional thought." Nathan scratched his beard. "I know if Samuel were alive, he would already be negotiating with the growers to secure their new contracts. However, I believe we should refrain from hiring a replacement at this juncture. If questions arise regarding contracts, we can then truthfully say we've been slowed down in the process due to Samuel's untimely death. What say you?" he inquired.

Once again murmurs filled the room, like the annoying hum of mating cicadas. Each man was intent upon discussing his view with a neighbor before reaching a final decision. Each one was hopeful he could sway a comrade to his own particular viewpoint. After waiting several minutes, Nathan pounded a gavel and restored order to the group.

"We can talk *after* the meeting. For now let's vote so those who need to return home may do so."

McKinley was not surprised when an overwhelming majority agreed with Nathan's proposal. They were usually in accord with his directives. Even those who voiced opposition during the meetings usually succumbed to the pressure to go along with the group. Like sheep, they nearly always followed their shepherd.

CHAPTER · 10

Early November 1857

JASMINE STEPPED into the library, her white kid slippers gliding across the carpet without a sound. Nolan's chair was turned toward the garden, but he was obviously engrossed in the letter he held in one hand.

"A letter from home or a business matter?" Jasmine inquired as she drew near his chair and gently grasped his shoulder.

Nolan started at her touch. "I didn't hear you approach," he said, placing the letter on his desk. "The letter is from Albert Cameron at the Lowell Savings Bank, along with a note from Paddy that he included."

"Is Paddy having problems with the farm?" she asked, taking a seat opposite her husband.

"No, nothing like that. Paddy could care for the farm and horses without a second thought. However, it seems the economy is much worse in the North—at least for the present time. Albert explains problems that have occurred and his prospects for the future. . . . It's rather dim, I fear. He says he recently reviewed a number of Southern newspapers and was surprised at the lack of coverage regarding what he describes as a full-blown panic that has now thrown large portions of the country into a recession."

"I've not heard or read anything that indicated the country was in a recession. Are we so far removed from the rest of the country that we have no idea what is transpiring at home? Surely Albert is exaggerating," she said.

"He isn't one to overstate his concerns, so I seriously doubt he would write unless he perceived this as a genuine problem. He says predictions of a quick recovery aren't forthcoming, and he also states that President Buchanan referred to the country's monetary interests as being in deplorable condition, though he does believe we'll make a complete recovery."

Jasmine stood up and moved to Nolan's side. "This makes no sense. Why would this information not be important to the Southern community? For the life of me, I cannot understand why such matters would be hidden beneath a cloak of silence."

Nolan smiled and patted her hand. "I don't imagine anyone is making a concerted effort to hide these issues. The newspaper editors have likely decided that since the Southern economy has not yet been affected, there is no reason to create panic among the gentry."

"So they're going to bury their heads until disaster swoops down upon them rather than preparing when they have the opportunity?"

"I believe they prefer to think the problem will not filter into the Deep South. And though I have serious doubts, they may be correct in their thinking."

"Oh, pshaw! There must be more to this than meets the eye. I'd guess someone in power made a decision to withhold the information from the South for as long as possible and for whatever reason. I would speculate that favors are being exchanged among the powerful and at the expense of the citizens."

Nolan gave a hearty laugh. "I believe your analysis of the situation may be more dramatic than the actual truth—whatever that may be."

Jasmine removed a small watch from the tiny pocket set in the seam of her violet day dress. "I didn't realize it was getting so late. I had best check on Spencer. I told Henrietta I would see that he completed his sums." She kissed him on the cheek. "I'd like to discuss this matter further when I've finished. I haven't yet heard what Paddy had to say in his note to you, and I want to read Albert's letter," she called over her shoulder.

The violet and gray silk fringe that edged the bodice and sleeves of the wool dress swayed in time with her steps as Jasmine hurried up the steps to the small room she had converted into a schoolroom for her son.

Spencer was leaning out the single window in the tiny room with only his lower body remaining inside the framework.

"That's a dangerous position, Spencer. Come back inside before you fall and hurt yourself," Jasmine warned. "Have you finished your lessons?"

"On the table," he replied as he wriggled his upper torso back inside. "Can I go fishing if they're all correct?"

"Do you never tire of fishing?" she inquired with a soft smile.

"It's the only good thing about being in Mississippi. It remains warm enough to fish nearly all year long, doesn't it?"

"Sometimes nature will play a trick upon us and we'll have unpleasant weather for a good deal of the winter," she said absently as she checked his figures.

"Will we be home for Christmas?" he asked.

"You know that's impossible, Spencer. I don't know why

you'd even entertain such a notion. Even if all of the cotton had been picked, we couldn't possibly prepare to return to Massachusetts by year's end."

His head drooped until it nearly rested upon his narrow chest. "I know, but I want to go home."

His plea wrenched Jasmine's heart. She knew her son was unhappy, and she couldn't blame him. Since the incident at school he'd become reluctant to leave The Willows. Even attending church had become a battle. Forcing him to sit in the same pew with some of those same boys who had raised their fists against him seemed cruel.

She tousled his brown waves and pulled him close. "I want to go home too. This is a difficult time for all of us, but we must complete what we came here to do. Once we return home, all of this will soon be forgotten."

The look in Spencer's eyes revealed he wouldn't soon forget the beating he'd taken, yet Jasmine knew both prayer and time could heal his internal wounds and make him an even stronger person. Suffering at Bradley's hands had made her stronger, and now she seldom thought of those frightful years when she was his wife. The same transformation could happen to Spencer.

"I miss Moses. I tried making friends with some of the slave boys, but they don't want to be my friend."

"They are no longer slaves," Jasmine corrected. "Most likely they are skeptical of your motives. Don't take it to heart. They will come around in time."

He didn't seem to hear her. Jasmine ached for her son's misery. She went to the table and quickly scanned his arithmetic.

"Wonderful!" she exclaimed as she wiped the slate clean. "If time at the pond is what you want, then off with you. But promise me you'll be home in time for supper."

His face brightened. "I promise. And maybe I'll bring some fish home with me."

The two of them walked downstairs together. Jasmine watched as Spencer ran off to fetch his fishing pole, and once he was out of sight, she returned to the library.

Nolan glanced up as she walked into the room. "That was a quick lesson."

"I was merely checking his work, not giving him a lesson. His answers were all correct, so now he's off to the pond to catch some fish. He's terribly unhappy and longs to go home," she said, sitting down opposite the mahogany desk that had belonged to her father.

Nolan tilted his head to one side. "I believe that's true for all of us."

"That's what I told him, but that fact doesn't lessen his own misery. He misses Moses and being in school with his other friends, not to mention being in familiar surroundings. He's been isolated since the episode at school. Even the former slave children want nothing to do with him."

"I realize that, my dear, but we can't change what is in the past or force friendships. Like most children, Spencer is resilient."

"He deeply resents that we brought him here," she said in a faint whisper.

"And you're now feeling blameworthy for what happened at school. We made the proper decision, Jasmine. The event at school does not change the fact that Spencer belongs with us. Please promise me that you won't continue down this path of self-recrimination."

"I promise—but it won't be easy." Her gaze fell upon the missive lying open upon the desk.

"What did Paddy have to say? Any good news?"

Nolan laughed. "It seems he's met a girl. He says she fancies herself quite the expert on horses. From the sound of things, he may have met his match, though he says she's a bit too high and mighty for his liking. Apparently she lives at Elinor's boardinghouse instead of in the Acre. When he offered to help her find a place in the Acre, she told him she'd live where she pleased and it wasn't in the Acre."

"Dear me! I can't imagine Paddy taking it upon himself to tell a young lady where she should live. No wonder the girl spoke her mind."

Nolan laughed. "That's not the worst of it. Seems he was having difficulty with one of the horses, and she told him how to correct the problem using Baucher's method. He had never heard of the technique, and she quickly put him in his place."

"And did he take her advice?"

"He did. And it worked! However, it seems she may have taken a liking to Timothy Rourke. Who knows? Our Paddy may be wed by the time we return to Lowell."

Jasmine clasped the fringed bodice of her dress. "Don't even think such a thing! We'll be home much too soon for any weddings to occur. In fact, given the tenor of Albert Cameron's letter, I think we should truly consider leaving at the earliest opportunity. I'm afraid we are going to be dramatically impacted by the events occurring at home. There are likely matters that need our attention even as we speak."

"What would you have me do? I see no alternative other than to complete the task at hand. Once the cotton is ready for shipment, we'll leave—even if we haven't sold The Willows. I know McKinley will object, but if selling the plantation is the only thing that prohibits our return home, we'll place it in the hands of someone we trust. Someone who will bargain for the best possible price."

"I am in complete agreement. And should McKinley find fault with our decision, then he may handle the sale himself. My hope is that we can return by spring. Poor Alice

Ann believes her pony will be all grown up before she returns home to ride the animal again."

"Yes. She's mentioned her concern to me on several occasions. But I told her she was going to have many years to ride her horse." Nolan walked around the desk and gently pulled Jasmine from her seat and into his arms. "Please don't fret about the children. Once we return home, their bad memories will fade. We've done the proper thing by coming here. Giving your father's slaves their freedom and enough money to begin a new life is worth the few sacrifices we've been forced to make."

Jasmine lifted her face and looked into Nolan's deep blue eyes. "Who could ever ask for a better man than you? No wonder I love you so much."

She closed her eyes and felt the warmth of his arms as they tightened around her waist. He captured her lips in a long, lingering kiss, and she knew she could never love another.

———————

Elinor poured two cups of tea—one for herself and one for Justin Chamberlain. Since his return from Maine, he had begun stopping by the boardinghouse regularly—once or twice a week—generally seeking advice regarding Reggie's behavior or requesting Elinor's assistance with a church function.

Through the weeks, they had formed a comfortable companionship, and Elinor now looked forward to his visits, particularly when they were discussing an idea for one of his sermons. Justin's visits helped provide balance to her life, an escape from her routine housework and meal preparation.

"You appear preoccupied," Elinor remarked after Justin had failed to answer her question.

"What? I'm sorry . . . my mind was elsewhere."

She laughed. "That's what I said—you appear pre-occupied. Is it something you'd care to discuss?"

Justin appeared rather sheepish as he looked up from his cup of tea. "Actually, I've come to ask another favor of you, and I've been searching for some way to broach the topic."

"There's no need for such tactics between friends. You merely need ask. If I can help, I will be pleased to do so," she said in her no-nonsense manner.

He gave a nervous laugh. "I need a place for Reggie to stay all next week."

"Why would you hesitate to ask? You know I'm fond of Reggie. If we didn't enjoy one another's company, she wouldn't stop here on her way home from school each day," Elinor said. "You need only tell me when she'll arrive."

"You are very kind. I must leave for Boston early Monday morning and hope to return Friday evening."

"In that event, it would be best if she stayed with me Sunday night. That way you can leave on the early train. In fact, why don't you and Reggie join me for supper Sunday evening—if you have no other plans," she added hastily.

"I fear your kindness causes me to impose upon you," he said sheepishly. "However, joining you for supper is very appealing. Are you certain you'll go to no trouble on our account?"

"I promise," she replied. "May I tell Reggie of our plan when she stops to see me after school today, or would you prefer to tell her yourself?"

Justin gave her a feeble smile. "She knows I must go to Boston. She said that if I didn't come and ask you today, she would do so herself. There was little doubt in my mind she would carry through with her promise."

"Then I will tell her the arrangements have been completed."

Reggie yanked on the needle and then emitted an exasperated sigh. "My thread knotted again," she lamented as she turned over the sampler and glared at the tangled thread.

"You try to save time by using a piece of thread that's much too long—that's what causes it to knot," Elinor quietly informed her as she sat down beside the girl and examined her handiwork.

"I use a longer piece because I don't like threading the needle."

"Is it because you don't like threading the needle or because you think it's quicker if you use a longer thread and don't have to stop so frequently?"

"Because it's quicker," Reggie replied with a giggle.

"But only if the thread doesn't knot, and usually—"

"The thread knots," she said, completing the sentence.

"Making a sampler isn't a test of speed, Reggie. Rather, it's intended to teach you the variety of stitches you can use in future fancywork. There! I think I've untangled it for you," Elinor said as she handed the piece of stitching back to the girl. "Your stitches have improved greatly. You should be very proud of what you've accomplished thus far."

Reggie ran her finger across the stitching. "Do you think my father will believe I made this all by myself?"

"Well, if he doesn't, I'll be the first one to come to your defense. I do believe your father is going to be *very* proud of you."

Shortly after Justin Chamberlain returned from Maine, Reggie had shown Elinor the sampler her mother had made before her marriage. The child was enchanted by the piece and expressed a desire to make one of her own. "So they can hang on the wall side-by-side," she had told Elinor before expounding upon the fact that Elinor would need to teach

TRACIE PETERSON / JUDITH MILLER

her well. After all, the stitching would need to be of a fine quality, for people would surely compare the two pieces of handwork, Reggie had advised.

And so they had begun the project. Each evening when Reggie stopped by the boardinghouse, she worked on the sampler while Elinor prepared supper and the two of them visited about their day—Reggie's ongoing struggle to fit in at school and Elinor's efforts to keep her house running smoothly.

Now, without the necessity of going home for the next week, Reggie was certain she could accomplish a great deal on her sampler while her father was away in Boston—at least that was the hope she had expressed to Elinor.

So while Elinor pared potatoes for the stew she would later be serving for supper, Reggie pushed her needle through the tightly woven muslin and then gently pulled the length of thread to the opposite side of the fabric. "I heard the girls talking last night," Reggie told her. "Ardith and Lucinda were crying. They're afraid they're going to lose their positions at the mill. Lucinda said the overseer in the weaving room told six girls to go to the office and collect their final pay yesterday. She thinks she'll be next. What do you think?"

"The only thing I know is that many of the girls are losing their jobs. Thus far, we've been most fortunate. There are very few boardinghouses where at least one or two girls haven't lost their positions. I suppose it was bound to happen, yet I've been fervently praying that those who are most in need of their wages will be protected."

"Lucinda said she didn't know how her family would survive without the money she sends them. Then Janet laughed and said she didn't know how she would survive without money to buy new shoes and jewelry, but she knew she wouldn't lose her position. Next, Ardith told Janet to keep quiet or leave the room, and then Janet said she didn't have to and then—"

"I believe I understand the gist of the discussion," Elinor said with a faint smile. "All the girls are concerned about losing their livelihood."

"Aren't you afraid? What happens if they all leave your boardinghouse? What will *you* do?" Reggie asked.

"Eventually I would be forced to speak to my brother, Taylor, and request his assistance, I suppose. However, I pray the financial problems of our country will be resolved before I'm required to take such a step."

"I thought you told Father your brother was moving to Maine."

"Yes. In fact, he's already done so. He bought part interest in a milling operation. I'm not sure his timing was the very best, but one never knows about such things."

Reggie's eyes opened wide. "You mean you would move away from Lowell?"

"If necessary, I would have to."

"But what would I do without you?" she asked, her eyes filled with concern.

"No need to begin worrying, Reggie. I'm confident this will all work out for the best."

The girl bobbed her head up and down, though she didn't appear convinced. "I don't like Janet—she's mean."

"Well, that was a quick turn in our discussion," Elinor commented as she removed the heavy white dinner plates from a shelf in the kitchen.

"I don't want to hear about you moving away, so I decided to talk about something else."

Elinor was touched by Reggie's reply. Knowing the girl had suffered through a lifetime of missing a mother gave her pause. She now questioned why she had been so forthright with the child. After all, Elinor had suffered through the

183

same feelings as a young child, and there was no need to cause the girl unjustified concern. Yet truth was truth, and if matters continued to spiral downward, she would have no choice but to move. There would be far too many women in Lowell seeking employment for her to remain.

"So you've decided you don't like Janet because of her remarks to Ardith and Lucinda?" Elinor inquired.

"Not just that. She appears to enjoy herself the very most when others are suffering. Have you noticed that about her? The last time I stayed here, Sarah received a letter from home saying her father had been severely injured in a farming accident. As she was reading the missive, Sarah began to weep. Without even asking permission, Janet took the letter from Sarah and began to read aloud all the terrible details contained in the letter. Even when Sarah covered her ears and begged Janet to stop, she continued. And all the time she had a cruel look on her face. I waited for a few moments and when no one else did anything, I grabbed the letter from Janet's hands and gave it back to Sarah. That's why Janet is always saying mean things to me."

Elinor dropped into the chair opposite Reggie. "How is it that I know nothing about any of this?"

Reggie shrugged. "I suppose because Janet always threatens the girls, and they're afraid to tell you what she's really like. Janet told Sarah she had better not complain to anyone or she'd be sorry."

"But what threat would Janet pose? The girls are all equal in this house."

"But not at the mill. That night Sarah said she didn't care what Janet said, for she was going to tell you about her improper behavior. Janet pushed me out of the room and told me to go downstairs. After she closed the door to their room, I clacked my feet on the top two steps like I was going downstairs, but instead I listened outside the door. I heard

Janet tell Sarah that if she said one word to anyone, she would tell the overseer and he would terminate Sarah," Reggie explained.

"Surely Sarah didn't believe such nonsense. The overseer isn't going to terminate Sarah merely because Janet makes such a request."

"From what I heard, it appears Janet and the overseer are very close friends. The girls said she receives special treatment all the time. Even Mary Margaret said it was true, and she rarely says much about any of the girls. Did you know Janet doesn't have to operate as many looms as the other girls? Mary Margaret says it's because she's friends with Mr. Wingate, the overseer."

"I am taken aback to think that Mary Margaret would relate such delicate information to a girl of your tender years," Elinor said.

"Oh, she didn't tell *me*. I heard her whispering with Lucinda and Ardith in the parlor one evening after the incident with Sarah. Janet is always making unkind remarks to Mary Margaret because she's Irish. Janet says Irish people shouldn't be permitted to live in the boardinghouses, and as soon as she can move to another room, she's going to do so."

Elinor tilted her head and began to rub her forehead. "You are a true fount of information, Reggie. However, I'm afraid the details you've related are not very heartening. I thought the girls were all quite happy, yet trouble has been brewing right beneath my nose and I didn't even smell a whiff. And I have always considered myself a relatively good judge of character."

Reggie laid her stitching on the edge of the table. "You must promise you won't breathe a word of what I've told you. Otherwise, I'll never be able to sneak about and hear their conversations again."

Elinor tucked a loose strand of Reggie's hair behind the

girl's ear. "I won't divulge your secret, but you must call a halt to your spying activities. You know such behavior is inappropriate, don't you?"

"Yes," Reggie replied in a disappointed voice. "But it *is* fun," she added with a sparkle in her eyes.

Elinor bit her lower lip so she wouldn't laugh at the girl's reply. "But you promise to stop?"

Her head bobbed up and down.

"Good! Now that we've settled that issue, I had best get back to supper preparations. The girls will be arriving within the hour."

"Would you like me to help you in the kitchen?"

"I believe I have everything under control. Why don't you continue stitching on your sampler."

"May I go outside for just a short time? I promise I won't go far, and I'll start home when I hear the final bell ring at the mills."

"That's fine," Elinor said. "There's a cool breeze. Be certain to wear your bonnet!"

The fresh air would do Reggie good, and Elinor needed a bit of time to digest the discomfiting news. Exasperated by what she'd been told, Elinor slapped her hand upon the table. How had she overlooked the manipulation and cruel behavior that bubbled beneath the surface of the girls' smiles and polite table conversation? And how long had Janet's meanspirited behavior been going on? She wrestled with the thought momentarily until she remembered Janet mentioning she was going to be promoted. When was that? At least a year ago. Elinor had been surprised when Janet made the announcement—especially since Janet had moved to Mr. Wingate's weaving room only a few weeks earlier. From all appearances, Janet had taken the wrong path when she accepted her new position.

Elinor had heard the stories of mill girls succumbing to

the advances of their superiors for special favors, yet she didn't think any of her girls would ever compromise themselves. Obviously, she had been incorrect. Now that she was aware of what was happening, she would be more observant. Deep inside she harbored the thought of greeting Janet with a notice to vacate her house this very evening. But she couldn't keep her word to Reggie and force Janet from the boardinghouse without furnishing a reason for her action. Janet was shrewd and would likely assume Elinor had learned of her behavior. If Elinor wasn't careful, Janet would blame one of the other girls, who would soon suffer her wrath.

As the girls entered the house after work, Elinor reminded herself to remain silent regarding the discoveries made this afternoon. She must bide her time with a listening ear and a watchful eye.

Except for Reggie, who for some unknown reason appeared particularly jovial, the mood around the supper table was somber.

"I pray that all went well at work today?" Elinor inquired as she passed the plate of bread.

Janet ladled a heaping portion of stew onto her plate. "No one was laid off today, though I believe there will be several tomorrow."

"Truly? And why would you think so?" Elinor inquired.

Janet glanced about the table with a self-satisfied look on her face. "I overheard some of the *men* talking today."

Elinor digested the reply before speaking. "I would think it very difficult to overhear a conversation while operating those noisy looms."

The girls smiled at Elinor's remark but said nothing. They watched Janet, obviously curious about how she would reply.

"I waited a brief time after the noonday bell had sounded—when the machinery was shut down for dinner break. Consequently, I had no difficulty whatsoever."

"I see," Elinor said, remembering that Janet hadn't appeared with the other girls for the noonday meal.

In fact, now that Elinor thought about it, there had been any number of days when Janet hadn't arrived for the noonday meal. This would provide a perfect opportunity for her to meet with Mr. Wingate, who was, after all, a married man. One who likely carried a lunch pail for his dinner yet would be expected home on time for supper.

"Where did you eat your dinner today, Janet? I missed you around the table," Elinor casually remarked.

"I took some ham and bread left over from breakfast. I wanted to spend the time visiting with some of my friends from the number four mill."

"I see. In that case, I hope you had an enjoyable visit."

"Yes, I did," she replied curtly. "Now if you'll excuse me, I want to fix my hair before I go into town. I saw a perfectly charming pair of earbobs at Whidden's. I don't believe I'll be able to sleep until I've purchased them."

A look of disgust was exchanged among the remaining girls, who soon excused themselves and moved to the parlor with Reggie following along behind.

"Come help me in the kitchen, Reggie. I think it's best if you remain with me."

"If Mrs. Brighton doesn't object," Mary Margaret said, "you can come up and visit with us after you've finished your chores. Would that be all right, Mrs. Brighton?"

"Yes, of course," Elinor agreed.

———

Although she was ready for bed by nine o'clock, Elinor sat reading a book in her small parlor near the front door. She never went to bed until all of the girls had returned from their evening outings, and Janet had not yet come home.

She looked up from her book as Reggie came running into the parlor with her nightgown flying about her legs.

"Janet's coming down the sidewalk," she announced.

"And how do you know that?"

"I was watching from the upstairs bedroom window," she replied with a giggle.

The words had no more than escaped Reggie's lips when the latch on the front door clicked.

"See! I told you," the girl whispered with a smug grin. "I believe I'll go to bed. Shall we say our prayers?"

During Reggie's previous visit, they had begun a ritual of saying their prayers aloud each night before going to bed, and Elinor was pleased Reggie wished to continue the practice. Elinor prayed and then nodded to Reggie to begin. Her prayer was much briefer than usual, and Elinor decided the child must be completely exhausted from the day's activities.

"I'll be back as soon as I make sure the front door is locked and there are no candles burning. You go ahead and get into bed."

After completing the nightly ritual, Elinor returned to her rooms. Reggie had followed her instructions and was already in bed with her eyes tightly closed. Using the brass candlesnuffer by her bed, Elinor extinguished the flame and slid between the bedcovers. Her thoughts wandered aimlessly, and exhaustion soon gave way to sleep.

"What was that?" Elinor shrieked, sitting straight up in her bed. Something had startled her out of a sound sleep. She covered her mouth and waited a moment.

A shrill scream sounded from upstairs. Fear gripped her and she grabbed her robe from the foot of the bed. It was then she heard Reggie giggle.

"You don't need to hurry upstairs—it's only a toad," she said. "I put it in Janet's bed."

"Who did this?" Janet screamed, her voice piercing the

quiet night. "Catch it! Somebody do something!"

Reggie lifted her knees to her chest and giggled until tears ran down her cheeks. "I knew she'd be afraid of a silly toad. I told Lucinda to sleep with Mary Margaret so Janet would be the only one getting into the bed. Then I put the toad in her bed before I came downstairs," she admitted.

"And that's why you were watching to see when she was coming home."

"Yes. I didn't want the toad to be frightened for too long," she said, stifling her laughter.

"It's good to hear you were at least concerned about the toad's welfare," Elinor said.

"Please don't be angry. We all thought it a fine joke and nobody got hurt. I'll apologize and tell her I'm responsible so she won't become upset with the others."

Elinor nodded. "I think catching the toad would set things aright even more than an apology. Let's go upstairs and see if we can find it."

By the time they reached the upstairs room, Janet was sitting atop one of the trunks with her feet drawn up underneath her. "You did this, didn't you? You are the most unpleasant child I've ever encountered."

"Truly? Then I must introduce you to some of those who would put me to shame," Reggie said. "I put the toad in your bed and I was going to say I'm sorry, but I'm not. If it weren't for Mrs. Brighton, I'd leave it here to frighten you all night."

Elinor pointed at the toad and Reggie quickly retrieved the creature. "Did it touch you?" Reggie inquired.

"Yes! It got on my legs and my hand."

"Then you'd best watch for warts. Toads are known to cause warts on people of foul disposition—such as yourself."

"And you!" Janet screeched. "You're holding it in your hand and you are a horrid little person, so you will surely get warts also," she said in a gleeful tone.

"But I don't care if I get warts, and you do," the child countered, then lifted the toad in front of her face and whispered words of praise to the creature while walking down the stairs. "I have to put you outside now. But if Janet is mean, I'll be sure to find you again," she promised.

Once the toad had been placed outside, Elinor pointed Reggie toward one of the chairs in her parlor. "We need to talk," she said as she gently closed the door.

"Are you going to tell Father?" she asked. "He'll never let me come and stay again if you do. Please don't tell him."

"I'm not going to tell him, but I think I have a better solution to the problem with Janet. Not as much fun perhaps, but I think it will prove much more beneficial to all of us."

"What is it?" Reggie asked, her eyes wide with anticipation.

"We need to pray for Janet."

"What? I don't want to pray for Janet. I don't like her."

"I know, and that's all the more reason we must do so. We need to pray that Janet will have a change of heart, and we need show her kindness. Only that way will we see a change in her."

Reggie frowned as she contemplated the suggestion. "I suppose I could *try*. But I think you'll need to pray for me too. Otherwise, I'll fail and have thoughts of placing a snake in her bed."

"In that case, I'll be praying very hard!"

When Justin arrived in Lowell late Friday afternoon, he was several hours ahead of schedule. At least as far as Reggie was concerned. A single row of stitching along the bottom of her sampler required completion, and she was intent upon completing the project. Consequently, his daughter had greeted him at the front door of the boardinghouse with an accusatory "You're early!"

"I thought you would be pleased to see me," he said, surprised by her outburst.

"But I thought you wouldn't be back until later in the evening."

Justin stood in the doorway, hat in hand, uncertain how he should respond. "Would you like me to leave and come back later?" he finally inquired when she didn't invite him inside.

Before Reggie could reply, Elinor strode down the hall, wiping her hands on a linen dish towel. "Pastor Chamberlain! How nice to see you. I trust you had a pleasant journey. Step aside so your father can come inside, Reggie," she said in an authoritative manner.

Reggie moved to one side and inched the door open for her father. "I'm not ready to go home," she announced. "I have *things* to finish."

"I see," Justin said, looking to Elinor for assistance.

"Why don't you see to your chores while your father and I visit in the parlor? Perhaps you'll be finished by the time he's ready to leave. If not, I'm sure he won't mind if you come home after supper."

Elinor's words seemed to resolve matters for Reggie, and Justin watched his daughter stride down the hallway as though she were on a mission of great importance.

"I can't believe the changes in Reggie since we've moved to Lowell. It's amazing. Now she voluntarily wears a dress and combs her hair, and her schoolwork is much improved. I must admit that you've had an astonishing influence upon her. I am most grateful."

"Reggie is an easy child to love," Elinor replied.

Justin laughed and shook his head. "That's not what most people say!"

"Then most people haven't taken the time to get to know her. Besides, Reggie and I share much in common. I think that's why I'm so easily able to influence her behavior."

Justin leaned back in the chair and gave his full attention to Elinor. "You've never mentioned having a common bond with Reggie in our previous discussions."

"I suppose I haven't, but Reggie and I have discussed it. You see, like Reggie, my mother died when I was but an infant. Unlike Reggie, I had my grandmother and other family members to help raise me, but I always felt different from the other children. Especially the girls when they would speak of their mothers taking them shopping or teaching them how to do a special embroidery stitch. . . . I felt set apart from them. So I began playing with my brother and his friends, doing the things they enjoyed: climbing trees, fishing, capturing snakes and spiders to scare the girls. The boys didn't judge me—they didn't care whether I had a mother teaching me how to sew and shop."

"And so that worked for you?"

"Until I began school. Once again I became an outcast because I didn't want to dress or act like a girl—until I met Bella, Taylor's wife. Taylor brought her to England after they married, and I thought her quite wonderful. As you know, they brought me here to America and I lived with them. Bella quickly influenced my behavior."

"Were you unhappy when she forced you to change?"

"Oh, she didn't force me. I admired Bella, so I attempted to emulate her in every way. Of course, I don't believe Reggie has changed because she wants to imitate me, but rather because I can relate to her experiences. I've not attempted to transform Reggie—merely offered her different options. And for the most part, she has been quite receptive. Now why don't you relax while I go to the kitchen and prepare a pot of tea."

Justin nodded and smiled as Elinor rose from her chair. She was an extraordinary woman, tender and kind yet filled with a strength he hadn't observed in most women—likely due to the losses she had suffered. One would be forced to develop inner fortitude in order to survive so many difficulties, he decided. And she had worked wonders in his daughter's life, and for that he would be eternally grateful.

With a practiced ease, Elinor placed the tea tray on the table in front of her and began to pour. "Biscuit?" she offered.

"Yes, thank you," Justin replied as he pulled a handful of coins from his pocket. "I am going to insist upon paying for Reggie's care. If you won't agree, then I'll have to make other arrangements in the future. In these difficult times, I will not add to your financial burden."

"My finances have not changed in the least. I have, in fact, been much more fortunate than many of the keepers. None of my boarders has lost her job, though I've heard talk of additional layoffs in the future. As for Reggie, having her here is my pleasure. Should her time with me ever become a financial burden in the future, I will surely tell you. For now, however, I simply cannot accept your money."

Justin placed the coins on the table. "I insist!" he said while maintaining a steady gaze into Elinor's thoughtful eyes.

"May I suggest we place the money in a benevolence fund? One that can be used solely for aiding the girls who lose their positions at the mills? There are many who help support their families with their wages, and losing their jobs will be devastating. If we could help in some small measure, I believe it would be a fine way to exhibit our Christian charity. What do you think?" she asked, scooting to the edge of her chair.

Her enthusiasm was contagious. "I believe a benevolence fund is a wonderful idea. The fund could be handled through the church, and I believe you would be the ideal person to take charge!" He leaned forward and took both of her hands in his own. "Would you be willing to accept such a challenge?"

"Yes, of course. I would be honored to do so."

"Look what I—" Reggie's words stopped midsentence.

Justin turned toward his daughter. Her gaze was fastened upon his hands tightly wrapped around those of Elinor Brighton. He froze in place, unable to move. There was a look of accusation in Reggie's eyes that forced him to remain transfixed. Fortunately, Elinor pulled back.

"You've finished?" she asked, her attention moving to the fabric in Reggie's hand.

She nodded. "Look what I made," she said, proudly holding up the sampler for her father's inspection.

"Bring it closer and let me see," he said. He took the sampler and carefully examined her sewing. "Am I to believe you made this all by yourself?"

"Mrs. Brighton taught me the stitches, but I did all of them myself, didn't I?"

"Every single stitch—and some of them twice."

Reggie edged onto her father's knee. "I want to put it in a frame and hang it on the wall."

"That's a fine idea. We'll put it in the parlor, where all our guests can see it when they come to visit."

"I want to hang Mama's sampler in the parlor too," she said carefully.

Justin knew she was watching for his reaction. Was it because he'd been holding Elinor's hands and she thought him disloyal to her mother's memory?

Reggie wriggled under the bedcovers, hoping to find a comfortable depression in the lumpy mattress. She'd been in bed for over an hour, yet no matter how she repositioned herself, sleep wouldn't come. Perhaps because it was the first night back in her own bed after a week at the boarding-house . . . or perhaps it was because she couldn't forget her father holding Mrs. Brighton's hands when she had walked into the parlor earlier this evening.

Oh, she liked Mrs. Brighton—in fact, she was quite fond of the boardinghouse keeper. Yet a troublesome suspicion had begun to grow ever since she walked into the parlor. She tucked the quilt under her chin and wished she could push the thought from her mind. Surely Mrs. Brighton's friend-ship was genuine. Reggie didn't want Mrs. Brighton to be another one of those women who used her in order to win her father's attention. Before coming to Lowell, she'd had her fill of women befriending her as a means to snag a hus-band for themselves.

"Please don't let her be like all the rest," she murmured into the darkness, hoping to push the unpleasant thought from her mind.

Yet no matter how she tried, the scene in the parlor played in her memory over and over again, like a squeaky violin that could not be silenced.

"Just like the others, I shall put her to the test!" she finally muttered.

The decision made, she rolled over and drifted into a restless sleep.

CHAPTER · 11

PADDY SHADED his eyes from the early morning sun and squinted hard as he attempted to make out the riders approaching from the east—two of them. He couldn't make out the riders from this distance, but he didn't recognize the horses. Strange to have visitors arrive this early in the morning. He had planned to take several of the Arabians out for their morning exercise. Since Mr. Houston's departure for The Willows, he'd had scant time for riding, which he truly loved, and was looking forward to a morning spent with some of their finest animals

The riders were proceeding at a slow pace, so he would have time enough to retrieve one of the beauties from its stall and lead it into the corral adjacent to the barn. He stopped to pat the nose of Alice Ann's pony, Winnie, as he passed by. The pony would be a good animal for the girl—if she ever got a chance to ride her again.

"Sure and I wish they'd come home," he muttered as he gave the pony one final pat.

The riders were within a short distance of the barn when

he finally led Glory's Pride out of the barn.

"I do hope that's one of ours," the rider called out as he approached Paddy.

Paddy gave a hearty laugh, for he recognized the speaker. Leland Bradford was a captain at West Point who had been to the farm on previous occasions. However, Paddy had never seen his companion.

"I do na think so. Glory's Pride is one of our finest studs. This fine fellow will na be leaving the Houston farm."

"Can't blame me for trying. How are you, Paddy?" The captain swung down from his horse and pulled off his glove before reaching to shake Paddy's hand.

"Fine, but I must admit I was na expecting visitors this mornin'. What brings ya to Massachusetts on this fine day?"

"This is Captain Ira Payne. He's in our main offices at the Point—helps take care of the finances," Captain Bradford explained as he made the introduction.

Paddy nodded. "Pleased ta meet ya, Captain. How can I be helpin' ya?"

Captain Bradford removed his hat and surveyed the surrounding area. Paddy didn't know what the man was looking for, but he waited patiently. Mr. Houston had taught him to be patient with their customers—especially the military, for Mr. Houston believed these men needed to feel they were in control.

Glory's Pride nudged Paddy with his broad nose, and Paddy turned to pat the horse. "Just a minute, boy," he murmured in a soft voice.

"We're interested in seeing the horses you're to deliver to the academy in the spring," Captain Payne finally told him.

"I do na recall ya ever doing such a thing before. Is there some problem?"

"With the *Houston* horses? Of course not!" Bradford declared. "We've merely begun a new procedure that includes reviewing the stock approximately six months prior to delivery."

Paddy thought the idea a waste of their time, yet who was he to argue with these military men. If they wanted to see the stock, he would give them what they wanted. "Simon! Harry! Michael!" he shouted.

The three men came running from different directions, all lurching to a halt in front of Paddy. "I need the horses scheduled for spring delivery to West Point brought into the far corral."

"All of them?" Simon asked.

"Aye, all of them."

"Gonna take a little while. Some of them's out in the far pastures."

"We have all day," Captain Payne said.

Paddy signaled for the men to round up the horses before turning his attention back to the visitors. "Could I interest ya in a cup of coffee or some tea? Me sister and her husband live here on the property, and I'm sure she'd be happy to have a bit o' company."

"That's a kind offer, but we were planning to talk with Mr. Houston. Is he about?" Bradford inquired.

"I do wish ya would have sent a telegraph or written before ya made yar visit. I could have let ya know Mr. Houston is in Mississippi, sir. I do na have an exact date for his return. However, he has left me with the authority to oversee the operation of the farm."

The two men exchanged a glance. "What business could Mr. Houston possibly have in Mississippi? Off searching for some new breed of horse?" Bradford inquired with a chuckle.

"Family matters," Paddy replied simply.

Captain Bradford directed his puzzled gaze at Paddy. "Family? Houston isn't from the South. He told me his parents hailed from England but he was born and reared in this part of the country."

"'Tis *Mrs.* Houston that has roots in the South," Paddy explained, uncertain how much information he should be parceling out to these men.

Bradford led his horse to the corral and glanced over his shoulder at Paddy. "Do you mind if we turn the horses loose in your corral while we talk?"

"Sure and that would be fine. Let me unsaddle them for ya."

"Since Mr. Houston isn't here and it's going to be a while before your men return with all of the horses, perhaps we should have that cup of coffee you offered earlier," Captain Bradford remarked.

"Aye. If ya'll follow me, it's only a wee stroll from here. There's a bit of a nip to the air, but I imagine you gentlemen are accustomed to being out in all types of weather."

Paddy quickly unsaddled the mounts and turned them into the corral before joining their owners. He was careful to observe the men's actions as they walked toward Rogan and Kiara's house. Although he could have entertained them in the main house, where Maisie would have been more than willing to serve the officers their coffee, he would feel more comfortable in Kiara's home. And something told him he needed to level the playing field. He feared there was more to this visit than merely assessing horseflesh.

"How has your business been faring these past months?" Captain Payne inquired as the men settled themselves in the parlor.

Paddy didn't know if the captain was simply making polite conversation while they awaited their coffee or if he was on a fishing expedition and hoped to elicit vital information of some sort.

"As well as can be expected, I suppose—can always be

better, don't ya know," he said with a grin.

Payne hunched forward in his chair. "These are difficult times. The North is suffering particularly hard, and I imagine it won't be long before the South succumbs to the economic downturn also. We've all been forced to take monumental steps in order to preserve our financial security. Even institutions such as West Point have been dramatically impacted by this latest panic. No doubt you're suffering the same consequences—certainly nothing to be ashamed of. After all, the purchase of horses is something a man can delay until there's a turnaround in the economy."

They were playing a game of cat and mouse—waiting for him to say the wrong thing, yet Paddy didn't know what the wrong thing might be. Mr. Houston always said to play your cards close to your chest and above all, don't speak unless you speak the truth.

" 'Tis true most are sufferin'. The bank closures are difficult for all and that's a fact. Ah, here's our coffee," he said as Kiara came into the room. He was thankful he could turn their attention to something other than his reply.

Captain Bradford settled back on the divan with his cup of coffee and riveted his steely eyes upon Paddy. "Have you had any purchasers renege on their contracts?" he inquired boldly.

"I would na discuss your contract with others, sir, and I can do nothing less for our other patrons. I'm sure ya understand—'twould be improper to do such a thing. But if it's additional horses ya're needin', I do na think I can be of assistance."

"I think I can take that statement to mean that your business has suffered very little. Apparently, like us, your clients pay six months in advance of delivery or have managed to find another method to meet their obligation."

Paddy took a gulp of his coffee and placed the cup on

the table. "Ta tell ya the truth, gentlemen, I'm not a man who enjoys playin' games with words. I prefer spending me time with those horses you've contracted to purchase. And there's nothin' I'd like better than to go out riding one of them. So understand me when I say that I do na mean to insult ya, but I'd like ta know just what it is ya're wanting. I don't believe you came all this way just to take a wee look at the horses."

Captain Bradford chuckled. "You're right, Paddy. We know we can always count on excellent horses from this farm. You and Mr. Houston have never disappointed us—in fact, you always exceed our expectations. Unfortunately, we've come today because we need to renegotiate our contract with Mr. Houston."

"Renegotiate?" Paddy's heartbeat quickened. "The West Point contract is valid for another two years. What is it ya're hoping to renegotiate?"

"Much like every other institution in this country, West Point is suffering from the poor economy," Captain Payne explained. "I'm pleased to hear that at least your business hasn't felt the impact. Hopefully, that will work to our advantage."

Paddy inwardly cringed. He'd been cautious in his conversation, yet it seemed he'd given them enough facts to use against him. These men were shrewd. Moreover, they had a history of negotiating contracts, while he had none. He could send for Albert Cameron at the bank or even McKinley Wainwright, yet he doubted they would strengthen his position. In fact, such a tactic could weaken his ability to negotiate—especially if they didn't agree with his opinion on how to handle the situation.

"You gentlemen have taken my words and attempted to twist them to yar advantage. Just because we have no additional horses ta offer does not mean we've not been hurt by the financial crisis or that we are in a position to rewrite our contract with the academy. I understand that with the banks closed, ya've likely na been able to transfer the money for the horses, and we have no problem with that."

"This is more than a matter of transferring funds," Payne said. "And while I understand you must protect the interests of this business, given the difficulties we're suffering at West Point, it is imperative that we receive the horses at a lesser price. Now I realize lowering the selling price of your animals isn't something you're anxious to do. However, we simply have no choice."

Paddy stared at him. "No choice? Of *course* ya've got a choice, Captain. Ya can honor your contract and if ya can na do that, ya can do the respectable thing and tell me ya can na purchase the entire herd ya've contracted for. We're not anxious for that to happen, but we're better off to sell our horses elsewhere."

Bradford stood up and began pacing in front of the divan. "The fact of the matter is we *need* all of the horses."

"But ya can na afford them. So tell me how many ya can pay for and that's what we'll deliver to ya come spring."

"West Point has done an excellent business with you in the past," Bradford pointed out. "I would think you'd be willing to accommodate us this one time."

"Then let me ask ya this, Captain Bradford. If I delivered all but ten of the horses you contracted for, would ya hand me money for a full herd? Would ya be thinkin' it didn't matter because I'd always met the terms of my contracts in the past? I do na think that's what would happen, yet it's exactly what ya're asking of me."

Bradford ceased his pacing and turned to face Paddy. "You are correct. I would not pay you for goods I did not receive. You, however, hold the power to help us equip men who will one day serve this country."

"I know ya're thinking I have no sympathy for yar situation. Nothing could be further from the truth. I wish there was some way I could help, but I can na sell the horses for less," Paddy replied quietly. "The truth is that the academy already receives the horses for less than anyone else we contract with—and I should na be tellin' ya that, but 'tis a fact. The profit we make on your horses is marginal at best, and we can na afford to be giving the animals away."

Captain Payne leaned forward and rested his elbows on his broad thighs. "And what would you do if we cancelled the entire contract and took none of your horses? Would you be equally willing to continue feeding and caring for all those horses, knowing you'll not find anyone to purchase them given the state of the economy? Now, we've told you we need those horses, and we've also told you we cannot afford to pay the entire price for them. We need something from you other than hearing there's nothing you can do!"

"To tell ya the truth, Captain, I could probably sell every one of those horses to the Virginia Military Institute for more money than we've ever received from West Point. But that's na what I want ta do. I understand ya need the horses and I want to provide them to ya, but yar threats do na serve ya well."

Captain Bradford sat down on the divan. "You're right. I apologize for our behavior, but we're placed in a difficult situation. We were told to return to the academy with a renegotiated contract for all of the horses."

"Would it ease yar financial problems if we agreed to accept payment for the horses in installments rather than in a lump sum? Payment is already past due on the herd, but I'd be willing to accept half now and half upon delivery in the spring. I'm hopeful Mr. Houston will return by spring, and if further negotiation is needed, he may be willin' to help ya further."

The two men exchanged a glance; then Payne nodded and smiled. "I apologize for my heated behavior. You've done less than we hoped for but more than we expected. You've a good head for business, and Mr. Houston is fortunate to have you in his employ."

Captain Bradford chuckled. "You should consider yourself highly complimented, Paddy. Captain Payne isn't liberal with his praise."

Paddy glanced toward the hallway and saw Kiara standing beside the parlor door. She winked and blew him a kiss. He could see the pride in his sister's eyes, and his heart swelled at the sight.

"Are ya certain Kiara won't mind if I'm comin' along uninvited?" Mary Margaret asked for the second time since they'd departed the outskirts of town.

Bridgett gave her friend a stern frown. "How many times must I tell ya the same thing, Mary Margaret? Kiara's not the type to think ya need an invitation in order to come visiting. Besides, it's not as though we're arriving unexpected. She knows Cullen and I are coming to pay a visit. She'll be pleased to see ya. Won't she, Cullen?"

"Aye," Cullen replied while keeping a tight hold on the reins and his eyes fastened upon the narrow path.

Cullen had borrowed the horse and buggy from one of the men at work, and from all appearances, he didn't have much experience handling either. The horse seemed to sense his anxiety and Mary Margaret thought the animal a wee bit skittish. She considered offering to take the reins, but Cullen might be offended by such a suggestion. So she clung to the side of the buggy and hoped the animal would trust its own instincts rather than Cullen's direction with the reins, which she noted he was holding much too firmly.

As they neared the house, Cullen yanked back on one of the reins with such fierceness the horse turned sharply, nearly overturning their buggy.

Without thinking, Mary Margaret began issuing orders. "Quit pulling back with your right hand and loosen your hold on the reins," she hollered, tempted to grab the reins from Cullen's hands. However, her good sense prevailed and she refrained from such unacceptable behavior. When the buggy was finally turned aright and the horse had settled, they stepped out of the wagon. Mary Margaret couldn't remember a time when she'd been so happy to be on solid ground.

"That didn't go so well, did it?" Cullen asked with a sheepish grin.

"I think ya did mighty fine, don't you, Mary Margaret?" Bridgett asked.

Mary Margaret knew she was expected to agree with her friend, yet she did not want to return to the city with Cullen McLaughlin handling the reins. "We've arrived safely, and for that I'm thankful. Are ya a wee bit afraid of horses, Cullen?" she inquired.

"I suppose ya can tell I've not been around animals very much."

"Aye, but there's no shame in that. Driving a horse takes a bit of instruction and practice, just like most things in life. I'd be pleased if ya'd consider permitting me to give you a bit of a lesson. In fact, if ya'd like, I could take the reins and teach you as we return."

"Could ya now? I did na know you were an expert with the horses."

"She's an expert and that's a fact," Paddy said as he drew near.

Mary Margaret couldn't tell if Paddy's words were spoken as a compliment or if he meant to ridicule her, so she kept her attention focused upon Cullen.

"Before I came to Lowell, I was around horses a great deal of the time," she told him. "My employer permitted me the use of his animals when I was not busy with my other duties, and I grew fond of them. I find them loyal and tolerant—unlike many humans."

She noted Cullen's glance toward Paddy before he answered. "I'd be pleased ta have ya give me a bit of instruction."

"Then it's settled," Mary Margaret said.

Paddy gave her a broad smile. "Bridgett, I believe my sister is expecting ya in the parlor. Cullen, I told Rogan we'd join him in the small barn out back. He's finishing up some carving for Liam. I believe he's nearly as good as Liam, but he denies there's any truth ta what I say."

Bridgett grasped Mary Margaret's hand, and they hurried toward the house while the men walked to the barn. Mary Margaret felt a sense of relief that the men were not joining them. She didn't want to spend her Sunday afternoon sparring with the likes of Padraig O'Neill.

"Where are Nevan and Katherine?" Bridgett asked as they entered the neatly appointed parlor.

Evidence of Kiara's skill with a needle adorned the room, and Mary Margaret wondered at the patience it must take to create such beautiful handwork.

"They've both gone to Simon and Maisie's to visit Moses. Poor Moses has been so lonely with Spencer gone that he comes almost every evening and asks if Nevan and Katherine can come for a visit. Although I believe it an imposition, Maisie insists her life is much easier when Moses has the children to play with."

"Children need one another for entertainment." Bridgett took a good look at her friend. "Ya're beginning to look a might uncomfortable."

"Aye. Only a few months until this babe is born, and none too soon for my liking. I'm ready to hold the wee one in my arms and be done with this," Kiara said, resting her arm atop her protruding stomach.

"And what do Nevan and Katherine think of having a new brother or sister? Are they excited?" Bridgett asked.

Kiara laughed. "Not nearly as eager as Paddy! I believe he's even more excited than he was when Nevan and Katherine were born—though I do na know how that's possible."

"Paddy?" Mary Margaret asked, stunned by the revelation. "I wouldn't think him a man who enjoyed children."

"Truly? I'm surprised you'd say that," Kiara said. "From the time he was a young lad, he's been caring and compassionate. He nearly died as a child, and then when we came to Lowell, we faced great adversity. Paddy and I came to this country as indentured servants, but through the grace of God we received our freedom. Know that I speak the truth when I tell you there is no finer man than Padraig O'Neill." Her eyes shone with pride.

Bridgett giggled. "And what would your husband be thinkin' of such a remark?"

Kiara blushed. "Other than my husband, of course."

"I do agree that Paddy is a fine man," Bridgett said. "It's with great fondness I remember sailing across the sea with you and Paddy."

"Aye. He wasn't afraid of anything then and he still isn't. I marvel at the man he's become. Why, only today I listened to him bargain with men from West Point concerning the fact that they couldn't afford to pay for the horses they'd already contracted to purchase. Once Paddy determined they were in financial difficulty and weren't attempting to take advantage of him, he offered a fair and compassionate compromise."

"Enough about Paddy now," Bridgett said. "I came here

to have ya show me how to correct the mistakes in the lace I've been making, and if we don't begin soon, Cullen will be telling me it's time to go home."

Kiara gave Bridgett a warm smile. "Let me see what ya've brought for me."

Bridgett pulled the piece of handwork from her bag and offered it to Kiara. Mary Margaret glanced at the lace and then at Kiara—she was certain she saw Kiara shudder at the sight.

"You'll be needing some help with this," Kiara said as she examined the stitches.

"There's no denying it's na a pretty sight, but for the life of me, I do na know what I've done wrong," Bridgett lamented.

"The weave is much too loose. Ya've used a pattern that's too large for this thread, and then ya've put too few twists between the stitches, making it even worse. Yar braids are not bad, though, so there's hope for ya. We'll get ya started with the proper thread. Would ya fetch me my basket?"

Mary Margaret listened closely as Kiara began the intricate lace-making instructions, but as the afternoon wore on, her thoughts wandered to Kiara's earlier discussion of her brother. Perhaps Mary Margaret had misjudged Paddy. Perhaps he really was a good person and she'd been overly distrustful. He was, after all, quite good looking, and by all accounts there were any number of girls who would be pleased to have him come calling. Truth be told, she might enjoy having him call on her!

CHAPTER · 12

REGGIE TAPPED lightly and then turned the doorknob of Mrs. Brighton's back door.

"Reggie! I was beginning to think you'd forgotten where I live. And you've come just in time to help me with these apple pies," Elinor said with a broad smile. "Take off your cloak. I'm happy to see you."

Reggie returned the smile before removing her cloak and hanging it on the iron hook by the door. "It doesn't appear you need any help," she said as she entered the kitchen. "The pies are ready to bake."

Five pies rested on the table, and Reggie knew from her stay at the boardinghouse that each piecrust was heaped full of tart apples mixed with sugar and cinnamon and then generously dotted with butter before being covered by the top crust.

"These are ready, but I have some extra dough and there's butter and cinnamon and sugar," she said, pointing at the crocks sitting on the table.

Unable to resist the temptation, Reggie lifted the ball of

dough from the bowl and slapped it onto the table. With the ease of someone who had been preparing piecrust for years, she began rolling the dough into a thin crust while Elinor set the pies to bake.

"I must say I'm impressed with how capably you've learned to roll a piecrust," Elinor said.

"Thank you." The compliment pleased her, but she forced herself to remain guarded.

Mrs. Brighton wiped her hands on the towel tucked at her waist, then turned her attention to the girl. "Where have you been all week? I've missed you."

"It's only Thursday," Reggie replied as she spread a thin layer of butter across the crust.

"But you usually come to see me every day after school. When I didn't see you for three days, I was beginning to think you must be ill. If you hadn't come today, I was going to come and check on you this evening after supper."

Reggie began to carefully sprinkle the sugar and cinnamon mixture over the buttered crust. "To see me or to see my father?" she asked with a sidelong glance, hoping to evaluate each word and look that the two of them now exchanged.

A frown creased Mrs. Brighton's face. "To see whoever could answer my questions about why you hadn't come to see me."

Without looking up, Reggie rolled the dough up into a long tube and carefully cut it into even slices, just as Mrs. Brighton had taught her. "Would you still want to see me if I told you my father has met a woman? I think he wants to marry her."

"Why would that change *our* friendship? Would you be leaving Lowell if he married?"

Mrs. Brighton appeared confused by the question, though Reggie thought it quite forthright.

"No. But I didn't know if you'd think I shouldn't come around if Father has a lady friend."

Mrs. Brighton cupped one hand under Reggie's chin and lifted her head until their gazes met. "I don't know why you would even ask me such a question, Reggie Chamberlain! You are always welcome here. But since we're revealing our thoughts, do you know what I thought when you didn't come to visit?"

"No," she replied as she neatly placed the circles of dough in a pan.

"That you'd wanted to be with me only until you completed your sampler. And since you had finished the sampler last week, you were finished with me also."

Reggie's eyes opened wide with surprise. "You thought *that*? How could you think such a thing?"

Mrs. Brighton shrugged. "It wasn't difficult. Each evening as I sat stitching, I wondered why you hadn't come by—it was the only thought that seemed plausible. However, it now makes sense. Your father wants you to spend time with his new friend so the two of you can become better acquainted."

A feeble smile was the most Reggie could muster. Now what? She didn't want to lie, yet she was still uncertain of Mrs. Brighton's motivation. This brief conversation was not enough to convince her of the older woman's loyalty. She'd learned long ago that she needed more than a few patronizing remarks—much more.

"I don't know if I want my father to marry anyone—not ever," she said, plopping down on one of the wooden kitchen chairs.

Mrs. Brighton sat down opposite her. "I understand the thought of another person becoming a part of your family could be frightening. After all, you don't want a stranger coming between you and your father. However, I don't think your father would be interested in a woman who wouldn't become a good mother for you. You need to give this lady an opportunity to become your friend. Show her the sweet young lady that you've shown me, and the two of you will become fast friends."

"My father isn't always the best judge of character. He doesn't know that people sometimes pretend to be something they're not. Besides, we're doing just fine without a woman in our house."

"I suppose that's true enough, but you must remember that your father is probably lonely. I know he has you and he has the members of his congregation, but that's not the same as having a wife. You should think of his happiness also, Reggie," she said softly.

"Why should he want to get married again? I thought you said it wasn't so terrible being without a husband. Didn't you say that?"

"Yes, I did. And for me, that's true. However, that doesn't mean it's the same for your father. He may be very lonely and want to marry again. Trust God to provide you with the perfect mother and He won't disappoint you. If you like, we could pray about this each day when you come to visit me. We wouldn't need to tell anyone else. What do you think?"

"I suppose we could pray that if he marries, he marries the woman I choose," Reggie replied with a giggle.

"If he's already chosen someone, don't you think we should pray for you to accept *her* instead?"

"Possibly . . ." She paused. "In fact, I believe you're absolutely correct."

The front door opened, and Elinor could hear the girls chattering as they hung their capes in the hallway.

"Smells like apple pie. Again! I would prefer some variety myself. We had apple pie earlier in the week."

Reggie peeked around the doorway into the dining room. "If you're tired of apple pie, then don't have any. I'll be happy to eat your slice and mine too."

"There *is* no slice that belongs to you, Regina Louise. In case you've forgotten, *you* don't live here," Janet said.

Elinor slapped a serving spoon onto the table, her irritation mounting. "And *you* do not decide who eats at my table, Janet. If you're unhappy with the fare I serve, then you're free to seek a room elsewhere. I have no hold on you or where you live."

"Unlike you, there are many keepers who have already lost boarders due to the layoffs. You need only speak to one or two of them to realize they are feeling the pinch of making ends meet without a full house. I'd think you would be anxious to keep *all* of us happy."

There was little doubt Janet's reply was a veiled threat. She would make every effort to influence the other girls to follow if she decided to leave Elinor's boardinghouse. It was clear Janet was attempting to intimidate her, and the very thought was infuriating. Even though the girls disliked Janet's meanspirited behavior, in her absence, they whispered about her ability to influence the overseer, so Elinor knew they feared her.

"Don't worry, Mrs. Brighton, she won't leave," Reggie said quietly. "You keep the best boardinghouse for the Corporation and everyone knows it—especially Janet."

Elinor smiled and tousled Reggie's hair. "I'm not worried, Reggie. Janet knows I strive to give my best effort in order to provide the girls with a good house."

Obviously the comment served only to annoy Janet, for she leveled a look of disgust toward Reggie as the girls seated themselves around the supper table. An uncommon silence permeated the room as the girls filled their plates and began to eat. Had her comments to Janet caused the other girls discomfort? Surely not. Yet she wondered at their lack of conversation. Elinor had grown accustomed to their silence during the noonday meals. After all, they had but half an hour to hurry home, eat, and then rush back to the mill. However, during supper, when there was no need for haste, the girls usually recounted the day's activities, and the room was filled with the sounds of their chattering and laughter. This evening, however, the mood remained somber and unusually quiet.

It was shortly after Janet's exit out the front door that the girls finally began to talk. They had gathered in the parlor, and after clearing off and washing the dishes, Elinor and Reggie joined them.

"I'm pleased to hear a bit of chatter," Elinor said as she sat down. "You were all so quiet during supper that I feared I had affronted all of you with my harsh remarks to Janet."

"You weren't harsh, Mrs. Brighton. You spoke only the truth," Helen said while fidgeting with a strand of her thin, mousy brown hair.

"Thank you, Helen, but I fear I was lacking in both manners and Christian kindness toward Janet."

"She doesn't deserve either," Mary Margaret chimed in, her bright blue eyes flashing. "Janet needs to be fallin' to her knees and askin' forgiveness from the Almighty for her behavior."

"Yet Janet's actions don't excuse my own behavior, Mary Margaret. I fear I only made matters worse."

"I do not see how things can get much worse with Janet. She's filled to overflowing with the power she holds over us. It's ironic that she should need her position at the mill less than the rest of us, yet she'll likely be working long after the rest of us have lost our jobs," Ardith lamented.

Tears pooled in Sarah's eyes, and she withdrew a handkerchief from her skirt pocket. "I don't know what will happen to my family if I lose my position. My father was severely injured in a farming accident and he's not been able to work. In each letter I receive from home, my mother tells me how they're struggling. She fears they'll lose the place," she mournfully related. "Without the money I send, her fear will become a reality."

"Aye," Mary Margaret agreed. "While others toil to keep food on the table for their families, Janet's off to town purchasing new baubles for herself each payday. She's a cheeky one."

Sarah nodded. "I don't approve of Janet's behavior with the overseer, but I dare not say anything against her. Just today there were five layoffs in number three and seven in number five. It's utterly frightening. I can barely sleep at night; then I'm so weary I have difficulty remaining alert at my looms."

"I know all of you are deeply concerned about losing your jobs. However, you gain nothing by embracing an attitude of fear. I believe you'll do much better if you'll remain calm and adopt an optimistic attitude," Elinor encouraged.

"That's easy enough for you," Sarah said. "You don't have a family that's depending upon you."

Helen folded her lanky arms across her waist. Her eyes appeared to bulge from their deep-set sockets as she bobbed her head up and down in agreement. "She's right, Mrs. Brighton. It's a terrible load having your family waiting to receive money from you every week. My father's dead, and without the money I send home, my sisters and brothers will go hungry. The burden weighs heavy on me, and there's no one to help any of us if we lose our positions."

Elinor leaned forward and looked into the faces of each of the girls. "Now, I want you to listen carefully to what I'm going to tell you. I am not a wealthy woman, nor do I think my life has been one of particular ease. However, God has blessed me in many ways, and I've been able to set aside a portion of my wages throughout the years. If your hours are decreased or you lose your position, I want you to come to me and I will help you. In addition, Pastor Chamberlain has set up a benevolence fund at the church—one that is solely for those of you who find yourselves unemployed and in need of assistance. I am overseeing that fund. All you must do is exhibit your need for assistance.

"And I hope you girls know that I would permit you to remain in the house so long as the Corporation offered no objection. I'll do all I can to help you remain in Lowell until this crisis is over, if that is your decision. We may have to eat a bit more sparingly, but we'll make do and see each other through this difficult time."

Sarah began to sniffle again. "Thank you, Mrs. Brighton. You're most generous."

Elinor patted Sarah's hand. "I trust all of you are keeping the economic situation in our country and at the mills in your prayers. In times of difficulty, our true power comes through prayer. We must remember that we have a heavenly Father who cares deeply about our every need. When others flail about in worry and torment, we should be leaning upon God, knowing He will see us through our tribulation. Instead of showing others the strength we have in our Lord and Savior, we often emulate the behavior of nonbelievers."

"Aye. 'Tis true the good Lord above can help if He's a mind to," Mary Margaret remarked. "But there's many an Irish family lyin' in their graves because God turned a deaf ear during the potato famine."

"Our ways are not God's ways," Elinor reminded her. "Many times we don't understand why tragic things occur or why God doesn't step in and make things better each time we cry out to Him. When that has happened in my life, I try to remember that Jesus didn't want to die on the cross either. Even though Christ cried out to God, it didn't change His death on the cross. Nor did it take away His pain and suffering. However, God was still there—as strength and refuge—just as He's here for us. You may still lose your position at the mills, your families may go without food, and you may despair. But when all is said and done, if you have Jesus as your Savior, you have what is most important—your eternal salvation."

" 'Tis true, but watching those ya love die is a hard thing to do," Mary Margaret said.

Elinor nodded. "Indeed! And I can't even begin to fathom what it must have been like for God to observe His beloved Son put to death—especially knowing that Jesus was perfect and didn't deserve any of the cruelty heaped upon Him. He had never sinned, yet He willingly suffered so that we might have eternal life. It truly amazes me each time I pause to think of the depth of God's love for us."

"Ya're right, o' course, but sometimes 'tis difficult to remember anything but yar own pain," Mary Margaret said quietly.

"For all of us," Elinor agreed, patting her arm. "Now if you girls will excuse me, I believe I'd better walk Reggie home before her father begins to worry."

"He won't worry," the girl said. "I told him I was stopping after school and that you'd likely have me stay for supper."

"But I don't imagine he planned on your being away until this hour. It's nearly nine o'clock. Let's hurry to the kitchen and wrap up the sugar-and-cinnamon crusts. You can pack them in your tin for a treat with your noonday meal tomorrow."

Reggie brightened at the offer and jumped to her feet.

"I like that idea," she said while leading the way into the kitchen.

A short time later they were on their way. Although Reggie insisted she was quite capable of walking home by herself, Elinor accompanied the girl after explaining a walk would give her the opportunity for a much-needed breath of fresh air.

"You're very nice to everyone. I like that," Reggie said, grasping Elinor's hand as they walked down the street.

"I appreciate the compliment, though you seem to forget that only this evening I was less than kind to Janet."

Reggie giggled. "You're nice to people who *deserve* your kindness."

"That's just the thing, Reggie. Those who deserve our kindness the least are the very ones whom we're called to show the most compassion. Unfortunately, I failed miserably with Janet. But I'll try to do better next time. And here we are—you're safely home." She handed the sweetened pie-crusts to the girl.

Reggie kicked a pebble down the street as they stopped in front of the frame house. "Can I come back and visit tomorrow?"

"Why, of course. I thought we'd settled that issue. I'll be expecting you after school. I'm going to begin embroidering squares for a quilt. Perhaps you'd like to work on one of your own?"

"Oh, that would be grand. I'll see you tomorrow," Reggie said, hurrying up the path to the house.

Elinor watched until Reggie had safely entered the house. As she turned toward home, Elinor's thoughts returned to her earlier conversation with Reggie. She had longed to ask for the name of the woman who had captured Justin Chamberlain's heart. However, she had forced herself not to pry. Not knowing would make it easier to remain optimistic—more capable of encouraging Reggie. After all, had Reggie revealed that her father was enamored by someone like Caroline Emory or Sarah Sanders, Elinor would find it impossible to remain positive.

Yes, she decided, there were some things best left unknown.

CHAPTER · *13*

THE ENTIRE DAY had been replete with problems. Clara had whined and cried throughout her waking hours, and on the few occasions when her tears ceased, Alice Ann teased her until the weeping again began in earnest. And Spencer's behavior had been no better. He had refused to complete his schoolwork, maintaining he was tired and didn't feel well.

Jasmine rocked Clara on her lap, hoping the child would take a nap. "Perhaps the children are ill. Have you heard whether there's any sickness on the other plantations?" she asked Prissy, who was rolling a ball across the floor to Alice Ann.

"You's worrying too much, Miz Jasmine. The plague's over with—we done with dat mess till next year," Prissy said as she tossed the ball back to Alice.

"There are illnesses other than yellow fever—ones that occur throughout the year," Jasmine replied as she rested her palm on Clara's forehead. "Come here, Spencer. Let me see if you're feverish."

Spencer placed his palm on his forehead. "I don't have a fever," he told her.

"I'll be the judge of that. Come here, please."

With a grudging look upon his face, Spencer moved to her chair and leaned down while Jasmine placed her hand on his forehead. "You don't feel warm," his mother conceded. "I can't imagine what's wrong with the three of you today."

"We want to go home," Spencer said as he flopped down on the divan.

"So do I. And we will. Every last person on this plantation is going to leave. But first we must get picking the final crop, and once it is ginned and baled, we can ship the entire crop to New Orleans."

Spencer formed his lips into a taut line and narrowed his dark brown eyes. "When that's done, you'll say we must remain until you complete something else. We're never going to leave, and I don't want to live here."

"Your father and I are perfectly aware of your wishes, Spencer, and if you don't cease your unpleasant behavior, you may go to bed."

"We haven't even had supper yet."

"Exactly!" Jasmine replied, her retort filled with exasperation.

"So you think we's gonna be leaving soon, Miz Jasmine?" Prissy asked in a trembling whisper.

Jasmine nodded. "Mr. Houston agrees that we will leave by February at the latest—whether or not the plantation has sold."

Prissy wrapped her arms around her knees and began to rock back and forth. "I don' wanna leave here, Miz Jasmine. I done lived here long as I can 'member, and dis here's my home. Don't wanna be leaving it. I always been thinkin' me and Toby would jump the broom and we'd grow old on dis here place. Now ever'thing's changing."

"There's nothing to be concerned about, Prissy. You and Toby are going to be just fine. Surely you want your freedom more than you want to stay here."

"I don't care nothing 'bout no freedom if I can stay here and have ever'thing stay the same as always."

"But it can't, Prissy. The Willows is going to have a new owner, and we have no idea who it might be—possibly someone like Mr. Wade from the Bedford Plantation. You wouldn't want to be here if that happened, would you?"

"No, ma'am. I just want things to go back to the way they was before Massa Malcolm died. Ain't nobody up there in the North gonna hire me to do no work."

"Of course they will, Prissy. You're a wonderful house-keeper and have much to offer—and so does Toby."

"They ain't gonna want me when they find out I'm gonna have a baby," she whispered.

Jasmine met Prissy's intent, frightened gaze. "You're . . ."

"Yessum."

"You and Toby should be married immediately. Why didn't one of you come to me?"

"Toby don' know either," Prissy whispered. "I was skeered to tell him."

Jasmine grasped Prissy's hand. "There's no need to be afraid. Toby is an honorable man. He'll want to be respon-sible for his child—he was already planning to marry you."

"Yessum, that's true."

"Then we need to see to this matter immediately. Is there someone special you'd like to perform the ceremony?"

"Ol' Samuel down in the slave quarters—he do the preaching and marrying for us," she said.

"I want you to promise me you'll talk to Toby this very evening. Then tell him I want to speak to him."

"Oh no, ma'am. Please don't be giving Toby no talkin' to—he'll for sho' be angry with me if you do that."

"I wasn't going to scold him, Prissy. I want to tell him that I'll be willing to help in any way necessary so the two

of you can be married as soon as possible," Jasmine said.
"And I want you to cease your worrying about finding a
place to work and live when we go North. Both you and
Toby can live at the Houston farm. There's plenty of work
on the farm that I'm certain Toby would enjoy, and you can
continue to help with the children. Everything is going to
be fine, Prissy."

"Yessum," she replied in a faltering voice.

Her agreement was unconvincing, and Jasmine knew
nothing she said was going to convince Prissy her life would
be better away from The Willows. The young woman would
have to see for herself. Once they were in the North, her life
would be filled with possibilities. There would be ample
opportunities for her and Toby as well as the baby she was
now expecting.

"I'm going to go downstairs and see if Mr. Houston has
returned. He said he would be bringing a land agent home
late this afternoon," Jasmine said as she placed Clara in
Prissy's arms. She walked toward the door and then turned
and glanced over her shoulder before exiting the room.
"And don't forget I want to talk to Toby later this evening."

Prissy nodded her agreement. However, she looked as
though she'd been told she was going to receive forty lashes.

Jasmine's friendship with Prissy had deepened since their
arrival at The Willows, and Jasmine truly enjoyed the young
woman's company. She wanted to believe Prissy trusted her,
yet the girl remained unwilling to embrace the thought of
moving North no matter what Jasmine said or did. Perhaps
Prissy was afraid to trust anyone—even Toby. After all, Toby
was more than anxious to leave the South and gain his freedom.

And why hadn't Prissy told Toby she was expecting his
child before now? Surely she didn't intend to wait until they
wed to tell him. Jasmine was certain Toby would have

married Prissy the moment he discovered her condition. And though Jasmine hadn't expressed her surprise to Prissy, she was somewhat taken aback by Toby's behavior. From the time he was a young boy, he'd always attempted to act in an honorable manner.

"I see you've arrived home," Jasmine greeted Nolan as she walked into the library. She glanced about the room expecting to see the land agent.

"Yes—a short time ago. If Mr. Turner is a punctual man, he should be arriving within the hour." Her husband stood and kissed her cheek. "You look particularly lovely today."

A lilting ripple of laughter escaped her, and she sat down beside him on the divan. "You say that *every* day."

"Because it's true," he replied. "How has your day been?"

"Difficult. The children have been out of sorts. Clara crying, Alice Ann teasing, Spencer unwilling to do his school lessons—I don't know what's gotten into them. Spencer says it's because they're homesick, but that's his reasoning for everything."

Nolan pulled her closer in a warm embrace. "We'll be leaving soon. We're all anxious to return to the farm, but poor Spencer wants to believe he's the only one who's truly unhappy. I'm sorry your day has been trying."

"I haven't shared the most surprising news of all," she said, turning to face her husband.

"Did you know that when you become excited, the golden flecks in your eyes sparkle like brilliant gold nuggets?" he asked before leaning forward and brushing her lips with a kiss.

She giggled and pulled away from her husband's embrace. "Nolan, stop that! I have something I must tell you."

He immediately drew her back into his arms and kissed her with increasing passion. "So tell me . . . what is your news?" He pulled away only far enough to whisper his question.

His breath tickled her lips, and she smiled while pushing against his chest. "I can't speak if you continue to smother me with kisses."

"All right. I promise to stop—at least for a few moments. I do hope your news warrants my sacrifice," he said with a grin.

"When Spencer was lamenting his woes about returning home, I told him that we would all be leaving soon. Then, as she normally does, Prissy said she didn't want to depart The Willows. I made every attempt to convince her that she would find suitable employment and she and Toby would have a good life."

"I believe I've heard this all before," Nolan said, giving her a sidelong glance.

"But not this part! She said no one would be willing to employ her because she's going to have a baby."

Nolan turned to meet her gaze. "Well, that *is* news. If she's speaking the truth, I'm surprised Toby hasn't already married her."

"She hasn't told him!"

"Seems strange she wouldn't tell him immediately—especially since they plan to marry. Did she say why she hadn't spoken with him?"

"She said she was afraid to tell him, which made absolutely no sense to me. Toby is gentle and kind—I have no doubt he will accept responsibility for his actions. Though I must admit I'm disappointed by his behavior."

"Don't judge him too harshly, Jasmine. We don't know the circumstances, and it's unfair to place blame."

"You're correct. Blame won't change anything. I told Prissy she was to tell Toby about her condition today and that I wanted to talk with him this evening."

Shifting on the divan, Nolan turned to give her his full attention. "I don't believe this is a proper topic for you to discuss with Toby, my dear. Tell Prissy to have him come and see me."

"I was merely going to tell him I thought they should marry immediately and ask what I could do to assist them."

"Still, I think it would be more appropriate for him to talk with me. Besides, he'll likely be more at ease speaking to another man, don't you think?"

Jasmine nodded. "Yes, of course. I did tell Prissy that she and Toby could come and live on the farm and work for us if she was fearful about their welfare. I do hope you don't disapprove?"

He laughed. "Have I ever disapproved of your lending aid to others? There's more than sufficient work to keep them both busy at whatever work they might choose to do. However, I believe we should permit Toby to have a say in the matter. I don't want him to feel we're forcing them to come and live at the farm."

"No, of course not. I made the offer because of Prissy's concern about finding work. Should they choose to go somewhere else, that's perfectly acceptable."

The quiet was interrupted and Nolan stood and peered out the window.

"Ah, I believe that is Mr. Turner's carriage approaching in the driveway," he said as he pulled out his pocket watch and snapped open the lid. "I'll go out and greet him."

"I believe I'll go to the kitchen and ask Martha to serve refreshments. I shouldn't be long."

Jasmine walked down the hallway and into the empty kitchen, then realized the servants were likely in the detached summer kitchen. During the heat of summer, the kitchen contained within the walls of the house was used merely as a serving kitchen for preparing coffee, tea, or lemonade.

She waved to Martha as she drew near the other kitchen. "Are you busy preparing supper?" she asked.

"Oh, I don't do much, Miss Jasmine. These ladies tolerate me in their kitchen just because I miss cooking," she replied.

"Ain't true, Miz Jasmine. Miss Martha's a mighty big help," Esther said, her black face gleaming like ebony.

"Is there something I can do for you," Martha asked, "or did you want to oversee the supper preparations?"

"Could you possibly prepare light refreshments and serve them in the library? Mr. Nolan and I are meeting with a gentleman for a short time. Though it's near suppertime, I thought I should at least offer him a light repast."

Martha's head bobbed up and down. "You go and entertain your guest, and I'll be in shortly."

The meeting proceeded more quickly than Jasmine had anticipated. In fact, there seemed little to negotiate. Mr. Turner agreed to handle arrangements for the sale of The Willows, and if a buyer was not secured by the time they departed, he would handle matters in their absence.

"My wife is unwilling to give you final authority on the sale price, Mr. Turner, but if you telegraph any offers, we will make every effort to reply promptly," Nolan said. "Of course, we remain hopeful you might locate a qualified purchaser prior to our departure."

Mr. Turner nibbled on one of the molasses cookies he'd placed on his saucer. "As I said, there's little likelihood you'll have a buyer any time in the near future—however, one never knows. There may be a potential purchaser who is anxious to invest in this fine plantation. Bear in mind, however, that the market is depressed at this time. Even though we've not suffered losses such as those experienced in the

North, we're now beginning to feel the repercussions of this economic downturn, and there are fewer men willing to take risk with their capital."

"The Willows isn't a risk," Jasmine asserted. "It has always turned a fine profit for our family."

Mr. Turner gave her a perfunctory smile. "I'm sure that's a fact, Mrs. Houston, and I'm going to do my very best to secure the highest possible price for your family's home. I merely wanted to warn you in advance that the sale might take longer than you would normally anticipate. So long as we're clear on that issue, I believe we can sign the necessary papers and I can be on my way."

Nolan and Mr. Turner took care of the necessary paper work, and Mr. Turner wished them a good evening.

"I don't particularly like Mr. Turner," Jasmine said to her husband after the land agent had departed the house.

"He seems as trustworthy as the other agents I spoke with. He bears a good reputation in the area, though I suppose he is rather negative," Nolan replied.

"Truly? I barely noticed," she said with a glint in her eye. "Anyone listening to him for long would find himself in a state of utter despair."

———

Nolan glanced up from his desk and motioned Toby forward. "Come in and sit down," he said while pointing his pen toward the chair opposite the massive desk.

Toby hesitated for a moment but finally dropped into the chair and stared into Nolan's eyes. "You wanted to see me, suh?" he quietly inquired.

"Yes. Please understand I'm not passing judgment, Toby, but given the circumstances, I would highly recommend you and Prissy marry immediately."

"Yessuh. Prissy told me 'bout the situation this afternoon. I told her not to be worrying—that we'd get ol' Samuel to marry us. Ain't no need for nothing more'n the three of us to get things taken care of. I'm going down an' talk to him soon as we's finished with our talk."

Nolan nodded. "Miss Jasmine asked me to tell you we would be pleased to help with any wedding preparations. Surely Prissy would prefer something just a bit more elaborate than repeating your vows before Samuel."

"No, we's agreed 'bout the marriage. Everything should be taken care of by dis time tomorrow," he said. "It's better dis way."

"If that's what you prefer. And did Prissy tell you that if the two of you want to come to our farm in Lowell, we'd be pleased to have you come and work for us? You're not obligated, but Prissy was concerned about finding work and there's plenty at the horse farm. You could stay until after the baby is born, and if you then decide you want to leave, we'll not have any objection."

Toby began to fidget at the mention of Prissy's condition, and Nolan regretted going into detail.

"You and Miz Jasmine is very kind. When da time comes to go north, we'd be proud to work for you, Massa Nolan."

"Good. And if you need *anything* for the wedding, please—"

"No, suh, we ain't gonna be needing nothin'—nothin' at all," Toby said. "We's jest fine. If we's through, I believe I'll go on down to the quarter and talk to ol' Samuel."

"Yes, of course."

Nolan was deep in thought when Jasmine entered the library a short time later. "Did you talk to him? What did he say?"

"I talked to him. They don't want any type of large ceremony. Toby has gone to speak to Samuel, and he advised me that they will be wed by this time tomorrow. He said he and Prissy are in agreement about wanting just the three of them present when they say their vows."

His wife exhaled and she frowned. "And here I was hoping for something cheerful to focus upon."

"I'm not certain Toby shares your enthusiasm. However, he did accept our offer of employment, so at least that much should please you."

"Yes. It pleases me they'll be with us and I'll have the pleasure of seeing their child," Jasmine replied. "If only *all* of life's problems were so easily resolved!"

CHAPTER · *14*

NOLAN ADJUSTED his silk top hat before lifting Alice Ann into the carriage and onto Prissy's lap. "I believe we'll have ample room in the carriage. Especially since Henrietta and Martha decided they weren't feeling well enough to join us," he told Jasmine.

"I do hope you don't mind going along with us this evening, Prissy. With Henrietta and Martha both ailing, I thought we might be forced to remain at home," Jasmine said. "But the children wouldn't have forgiven us if we attended the festivities without them."

"It's fine, ma'am. I's glad to help." Prissy peered at the house. "Where's Henry? Ain't he gonna drive the coach?"

"Henry's ailing too," Nolan said. "I told him to remain abed and perhaps he'll be better by morning. Besides, I enjoy driving my own coach from time to time. It will give the gentry of Mississippi yet another grievance against me," he said with a grin.

Jasmine stroked Clara's soft hair. "Clara and Alice Ann will likely be asleep soon after we arrive."

"I won't sleep. I'll remain awake until we return home," Spencer promised. He was sitting beside his father and obviously feeling quite grown up.

"Personally, I would have been happy to remain at home," Jasmine told her husband. "Besides, I find it strange that we received an invitation to the gathering at Rosewood. After all, we've been excluded from every other social function since our arrival. Why would the Woodsons invite us to their party celebrating the final picking? After all, there's no denying the fact that John Woodson dislikes us intensely."

"He's extended an olive branch, my dear. The least we can do is reciprocate in kind. And the children haven't had an opportunity to participate in any festivities. Christmas, after all, was quite glum this year."

"You're right, but services at the church were quite nice, I thought," she said as they made their way down the lane. "And I'm completely surprised you want to attend tonight, Spencer. I feel certain some of your schoolmates will be among those invited."

Spencer flashed a smile at his mother. "Since we're leaving next week, this will give me a chance to tell all of them what I truly think of their deeds."

"Now, son, I expect you to be on your best behavior," Nolan warned. "No rowdiness."

He nodded. "Not unless they start it."

"No fighting whatsoever!" Jasmine insisted in a stern tone. "If you encounter any difficulty, you must come directly to your father or me for assistance."

"All right," he begrudgingly agreed. "Do you think it's snowing at home?"

"Probably so," she replied absently.

Spencer scooted around in his seat and directed his attention to Prissy. "Just wait until you move up north. One morning you'll wake up and look out your window, and you'll see piles and piles of white snow covering the ground."

"We had us some of dat white stuff one or two times. It come fallin' from da sky in little white flakes, but it melted to water when it hit the ground—didn't do no piling up," she said. "Massa Wainwright told us snow was for up north, where it be cold and unpleasant, an' rain is for in da South, where it be warm and agreeable."

"That sounds like something my father would say," Jasmine commented. "However, the North is not unpleasant, though it does grow cold in the winter. But you'll soon learn to love the North."

"I s'pose," Prissy said, although her voice lacked enthusiasm.

"Here we are," Nolan said as he pulled back on the reins and the horses brought the carriage to a halt outside the main entrance of Rosewood.

Festive decorations adorned the foyer of the big house, where both John and Ramona Woodson stood near the entrance greeting their guests. Mrs. Woodson immediately directed one of her house slaves to escort Prissy and the children upstairs, where they were to be entertained.

"We're pleased you accepted our invitation," Mr. Woodson said as he pointed to another slave to take their wraps.

Jasmine directed a dutiful smile toward their host. "We were pleased to be included."

Mrs. Woodson whispered to a butler, who stepped forward and ostentatiously announced their arrival to the many guests gathered in the loggia, where music was playing and the guests were beginning to dance.

"Shall we?" Nolan asked as he led Jasmine to the dance floor.

"Seems everyone in the area is in attendance," Jasmine said as they circled the floor. "It's been years since I've attended one of these parties, yet most of the faces remain familiar. It appears as if few of my generation have departed this area. You'd think they would want to strike out and see another part of the world."

Nolan led her in a wide circle toward the rear of the dance floor. "I'm certain they do see other parts of the world. Most everyone here is widely traveled. But unlike you and McKinley, they chose to return."

"They travel, yet they've not yet become enlightened," she remarked.

Nolan cocked one eyebrow. "I believe they would quite disagree with you, my dear. In fact, I believe you'd find they think *you* are the one who is unenlightened."

"No doubt."

The music proved quite delightful, and Jasmine spent much of the evening dancing with Nolan and a few of her schoolmates from years ago. Throughout the evening, she watched the doorway closely, almost expecting to see Spencer emerge with a bloody nose, but such was not the case. Instead, he remained ensconced upstairs until after midnight, when they were preparing to depart for home.

"From all appearances, you and the other boys got along well this evening," Jasmine commented as she settled Clara into a nest of blankets in the back of the carriage. Prissy helped Nolan settle Alice Ann in beside her sister.

"Yes. They were quite friendly—even apologized for their behavior and said the issue of slavery was one that should be settled by our parents."

"I'm pleased to hear their parents have spoken to them and explained their actions were inappropriate," she replied.

"Did you enjoy yourself, my dear?" Nolan inquired as the carriage rocked to and fro on the uneven road.

"The evening was tolerable, though I didn't find it as jovial as I remember from my childhood. And what happened to all of the men? One moment the dance floor was filled with more couples than one could imagine, and suddenly it seemed as if all of the men had disappeared and the women were standing about fanning themselves and drinking punch."

Nolan nodded. "I wondered at that myself. I even commented to Woodson about his missing guests. He said they'd gone into his library to conduct business of some sort. Rather rude, if you ask me. Seems they could conduct business somewhere other than a social gathering that occurs but once a year."

"Indeed you would think so. I thought Lydia looked quite lovely this evening, though she and Rupert both were somewhat aloof, didn't you think?" Jasmine asked.

"Jasmine! Look up ahead! Is that glow of red coming from the direction of The Willows?" Nolan's voice was an urgent plea begging for a denial from his wife.

She stretched to the side and leaned out the carriage window. "Oh, Nolan! The Willows is on fire! Hurry! Hurry! It appears to be the house. Martha, Henrietta, and the other house servants are in there."

Nolan flicked the reins and urged the horses into a gallop. "It's more than the house. The entire sky seems lit up. It's coming from all directions. It appears that nothing has been spared. I fear the entire plantation is afire."

"Surely not. Dear God, let this be a dream!" she cried out.

———

Jasmine leaned heavily against Nolan's chest, clutching his arm, as they surveyed the plantation, unable to believe the devastation that surrounded them. Fires burned in varying degrees throughout the plantation. Unremitting flames snaked across the acreage, licking and scorching every vestige of habitation lying in their destructive path. Smoke curled upward and spread across the sky like a giant blanket that had been unfolded to hide the starlit heavens. The heavy stench seeped downward and filled their nostrils—a continuous reminder of the fire's catastrophic obliteration.

Fear swelled through Jasmine, clawing at her with an unrelenting insistence. "We must see if anyone has survived. All of the servants were in the house, even Martha and Henrietta." Her voice was shrill and cut through the February air. "There doesn't appear to be anyone attempting to put out the fires."

Nolan wrapped her in a protective embrace. "We can't possibly contain these fires. It's much too late for that. The most we can hope for is to find the servants alive."

"Look over dere, Miz Jasmine," Prissy exclaimed. "Someone's wavin' a white cloth from behind da tree."

Nolan cupped his hands to his mouth. "Who's there? This is Nolan Houston—come out and show yourself."

Jasmine squinted as she attempted to make out the figure running toward them. "I believe it's . . . Yes! It's Henrietta. Henrietta!" she called. "Praise God, you are safe! Where are the others? Martha? The house servants? All of the former slaves that were down in the quarters? Can you tell us anything?"

Henrietta dropped to the ground and began to weep in deep inconsolable sobs, her body heaving up and down as she clung to the hem of Jasmine's gown.

Nolan hurried to where she sat and helped her to her feet. "Let me assist you into the carriage, where you and Jasmine may sit and talk," he urged.

"You're safe now, Henrietta," Jasmine whispered as she pulled the woman close and patted her back. "Please tell us what happened. You're the only person we've been able to locate."

Henrietta nodded her head up and down as she appeared to choke back her sobs. "It was terrible, Miss Jasmine, just terrible. Martha was overcome by the smoke. I pulled her out of the house, but I don't know if she's alive. I'm ashamed to say I was afraid to remain. After all, what could one woman do against all that? I ran out here to hide," she cried, beginning to weep once again.

"It's all right. You did the right thing, Henrietta. What about the others? Did any of them survive?"

"The men took all the colored folks from the house and the quarters. I heard a gunshot, and then someone yelled that they'd shot Mr. Draper. I don't know if it's true—I've been afraid to show myself for fear they would kill me too."

"What do you mean the men took all the colored folks?" Jasmine asked. "What men?"

"The men that started the fire," she gasped.

Jasmine and Nolan exchanged a worried look, but it was Nolan who spoke. "You say they took the coloreds—did they not put up a fight?"

"Those men had guns, Mr. Houston, and I heard them yelling back and forth. They put all of them in chains so they couldn't run off. I kept praying you would return or that one of the neighbors would come down the road on their way home. I kept praying someone, anyone, would come and help."

"What did these men look like, Henrietta. Did you know them?"

"They were white, riding horses—a few carriages too, but mostly on horseback. They were dressed in fine clothes, but I don't know folks from around these parts. I heard one of them laugh and say something about paying a neighborly visit."

Nolan slapped his top hat on his leg. "This is an outrage! There's no doubt these fires were set by the very men who

241

were at that party this evening. I'd venture to guess they weren't in John Woodson's library at all—they were out setting fire to our plantation while they knew Woodson would keep us occupied at his party. Every one of them took part in this travesty."

Prissy leaned forward from the rear seat of the carriage, tears lining her cheeks. "D'ya know what happened to my Toby, Miz Henrietta?"

"They took him—they took all the house servants first and put them in chains. Some of the riders had gone to the slave quarters, and that's when I heard the gunshot. Soon after they brought all the others back to the main house, where they chained and put them in the wagons. I was still hidden near the house and knew I had to get away from there before they spotted me." A look of terror sparked in her eyes and she hesitated a moment. "Do you think they took Martha?"

Nolan slowly shook his head back and forth. "No. I don't think they would take a white woman. They came with shackles and chains in order to steal the coloreds and force them back into slavery. I'll go and see if I can find Martha. You say she was outside the rear of the house?"

"Yes, sir. Behind the big trees along the path to the water troughs."

Jasmine grasped Nolan's arm. "Wait a moment, please. It sounds as though a rider's approaching—or is it my imagination?"

"You're right; someone is coming down the road. I'd best wait and see who it is. I'd like to think it's someone coming to lend a hand, but I don't know who that would be since it appears as if all of our neighbors took part in this devastation."

"Looks like it might be Rupert—and I'd guess that he smells like smoke." Jasmine climbed out of the carriage at the same time that Prissy grabbed a blanket from off the front carriage seat and scooted into the far corner beside the children, being careful to pull the cover over herself. Fortunately, the girls were sound asleep, and Spencer was watching in wide-eyed silence.

"Are you cold, Prissy?" Jasmine asked.

"No, ma'am, just wantin' to stay out of the way," the girl meekly replied only moments before Rupert reined his horse to a halt beside the carriage.

He tipped his hat and directed a wide grin at Jasmine. "Cousin," he greeted. "Appears you've been forced out of this place."

"These fires were intentionally set, and we know that you and your friends are responsible," she accused, "and to think you call yourselves gentlemen. You're all a disgrace to mankind."

"Careful, Jasmine. You've already made enough enemies in these parts with your judgmental attitude and quick tongue. Just as these fires were meant to deliver a message, I'm here to enlighten you. You and your kind are not wanted in the South—it's best you realize that before it's too late." He reached into his coat pocket and pulled out some folded papers.

She emitted a wounded laugh. "Too late for *what*? There is nothing remaining, *cousin*. You and your legion of pathetic followers have already destroyed or taken everything we own, so you may feel free to tell your cohorts we will leave when we are ready and not a moment before. And merely as a matter of curiosity, what does Lydia think of your behavior? Even through the most difficult times, the Wainwrights have protected and defended one another. Does she know of your involvement in this unspeakable affair?"

"Indeed, Lydia *is* a Wainwright, and though both Lydia and I hold familial ties to you, our Southern heritage and beliefs go beyond a loyalty to family bloodlines—especially when the family members involved have pledged their allegiance to the abolitionist North. And you, my dear cousin, are no longer a Southern Wainwright—you are a Yankee Houston," Rupert retorted, his face now contorted with anger. "So far as we're concerned, you need to take your family and abolitionist ideas and return to where you came from."

Nolan stepped forward and positioned himself between Rupert and Jasmine. "You need to remember whom you're talking to, Rupert. I'll not tolerate any more of your abusive behavior. I demand the immediate return of the people you kidnapped from this plantation."

"*People? Kidnapped?* You mean those slaves? They've been taken to other plantations where they belong *and* where their labor is needed."

"They are *not* slaves. Jasmine has signed their papers—every one of them is free, and you have no more right to hold them than you would me."

"Don't tempt me, Nolan," Rupert sneered.

"If they are not immediately returned, I shall take this matter to the law. I intend to see each person who participated in this heinous deed prosecuted to the fullest extent possible."

Rupert's laughed was filled with a sadistic ring. "Do you now? Well, before you go and make a fool of yourself, let me tell you that it was the law that helped plan and carry out our strategy. You can rest assured you'll receive no help from any lawman in these parts."

"You've delivered your message. Now I'm telling you to leave our property."

"Well, that is another matter entirely. You see, I have papers here that show you've agreed to turn the property over to me. After all, the fire destroyed everything of value and you have no reason to hold the property any longer." Rupert grinned as he threw the papers at Nolan's feet.

"We've agreed to no such thing," Jasmine protested. "I'll not give you The Willows. Not now—not ever!"

"But my dear, you already have. I have witnesses who will vouch for that fact—testify under oath—that they saw you willingly sign those papers."

Nolan picked the papers up. It was impossible to read them, but Jasmine quickly went to see what they might say. "You won't get away with this. I'll go to town and tell the judge everything that has happened."

"You do that, cousin. You'll find, however, if you look those papers over, Judge Weston is one of the people who witnessed our transfer of ownership." Rupert gave a maniacal laugh.

"You've said what you wanted to say. Now leave," Nolan commanded.

"Not without Prissy. Come on out of there, girl," Rupert called. "I see you hiding under the cover. Don't be making me wait—get on out here."

"Prissy isn't going anywhere with you. Get out of here," Jasmine ordered, her fists balled in anger.

"Why don't you let Prissy answer for herself? Come on out, Prissy, and I'll take you to that fellow you're so fond of—Toby, isn't it? I know you don't want to see him take a lashing, so why don't you hurry out of there," Rupert said with a cruel smile curling his lips.

Jasmine rushed to the carriage as Prissy dropped the blanket and stepped out. "You're not thinking of going with him, are you?" she whispered while grasping the girl by her thin shoulders.

Tears streaked Prissy's cheeks. "I don' want Toby gettin' no lashing on my account," she murmured.

"Don't you see he's lying to you, Prissy? He's not going

to take you to Toby. He's not going to do what any of us want. He'll either keep you or sell you to the highest bidder, but he's not going to reunite you with Toby. Rupert Hesston isn't going to do anything that would please anyone except himself. Have I ever lied to you, Prissy?"

"No, ma'am, but iffen I can help Toby . . ."

"That's just it, Prissy. You can't help Toby. None of us can. Think of your baby," she whispered. "Toby wouldn't want his baby to grow up in slavery. Would he?"

"No. But I don' care nothing 'bout this child right now; I care 'bout Toby," Prissy insisted.

"There, you see—she wants to come with me. Let her be, Jasmine. You say she's free, yet you attempt to hold her against her will," Rupert said. "Apparently you haven't truly freed your slaves."

"We's free," Prissy hissed. "She's jest tryin' to make me see what's best."

"You know what's best, Prissy," Rupert said with an evil look in his eye. "Now get over here."

She stiffened. "No, suh, I ain't going, and you can't make me." Her voice was trembling with fear as she took cover behind Jasmine. "He can't, can he?" she whispered.

"I want you off this property immediately!" Nolan commanded. "Get out and don't ever return."

"Prissy belongs to me. I won't leave without her."

"You'll leave now." Nolan stepped forward, his hand going to the inside pocket of his coat. Jasmine wondered at his actions. Nolan never carried a gun, but it appeared he was about to draw one now.

"Very well. I'll leave, but I'll be back. And when I return, I'll have help with me. You think you have nothing left? Remember, you still have your children—but perhaps not for long. You have your lives as well. You're going to be sorry for your actions here tonight," he threatened. "You have my word. We'll be watching you. When you come to town, I'll get Prissy then and no threat of yours will stop me. You'll be lucky if you even make it as far as town."

He mounted the bay gelding, jerked on the reins, and kicked his heels into the horse's flanks. They stood watching as the horse carried him down the road at breakneck speed.

"Why is he so insistent upon having Prissy?" Jasmine asked. They both looked to the girl who was now backing up toward the carriage.

Jasmine realized there would be no answer from her and turned her gaze once again to her husband. "He's taken The Willows and everyone else. Nolan, he surely means to see us in complete defeat."

"No, I believe he very well means to see us dead," Nolan said in a whisper only Jasmine could hear.

CHAPTER · 15

JASMINE STARED into the carriage, where the girls were still sleeping soundly. Thankfully, Spencer had remained a silent observer. No telling what her cousin might have said or done had her son attempted to enter into the quarrel, especially in light of his final threat toward their children. Jasmine shivered as she recalled Rupert's parting words.

"I've failed miserably," she said as Nolan wrapped her in a comforting embrace. "Nothing has gone as we hoped. Because of me, every one of our former slaves has been forced back into slavery. And likely into the hands of owners and overseers who will abuse them for no other reason than the fact that they come from The Willows."

"I must go and check on Martha. Once we know her condition, we're going to need to formulate a plan. Stay here with the children, and I'll return as quickly as possible. If I attempt to take the horses any closer to the fire, they'll only become skittish. I don't want a runaway carriage—especially since it's our only means of transportation."

"Hurry, Nolan—and take Prissy with you, just in case

Rupert didn't actually leave. Should he return and you weren't here, there's no way I could protect her."

Jasmine climbed into the carriage and settled in beside Henrietta. They sat watching the roadway, both of them praying Nolan would return before they spied any sign of a rider coming in their direction. Jasmine tried to calculate what should be done next, but her mind refused to work. These past months had been the hardest of her life, losing first her father and brothers and now The Willows and all the people she had hoped to free.

"Can we hope to find the others?" Henrietta asked softly.

Jasmine saw Spencer watch her as if intent for the answer. "I don't think so. The law won't be any help to us, and other plantation owners will simply hide our people away until we give up. To push them for answers might even result in the death or removal of them all together." She shook her head. "I just wanted to do a good thing here." Spencer reached out and touched her hand, and Jasmine clung to it gratefully.

"I sure hope they won't take long to find Martha," Henrietta suddenly declared. "I don't know what might happen if they don't come right back."

"Don't be afraid, Henrietta. The Lord is with us. He is watching over all of us."

"Was He watching earlier when those men came?" Spencer asked seriously.

"Yes, I suppose He was," she said. "I believe He sees everything."

"Then why didn't He stop them?"

"I don't know, Spencer. I wish God would have stopped them, but apparently He has something else in mind."

"Maybe He just wants us to go home. There's nothing to stop us from going now."

Jasmine nodded. Her son was right on that account. In

fact, if they didn't go now, they might very well risk their lives.

They didn't have to wait long, for a short time later, Prissy and Nolan hurried toward them. Martha was very evidently absent.

"I'm sorry, dear, but Martha . . . was obviously overcome by the smoke." Nolan met Jasmine's gaze hesitantly. She felt sorry for her husband. He no doubt feared she might be unable to withstand yet another blow. She nodded at him, hoping it might ease his concern.

"If it helps at all," he continued, "she appeared peaceful, as if she'd merely fallen asleep. I would like to remain here and bury her, but I fear Rupert's threats were real. If so, he may return later tonight or at daybreak. We must leave, Jasmine. I can possibly return tomorrow and bury Martha, but right now we must get the children to safety."

"I agree," Jasmine managed to say, though she felt as if she were in a daze. How could things have appeared so peaceful, so good, only hours ago? "If Rupert returned, we would be defenseless against him and his treacherous friends."

"Think, my dear. Do you know *anybody* who would help us? Even if only for a short time, we need a place to hide until we can make arrangements to leave. If Rupert is determined to have Prissy, I'm convinced he'll follow us."

Jasmine realized there was no time to mourn any of the losses she'd sustained. There never really had been a time— had there? She squared her shoulders and pushed aside her grief. There had to be someone who might help.

Prissy began to weep. "I don't want yo' babies getting hurt, Miz Jasmine. You leave me here. I ain't gonna put them in harm's way. Massa Rupert will have to find me first, and I know some good hiding places 'round these parts."

"He'll put the hounds on you, Prissy. I'll not have that!

You're coming with us," Jasmine insisted.

"What about the preacher in Lorman?" Nolan asked. "Any chance he might help?"

Jasmine wrung a handkerchief through her fingers. "I doubt he'd be willing to chance losing his biggest contributors. Besides, he's pro-slavery and doesn't understand us or our beliefs. He thinks we're fools and he's told me so."

"Isn't there a soul you can think of?"

"Wait! When Mr. Forbes came to Lowell and talked to us, he mentioned my cousin Levi had survived. Now that winter is upon us, I'm guessing he should have returned home."

Nolan drew closer and took her hands in his own. "Can we trust him? Once he discovers our beliefs, will he betray us?"

"Levi has always been a free spirit—never one to conform to others' beliefs. Yet I haven't seen him in years and can't speak with authority on whether he'd be willing to lend aid. However, I don't see that we have any alternative other than to throw ourselves at his mercy."

Nolan nodded. "I'll approach him with the option of turning us away if he doesn't want to become embroiled in this matter. Of course, I'll seek his promise not to tell anyone we requested his assistance. However, if he agrees to help us, we'll have to trust that he is willing to embrace the cause. We have no other choice. How far is it to his home?"

"At least ten miles," Jasmine replied. "He doesn't live in Lorman."

"Although I dislike having to travel ten miles at this time of night and under these conditions, it's to our advantage Levi lives in a secluded area. Someone would surely see us if we were attempting to hide in town. We must leave and get as far from here as possible before daybreak."

Nolan and Prissy climbed into the carriage, and they

were soon on their way. Jasmine stared at The Willows until it was gone from her sight. She then focused on the road before her, attempting to remember the proper turns and directions that would best deliver them to Levi's door. She prayed he would be home. What if he was visiting relatives, or what if he turned them away? *Quit borrowing trouble,* she silently chastised herself, though it was difficult to push the disturbing thoughts from her mind.

"I believe we need to take the path that veers off to the right just up ahead," she told Nolan.

"You *believe*?" he asked, slowing the horses.

"I haven't been to Levi's home in years, and it's dark, Nolan. I'm doing the best I can," she replied while attempting to hide her own concern.

"I know you are, my dear. I'm sorry; the stress is beginning to wear on me. Forgive me?"

"Of course," she said as they turned down the road. They'd traveled only a short distance when Jasmine said, "Yes, this is right. I do remember. We'll take another right turn, and then it's only three or four miles."

"Good. It's soon going to be daybreak, and I'd like to have the carriage safely hidden and the family inside Levi's house before the sun rises."

"I do hope he remembers me," she said quietly.

"Of course he'll remember you."

"I haven't seen him for years. Since my marriage to Bradley—he attended the wedding."

Nolan gave her a lopsided grin. "At least your name remains Houston. Surely your father has visited with Levi throughout the years and informed him of the many happenings in your life."

She shrugged. "Who knows? Father would have willingly offered the information, but I don't know that Levi would have been interested. As I said, he's nothing like the rest of the family."

"Hopefully, that will be to our advantage."

"But being different doesn't ensure his help."

"Well, we will soon find out." Nolan pulled back on the reins and the team came to a halt near the front entrance of the hulking, poorly maintained frame house sitting a distance from the road. The house was surrounded by leafless oaks, and a substantial barn was located to the distant rear of the house.

"The rest of you remain in the carriage while we go up and speak with Cousin Levi," Jasmine said with a cheery smile. "We shan't be long."

The girls remained asleep and the others appeared quite content to remain in the carriage while someone else secured provision for their safety. Truth be told, Jasmine longed to remain in the buggy with them. She disliked having the group reliant upon her to find the proper accommodations; there was much at stake.

She tapped upon the door—lightly at first and then more forcefully. "I forgot that he's a bit hard of hearing," she said to Nolan as they stood on the wraparound front porch.

A frazzled-appearing servant finally answered the door after peering out from behind the lace curtains at the front windows. "May I help you?" she asked, opening the door only wide enough to extend her beak of a nose through the crack.

Jasmine nearly giggled at the sight. "Good morning. My name is Jasmine Wainwright Houston—I'm Levi's second cousin. Is he in?"

"You've come calling at this time of the day? He's not even had his breakfast."

"Well, nor have we, and we would be most happy to join him if you'd tell him we've arrived. Actually, there are seven of us. Our three children, two servants, and the two of us," she added with what she hoped was a pleasant smile.

"I'll go and tell Mister Levi you're here. You may wait on the porch."

"Perhaps we could at least enter the foyer," Jasmine said. "I assure you we're harmless." If they were already in the house, it would be much more difficult for Levi to send them on their way—or so she hoped.

The servant opened the door a bit farther and peered at the wagon with a frown on her face. "I suppose it wouldn't hurt," she conceded begrudgingly.

"Thank you. I'll go and fetch the others while my husband moves our carriage and horses into the barn," Jasmine said as she and Nolan turned and stepped from the porch.

"I'm not certain . . ."

"Not to worry—I'll explain to Cousin Levi," Jasmine said without giving the woman any further opportunity to protest.

"Handled quite nicely," Nolan complimented as they hurried to the carriage.

"Thank you. I hope the meeting with Levi goes as well. As I recall, he's fond of children—at least he always treated me well as a child. Let's hope he still looks kindly upon youngsters. Some older people don't, you know," she added in a hushed voice.

Nolan laughed. "Yes, I do know, my dear. My own father was one of them. I'll be in as soon as I've cared for the horses. Don't let him pitch you out on your ear before I return."

"I'll do my best. He may not be down for breakfast until after you join us," she hastily added as she helped the women, each one carrying a drowsy child, out of the carriage.

Although the notion gave her comfort, her hope was

dashed when the small group entered the front door. Cousin Levi stood at the bottom of the stairway with his hand resting upon the oak balustrade, looking as though he expected royalty to enter his presence.

The old man adjusted his spectacles and peered at the group, his eyes traveling from head to toe as he examined each one. "A bit overdressed for a morning call, aren't you?" he inquired as his gaze finally settled upon Jasmine, who was still attired in her ball gown.

Jasmine glanced at her mauve satin gown with its puffed trim across the bodice and hem. The silk roses and fichu adornment further served to make the gown appear completely inappropriate for morning wear. "Yes, we are. However, my family attended a gala at Rosewood Plantation last night, and we now find ourselves in quite a quandary. I'm hopeful you'll be willing to help. If I might have a few moments of your time, I can explain."

"Since the children are still in their party wear, may I assume they've not eaten breakfast, either?" he inquired.

"No, they haven't," Jasmine replied.

"Maude!"

The beak-nosed servant rushed into the foyer with her cap askew. "Yes, sir?"

"Take the children and servants and feed them breakfast."

"At the dining table?" she asked, her gaze clearly fixed upon Prissy.

"Yes, at the dining table, and quit staring. I'm certain the colored girl knows how to use a fork as well as you and I. Off with you now, and take them along."

"I's willin' to eat in da kitchen or even help prepare da food," Prissy offered.

"Nonsense. Go and eat," Levi ordered.

"You're very kind," Jasmine said.

"I'm a grumpy old man. Now come into the parlor and

let me hear your tale of woe." He slowly edged himself into one of the overstuffed chairs. "My rheumatism kicks up from time to time. Probably a storm moving in," he explained as he scratched his thinning white hair. "I'm trying to remember what it was your father told me about you. Ah, yes. Your first husband died and you married his brother, isn't that it?"

"Yes. And I live in Massachusetts," she added.

"Right . . . an abolitionist. Your father mentioned that too. I was surprised he'd come to accept the fact that you and McKinley had turned against the South."

Jasmine cringed at his characterization of her beliefs. "We didn't turn against the South, cousin. We are abolitionists, but we continue to love the South and many of the people who live here. However, we find it impossible to embrace slavery—which is what brings me here."

A startled look crossed his face. "I don't own any slaves, so you have no argument with me."

Jasmine smiled and leaned over to pat his hand. "This has nothing to do with whether you own slaves, Cousin Levi." Clearly and concisely, she explained their dilemma, leaving few details to the imagination. Levi gave her his full attention without once interrupting her explanation. She had nearly completed reciting the facts when Nolan entered the front door.

"Do permit me to introduce you to my husband, Nolan Houston."

"You're a fellow artist, I understand," Nolan said.

"Ah, you paint?" Levi inquired.

"In my early years I spent a great deal of my time writing and sketching. My passion, however, was poetry. Now, I no longer have time to indulge myself. Perhaps when the children are grown and life has settled a bit."

Levi laughed as he shook Nolan's hand. "Don't wait too

long, my boy, or you'll never return at all. I know many people frown upon artists. They think us lazy and unwilling to adhere to *their* idea of honorable work. Little do they realize how difficult it is to place paintbrush to canvas or pen to paper and deliver a work of beauty. But those of us who are blessed with creative gifts have an obligation to God and mankind to use that ability. Don't waste your talents! From what your wife tells me, you have been given much that you could write about."

"Unfortunately, none of it heartening," Nolan replied.

"True. Nonetheless, much art is communicated through pain and suffering. Remember that when you return to your home. However, the problem at hand is of greater import than your artistic endeavors. Jasmine says you need protection until you can formulate a plan for you and your family to flee back to the North."

"Are you willing to assist us? I'd like to say we won't be placing you in danger, but such a statement may not be truthful. Men who would threaten the lives of young children will care little if they injure you also. I want you to be fully aware of the possible harm that may befall you."

"I'm an old man, Nolan. Death does not frighten me. As for the slavery issue, I was born and raised in Mississippi, but unlike most folks around here, I've lived in other places. Certainly, some of my neighbors have traveled abroad or gone north for short periods of time, but they've never actually immersed themselves in other cultures and social settings. As I told your wife, I own no slaves. In fact, I never have. I hire servants to assist me as needed—white folks. There aren't many freed men around these parts or I'd be willing to hire them."

"Then you agree with our stand against slavery?" Nolan inquired.

"I don't participate in slavery, but I *do* believe in the right to make a choice. Not quite the same thing you folks believe. Let me add, however, that I strongly oppose the tactics being used by Rupert and his cronies. I stand willing to assist your family, though, if you believe Rupert's threats to be real. I suggest we reason together and develop a well-thought-out plan—after breakfast," he said with a broad grin. "Man cannot work on an empty stomach. Let's join the rest of your family in the dining room."

Once breakfast had been completed, Henrietta and Prissy were shown to a room where they could tend the children, and Levi escorted Nolan and Jasmine to his library.

"Why don't you specify your priorities and what you need from me so that we may begin to formulate a plan," Levi said, taking up his pen.

Jasmine sat opposite Nolan, grateful that the older man was taking charge. "We had given all of my father's slaves their freedom, cousin. They are now freed men and women. We told them we would divide the money we received for the crop they were harvesting so they would have enough to begin their lives and become established in the North."

"Mighty generous of you," Levi remarked.

"Perhaps, but none of that is now going to occur. The Willows has been stolen from me. Rupert has some forged documents that everyone for miles around will attest to being bona fide. The cotton, ready for shipping, has been burned, and worst of all, all of our former slaves have been hauled off by Rupert and his men and are being sold back into slavery. Do you think there's any way we can help them regain their freedom before we depart?" Jasmine asked as she attempted to hold her emotions in check.

"Now, it's not going to serve us well if you become distressed. We need to keep our wits about us if we're to accomplish our mission. Concerning the slaves . . . I don't know how your husband feels about this issue, but I believe our first priority should be getting all seven of you to safety," Levi said.

"But I fear if we leave the field hands, they'll never escape bondage," Jasmine said, dabbing her eyes with a lace handkerchief. "I know we don't have the law on our side, nor the sympathy of our neighbors, but it seems we should at least try."

Levi leaned back in his leather desk chair and clipped off the end of a cigar. "I'm not going to sit here and tell you I think you're going to have much success with such a venture either now or in the future. Frankly, your first responsibility is to those three children. Once they're safely returned home, use your own judgment about coming back and helping the others gain their freedom," he said while puffing on the cigar.

"Your cousin is absolutely correct, Jasmine. I abhor these ghastly happenings, but the children cannot remain in Mississippi while we go searching about the countryside. You know as well as I do that our chance of finding any of the former slaves is miniscule."

"And if you find them," Levi added, "your attempts to regain their freedom will be thwarted at every turn. These men are shrewd, and they'll quickly assist one another in their scheme."

"Yet our former slaves are depending upon us—I know they are," she lamented. "We'll be like all the rest: we'll leave them disappointed and reinforce their belief there are no whites who care for them."

Nolan leaned forward and grasped her by the shoulders. "Jasmine, we *cannot* remain here. You would never forgive yourself if something were to happen to our children."

"I know, I know," she finally conceded in a hoarse whisper. "Yet I feel as though I've betrayed all those people."

"No, my dear. You haven't betrayed them—it's Rupert and his cronies who have made a mockery of the law and justice. And one day he will pay dearly for his actions," Nolan assured her.

Levi leaned forward and rested his arms upon the massive desk, ocher spots showing prominently on his aging skin. "Now that we've settled the issue of the slaves, let's move on. Have you booked passage for your transportation home?"

"Yes. We should be able to exchange Martha's passage for Prissy's use. However, Rupert knows our plans. When he came to visit, he asked about our journey and then inquired if we would take the same route home. We told him that we had made arrangements with Captain Harmon to sail home on the *Mary Benjamin,*" Nolan replied. "Knowing Rupert, he'll surely be on the lookout at the docks in Rodney. He and the rest of the men realize it's the ideal place for us to board a steamboat to New Orleans. And he did say he'd be watching us."

"I realize the journey would be difficult, but I think you'd be wise to travel north by foot for a time—get yourselves to Vicksburg, then take a steamboat north and make train connections for the remainder of your journey. If Rupert believes you're going to sail out of New Orleans, he'll have his men stationed in Rodney and Natchez."

"True," Nolan agreed. "And he'll be expecting us to sail south toward New Orleans rather than north. We can make our way along the river until it appears safe."

"Rupert is clever. He may send men in *both* directions, so your journey is going to be treacherous until you're safely beyond Vicksburg. I doubt they'll search any farther north than that," Levi said thoughtfully. "I can furnish you with food, and I'll have Maude see if she has something you can wear other than that . . . that . . ." He flitted his hand toward Jasmine's gown.

"Ball gown," she said, completing his sentence.

"Yes. You'll need something more substantial—and shoes made of something other than cloth, I suspect."

"Maude!" he shouted while ringing a small brass bell that had been resting on his desk.

"Yes, sir?" She edged into the room like a frightened bird.

"Mrs. Houston is going to need clothes in which to travel. This, of course, will not do." He once again waved his hand up and down. "Do you think you can be of assistance?"

The older woman's eyes traveled up and down Jasmine's body as though she were taking measurements. "My clothing would not fit her, sir. She has more meat on her bones than I, but I suppose I could go into town and make some purchases if you like."

"Would such purchases arouse suspicion, do you think?" Jasmine inquired.

"Why would anyone care if I was purchasing a traveling suit for Master Levi's relative?" she asked.

Jasmine flinched. "That's the point, Maude. We don't want anyone to know I'm here or that I'm leaving."

Maude stared at her as though she'd taken leave of her senses.

"It's private information, Maude. Not a word to anyone. Understand?"

"Indeed, sir."

"But will it cause suspicion?" Jasmine insisted.

"I sometimes make clothing purchases to send to my family. Should anyone inquire, I'll say my sister is in need of a traveling suit and there's nary a decent shop to be found near her home. 'Tis the truth anyway."

"Your sister is traveling?" Levi inquired.

"*No!* The part about having no decent shops in Ken-wick," Maude said in an exasperated tone.

"I see," Levi said. "I want you to hasten off as soon as possible. Don't dally, but find both shoes and a dress, along with a change of clothes for the children, if possible. Put it on my account," he added.

Jasmine stood and motioned to Maude. "I'll go to the other room and give you some measurements, Maude. If you gentlemen will excuse me for a short time?"

"Of course," Nolan replied. "We'll work on the additional arrangements. We should likely plan to leave at first light, don't you agree?" he asked Levi.

"You may want to leave under cover of darkness. I'd suggest you leave well before daylight so you can be away from this area before sunrise. I'm concerned Rupert may come here searching for you—I want you to be well on your way if that should occur."

"Rupert calls on you?" Jasmine inquired as she and Maude reached the doorway.

"Not on a regular basis, but we see each other from time to time. And now that there is so little family remaining, he's bound to wonder if you thought to come here."

Jasmine frowned. "I suppose you're correct. I hadn't thought of Rupert considering we might come here, though I don't know where else we could have gone. Maude and I will see to the clothing while you assess our other needs—and I think we should travel to Vicksburg by wagon, not on foot."

Levi gave a brief laugh as he stubbed out his cigar. "I'm sure you do. However, you won't be safe traveling on any roads that will accommodate a wagon. You're going to need to keep to the woods if you're to stay out of sight. You may be able take a coach once you're twenty or thirty miles north, but remember—each person who sees you is one who may betray your whereabouts."

"There's one more thing," Nolan told Levi. "Our hired woman was killed in the fire. She still lies near the back door of the house. Can you see to her proper burial?"

He nodded. "Be assured of it."

Jasmine sighed. It would have to be enough. They had no other choice.

———

That night, with Clara hoisted into a sling on Nolan's back and each of them carrying provisions to sustain them until they reached Vicksburg, they stepped out into the crisp air.

"Thank you for everything! I pray we haven't placed you in any danger," Nolan said. "Make some arrangement to rid yourself of the carriage and horses; I'm afraid Rupert would recognize them."

Levi nodded. "Don't worry about me—you've got more than enough to concern yourself with. You'll all be in my prayers." Levi's eyes shone with emotion as he picked up his worn leather Bible and tucked it into Jasmine's satchel. "I want you to have my Bible as well as the money I placed inside the front cover. Don't refuse me; you'll need both the money and God's Word to sustain you throughout your journey."

Jasmine leaned forward and placed a kiss on her cousin's cheek. "Thank you for your kindness. I'll write once we've arrived home."

"Remember to keep to the woods. So long as you can hear the river and you're headed due north, you'll remain on course." Levi took hold of Jasmine's arm. "And don't fret about The Willows. I, too, have friends in these parts. I may not be able to get your slaves back, but I feel confident between my friends and what I know of Rupert Hesston, we'll secure The Willows for you and McKinley. Now hurry on."

Jasmine felt only moderately relieved at this thought. "Thank you so much."

Nolan waved, and their small band walked away from the house with Alice Ann holding tightly to Jasmine's hand. Henrietta and Prissy walked side by side. Spencer brought up the rear, listening for anyone advancing from that direction.

"I don't like this," Alice Ann whined as she tripped on a fallen branch.

"You're fine. You didn't fall. So long as you hold my hand, nothing will happen to you," Jasmine said in a reassuring voice. "We're on a great adventure, Alice Ann. One you can tell all your friends about once we get home."

"I'm going to tell Winnie first thing," she said.

"A horse can't understand you," Spencer told her.

"Shh!" Nolan warned. "Let's keep our voices down. We're close to Rodney, and there may be rowdies out and about in these woods."

Alice squeezed Jasmine's hand more tightly. "Is somebody going to hurt us?"

"No. Your papa won't let anything happen to you, Alice Ann, but you must do as you're told. Try to keep quiet unless it's very important."

They moved slowly, silently picking their way through the stand of woods that flourished not far from the banks of the Mississippi. The raw, fishy stench of the river mingled with the lapping sound of the water as it licked the dry riverbank—sounds and smells that directed their path when vision failed them. For a short time they floundered in the darkness, but their eyes quickly adjusted to the shadowy surroundings and they picked up their pace. All but Alice Ann, who was shifted to Nolan's back while Henrietta and

Jasmine took turns carrying Clara. There was little doubt this would be a grueling journey.

The night was filled with the sounds of croaking frogs and hooting owls while the distant moon cast eerie shadows in all directions. Giant tangles of Spanish moss hung from the trees like thick spider webs waiting to lure their prey. Jasmine swallowed her fear and followed closely behind Nolan as she wondered about the terror of all those runaway slaves who had stumbled through these woods before them. Runaways with dogs sniffing and yelping in the distance and then growing closer and closer, nipping at their heels until surely the bile of fear would rise in the throats of those slaves and nearly choke them. How did they manage to stop breathing and listen for the snap of a twig or the sound of a footstep on the forest floor when everything within them ached to run like the wind? How did they withstand the pure terror of being at the mercy of both the elements and their cruel captors? Though she feared for her family, her terror could be nothing compared to those brave slaves who dared to run for freedom.

"I think I hear something," Spencer hissed.

Nolan quickly gathered them together behind a growth of bushes. "Don't anyone say anything," he whispered.

Jasmine's heart hammered with the violence of pounding thunder on a stormy night as they hunkered behind the overgrowth. The voices were coming from the direction of the river—not from behind them, as Spencer had thought. Jasmine shrunk back as the voices grew louder.

"I'm not going any farther," a man said. "If Rupert wants to chase after that colored girl, then let him come and get her."

"He wants *all* of them—not just the darkie."

"Says he wants to prove to them that they've got to show him proper respect."

"This is mad. I'm not going to stay out here any longer just so Rupert can force someone to show him some respect. Besides, if they were headed north to Vicksburg, they would have been on the last boat. There's another one due in the morning. I say we go back to Rodney and, come daybreak, wait at the dock to see who boards the boat."

The other man grunted his agreement.

Nolan signaled them to remain where they were until long after the men could no longer be heard and then emitted a sigh. "I think it's safe for us to continue now," he whispered.

Jasmine clutched his arm. "From what those men said, I believe we'll be safe once we arrive at Grand Gulf. Let's pray we don't have to continue on foot to Vicksburg. I don't believe I could make it," she said wearily as she again wondered how runaways had endured their flight to freedom under circumstances much harsher than the conditions she was now being forced to experience. Suddenly she felt dreadfully inadequate.

CHAPTER · *16*

MARY MARGARET hoisted her skirts a few inches and made her way across Merrimack Street, carefully avoiding the pools of mud that were a vivid reminder of last week's snow. She was thankful the weather had warmed a bit, yet the muddy remains made getting about perilous. Even the carriages were having difficulty navigating the streets.

"Careful. That mud is as slick as the snow preceding it."

Mary Margaret looked up at the warning. "Paddy! What brings ya to town this evenin'?"

"I was attending a meetin'—we were havin' discussions about the St. Patrick's Day festivities," he replied, taking a few steps closer.

"Truly? And were ya able to complete the plans?"

He laughed and shook his head, surprised by Mary Margaret's conviviality. " 'Twill take more than one meeting for this group ta make any decisions."

"Bridgett tells me the decisions for the dance have already been made and the ladies have begun work already."

"Aye—but it's the women that have taken charge of the

dance. Men are a wee bit slower in making arrangements for parades and such—they want to make sure everything is exactly correct."

She laughed. "Get on with ya, Paddy. We all know it's the women that are slow to make decisions but quick to set their hands ta work once they've a plan, while 'tis the men who are quick to decisions but slow to beginning their task. If ya ask me, the men were likely anxious to get out to the pub and tip an ale or two instead of makin' plans for a parade that's more than a month away."

"Quick to pass judgment, are ya?"

"Just telling the truth about what I figure happened. Are ya tellin' me I'm wrong?"

A faint smile crossed Paddy's lips. "Sure and ya know exactly what happened. But they all agreed that we'd make our final decisions at the meeting next week," he quickly added. "I was thinkin' to walk over and see Bridgett and Cullen before headin' back to the farm. Are ya off to do some shopping?"

"No, just wanted to leave the house for a while and get a breath of air. Another one of the girls in our boarding-house lost her position at the mill today. Rather gloomy at the house, so I thought I'd take a walk."

"Well, then, would ya be wantin' to accompany me? If ya do na mind the walk, that is. The wagon is at the black-smith having a new wheel put on, and I'm to pick it up later. But if ya do na mind traveling by foot, ya could visit Bridgett for a bit before returning home."

There was a slight hesitation in his voice. Mary Margaret was unsure if he truly desired her company or if he was merely being polite. But no matter. Since learning more about Paddy from his sister, she was interested in becoming better acquainted, though she didn't want to appear overly anxious.

"I'm not certain," she tentatively began as she clicked open the small watch attached to her jacket and glanced at the time. "I do suppose I could, so long as I'm back to the boardinghouse by ten o'clock."

"Aye. I'll be sure ya're home on time. So ya say one of the girls lost her job today. I hope you and Bridgett do na have to face such a terrible thing," he said as they began walking.

"Bridgett should be safe unless the economy gets much worse. They're terminatin' by seniority, though they've made a few exceptions and let some girls go who they said didn't turn out as much work," she said. "That's what happened to Helen today. She's been with the Corporation longer than I have, but she's sickly and can na work so fast. I'm hoping she will na be bearing a grudge toward me, for it was na my doing."

"Did ya try discussin' the matter with her?" Paddy asked.

"Aye, but she said she didn't want to talk, so I left her to her thoughts. Mrs. Brighton said she could stay at the house, but there's no tellin' if she will. She's a quiet girl that came to our house because she was ill-treated at the place she had lived before. Mrs. Brighton has been kind to her, though Helen seldom has a word to say. At supper Mrs. Brighton told Helen there might be work for her someplace other than the textile mills."

"Does she have some other skills ta offer at one of the other companies?"

"I do na know, but Mrs. Brighton mentioned the company that's begun manufacturing shuttles and bobbins. She said she'd heard there might be a few positions there. She also suggested Helen talk to the owners of some of the shops in town to see if they might be needin' help, but I do na think there's much of a chance for that. Helen's na the type to be greeting customers in a dress shop or stationery store—she's too fearful of approachin' strangers."

"Ya never know what hunger will do for a person," Paddy said. "She may find she's able to handle such a position if it's all she can locate."

"It's a fact her family's needin' her money, so I do hope she finds work. Mrs. Brighton's willing ta seek aid for her through the benevolent group at her church. She's a kind woman, that one."

"Aye, so I've been told."

Mary Margaret took a deep breath to bolster her courage before speaking. "Are ya making plans to attend the St. Patrick's Day dance?" she asked as they neared Cullen and Bridgett's home.

Paddy turned to glance at Mary Margaret. "Sure and I always attend the dance. What good Irishman would remain at home on such a festive day?"

He didn't give the answer she had hoped to elicit, but she wasn't deterred. She would ask him again as they walked back to the boardinghouse. However, this time she would phrase her question a bit differently.

———

Paddy was certain he'd heard Bridgett whisper a remark about the St. Patrick's Day parade to Mary Margaret and then giggle as they were preparing to depart.

"I'm wonderin' why the two of them are discussing the parade when what they need to concern themselves with is the dance," he said to Cullen. "Next thing ya know they'll be tryin' to take over the parade."

"To be sure," Cullen agreed. "Bridgett's quite the organizer. She'll be havin' our work done for us if we leave 'er to it long enough."

"Still, they needn't be doin' our job. Although I'm sure

Bridgett would get the work done."

Cullen gave a hearty laugh. "Aye, to be sure. But women would na be women if they did na put themselves in the center of all of our plans. Besides, if I know Bridgett, they're likely discussing the latest fashions they'd like to be wearin' rather than interfering into yar plans, Paddy. Do na worry— there will be plenty for ya to attend to before the seventeenth of March arrives." The women moved closer to the front door. "Best be fetchin' yar jacket. Looks like the lass is ready to leave."

Mary Margaret had her cape fastened and her reticule in hand. She directed a warm smile in his direction, and for a moment Paddy wondered if there might be someone behind him for whom the smile was intended. After all, this lass had been nothing but agitated with him when they'd encountered each other in the past. He'd been taken aback when she agreed to spend time with him this evening; now she was smiling at him as though she'd missed being in his company. He was not a man given to second-guessing people's motives, but Mary Margaret was indeed cut from a different cloth than were the lasses he'd encountered in the past. Why was she now so affable?

She appeared to listen intently as they walked home and Paddy talked of the farm and the horses that would soon be ready for their new owners at West Point and the Virginia Military Institute. He spoke of several of the animals that had been sick and the fact that he missed Mr. Houston's presence at the farm, and he admitted he was sometimes overwhelmed making the many decisions needed in order to run such a fine operation as the Houston farm.

"I have little doubt but what ya're doin' a wonderful job. Mr. Houston has paid you a fine compliment by placin' you in charge during his absence," Mary Margaret said sweetly as she patted his arm.

"Aye, that he has, and I do na want to disappoint him," he said with his gaze fixed upon her hand as she continued to lightly grasp his arm.

"I do na think that would be possible." Her voice sounded thick and sweet like the honey he used to pour on his pancakes when he was a wee lad living in Ireland.

"Bridgett and I were discussin' the St. Patrick's Day dance. She was tellin' me about the new dress she's makin' for the dance."

"That's nice. I'm thinkin' she'll look lovely whether her dress is old or new."

"But having a new gown to wear to a dance always makes a woman feel special."

He didn't know what she wanted him to say. Surely the lass knew he had no knowledge of dresses and sewing, and there was little more he could add to a discussion of dress for the St. Patrick's Day dance—or any other dance, for that matter.

"Will ya be purchasing new trousers and shirt for the dance?" she finally inquired.

Paddy scratched his head. "I do na think so. I do na give much thought to such things until the time is upon me. Unlike you women, I do na plan to be doin' any sewing."

"Of course, if a lass wanted to make a new gown for the dance, she'd have to know some time in advance that she was going," Mary Margaret said.

"Anyone can go to the dance. Ya do na need a special invite," he said. "Well, here we are—I've gotten ya home well before ten o'clock, and now I must be hurrying off before Jake beds down for the night. He will not look kindly on me if I wake him up needin' my wagon."

He tipped his hat and nodded. "Good night to ya, Mary Margaret. I enjoyed spending the evenin' with ya."

"Good night," she replied, giving him another of her sugary smiles.

The girl was a puzzle—of that there was no doubt!

Kiara rounded the table and placed a plate of eggs and sausage in front of Paddy. "Get busy with yar breakfast," she ordered Nevan and Katherine, who were busy annoying one another rather than eating the food their mother had placed in front of them.

"You do na have to tell me more than once," Paddy said, picking up his fork. "Has Rogan already eaten and gone with Liam?"

"Aye, about five minutes ago."

He nodded. "I thought I saw him go by when I was mucking out some of the stalls. And how's that fine babe doin' this mornin'? Seems little Aidan is always sleepin' when I come in."

"That's what babies do. They sleep. And thankful we are that they do. He's nearly six weeks old now, Paddy. He'll soon begin to stay awake a wee bit more. Were ya able to get the wagon repaired?" she asked.

"Aye, it's back in the shed if Rogan's needin' it for anything."

"And did ya stop by and see Cullen and Bridgett?"

"Aye, along with Mary Margaret O'Flannery."

"Is that a fact, now? Do tell me how ya happened to be keeping company with Miss O'Flannery," Kiara said as she wiped the apron that covered her green chambray skirt.

Paddy related the entire episode in between bites of breakfast. "If ya do na begin eating that food, Nevan, I'm going to clean yar plate as well as me own," he said to the boy with a grin. "Now, where was I?" he asked, turning his attention back to his sister.

"Where she's talkin' about the dance," Kiara said impatiently.

"Aye. Well, if I did na know better, I'd think the lass was wantin' *me* to ask her to the dance," he finally said.

"And why would that be so hard ta believe? Ya're a fine young man that any lass would be lucky ta have!"

"Ya saw how she acted when she and Bridgett were over here—her nose up in the air as though she did na think much of me. Yet last night, she was sweet as a peppermint stick. I do na understand the mind of a lass," he said, wiping his mouth. "I best get back out to the barns. There's much ta be done today. And I hope the two of ya are done with yar breakfast by the time I come in for the noonday meal," he added with a wink at his niece and nephew.

———

Kiara began to clear the table while contemplating the information her brother had imparted. 'Twas true Mary Margaret appeared to think Paddy a wee bit full of himself, but Kiara thought she'd noticed the girl's feelings soften—especially when Bridgett was telling her about their voyage from Ireland. Perhaps what Mary Margaret and Paddy needed was a little more time together. Time to get to know one another a bit better in a friendly environment. Perhaps she'd extend a dinner invitation to Mary Margaret—and the sooner the better, for St. Patrick's Day would soon be arriving.

CHAPTER · 17

THE WOMEN AND children were huddled in a small circle, praying Nolan would return with the news they could board the boat. Jasmine had begged Nolan to go into Grand Gulf the preceding night and rent a room at the hotel, but he had refused, saying they would raise too much suspicion and would be too easily remembered should Rupert or his men come looking for them. She knew he was correct: one man, three children, and three women—one of them colored. There was little doubt they would raise eyebrows, especially in their filthy condition. So now they waited, Jasmine leading them in yet another prayer for safe passage home.

"It's Papa," Spencer whispered as they heard footsteps drawing near.

"Shh. Stay quiet. We can't be certain," Jasmine whispered into his ear.

She captured a glimpse of Nolan's brown wool coat as he edged through the thick brush. "Jasmine, it's me—Nolan," he called. He greeted her with a hand to her shoulder. "I talked with a number of men along the docks and some of the merchants doing business near the wharf. None of them had seen strangers loitering near the docks."

"Did you book passage?" she asked excitedly.

"Yes, though I pray I didn't make a mistake. I continue to wonder if we should wait until we reach Vicksburg to board a vessel."

"You may place the responsibility on my shoulders, Nolan. I truly can go no farther, nor can the children. If any of Rupert's men board the ship looking for Prissy, we'll hide her, but I honestly believe they've given up by now."

Nolan glanced about the weary group. "Do you all agree?"

"Yes," they replied in unison.

"Then we shall board. It's not what you're accustomed to, my dear. In fact, we'll have little space since the boat is already loaded with cotton."

"You'll hear no complaint from me so long as I don't have to walk another mile in these uncomfortable shoes. I have blisters on top of blisters," she said while bending over to rub her tender feet.

"We have no time to tarry, for the captain tells me they're preparing to lift the gangplank within the hour. If we're not on board, they'll sail without us." Nolan lifted Alice Ann to his hip. "Can you manage Clara?"

"Yes, of course. Spencer, please help Prissy and Henrietta gather things together and let's be on our way," Jasmine instructed.

Nolan quickly surveyed their camp to assure himself they'd left nothing behind. If Rupert or his supporters searched these woods, they didn't want any evidence to remain that their family had been there. It would take only a piece of fabric or a small toy of Alice Ann's to alert Rupert's men, convincing them to continue their search. When Nolan had finally completed his appraisal of the campsite, he motioned for them to follow.

"God has heard our prayer," Jasmine told Henrietta and Prissy.

"Don' be too sure—we ain't out of here yet, Missus," Prissy said as she hoisted one of the satchels under her arm.

Jasmine ignored Prissy's gloomy response. She could feel God's hand guiding them, so she would not be deterred by anything Prissy or anyone else might say. In her heart she knew they would arrive home safely—all of them.

The dock bustled with stevedores and roustabouts unloading packet boats heavy with freight destined for Vicksburg, while other dock workers hauled cotton bales and freight onto boats destined for Memphis and St. Louis.

"This way," Nolan directed, hurrying the bedraggled group toward a steamer at the far edge of the riverbank. The boat was laden with cotton bales that filled the lower deck of the boat and were stacked high around the front and sides.

Jasmine hesitated as Nolan headed for the gangplank. "Come along, my dear," he said, motioning her forward.

"The bales are stacked so high we won't be able to see a thing unless we go to the upper deck, which, I might add, looks none too safe." She eyed the vessel from the top of the tall black smokestacks and back down again. "They should have a higher railing up there. I truly wonder if this boat is actually seaworthy—especially with so much cargo on board. It doesn't appear well maintained."

Nolan turned to face her, Alice Ann clinging to his neck, and leveled a look of utter exasperation in her direction. "I didn't ask to review the maintenance log. I thought it more important to locate a boat going to Vicksburg that had space for us. As I recall, you said you couldn't walk another mile," he reminded her.

"That's true, but from all appearances, this boat has picked up all the cargo it can possibly carry."

"I told you there would be little space. I believe the boat is safe, but if you prefer to wait for another, we can go back to the woods."

"No, Mama. Please let's get on the boat," Spencer urged. "It's safe. I just want to go home."

Prissy was wringing her hands as her gaze settled on the murky water. "You think we's gonna end up at the bottom of that river, Miz Jasmine? I sure don' know how to swim. I never did like being 'round no water deep enough to drown in. You remember ol' Elijah what lived in the slave quarters?"

Jasmine shook her head. "No, I don't think I knew him."

"Well, he never did learn to swim neither. And one day when he was fishing in the pond down by the quarter, he done fell in and drowned hisself. I sho' don't want that happening to us," she said, her eyes shining with terror.

"We're not going to drown, Prissy," Nolan assured her. "This boat is perfectly sound. Otherwise, the plantation owners wouldn't use it to transport their cotton. Come along now—we're all going to be fine."

A short time later the boat released a long, shrill whistle. They watched from the upper level but well out of sight of anyone who might be watching from the shore as the gangplank was lifted and the boat began to move slowly away from the levee.

"We're going home, Alice Ann," Spencer said brightly. "You'll soon be able to ride Winnie, and I can ride Larkspur once again. Do you think Larkspur will remember me, Papa?"

Nolan tousled Spencer's disheveled hair. "I'm sure he will."

"When Reggie last wrote to me, she said Moses was exercising Winnie and Larkspur every day. I wonder if Larkspur will want Moses to ride him more than me when I get home."

Nolan gently clasped Spencer's shoulder. "I wouldn't worry. It may take a few days, but Larkspur will soon remember you and be happy to have you back home."

A scruffy-appearing seaman approached as the boat began to gain speed and move farther away from the bank. "Captain says to tell you there's a small cabin of sorts that you can use if ya've a mind to—ain't much, but it'll give you a little privacy. Follow me. It's back this way," he said. "Call out if you think you smell anything burning. Don't want this load going up in smoke. Fire's always a problem when we're carrying a big load of cotton. We have one most every voyage, what with all the wood to fire the boilers and all this cotton—guess it's to be expected."

"Then it's good you's got all dis water around," Prissy said as the group followed the man through the narrow passageways.

The crewman laughed at her remark. "If this cotton gets going, that river ain't gonna help us much, except to swallow up the boat when she sinks. Gotta catch 'em early or there's not much hope. Here's the cabin," he said as they came to a stop in front of an open doorway.

Jasmine surveyed the room and though she thought the captain had taken great leniency in calling the space a cabin, she didn't say so. "Do thank the captain for his thoughtfulness," she said instead.

"I don't want to stay here," Alice Ann said tearfully. "I'm afraid we're going to burn in the fire."

"What are we supposed to do when the fire starts?" Spencer asked, his voice quivering.

"There isn't going to be a fire," Nolan asserted.

"That man said there's a fire almost every time they go

on the river," Spencer said. "Now I wish we hadn't come on this boat."

Nolan attempted to calm the children, but both of them were insistent upon further talk of fires or drowning, continuing their questions until their fear was palpable.

Jasmine pulled her satchel close and rummaged through until her fingers touched upon the leather-bound Bible. She pulled it out and handed it to Nolan. "Perhaps you could read to the children about Jesus calming the storm," she suggested.

"Excellent idea," he said and opened the Bible to the Gospel of Luke. "Come sit close while I read these verses. They are very powerful words about a time when Jesus was out in a fishing boat with His disciples."

"Is this a fishing boat?" Alice inquired.

"No, but I suppose it would be easy enough to fish from this boat," Nolan replied. "Now come sit on my lap while I read to you."

They created a tender picture for Jasmine: Alice Ann on her father's lap, Clara on Henrietta's lap, and Spencer between the two—all of them focused upon God's Word. Nolan quietly began reading, the children's eyes growing wide as Nolan read about the storm that suddenly arose at sea and how the disciples hastened to awaken Jesus, who was sleeping in the boat.

"What did Jesus do?" Alice Ann asked, her dimpled chin turned upward as she looked into her father's eyes.

"I'm going to tell you in this next verse—listen closely. 'He got up and rebuked the wind and the raging waters; the storm subsided, and all was calm. "Where is your faith?" he asked his disciples. In fear and amazement they asked one another, "Who is this? He commands even the winds and the water, and they obey him."'"

"You must remember that Jesus is in this boat with us

right now," Jasmine said. "He's our protector, just as He was for the disciples."

"But I can't see Him," Alice Ann said.

"Because He's in your heart—and you must not ever forget He is with you," she explained. "It's a beautiful day. The sun is shining and it's not overly cold. Perhaps your father would agree to a short walk around the boat so you can become more comfortable with our new surroundings."

The children agreed, even convincing Henrietta to join them on their brief tour while Jasmine and Prissy set about arranging their belongings.

"You truly believe what you tol' your younguns 'bout Jesus being with us and being our protector?"

"Yes, of course. Don't you believe Jesus is watching over you, Prissy?"

"I ain't so sure. Maybe I jes' don't have enough faith, 'cause I sure has had some mighty bad things happen to me. I called out to Jesus, but them bad things jes' kept on happening. Seems like maybe He jes' don't care much 'bout me."

Jasmine reached out and gently grasped Prissy's hands in her own. "God loves you, Prissy. There was a time in my life when I thought God had forsaken me. I was truly unhappy and suffering more than *I* thought fitting for a person who loved the Lord. Eventually, however, my situation changed and my life significantly improved. Our timing is not always the same as God's timing."

"Maybe that's true, but jes' about the time I think things is getting better, then I get slapped back down again. Like me and Toby getting married—now that was a good thing, and I was mighty happy 'bout that. But now Toby's gone, prob'ly sold at the auction to some new owner, and we'll likely never see each other again. And me gonna have dis baby don't make things no better," she lamented.

"I know that's how it must seem now, but you need to keep believing that God is going to see you through this difficult time. I promise we'll do everything we can to find out where Toby is and have him join you. As soon as we arrive in Lowell, I'll pen a letter to my cousin Levi and ask his assistance. I believe he'll agree to help us, and I know we can trust him. Why don't we agree to earnestly pray about this every day? What do you think?" Jasmine asked.

They sat face-to-face, Prissy staring deep into Jasmine's eyes. "I guess we can try, but I jes' don' know if it'll do any good," Prissy replied in a soulful voice.

"We'll both pray, and I'll believe for *both* of us until you gain enough strength to believe for yourself."

Prissy nodded her head up and down, her tawny skin shining like pulled taffy in the warm afternoon sun. "You's a mighty fine woman, Miz Jasmine. You is one of the *good* things God done give me."

"Thank you, Prissy. And I'm going to trust God to send you more good things too."

———

Kiara wiped her hands on her apron, wrapped an old shawl around her shoulders, and walked out the back door toward the stables. Both Aidan and Katherine were napping, and Nevan was off to school. She hoped to make good use of the free time to begin supper preparations, but first she wanted to find Paddy. Simon came out of the stables leading one of the fine Arabians, the horse stomping and snorting in the cold afternoon air. She could not help but admire the horse's beauty. *A fine animal,* she thought as she waved her arm to gain Simon's attention.

When he finally looked in her direction, Kiara cupped her hands to her mouth. "Ask Paddy to come and see me when he has a minute."

Simon waved his hat. "I'll do that, Missus," he called.

"Thank you!" She rubbed her arms under the woolen shawl. "It's cold out here," she muttered while hurrying back indoors.

She was pleased she had decided upon mutton stew for supper. Upon entering the warm kitchen, Kiara checked the dried apples she had earlier placed in a bowl of warm water. The apples were ready to be used in her apple cinnamon cake, one of Rogan's favorites.

"I hear ya're wanting to see me," Paddy said as he burst through the kitchen door.

"Close that door—ya're bringing all the cold air in with ya," Kiara scolded.

He gave the door a shove. "It's closed," he said with a grin. "Now what is it ya're calling me away from my work to discuss?"

"I was wondering if ya would like to join us for supper tonight."

Paddy pulled off his cap and ran his fingers through the dark curls that fell across his forehead. "It's an inviting offer, but I do na think so. I've a lot of work to finish today, and I'll likely work until late."

Kiara glanced over her shoulder and gave him a haughty look. "Since ya have yar own house, ya never seem to have any time for yar sister and her family. Poor Nevan's soon goin' to forget he has an uncle."

"Go on with ya, lass. Ya know I spend far too much time at yar house, and Nevan's out to the stables every day after school, so I do na think he's going to be forgetting me."

"That does na change the fact that I would enjoy havin' ya join us for supper tonight. I'm fixing a fine mutton stew—ya won't want to be missing that, will ya?"

"Ya do know how to win yar own way. I will na promise ta be here, but if I finish all my chores and paper work, then

I'll join ya," he said as he helped himself to a piece of her soda bread.

"Ya should have more than enough time, for I do na plan ta serve supper until seven-thirty."

"Rogan working late, is he? I'll do my best." He pulled his cap back onto his head and opened the door.

He didn't wait for an answer before hurrying off, and for that she was thankful. After all, she did not want to tell her brother an untruth. Nor did she want to reveal her plot to have him spend the evening with Mary Margaret.

The children were cooperative, and Kiara's supper preparations moved forward according to plan. "Go and wash up—we're having company for supper," she told Nevan when he came in from the stables with a piece of straw tucked between his lips. "And take that straw out of your mouth," she said in a stern tone.

"Uncle Paddy does na care if I wash up," he muttered.

"Uncle Paddy's not the only one comin' for supper. Did he say he was comin' for sure?"

"No, he said he was going to try, but he was runnin' behind. Mrs. Houston's brother came to see 'im this afternoon, so he's even further behind with his work. Who else is comin' to supper?"

"Mary Margaret O'Flannery. The lady who works with Bridgett—she's been here to visit several times. Do ya remember her?"

Nevan's brow creased for a moment. "Is she the one that watched ya showing Bridgett how ta make the lace?"

"Aye, she's the one."

"Has Da come home yet?"

"He has, and he's already washed up and tendin' to Katherine."

"Can we be expectin' ta see Bridgett and Cullen at supper too?"

"No. Just Mary Margaret. Now stop with yar questions and get yarself presentable."

He gave her a quizzical look. "Sure and supper is smelling fine," he hollered over his shoulder as he hurried off.

She smiled at her son's remark. Nevan was like his da—he enjoyed a satisfying plate of food and a hearty laugh when he sat down to supper each night. Kiara pulled off her apron and peeked out the kitchen window, checking to see if she could see Paddy, but there was no sign he'd yet left the barns. She sighed, hoping her plan wouldn't run afoul. The good Lord knew Paddy had reached the age at which he needed to wed a fine Irish lass. But, like most men, Paddy was not yet aware of his need. She hoped this evening would be just the thing to heighten his awareness.

"I may just have to go out and yank him in here by the ear if he does na soon show up," she muttered. She glanced at the mantel clock as she passed through the parlor on her way up the stairs. She had only a few minutes to make herself presentable before Mary Margaret's arrival.

"Would ya take Katherine downstairs and keep a listen for Aidan? He should na be waking up, but ya never know," she remarked as she stood in the doorway of the children's room, where Rogan was reading to Katherine. "Mary Margaret should be arriving, so can ya keep a listen for the carriage also? I'll only be a few minutes."

"Aye. Sure and ya seem to be making this supper into an important evening. It's only one young lass coming to have a meal. I do na understand why ya're rushing about like ya're fixing supper for nobility."

"I'm na acting any different than any time when I invite company for supper," she defended.

Rogan swooped Katherine up onto his shoulder. "Say what ya will, lass, but I know different," he said with a wide grin. "Duck yar head, Katherine," he instructed before walking through the doorway.

———

Mary Margaret turned in front of the mirror. However, the small oval looking glass prevented her from seeing much more than a limited portion of her body at one time. Exasperated, she ran down the stairs and into the dining room, where Mrs. Brighton was clearing off the supper dishes.

"Do I look presentable?" she asked, doing a brief twirl in front of the older woman.

"You look quite lovely. You can be sure Mr. and Mrs. Sheehan will think so too. Have they invited you for supper to celebrate some special occasion?"

"I do na think so. I received a note asking me to come to supper, and that's as much as I know. I must hurry or I'll be late. Kiara said she would delay supper to accommodate my workin' hours, but I do na want her children to become overly hungry because of me. She's even sent a buggy for me."

"Then you had best be on your way. Have a nice time," Mrs. Brighton said.

"Sure and I'm hopin' to enjoy some Irish food and stories," Mary Margaret replied as she scurried down the hallway. She slipped into her woolen cape and then stopped to give Mrs. Brighton a quick wave before departing.

She couldn't imagine why Kiara had invited her to supper, but she intended to use the matter to her advantage. She couldn't be sure that Paddy would join them for the meal, but if he proved to be absent, Mary Margaret might very well ask to see the horses. Surely that wouldn't seem odd to anyone; after all, she had proven herself to be interested in the beasts. And their trainer.

Kiara moved swiftly to tidy her appearance. Within minutes, she looked as though she'd been doing nothing but sitting in the parlor and reading or sewing all afternoon. She walked down the steps and hurried to his side as Rogan started to answer the door.

"Mary Margaret, we are so pleased to have you join us this evening," Kiara greeted. "Do come in."

"I'm delighted. It's most kind of ya to invite me. I hope I haven't caused yar family too long a wait for their supper," she said as Kiara took her cloak.

Rogan laughed. "I do na think it would hurt any of us ta go without a meal or two," he said, patting his stomach.

While Rogan and the children entertained Mary Margaret in the parlor, Kiara took her leave and hurried to the kitchen. After ladling the stew into a large crock, she again checked to see if Paddy was on his way. Simon appeared to be headed for home, but there was no sign of Paddy. If she sent Nevan to fetch his uncle, he would surely reveal that Mary Margaret was joining them for supper. Best to wait a wee bit longer, she decided.

The back door opened just as she was slicing a round of warm caraway rye bread. "I believe I'm smelling rye bread," Paddy said as he walked into the kitchen.

Kiara stopped, knife in midair. "Look at ya! Did ya na think to wash up before comin' from the barns? Ya smell as bad as those stables ya've been mucking. I'll fetch one of Rogan's shirts for ya."

Mouth agape, Paddy stared at her for a moment before regaining his wits. "Ya told me to come for supper. Ya did na say to clean up before I came. I hurried down here hoping I'd na be causing yar supper to be late. There's no pleasing ya, Kiara."

She stomped her foot and pointed to the other room. "And hurry!" she ordered before stepping to the parlor door and motioning to her son.

"Run upstairs and fetch one of your father's shirts. Bring it to me in the kitchen—and don't ask any questions. Just do as ya're told."

As Nevan scurried off, Kiara told the others that supper would be ready in just a wee bit.

"I'd be happy to give ya a hand with the preparations," Mary Margaret offered.

"I won't hear of it. Ya sit there and enjoy yarself," she said, hurrying off before Mary Margaret could argue the point.

After placing the food on the dining room table, she surveyed the kitchen to make certain she'd not forgotten anything.

"Do I pass yar inspection?" Paddy asked as he returned to the kitchen.

"I suppose ya'll have to do, but ya could have dried yar hair a wee bit. Supper's waiting—put on this shirt and come along with ya."

Paddy shrugged into the shirt and fastened the final button as he followed Kiara into the dining room. "Ya're acting strange. I do na see what all the fuss—"

When her brother stopped midsentence, Kiara knew he'd spied Mary Margaret sitting in the adjacent parlor. Stepping to one side, she pulled Paddy forward. "I'm sure ya'll be remembering me brother, Paddy," she said to Mary Margaret.

"Aye, that I do. Good evening, Paddy," she said.

"Good evening. I did na know Kiara was entertaining this evening or I would have dressed for the occasion," he said, giving Kiara a frown.

"Sure and I think ya look quite presentable," Mary Margaret said.

Kiara was pleased to see the sparkle in Mary Margaret's eyes as she spoke to Paddy. And though Paddy might have been reluctant to admit such a thing, there was an undeniable attraction between Mary Margaret and her brother. With a feeling of smug satisfaction, she directed the family into the dining room, being careful to seat Paddy and Mary Margaret side-by-side.

Once the children were settled around the table and Rogan had said grace, Kiara passed the stew to her husband. "Would ya be so kind as ta serve?"

"Aye," he replied, taking the bowls as she handed them to him. "So ya had a busy day did ya?" he asked Paddy while ladling stew into one of the white stoneware bowls.

"That we did. I knew 'twould be busy, but Mr. Wainwright unexpectedly came by to visit and completely ruined my schedule. Na that I wasn't pleased ta see him, mind ya," he quickly added.

"And what brought McKinley Wainwright to the horse farm?" Rogan inquired as he finished serving the stew.

"He had a telegram from Mr. Houston and wanted to tell me that they're on their way home."

Kiara handed the plate of bread to her husband. "That's wonderful news ta be hearin'. I've missed my visits with Jasmine. When will they be arrivin'?"

"They didn't say exactly. Mr. Houston told me the telegram seemed somewhat strange—as though they were afraid to give details."

"Why would they be afraid ta say when they're comin' home?" Kiara asked.

Paddy shrugged. "The telegram said they'd met with some kind of difficulty. They didn't say what and they didn't say when they'd be here—just that they were on the way and anxious to be home."

"Those people down South probably give them a hard time for not believing in slavery or some such thing," Rogan said.

"I'm hoping they'll be back before there's further negotiating to be done with the customers," Paddy said.

"Kiara tells me that ya've done an excellent job taking over for Mr. Houston during his absence," Mary Margaret said, "and ya've shown a deep kindness toward the customers ya've been dealing with."

"Has she now?" Paddy asked as he gave his sister a suspicious look.

Kiara jumped to her feet before her brother could say anything further. "I'm guessing ya all would like a piece of apple cake. I'll be off ta the kitchen for only a wee bit."

"Let me help," Mary Margaret offered.

Paddy pushed back his chair. "Ya should na be helping, Mary Margaret. Ya're a guest. I'll be pleased ta lend a hand."

Kiara wilted. She knew she'd catch an earful as soon as they were in the other room unless she immediately took the offensive. "I was telling Bridgett of your accomplishments with the gentlemen from West Point," she started as soon as they were out of earshot, "and Mary Margaret merely overheard the conversation. Do na think I spend my time telling of my brother's accomplishments to all who will listen."

"Ya do na fool me even a wee bit, Kiara. It's matchmaking ya're trying yar hand at, and I do na need help finding a lass—*if* I've a mind to."

"I see little evidence of that! Ya keep ta yarself like a hermit. Mary Margaret is a fine lass, and ya could do no better even if ya tried on yar own."

"She's nice enough," he admitted.

"Then go out there and talk to her," Kiara said. "I'm

capable of servin' cake on me own, ya know."

"I do na need yar meddling. Nor do I like it."

"Off with ya and take the cake platter with ya. And *talk* to her," she hissed as they walked through the doorway.

"Mary Margaret tells me she's on the committee to help with the St. Patrick's Day dance," Rogan said before taking a bite of the cake.

"From the sounds of things, 'tis going to be a fine celebration," Kiara said. "Paddy's helping with some of the festivities also. Aren't ya, Paddy?" she urged.

"Aye."

"And how are the plans coming?" Kiara asked, wishing she could kick him under the table.

"Fine."

She sighed. Obviously Paddy was going to do his best to prove that he didn't want her assistance. By the time they'd finished supper and visited for a short time, she knew her assessment was correct. Paddy hadn't entered into the conversation except when absolutely required.

"It has been a lovely evening, but I must be getting back to the boardinghouse," Mary Margaret finally announced.

"I'm supposin' Paddy would be willing to drive ya back," Rogan said without waiting for Paddy to comment. "The buggy's out front."

Paddy nodded his agreement, clearly unwilling to cause Mary Margaret any embarrassment by refusing Rogan's request.

———

Mary Margaret settled into the leather buggy seat and attempted to hide her delight. From the moment he had entered the dining room with his damp black curls clinging to his forehead, she had longed to spend at least a few moments alone with Paddy. He'd been particularly quiet during the evening, but now she would have the entire ride back to the boardinghouse to visit with him.

"I do hope ya do na find this too much of an inconvenience," she said as he sat down beside her.

He unwound the reins and flicked them with a practiced ease. "I do na mind—my day has been filled by one unexpected event after another—the evening should be no different."

"I do na know if I should consider that good or bad," she said quietly.

He glanced in her direction and then gave her a lopsided grin. "'Tis na a bad thing, just unexpected."

"'Twas nice to spend the evening with your sister's family—she's very kind."

"Aye. A wee bit meddlesome from time ta time, but there's no denying she's got a good heart." A moment passed, quiet but for the creaking leather and horses' hooves. "Do ya still like livin' in the boardinghouse?"

"'Tis fine, though things are becomin' difficult in the mills. Many of the girls have lost their jobs, and it does na look as though things are going ta get much better in the near future."

"Aye, so I've been told. The men are suffering as well. This downturn in the economy has many facin' difficult situations."

"At least my mind is na on the economy when I'm helpin' to plan the dance," she said. "We all have fun while we're at the meetings and do na discuss our work and such. Is it the same with the men? When ya're planning the parade?"

"Aye—'tis a good place ta forget yar worries," he agreed. Paddy gave her a sidelong glance. "So what kind of plans do ya lasses have? Are ya plannin' something more than in the past?"

"For the dance? The plans seem no different than for most parties. Most of the ladies only say that they're looking forward to an evening of dancing and hoping that there are enough men to dance with. They hope, too, that the downturn does na spoil the festivities."

"I think it would take more than the economy to ruin St. Patrick's Day."

Mary Margaret nodded. "Some of the girls I work with who live in the Acre have already bought fabric to make their dresses. They said they'd do without other things before they'd go without a new dress for the dance."

The dance. It seemed as if every conversation with Mary Margaret turned into talk of the dance. He didn't know why he hadn't yet asked her—after all, she was a pretty lass with a sweet smile, and she would likely say yes. And it wasn't as though he had anyone else whom he wished to escort. After all, if he waited much longer, someone else might ask her. Quite obviously, there was no reason to delay.

He pulled back on the reins as they neared the boardinghouse. When the buggy came to a halt, he turned to face her. "I was wondering . . . if ya might . . ." he haltingly began. "That is ta say, if ya do na already have plans . . ." He hesitated once again.

"Yes?" she asked encouragingly.

"Do ya think ya might . . . like ta—" he swallowed hard—"go ta the dance with m-me?" he finally stammered.

"Aye, that I would!"

She replied so quickly it nearly took his breath away. "Ya *would?*"

"Of course I would. I was hoping for an invitation—from you," she hastily added.

"Then I suppose it's settled," he said as he walked her to the door.

"Aye, that it is," she replied sweetly before disappearing behind the door of the boardinghouse.

Paddy hoisted himself onto the buggy seat and flicked the reins. For a brief moment he was proud of himself—pleased he'd had the courage to ask Mary Margaret to the dance and that she had so readily accepted. Yet his thoughts quickly returned to previous conversations with the lass. There was no denying her beauty and the fact that she could be pleasant. On the other hand, she had a stubborn streak a mile wide and a large portion of unbridled determination. She reminded him of his sister! And unlike Rogan, he wasn't certain he could tame Miss Mary Margaret O'Flannery!

"I hope I've na made a mistake this evenin'," he muttered.

CHAPTER · 18

FEELING SOMEWHAT uncomfortable, Elinor rapped on the front door of the parsonage. Somehow it seemed improper to be calling on the pastor. Yet when she'd mentioned the need to discuss issues regarding the benevolence fund as she exited church earlier in the day, Pastor Chamberlain had suggested she stop by the parsonage so they could discuss the matter in private. Of course, Reggie would be present, yet if any of the church ladies discovered Elinor was making a personal call upon the pastor, there was little doubt she'd be the topic of discussion for weeks to come—or at least until some other matter captured their interest.

"Mrs. Brighton! Come in, please," Reggie said with an infectious smile.

"Thank you, Reggie. And may I say that your manners are quite lovely today."

She giggled. "Father didn't tell me you were coming to visit."

"Perhaps he wanted to surprise you."

"Exactly!" Justin said as he entered the hallway. "Good

297

to see you, Elinor. Why don't we go into the parlor. I do hope it wasn't an inconvenience asking you to come here. I had several matters that needed my attention," he added as he led her into the sitting room.

"Of course not. I enjoy a change of scenery, and it's always nice to spend time with Reggie."

Reggie plopped down beside their guest and scooted close.

"Reggie, I need to speak privately with Mrs. Brighton. Could you leave us for a short time?" her father asked.

The girl frowned momentarily, then brightened. "I'll fix us tea. Would that be good?"

"That would be wonderful," her father replied. "By the time you serve tea, we should be through with our discussion."

Elinor stared after Reggie as the girl hurried off to the kitchen. "She's turning into quite the little lady, don't you think?"

"Absolutely, and I have you to thank for the dramatic changes in her. I truly don't know how you've worked such wonders. I knew Reggie needed a woman's influence in her life, yet I was perplexed as to how to find someone willing to take on the challenge. The moment you entered her life and began tutoring her in proper manners and etiquette, she was receptive. Tell me, how have you done it?"

"I've not attempted to change Reggie. I've merely included her in my life. The transformation that has taken place is of Reggie's own doing. Change usually occurs when a person is truly desirous of doing so, not when one is forced by others. Don't you think?"

Justin nodded. "The old adage of leading a horse to water?"

"I believe so. In any event, Reggie seems receptive to having a woman in her life, and I'm confident she will accept your new wife with enthusiasm. At least I've encouraged her to do so. I might add that I'm looking forward to meeting your fiancée as well."

"As am I," Justin said with a startled look on his face. "Wherever did you get the notion that I plan to wed?"

Elinor hesitated. She didn't want to say anything that would cause Reggie a problem, yet she needed to reply. "Well, I-I . . ."

"No need to say any more. The church ladies must have been gossiping again," he concluded. "You can disregard anything you've heard. I have not made any plans to marry. I'm truly astonished at some of the stories that have circulated since our arrival."

"No doubt," she said as a surprising sense of pleasure flooded over her. She was actually *delighted* to hear Justin Chamberlain had no wedding plans. Yet the thought frightened her. Never again did she want to have feelings of love for another man. Long ago she had vowed she would not go through the pain of losing one more husband. Yet her heart had quickened at his words, and she enjoyed his company far too much. Was she becoming like some of those church ladies who were secretly hoping to find themselves a husband? At the thought, she felt the heat rush to her cheeks.

"Is it overly warm in here? You suddenly appear flushed—I do hope you're not becoming ill. I shouldn't have requested that you walk over here in this cold weather," he said.

"No, I'm fine, thank you. Don't concern yourself. Now then, I believe we were going to discuss the benevolence fund."

"Ah, yes. You mentioned you've had additional applicants."

"Indeed. I have three girls who have come to me—two from other boardinghouses and one from my own. I believe their requests are valid. They've all shown me their separation papers from the mill. I had hoped to refrain from using the benevolence fund until it had grown larger; in fact, I had been using my own savings to help some of the girls. However, I fear I used the last of my funds this week."

"By all means, we'll see that they receive assistance. If you'll give me the information, I'll withdraw the funds. But it would likely be less embarrassing for the girls if *you* delivered the money."

"I'd be happy to do so," Elinor replied. "I also received word this week that my boardinghouse may close. Since I've used all of my resources, I'll likely be required to leave Lowell."

"Leave Lowell? Where would you go?"

"My brother Taylor and his family are in Maine. They would welcome me," she said. "I surely find that God sometimes has a strange sense of humor. I had hoped to help others not lose their homes, yet in the process it appears as if I'll lose my own."

"We must put this matter to prayer," Justin said. "I can't believe that you are meant to leave Lowell."

"*Leave?*" Reggie screeched. "Where are you going?" she asked, dropping the tea tray onto the table.

Elinor quickly leaned forward and placed a hand on the teetering china. "It's not definite yet, Reggie. That's why I hadn't told you. I received word this week that my boardinghouse may be closed—I don't know when it may occur. I'm praying it won't happen at all."

"Absolutely. We must all pray for intervention," Justin stated.

Reggie ignored her father's remark. "Would you go to Maine and live with your brother?"

"Yes, if the boardinghouse closes. But I don't—"

"You said you didn't want to go there," Reggie said

without waiting for Elinor's full reply.

"That's true; I don't. But if the boardinghouse—"

"You could come and live with us. Couldn't she, Father?" Her eyes were filled with a mixture of fear and anticipation.

"I couldn't possibly do that, Reggie," Elinor said. "My family would expect me to come to Maine."

"It doesn't matter *what* they expect. You should be able to stay here if you want. Shouldn't she, Father?"

"Well, yes," Justin replied. "And we are going to pray about the situation, Reggie," he promised.

"I'm sorry to upset you, Reggie. I hadn't planned for you to hear me. There's no need to upset yourself, for it's still uncertain whether I'll have to move. Why don't we have our tea? Did you bake those fine-looking cookies all by yourself?"

Reggie nodded, but there was no smile. "It's your recipe for lemon cookies."

"Then I must have one." Elinor took a bite of the cookie, chewing slowly and nodding approvingly while Reggie watched. "I believe they're even better than the ones I bake."

"Truly?" Reggie asked with a grin.

"Truly! They are excellent. You should be most proud of yourself, young lady."

When they had finished their tea, Elinor patted Reggie's hand. "I would be quite pleased if you'd walk me home and stay for supper."

"May I, Father?"

"Yes, of course. Though I must say I'm a bit envious."

Elinor tilted her head and gave him a thoughtful look, unsure what his remark truly meant. "Would you like to join us for supper? I know you mentioned you have several matters needing your attention. Perhaps you could attend to them and then join us at seven o'clock," she suggested.

Justin gave a hearty laugh. "Well, since you insist."

"Absolutely! Reggie and I will expect you at seven," she said as they stood to retrieve their coats.

"I promise to be on time," he said. "Behave yourself, Reggie," he reminded as they walked onto the porch.

"I *know*," she said, giving her father a look of exasperation.

Reggie reached for Elinor's hand and grasped it tightly as they set off down the street.

"Your father tells me he has no plans to marry and was shocked that I had any such idea," Elinor casually remarked.

Reggie's face turned ashen and her shoulders slumped. "You told him I said he was to be married?"

"No, not exactly."

"What did you tell him?" she asked, her eyes glistening with fear.

"I told him I thought you would be most accepting of his new wife. He said he was not planning to wed and then asked how I had conceived such a notion."

"Did you tell him it was me?"

"Before I could answer, he assumed I'd heard some of the church ladies gossiping. I didn't agree with or deny his assumption."

"Thank you!" Reggie sighed and straightened her shoulders. A wide smile curved her lips as though she believed the entire incident now totally resolved.

"Why *did* you lie to me, Reggie?"

A startled look returned to the child's face. "I didn't lie. I said my father met a woman and I *thought* he wanted to marry her. I guess he doesn't."

"Reggie Chamberlain! I do not for one minute believe what you're telling me. Now out with the truth!"

"It was a test."

"A test? What on earth are you talking about?"

Reggie gave her a sheepish look. "I wanted to see if you were truly my friend or if you were like all the others—just being nice to me so my father would like you."

"Is that truly what you believed all the time we were together?"

"No, but I had to be positive. Don't you understand that I had to know for sure that somebody liked me just for me and not because they wanted to marry my father?"

"I suppose I do understand, Reggie, but I can't say I'm not disappointed."

"Because I lied?"

"Because you lied and because you didn't realize my feelings had everything to do with you and nothing to do with your father."

"I'm sorry," she said. "Will you forgive me?"

"On one condition. In the future if you have concerns, I want you to talk to me truthfully. I promise I will give you honest answers in return."

Reggie grinned and squeezed Elinor's hand. "I promise."

The parade had proceeded on schedule. Although there were those who said the previous parades had been larger, Mary Margaret was impressed with the entries and those who had lined the streets cheering them on. Two marchers carrying enormous green banners had set off the procession. One of the banners was inscribed with an Irish harp and the words *Erin go Bragh,* and the other sported an American eagle. The members of the Irish Benevolent Society had followed the banners, each member adorned with a long green silk scarf surrounded by a rosette of green and white.

Even the weather had cooperated, the day dawning sunny and warm. The remainder of the afternoon was spent listening to the numerous speeches that both attacked Britain and argued for the repeal of the union or spoke of gratitude for the blessings and advantages enjoyed in this adopted country. And, of course, there were the goodly number of men who happily downed quarts of ale as they cheered their agreement or shouted their disapproval to the speechmakers.

The day had been exhilarating, especially since Paddy had come to sit with Mary Margaret during the speech-making. Afterward, he had even walked her home with a promise to return at seven o'clock and escort her to the dance.

"Did you have a nice afternoon?" Mrs. Brighton asked as she walked into the house.

"Aye. 'Tis a surprise that the Irish were given the day off from work in order ta celebrate. I wish that all the girls had been able to enjoy the parade." She followed Mrs. Brighton into the kitchen. "Were you able to attend?"

"No, I had the noonday meal to prepare, but I'm pleased you had a good time."

"I'm feeling a bit guilty going off to a dance when things seem so bleak for some of the girls."

"Nonsense. Whether you attend the dance or remain at home does not change anyone's circumstances," Mrs. Brighton said as she started peeling some potatoes. "You had best take a few minutes to rest. I'm guessing you'll be tired after an evening of dancing."

Mary Margaret waited until the other girls were eating supper before donning her dress for the dance. Bridgett had loaned her a green plaid silk gown with black piping that edged the bodice and waistline. She tied a wide black ribbon around her throat and another around her red curls before looking in the mirror.

"It will do just fine," she told herself before rushing downstairs.

She remained in the hallway until Paddy arrived and then called her good-nights to the girls.

"I can wait while ya go and bid them a proper good-night," he said.

She shook her head and hurried him out the door. "I feel a wee bit of discomfort going out ta have fun when some of the girls have fallen upon such hard times. I do na want ta go prancing in front of them all dressed for the dance. It does na seem proper."

"Ya have a kind heart, Mary Margaret."

"Thank you," she said as a faint blush colored her cheeks.

When they arrived at the hall, many of the Irish celebrants were already shouting for the music to begin. The music of fiddles and accordions soon filled the air and couples took to the floor, some dancing jigs while other enjoyed a polka or hornpipe.

"Would ya care ta dance?"

"Aye," Mary Margaret replied.

They twirled around the floor with Paddy holding a firm grip around her waist as they performed the intricate steps in time to the music.

"Ya're looking a wee bit warm, Paddy," Timothy Rourke said as he drew near. "Perhaps I should take Mary Margaret as my dancing partner." He attempted to take hold of her hand.

"I do na think so," she told him. "I've been escorted to the dance by Paddy, and I do na wish ta be dancing with another."

"I canna believe ya'd turn down the likes of me for Padraig O'Neill," Timothy said mockingly.

"Ya best believe it, Timothy Rourke. I'll na be having any dances with ya this night," she replied haughtily before turning her attention to Paddy. "I'm a wee bit thirsty. Shall we get something cool ta drink?"

"Aye. That sounds fine," he said, grasping her elbow and leading her to a table where a group of women were serving punch and cookies directly across from a counter where several men were serving ale.

Paddy ordered two cups of punch and picked up several cookies. "We can sit down over there," he said, nodding toward a row of wooden chairs.

"Thank ya for turning down Timothy Rourke," he said. "Though I do na expect ya to turn down every lad asking for a dance, I canna deny I was pleased ta have ya turn him down."

"Ya're welcome. I have no interest in dancing with anyone else, Paddy." She took a sip of her punch. "Have ya been busy at the farm?"

He nodded. "'Tis always busy, but as spring begins to arrive there's always more ta tend to. We've a lot of horses ready to foal, and it's always a worry—ya do na want to lose the mare or the colt."

"And what of Mr. and Mrs. Houston? Have they returned home?"

"We expected them at least two weeks ago, and I was beginning to get a wee bit worried thinking something might've happened to them—what with them saying in their last telegram they'd met with troubles. But I stopped to see Mr. Wainwright when I was in town a few days ago, and he said he'd received another telegram that morning. He said the Houstons will be arriving in the next couple of days."

"That's good news for ya then," Mary Margaret said.

"Aye. It's been a load of responsibility for me while they've been gone. I'm na complainin', mind ya, but still I'll be glad to have them home."

"Mr. Houston is lucky to have someone like ya to depend upon."

"Thank ya," he replied. "The band's warming up ta

begin. Shall we try another dance?"

"Aye," she said, taking his hand.

Above the music, the sound of laughter and chattering voices could be heard throughout the hall. They danced and talked and then danced even more as the hours quickly passed. They were stepping onto the dance floor when they turned at the sound of an angry shout. A mug of ale came flying through the air and crashed to the dance floor, and the rest was a haze—men shouting and throwing punches, glass breaking and women screaming.

"Take hold of my hand and don't turn loose," Paddy shouted above the din.

She grasped his hand and followed close on his heels—down the stairway and out the front door into the cool, star-lit evening. They stopped and looked at the upper windows of the building, where flying fists could be easily detected.

"I hope no one comes crashing through one of those windows," Mary Margaret said.

"We best move from here; I would na want to be the one to break a lad's fall should such a thing happen."

They walked a short distance down the street as other couples began to exit the building, likely afraid they, too, would become injured in the donnybrook.

"If ya had not escorted me to the dance, ya could have remained upstairs instead of waiting down here and wonder-ing what's happening up there," Mary Margaret said.

Paddy grinned and gently pulled her into a warm embrace. "I think I'm more interested in the one who's standing right beside me. We can have our own good time down here."

Before she could reply, he drew her closer. She gazed into his eyes and felt the blood course through her veins as he lowered his head and caressed her lips with a tender kiss.

She leaned heavily against his broad chest and knew she was both safe and protected. How she could have ever thought this sweet man anything but gentle and kind was now beyond logic.

CHAPTER · *19*

"JASMINE! NOLAN! Over here," McKinley shouted while waving a hand above the crowd gathered on the train platform.

Jasmine spotted her brother and waved in return before leaning down and whispering to Spencer. "Do you see Uncle McKinley? Run over—he's brought a surprise along with him."

She watched her son run fleetingly through the crowd, knowing she was presenting him with the greatest of pleasures upon his return home—seeing his very best friend. Above the train's whistle and commotion of passengers, she could hear her son's shouts as he called out Moses' name. This one thing had gone as planned, and her heart was filled with abundant joy.

They worked their way through the throng, finally reaching McKinley's side several moments later. "McKinley! I can't tell you how wonderful it is to see you," she said while pulling her brother into a warm embrace.

"It has been far too long," he agreed. "Nolan!" he

greeted, grasping his brother-in-law's hand warmly and then swinging Alice Ann up into his arms before planting a giant kiss upon her cheek. "How is Clara?" he asked, noting the sleeping child in Henrietta's arms.

"She's fine. We all are—especially now that we're back in Lowell," Jasmine replied.

"And who is this?" he asked, nodding toward Prissy.

"Prissy; she was one of Father's house slaves. She is married to Toby," Jasmine explained.

"Truly? It doesn't seem possible Toby is old enough to take a wife. Did you not bring him also?"

"No. We were unable to do so. Once we get home to the farm, Nolan and I will explain the difficulties we encountered. I do hope you have ample time—it's quite an adventure and one that is not yet over, I'm afraid."

"I've been intrigued ever since I received your first telegram, but I must say you all appear in good health and certainly in the height of fashion," he said while appraising Jasmine's traveling suit.

Jasmine gave a harsh laugh. "Your opinion would have differed greatly had you met us in Boston. I fear even the hotel clerk had not seen such a beggarly-appearing group in a long time. Nolan thought it best we telegraph you and then spend a few days in Boston recuperating from the journey. We purchased our clothing while we were there."

"I see. The carriage is out in front of the depot. I had one of your men bring a wagon for your trunks."

"There are no trunks, McKinley. We have only what we're carrying," Jasmine told him.

McKinley's confusion was evident, but he didn't question them. "I'll send the driver back home then and join you in the carriage."

The ride home seemed endless. When the carriage finally rolled to a stop in front of their house, Jasmine felt as though they had been away for years. The house appeared unchanged yet strangely foreign as she walked through the doorway. She smiled broadly at the group awaiting their arrival. Kiara and Rogan, along with Paddy, Maisie, Simon, and a host of servants, cheered their arrival.

As Jasmine circled the group, hugging each one, she stopped several times to silently thank God for their safe arrival home. The journey had been treacherous, and both she and Nolan knew that without the hand of God upon them, they would never have safely returned to Lowell.

"We've prepared a feast ta celebrate yar homecoming," Kiara said. "We did na want to overwhelm ya, so we thought to wait a few hours before the celebration," she added.

"Thank you all so much," Jasmine replied. "Mr. Houston and I do need to spend some time alone with my brother, but before we go into the library, I want to introduce you to Prissy. She was a house slave at The Willows, but now she is free. I would be appreciative if you'd show her the house and make her feel welcome."

Maisie stepped forward and embraced Prissy. "D'you 'member me, Prissy? Me and Simon was at da big house for a little while right after you come dere to work."

Prissy stared hard at Maisie and then looked at Simon. "You was in the kitchen," she said.

Maisie nodded. "Dat's right. I'm right glad to see you, chile. You gonna be mighty happy here. Come along and I'll show you around, and den we'll go out to our house and have us some coffee. Moses, you and Spencer go on over to da house with your pappy. I be along soon."

Jasmine smiled at the boys as they hurried toward Simon. "Can we go see Larkspur before we go to the house?" Spencer asked.

Simon gave them a toothy grin and nodded. "We's gonna go there right now."

McKinley and the Houstons went into the library. Once the doors were closed, the three adults settled into the leather chairs.

Jasmine hesitated a moment before addressing her brother. "I'm trying to think of where I should begin," she said.

It took nearly an hour to relate all that had occurred throughout their time at The Willows and during their journey home. McKinley listened intently as the story unfolded, never interrupting. When Jasmine finally leaned back in her chair, emotionally exhausted from the telling, her brother hunched forward and gazed into her eyes.

"Am I to understand that both The Willows and the entire crop were completely destroyed in these fires? That you've returned with *nothing*? No money from the sale of the crop, no money from the sale of the plantation—*nothing*?" he asked, his voice frantic.

"We've returned with our lives," Nolan replied. "I count that alone a miracle and worth more than any amount of money!"

"Yes, yes, of course. I didn't mean to imply your safety was worth nothing, but I was relying upon those funds."

"I'm sorry, McKinley," Jasmine said. "Though the plantation was in the hands of a broker, Rupert forged my name on documents to suggest that we had given him the property. Cousin Levi promises to help, but I do not expect we'll see anything for some time—if ever. There is grave hostility toward us. Surely you understand that by now."

"Yes, but it is difficult for me to believe Rupert would be in the midst of this. Surely you've misunderstood. He would never forge documents or threaten our family. I'm convinced you were both distraught with the circumstances and misunderstood his intentions. We were, after all, boyhood friends as well as cousins. Rupert and I enjoyed a closer kinship than I had with either of our brothers when we were growing up. I'm certain if I go to Mississippi, I can reason with him. We need to take back what is lawfully ours," McKinley insisted.

Jasmine looked at her brother in great frustration. "Believe what you will, McKinley, although I would have expected you to believe your own sister over a cousin who's had nothing to do with you since you've come north. Both Rupert and Lydia have changed. They are not the same people we knew as children—no more than you and I remain the same. And what is it you hope to gain by going to Mississippi? You can't regain a mansion and crop that have been burned into nonexistence. Do you think you can convince these men to pay you for their dishonorable actions? Surely you don't believe men who have acted in such a manner will now step forward and offer you money for their unjust deeds."

"Then what is it you referred to when you said you feared this matter was not yet finished?" he asked.

Nolan stood up and walked to the doors leading to the garden. He looked outside for a moment before turning toward McKinley. "The slaves. We signed over the papers granting all of them their freedom. In addition, we promised to divide the funds from the cotton crop among them in order to assist them with their new beginning in the North. But as your sister told you, except for Prissy, they were all taken away in shackles and have been either enslaved by the men who committed these crimes or turned over for sale in the New Orleans market. Either way, we are determined to regain their freedom."

"If we can find a way to reason with Rupert, perhaps we can do so," McKinley said, rising to address Nolan face-to-face. "If we agree that we will not bring charges against the men who committed these crimes, assuming they are willing to return the slaves and compensate us for the damages, this matter can be brought to a suitable resolution for all concerned."

Nolan gave a sorrowful laugh. "Do you not understand that these men do not fear the law? In fact, the men who mete out law and justice are among the number who committed these crimes against our family. Like us, you'll find no assistance by placing your hope in the lawmen."

"This issue of slavery goes far deeper than you realize, McKinley. Matters are worsening by the day," Jasmine said. "Soon slavery will divide more than families; it will divide this nation so deeply we will find ourselves entrenched in war."

McKinley shook his head. "I understand you've had a harrowing experience, but I believe you're overdramatizing the entire issue."

"Think what you will," Jasmine said, "but you were not there to see the ugliness that is being called honorable and patriotic by many Southerners. Mark my words, McKinley: you are naïve if you believe the issue of slavery will pass away or be resolved without a real fight."

CHAPTER · 20

September 1, 1858

MCKINLEY EAGERLY opened the thick envelope and sat down in his office to read the missive he'd picked up at the post office a short time ago. Though Jasmine remained unaware of his contact with Rupert, McKinley had been communicating with his cousin since shortly after his sister's return to Lowell. And though he'd had a recent telegram from Rupert, McKinley was anxious for a detailed reply to his latest letter, for he wanted to receive both explanations *and* remuneration. To date, it appeared Rupert was the only answer to his needs. After all, McKinley had never believed Jasmine's story about forged documents, even though Nolan had stood in agreement that this was exactly what had happened. He figured them both to be simply victims of the moment. Rupert's correspondence had proven that thought to be correct. Even Jasmine admitted, after receiving a missive from Cousin Levi earlier in the summer, that the property remained in their care. So whatever misunderstanding there had been about forged documents and property being stolen was behind them now.

Still, McKinley had been careful to keep his correspondence a secret from everyone, including his wife. After all, Violet would wonder at his fierce determination to recover the funds, and he could not bear to tell her of their financial losses. Then too she might say something to Jasmine, and McKinley definitely didn't want his sister to know the truth. At least not until much later—after everything was settled. Jasmine might again misinterpret the matter, and she absolutely wouldn't understand McKinley writing to Rupert.

Thus far Rupert's correspondence revealed what McKinley had believed from the time his sister returned home: she had exaggerated the entire incident at The Willows. With great kindness, Rupert had sent several lengthy missives answering McKinley's myriad of questions and advising him that the entire ordeal had been a complete misunderstanding on Jasmine's and Nolan's part. Rupert had eloquently explained that because both of them had become so completely indoctrinated by Northern dogma, they had hastened to recount inaccuracies.

Rupert's initial letter of explanation had gone on to state that he was confident McKinley knew him to be a true Southern gentleman and that his visit to The Willows after the devastating fire was never meant as a threat to Nolan and Jasmine. His sole purpose in going to them had been based upon his deep love and concern for Jasmine and her family. He had simply wanted to warn them of the possible impending danger.

McKinley's excitement increased as he read the most recent letter. Rupert wanted to purchase The Willows, and he would soon be arriving in Lowell to finalize their agreement!

He reread the final sentence: *"Do not tell anyone of my plan to purchase The Willows or my visit to Lowell. As you know, your sister tends to think the worst of any Southerner, and I do not want anything to destroy this final opportunity for both of us."*

"Nor do I, cousin; nor do I," McKinley murmured as he carefully refolded the letter.

———

Jasmine reached into an old trunk that had been stored in the attic and pulled out a stack of Clara's outgrown dresses and gowns. One by one, she scrutinized each tiny article of clothing, knowing it would likely fit little Emily now that she was more than a month old. Prissy had experienced an easy birth but now seemed to be languishing in a form of melancholy. She nursed the baby with little enthusiasm and appeared hopelessly uninterested in the child.

Upon her arrival in Lowell, Prissy had eagerly embraced the idea of becoming the head seamstress for the Houston farm, and Jasmine had been delighted by the young woman's abilities. Prissy, along with several other women, had been hired to operate the sewing shop. With the many workers employed by the farm, it had proven economical to make and furnish clothing to their employees rather than to increase wages. So talented was Prissy at fashioning clothing that the women of the community were soon seeking her services. Jasmine had watched Prissy flourish throughout her pregnancy, though she never did appear enthusiastic about the impending birth.

"Perhaps these clothes will boost her spirits," Jasmine muttered as she closed the trunk and descended the narrow stairs leading down from the dusty attic.

"Whatever were you doing up there?" Nolan asked as he walked out of their bedroom.

She held up the stack of baby clothes.

"Are you . . ."

Jasmine giggled. "No, my dear. You may breathe easy for a while longer—there's no baby in our future just yet. I'm taking these to Prissy. I thought she might enjoy dressing Emily in something other than the few plain gowns she made for her. I'm hoping it will cheer her a bit."

"That's kind of you, Jasmine. She still doesn't appear to enjoy being a mother, I take it?"

"No, and I do not understand her behavior. Emily is a beautiful child, though she doesn't resemble Toby or Prissy in the least—she's so *white*. I believe she's as white as Moses. In any event, Prissy's behavior surprises me. Although I knew she missed Toby, she appeared to adjust so well. I suppose I assumed she would do the same with her baby."

Nolan placed his arm around his wife. "Do remember, my dear, that having the child has likely caused her to dwell even more upon Toby's circumstances. To be without the man you love when your child is born would be difficult. Poor Prissy doesn't know if she will ever see her husband again or if Emily will ever know her father. And now that she's not busy with her work, she has more time to dwell upon those thoughts."

"You are a very wise man, Nolan Houston. No wonder I love you so much."

He leaned down and kissed her. "I believe I had best be off to the stables. We're to have visitors from West Point today."

She walked down the wide staircase beside him, their arms entwined. "Paddy should be pleased to see them once again," she remarked.

"Yes. He's looking forward to their visit. I can't tell you how proud I am of that young man. He has exceeded my greatest expectations with both the horses and the customers."

"And I think it only fitting that you rewarded him with an interest in the farm. He's added much to the business."

The couple walked together until they reached Simon

and Maisie's house. "I'll leave you to your meetings," she said.

Nolan arched his eyebrows. "Prissy is still living with Simon and Maisie?"

She nodded. "She doesn't want to go back to her little house, and Maisie doesn't believe she should just yet."

"I see," he said. "Well, let's hope those clothes cheer her."

He leaned down to kiss her cheek, then Jasmine watched as he strode off toward the barn before she knocked on the front door of Maisie's house.

"Come on in," Maisie said with a broad smile. "I was jes' fixing me and Prissy a cup of tea. Sit down."

"I brought some clothes for Emily," Jasmine whispered. "I'm hoping they'll bring a bit of pleasure to Prissy."

Maisie shook her head. "I tell you it's a battle getting dat gal to show interest in anything, Miz Jasmine. I can hardly force her out of bed all day long. I told Simon I'm beginnin' to git worried 'bout whether she's ever gonna come around. I has to force her to put that baby to her breast. It's a shame—sech a sweet little thing too. Don' hardly never cry. I keep her out here in da cradle near me. I tried leaving her in da bedroom wit Prissy, but she jes' ignored her cries."

Jasmine crouched down by the cradle and stroked the sleeping baby's soft hair. "Such a beautiful baby. I told Nolan she's as white as Moses—don't you think?"

"Oh yessum—sho' enough."

The baby wriggled and her eyelids fluttered open. "May I hold her?" Jasmine asked.

"'Course you can. Dat chile can use all the loving she can get."

Jasmine lifted the baby into her arms and smiled as Emily began to suck on her own fist. Jasmine stared at the child, her mind beginning to turn cartwheels as she concentrated on the child's coloring. Suddenly she felt the blood drain from her face.

"Maisie, do you think there's any possibility this child could have been fathered by a white man rather than Toby?" She swallowed hard as she watched Maisie's reaction.

With a tilt of her head she met Jasmine's questioning eyes with a steady gaze. "Ain't no doubt in my mind at all. That ain't Toby's baby, an' I figure that's why Prissy rejected the child." Maisie paused and stared at Jasmine. "What's wrong with you, Miz Jasmine? You feeling poorly? You done lost all the pink out of yo' cheeks."

Jasmine didn't want to ask, yet she could not stop herself. "Maisie, tell me the truth. Do you think my father or my brother Samuel could be the father of this child?" she whispered.

"Oh, mercy me! No, ma'am, I ain't even given that a passing thought. Neither one of dem would have ever done such a thing—and dere's nobody could convince me no different. This baby ain't no Wainwright, Miz Jasmine."

"Has Prissy told you that? Has she even told you Toby's not the father?"

"No, she ain't told me nothing 'bout the father, but I know sure as I'm standin' here afore you that the father of dat baby is white. After she was here at the farm for a week or so, I 'member her watching Moses when he was out in the yard playing with Spencer. She ast me how I come to have such a white chile. I told her about Moses' real mama and papa. She kept staring at him, and finally she rubbed her belly and said, 'So dat's what I got to look forward to.' I didn' know what she was talking 'bout den—but I surely do know now."

Jasmine placed the baby back in the cradle. "May I go and talk to her?"

"'Course you can. I'm gonna take this tea in there and

see if I can get her to drink it. You come on along."

"Why don't *I* take it to her?"

"Dat would be mighty kind of you. You want me to put two cups on da tray so you can have some tea with her?"

"Yes, thank you. In fact, let me take care of that. I'm certain you have other matters that need your attention. The least I can do is prepare the tea."

Maisie didn't argue, having learned long ago that Jasmine was quick to help herself and slow to expect others to wait upon her. "Will you keep a listen for the baby while you's visiting with Prissy? I can go ahead with my washing if I know somebody's in here with the two of dem."

"Of course. I'll leave the door to Prissy's room open so I can hear. You need not worry about a thing while you're outdoors."

Jasmine was pleased she could relieve Maisie in some small way. Moreover, knowing she was alone in the house would permit her to speak openly with Prissy. She stopped in the kitchen to get a second cup and then, carefully balancing the tray upon the stack of baby clothes, Jasmine went to Prissy's room. After tapping lightly on the door, she paused a moment and then entered.

"Good morning, Prissy! It's a beautiful day outside. I've brought you some tea and thought we might visit for a spell. In fact, it would be nice to go outdoors with you after a bit—the sunshine is glorious. I think it's warm enough we could take Emily with us if she's wrapped in her blanket."

Prissy scooted up in the bed and rested her back and shoulders against the wall.

"Shall I pour?"

"I'll drink me a cup of tea, but I don' think I'll be gettin' out of dis bed."

Jasmine poured the tea and added cream and sugar before she offered the cup to Prissy. "I do hope you like cream and sugar," she said with a bright smile.

"Um, hum, that's fine. I'm sure you got better things to do than come over here an' serve me tea," she said, slowly lifting the cup to her lips.

"There are certainly other things I *could* be doing, but nothing I'd *rather* do," she replied. "I went up to the attic this morning and found some of Clara's clothing. She outgrew these things long ago, and I thought they would be perfect for our little Emily."

Prissy glanced at the clothes but showed little interest even as Jasmine began to unfold the items for her inspection. "Them's real nice. Thank you. You can give 'em to Maisie. She sees to washing and dressing the baby," she said in a monotone voice.

"Yes, I know, but I think it's time you began to care for Emily yourself, Prissy. And you need to get out of this bed," she said as she walked to the windows and pulled open the curtains.

Prissy blinked against the sunlight and quickly covered her eyes with one arm. "I like dem curtains closed. Don' like it bright in here."

Jasmine shook her head back and forth. "Darkness breeds depression and sadness."

"What *you* know 'bout depression and sadness?" she rebutted bitterly.

"I've had my share of heartache, Prissy, and I also had a mother who suffered from severe headaches and phobias that sent her into the depths of depression. Don't make the mistake of imprisoning yourself with a desire to withdraw from the world, Prissy. There is nothing so great that God won't see you through. You do believe that, don't you?"

"I ain't so sure 'bout God helping me. I been calling on the name of Jesus ever since I was a youngun, but it ain't done me much good."

Jasmine pulled a chair close to the bed and sat down. "I would guess you've had a very difficult life, Prissy, but if you will take your mind off the bad for a moment, you will see that you have been blessed with good things too. You fell in love with and married Toby, and although he's not with you now, we're still praying he'll join you one day. You are freed from slavery and you enjoy earning wages as a seamstress . . . at least you told me that was true."

"That's true; I do like sewing in dat little shop Massa Nolan fixed up for us. I feel more at home there than any-place."

"And you have a beautiful, healthy little girl."

"That child ain't no blessing—she's a *curse*," she hissed through clenched teeth.

Jasmine recoiled at the venomous response. "She is *not* a curse. She's an innocent baby who had no say in her birth."

"Well, neither did I, 'cause if I'd had any say, she wouldn't be here, an' you can believe dat for sho'."

"Toby isn't Emily's father, is he?"

Prissy shook her head. "That's easy enough to see. Just look at her—she's as white as dem clouds floatin' out dere in the sky. She's too white to be my chile."

"Prissy, that's not true. Emily *is* your child. Will you tell me who fathered her?"

"No, ma'am, I'll not be telling that, but we best all hope da child don' turn out nothin' like the man who be her true pappy."

"Do I know him?"

"I ain't sayin' no more, Miz Jasmine. Toby knew the baby wasn't his 'cause he never touched me afore we was married. He asked if I was forced against my will, an' I told him I was. He didn't ask me if it was one of da other slaves or if it was a white man. He jest nodded, and we never talked 'bout it again."

"I've known Toby since he was very young, Prissy, and I believe that since he willingly married you, he was also willing to accept your baby no matter who had fathered her. I don't understand your reluctance to even feed her."

Prissy's face contorted in pain. "I hate that man and what he done to me. I can't love no baby that comes from his seed."

Jasmine poured a cup of tea for herself, then settled back in the chair. "Do you believe Jesus saved you?"

There was a look of surprise on Prissy's young face. "'Course I do. I took Jesus into my heart when I was thirteen years old. Ol' Samuel took me to the big pond and baptized me—I thought I was gonna drown he held me under there so long. Never liked the water much after that. You know I didn't like traveling on those river boats coming back here," she added.

"Yes, I remember," Jasmine replied with a smile. "When Samuel talked to you about taking Jesus into your heart, did he explain that Jesus' death wiped the slate clean and our sins were forgiven?"

"Um-hmm. He told me dat. I told all them folks standing 'round the pond that I was asking Jesus into my heart and wanted Him to forgive me of my sins. After that, Ol' Samuel dunked me in da water."

Jasmine hesitated a moment. "You know, Prissy, when we accept Jesus as our Savior, He adopts us into His family and we become one of His children."

"Um-hmm, I know dat."

"And even though we're soiled and stained from our sins, He wipes us all clean and pulls us close and loves us because we're part of His family. He treats us as though we were spotless and perfect all of our lives."

Prissy eyed her warily, obviously wondering where this

conversation was leading. "I s'pose dat's true enough," she agreed slowly.

Jasmine grasped Prissy's hand in her own. "You and I were sinners, yet Jesus died so we could be adopted into His family. And now here you are with this purely innocent little baby who has done nothing to deserve your disdain," she said as the baby started whimpering in the other room. "I believe it would be most pleasing to God if you accepted this blameless child and adopted her into your heart. There is no doubt He loves little Emily as much as He loves you and me."

A single tear rolled down Prissy's cheek, and Jasmine reached to wipe it away. "Think about what I've said, Prissy. I can't make you love Emily, but she *is* your child. Reject her and you'll dwell in self-pity and despair; love her and you'll reap untold blessings."

The baby's whimpers soon gave way to a lusty cry, and Jasmine rose from the chair. "Shall I bring her to you?"

Prissy nodded. "Guess so. She be hungry—I can tell her cry when she wants to nurse." She turned her sad eyes to Jasmine. "Don' know that I can be a good mama to her, Miz Jasmine."

"But you will try, won't you? At least think about what I've said? After all, Emily didn't choose to come into the world this way. She's as innocent of this mess as you are. Perhaps thinking of it that way will help you to love her."

"Guess that's so." Emily's cries increased and Prissy drew a deep breath. "I's ready for her now."

Jasmine left the room uttering a silent prayer that God would continue to melt the ice that had formed around Prissy's heart.

McKinley removed his pocket watch and clicked open the gold case. He'd best leave for the depot in the unlikely event the train arrived early. He didn't want to chance Rupert's being seen in Lowell. Not many folks in town would know him, yet there was always the possibility that Henrietta or Prissy might be in town on errands. And the thought that Jasmine or Nolan could be in Lowell conducting business was worrisome indeed.

"I must remember to be particularly careful. I can't afford for anything to go wrong," he muttered as he drove the buggy through town.

He heard the train whistle in the distance as he pulled back on the reins and jumped down from the buggy. The train would be arriving on schedule. With what he hoped was a casual gait, he walked into the station and mingled with the crowd, some of them awaiting arrivals and some of them departing. He surveyed the depot and sighed with relief when he didn't spot anyone who might know Jasmine or Nolan.

McKinley relaxed and walked to the platform as the train screeched and panted to a halt. He was straining to see above the crowd, hoping to catch sight of Rupert's familiar face when he felt a friendly slap on his shoulder. He turned and was face-to-face with Paddy.

"A fine day, is it not?" Paddy asked as he gazed toward the blue sky lined with filmy threads of pristine white.

"In-indeed . . . yes, yes it is," McKinley stammered, the words sticking in his throat.

"Are ya na working today?" Paddy inquired.

McKinley struggled to organize his thoughts. "Yes, yes I am. I came to escort a gentleman to the Appleton—he's interested in conducting business with the Associates and is meeting with Mr. Cheever."

"I'm doin' the same. The gentlemen from the Virginia

Military Institute are arriving on this train, and I've the privilege of escorting them back to the farm."

McKinley nodded and then moved a few steps away, hoping to distance himself from the young man.

"And there they are, looking distinguished in their military garb." Paddy grinned at McKinley before waving to the uniformed men. "I best be off."

"Yes, you don't want to keep them waiting," he said as he caught sight of Rupert walking toward him. Relief washed over McKinley as Paddy hurried off to meet his guests. He was still watching after the young man as Rupert approached.

The two men quickly exchanged greetings. "I think it best we leave for my home as soon as possible. It wouldn't be wise for Jasmine or Nolan to learn you've come here. I still do not understand why you wouldn't agree to meet elsewhere. This is dangerous," he said as the two men neared the buggy.

"What's life without a bit of danger, McKinley? I don't remember your being so anxious—you need to relax."

"Appears our buggies are side-by-side," Paddy said as he and the three uniformed men drew near. Paddy looked directly at Rupert before turning his gaze to McKinley. "I hope yar business dealings go well."

"Thank you. Give my regards to Jasmine and Nolan," McKinley replied.

"Aye, I'll be sure ta tell them."

"Irish?" Rupert asked.

"How could you possibly guess?" McKinley asked sarcastically. "Nolan has placed him in a position of authority at the horse farm. In fact, Paddy capably operated the business during the months Jasmine and Nolan were in Mississippi."

Rupert laughed as he settled himself in the buggy. "Then

it appears we have come face-to-face with the danger you anticipated."

McKinley stared at him in utter disbelief. "Do you *want* them to know you're here?"

"Not particularly. However, I'm not going to tremble in fear. Besides, the boy has no idea who I am. What harm is done? None!"

McKinley shook his head. "Quite frankly, I have too much at stake in this matter. I've told you in my letters that I must secure funds in order to repay loans. I've taken a beating during this economic downturn. My wife is beginning to question me, and before long, her father will also be inquiring into our affairs. Therefore, it is my sincere hope you came here to conduct business."

"Rest easy, good man. We do, after all, have *nearly* the same goals."

C H A P T E R · *21*

ELINOR READ the precisely penned notice one final time, then tucked it into her skirt pocket. She should have known this would come. After all, it was the way of things with her. God had granted her a brief respite—time to believe she might enjoy an ordinary life. But now her normal life would be snatched away.

Though deep in the recesses of her mind she had known this would happen, Elinor hadn't remained alert enough to protect herself. She had let down her guard and permitted Reggie and Justin Chamberlain into her heart. Throughout the summer, she had taken delight in their company, enjoying the picnics and fishing, long walks, enlightening conversation, and laughter—joyful laughter. Brick by brick, her inner protective wall had crumbled and had slowly been replaced by an abiding fondness for both Justin Chamberlain and his daughter.

"Fondness? What I feel is not fondness. It's love," she angrily admitted as she began to knead the bread dough with a vengeance. "This is what I receive in return for opening my heart to a little girl and her father," she railed while punching her fists into the soft dough.

"And now what? I must leave Justin and Reggie, this house, these girls, this town—everything and everyone I've come to love. Where is your kindness and mercy, God? Is it reserved for all but me?" she questioned. Defeated, she dropped to one of the wooden chairs and gave herself over to the pent-up tears and pain—the loss and desperation that filled her soul.

She didn't know how long she had been sobbing when she felt the touch of a hand on her shoulder. Elinor lifted her swollen, tearstained face. She hadn't heard the child come in the door. She looked up into Reggie's frightened eyes.

"What's wrong? Why are you crying?" Reggie asked in a trembling voice.

"It's nothing," Elinor replied. "I'm feeling a bit melancholy . . . nothing more."

Reggie shook her head vigorously. "I don't believe you. You told me a long time ago that if I came to you with questions, you would tell me the truth."

Elinor gave her a feeble smile. "You're right. I did promise you I would be honest with you, but I'm not certain this is the proper time."

Reggie folded her arms across her chest like a commanding schoolmarm. "If it's bad news, there is *never* a good time."

"I suppose that's true. You've grown very wise in your old age," she teased.

"Does that mean you're going to tell me what has made you cry?"

Elinor reached into her pocket and removed the notice that had been delivered earlier that day. "I've received notice that my boardinghouse will close at the end of this month."

Reggie fell to the empty chair alongside Elinor. "You

can't go. I won't let you," she said, tears trickling down her cheeks.

Elinor drew her into an embrace. "Dear, sweet Reggie. Please don't cry—I've shed more than enough tears for both of us. It will change nothing."

Reggie sniffed loudly, then wiped her nose on a ragged hanky she pulled from her pocket. "We must go and talk to Father. He'll know what to do."

"There is nothing anyone can do, Reggie. And I can't leave right now—the girls will be home for supper soon, and I've been sitting here feeling sorry for myself rather than preparing their meal."

Reggie grasped Elinor's hand in a death grip. "Promise you'll come and talk to Papa this evening after supper."

"I'll see," Elinor replied vaguely. She avoided making a promise, for she sincerely doubted she would go anywhere but to her rooms after the evening meal.

Reggie gave her a suspicious glance. "If you don't appear by eight o'clock, I promise Father and I will come here to see you."

From the determined look in Reggie's eyes, Elinor knew the girl would carry out her promise. "You might consider giving me until eight-thirty. I'll need to wash and dry the dishes and complete some preparations for tomorrow's breakfast."

Reggie gave a quick nod. "Eight-thirty," she said with authority.

They walked to the door, and before turning to leave, Reggie wrapped her arms around the older woman's waist. She hugged her with a fervor that surprised even Elinor. "We'll find an answer—I just know it," Reggie insisted.

Elinor returned the hug but remained silent. She didn't want to build Reggie's hope, for she already knew the answer. Come the end of September, she would be packed and on her way to Maine. In fact, she decided, she must pen a letter to Taylor and Bella first thing in the morning.

———

Reggie ran home at breakneck speed and rushed into her father's cluttered library. She came to a skidding halt in front of his desk and deposited her lunch pail atop one of the many stacks of papers covering his writing desk.

"We must do something about Mrs. Brighton," she panted, doubling forward to catch her breath.

Her father jumped to his feet and rounded the desk. "Is she ill? What's happened?" he asked while grabbing his felt hat from a hook at the doorway.

"She's not ill—she's leaving."

The hat slipped from his fingers and dropped to the floor. "*What?* Who told you such a thing?"

Reggie sat down in one of the uncomfortable wooden chairs. "Mrs. Brighton—just now. I stopped after school and she was crying. She received a notice from the Corporation this morning that her boardinghouse will close at the end of the month. She says there's nothing left for her to do but move to Maine."

Her father picked up the hat and dropped it back over the hook before sitting down. He rested his face in his hands and said nothing.

"Are you praying?" she whispered.

"I'm thinking . . . though I *should* be praying," he replied, lifting his face and meeting her intent gaze.

"We've prayed every night that Mrs. Brighton's boardinghouse wouldn't close, but God isn't listening."

"He's listening, Reggie. Remember what I've told you over and over? We don't always receive the answers we want—and perhaps this isn't even God's answer. Mrs. Brighton's outcome isn't determined just yet."

Reggie looked straight into her father's eyes. "I don't want her to leave—I love her. Besides you, she's the only one who has ever really cared about me since Mama died. We need to think of some way to keep her in Lowell. I told her you would find an answer and that she must come here this evening."

Her father startled to attention. "You believe I'll have a resolution for this dilemma by seven or eight o'clock tonight?"

"Eight-thirty," she said with a broad smile. "That gives you even more time than you expected."

"I certainly feel much better with that extra half hour," he replied as he glanced toward the ticking clock on his desk.

Reggie stood up and grasped her lunch pail in one hand. "I'll go begin supper and you can begin thinking—and praying," she added quickly.

"If you expect an answer by eight-thirty, *you* had best pray also," he called after her.

She giggled. "I'll pray while I peel the potatoes, but I'll keep my eyes open."

"I'm sure God will not object to your safety measures."

The girls had completed their evening meal when Elinor sat down at the head of the table. "Before any of you rush off, I want to share some news with you."

Mary Margaret looked up from her plate of half-eaten food. "Sure and I'm hopin' it's something good. I do na think I can bear more bad news today."

"Did you have problems at work today?" Elinor inquired.

Mary Margaret nodded as she toyed with the food on her plate. "Aye. Mr. Dempsey gave me my termination papers as I was leaving today. He said I'm na to come back after I pick up my pay on Saturday. He had other papers in his hand, so I know I'm na the only one, though I was pleased ta know Bridgett did na lose her position."

"I'm so sorry, Mary Margaret. I fear when you need assistance the very most, I'll not be able to lend a helping hand. My boardinghouse will be closed at the end of this month. For those of you still holding positions at the mills, you'll need to find another house—and that should prove easy enough with so many girls losing their jobs. And for those of you who have remained here since your termination, I fear you must seek other accommodations here in Lowell or depart for home."

There was a collective hum of disapproval toward the Corporation and sympathetic encouragement for both Elinor and Mary Margaret.

"If the Corporation closes a boardinghouse and we're required to move, I think they should send someone to move our trunks for us," Janet said while clicking open the jeweled watch fastened to her bodice.

Elinor stared at the girl. Although she and Reggie had been steadfastly praying for Janet, there appeared to be little change in the girl's heart. Obviously much more prayer was needed! Elinor gathered a stack of dishes and strode off to the kitchen, silently uttering a prayer for Janet. She was about to return when she heard Mary Margaret confront Janet.

"Ya're worried about someone ta lift yar trunks while the rest of us are concerned about losin' our livelihood?"

"Moving heavy trunks up and down all these steps is difficult," Janet whined.

"Have ya considered asking yar friend Mr. Dempsey ta help ya?" Mary Margaret asked. "I'm thinking he oughta be pleased to lend ya a hand."

"What does *that* mean? Are you insinuating Mr. Dempsey shows me favoritism?"

"I'm thinking ya both perform too many favors for one another—especially with him being a married man as well as your supervisor," Mary Margaret replied hastily.

Elinor heard the scraping of a chair against the floor. Janet's angry voice followed. "The Corporation should never have begun hiring *your* kind in the mills."

"Ya do na like me because I speak the truth. But since I no longer have a position at the mills, I can speak without fear of retribution. So if ya're embarrassed to have the truth spoken aloud, Janet, then ya ought change yar ways," Mary Margaret stated, her voice rising in volume.

Elinor entered the room to find three of the girls applauding while another giggled as Janet trounced off. There was little doubt they were pleased someone had finally confronted Janet about her inappropriate behavior. But an air of gloom quickly replaced their giggles. Although Janet had received her comeuppance, they still faced troubling circumstances.

Elinor began to gather another stack of dishes. "Have you any plans, Mary Margaret?"

Her red curls swayed back and forth as she shook her head. "I have na told anyone else. Paddy is ta call on me later tonight. I'm hoping he can give me some advice."

"I'm sure he can." Elinor glanced around the table. "Has Janet already left for town?" she asked, hoping no one would realize she'd eavesdropped on the group earlier.

"I'm na certain if she's left or still upstairs primping," Mary Margaret replied.

Elinor ignored Mary Margaret's curt remark as she surveyed the group of worried boarders gathered around the dining room table. "I want all of you girls to know you will be in my prayers. I trust you will pray for each other and for me as well. I have an appointment later this evening, and I must finish washing these dishes before I depart."

An hour later, Elinor removed her stained apron, patted her hair into place, and removed her cape from the wooden hook inside the doorway. Confusion jumbled her thoughts as she made the short walk to the parsonage. The front door swung open as she reached the top step. Before her stood Justin and Reggie sporting their coats and hats.

Reggie smiled broadly as she caught sight of Elinor. "I thought you weren't coming."

"You were leaving to come to the boardinghouse?"

"I told you if you weren't here by eight-thirty, we would come."

"But it's just now eight-thirty."

"I knew we'd see you along the way if you had already left the house," she said with a shrug.

Elinor laughed at the child's determination as she followed the two into the house. Reggie took Elinor's cloak and carefully hung it alongside her father's coat and her own blue cape.

"All of our coats hanging in a row look very nice together," the child commented. "Why don't you and Father go into the parlor, and I'll bring our tea. I had begun to prepare it earlier, but then when I thought you weren't coming . . ."

"Tea would be lovely, thank you," Elinor said.

Elinor and Justin sat down in the parlor as Reggie scurried to the kitchen.

"Reggie tells me you received notice the boardinghouse will close this month," Justin started. "I'm sure you haven't come to a decision, and I think it would be wise if you would take these final days to consider all of your options before immediately hurrying off to Maine."

"*All* of my options? I can't possibly remain in Lowell

now. With the decline of the mills and so many women out of work, there are no positions available for anyone with my skills in the immediate area." Elinor could see Reggie's arm as the girl stood just on the other side of the doorway.

"There must be something. You've said in the past that you truly do not want to move and that you're not anxious to move into your brother's household."

"All of that is true, yet I see no alternative."

Reggie stepped through the doorway and announced, "I prayed while I was fixing supper, and God gave me the answer." She plopped down beside Elinor.

Justin appeared as surprised as Elinor was. "Why didn't you tell me?" he asked.

"Because it's better to tell you when we're all together."

They both stared at her, waiting.

"Well?" Justin finally inquired.

"We're going to get married." Her eyes shone with delight as she looked back and forth between them. "I love both of you and you both love me and you love each other, so we should get married," she said in a rush.

Elinor looked at Justin, wondering what he must be thinking at this moment—yet unsure if she truly wanted to know.

Reggie held up her hand. "Nobody can say anything yet. First I have to tell you *all* the reasons. Besides all of us loving one another, if you two marry, I will have a mother right here at home to help me with my schoolwork and teach me all the things you want me to learn about being a proper lady," she said while looking at her father.

Then she turned toward Elinor. "And if you marry my father, you will have a house of your very own, and we won't have to share you with the girls at the boardinghouse. *And* you will have me and Father right here so you can still bake and cook and go on picnics and fishing—and take care of us," she added softly.

Reggie glanced back and forth between the two people she loved most in the world. "Well, didn't God come up with a wonderful answer?"

"Indeed He did," Justin replied. "At least I think so. What about you, Elinor? Would you consider becoming Mrs. Justin Chamberlain? As Reggie so adeptly pointed out, I do love you," he said softly. "And I would be proud to have you as my wife if you'll have us."

Reggie giggled and applauded as Elinor clasped her bodice, deciding whether to laugh or cry. Surely this wasn't happening. Justin Chamberlain had just declared his love for her—love she surely returned. A nudging doubt crept into her heart. *If he loves me so much, why didn't he say so before?* She pushed the thought aside. *I love him. Despite my fears, I cannot deny that one thing.* "I would be honored to become your wife *and* Reggie's mother," she whispered.

"And a little child shall lead them," he said, grinning at his daughter. "Now why don't you fetch that tea you promised us so that we may have a few moments alone."

"I'll be in the kitchen for at least fifteen minutes, and I promise not to peek if you want to kiss her," Reggie sang gleefully as she skipped out of the room.

A moment of awkward silence filled the room after Reggie had departed. "Elinor, I want you to know that although it required my daughter's prompting, I have been in love with you for some time. However, I was afraid to express my love because I knew you had vowed never to marry again. I feared if I hinted about my feelings, you might withdraw from my life—and I knew I couldn't bear to lose you. Unlike Reggie, I didn't have the courage to speak of my love."

A faint smile crossed Elinor's lips. "How could you have known that you had broken down the barricade that surrounded my heart? Like you, I was afraid to hope for anything more than friendship. Until today, I had not even acknowledged my love."

He clasped her hands and brushed each palm with a featherlike kiss. "I don't want you to change your answer, but I do want you to be certain this is what you want and not a marriage forced upon you by circumstances—or my daughter," he said. "I want you to come to me because it is your heart's desire."

"There could be no other way," she whispered as he tenderly gathered her into his arms and kissed her with an ardent longing that spoke of his love.

Slowly he pulled back, and she gazed into the depths of his greenish-blue eyes, her heart pounding with the force of a blacksmith's hammer striking his anvil. Suddenly Elinor knew she had underestimated God's plan for her future.

"With the boardinghouse closing in less than two weeks," he said, "I see little reason that we should wait to wed—unless you want time to plan an elaborate wedding."

She laughed softly. "No. I believe all we need is a minister, Reggie, and the two of us."

"Good," Reggie said as she reentered the room and placed the tea tray on a small walnut table. "Spencer and I rode Larkspur over to Billerica earlier this evening. Reverend Foster said he would be pleased to marry you on the last Saturday of the month at seven o'clock in the evening," she proudly announced. "I told him we'd be sure to arrive on time."

It was impossible not to laugh. In a matter of only three hours, Reggie had arranged their marriage. "Have you also decided what I should wear for the wedding?" Elinor inquired.

"I think your peach-colored gown with the ivory lace

would be very nice," she replied without hesitating for even a moment.

"In that case, it appears as if the arrangements have been decided, and we need only relax until then," her father remarked.

"Oh, Father!" Reggie said in an exasperated tone. "We must have a reception after the wedding, but you need not worry about that either. Spencer's mother said she would be delighted to host the reception at their house. She said not to worry about a thing."

"You asked Mrs. Houston to host a reception before you knew whether we were actually going to wed?" her father asked.

"Spencer told his mother about the wedding before we went to Billerica; he needed permission to take Larkspur," she explained nonchalantly. "And I didn't ask—she offered."

"I couldn't possibly put Jasmine to such an inconvenience," Elinor protested. "That is far too much to expect of anyone, Reggie. Besides, your father and I don't need a reception."

"Mrs. Houston said you would fuss and argue, but to tell you that once the church ladies got wind of the marriage, they'd plan their own reception for you. She thought you might find her party more enjoyable."

Elinor bit the inside of her bottom lip to keep from smiling. Jasmine was correct; she didn't want Martha Emory and Nancy Sanders planning a party for her. They'd be angry enough when they discovered the pastor was no longer an eligible candidate for either of their daughters!

"Mrs. Houston is right," Elinor said. "I'll go and visit with her tomorrow."

Reggie beamed. "We're going to have a grand wedding, aren't we?"

————

Mary Margaret was waiting inside the front door, and at the sound of Paddy's voice commanding the horses to a halt, she ran down the front step to greet him.

"It looks like ya're a mite anxious ta see me," he said with a grin.

"Aye, that I am. Do ya think we could take a walk? I have something to tell you."

"Just let me tie the horse and we'll walk down toward the river. Ya're looking a wee bit worried, lass. Is something wrong?"

She nodded her head. "I've troubles more than I'm able ta solve on my own, Paddy. I'm needing some sound advice."

"Then I'll do my best," he said while offering her his arm.

She rested her hand inside the crook of his arm and immediately felt less frightened about her circumstances. "The day I've been fearing for quite some time arrived today. I went into work, and all was fine until we shut down the looms for the evening. I was one of the first to pass by Mr. Dempsey, and he handed me my notice. I've lost my job, Paddy. I do na know what I'm ta do. I was na so terrified at first, for I knew Mrs. Brighton would let me stay on at the boardinghouse." Her words were bursting forth like flood-waters. "But then I get myself home, and she sits herself down to the supper table and tells us she was served with a notice to close the boardinghouse at the end of the month."

"Take a breath, lass," Paddy said as he stroked her hand. " 'Tis na such a bad thing that's happened. I did na want my wife ta be working anyway."

"There ya go again with telling me what I can and can na do. I'm the one ta be deciding if I want ta be . . . Did ya say *wife*?" she asked, jerking on his arm and pulling him to a halt.

"Aye. I said *wife*. Ya're gaping at me as though ya're surprised, when I know ya've been wondering if I was ever going ta ask ya," he said with a lopsided grin.

Her eyes sparkled with anticipation. "Are ya really asking me ta marry ya, Paddy?"

"I do na know what it's gonna take ta convince ya, lass! Let me try this: Mary Margaret O'Flannery, will ya marry me and be me lovin' wife?"

She wrapped her arms around his neck and kissed him soundly on the lips. "Aye," she whispered. "There's nothing I'd rather do than become Mrs. Padraig O'Neill."

"Ya see? There's no problem at all. I'll talk to Kiara—she and Rogan have plenty of room in their house. Ya can stay with them until the wedding, providing the two of ya won't start making elaborate wedding plans that will delay our marriage. I do na want ta be waiting much longer for ya ta become my bride," he said with a wink.

CHAPTER · 22

"JASMINE! WHAT A pleasant surprise," Violet greeted. "I was just preparing to have tea in the garden. Won't you and Alice Ann join me?"

"I imagine Alice Ann would much prefer a visit with her cousin Zachary. Is he outdoors?"

"Indeed he is. I cannot keep that child in the house until the dead of winter sets in—and even then it remains a difficult task. I'm disappointed you didn't bring Clara along."

"I had a number of errands to accomplish and promised Alice this could be our special day together, but I'm anxious to see the baby. I'm sure little Mattie Rose has grown inches since last I saw her."

"Unfortunately, she's hardly a baby any longer. Children seem to grow up in the blink of an eye, don't you think? Why, she's already pulling up to a stand and toddling about while we hold on to her fingers," Violet proudly announced. "It has been far too long since we've seen you," she continued while looping arms with Jasmine as they walked outside. "Have you and McKinley argued? He denies there are any ill

343

feelings between the two of you, yet since your return from Mississippi, I feel he hasn't made any attempt to socialize with you and your family."

Jasmine hesitated for a moment and watched as little Zachary and Alice Ann embraced each other before hurrying off to inspect the late fall blooms in Violet's garden.

"We haven't argued. His days are likely filled with problems relating to the mills. After all, this is a difficult time," Jasmine said. "However, you might mention that there is a matter I need to discuss with him in the near future."

Violet brightened. "As a matter of fact, he's in the library. Why don't I look after Alice Ann and Zachary while you visit with McKinley? We'll have tea when you return."

"Are you certain he won't mind the interruption?"

"Of course not. He was working on his ledgers when I went outdoors and said he wouldn't be going to the mill until after the noonday meal. Do go and see him," she urged.

After quickly telling Alice Ann to behave during her absence, Jasmine entered the house, crossing through the parlor and turning down the hallway toward her brother's library. The sound of men's voices floated from the library. Jasmine hesitated outside the partially open door. She didn't want to interrupt if McKinley was conducting business, yet Violet hadn't said he was entertaining any visitors.

Her brother was discussing the finalization of a sale as expeditiously as possible. She listened intently to the voice of the man now responding. The deep southern drawl sounded strangely familiar. Her brows furrowed as the man continued to speak. *Cousin Rupert!*

What was *he* doing in Lowell? In McKinley's home? Without her knowledge? And they were discussing the sale of something. . . . *The Willows!* McKinley had gone behind her back and was making arrangements to sell the plantation to that dreadful excuse of a man. How dare he!

"How will you ever get your sister to agree to this sale?" Rupert questioned. "After all, she is part owner, and the sale will hardly be legal without her signature. And," he chuckled, "we don't want any more misunderstandings about my trying to forge her name on papers."

"I'll deal with Jasmine," McKinley declared.

"Well, you also need to deal with a couple of other things. I have some concerns about the contract to purchase."

With every fiber of her being, Jasmine wanted to burst through the door and condemn their appalling behavior. Instead, she forced herself to remain calm and keep her wits.

"I thought we had reached a satisfactory agreement," McKinley said.

"After further consideration, I believe there are a few conditions that I can't possibly agree to."

"And what would those be?"

Rupert's voice lowered and Jasmine strained to hear. She heard him mention buying the slaves and then McKinley replied, yet she couldn't hear his comment. Oh, why wouldn't they speak up—especially now when she wanted to hear what they were saying about the slaves?

Jasmine remained outside the door as they continued to speak in muffled tones. She had no choice but to go inside the room and make her presence known. After all, Violet would certainly ask questions when she returned to the garden. She inhaled deeply and knocked on the door.

"Come in," McKinley called.

She opened the door, prepared to give the acting performance of a lifetime. Neither of them would know she'd heard a thing!

McKinley's eyes opened wide as she walked into the room. "Jasmine! I wasn't expecting you," he blurted.

She smiled sweetly and turned her attention to Rupert.

"Why, Cousin Rupert! Violet didn't tell me you were visiting. She said McKinley was working on his ledgers. When did you arrive?"

"Yesterday. And I'll be in town only briefly. I assumed you'd have little time available, what with your *social* involvement," Rupert said eyeing her cautiously.

Jasmine only offered her most pleasant Southern belle face. She watched her brother begin to fidget as she sat down opposite Rupert. "I'm so surprised you would come north." She held her tongue, not saying the things she really wanted to say. So many times McKinley had told her he thought her reaction and feelings toward Rupert were based solely upon a misunderstanding. Especially after Cousin Levi wrote to say that he had managed to clear up Rupert's supposed takeover of The Willows. She steadied her nerves and looked her cousin in the eye. "So what brings you to Lowell, Rupert?"

"Ah . . . well . . . I'm interested in the possibility of investing in the mills. McKinley extended an invitation so that I might gain firsthand knowledge about the operation. I don't like going into any investment without have a thorough knowledge of the business venture."

His smugness and deceit annoyed her. "I'm surprised you'd be looking to invest in the mills at this time. The outlook is rather bleak right now for investment purposes, wouldn't you think?"

"Not at all. Investing during a downturn can yield huge returns when the economy stabilizes."

"So long as one invests properly," she added.

He smiled at her as though she were a young child to be tolerated for a short time. "I believe my assets show I've had no difficulty in that regard. Speaking of assets, how is my little Prissy faring these days?"

Jasmine grasped the chair arms, her knuckles turning white as she forced herself to remain civil. "Prissy was never *yours,* Rupert. However, she is doing quite well as a free woman. And how is Toby?"

"I really wouldn't have any idea," he said caustically.

McKinley rose from his chair. "I'd like to continue this reunion. However, Rupert and I are expected at the mills within the next half hour."

"Feel free to take your leave. After all, I wouldn't want to keep my dear cousin from investing his money in our *Northern* mills."

Rupert cast an irate look at Jasmine as he departed the room. She waited until the front door closed and then sank back into the chair, her mind reeling. She didn't know if Rupert had actually come to discuss investing in the mills, but there was little doubt he and McKinley were negotiating the sale of The Willows—and possibly even the slaves. And why had Rupert shown such interest in Prissy? She had noted a contemptible glint in his eyes as he had spoken of the girl. Remembering his attempts to take possession of her when they were in Mississippi, coupled with his question this morning turned her thoughts to baby Emily.

She covered her mouth to stifle the scream threatening to escape her lips. *Rupert Hesston* had fathered Prissy's baby!

———

Jasmine kissed the children good-night, then hurried back downstairs to the parlor. Before supper, she had spoken with Nolan and related the details of her morning visit to McKinley's home. When she had completed the distasteful tale, she had asked for his advice. But instead of taking her side and condemning McKinley, he had requested additional time to think on the matter. After pressing him further, Nolan had agreed they would talk after the children had gone to bed for the night.

"Have you come to any conclusions?" she asked as she

sat down in her rocker and picked up her stitching.

"I think the only answer to this entire dilemma is truthfulness. You need to tell McKinley you overheard a portion of his conversation with Rupert. Tell him of your suspicions. Explain that you abhor thinking he could turn against the abolitionist movement and that you have a deep concern that he is planning to sell The Willows without consulting you and perhaps even deal in the sale of the slaves. If you approach him honestly, I believe he will feel obligated to answer you in kind. Your brother is a devout Christian man who has renounced slavery, Jasmine. I can't believe he would so easily turn against his beliefs."

Jasmine shrugged, not sure she agreed. "I hope you're correct. I'll go to him tomorrow."

"I'd wait until you're certain Rupert has departed."

She nodded. "When we spoke earlier, I failed to mention that Rupert asked about Prissy. From his behavior regarding her, I've grown to believe he is Emily's father."

Nolan sighed. "It's true his obsession with her was odd. When we were in Mississippi, I truly feared his interest in her went beyond proper boundaries, and I don't doubt your assumption. However, with your capable intervention, Prissy has made great strides in accepting the baby, and we don't want to do anything that would disrupt their bond. No one need know of our suspicions."

She carefully knotted her thread before meeting Nolan's gaze. "I agree. I want to honor Prissy's wishes. It was clear she did not want to name the father, and I now understand why."

It was midafternoon on Thursday when Jasmine approached the offices that fronted a row of brick textile mills. Nolan had suggested she visit McKinley at his office, thinking it best to keep Violet unaware of any possible problem. And Jasmine knew he was correct. This was a matter that was best resolved on neutral ground, away from friends and family.

Her brother's name had been printed upon the glass pane in his open office door—bold black letters surrounded with gold, proclaiming that the office belonged to McKinley Wainwright. He glanced up as she approached, and she noted his look of surprise as he motioned her in.

"I hope you don't mind my calling on you unannounced," she said.

"No, this is fine. Is there some problem?" he inquired cautiously.

"Actually, there are several. May I?" she asked while pointing at one of the wooden chairs.

He jumped to his feet. "Yes, of course. Please be seated."

"Let me begin by saying that I have an admission to make."

He stared at her intently and waited. "Go on," he urged.

"When I visited you at your home the other day, I had been standing outside the library for a short period of time before I entered."

"Eavesdropping?"

"Not intentionally—at least not at first. But as I stepped to the door, I heard you discussing a sale and then I recognized Rupert's voice. The two of you were discussing The Willows—and the slaves," she added.

"If you remained by the door once you knew we were in private conversation, you *were* eavesdropping. Not an admirable quality. I'm surprised you would conduct yourself in such a manner," he said heatedly.

Her eyebrows arched and her jaw went slack. "*You're* surprised by *my* conduct? You've entered into the business of selling our inheritance to a man who tried to steal it and then deal in the buying and selling of human flesh, and *you're* surprised by *my* conduct? Come now, McKinley! You can't believe you're in good standing to take the offensive in this argument."

"I believe that I am, dear sister. You know I have been in dire straits, what with my financial losses and the . . ."

"There is no explanation you can provide that will excuse your behavior, McKinley!"

"Will you let me finish at least a sentence before you interrupt?"

Jasmine fastened an unyielding gaze upon him. "I'm listening."

"As you know, I have been desperate for The Willows to be sold, and that land agent you hired has been of no assistance whatsoever. Even you must admit he's useless."

"I will *not* agree Mr. Turner is useless. I believe he's made every attempt to sell the plantation, and I've notified you each time I've received word from him," Jasmine countered.

"And each time his report is the same. That man will never find a buyer for The Willows. In any event, shortly after you received Mr. Turner's first letter, Rupert and I began exchanging correspondence. I asked for an explanation of all that had occurred while you and Nolan were in Mississippi."

She opened her mouth to speak, but he motioned for her to remain silent.

"As we corresponded, Rupert explained that there had been misunderstandings on both sides. He never meant to threaten you or cause you to believe he was taking The Willows by force."

"He's a liar."

McKinley shook his head. "Perhaps, but it doesn't matter now. Other things have happened. Rupert expressed a desire to purchase the property and said he would also be willing to pay me a tidy sum for the slaves—provided I would return Prissy to him. His offer was extremely generous. My share would be more than enough to free me of any financial woes for many years. The offer was tempting, and I admit I wrestled with accepting his offer. However, after much prayer, I knew it was far more important to free our people than secure my finances. I told him I could not accept his offer. So you see, this wasn't exactly as you thought."

Jasmine's features had softened as he spoke. "I am so very proud of you, McKinley, and I'm sorry I ever doubted you. Can you ever forgive me?"

"Yes, of course I forgive you."

"How do matters now stand between you and Rupert?"

"We've reached another agreement. I have agreed to sell the plantation at a reduced cost in exchange for the slaves."

"And he agreed?"

"Yes, he agreed. He says there may be one or two he cannot locate, but the remainder will be turned over."

"What can I do to assist? While I dislike the idea of Rupert owning the land, if it means freeing our people, I must relent. Do you want Nolan and me to travel south and escort them back here? Or perhaps I can write to Rupert and express my thanks and offer to send clothing and supplies for the journey north," she suggested.

"No, Jasmine. What you must do is remain completely uninvolved in this process. Rupert and I have a history that goes back to our childhood days. I can deal with him much more easily on my own. You will only complicate matters. There is far too much animosity between you and Rupert."

"But I want to help!" she proclaimed insistently.

"What is more important, sister? That you be involved or that our people regain their freedom?"

"You're right. I'll stay out so long as you promise to advise me if there is any way I can lend assistance."

"I promise."

"One other thing: since your inheritance will be greatly diminished by the bargain you've made with Rupert, I'm going to insist you retain all of the money from the sale. Nolan and I have been most fortunate in our business dealings, and I can well afford to give up my portion of the inheritance. It is the very least I can do."

McKinley shook his head. "No, I won't consider such charity. Father intended for you to have a portion of the inheritance."

"I admire the sacrifice you are making by selling the plantation at a reduced price, McKinley, and I *want* to help you. Remember that the Bible tells us we are to bear one another's burdens. You don't want to defy *any* of God's directives, do you?" she asked.

He leaned back in his chair and laughed. "You have always been good to me, Jasmine."

"We have been good to each other—that's why God created families: to love and support one another in the good times as well as the bad."

"And I'm very thankful for you," he said.

———

Elinor took one last look in the mirror. The pale peach cashmere dress was truly lovely, and she was genuinely pleased Reggie had suggested it.

She turned toward the door leading to the hallway and clasped a hand to her chest. "Helen! You startled me. I didn't hear you come down the stairs."

"I'm sorry. I truly didn't mean to alarm you."

"It's all right, Helen. Are you finished packing?"

The girl gave a sad nod. "Your dress is lovely, Mrs. Brighton. I came down to see if you needed any assistance preparing for the wedding."

There was such expectancy in her face that Elinor motioned Helen into the small sitting room. "If you could fasten this around my neck, I'd be most appreciative." Elinor handed her a wide velvet ribbon she'd embroidered with peach and green flowers to match the dress. Helen carefully fastened the ribbon with a small gold brooch that had belonged to Elinor's grandmother.

"Will your brother and his wife be attending the wedding?" Helen inquired.

"No, though I know they wish they could be here. I sent a telegram advising them of my plans. I received their regrets—their children are in school and there was insufficient time to make proper plans. However, they invited us to come visit at our earliest opportunity. I believe we'll wait until school is out next summer," Elinor explained. "I think Reggie would enjoy meeting all of my nieces and nephews."

"That will be nice. I wanted to tell you that I appreciate your kindness since I've been in your house, and I'm sorry to leave here. However, I'm very happy for you. I do hope Reggie knows how fortunate she is to gain you as a mother."

"Why, thank you, Helen. I've enjoyed having you as a part of my boardinghouse family. You *are* planning to attend the reception, aren't you?"

The girl's face glowed. "Oh yes! I wouldn't miss it. Mary Margaret said Paddy is coming to fetch all of your former boarders who live here in town and want to attend." At the sound of an approaching buggy, Helen hurried to the window in Elinor's room. "It's Pastor Chamberlain," she announced excitedly.

"Thank you, Helen. I'll look forward to seeing you at the reception later this evening," Elinor said as she lightly kissed Helen's cheek. The young woman scampered toward the stairs as Elinor checked her appearance once more before going to the front door.

She opened the door to Justin, who was holding his tall silk hat in one hand and a nosegay in the other. "Reggie insisted that you have flowers," he said, handing her the cluster of ivory mums mixed with an assortment of greenery.

Elinor was mesmerized as he stood before her in his black double-breasted wool morning suit. The points of his heavily starched white collar perfectly accented the wide gray-and-blue striped cravat he had chosen to wear.

"May I come in?" he finally asked.

"Yes, yes, of course," she said, regaining her voice.

"You look lovely, Elinor. That color becomes you."

She felt a blush rise to her cheeks. "Thank you. And may I say you look most handsome yourself."

He grinned at the compliment. "Reggie says we must hurry or we'll not arrive in Billerica by seven o'clock. I couldn't even convince her to come in—she said there was no time."

Elinor picked up her cape and reticule. "Then we had best be on our way. We ought not keep the preacher waiting—or Reggie."

"Absolutely not!"

Glancing over her shoulder, Elinor caught sight of Helen standing on the stairway. "We'll see you after the wedding, Helen."

The young woman brightened and waved as they walked toward the carriage.

Reggie giggled as Elinor settled beside her in the buggy. "In only a short time I can call you Mama instead of Mrs. Brighton, can't I?"

"If that's what you'd like to call me, I would be honored." Elinor was thrilled by the child's desire to immediately use the endearing term.

Reggie glanced up at her father. "The dress is very pretty, don't you think?"

Justin nodded his agreement. "The dress is lovely, but not nearly so lovely as the lady wearing it."

Reggie covered her mouth and giggled, and Elinor pulled the child close, almost afraid to believe the goodness God had showered upon her. She would have not only a wonderful husband with whom to share her life, but also this delightful child whom she had already grown to love and cherish. She released Reggie and leaned back into the cushion, offering a prayer of gratitude and thanksgiving that God had sent them both into her life.

The wedding ceremony was simple, but much to Elinor's liking. And to her great delight, after Justin vowed to take her as his wife, Reggie also stated her desire to have Elinor as her mother.

When Reverend Foster asked if she would take Justin as her husband, Elinor promptly replied, "I do, and I take Reggie for my daughter as well."

A short time later they arrived at the Houston farm, where buggies lined the driveway. Two servants stood waiting to greet them. "Go tell Miss Jasmine they've arrived," the man ordered as the other servant immediately raced into the house.

The trio followed the servant up the steps and into the foyer, where a maid quickly took their wraps. "Please follow me," the woman said, motioning them forward.

They moved to the doorway of the large sitting room, where the guests awaited their arrival. "Reverend and Mrs. Justin Chamberlain and daughter, Reggie Chamberlain," he announced in a resounding voice.

The applause was deafening as they stepped into the room. "Thank you all for attending," Justin called out loudly as he motioned the crowd to stop clapping.

Nolan signaled for the music to begin and then he and his wife turned their attention to the new family. "Can we assume all went well with the marriage ceremony?" Nolan asked Justin.

"Absolutely. Reverend Foster did a fine job, though his part in all of this was much less difficult than the lovely party you have arranged," he said, taking in the elaborate decorations about the room. "You shouldn't have gone to all this trouble."

"It was our pleasure," Jasmine replied. "We would have it no other way. Spencer and Moses are upstairs if you care to join them, Reggie. In fact, you may tell them they can come downstairs with you if they promise to be on their best behavior."

"I'll tell them," she said before hurrying out of the room.

"You'll be pleased to see many of your church members as well as girls from the boardinghouse among the crowd," Jasmine told them. "Now, do come fix a plate of food so that the others can begin to eat."

Elinor and Justin followed her to the dining table. Alice Ann was holding a stack of perfectly folded white linen napkins while three maids hovered nearby, prepared to refill the trays with an array of wondrous treats.

"It's abundantly obvious you have outdone yourself," Justin commented as he began to fill his plate with several sweet delicacies. "It's going to be difficult making my choices."

"Then you must come back until you've tried some of everything," Jasmine suggested before turning her attention to the bride. "Do have one of my raspberry tarts, Elinor. I prepared them especially for you. As I was planning what to serve, I suddenly remembered they're one of your favorites."

Elinor placed two of the small tarts on her plate. "Seems the church ladies have gathered for a private conclave," she whispered to Justin.

He winked at her and when he had filled his plate, he

strode to the cluster of women. "We're pleased to see so many of our church members in attendance. Do help yourselves to some of this fine food, ladies. There are many selections to please your palate."

Reggie, Spencer, and Moses positioned themselves in a small nook where the heavy parlor drapes hid them from view yet provided them with an excellent vantage point. They had come down the stairs and circled through the dining room in order to secure the perfect spot. It wasn't until the church ladies gathered in front of the draperies that their view of the guests became somewhat obscured.

"I wish they would move. Now I can't see my mama." Reggie said the last word tentatively, as though she were trying it on to see how it fit.

Martha Emory poked Nancy Sanders in the arm. "Just look at her smiling like the cat that caught the canary. I told you from the beginning that she was out to snag him. *Didn't* I, Caroline?" she asked, now looking at her daughter.

"Yes, Mama," Caroline answered meekly.

"And didn't I tell you that if you'd just assert yourself, you'd have yourself a husband?"

Caroline bobbed her head up and down. "Yes, Mama."

"I believe he was interested in my Sarah until Elinor set her cap for him," Nancy told Martha. "Of course, my Sarah is too much of a lady to throw herself at a man. Unlike Elinor, she could never behave in an unladylike fashion in order to gain a man's attention. Surely you all remember how Elinor marched into that parsonage and took charge— ordering everyone around, just like she owned the place."

Cecile Turnvall was focusing on Jasmine Houston. "For the life of me, I cannot understand why this reception is being hosted by the Houstons. It's as though they didn't think the ladies of the Congregational church could provide them with a reception that would meet their standards. The Houstons are *Episcopalians!*"

"Episcopalian or not, any reception we would have hosted would pale in comparison to this," Winifred Mason remarked. "I imagine it's Elinor who wanted this fancy party—Pastor Chamberlain isn't one to put on airs." She leaned closer to the other women. "Of course, unlike the rest of us, the Houstons appear to lead a charmed life. Even the economic problems don't seem to have affected them."

"I think it's a wonderful party," Caroline offered. "The food is excellent, and I particularly like the music."

A slap of her mother's fan caused Caroline to flinch. "You see! That's exactly why you're going to spend your life as a spinster! Instead of evaluating why you aren't on the arm of Pastor Chamberlain, you're enjoying his wedding reception."

"Sorry, Mama," Caroline said, casting her eyes downward.

"See what they're like?" Reggie whispered to Spencer and Moses. "I told you, but you didn't believe me."

"I feel sorry for dat Caroline lady," Moses whispered. "Her mama is mean."

The young trio sat listening for a short time longer before Reggie decided to take matters into her own hands. She poked Martha Emory lightly in the back and waited until the older woman turned before stepping from behind the burgundy-fringed draperies.

"Good evening, Mrs. Emory, Mrs. Sanders, ladies," she said as though she were a politician preparing to address a group of prospective voters. The women were visibly startled. "The three of us have been sitting here listening to your very cruel remarks. I'm going to kindly request that you immediately cease your disparaging remarks regarding my mother, or I'll be forced to tell my parents everything you've said here tonight," she said in a firm but gentle voice. "I truly don't think you'd want me to do such a thing."

"No, no, of course not," Nancy Sanders sputtered. "We're very pleased for both you and your father."

"That's nice to know, because if you are pleased for me and for my father, I know you'll also be pleased for my mother. After all, she is the one who has brought joy to us."

"Yes, yes, of course," Mrs. Emory stammered as she grabbed Caroline by the arm. "Come along, ladies, we must try some of that punch. It looks delightful."

Giggles emanated from behind the draperies as the women hurried across the room toward the punch bowl.

C H A P T E R · *23*

Late October 1858

JASMINE OPENED the door as her brother bounded up the front steps.

"You must have been watching for me. Am I late?"

"No. You're exactly on time," she replied. "I have tea prepared and waiting in the parlor."

"Good! It's turned colder since I left home this morning, and I noticed the skies have taken on a somewhat ominous appearance. We could be in for a snowstorm later today."

She shivered. "I know a deep layer of snow would delight the children, but I don't look forward to the biting chill created by these Massachusetts winter storms."

McKinley laughed. "It's our Southern blood. I don't think it's ever going to thicken enough to guard us against this cold weather."

"Perhaps you're correct," she said as she hung his hat on a peg.

"I do hope you've developed a plan. I fear I've had little time to concentrate on the problem of housing the former slaves."

"I told you I would take responsibility for those issues. You're the one who insisted upon remaining involved."

"I know, I know. However, if Rupert questions me, I want to be prepared with accurate answers. I don't want him to suspect you've been involved in our business dealings."

Jasmine sighed. "That's just it, McKinley. I haven't been involved in the business dealings, and Rupert isn't going to care in the least whether we've made adequate arrangements for the former slaves once he gives them over to your care."

"I'm certain you're right on that account. But I'll be more comfortable in my dealings with him if I'm aware of all aspects."

"As you wish," she replied.

McKinley poured a dollop of cream into his tea and then took a sip. "Now, tell me of your idea."

"Actually, it's more than an idea. I've already set to work, so at this point there's no room for objection on your part."

"Why am I not surprised?" he asked.

She shrugged and flashed a sheepish grin. "After reviewing the number of people we could adequately care for here on the farm, I began making inquiries among our abolitionist friends and the colored people already settled in this area. All have agreed to take in at least three and some many more. From the ledger Nolan and I maintained when we freed the slaves, it appears Rupert should deliver nearly one hundred. I've made up a list of where they will be housed until they make final decisions regarding their future."

McKinley shook his head. "There is no stopping you once you've been presented with a challenge."

"It wasn't a difficult assignment. Even in this time of economic depression, the good people of Lowell have opened their hearts and their homes. Nolan and I have agreed to give financial aid to those families who so willingly offered space in their homes but do not possess the adequate financial resources to feed additional mouths. When the former slaves finally arrive here at the farm, we will know exactly where each one will be housed and cared for."

McKinley downed the remainder of his tea. "How could I possibly find fault with such a plan? It seems you've thought of everything."

"We're ready to receive them if Rupert will merely agree upon an exact date for the transfer to take place. That, dear brother, is the task you must complete—and quickly," she added.

He placed his cup and saucer on the tray and rose to his feet. "Let's pray I'll be as successful as you have been."

———————

The servants buzzed about the house, cleaning and polishing while Jasmine and Kiara once again reviewed the list of wedding guests.

"Ya've become quite the hostess these last couple of months," Kiara commented. "First the party for Pastor and Mrs. Chamberlain, and now this lovely reception ya've been planning for Paddy and Mary Margaret. Do ya truly think ya want all this work—not to mention the expense?"

Jasmine laughed. "Nolan and I would have it no other way, Kiara. I don't know what we would have done had Paddy not been here to take care of the farm while we were away. He's grown into such a fine young man, and I know you're very proud of him."

"Aye, that I am, and had it na been for the famine, we'd still be struggling in Ireland. 'Tis strange the twists and turns life takes. I'm still amazed how God takes the tragedy in our lives and turns it into something good. Ya know, when our ma and da died, I thought for sure God had deserted me, but then He saved me and Paddy and we came to this wonderful country. And then when things was so bad between me and your first husband, again I thought God had turned His back on me. Them was hard times for all of us, but God took those terrible things and brought good from them. We have truly been blessed to have the good Lord lift us out of such tragedy and restore our joy."

Jasmine's eyes clouded as she remembered those days when Kiara and Paddy had first arrived in Lowell and the heartbreak that soon followed. She, too, had suffered at Bradley Houston's hands; she, too, had wondered if God had deserted her. Yet God had victoriously delivered them through their circumstances. Now she prayed their former slaves would taste that same victory and be delivered from Rupert's evil hold.

The touch of Kiara's hand caused Jasmine to startle. "Ya look so far away suddenly, Jasmine. Are ya na feeling well?"

"I'm fine. I was merely lost in my own thoughts for a moment. Now what were you saying about the food preparations?"

"Mary Margaret has enlisted Bridgett to take charge of preparin' some special Irish fare, and Maisie and Prissy asked if they could help. Henrietta 'as agreed to keep the younger children in the nursery. I completed Mary Margaret's gown last evening—stitched on the final lace and had her try it on. She looked lovely with that gorgeous red hair and creamy complexion. Paddy's going ta be speechless when he sees her in that gown."

———

"They're coming! They're coming!" Spencer shouted as he rode Larkspur to the front of the house. He delivered his message to Alice Ann, who immediately raced into the house, nearly tumbling into one of the servants carrying a beautiful cut glass punch bowl.

"Mama, Spencer says Paddy and his bride are here," she

shouted as she rushed into the parlor.

"Thank you for the message, but please cease running through the house. If you don't, there's bound to be an accident," Jasmine warned.

Alice danced from foot to foot. "Can I help, Mama, can I?"

Jasmine smiled at her daughter. "I don't think there's anything you can do."

The child's lips began to quiver as Prissy walked into the parlor.

"It would be a mighty big hep if someone could hand folks their napkins," Prissy said. "I jes' can't seem to make enough room for dem on the table, Miz Jasmine. Can you think of someone who could do dat for me?"

"I could, I could!" Alice Ann squealed in delight.

Prissy grinned at Jasmine and then gave the child an appraising look. "I don' know . . . you sho' you'd be careful to make sure *each* guest gets a napkin?" she asked.

Alice Ann's chestnut brown curls danced up and down as she bobbed her head. "I promise," she said. "I did that for Mrs. Brighton . . . I mean Mrs. Chamberlain's party."

"All right, then. Come along with me and git into place afore them people get in here," she said, taking Alice Ann by the hand. "They's bound to be hungry, so you best be having dem napkins ready."

"Thank you, Prissy," Jasmine said gratefully.

Prissy nodded. "When she gits tired of handin' out napkins, I'll send her upstairs to Henrietta."

The rooms soon filled with an array of guests, and the small group of Irish musicians began to play their fiddles while the guests filled their plates with a variety of tasty treats. Paddy and Mary Margaret briefly visited with their guests before Paddy took her in his arms and they circled the room in a wedding dance. Moments later, the fiddlers scratched their bows in rapid motion, plucking out an Irish jig while the guests clapped in time to the music.

The music went on for hours and everyone seemed to have a wonderful time. Jasmine watched the Irish celebration and found it all to her liking. She knew there had been a time in her life when her path would have never crossed with these people, but she was glad changes had come.

"A bit weary?" McKinley asked when he found Jasmine resting in the parlor.

"One dance too many, I fear," she told him. "These Irish dances take more physical exertion than I had imagined."

He laughed. "I tried one of the jigs, but I don't believe my feet will move that quickly. I think unless you've grown up performing those dances, you'll not learn as an adult."

She unfolded her silk fan and began to stir the air as she flipped it back and forth in rapid motion. "I must admit I had fun trying. Where is Violet?"

"She went upstairs to check on the children. She'd rather be in the nursery than dancing." He nodded toward her hand. "I was thinking that your fan reminds me of Toby and how he used to swing that big feather fan over the dining room table at The Willows."

"That seems a lifetime ago, doesn't it?"

"Yes, so it does. Strange how some things seem to have happened only yesterday while at the same time so far in the past."

A faint smile curved her lips as she nodded. "And speaking of Toby, what do you hear from Rupert? It seems he's done nothing but make excuses. Do you believe he intends to keep his word?"

"He continues to change the date when he's going to send the slaves, but I remain optimistic. His last missive stated there were another five that he had located and he was in the process of making proper arrangements. It seems that each time we agree upon a date, he locates another slave or two. I want to believe the delay is because he's taking pains to locate as many as possible rather than merely prolonging the entire process."

"I truly do not trust him," Jasmine expressed.

"I know he doesn't share our beliefs, but I want to give him the benefit of the doubt and believe he's doing the proper thing. He's agreed they should arrive before year's end."

"Year's end? That's two months away. Surely he can do better. Perhaps if I telegraphed him and—"

"Jasmine! You agreed I would handle the negotiations without interference. Rather than helping matters, a telegram from you could possibly ruin the progress I've made."

She folded her fan and placed it on the side table with a purposeful thwack. "I grow weary of tiptoeing around Rupert and his detestable behavior. However, I will keep my word. Has he mentioned Toby? You tell him that I expect to see Toby leading the group when they arrive!"

"Your demanding tone is exactly why I don't want you dealing with Rupert. But in answer to your question, I asked for the names of those currently in his possession, and Toby is listed among the group. Now, enough of this talk. The musicians are finally playing something I can actually dance to, so let's not miss the opportunity," he said as he offered his sister his hand.

Waving a telegram, Nolan strode into the parlor. "Telegram from your cousin Levi," he said, handing the message to his wife.

Jasmine looked up from her sewing. "This is quite unexpected; I hope he hasn't taken ill. But perhaps he's planning a visit. Wouldn't it be wonderful if he'd come to Lowell and spend the Christmas season with us? In my last letter, I asked him to consider the possibility. Perhaps he's decided to accept my offer," she eagerly speculated.

"Perhaps you should read it and find out," Nolan said with a grin.

She waved the telegram back and forth. "Part of the enjoyment is guessing what's in a letter or package—or, in this case, a telegram." With an air of anticipation, she placed the telegram on the table beside her.

Nolan shook his head and then turned to leave the room.

"Wait! Where are you going?"

"Please feel free to enjoy this period of expectation. However, I have work that needs my attention. I'll look forward to hearing what Levi has to say at supper this evening."

"Oh, all right, I'll open it! I wasn't going to wait but a few minutes, anyway," she admitted.

Nolan sat down beside her as she ripped open the telegram and began to read.

Her eyes narrowed, and the color drained from her already pale complexion. "He's done it again!" she seethed. "He's a lying, despicable excuse of a man."

"Cousin Levi?"

Her husband's shocked appearance nearly made her laugh—nearly. In fact, under normal circumstances, Nolan's reaction would have caused her to burst into laughter. But not now—when she knew Rupert was again attempting to deceive them.

"It's Rupert! Levi discovered Rupert has devised a convoluted plan to actually send our former slaves but then have them recaptured by men posing as bounty hunters. Likely the same group that placed them in shackles when they burned The Willows! He'll not get away with this—I'll see *him* in shackles first!"

"Becoming overwrought will serve no purpose, Jasmine.

The first thing we must do is go to McKinley and learn whether Rupert has sent him any details about when we may expect the arrival of our former slaves. If so, we can then begin to devise our own plan."

"I'll fetch my coat and hat," she said.

"I didn't mean we need to go this very minute."

"But of *course* we must. We don't know when Levi received this information. By now, Rupert may have departed with the slaves."

"As you wish. It's true they may be on their way as we speak."

When Jasmine settled into the buggy beside Nolan, she hoped she'd not be forced to argue with her brother about the necessity of taking immediate action. She would no longer listen to McKinley's concerns—she cared not at all if her interference offended Rupert. If their former slaves were going to reach freedom, McKinley could no longer believe Rupert Hesston.

"Shall I go directly to his office, or do you think we should go by the house first?" Nolan inquired as they approached town.

"I don't think he would be home at this time of day. In any event, I'd rather speak with him at his office. Poor Violet becomes overly upset whenever she thinks there are difficulties on the horizon. While she attended the antislavery meetings and was marginally involved in the movement, she never was completely devoted to the cause. And though I've long ago forgiven her, I've not forgotten her behavior when I proposed to rear Moses. You'll recall she drove a wedge between McKinley and me with her failure to support my position."

"Then we'll hope that he is here," Nolan said as he assisted her down from the buggy. "In fact, there he is coming out of the counting house." He waved to his brother-in-law.

McKinley hastened toward them, bowing his head against the cold north wind. He rubbed his hands together as he grew closer. "To what do I owe this visit?" he asked in a tentative voice.

"Not good news, I fear," Jasmine replied. "We must speak privately. May we go to your office?"

"Of course," he said, leading the way. "Nothing wrong at the farm, I hope?"

"No, it concerns the transfer of the slaves," she said. They entered the building and walked directly to McKinley's office.

"I thought you had agreed to remain detached from the negotiations," he said while removing his coat.

"This is not of her doing, McKinley. Jasmine has received a disturbing telegram from Cousin Levi," Nolan defended.

"More than disturbing," Jasmine interjected. "Rupert is planning to have the slaves recaptured. Have you received any word about arrangements for delivery of the slaves?"

"One moment, Jasmine. You say he's made plans, and I assume you've received this information from Levi."

"Yes, of course. Rupert has hired men to disguise themselves as bounty hunters," she explained.

McKinley looked at her as though she'd taken leave of her senses. "This sounds a bit preposterous. Why would he go to such elaborate measures?"

Jasmine crossed her arms and leaned forward to look directly into her brother's eyes. "*Because he is a cunning man.* Unless he makes a genuine attempt to deliver the slaves—an attempt that can be substantiated by disinterested individuals, he knows we won't believe him. At least he knows *I* won't believe him. If he can prove he's traveled a portion of the way north—with the slaves in tow—he will maintain he's upheld his part of the bargain and insist you uphold your bargain to sell The Willows for the reduced price."

"I believe she's correct, McKinley, and we truly must have more details regarding the transfer. Has Rupert forwarded additional details to you?"

"Yes. I had planned to surprise you by having them arrive shortly before Christmas—as a special gift to you. Obviously, that isn't going to be possible now. Rupert sent me a missive outlining their travel plans, though there's no way of determining if he was truthful."

"Where were you to take possession?" Jasmine asked.

McKinley pulled the letter from his desk drawer and handed it to his sister. "He agreed to bring them up the Mississippi on a riverboat. They'll disembark at St. Louis and travel by foot the short distance to Alton, Illinois. I want the exchange to take place in a free state. And I know he's made the arrangements. I received verification only yesterday of their paid passage from the riverboat company. I doubt even Rupert would expend such a large sum if he didn't intend to bring them."

Jasmine nodded. "He also knows you will expect corroboration from those who would see them traveling that particular route, so he'll surely choose someplace that is heavily populated. Obviously, he won't wait until he crosses the border into Illinois, for he'll want his reprehensible deed to occur in a slave state. However, I fear it's a guessing game as to exactly where he's decided upon."

McKinley rubbed his forehead and glanced toward Nolan. "Any suggestions?"

"I believe we should telegraph Levi and request his assistance. He may be able to discover more details that will aid us." Nolan shifted to the edge of his chair. "I'll specifically ask if he can learn the location where Rupert plans to have this spurious attack take place. If they haven't yet departed

Mississippi, we may still have a little time to develop a strategy."

"Very little," McKinley commented.

"Jasmine and I will go directly to the telegraph office. Why don't you come out to the farm tomorrow and we'll talk further. In the meantime, we can all attempt to formulate some plan of attack."

McKinley agreed and escorted them to the street. "I'm sorry. I shouldn't have been so trusting," he apologized as Jasmine stepped up into the buggy. "I suppose everything you told me about him was true."

"There is no need for an apology," Jasmine said. "Had he been dealing with me, he would have done the same thing."

"Yet you would have questioned him and been more cautious."

"It matters little what I would have done. At this juncture, our energies need to be directed toward dismantling his plans." Jasmine leaned from the buggy and kissed her brother's cheek. "Don't be so hard on yourself, McKinley. If we remain steadfast in our prayers, I'm going to trust that God will see us through to victory. After all, He has overcome circumstances much greater than these."

"I suppose you're right," he said tentatively. "If God could deliver the Hebrew children from the pharaoh, He can certainly deliver our former slaves from Rupert Hesston."

Jasmine turned slowly while Prissy marked the edge of her ocean blue merino dress. "Dis black velvet is gonna look mighty fine along da hemline. I should have it done afore Christmas. You can wear it for Christmas Eve church services."

"I believe I'd enjoy that very much," Jasmine said as she turned a few more inches.

"Jes' can't believe Massa Nolan having to leave on business at dis time of year. He shoulda sent Paddy or one of them other men what works for him. The chillens gonna be disappointed if he don' make it home afore Christmas."

"I'm trusting that he'll return soon. If not, we'll celebrate upon his return. The children and I can still attend services at the church. Christ's birth is what we're celebrating, after all, and Nolan knows we'll be thinking of him no matter where he might be."

"I sho' know how that be. I spend lots of my time still thinking 'bout Toby. Sometimes I wonder if he still thinks about me."

"I'm confident he does. And I believe the two of you will be together again," she said as she patted Prissy's shoulder. How she longed to tell Prissy of Nolan's whereabouts. But if he should meet with failure and return home without Toby, Prissy would be devastated. Better to remain silent and pray for the safe return of Toby and the rest of the slaves.

"I done give up on that idea a long time ago," Prissy said dryly.

"Mama! Mama! Come quick!" Spencer yelled as he tore through the house. "Papa's arrived and there's lots of people with him!"

Jasmine grabbed Prissy's hand. "Come on! Let's go see."

Prissy yanked on Jasmine's hand. "You cain't go outside in dat dress. I ain't finished taking up the seams an' marking the hem."

"This is more important, Prissy. Come along and don't worry over the dress."

Jasmine pulled Prissy along, hope filling her heart, as they followed Spencer out onto the porch. An irresistible joy besieged Jasmine as she gazed into the sea of dark faces. Men with their feet wrapped in rags to help ward off the cold walked alongside the wagon; others followed behind and formed a snaking procession that continued to inch its way toward the house. The women and children were piled in the wagon behind Nolan, most of them wearing the coats she'd forced Nolan and McKinley to take with them. They were a cold and bedraggled appearing lot, yet even from the porch she could see the hope that shown in their eyes.

Jasmine spotted Toby sitting directly beside Nolan atop the wagon seat as the wagon moved slowly down the driveway. She grasped Prissy by the shoulders and pulled her forward. "Look, Prissy! Look who's in that wagon!"

Prissy's face registered disbelief as Toby waved and called out her name. She looked at Jasmine and then back at Toby. "Am I dreaming, Miz Jasmine?"

"No, Prissy. Your husband has finally come home. Go and greet him," she said as Nolan pulled back on the reins and the wagon came to a stop in front of the porch.

The young couple ran toward each other with sheer abandon and united in a warm embrace. The onlookers all began to applaud as Toby leaned down to kiss his wife.

"Where's your coat? You're going to catch your death of cold," Nolan said as he hurried up the steps and pulled Jasmine close, rubbing her arms.

"How could I possibly be cold with such a sight before me?" she asked, her face aglow.

"And with your husband to keep you warm," he said, pulling her close and kissing her soundly. "It is so good to be home!"

"And it is so good to have you back again. I can see you were victorious is reclaiming freedom for the slaves, but I must admit I'm anxious to hear all of what occurred during your journey."

"McKinley is following with another wagonload of folks. Let's wait until he arrives, and then I'll give you all the details. But first you go back in the house while I fetch

Simon and Paddy. They have the list of families who agreed to provide temporary homes when we arrived."

Prissy turned to Jasmine. "Did everyone know 'bout this 'cept me?"

"There may have been a few others. Please don't be angry with me. We didn't know if our plans would succeed, and I didn't want you to be disappointed if Toby wasn't rescued."

A lopsided grin curved Prissy's lips. "You done the right thing," she said and gave her husband another squeeze. "You best get out of that dress, Miz Jasmine, 'cause I don' think I'm gonna be doing any more alterations this evening. I's gonna be introducing Toby to our little Emily and showing him his new house."

"I believe the dress can wait as long as necessary!" she assured her.

Nolan leaned down and placed a kiss on Jasmine's cheek. "Go inside. I'll soon be back and give you my full report. It is better than even *you* could have hoped for."

———

Jasmine fidgeted with the fine lace that edged her handkerchief as she awaited Nolan and McKinley's arrival. Eager to hear Nolan's report, Jasmine patted the settee cushion the moment the two men entered the room.

"Do sit down and tell me everything," she said, giving the men her complete attention.

Nolan rubbed his hands together. "The entire process could not have gone any better. We could truly feel your prayers throughout the journey, and we knew God was in control. How else could we possibly have found lawmen in a pro-slavery state willing to assist us?"

McKinley nodded and laughed. "In fact, when Nolan

and I located those lawmen, we told them they were an answer to prayer."

"I *told* you that prayer was the solution!" Jasmine exclaimed.

"Of course we had no choice but to rely on Levi's information that the subterfuge would occur in St. Louis," Nolan said. "Upon our arrival, I found a lawman who, after listening to our story and reviewing the ledger listing the names of our freed slaves, agreed to help us. He recruited a number of men, and we stationed ourselves on the wharf and then waited for the boat to dock."

"I truly believed Levi was incorrect about St. Louis," Jasmine said. "In fact, I'm still surprised Rupert decided the incursion should occur in such a busy place. I thought he would choose some outlying town along the river."

"I think he worried something might go amiss in a small town," McKinley said. "Perhaps he feared passersby might overhear or actually see what was occurring or possibly even believe the slaves if they spoke out. However, the docks in St. Louis are teeming with people and activity. He brought the slaves off the boat in shackles in order to contain them for his men and also give the appearance that he was delivering slaves. Fortunately for us, he had only three men appear to claim the slaves. You should have seen his face when he spotted us."

"Did he attempt to fabricate a lie in order to cover up his deeds?" she asked as she moved to the edge of her seat.

Nolan nodded. "He said he knew the men, but he had no idea they had plans to capture the slaves. However, his story soon crumbled. The other men were unwilling to take the blame for the part Rupert played in the scheme. We showed our proof that the slaves were ours, and because of Rupert's deception, it was decided that the entire arrangement was null and void."

"What does that mean?" Jasmine questioned.

"It means that Rupert gets nothing," her husband replied. "He's lucky he wasn't arrested. Had we been willing to press charges, it could have gone very bad for him. But he denied everything right up until we left for home. In fact, he was still blaming the others."

"You mean he actually denied knowledge of his own nefarious plot and pointed a finger at his fellow cohorts in crime?" Jasmine asked indignantly.

"Absolutely!" McKinley said. "I fear I completely misjudged Rupert and his intentions from the very beginning."

"Did you not bring any charges against the men?" she inquired.

"No. I didn't want to remain and attempt to bring legal action against them," McKinley explained, "and the sheriff said since they had not yet committed a crime, it would be a difficult battle—especially in Missouri. The court would not look favorably upon our claim."

Jasmine smiled at her husband. "It's better this way. The men he so quickly accused will likely spread word of his cowardly actions throughout the region. His neighbors will have little use for a man who is unwilling to take the blame for his own deeds. I have little doubt that Rupert will be treated with disdain."

"As well he should be," McKinley said. "How can I possibly thank the two of you for all you have done—for the slaves and for me? I pray that one day I'll be able to repay you."

"I think that may soon be possible," Nolan replied with a quirk of his eyebrow.

McKinley's gaze was filled with puzzlement. "How so?"

"The Willows still belongs to you and Jasmine. And Cousin Levi's telegram stated he knows someone who may be interested in purchasing the land. He said he would send the information to the land agent, depending upon the final outcome in St. Louis."

McKinley shook his head back and forth, his eyes growing moist. "This is wonderful news."

"You see? God has blessed us beyond our highest expectations. His grace makes it difficult to question the abiding love He has for each of his children, don't you agree?"

"I do agree," McKinley said. "However, during difficult times, I fear I, too, quickly forget God's faithfulness."

Jasmine moved close and embraced her brother. "Then in the future, I shall take full responsibility for reminding you."

CHAPTER · 24

December 25, 1858

JASMINE LOOKED out the bedroom window and smiled. Nolan had predicted the children would enjoy a sleigh ride on Christmas morning, and now a heavy blanket of snow covered the ground. She squinted against the blinding intensity of the sun's rays as they reflected off the pristine layer of white.

"Did you see? Did you see?" Alice Ann squealed delightedly as she ran into her parents' bedroom. She dove onto the bed and landed on her father with a vigor that caused him to groan. "It's snowing, Poppa, just like you promised. How soon can we go on our sleigh ride?"

He struggled to a sitting position as he lifted Alice Ann off of his chest. "Not until after breakfast, remember? I believe I hear Henrietta calling your name. You had best hurry to your room and get dressed."

The child slipped off the bed and gave Jasmine a fleeting hug before scurrying out of the room and down the hall.

"Oh, for a portion of that youthful energy first thing in the morning," Nolan said as he grinned at his wife. "Did we have a good snow?" He threw back the covers and stretched.

"More than I want to see," she replied with a shiver.

He laughed. "*Any* snow is more than you want to see, my dear, but it doesn't seem like Christmas unless there's at least a smattering."

"This is much more than a smattering." She peered out the window again. "I hope it won't ruin our Christmas celebration. I'll be disappointed if McKinley's family is unable to join us."

Nolan walked to the window and looked for himself. "From the way you talked, I thought we'd had a blizzard." He rubbed his hands together. "This is perfect. Your party will go on as planned, my dear. McKinley will have no difficulty maneuvering a sleigh through these few inches of snow."

Jasmine took up her brush and began to style her hair in front of the mirror. "The party is not as important as having our family together. There are so few of us that it suddenly seems almost critical to me. I suppose it's the reality of losing so many family members in such a short period of time. I had always taken family for granted, but now I realize how precious those ties become as we grow older."

"In some respects, Rupert did you and McKinley a service," Nolan commented.

Jasmine swung around to face her husband. "Rupert? How is that?"

"You and McKinley have drawn much closer to one another. I don't know if that would have occurred without the problems the two of you faced and resolved during this past year."

Jasmine nodded thoughtfully. "I suppose I hadn't thought of it in such a manner, but you're correct. And I'm certain such a thought would cause Rupert severe displeasure."

He laughed. "Indeed! Cousin Levi's last missive is testimony to that fact. Rupert continues to blame everyone but himself for his current situation. I presume he isn't enjoying his life as an outcast from Southern society. It seems a man so incapable of keeping his word is much scorned." He pulled his shirt on and started securing the buttons. "As I understand it, many promises were made by Rupert to his neighbors, and when those promises proved false, well, most folks wanted nothing to do with him."

"In time his friends will forget his misdeeds, but for now he is reminded daily of his despicable behavior. To my own astonishment, I've begun to pray for him—and Lydia also," Jasmine said. "Lydia is surely suffering along with her husband, and it's hardly her fault that Rupert's deception and conniving have put them in this fix."

"I'm proud of you. I shall attempt to follow your example, for there's little else that will cause a change in Rupert." He pulled on his trousers and tucked his shirt in.

"I'm also praying for the strength to forgive him, but I've not yet reached that lofty goal. Sadly, I don't think Rupert feels a need for change, but perhaps in time he will come to that realization. And, perhaps in time, I will be able to forgive him for the wrongs he committed against so many," she said, her voice trailing off as she stared into the mirror.

Nolan stepped behind his wife and wrapped her in a warm embrace. "This has been a monumental year. . . . Much sadness, yet much happiness also," he said, gazing at their reflections.

She smiled warmly at her husband. "Yes, *much* happiness. For we have been able to share in giving a wondrous gift to many—the gift of freedom."

THE DOOR HAD BEEN closed on the past, but opening it was the ONLY WAY FORWARD...

TRACIE PETERSON

What she left for me

A NOVEL

God's forgiveness and true healing are at the heart of this moving family saga. When Jana returns home from a mission trip to find her husband and bank account gone, she reluctantly turns to her mother, Eleanor. But Jana's presence is a daily reminder of her mother's secrets from the past. Eleanor is haunted by the pain and guilt of the memories she keeps hidden away. Can an eccentric aunt bring together these women and remind them they have a future filled with love?

What She Left for Me by
Tracie Peterson

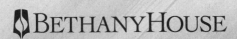

BETHANYHOUSE

FREEDOM'S PATH

Stories of *Courage, Faith & Love* on the Kansas Plains

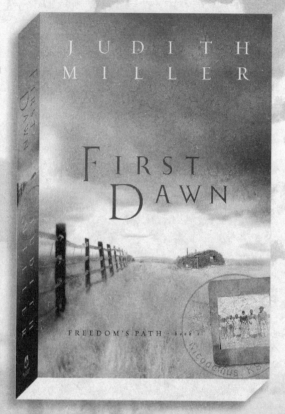

JUDITH MILLER

FIRST DAWN

FREEDOM'S PATH · book 1

*L*ured by the promise of true freedom and a new town to call their own, sharecroppers Ezekiel Harban and his three daughters leave behind remnants of slavery in the war-torn South and set off with a wagon train for Nicodemus, Kansas. Their hopes are crushed when they find nothing but open prairie where the town should be. Dr. Boyle, a newly arrived doctor in neighboring Hill City, is called to deliver a baby in Nicodemus. When the lives of these two families intersect, neither town will ever be the same.

First Dawn by Judith Miller
FREEDOM'S PATH • book 1

◆ BETHANYHOUSE

A LOVE
WOVEN TRUE

Books by Tracie Peterson

www.traciepeterson.com

The Long-Awaited Child • Silent Star
A Slender Thread • Tidings of Peace
What She Left for Me

BELLS OF LOWELL*
Daughter of the Loom • A Fragile Design
These Tangled Threads

LIGHTS OF LOWELL*
A Tapestry of Hope • A Love Woven True
The Pattern of Her Heart

DESERT ROSES
Shadows of the Canyon • Across the Years
Beneath a Harvest Sky

HEIRS OF MONTANA
Land of My Heart • The Coming Storm
To Dream Anew • The Hope Within

WESTWARD CHRONICLES
A Shelter of Hope • Hidden in a Whisper
A Veiled Reflection

RIBBONS OF STEEL†
Distant Dreams • A Promise for Tomorrow

RIBBONS WEST†
Westward the Dream • Ties That Bind

SHANNON SAGA‡
City of Angels • Angels Flight • Angel of Mercy

YUKON QUEST
Treasures of the North • Ashes and Ice
Rivers of Gold

Books by Judith Miller
www.judithmccoymiller.com

FREEDOM'S PATH
First Dawn

*with Judith Miller   †with Judith Pella   ‡with James Scott Bell

05C

TRACIE PETERSON
AND
JUDITH MILLER

A LOVE
WOVEN TRUE

BETHANYHOUSE
PUBLISHERS
MINNEAPOLIS, MINNESOTA

Published by Bethany House Publishers
11400 Hampshire Avenue South
Bloomington, Minnesota 55438

Bethany House Publishers is a division of
Baker Publishing Group, Grand Rapids, Michigan.

Printed in the United States of America

ISBN 0-7642-2895-1 (Trade paper)
ISBN 0-7642-0010-0 (Large Print)

Library of Congress Cataloging-in-Publication Data

Peterson, Tracie.
    A love woven true / by Tracie Peterson and Judith Miller.
        p.   cm. — (Lights of Lowell ; bk. 2)
      ISBN 0-7642-2895-1 (pbk.) — ISBN 0-7642-0010-0 (large-print paperback)
      1. Conflict of generations—Fiction. 2. Fathers and daughters—Fiction.
3. Women landowners—Fiction. 4. Textile industry—Fiction. 5. Lowell (Mass.)—
Fiction. 6. Abduction—Fiction. 7. Freedmen—Fiction. 8. Widows—Fiction.
I. Miller, Judith. II. Title. III. Series.
    PS3566.E7717L688   2005
    813'.54—dc22   2004020014

To Gerry Perry
a woman I greatly admire

TRACIE PETERSON is a popular speaker and bestselling author who has written over sixty books, both historical and contemporary fiction. Tracie and her family make their home in Montana.

Visit Tracie's Web site at: *www.traciepeterson.com*.

JUDITH MILLER is an award-winning author whose avid research and love for history are reflected in her novels, many of which have appeared on the CBA bestseller lists. Judy and her husband make their home in Topeka, Kansas.

Visit Judy's Web site at: *www.judithmccoymiller.com*.

C H A P T E R · 1

October 1849, Lowell, Massachusetts

JASMINE HOUSTON trembled uncontrollably. Surely her brother-in-law was mistaken!

"I'm to return home to The Willows immediately? Please," she said, extending her shaking hand in Nolan's direction. Her voice sounded strangely foreign to her own ears, and she cleared her throat before attempting to once again speak. "Permit me to read the missive for myself." The high-pitched quiver remained in her voice, ruining any hope of appearing unruffled by Nolan's news.

Nolan's brow furrowed into deep creases. "I'm sorry. In my haste to arrive, I failed to bring the letter with me."

She lowered herself onto the ivory brocade settee and met her brother-in-law's concerned gaze. "Does my father say why he penned the missive to you instead of corresponding directly with me? And why did Samuel say nothing of our mother's failing health when he was in Massachusetts? Surely if Mother's health hung in the balance, Samuel would have sent word." Giving Nolan a feeble smile before continuing, she said, "Perhaps Mother is merely languishing since suffering with yellow fever this summer. What with her bouts of melancholy, she tends to be somewhat slow in healing from any illness. I suspect Father is hoping a visit from little Spencer and me will cause her to rally."

"It certainly could do no harm."

Jasmine gave an emphatic nod. "It will take time to make preparations for the journey. Traveling with a child of nearly two is not quite as simple as one might think. And, of course, I'll need to make inquiry concerning when a vessel will be sailing. Also, I must see to Grandmother Wainwright. She's been ailing this past week." She hesitated for a moment. "And you say Mammy isn't well either?" Her thoughts were jumbled, and she now realized her words had poured forth in a mishmash of confusion.

"That's what your father indicated in his letter," Nolan softly replied.

"I must admit I am exceedingly surprised to hear that piece of news. The fact that Mammy would remain in a weakened condition after her supposed recovery several months ago is disconcerting. She's always been strong and healthy. Perhaps Father was overstating matters in order to ensure my return to The Willows for a visit."

"There is always that possibility. And your grandmother? What ails her? I thought she might give consideration to making the journey as well."

Jasmine began pacing, quickly covering the length of the parlor and returning several times. "The doctor fears she may have pneumonia. Grandmother says it's merely an attack of ague and will soon pass. However, she does have a troublesome cough, and I doubt whether she's strong enough to travel. Then again, she's a stubborn woman. Who knows what she may decide. But unless she makes a quick recovery, I believe she should remain in Lowell."

"You're likely correct on that account. The journey from Massachusetts to Mississippi could prove harrowing for her. Hearing of her condition only serves to confirm the decision I made upon receiving your father's letter," Nolan said.

Jasmine glanced over her shoulder as she continued crisscrossing the room. "And what decision would that be?"

"I plan to accompany you and Spencer to The Willows."

Her pacing came to an abrupt halt at the far end of the room.

Turning toward him, Jasmine flushed at the overwhelming sense of warmth she felt for Nolan. His obvious concern touched her. "I can't ask you to do such a thing, Nolan. The commitment of time required to make the journey is unreasonable to ask of anyone—other than a family member, of course."

His gaze fell. "Am I not family?" His question was barely audible.

"Oh, what have I said? Of *course* you're family. My comment was directed toward Father's request that Spencer and I make the journey." Taking several quick steps, she came to a halt in front of him before meeting his questioning gaze. "Surely you realize that Spencer and I couldn't have survived since Bradley's death without you. Spencer has come to look upon you as his very favorite visitor. In fact, he often demonstrates his displeasure over the fact that you live in Concord rather than Lowell. He would, of course, prefer more frequent visits."

Nolan gave a slight nod, but his lips remained fixed in a taut, thin line. She feared he was weighing her response much too critically, so she hastened to explain further. "I find the fact that you would be away from Massachusetts for such a long period of time to be a matter of grave concern. I can't expect you to make yourself available every time difficulty arises in my life."

His gaze softened. "Of course you can. That is *exactly* what I want. You and Spencer are my only remaining family. How could I ever consider any request from you a burden? Besides, you *didn't* ask me—I offered to accompany you. As for my work, you may recall I can write as easily at the plantation as I can in Concord— or anyplace else, for that matter."

"Yes. In fact I remember quite well." A faint smile crossed her lips as she recollected the antislavery articles Nolan had penned after his first visit to The Willows. Words that had stirred the hearts of abolitionists and also drawn the fiery criticism of the pro-slavery movement. Words that had set Nolan at odds with his brother, Bradley, and provoked a seething anger from her father and other Wainwright men. And it had been Nolan's words that had convinced those same men their anger was misplaced. With carefully chosen words, he had cajoled them into admitting they supported free speech and, in turn, his right to argue against their stance on the slavery issue. Finally they had decided to call a truce. With the distinct understanding, however, that such an agreement merely served as permission for all of them to disagree in a civil— and silent—manner over their personal feelings on the topic of slavery.

"I imagine you do," he said, returning her smile. "Incidentally, I hope you won't think me intrusive, but I did take the liberty of sending word to Mr. Sheppard at Houston and Sons that you will be sailing as soon as preparations have been completed for your journey. I have little doubt there will be a ship awaiting us when we arrive in Boston."

"I'm certain your foresight will prove helpful in expediting our voyage," she replied, giving him a pensive gaze. Jasmine knew they would be traveling after the first picking, and any slowdown in cotton shipments could prove costly. "Let us hope our journey won't interfere with the crop shipments. No doubt harvest will have begun in earnest by the time we arrive, but I wouldn't want my personal travel to be the cause of any delay."

"Your father requested your presence at The Willows. I'm certain he values your visit more highly than the cotton crop. Please don't fret over any possible delay with the ship's voyage to New Orleans."

"So long as it's Wainwright cotton, I suppose you're right. However, I doubt any of the other producers would be so forgiving should their shipments be hindered. Did you happen to inquire regarding their future schedules?"

"As a matter of fact, I met with Mr. Sheppard last week to examine the books of Houston and Sons, and he gave me what he hoped would be a final plan for the upcoming month. Our travel should coincide nicely. By the way, you'll be pleased to know that all is in order with the shipping company. It continues to turn a nice profit, and the investments you're setting aside for Spencer are accumulating handsomely. Of course, the cotton shipments between New Orleans and Boston provide our greatest profit."

"Thank you, Nolan. Since Bradley's death, I've never once worried about Houston and Sons Shipping Line. I know you've performed the necessary duties to keep everything operating smoothly. And I'm pleased you retained Mr. Sheppard. I think he feared losing his position when you assumed management of the business."

He chuckled. "We both know that would have been a disaster. I would be miserable attempting to operate any business on a daily basis. This arrangement has succeeded nicely for all of us. In fact, his work load has increased steadily as the business has grown. I'm amazed at the amount of cotton the company is now shipping. A mixed blessing, I suppose."

She nodded in agreement. "I understand what you're thinking. It's a complicated situation I find myself thrust into. With much of the cotton being grown on Wainwright plantations, I feel somewhat the hypocrite when I attend the antislavery meetings or when I state my opposition to the Southern bondage. Speaking of the Southern mindset, you still haven't told me why Father wrote his letter to *you*."

Nolan directed her back toward the settee and then patted her hand as though she were a fragile piece of china that might fracture at any moment. "I believe your father worried you would be overly distraught receiving news of the ongoing illnesses of both your mother and Mammy. He decided his concerns might be less worrisome if delivered personally—knowing someone would be with you when you actually heard the news. As for your questions regarding your brother Samuel, you must remember his schedule is continually filled with business meetings when he is in Lowell. Besides, with all of his traveling, I doubt he has been able to spend much time at The Willows during these past months."

Jasmine wrung a lace-edged handkerchief between her fingers and frowned at Nolan. In spite of October's chilly sting, she blotted the linen square to her cheeks and forehead. "It's terribly warm in here, don't you think?"

"As a matter of fact, I thought the room rather cool and drafty. I hope you aren't taking ill. Are you feeling faint?"

"Of course not! You're beginning to sound like Father, always thinking women will faint at the first sign of bad news," she replied while continuing to dab her face. "I'm perfectly fine. Now tell me more of what Father said in his letter." Before Nolan could answer, Jasmine's gaze shifted toward the stairway. "It sounds as though Spencer has awakened from his nap. If you'll excuse me," she said while tucking her handkerchief into the pocket of her apricot merino dress.

"Please," he said, immediately jumping to his feet, "let me go and fetch him. It's been nearly two weeks since my last visit. I'm anxious to see my nephew."

She resettled herself on the settee. "As you wish."

Nolan's pleasure was obvious as he bounded toward the stairway. "He's likely grown at least an inch during my absence," he ventured, his words floating into the parlor.

"I don't believe he's grown quite that quickly, but there's little doubt your presence will bring him great delight," she called back toward the hallway.

The sound of Nolan's footsteps grew fainter as he hastened up the stairs. Had Bradley ever hurried in such a fashion to see his own son? If he had, Jasmine could no longer remember. Of course, Spencer had been only an infant when Bradley died; her comparison was doubtless unfair. Yet that realization didn't quiet the longing that stirred deep within her. In only moments she would hear Spencer's unbridled cries of joy burst forth like a heralding trumpet. How she longed to have a father for her son— how she longed to have a loving husband's arms embrace her . . . and to lovingly embrace a husband in return.

Regrettably, she harbored only unhappy recollections of her marriage to Bradley. Oh, he'd professed to love her in the beginning, but even then she'd known their marriage was no more than a profitable liaison between the Wainwrights and himself. The true desires of Bradley's heart had been power and money. The Wainwright family had provided a viable connection to the cotton Bradley needed to procure for his success—and their marriage had sealed the much-needed link to secure his lucrative future. Unfortunately, their union had been a fraud from the beginning.

When Bradley met with his untimely demise, most who knew him felt either pity or revulsion for the life he'd led. As for Jasmine, she had experienced a little of each, but her focus had remained on Spencer. He was her joy: the light of her life, the pure pleasure God had given her. Spencer had burst forth from a dismal marriage like a single rose unfolding each petal and coming into full bloom after an unforgiving drought. His tiny life had given her more pleasure than she imagined possible, and had it not been for Spencer, Jasmine would likely have harkened to her father's plea and returned to live at The Willows.

Her nerves had been taut with anxiety. How could she suitably explain her decision to remain in Massachusetts without causing her family sorrow? After all, most people would view a young widow's return to the bosom of her family quite appropriate—would even expect it. In addition to being a youthful woman set apart by her widow's weeds, she was a misplaced Southerner living amongst Yankees, both facts that her father would quickly draw to her attention. She had carefully prepared, however, her words judiciously framed as she pointed to Grandmother Wainwright's increasing dependency upon her as she grew older and her health began to fail. She'd also explained that the rigors of making such a move would likely prove an overwhelming task so soon after Spencer's birth. However, the truth had been that Jasmine didn't want her son reared in a culture that perpetuated slavery. Making such a statement to her father would have breached their relationship—perhaps permanently, a risk she was unwilling to take. Although Jasmine fervently disagreed with her family's views on slavery, she would never intentionally damage her relationship with them. She disagreed with her family, but she loved them in spite of their beliefs.

And now the news in her father's letter. She stood and began to once again pace the length of the room. It was difficult to believe both her mother and Mammy suffered from illnesses to such a degree as to summon Jasmine to their bedsides. She wanted to believe her father was merely anxious to see Spencer and have the two of them come to The Willows for a lengthy visit. Yet Malcolm Wainwright was not a man to use such methods to draw his family home. He would have been straightforward in his request. A hollow feeling edged into her consciousness, then yielded to fingering tendrils of fear that slowly crept into her thoughts and began to take root.

"What if one of them should die before I arrive?" she murmured. Her fingers spread wide as she placed an open palm against her chest and dropped onto the brocade divan. Giving voice to her fears now caused her to face the possibility that one or both of the women she loved might be dead before she arrived home. "Oh, surely not! If I'm not careful, I'll soon become as histrionic as some of Grandmother Wainwright's acquaintances," she muttered.

"Mama!" Spencer screeched from the hallway. The boy pointed a chubby finger in Jasmine's direction before turning back to hug Nolan's neck in a tight bear hug.

Jasmine gazed up at the two of them, warmed by their obvious affection for each other—a devotion that was obvious to even the casual observer. So much so that Velma Buthorne had taken exception to Nolan's relationship with Spencer upon her first visit to Lowell, as well as on each of her two subsequent visits. It had been during her final visit six months ago that she had given Nolan an ultimatum—choose Spencer or choose her. He had quickly chosen Spencer, deciding that if Velma's security was threatened by a mere child, she was not a woman with whom he wanted to build a future. And now with the news of this imminent journey to Mississippi, Jasmine was exceedingly thankful she could accept Nolan's offer of assistance without worry of offending Velma.

Nolan sat down beside Jasmine and adjusted Spencer's wriggling body on his lap. "I shouldn't have left you alone for so long. You've obviously done nothing but fret since I went upstairs. There's not a drop of color in your cheeks. Shall we go outdoors and get a breath of fresh air?"

Nolan's suggestion elicited an immediate reaction from Spencer, who instantaneously attempted to wiggle off his uncle's lap.

"Out, out!" he cried, pointing toward the doors leading into the garden.

Spencer's enthusiasm brought a faint smile to Jasmine's lips. It was difficult for unhappiness to reign while young Spencer Houston was up and about. The child pulled at her fingers, tugging as though certain his efforts would bring his mother to her feet. "All right. We'll go outdoors, but first you'll need a coat." She grasped his plump hand in her own, and he toddled alongside while they fetched his jacket and cap.

Nolan remained at her other side, holding on to her elbow. She glanced toward him and said, "I promise I'm feeling better. You need not fear for my well-being. If you'll take Spencer's hand, I'll gather my cape."

"I will admit your color has returned, but I don't want to take any chances," he said, his features a strange fusion of apprehension and cheerfulness.

"I'm fine," she insisted, careful to speak in a firm and confident tone.

The three of them walked into the small flower garden that had recently been given over to Spencer as a play area. Jasmine no longer fretted over the trampled or picked flowers. The perennials would shoot up voluntarily again next year, and she'd be required to choose new annuals next spring anyway. In the end, Spencer would remain a toddler for only a short time, and if his wobbly feet carried him into the roses, mums, or azaleas, so be it. Truth be told, she enjoyed his occasional offering of a partially defrocked rose or daisy.

"You appeared deep in thought when I came downstairs," Nolan commented, though his gaze was still fixed upon Spencer as they sat down on one of the benches. "Were you worrying over your mother's condition?"

She followed his line of vision toward the tiny, robust child, who was examining a newly fallen leaf. "To be honest, I was thinking about Velma Buthorne—rather, I was feeling somewhat thankful that Velma is no longer a part of your life. I was selfishly grateful." She leaned down and picked a handful of golden mums that bordered the walkway.

"Were you?" he asked. His tone was almost playful. "And why is that?"

She met his gaze and then quickly looked back across the garden. "Because Velma would have objected to your offer to accompany us on the trip."

"Hmm. Only a short time ago, you told me you didn't want to impose upon me, and now you're pleased I'm making the journey?"

"I was merely being polite when I said I didn't want to impose," she said, giving him a sheepish grin. "There is no doubt that having your assistance will prove invaluable, and I know Spencer will find the journey much more to his liking with you along."

"It's my desire that my presence will make the journey more pleasant for *both* of you. And since we're discussing the voyage, have you come to any decision regarding when we might sail?"

"I can be ready by week's end. I hope that will give you sufficient time for your return to Boston to make preparations—if you still intend to accompany us," she hastened to add.

A sheepish grin tugged at his lips. "I made my preparations before leaving Boston. I had Paddy take my trunk out to the barn when I arrived."

His words brought back the reality of the situation. Surely Nolan must believe the circumstances ominous if he had already prepared to make the journey. Her thoughts were in a state of unrest—one minute calm and collected, the next fearful and apprehensive—uncertain what to expect when she arrived at The Willows. "I see. Well, then, I suppose I had best begin packing. With Kiara to assist me, I think everything should be in readiness by the day after tomorrow."

"Why don't you go inform Kiara of the news and I'll remain out here with Spencer? I'm certain he'll be happier playing outdoors."

"And likely will sleep better tonight," she replied. "Thank you."

Nolan reached into his jacket and pulled Malcolm's letter from the inner breast pocket while he watched Spencer tug at a small purple bloom. The child appeared to be completely engrossed with the blossom, unaware of the activity that swirled about him. Nolan held the envelope between his thumb and index finger, his guilt beginning to take root as he stared at the missive. It went against his nature to tell untruths. In fact, all his life he'd prided himself upon his truthful nature.

"It was a kindness to withhold the truth," he muttered. Revealing the full contents of her father's letter would have been nothing less than cruel. After all, Malcolm had written to him instead of Jasmine in order to protect her from the truth—at least until her arrival at The Willows. And Nolan didn't intend to second-guess Malcolm Wainwright's decision. He unfolded the missive and reread the carefully scripted second paragraph.

> *I fear my wife's condition hangs in the balance. The doctor has not given me hope that she will live much longer. However, knowing that Madelaine's life is in God's hands, I believe the possibility exists she may rally. Therefore, please do not convey the gravity of her mother's illness to Jasmine. It is useless for Jasmine to spend the entire voyage fretting over her mother's condition. Try to assure her that although I've summoned her home, she should remain calm. Being unduly distraught over Madelaine's condition will serve no useful purpose.*

Nolan believed Mr. Wainwright's position was the correct one. However, his confidence waned as he considered how Jasmine might react once confronted with her mother's condition or possible death. Perhaps his thoughts were selfish, but he didn't want to be the object of Jasmine's anger when she discovered he'd withheld information from her. Yet he felt an obligation to honor Malcolm Wainwright's request. For now he would say nothing further and continue to pray for Madelaine Wainwright's recovery.

Spencer struggled to remain upright as he wobbled across the uneven terrain of the small garden. A winsome smile tugged at his bow-shaped mouth. Reaching Nolan's side, he extended his chubby hand to offer a large fall mum, now minus its leaves and the majority of its purple petals. "Well, thank you very much," Nolan said while taking the fading bloom from the child's hand. "Why don't we take your flower into the house and see if we can revive it with a vase of water."

"Wa-der," Spencer said in a childish attempt to mimic his uncle.

"Yes, water. I fear you may be seeing more water than you'd like in the next several weeks. But we won't worry about that for the time being. For now, we'll get your flower a drink."

CHAPTER · 2

JASMINE EXTENDED her gloved hand. "Thank you for your assistance throughout our voyage, Captain Harmon. I know having us aboard has caused delays in your schedule that will require you and your men to make a return trip in record time. My prayers will be with you for steady winds and clear skies."

The bewhiskered captain appeared embarrassed by her gratitude but quickly recovered. "It's been an honor having you sail aboard the *Mary Benjamin* once again, ma'am. And it appears we've made a sailor out of young Spencer too," he said, tousling the boy's thatch of soft brown curls. "I hope you find your mother's health much improved, and I look forward to returning all of you to Boston whenever you're prepared to depart. I've had one of my men take your trunks to be loaded on the *River Queen*. Once you reach Rodney, the smithy should have a carriage available to take you to the plantation."

Hoisting Spencer into his left arm, Nolan extended his right hand to the captain. "Thank you, Captain Harmon. I'll send word once we've finalized the plans for our return."

Spencer soon grew restless aboard the *River Queen*, entirely weary of being restrained. "Only a little longer," Jasmine promised as the boat finally neared the dock.

"We're going to ride in a carriage for a little while and then we'll see your grandpa," Nolan added.

"Horthie," the boy excitedly yelped.

Jasmine smiled at Nolan. "At this point, even a carriage ride sounds appealing to him," she said with a laugh.

They disembarked the moment the captain gave his permission, Spencer more wobbly than usual when he finally was able to walk about on dry land. He giggled as he tottered around, attempting to remain upright.

"He looks like he's imbibed a bit too much," Nolan said with a hearty laugh. "I'll check on the carriage, and by that time they should have our trunks unloaded and we can be on our way."

When the carriage finally arrived at the plantation, Jasmine was exhausted and frightened at what news might greet her. She scanned the front of the mansion, praying there would be no black shrouds draping the expansive front porch or gallery.

She gazed at Nolan and nodded toward the house. "Either they've elected to await our arrival before shrouding the entries or death has not descended upon the household."

Nolan's eyes widened. "You expected your mother to be dead before we arrived?"

"The thought certainly entered my mind. I wondered if perhaps you and Father were attempting to protect me until my arrival. Forgive me for misjudging you."

"Of course that possibility could exist," he ventured. "It's been nearly two months since your father wrote his letter."

She adjusted her bonnet, her brow furrowing ever so slightly. "Then you *did* anticipate Mother's death?"

Nolan nervously brushed at some unseen spot on his pant leg. "With lingering illness, death is always a possibility, isn't it? However, I was praying all would be well and that both your mother and Mammy would be much better by the time we arrived."

The carriage came to a halt in the circular driveway fronting the Wainwrights' balconied Greek Revival mansion. And although Jasmine couldn't be certain, she thought Nolan emitted a loud sigh of relief as he jumped down from the carriage. She assumed he was pleased to have their discussion come to an end. Before she could say anything further, he held out his arms for Spencer and then assisted her down.

"Look who's arrived!" her brother David bellowed as he hurried out the front door and down the steps. Her father and her younger brother, McKinley, followed close behind.

"Jasmine! How good it is to see you," her father greeted. He pulled her into an embrace, then turned his attention toward Spencer. "And how this young man has grown. He looks much like McKinley did as a child, don't you think?"

"Yes, of course. How is Mother? May I go up and see her?"

Malcolm's smile faded and his mood abruptly turned somber. "Of course you may see her, but don't expect much response. She's not spoken for days now, and although I don't claim to be a physician, she appears to shift in and out of consciousness," he said, but quickly added, "but perhaps she's merely sleeping."

"Perhaps seeing Spencer would help," Jasmine suggested.

"Why don't we wait until you've had some time alone with your mother. We can take Spencer up after he's had an opportunity to eat and play for a short time."

"I'll be happy to attend to him—unless you'd like me to accompany you upstairs," Nolan offered.

"Spencer will likely be more content if you remain with him," she said before turning her attention back toward her father. "And Mammy? How is she faring?"

"She remains the same. I told her you'd be arriving, and she's anxious to see both you and Spencer. The doctor assures me there's no possibility of contracting illness from either your mother or Mammy."

"I'll visit her once I've seen Mother," Jasmine said, quickly moving up the front steps of the house, then stopping and turning toward her brothers. "There's plenty of baggage to be unloaded if the two of you would be so kind."

"Of course," McKinley said. "You go on now."

"She's lived in the North far too long," David muttered. "I'll have Solomon fetch the trunks. My sister has apparently forgotten we have slaves."

"Quite the contrary," Nolan replied. "I don't think she forgets for a moment that the South is filled with slaves."

Jasmine stood outside her mother's bedroom door for a moment to prepare herself. Should her mother be awake and detect any sign of concern, she'd likely become overwrought. Jasmine tapped lightly on the door and then entered the room. The heavy green velvet drapes had been pulled to prevent the infiltration of daylight, and Jasmine hesitated until her eyes adjusted to the darkened room before tiptoeing to her mother's bedside.

She leaned close to her mother's ear and whispered, "Mother, it's me, Jasmine. I've come to visit with you. Can you open your eyes? Mother?"

The only response was the chirping of a bird outside the window. Jasmine pulled her mother's rocking chair close to the bed and sat down. Grasping her mother's limp hand in her own, she began quietly telling her of the journey with Nolan and Spencer, of Spencer's antics on board the ship, and of the news that he was now downstairs in the parlor being entertained by McKinley and David. "He is quite the little boy. I know you will enjoy him," Jasmine said. "When you awaken from your nap, I'll bring him up to see you if you'd like." She fought back the tears that began to form.

She didn't know how long she'd been sitting by her mother's bedside, but when she could think of nothing else to say, she leaned back in the chair, still holding her mother's hand, and began to sing the lullaby her mother had sung to her when she was a little girl. She closed her eyes and repeated the tune over and over again in her sweet, soft soprano voice. A faint tug of her fingers caused Jasmine to startle.

Although her eyes were barely open, her mother's lips curved into a feeble smile. "Jasmine," she whispered, her voice barely audible.

"Yes, Mother, it's me—Jasmine. I've come all the way from Lowell just to be with you. And I've brought Spencer too."

Her mother stared back at her with dull, lifeless eyes. "Water."

"Yes, of course." Jasmine jumped up from the chair and, propping her mother in the crook of her arm, held the engraved goblet to her lips.

When she sputtered and coughed after only a few sips, Jasmine lowered her mother back onto the pillow. "Would you like me to wash your face and perhaps brush your hair, Mother?"

"Later. I need to rest," she whispered. Her eyes closed, and the rasp of her shallow breathing began to once again fill the room.

"Yes, of course. I'll come back and see you in a little while," Jasmine said, feeling compelled to announce her departure, yet knowing her mother did not hear.

She walked from the bedroom and closed the door softly behind her. Spencer's childish jabbers floated up the staircase, and Jasmine smiled as she peeked over the balustrade at the enchanting scene below. Young Spencer was seated in the center of the parlor floor playing with a set of carved horses that had been McKinley's favorite toys as a young boy. Nolan and her father, however, appeared to be engaged in a serious conversation.

Both men stood as she entered the room, their discussion coming to an abrupt halt. "I do hope you two haven't discussed Mother's condition without me. If so, I fear you'll need to repeat everything you've already said," Jasmine remarked, her gaze directed toward her father.

"Please join us, my dear. I'm sure you'd enjoy some refreshment. I was beginning to wonder if you were going to leave your mother's bedside," the older man said, walking to the corner of the room and pulling down on a thick gold cord.

"When did you have the bell cords installed?" Jasmine inquired.

Before her father could answer, a young light-skinned girl scurried into the room. "Yassuh?"

"Bring the tea tray," he ordered.

Jasmine smiled at the girl. "Please," she added.

"Please?" There was a note of irritation in her father's voice. "Since when do you say *please* to slaves?" He didn't await Jasmine's answer. "Dr. Borden is due at any time. He's been stopping to see your mother every afternoon. I'm certain he'll give you a full report."

"And you, Father? What is *your* report? You know Mother better than anyone else. Do you believe this is simply a reoccurrence of her chronic malaise, or has she not fully recovered from the yellow fever?"

Nolan sat down beside Jasmine. "Your father is obviously uncertain; that's why he wants you to wait and talk to Dr. Borden."

"Nonsense. My father has an opinion about everything—especially where Mother is concerned."

The older man gently tugged at his collar. "If you're going to force me to render a judgment, I'd say it's a combination of both. I don't think she ever fully recovered, but that could be due to her ongoing propensity toward melancholy."

Before Jasmine could further question her father, a knock sounded at the front door. Jasmine stared in disbelief as her father jumped up and hurried to the door.

"It's become quite obvious Father is trying to avoid me," Jasmine said quietly to Nolan. "I've *never* seen him answer the door. The servants are likely going to spend the afternoon worrying they'll receive punishment for not moving quickly enough."

Jasmine listened to the muffled voices in the vestibule for several minutes before Dr. Borden finally appeared in the parlor doorway. "Your father and I are going upstairs to see your mother. I look forward to visiting with you when I come back down. It's nice to see you, Jasmine," he added almost as an afterthought.

She knew she had been intentionally excluded. However, she would honor her father's wishes—at least for the time being. "If you don't mind watching after Spencer a little longer, Nolan, I believe I'll look in on Mammy. Father, am I correct to assume she's still in the same bedroom off the kitchen?"

"Yes, of course."

"You go and see her," Nolan said. "Spencer and I will be fine."

Jasmine offered her thanks and then hurried off to the rooms used by members of the kitchen staff. She greeted each of the slaves by name before making her way into the small room where Mammy lay upon a narrow rope-strung bed that sagged under her weight. Safra, one of the kitchen slaves, hurried into the room carrying a straight-backed wooden chair.

Jasmine offered the woman a smile and took the chair. "Thank you, Safra. The next time Mammy is out of bed, could one of you tighten the ropes on this bed? The mattress is barely off the floor."

"I's sorry, ma'am, but she don' git outta dat bed long 'nuf for no rope tightenin'. We's lucky to get clean beddin' under her."

Jasmine nodded and took Mammy's hand. It was the second time this day that she'd held the limp hand of someone she loved. "Mammy, it's Jasmine. I've come home for a visit."

The old woman's eyes remained closed, but her parched lips opened ever so slightly. "Chile, I's glad you come home. You need to be tendin' to your mama. When she's better, you come and see me."

"The doctor is with Mama right now. Has he been caring for you too?"

She gave a slight nod of her head. "Yes'm, but there ain't nothin' no doctor kin do fer me. I'm just waitin' here for da good Lord to come and take me home."

"Now, I'll hear no more of that kind of talk. I've come all this way to see you, and you tell me you're just going to lie here until you die? Why, I've even brought little Spencer along, and neither you nor Mother can hold your eyes open long enough to see him." The words sounded cruel to her ears, but Jasmine hoped to startle Mammy into fighting for her life.

Mammy's eyes opened, and her dry lips cracked as the beginnings of a smile began to form. "You is still a sassy chile. Now git upstairs and see what dat doctor got to say 'bout your mama. You can bring yo' baby in to see me after you find out what dat doctor has to say. I want a report. Ain't nobody willing to tell me nothin' about her."

Jasmine nodded her agreement before standing. "I'll be back after I've talked to Dr. Borden." Carrying the chair under one arm, she deposited it in the kitchen and headed up the back stairway to her mother's room.

"You know she's dying, Malcolm. It's likely going to be only a matter of days before you'll have to bury her."

Jasmine clutched the doorframe, her fingernails digging into the hard, cold cypress wood. "What are you saying?" she nearly shouted. "My mother isn't going to die. You're a doctor—do something to make her well. My father engaged you to heal her, not to issue a death sentence." She inveighed against him as though her very words would serve to strengthen his medical prowess. "Tell him, Father." She hissed the words from between clenched teeth, her gaze riveted upon her mother's lifeless form. "Tell him to make her well."

"Come with me, Jasmine," her father said, firmly taking her by the arm. "We'll discuss this matter downstairs."

Jasmine leveled an accusatory stare in the doctor's direction. "You *will* be joining us, won't you, Dr. Borden?"

Her father tightened his hold on her elbow. "Of course he will. And you need to remember your manners."

"Manners? He's just said that Mother is dying. I'm not concerned about manners; I'm concerned about my mother," she rebuked.

"As am I," he came back in a hushed voice. "Do you think you are the only one feeling pain and sadness? If so, you are very mistaken. The thought of living the remainder of my life without your mother is unbearably distressing. Yet I would prefer Dr. Borden's honesty to false platitudes. I've asked him to be forthright."

It was obvious these past months had taken their toll on her father. He had grown thinner, and his once taut skin now sagged, mapping creases and folds that hadn't been evident a year ago. A dull weariness had replaced the glint of joy and excitement she'd grown accustomed to seeing in his eyes.

"Of course, Father. I apologize. I've been here only one afternoon, and I'm passing judgment on everyone who has spent these
many months worrying and caring for Mother. It's just—difficult."
A lump rose in her throat and tears threatened to spill at any
moment. She dared not say anything more or she'd fall into her
father's arms weeping, and that was a burden he didn't need. What
he did need was a family that would be strong and supportive.

"Difficult. Yes," he said, patting her hand. "But with God's
grace, we'll get through this. Now let's go down to the parlor."

Dr. Borden's report was exactly what she'd expected: Her condition was weaker today; nothing more to do; wait; pray; he would
return tomorrow; he would check on Mammy.

His final words brought Jasmine to attention. "After you've
seen Mammy, will you tell me how she is faring?"

The doctor gazed down at Spencer making a stack of wooden
blocks and massaged his forehead. "Unless something unexpected
has occurred since yesterday, I can tell you her condition is quite
similar to that of your mother. To be honest, Mammy's illness was
one of the worst cases I've seen. I didn't expect her to make it
through the first weeks. However, whether it's because she was a
little stronger or because she had the will to live, I'm not certain.
But I do know that from time to time she speaks about the need
to hang on a little longer."

"For *what*? Has she said what it is she needs?" Jasmine asked,
hope beginning to kindle in her heart. Maybe she could supply
whatever it was Mammy wanted and the old slave would be mirac-
ulously healed.

The doctor shook his head back and forth. "I have no idea.
She hasn't confided in me, but whatever the reason, it seems to
have sustained her for now. I'll look in on her and stop to see you
before I take my leave."

"Thank you." Jasmine waited only a moment before turning
to her father. "Mammy will tell me what it is she needs. Whatever
it is, we'll see to it for her, won't we, Papa? We'll be able to help
her regain her health."

"Or give her the freedom to rest easy and die."

TRACIE PETERSON / JUDITH MILLER

Jasmine slumped down into the chair. "Is *that* what you think? If we help her, she will give in and die?"

"I don't know, Jasmine. I have no answers for you."

Jasmine's brothers came into the parlor and looked at the subdued group.

"If I knew how to resolve any of this," Malcolm continued, "it would already be accomplished. But I do know the doctor is correct. While your mother appears to have no will to live, Mammy has fought to survive, especially when I told her you were coming home." A tear glistened in her father's eye. "I wish it would have had the same effect upon your mother. I'm not certain she even heard me when I told her you and Spencer would be here for a visit. I've not been much use around the plantation. I've relied upon your brothers to take care of things."

"And we've been happy to do so," McKinley said. "If nothing else good has come from this, both David and I have learned a great deal about the business."

Her father gave a weary nod. "There's truth to that statement. And you've both performed admirably. And from what the Associates report, so has Samuel," he said, glancing toward Nolan.

"Other than through Jasmine's shipping business, I know little of what goes on with the Associates, Mr. Wainwright. However, if anything were amiss, I'm certain you'd receive word. I do know Samuel's schedule is very busy."

"I can attest to the fact that he's busy, for we seldom see him when he's in Lowell on business," Jasmine added.

"I'll discuss that situation with him. Business is important, but keeping strong family ties is even more essential. I fear I learned too late in life just how important my family is to me," her father said with a sad ache in his voice.

The sound of Dr. Borden's footsteps caused all of them to look toward the doorway. "She's much the same, although she remembers you are here, Mrs. Houston. She told me you'd brought your baby and come home to visit. I take that as a positive sign," he said while giving Jasmine a tentative smile. "However, please don't interpret my remarks to mean she is recovering. I'm merely saying that I'm somewhat encouraged that she spoke to me and that she remembered talking to you a short while ago."

"Of course," Jasmine replied, her lips bowing into a radiant smile. Hiding her elation would be as impossible as telling the sun not to rise in the east. If Mammy's condition worsened in the future, she'd deal with it then. But for now, she would take the doctor's words of encouragement and be thankful for this moment of joy.

By day's end, Jasmine was exhausted. She'd run back and forth between the bedsides of the two women she loved, attended to Spencer's supper and readied him for bed, eaten a late supper with her family and Nolan, and then fallen into bed consumed with guilt because she hadn't been at home to assist in her mother's care and also with fear that two of the most important women in her life would soon be gone from this world. Unbidden dreams plagued her sleep. When Spencer tugged at her hand the next morning, Jasmine could only moan in acknowledgment. The child finally resorted to crawling into her bed and prodding open her eyelids with his small fingers until she'd finally succumbed and forced herself to awaken.

The morning passed quickly, and after quieting Spencer for his afternoon nap, Jasmine sat down in the parlor with Nolan. Following last night's restless sleep, a brief period of relaxation would serve her well.

"I'm pleased to see you're going to take a few moments to yourself," Nolan said. "You need to take care of yourself or *you'll* be taking ill."

Before Jasmine could utter a response, a sharp rap sounded, followed by the incessant ringing of the servant's bell above the front door. "Who can that be, and why don't they give us an opportunity to come to the door? That bell is going to awaken Spencer," Jasmine said as she hurried from the room, unwilling to wait for one of the servants.

Yanking open the door, her look of anger and exasperation immediately wilted. "Cousin Zachary . . . I mean, President Taylor," she stammered.

"Jasmine, my dear, has your father relegated you to the position of housekeeper?" the president asked with a grin.

"No, of course not. Do come in," she said, stepping aside. "What a pleasant and unexpected surprise."

"Why is it you're answering the door here at The Willows? I thought you were living in Massachusetts."

She took his hat and handed it to Bessie, who was now scurrying into the hallway. In a hushed whisper she told the girl, "Go tell my father that President Taylor is here." Then turning to the president, she squared her shoulders. "Quite honestly, I didn't wait for one of the servants because I feared the ringing bell would awaken my son from his afternoon nap," she replied with a grin. "And I do live in Lowell. However, Mother's failing health brings me back to The Willows."

"Yes, your mother's health. Exactly why I've come," he said, striding into the parlor with an ease that spoke volumes. "Zachary Taylor," he said, extending his hand to Nolan.

"An honor," Nolan said, standing quickly and obviously stunned by a visit from the president of the United States.

"Do sit down. I'm not royalty and I'm no longer a general— merely the president. You need not remain standing in my presence," he said with a hearty laugh. He glanced toward Jasmine. "Is your father close at hand?"

"Yes, of course. I told Bessie to fetch him. He should be here any moment. I'll ring for tea. Do promise you'll stay for supper. I know Papa will be disappointed if you refuse."

"What will disappoint me?" her father asked as he rounded the corner and entered the parlor. "Zachary! What a wonderful surprise. Tell me what brings you to Mississippi. Nothing unpleasant, I hope."

Jasmine watched as the two men clasped hands and then embraced. They were relatives by marriage, a bond that had subsequently developed into a deep friendship.

"Visiting Mississippi is always a pleasure, Malcolm. Even when I'm greeted with unpleasant circumstances," he said with a brooding look in his eyes. "There were matters that needed my attention

at the plantation. I made mention of them, and my dear Peggy
insisted I personally attend to them. I didn't understand her resolve
until she read me a letter she had received from Madelaine saying
she'd contracted yellow fever. Peggy's concerns have continued to
mount as time passed with no further word from her cousin."

Her father briefly closed his eyes and nodded. "I didn't realize
Madelaine had written. I know Peggy's condition is tenuous, and
I didn't want to cause her undue concern, Zachary. However, I
fear anything I would have written could have only served to
worry Peggy further."

"My wife is an amazingly strong woman," Taylor said in a bittersweet manner. It left Jasmine wondering exactly what ailed the
president's wife.

"I wish I could say the same about Madelaine."

"So she is no better?"

"Dr. Borden says her prospects are grim. She appears to have
lost the will to live."

Zachary frowned. "Unfortunately, both of our wives have
been plagued by melancholy throughout their lives. Since taking
up residency at the White House, Peggy has retreated to her
upstairs rooms. I rely upon our daughter Betty to act as my hostess
at formal functions and, I must admit, she is becoming quite
accomplished at the task. I'm thankful for her assistance."

"And her husband—he's a colonel now, isn't he?" Jasmine
asked.

"Indeed. A fine man. Fortunately, we became fast friends from
the very beginning. I heartily approved of Betty's marriage to
Colonel Bliss."

"Unlike your daughter Knox. Her marriage to Jefferson Davis
was a bitter pill for you to swallow, wasn't it, Zachary," Malcolm
stated.

Nolan glanced toward President Taylor. "I didn't realize one of
your daughters married Jefferson Davis."

"Against my wishes. She died of malaria three months after
they wed. Jefferson and I finally settled our differences when we
fought together in Mexico. I know it would have pleased Knox. I

only wish our reconciliation had occurred before her death. However, it was important to set aside my pride, so I extended an olive branch. Jefferson accepted. I learned a difficult and valuable lesson through that ordeal: I don't let the sun go down on my anger with any member of my family. They come first in my life."

"I've certainly been much more taciturn in that regard. For far too long, I placed my business and financial concerns before anything else—even to the detriment of Jasmine's welfare."

Jasmine watched a look of despair etch itself upon her father's face. If the conversation continued down this path, he would soon be miserable. Jumping to her feet, she extended a hand toward the president. "Why don't I take you up to see Mother before Spencer awakens from his nap? Once he is up and about, I doubt there will be much peace for any of us."

"Yes, of course," he replied, accepting her hand. "Peggy will expect a full account upon my return to Washington."

CHAPTER · 3

LATER THAT EVENING, President Taylor escorted Jasmine into the dining room, followed by Nolan. The president pulled out one of the ornately carved mahogany chairs for Jasmine and greeted her brothers and father, who were already seated around the end of the table.

"Tell me about life in Massachusetts, Jasmine," the president said. "Unfortunately, I've not yet had the opportunity to visit Lowell." He sat down beside her, obviously interested in what she had to tell him.

"I hope you'll come and visit one day soon. In my estimation, the town is quite progressive and has much to offer. The textile mills are the primary industry, although locomotives are now being manufactured in Lowell, aren't they, Nolan?"

"Indeed. Both ventures have proven to be financially successful for those involved. And of course most of the other machinery and tools used directly in the mills are manufactured in Lowell as well," Nolan replied. "And it appears one of the most recent undertakings is patent medicine. From all appearances, Lowell is beginning to diversify, which is good for the economy."

The president helped himself to several pieces of crisp fried chicken and a generous portion of creamed peas before heaping a mound of roasted potatoes and a slab of corn bread onto his plate. "You live in Lowell also, Mr. Houston?"

Nolan shook his head. "No. I make my home near Boston, but I do visit Lowell frequently. I don't want my nephew growing up without knowing me," he said with a grin.

"Good for you," the president said. "You and young Spencer will both be the better for it. Time spent with children is a sound investment in their future."

"Nolan also oversees the shipping business that was owned by my late husband, who was Nolan's brother," Jasmine added. "His assistance has lifted a great burden from my shoulders."

"Ah, yes. Your late husband was responsible for pursuing the purchase of cotton from our Mississippi and Louisiana planters on behalf of the Boston Associates, wasn't he?"

"Yes, although Samuel had taken over that particular aspect of the business prior to Bradley's death."

"I understand your brother is doing an excellent job—at least where my plantation is concerned," the president remarked.

Nolan took a drink of coffee and leaned forward to meet the president's gaze. "I hope you won't think me boorish for asking, sir, but I do wonder if you would tell me how you've managed to win the *Northern* vote when you own a plantation and more than a hundred slaves."

President Taylor shrugged. "There are those who say it was my military record that appealed to the Northerners, while my slave ownership lured the Southern vote. I'm not certain if that's true, but in retrospect, I suppose each side chose to believe I was loyal to their camp. Neither gave consideration to the fact that I am my own person. I place my loyalty where I feel it best serves the nation's interests and welfare, though I know there are many around these parts who consider me a doughface in reverse."

Jasmine saw a twinkle in the president's eyes when Nolan's brow furrowed. President Taylor obviously realized Nolan was confused by his remark.

"A *Southern* man with *Northern* principles," Taylor explained. "Believe me, I heartily disagree with those who would characterize me in such a manner. I consider myself a patriot and, fundamentally, I believe in the Union."

"Please don't think me impertinent, President Taylor, but if you consider yourself a Unionist, how do you justify slave ownership?"

"Justify? Why would I feel a need to do so? Never have I attempted to hide my ownership of a cotton plantation and slaves. You must remember that I was a slave owner before I was elected president. Although there are many who abhor the thought, I shall be a slave owner when I leave the presidency. And I might add that the owners and workers of those famous textile mills in Lowell are more than a little dependent upon our Southern cotton."

"True enough, yet there is valid argument that the slaves should be given the freedom to choose whether they desire to remain on the plantations or seek a life of their own in some other place. Does it seem fair and equitable that one man has the freedom to choose while another does not?" Nolan asked while spreading apple butter onto a warm piece of corn bread.

President Taylor speared another piece of chicken and then leaned back in his chair. "There are many things in life that are unfair, Mr. Houston, for both Negroes and whites. Surely you don't desire *or* expect the men in Washington to solve every injustice."

"No, I don't, but I *do* expect the government to resolve issues that threaten to tear apart the very fabric of this country."

"Then rest easy, my boy. I will not permit such a thing to occur," President Taylor replied easily.

Jasmine glanced toward her father as he straightened in his chair and then loudly cleared his throat. The tension in her neck began to relax as she realized her father was going to call a halt to any further political discussion at the supper table.

"Word down here is that you've forsaken us, Zachary. We hear you're urging settlers in New Mexico and California to draft their own constitutions and apply for statehood, that you've advised them to bypass the territorial stage. But don't think for a minute we're oblivious to the negative effect that piece of advice will have upon the South," her father candidly remarked.

Jasmine stared at him in disbelief. Obviously *any* topic was now considered acceptable table conversation.

McKinley nodded and smiled. "They'll come in as free states since neither of them is likely to draw a constitution permitting slavery."

Jasmine stared at McKinley, surprised at the seeming pleasure in his tone.

"Exactly! And don't think your behavior is going to sit well with Congress, Zachary," Malcolm added. "They don't like having their policy-making prerogatives usurped by anyone, not even by the president. If you continue in this manner, you're going to alienate the entire country."

"There's no way to make everybody happy over the slavery issue. Why, I daresay there's no way I could please even the few gathered in this room. Ultimately there will be those who will be unhappy, no matter what the decision," President Taylor said while glancing around the table. "Why, I'm sure they're quite unhappy to find me absent from Washington. I know the men who traveled with me were surely displeased to awaken this morning and find me gone, but I am fully capable of seeing to myself. And I won't worry overmuch about wooing them into better humors when I return. Just as I cannot concern myself with wooing each and every voter whose nose is out of joint."

"Well, I think you would at least attempt to woo your Southern brothers who placed their faith in you," Malcolm fumed.

The president emitted a loud guffaw. "And the Northerners who voted for me think I should take a harsh stand against slavery. Should any of you young folks have a hankering for politics, you should remember your allegiance likely will be called into question on a regular basis. I constantly find myself in quite a quandary."

"I don't think I would ever aspire to a political future," McKinley commented. "There is little doubt repercussions will be forthcoming no matter what the outcome of the slavery issue. And should Congress pass a law requiring the return of fugitive slaves, I doubt that even the freed slaves up north will be safe."

"What law is this you're talking about?" Nolan inquired.

"McKinley is speaking out of turn. There have been rumors, nothing more," David retorted.

"Not so!" McKinley protested. "Matters have moved beyond rumor. I hear there are men who have already drafted legislation in the event California and New Mexico follow the president's advice to avoid becoming territories and move forward with statehood."

Nolan turned his attention to McKinley. "And what are the provisions of this possible legislation?"

President Taylor pushed his dinner plate aside. "In answer to your question, Nolan, it appears there are those who desire a law that would make it the responsibility of every person to return runaway slaves. I would tend to agree with McKinley. The possibility has moved beyond rumor for I, too, am privy to the information."

McKinley nodded vigorously as he met Nolan's gaze. "Yet it goes far beyond the mere return of slaves: this law would actually mandate the involvement of every citizen who encounters a possible runaway."

"Which is as it should be," Malcolm replied. "Think of the financial investment. The North wants abolition and the president obviously isn't going to take a stand for slavery. We must have some sort of protection for our investment. Expansion of the Underground Railroad continues with Northerners not only aiding runaways but practically encouraging slaves to leave their owners—and the antislavery do-gooders seem to be increasing their numbers daily."

Jasmine frowned and discreetly shook her head when Nolan glanced in her direction. She prayed he would heed her warning and remain silent. Continuing down this path would only cause her father to become more distressed.

"I see many problems with such a law," McKinley commented.

Startled, Jasmine tilted her head to one side and briefly contemplated her brother's behavior. His actions this evening appeared completely out of character. She'd never seen him enter into a passionate discussion on any topic other than finances. "What difficulties do you predict?" No sooner had she uttered the question than she wished she could recall the words. There was little doubt further explanation by McKinley would only serve to inflame her father.

McKinley didn't hesitate for a moment. "Such a law will make men greedy. They will accuse freed men of being escaped slaves, and they'll find disreputable Southerners willing to look the other way if they can pay a lesser price for another healthy slave. They won't take the time or energy to see if there's validity to the Negro's claim."

"Absurd!" Malcolm retorted, his cheeks flushed in anger.

Unfortunately, her father was reacting exactly as Jasmine had anticipated—he couldn't seem to hold his temper in check when it came to the issue of slavery and those who opposed it. However, McKinley's views *had* come as somewhat of a surprise to her. Granted, her youngest brother had always been kind to the household staff and, unlike Samuel, McKinley abhorred going out into the fields or to the slave quarters. Instead, he remained close to the big house, working on the accounts and honing his skills to become an astute businessman. Was he beginning to see the evils of slavery? His comments this evening seemed to indicate he was at least giving consideration to antislavery sentiments. If so, he might prove to be an excellent Southern connection for the antislavery movement in Lowell. Trusted Southerner antislavers were in demand. Jasmine touched the linen napkin to her lips and wondered if her father would later take McKinley to task for speaking his mind this evening.

David's knife clanked onto his plate with such force Jasmine thought the china would surely be chipped or cracked. "You're absolutely correct, Father. As usual, the Northerners are attempting to force their will upon the entire nation. They have always considered themselves superior to the genteel people of the South, quick in their attempts to force their choices upon all of us."

Although David had offered little to the dinner conversation this evening, Jasmine knew his loyalty would unfalteringly remain with their father and the South. She was keenly aware of his life-long struggle to gain their father's attention. Even at an early age, Jasmine had recognized her brother's longing to be noticed by their father. Always anxious to please, David never disagreed with their father, never voiced an independent idea, and never failed to do exactly as instructed. Consequently, he remained the over-looked middle son, still attempting to gain some glimmer of rec-ognition.

"True enough. As far as I'm concerned, they speak from both sides of their mouth. On one hand, they want our cotton, but on the other, they wish to do away with the slaves needed to raise the crop. Ridiculous!"

"No need to get into a heated political debate over supper, Malcolm—bad for the digestion," the president said calmly. He turned toward Jasmine and graced her with an affable smile. "Tell me, my dear, how is it that you chose to remain in Lowell rather than returning to Mississippi—especially since you have Mr. Houston to assist with your business interests in Boston."

Jasmine sighed with relief. The conversation was finally taking a turn for the better. She gave the president a radiant smile. "You may recall that Grandmother Wainwright lives in Lowell?"

"Ah yes, now that you mention it, I do seem to remember the fact that Alice went north. After your father's death, wasn't it, Mal-colm?"

Her father nodded.

"Having Grandmother Wainwright in Lowell was a true bless-ing, for a move after my husband's death would have been difficult. Spencer was a mere infant. However, since that time I have expanded my interests by purchasing a horse farm, where Spencer and I are now living."

"A horse farm? Now that's an unusual investment for a young woman with no husband. How did you happen to become involved in such a venture?"

"My husband had purchased several fine horses before his death—beautiful animals. When an unforeseen opportunity arose to purchase a farm several miles out of town, I immediately made a bid on the acreage. There was no way I could have expanded the horse business on the property I previously owned. My bid was accepted, and we moved to the farm a month later."

"I'd say your daughter has some of that same spunk you had when you expanded your cotton business, Malcolm."

Her father appeared to soften at the president's praise. "Once she had all the facts and figures, she wasn't afraid to move forward. And from what I've seen and been told, she made a wise decision."

"Thank you, Papa. We've increased our stock and have earned a good reputation. In addition, we've gained the trust of the locals, and that's always helpful."

"Perhaps I'll have to make that trip to Lowell in the very near future. I've been looking for a pair of carriage horses. I'm thinking you might have something you could recommend to me."

"Better yet, something she could *sell* to you," her father said with a loud guffaw.

Jasmine blushed at her father's assertion. "I would be honored to discuss my horses with you, President Taylor. And should Cousin Peggy's health permit, it would be my privilege to have the two of you be my guests in Lowell."

"I'll discuss that possibility with her, my dear. She hasn't been inclined to do much visiting and, as I mentioned, Betty sees to formal functions at the White House. However, I've been encouraged by the number of friends and kinfolk Peggy has welcomed to her upstairs sitting rooms. She regularly worships with the family at St. John's Episcopal Church, even though she steadfastly refuses to become involved in the Washington social functions. So there is a good possibility she might consider a visit to Lowell. Now tell me more about your horses."

"Why don't we adjourn to the sitting room, and I'll tell you about my farm," Jasmine suggested.

"We'll join you in a few moments, my dear," her father stated. "I'd like to have a glass of port and a cigar. I'm certain the other gentlemen will want to join me."

"Yes, of course. Since Nolan doesn't partake in cigars, I'm certain you'll excuse him. He promised to make a final visit to Spencer's room."

"Surely the boy is in bed by now," the older man said.

Nolan rose from his chair. "He's likely asleep, but I'll go up and make certain. I don't want to break my promise."

Malcolm nodded and gestured for the others to follow. "Whatever you think best—we'll be in my library if you want to join us once you've looked in on Spencer."

Jasmine waited only a moment before pulling Nolan aside. "I know we didn't have an opportunity to talk prior to supper, but I do wish you hadn't begun a discussion of the slavery issue with President Taylor. Surely you realized the topic would be unpredictable."

Nolan gave her a sheepish grin. "I suppose that's a correct statement. However, I wanted to see for myself where the president's loyalties are placed. I must admit he surprised me. I assumed he would hold fast to the Southern ideology. When he stated he was a Unionist, I was taken aback. I gathered from his comments that he's willing to do everything in his power to stop any talk of cessation. He's against slavery expansion, yet he supports its continuation in Southern states, all the while saying the fugitive slave laws should not be more stringent. It's obvious he doesn't intend to bow to Whig leadership in Congress."

"And it's also obvious my father disagrees with him on almost every account. Nolan, I would prefer this be a gracious visit. Mother's illness leaves Father weary and quick to temper, and I don't know when the president will be able to return for another visit. For approximately four years they spent a great deal of time on their plantation across the river in Louisiana, and we would visit several times a year. However, the Mexican War put an end to those visits. And now that they live in Washington and neither Mother nor Cousin Peggy is in good health . . ."

"I understand. I apologize for my thoughtless behavior. Of course, I could argue that McKinley added to the strife—and even you asked a few leading questions."

"You're correct, and if I could have snatched back my last

question to him, I would have done so." They stopped then and stood side by side, very close. Jasmine became very aware of Nolan's presence—the scent of his cologne, the rich blueness of his eyes. Realizing she was staring, Jasmine cleared her throat and headed for the door. "We had best go up and check on Spencer."

"Yes, of course," he agreed, following her into the foyer. "I must say I was astonished to have the president appear at your front door. How is it you never mentioned being related to him?"

"Mother and Mrs. Taylor are second cousins, so I'm not actually related to President Taylor. I'm barely related to his wife," she said with a giggle. "But I always enjoyed visits with the Taylors and their daughters. I was especially fond of Sarah. The family called her Knox, but I always thought the name Sarah much prettier. Betty and I were both withdrawn, while Sarah was full of vigor, always a leader. We were quick to follow."

The two of them stood in the entryway to the bedroom. Spencer was fast asleep, and Bessie was sitting nearby in a wooden rocking chair mending the torn pocket on her apron. "He wen right to sleep, ma'am," she whispered.

"Thank you, Bessie. Would you consider remaining with him until I come upstairs for the night?"

The older woman gave her a toothy grin. " 'Course I'se gonna stay. You go on now. I'm mo' than happy to sit here."

"I believe I'll look in on Mother while I'm up here, Nolan. Why don't you join Father and the others?"

"If you're sure you don't want me . . . to come with you?"

There was something akin to longing in his expression, but Jasmine quickly looked away. "No. I'm certain she's sleeping, but I'll feel better if I stop in and check on her. I'll come down momentarily."

Jasmine met her father's questioning gaze as she entered the parlor some time later. "She's asleep. Her breathing seemed rather shallow, but she didn't appear to be in distress."

Her father sighed, obviously relieved to hear the brief report, while the others settled back in their chairs.

"While we were enjoying our glass of port in the library, your father mentioned you have some Arabians, Jasmine. I'm interested in hearing how you came to own them. They are, after all, rather rare here in America, and quite honestly, one of the most beautiful animals in God's creation."

"I couldn't agree more, President Taylor. However, I didn't realize you would be interested in anything so . . ."

"Costly?" he asked with a wide grin.

"Well, they are expensive, but Arabians are also quite showy."

"Exactly! Sitting astride one of those beauties could make anyone appear grand and powerful. President Washington is patent confirmation of my observation. Have you viewed the paintings of him astride his Arabian? He looks absolutely magnificent—like a powerful warrior. Why, if I'd been riding one of those magnificent animals in Mexico, I would have given serious thought to prolonging the war just for the pure pleasure of riding the beast into battle!" He slapped his knee and emitted a loud guffaw.

Jasmine smiled, certain the president was joking—at least about the Mexican War. "I assumed you were looking for animals that are more unpretentious."

"I care little whether others find my choice of horses pretentious—and I *expect* to pay dearly for fine horseflesh."

"In that case, I'm certain we can accommodate you," she said, "but if you've set your mind upon Arabians, I would truly encourage you to visit us before you make your final decision, as we do have some others you might find entirely suitable."

He scooted forward on his chair and bent forward, resting his arms upon his thighs. "Tell me, how is it you happen to own Arabians? Quite frankly, I didn't realize anyone was breeding them here in America."

"Interest in the Arabian breed continues to increase and, truth be told, there have been occasions when we've been unable to meet all requests."

"How did you happen to develop an interest in Arabians?"

Jasmine glanced toward Nolan. "Actually, it was my deceased

husband who first acquired the Arabians with a thought toward breeding. A relative in England assisted him in securing the animals."

"Who has taken charge of the horse business since your husband's death?" the president inquired, looking in Nolan's direction.

"Bradley didn't actually enter into the care and breeding of the horses," Jasmine explained. "He was more an admirer and entrepreneur. Frankly, we had excellent help with the farm prior to his death, and those employees have remained with me. Our stable master has trained young Paddy O'Neill. Paddy is an acquisition from Lord Palmerston, a distant relative of Bradley."

The president's eyebrows arched like two woolly caterpillars. "How so?"

"Paddy and his sister, Kiara, were both sent to our home as the result of a game the elite gentry visiting Lord Palmerston had devised. Paddy and Kiara's parents died in the potato famine, leaving them penniless and starving. The small parcel of land where the O'Neills farmed was owned by Lord Palmerston. He was in Ireland on holiday when Kiara went to his manse seeking aid. As part of that game or wager, Kiara and Paddy were sent to my deceased husband as indentured servants."

"Surely you jest!" Taylor exclaimed.

"Unfortunately, the story is true, and I fear that the two of them might have starved to death if they'd been left to their own devices in Ireland. However, I heartily disagreed with keeping indentured servants and made my distaste known to my husband. When Bradley died, I granted both Paddy and Kiara their freedom. Since Bradley's death, Kiara has married Rogan Sheehan, and they live in a small house on my acreage. Paddy remains with me, working in the stables. His ability with the horses never ceases to amaze me."

"I'm pleased to hear matters have ended well for both of them. But I am surprised your husband didn't see fit to grant them their papers when they arrived. Releasing them from their indenture would have been the more Christian thing to do."

"There are those who would say that freeing the slaves is the more Christian thing to do, also, but we know that's not what folks in Mississippi and Louisiana believe," McKinley remarked.

Jasmine frowned at her brother. Once again, he had startled her with his stance, but more importantly, she worried his reply would cause another inflammatory discussion regarding slavery if she couldn't turn the course of the conversation.

"I believe you would find a journey to Lowell time well spent," Nolan said. "Not only would it give you ample opportunity to view the horses, but you could also tour the textile mills."

"I know you would find the mills fascinating," Jasmine's father agreed.

"Absolutely!" Jasmine graced Nolan with a pleased smile, thankful he'd prevented further turmoil.

The president stood and began pacing in front of the fireplace as though formulating a plan. "I do believe I could fit Lowell into my schedule, although it might not be as soon as I would like. And you're correct, Nolan: a visit to the mills could prove advantageous in many ways. Speaking of activities in Lowell, I would surmise the gold rush west has created a changing face upon the workforce. Have you noted any consequences?"

"More than the Boston Associates care to acknowledge," Jasmine replied. "At several meetings of our Ladies' Aid Society, the women say their husbands are gravely concerned. The loss of skilled mechanics is disquieting, and there is anxiety over—"

The sound of footsteps could be heard scurrying through the upstairs hallway. Jasmine leaned forward and met Bessie's wide-eyed gaze as the servant hurried toward her.

"Miz Jasmine, you best come with me. You, too, Massa Wainwright," she said. "Ain't lookin' none too good for the mistress." The black woman wrung an old handkerchief between her fingers as she spoke the soulful words.

Jasmine jumped to her feet and fled toward the stairway, her heart pounding wildly. "Not yet, Jesus, not yet. Please don't let her die. I'm not ready." She whispered the words over and over until she reached her mother's bedside. Leaning down, she embraced her mother's body before placing a kiss upon her ashen cheek. Backing away from the deathbed, Jasmine glared upward as though looking through a window into heaven. "Didn't you hear me? I'm not ready!" she accused, but only a deafening silence replied.

CHAPTER · 4

ELINOR BRIGHTON peered into the hallway mirror, straightened the ribbon on her hat, and exited the boardinghouse. Giving an extra tug on the doorknob, she listened as the metal latch gave its familiar click. Nodding in satisfaction, she marched down the two front steps and off toward the regularly scheduled meeting of the Ladies' Aid Society. Her final determination to attend hadn't been made until after preparing and serving the noonday meal. However, neither the substance of the meeting nor anyone who might be in attendance had influenced Elinor's decision. Her choice to attend had been based solely upon whether there would be sufficient leftovers for the evening meal.

Likely the girls would protest eating repeated fare for the evening meal, but Elinor had listened to their tiresome complaints before. They grumbled if the food was too hot or too cold, if they disliked a particular vegetable or meat, if they thought their sleeping space was too small, or if another girl snored—she had heard all manner of whining since she'd become a boardinghouse keeper for girls working in the mills. While listening to each petty grievance, she always maintained her silence, although she yearned to lash out at their triviality. She loathed feeling as though she were *their* servant, at *their* beck and call and constantly required to perform on their behalf. But as much as she disliked her position as a boardinghouse keeper, she knew she would remain, for she had no choice.

The silly-minded mill girls had no idea what it was like to experience the cruel hardships of life, but their day would come. Years ago she'd thought life was good and the world was hers for the taking, back when she'd sailed from England to make her home in Lowell with Taylor and Bella Manning, her brother and his new bride. That had been a lifetime ago, or so it now seemed.

Perhaps if she had remained in England and had not married at the first opportunity, things would be different now. But her past couldn't be changed, and her future appeared bleak. While the sun consistently shone upon others, her life continually filled with heartache and failure. A gust of wind whipped at her cape and Elinor shivered, longing for the warmth of her long woolen cloak.

In the distance she could see several buggies and carriages lined in the circular driveway that fronted the Donohue home. Perched upon a small knoll, the house was surrounded by several large trees. Elinor watched a curling trail of smoke rise from the chimney and blotch the horizon with a fading charcoal stain. The reminder of a warm fireplace beckoned her onward, and she bent her head against the wind until reaching the front door. She thumped the brass knocker and pranced from foot to foot in an attempt to ward off the chill that now permeated her entire body.

The door swung open, and Daughtie greeted her with a bright smile. "Elinor! It's so good to see you. You look lovely, as usual. I feared you weren't coming when the hour grew late."

Elinor removed her cape. "I had to prepare and serve the noonday meal for my boarders, clean the kitchen, and then walk to your house. Unlike many of your members, I have daily duties that require my time and attention. And, of course, I don't have a buggy at my disposal either. I suppose you should expect that I will always be late."

"My words weren't meant as a condemnation, Elinor. I'm pleased you chose to join us. Come in. We're just beginning the meeting. Let me get you a cup of tea to warm yourself," she said, leading Elinor into the parlor.

"No. I don't want to make a spectacle of myself. I'm already late arriving. I'll wait and have tea with everyone else. Please," she said firmly.

"Very well. Ladies, I believe we can now begin our meeting. I'm excited to report that all of the donations have been put to good use. However, with the onset of winter, we will need to collect even more warm clothing and blankets. Most of the runaways have only the clothes on their backs, and they are generally of a lightweight fabric. When these winter escapes take place, the people are ill-prepared for the cold weather that greets them as they proceed north. I'd suggest we work diligently both at our meetings and in our homes to help meet the needs that will soon face us. I hoped we could choose to either set a personal goal for contributions or set a goal for our group as a whole. What do you think?"

Mrs. Harper reached into her bag and pulled out a piece of embroidery work. "I've brought along some sewing to work on while we talk. If we all would stitch while we conduct our meetings, we could accomplish more," she proudly suggested.

Elinor glanced at the handiwork and gave a disgusted groan. "She's doing fancywork for runaway slaves."

Nettie met Elinor's reproving stare. "Better to create something of beauty than contribute nothing at all." She poked her needle into her fabric.

Elinor's eyes flashed with anger. "Why, whatever do you mean, Nettie Harper?"

"I may take longer to complete my projects because I value quality over quantity, but you appear to value neither. I haven't seen you making *any* donations to the cause."

"I don't have the freedom to sit at home and perform charitable work all day while my maid completes the household duties. You seem to forget that I actually work to support myself," she bristled.

Nettie looked up from her stitching. "We're all aware of your station in life, Elinor. You've made your situation clear to all of us—again and again."

Daughtie moved to gracefully position herself between the two women. "As I was saying, I think if we could set reasonable goals, it would be helpful. I'm concerned about our lack of preparation. Most of our runaways continue onward to Canada. In the middle of winter, it's a cruel journey, especially for those not accustomed to our cold New England weather."

"It would appear best for all concerned if they waited until spring," Elinor offered.

A small gasp circulated throughout the room. "Slaves must take any opportunity available, whether it comes in the heat of summer or dead of winter," Daughtie gently replied. "If they don't run when the opportunity arises, they may never again have a chance at freedom."

Elinor tilted her head and gave a slight nod. "I cannot disagree with your argument, Daughtie. But you must remember that it's easy to offer an extra measure of charity when you're prosperous. Try doing the same when you're struggling to make ends meet. What you ask is too much."

"Daughtie contributed profoundly when she was still a mill girl," Lilly Cheever put in. "Perhaps more with her time than her money, but her dedication and hard work were worth more than any money the rest of us donated."

"Don't speak on my behalf," Hannah Peabody said while leaning forward to make eye contact with Elinor. "I'm like you, a boardinghouse keeper. Even though I don't have much money, I can still be of assistance and help to free slaves by donating my time and energy."

"I don't see how you can donate much time or energy if you're keeping a decent boardinghouse."

Daughtie sighed and patted Elinor's hand. "Why don't we talk later, Elinor?" she whispered. "I'd like to move forward with the meeting."

Elinor shrugged and glanced heavenward. "If that's what you'd prefer. It's your meeting."

Cupping a hand close to her lips, Nettie leaned toward Daughtie. "I don't think Elinor is committed to freeing the slaves. Discussing confidential issues in her presence may prove to yield disastrous results," she said in a hushed voice.

"I heard your whispered accusation, Mrs. Harper. I resent your implication that I might divulge information that would place runaways in jeopardy. When I joined this group, I signed the same pledge as you." The volume of Elinor's voice escalated as she continued arguing her defense. "I've never broken my word to any of you, and I resent the unseemly attack you've made against my morals."

"I don't think she meant her remark as an accusation," Daughtie stated in a hushed tone.

"No need to whisper. Everyone in this room heard Nettie accuse me of disloyalty. The entire group may as well enter into the discussion. Perhaps you'd like to bring the topic of my ouster before the group, Nettie?" Elinor asked, straining her neck to catch Nettie Harper's eye.

"I was merely expressing what I thought might be a valid concern," Nettie said, glancing around the room.

Elinor clenched her hands into tightly coiled fists and momentarily wished she were a man. She would poke Nettie Harper right in her pompous nose. "I have a right to express my views without my loyalty being accused. Although I do not contribute as much as some, I will not break my word."

"I believe we should move along to the real reasons why we've gathered," Daughtie interjected. "Since I'm in charge of the meeting, I'm requesting that you both hold your tongues."

Nettie squared her shoulders and pursed her lips into a tight knot while several other women arched their brows or nodded their heads in obvious approval.

"Fine with me," Elinor muttered.

Daughtie looked in her direction and gave a slight shake of her head before continuing. "As I mentioned earlier, we're expecting a number of runaways throughout the winter. Liam and I have reason to believe our farm is being watched. We're not certain, but we've seen enough indication that we must be careful—especially in light of the difficulty with the group that came through earlier this month."

Elinor turned and was met by Nettie's accusatory gaze. "Did *you* know when the last group of runaways was coming through?" she hissed.

"As a matter of fact, I did," Elinor muttered.

"Ladies, *please*! You are trying my patience," Daughtie admonished.

"I didn't know there was any problem. Why wasn't I told?" Hilda Schultz complained.

Daughtie briefly massaged her temples. "There was no need, Hilda. We've all agreed that the less discussion regarding particulars, the better. Suffice it to say there were a number of us who were nearly discovered while moving runaways to the next station. Now that I've explained our problem, I hope there will be a few of you willing to open your homes and become stations for the runaways, at least on a temporary basis. Once we're certain our house is no longer under surveillance, Liam and I will renew our efforts."

Hilda clasped a hand to her chest. "After hearing what you've related about difficulties with the last group as well as your concerns that you're being watched, I don't think I could possibly offer my house. Especially since I'm a widow. Why, I'd have no one to protect me if something went amiss," she said, dabbing a handkerchief to her eye.

Elinor gazed at Hilda, wondering if the older woman had any notion of her good fortune. Widow or not, Hilda possessed a home and sufficient finances to care for herself. The old woman had never wanted for anything since her husband's death; she'd never been required to seek employment or consider taking refuge with relatives. Harvey Schultz had been dead for more than ten years, yet Hilda spoke of her widowhood as though her husband had died only a few months earlier. Besides, Hilda should expect widowhood—she was probably every bit of forty and five years.

The woman's behavior stuck in Elinor's craw like an ill-placed hat-pin.

While Hilda sat in her fine home stitching fancywork, Elinor scrubbed floors and prepared meals for a household of ungrateful girls who were nearly as unappreciative of their good fortune as Hilda Schultz. Elinor watched as the mill girls freely spent their pay on fancy ribbons, fabric, earbobs, and other whims. They attended lyceums and weekly French and music lessons and, of course, there were the gentlemen callers. The girls would descend the stairs with their new hair ribbons and fine dresses to sit in the parlor and bat their eyelashes at one of the mechanics or salesmen who came calling, while Elinor remained in the kitchen washing their dirty dishes and setting bread to rise. And when she was done, she would fall into bed, only to awaken the next morning and begin again. If she were Hilda's age, perhaps it wouldn't seem so dreadful. But at twenty and five, her future loomed before her like a long, dark shadow, her youth and beauty fading and then dying a little each day.

"It's settled, then!" Daughtie said, startling Elinor back to the present.

"Mary and Jacob Robbins' home will be the new station until Liam is certain our house is safe. You're certain Jacob is in agreement? I can wait to tell Liam until you've had an opportunity to talk with him."

Mary's lips turned up in a gentle smile. "Jacob told me that should the need ever arise, I had his permission to offer our home. In fact, we've even created a hiding space and have some extra provisions," she announced.

"Wonderful!" Daughtie exclaimed. "There's little doubt God's hand is at work in this, Mary. Give our thanks to Jacob. And now I'm certain everyone is ready for a cup of tea."

Elinor checked the time on the walnut mantel clock and jumped to her feet. "If you'll excuse me, Daughtie, it's late and I have the evening meal to prepare for the girls. By the time I get home—"

"Please stay. I'm certain there's someone here who would be

happy to take you in her buggy. And if all else fails, Liam will be home in sufficient time to take you home."

"No, I'd best take my leave. I believe the remainder of your afternoon will be more pleasant if I'm gone. If you'll get my cape," Elinor insisted while moving toward the foyer.

She donned her cape and hat while Daughtie enumerated a myriad of reasons why she should remain. "You know your early departure will merely serve to set tongues wagging."

Elinor secured her hat and turned to face Daughtie. "Of course! We both realize there must be some exciting topic of conversation at each of these meetings. Today it will be my insufferable behavior and bad manners. I imagine my departure will give Nettie sufficient bravery to actually suggest my expulsion."

"Then remain and defend yourself," Daughtie urged.

"I haven't the time nor energy. If the group feels I'm untrustworthy or my contribution is insufficient, then I'll quietly withdraw. I care little what most of them think. However, I want to assure *you* that I would never do anything to compromise the runaways or anyone who is lending aid on their behalf. However, I realize my comments are sometimes harsh."

"I hope I'm not overstepping my boundaries, Elinor, but I fear you're permitting your past difficulties to ruin your future happiness. You are so filled with anger and resentment that you seem to alienate anyone attempting to befriend you. Yet I'm certain that's *not* your intent," she said softly.

Elinor tugged at her kid gloves, carefully adjusting each finger before meeting Daughtie's concerned gaze. "Perhaps it's not my intent, but I have little time for friends, so I see no need to tiptoe around a group of women who have already judged me unworthy of their confidence."

"Nettie means well. Unfortunately, she's a bit high-strung and tends to fret overmuch. Both Nettie and Hilda are good women who, like the rest of us, want to help the runaways."

"Thank you for your kindness, Daughtie, but I must be on my way. I've supper to prepare and serve and a multitude of other duties awaiting me."

"I understand, but please promise you'll come to the next meeting."

"We'll see," she said. "Please go take care of your guests. I can see myself out the door."

With a smile and brief hug, Daughtie hurried back toward the parlor, and Elinor exited the Donohue home, glad to be back in the fresh air and away from the unpleasant atmosphere. "They likely think *I'm* the one with the biting tongue," she chuckled aloud, certain the women had already determined that her quick exit was due to a guilty conscience rather than their own unpleasant attitudes.

Red and yellow leaves swirled along the path as Elinor trudged toward home with Daughtie's parting remarks churning about in her head. Obviously Daughtie believed Hilda and Nettie to be kind Christian women with only goodness in their hearts. If so, she was an extremely poor judge of character and much more naïve than Elinor would have thought.

"I suppose we can't all have the ability to see others clearly," she muttered. The wind stung her cheeks, and she burrowed her head closer to her chest, concentrating on the final leg of her journey.

When she finally turned the corner and headed down Jackson Street, her face and fingers were nearly numb. "I should have set aside my pride and accepted Daughtie's offer of a buggy ride," she chastised herself aloud as she neared the front door of the boardinghouse.

"Excuse me?"

Elinor gasped and jumped back a step. "Who are you, and *why* are you on my doorstep?"

"Oliver Maxwell. My apologies," he said, bowing and sweeping his hat in front of him in an exaggerated gesture. "I didn't mean to startle you, good lady."

It took only a moment for Elinor to notice his case. "You're a peddler, I see. Obviously you know the girls haven't returned from work yet. No guests and no salesmen until after supper—house rules."

He stroked his narrow blond mustache. "I'm a shoe salesman," he replied, clearly not bothered by the sharp, cold wind. "Frequently the girls keep me busy when I come calling in the evening, and I don't have an opportunity to visit the boardinghouse keepers. Consequently, I decided to make some early calls while I'm in Lowell for that very purpose. A good pair of shoes is a necessity in cold weather, and winter will soon be here."

"It feels as though winter has already arrived. I really must go indoors. If you want to return at eight o'clock, there should be any number of girls anxious to purchase a new pair of shoes."

"And *you,* dear lady? Could I not interest you in a pair of shoes? I'd be delighted to take your measurements before the girls return home, and then I'll be on my way."

He was charming with his blond hair, wool frock coat, and proper manners, but Elinor really couldn't afford a pair of new shoes. She couldn't afford even a new ribbon. "It's the mill girls who have money to spend on themselves, not the keepers," she replied.

He nodded and smiled, radiating a kindness she'd not seen for far too long. "If you're truly in need of a pair of shoes, I'm certain I could find something within your budget. And although I require the girls to pay in full when they place their orders, in your case, I would be willing to arrange for payments."

"Why don't you come inside," she said after a moment of silence. "It's much too cold outdoors."

"Well, if you're absolutely certain. I don't want to keep you from your chores," he said, his voice as smooth as cream.

"Not at all. Come in," Elinor said while turning her key in the lock. She took his hat and coat and hung them beside her own on the wooden pegs inside the front door. The sight of a man's coat next to her own appeared strange and yet achingly familiar. "Why don't you sit down in the parlor while I make a pot of tea. A cup of hot tea would help ward off the chill, don't you agree?"

He rubbed his hands together in quick, exaggerated motions. "Indeed. Something warm would be most satisfying."

Mr. Maxwell had opened his case and was removing the contents when Elinor returned with a tea tray. She settled herself on the couch and poured him a cup of tea while glancing at his samples. "You have some lovely shoes," she said, offering him the cup.

"I'm pleased you think so. I pride myself on the quality and variety of shoes I sell. Have you decided to take me up on my offer and order a pair?"

"I believe I will," Elinor replied, pointing toward a soft kid boot.

He graced her with a charming smile as she extended her foot. "An excellent choice. Now I need only measure your foot." Mr. Maxwell wrapped his fingers around Elinor's ankle as he carefully removed her shoe. His fingers trailed the length of her foot before he placed it atop the measuring paper. Her eyes widened as an unbidden tremble coursed through her body.

CHAPTER · 5

JASMINE SAT STARING at the distant horizon in a trancelike stupor, feeling as though someone else had inhabited her body and rendered her immobile. She should be getting dressed, yet her limbs were heavy, weighed down by an intense aching sorrow—a sorrow she hadn't anticipated. The entire family had expected her mother's death, known it was coming, and in the end, waited upon it. Yet when death finally had its way and sucked the last remnant of breath from her mother's body, an unexpected pain had seared Jasmine's heart, for she knew that her life would never again be the same.

The bright, sunny morning seemed strangely out of place—not the type of day one envisioned for a funeral. Nolan had taken Spencer downstairs several hours earlier, likely thinking she would immediately don her mourning clothes and join the rest of the family. But she had no desire to enter the parlor, where her mother's body lay awaiting the undertaker's hearse. Better to let the coffin be closed without once again staring down at her mother's lifeless face—a picture that had already etched itself into her memory. She had listened and watched as their friends and neighbors attempted to impart comfort, yet there was nothing they could say or do that would assuage her grief. Most of them knew little of her mother. Visitors had not been encouraged in later years, at least not by the mistress of The Willows. However, now they needed no invitation to call; now they came because it was proper.

Somewhere in the distance she heard her name but pressed her face closer to the window, wishing it were springtime and the magnolias were in bloom. Her mother had loved magnolias. Instead, it was November and her father was as concerned over the cotton harvest as his wife's death—or so it appeared. She had listened while he'd discussed his disappointment over the prices with Uncle Franklin yesterday. Instead of lamenting his wife's death, they had talked of cotton and the prices they had hoped to receive with this crop. Never once did she hear either of them mention their remorse over her mother's death. She'd not yet seen her father shed a tear—and each time someone grew near and offered condolences, he would cover his face in a mask of grief, only to be replaced by his normal appearance once they turned away.

"Jasmine! Have you not heard me calling?" Her father's voice was followed by several loud raps. "Are you ill?"

"Come in," she said, still unable to force herself away from the window.

"I was concerned . . ." He hesitated, staring at her. "You're not dressed for the funeral. People have begun arriving. Thankfully, Samuel has finally arrived. You can't wear that dress. Change into your black gown and come downstairs. I've given Spencer over to Bessie's care for the remainder of the day. You need to gather your wits about you and behave like a grown woman, Jasmine. I need you to act as my hostess."

"Hostess? This isn't a party, Father. You don't need a hostess at Mother's funeral." She choked out the words and flung herself toward him. "She's *dead*! Don't you care?" Hot tears rolled down her cheeks as she pounded his chest.

He wrapped his arms tightly about her, holding her until the sobbing subsided and she relaxed in his arms. "Of course I care. She was my wife and I adored her, but I can't bring her back. And no matter how deep my grief, there is a funeral about to take place. I would greatly appreciate it if you would get dressed and join us in the parlor." He released his grasp and looked deep into her swollen brown eyes. "I apologize for my choice of words. You're right. I don't need a hostess. However, I do want my daughter to join me—I need to be surrounded by my family."

She saw the glisten of tears in her father's eyes and, for the first time since her mother's death, realized his pain was fresh and raw—hidden from view, yet as absolute and deep as her own. "I'm sorry, Papa." She drew him into a brief embrace and then leaned back to meet his gaze. "I thought because you and Uncle Franklin have been consumed by business discussions since Mother's death, you weren't feeling any loss."

"We all grieve in different ways, my dear. I prefer to remain composed in front of others, and the only way I can accomplish that feat is to talk of the crops or weather or some other mundane topic that won't remind me of your mother and the fact that now she is gone. At night I remind myself that one day we'll be together again. But for today, we must give your mother a proper burial, and I would very much like you by my side."

Jasmine nodded. "I'll join you as soon as I've changed clothes."

Her father leaned forward and placed a kiss on Jasmine's fore-head. "Thank you, my dear."

———

When the last of the visitors finally departed, Jasmine turned to Nolan. "I must look in on Mammy. I promised to share the details of Mother's funeral with her, and I've not yet been to see her today."

"Shall I go with you?"

Jasmine's shoulders sagged a bit, and she forced a weary smile. "It's probably best that I go alone, but thank you for your kind offer."

"Promise that if Mammy's asleep, you'll return and get some rest yourself. I'm worried about you, Jasmine. You're going to become ill if you don't take care of yourself."

"You have my word."

Jasmine inhaled deeply as she walked down the hallway and neared the small room off the rear of the kitchen. Unfortunately, it didn't help. She honestly doubted there was anything that would calm the roiling tumult of fear that had taken up residence deep within.

She tiptoed into the room and sat down on the marred wooden chair beside Mammy's bed. There was no sign of life in the old woman. However, before she would permit panic to clench a final hold over her, she held her hand above Mammy's face. A faint rush of warm air tickled her palm.

"What you doin', chile? Plannin' to smother me?" Mammy asked with a hint of a smile on her cracked lips.

"I couldn't see you breathing, and I was frightened," Jasmine admitted. A tear trickled down her cheek as she leaned against the wood slats that backed the chair.

"Ain't no need to be cryin'," Mammy said, reaching for Jasmine's hand. "Now tell me 'bout your mama's buryin'. Did the preacher say fine words over her?"

Jasmine nodded and squeezed Mammy's hand, unable to push any sound around the large lump that had risen in her throat.

"She's in a better place, Miz Jasmine. You got to remember dat."

"I know, but with Mama gone and you so ill, I feel as though my whole world has turned upside down. I don't think I could bear it if you died. Promise me you'll get well," she begged.

"Umm, um, chile, you know I can't be promisin' such a thin' as dat 'cause the good Lord, He be callin' me home. But you listen to your ole mammy and you listen good. You need to be lookin' to the Lord to fill dat place inside o' you. He's the only one dat'll pull you through the hard times, the only one dat's always there when you need Him, the only one who never changes—He's faithful and true and won' never leave you, chile. So it's *Him* you need to keep fixed on—not your ole mammy. You understan' what I'm telling you?"

Jasmine folded her arms around herself and rocked back and

forth on the hard wooden chair. The slats jarred her spine and caused a pain as real as the ache in her heart. "I know what you say is true, Mammy, but my prayers seem like vapor. I wonder if God even hears them. I pray and pray, but I don't feel His presence. I don't think I can bear any more loss."

"The Lord is always with you, chile, even when you don' feel Him. Been lots a times in my life when I thought I couldn't bear no more pain, but da hurt came and the Lord saw me through, just like He will now. You keep yo' faith in God. Ain't nothin' more important in dis life. I want you to remember dat when I'm gone. Will you do dis for me?"

"I'll try," Jasmine whispered.

"Good. Now, why don't you get your ole mammy a drink of water. I gots somethin' I needs to be askin' you, and I'm thirstin' mighty bad right now."

Jasmine jumped up and fetched the old woman a drink from the bedside table. "I'm so sorry. I should have gotten you some water as soon as I arrived," she said while cradling Mammy's head in the crook of her arm.

"Umm, dat sure tastes good," she said, running her thick tongue along her parched lips. "Now sit back and listen to your ole mammy 'cause I'm fixin' to ask you somethin' important. Way back when you was jest a baby, your pappy bought me and brung me here to De Willows."

"Yes, I know. Mother told me how Father looked everywhere to find a wet nurse for me because she was sick after I was born and couldn't nurse me. She said he had a hard time finding someone."

Mammy nodded. " 'Cause your pappy weren't willing to separate families."

"Mother said your baby died and your husband had been sold to another plantation, so Papa bought you to be my wet nurse."

"Dat's right, only dat was a lie I been livin' with all these years."

Jasmine bent close to hear her words.

"My baby *weren't* dead. He was a big strong boy 'bout half a year older than you. He had a smile bright as all outdoors."

"But why didn't you tell Father? He wouldn't have bought you, Mammy."

"Ole Massa tol' me he'd kill my baby iffen I didn't go or iffen he found out I tol' I had a chile. He said I better *never* tell 'bout my Obadiah."

"That's your baby's name, Obadiah?"

"Um hum. Dat name come straight outta da Bible. 'Course I don' know if the massa let him keep dat name or not, but he promised me he'd keep da boy safe on his plantation so long as I didn't tell. Miss Jasmine, I wants you to find my Obadiah and see if you can set him free. I don't want to die knowin' I never did nothin' to help my boy outta da shackles of slavery."

Questions flooded Jasmine's mind. "How have you been able to remain silent all these years, Mammy? How could you bear knowing you had a child you'd never see again and not ask for help before now?"

"Dat's what I been tryin' to tell you, chile. You can bear da pain if you got Jesus holdin' yo hand. And dat's what you gotta do from now on: reach out and take hold of Jesus with all yo might. Weren't hard to keep my mouth shut 'cause I knew if your pappy went back to try and buy Obadiah, ole Massa woulda killed him right in front of your pappy and all the other slaves jest to make sure they all understood what would happen to dem if they disobeyed. Couldn't take that chance with my baby's life. Better he be raised without me than to have him die."

"Couldn't Papa have bought you both?"

"No," she whispered. "Ole Massa never turned loose of big, healthy boy babies. He raise dem up like prime stock. He didn't care none 'bout losing me. I 'most bled to death birthin' Obadiah, and he knew my days fo' having babies was past. 'Sides, he had other young slaves to wet-nurse my boy, and your pappy was willin' to pay a high price fo' your ole mammy."

Jasmine's stomach wrenched in pain. "It's because of *me* that you were forced to leave Obadiah."

"Now don't you be dwellin' on dat. I only tol' you bout Obadiah so's maybe you could help set him free. Would you try and help him for your ole mammy?"

"You know I will. Do you remember anything about where you were or any names that will help us?"

"I's hoping he's still with Massa Harshaw. Dat's where I was— at Harwood Plantation, but I can't tell you how to get there. Don't seem like it took us terrible long to get to Da Willows, but I was so sad, I don't 'member much about da journey from one place to da other."

"But you're certain it was Harwood Plantation and the owner was Mr. Harshaw?"

"Dey used to call it Harshaw Plantation, but when ole Massa married, he changed de name to Harwood to make the new mistress happy," she explained.

"I'll do everything in my power to find Obadiah, and when I do, you can be certain I'll buy his freedom. Now I want you to get some rest. I'll be back to see you in the morning."

The old woman's lips formed a faint smile and she closed her eyes. "I'm gonna do jes' dat, chile. I'm gonna rest in the arms of Jesus."

Jasmine brushed a soft kiss onto Mammy's fleshy cheek before leaving the room. The hour was late and her body ached with an overpowering weariness, yet she felt a determined purpose as she ascended the rear stairway to her bedroom. She would find Obadiah and bring him to meet his mother. Seeing her son would surely cause Mammy's health to rally. The thought made Jasmine smile, and when she finally slipped into bed a short time later, she thanked Jesus for this opportunity to help Mammy. She fell asleep with renewed optimism and enthusiasm for the task with which she'd been entrusted.

Jasmine caught sight of Nolan talking quietly with her brothers and father in the parlor as she descended the stairway the next morning. The group stood shoulder to shoulder in a tight half circle surrounding the hearth like a decorative fire screen.

She entered the room and met their somber gazes with a gentle spring in her step and a gleam in her eyes. "I slept well last night, although it appears the five of you could use more sleep," she commented. "Shall we go in to breakfast?"

"Sit down, my dear," her father requested while gently leading her to the divan.

"This sounds ominous," she said. The others lingered in front of the fireplace, staring at her. With their arms locked behind their backs, they reminded Jasmine of toy soldiers set in place to guard an imaginary fort. The spectacle unsettled her, and little by little, she could feel her joy slipping away.

Her father reached out and took her hand, and she noticed his hands were shaking. "I don't want you to become unduly upset, but I fear it is left to me to give you more sad news. Mammy died during the night."

Jasmine stared at him, unable to speak. She heard the slaves talking in the kitchen, their voices muffled and distant, echoing as though they were calling to her from a deep cavern.

"Jasmine! Open your eyes. It's Nolan."

He was dabbing her face with a cool cloth. She willed her eyes to open. Nolan was kneeling beside her, peering directly into her eyes. "What happened? Please tell me I didn't faint. I abhor fainting women," she said, pushing herself up on one elbow.

Nolan laughed. "I fear that's exactly what you did. Fortunately, you were on the sofa and didn't hurt yourself."

But now she remembered the reason for her disquietude. Her father's words came rushing back and invaded her mind. "Mammy . . . she's—"

"Yes," Nolan whispered. "Bessie said she went peacefully during the night."

"I should have known. We talked last night, and when I bid her good-night, she said she was going to rest in the arms of Jesus. She was telling me she knew her time on earth was over, but I was too foolish to understand. I should have remained with her through the night."

Her father tenderly embraced her. "Don't be so hard on your-self, Jasmine. Mammy wouldn't have wanted you sitting in that room all night long. We both know that."

"Sitting up one night is the least I could have done. Think of the many nights she remained awake caring for me when I was a child. She was always there when I needed her. She even came to Lowell when I married Bradley, even though she didn't want to leave Mississippi. I want her to have a proper burial, Papa."

Her father's eyes widened as he pulled away from her. "When have I ever *not* given my slaves a proper burial? I'm not akin to those who would hearken to any less."

"I know, Papa. I'm sorry if my words hurt you."

"I'll take care of the funeral arrangements, and everything will be very special, if you'll promise to come in and eat some break-fast. You can go upstairs and rest as soon as you have something to eat."

Jasmine sat in the carriage beside Nolan. The funeral had been the finest ever held for any slave at The Willows—likely for any slave in all the South. But a fine funeral wouldn't fill the void of Mammy leaving this world.

"Time will heal the loss of your mother and of Mammy. I hope you find comfort in the fact that you were able to spend some time with each of them."

She nodded and gave him a faint smile. "I need to discuss something with you, Nolan. Something Mammy asked of me, a deathbed request that I promised to fulfill. I'm hoping you'll agree to help me."

"Of course. Anything. Surely you're aware you need only ask. What is it she requested?"

Nolan listened intently as Jasmine explained Mammy's heart-rending tale of being separated from her son when he was a mere babe. "And she asked you to find this son and purchase his free-dom?"

"Exactly! But I've never heard of Harwood Plantation. Of

TRACIE PETERSON / JUDITH MILLER

course, I'm certain there are many plantations in Louisiana and Mississippi that I've never heard of, but I'm not certain how to locate the place without arousing interest. I don't want to answer a multitude of questions, especially from my father. Mammy didn't want him to ever find out about what had occurred. She said it would serve no purpose at this late date. I suppose she's correct. Papa would be either angry that Mr. Harshaw had lied to him or distressed that he'd separated a family."

"Or both," Nolan remarked.

"True," she agreed. "Can you think of any way we might easily be able to secure the information? I don't want to alert anyone in the family of our plan."

He rubbed his jaw. "Let me take care of it. I'll think of something," he said as he drew back on the reins and the carriage came to a halt in front of the house. "Now let's go inside. I believe your father expects all of us to have dinner together."

"I want to check on Spencer; then I'll join you in the parlor," Jasmine said as she passed through the foyer.

After assuring herself the boy had eaten and was taking his nap, Jasmine once again entrusted him to Bessie's care and hurried back downstairs. "I hope I didn't delay dinner," she said, glancing toward the dining room, where the servants were busy placing food on the oversized serving buffet.

"No, we were just preparing to go in. I trust you found everything satisfactory at the service?" her father inquired.

"Yes. In fact, I wanted to tell you that several of the slaves expressed their gratitude for your kindness in seeing that they always receive proper burials."

The comment appeared to please her father. Jasmine's preference was to have all of the slaves freed, but she knew it would do no good to speak of that matter.

"I trust you're still enjoying your work for the Associates, Samuel?" Nolan inquired.

"Absolutely. I regret the fact that it keeps me away from The Willows so much, but it seems I'm traveling most of the time."

"You certainly haven't had much time to spend visiting with

me or Grandmother in Lowell," Jasmine said.

Samuel grimaced at his sister's remark. "I apologize. However, most of my business is in Boston. I venture into Lowell only on rare occasions upon the specific request of the Associates, and I've attempted to see you on each of those visits."

"Lowell is not so very far from Boston, Samuel, and Grandmother isn't getting any younger," Jasmine said. "I'm certain she would have appreciated a visit during her recent bout with pneumonia. Stopping for a cup of tea from time to time wouldn't take long."

"Duly noted, sister. I shall consider myself thoroughly educated on proper etiquette," he said with a grin.

Jasmine set her glass down with a force that caused the contents to slosh over the rim and onto the linen tablecloth. "I'm not speaking of etiquette, Samuel. She's your *grandmother* and soon she's going to die too. You should spend more time with her while you have the opportunity," she said, her voice laced with emotion.

"I'm sorry. I didn't mean to make light of your request. I'll make an effort to visit more often," Samuel replied with his gaze focused upon his dinner plate.

"Have you been able to expand any of your markets here in Mississippi?" Nolan inquired, giving Jasmine a sidelong glance. He was obviously intent upon defusing the attack upon her brother.

Samuel sighed and directed a visibly appreciative smile toward Nolan. "As a matter of fact, I was telling Father only yesterday that I signed on two new growers three months ago: one in Mississippi and one in Louisiana. Both of them have large plantations that yield as much cotton as The Willows. I plan to leave The Willows tomorrow morning and call at a number of plantations before I leave. I've been negotiating with the owners and hope to have at least one of them sign a contract before I board ship for Boston next month. My discussions with all of them appear promising."

"Sounds as though you've been very successful. Have you heard mention of Harwood Plantation? I seem to remember someone saying they were known for huge cotton crops years ago."

Samuel nodded enthusiastically. "Not only years ago. Jacob Harshaw currently operates one of the most prosperous plantations in Louisiana. In fact, I successfully negotiated a contract with him only this year. Although we weren't able to agree upon a price for this year's crop, we will be purchasing his entire crop next year."

"Well, that *is* quite an accomplishment. I'm certain the Associates were elated over your ability to win over Mr.—did you say Harshaw?"

"Yes, Harshaw. His plantation is located across the river in Louisiana and about thirty miles south, not too far from the river—good fertile land. He's well known among the southern Louisiana growers. You've met him, haven't you, Father?" Samuel asked.

Jasmine glanced toward her father, who had placed a finger alongside his cheek as though attempting to recall the name before he answered.

"Yes, as a matter of fact, I have. I've talked with him on several occasions at the docks in New Orleans. Not a man I'm particularly fond to know on a social level—rather crass and uncouth, although I'll give the devil his due. His crops are exceptional."

"Have you ever seen his plantation?" Jasmine ventured.

Deep ridges creased her father's brow. "Yes, I have." He hesitated a moment and rubbed his forehead. "Seems strange discussing Jacob Harshaw today, of all days. You see, Harwood Plantation is where I purchased Mammy."

"Really? Peculiar how a topic will arise at the most unexpected moment," Samuel said. "From what I observed at Harwood, I'd say Mammy was very fortunate you purchased her. Unlike The Willows, the whip is used freely by Jacob Harshaw on all of his slaves."

Jasmine gave an involuntary shudder. She wondered how many lashes Obadiah may have taken from Master Harshaw's whip.

CHAPTER · 6

December

THE TIME FOR DEPARTURE had arrived. Jasmine could no longer delay leaving her father and brothers. The trunks sat in readiness beside the front door, and the family was waiting downstairs. Picking up her reticule, she checked her appearance in the mirror and glanced about the room one last time, as though she must commit each item to memory. She detested good-byes, especially now. Farewells seemed much too final. What if her father took ill before she saw him again—or one of her brothers? Suddenly life seemed very fragile.

Spencer was tugging at McKinley's pant leg and begging for a horsey ride when Jasmine entered the parlor. She smiled and shook her head. "You've spoiled him with those rides around the house, McKinley. I'll never be able to handle him once I get home," she said, giving her brother a wide smile.

"Then I suppose I'll have to come to Lowell and entertain him for you."

"Oh, *would* you? Come for a visit, I mean? I would truly love that, and it would give us something to plan and look forward to," she said, feeling a renewed enthusiasm. "You'll come too, won't you, Father? And you, David! *All* of you."

Her father laughed and wagged his head back and forth. "And

71

who will tend to this place if we all go traipsing off to Lowell?"

"Uncle Franklin and the slaves," she replied. "Please say you'll come."

"I won't promise we'll all come at the same time, but we'll all come for a visit. How's that? Besides, if we spread out our visits, it will continually give you something to anticipate."

"Either way, I won't argue. Just so you come," she said while accepting his embrace.

Her father took hold of her arm. "I'd like to have a few words alone with you before you depart, Jasmine. I'm certain your brothers and Nolan can look after Spencer."

"What is it, Papa?" she asked as they walked into her father's library.

"I know we haven't always seen eye to eye on things, and I still regret forcing you into a marriage with Bradley, but . . ."

"That's all in the past, Papa. You apologized long ago, and I forgave you. Besides, had I not married Bradley, I wouldn't have Spencer now, and he's the joy of my life. You know that. Please don't worry yourself with regrets over my marriage any longer."

"It's not just the marriage. I feel as though I failed you—both you *and* your mother. Perhaps if I had left this place long ago, things would have been different. I fear I was so busy becoming prosperous, I didn't give your mother the attention she deserved."

"Papa, that's all behind us. There's no way to change the past. If you regret where you've placed your values in the past, you have the rest of your life to make changes. I know your life is going to be very different without Mama. However, you'll have ample opportunity to evaluate how best to live your remaining years— and you can begin by coming to visit Grandmother, as well as Spencer and me."

"You're right," he said. "Perhaps I'll even journey to the capital and stop for a visit with Zachary and Peggy. What do you think of that?"

"I think a visit to Washington would be a splendid beginning."

He pulled her into an embrace and placed a kiss upon her forehead. "Always remember I love you, Jasmine. While I don't have high expectations, please remember that I would look favorably upon having you and Spencer move back to The Willows."

Jasmine stood on tiptoe and kissed his cheek. "I think it's wise of you to keep expectations of me returning to The Willows *very* low."

"I know, I know, but you can't fault me for trying," he said. "I suppose we had best get your trunks onto the carriage if you're going to get on the road before nightfall."

After all the good-byes were finally said and the carriage pulled away from the plantation, Jasmine leaned back against the leather-upholstered seat and sighed. Spencer wriggled onto her lap and, wrapping his chubby arms tightly around her neck, placed a wet kiss upon her cheek. "Thank you, sweetheart," she said, ruffling his curls. "A kiss is exactly what I needed."

"Had I known, I would have come to your rescue long ago," Nolan said with a roguish grin.

A blush colored Jasmine's cheeks. "Nolan Houston!" she said with a giggle. Her heart began a rapid beat that suggested more than girlish amusement.

Spencer quickly moved to take his place between them on the cushioned seat, and Nolan momentarily gazed out the window before turning back to face Jasmine. "About Obadiah," he began.

"I think we should attempt to find him before our voyage home. Do you think we have sufficient time?"

"It's not far out of our way; I was planning exactly the same thing. We can go down river the thirty miles and then hire a conveyance to the Harwood Plantation. If we're fortunate, we'll easily locate someone who knows Jacob Harshaw. If his reputation is what Samuel has indicated, we should have no difficulty."

"Let's pray all goes well. From the little Mammy told me, I doubt we'll have an easy time convincing Mr. Harshaw to sell Obadiah."

"*If* Obadiah is still there. However, there's no need to worry yet," he said. "As you said a moment ago, perhaps a word of prayer is what we need."

The smell of dead fish and wet moss filled Jasmine's nostrils as the carriage neared the river at Rodney. When the horses came to a stop near the dock, Nolan jumped down and quickly assisted Jasmine and Spencer while the driver unloaded their trunks.

"Thank you for your help, Louis," Nolan said. "You can return to The Willows and tell Master Wainwright you saw us safely to the docks at Rodney."

"Yessuh," the black man replied. "Been good seein' you, Miz Jasmine. You have you a safe trip back home, ya hear?"

"I will, Louis, and you take care of yourself—and Bessie," she added.

"I be doin' dat fo' sure," he said with a toothy grin. He clucked at the horses and turned the carriage. Jasmine watched as he waved and headed back down the road.

"I'll go to purchase tickets and see if anyone knows where we should go ashore if we're planning to visit the Harwood Plantation."

"I believe I'll take Spencer for a short walk near the river. He'll be intrigued with the water, and I'm hoping the walk will tire him. Hopefully he'll take a nap once we depart," she said, giving way to the two-year-old's insistent tugging at her hand. "We'll meet you on the dock or in front of the general store if it doesn't take long to purchase the tickets."

"Is that quite safe? I mean . . . to go unescorted."

Jasmine smiled. "I'll be fine. This is the land of my birth—I know it well. Besides, a lady needn't worry about being accosted—at least not in the same manner that she might in the North. Southern manners and etiquette generally keep the rogues at bay. Still, you won't be that far away should the need arise to rescue me."

Nolan nodded his agreement and strode away while Jasmine turned Spencer by the shoulders in the direction of the dock. "Come along, Spencer. Let's go see the water."

The child needed no further encouragement, and Jasmine was immediately thankful she had placed a tight grasp around the boy's tiny hand before making the suggestion. Spencer was delighted to splatter his hands in the murky river water and watch as the twigs he dropped made a tiny splash and floated off.

Jasmine thought of the long trip home. She longed for Lowell and the farm, yet she knew a certain sadness in leaving the South. It was a bittersweet hurt. Her mother would say she was waxing nostalgic, but Jasmine couldn't help it. So much had happened on her visit. Her mother and Mammy had both departed, leaving her regretful for all the time and distance that had separated them. What if she returned to Lowell to find her grandmother gone as well? What if her father were to die before he could journey north to visit her again?

Spencer laughed with glee as he dropped a rock into the water. His revelry forced Jasmine to leave off with her sorrowful ponderings. Life was fragile. It was but vapor—a mist, as the Bible suggested. Here and then gone. Smiling at her son, Jasmine knew that the past could not hold her captive. Not when Spencer was her future.

Jasmine turned at the sound of approaching footsteps. "You certainly weren't long," she said, gracing Nolan with a pleasant smile.

"I paid for our passage and was able to gain information without any difficulty. It didn't take long to locate someone who was familiar with Jacob Harshaw and his plantation. But I must admit the comments weren't particularly flattering. Seems Mr. Harshaw is a bit abrasive, and when he's in his cups, I'm told he's an odious man."

"Then we'd best pray he's sober when we arrive. I'm going to remain optimistic."

Nolan lifted Spencer into his arms and pointed toward the water. The boy watched and then giggled as Nolan skipped a pebble across the water. "If Obadiah is at Harwood, we'll find him. And there's little doubt in my mind you'll somehow convince Mr. Harshaw he should sell Obadiah to you."

"Are you saying I'm somewhat overbearing?" she asked with a grin.

Nolan chuckled. "Oh, not at all. However, I would say you have strong powers of persuasion." He glanced toward a group assembling on the dock. "It appears as though the captain has begun gathering the passengers to board."

"Then we best not keep him waiting. Were you able to gain specifics on how far we'll be required to travel after disembarking?"

"Indeed. It won't be long at all compared to our journey upriver, and then we'll travel another hour or two by carriage—perhaps longer if the roads are muddy and difficult to traverse."

"Let's hope it's less. I wouldn't want to spend the night as Mr. Harshaw's guest. Do you know if there will be another boat coming to the landing before nightfall?"

"Only one, and I have my doubts we'll be able to return by then. We'll see how things progress at Harwood Plantation. If we're required to find accommodations elsewhere, we'll do so. However, it was my understanding you were intent upon finding Obadiah. . . ."

"You're right. I shouldn't be creating a problem before one exists. Forgive me. I can certainly push aside any ill feelings I might have toward Mr. Harshaw if it means we'll be able to find Obadiah and secure his freedom."

The instructions Nolan received were accurate. The boat reached Pappan's Landing early in the afternoon. By the time they arranged for a carriage and entered the driveway to Harwood Plantation, it was approaching three o'clock. Two large dogs loped alongside the carriage and remained on either side until their coach stopped in front of the main house. A large man carrying a coiled whip called the dogs to heel. A deep, jagged scar lined the man's cheek, and his clothing bore evidence of more than several days' dirt and grime.

"Do you think that's Mr. Harshaw?" Jasmine whispered.

"I have no idea. Let us hope not." Nolan quietly replied before leaning forward and waving to the man. "Is it safe to alight from the carriage, or will your dogs consider me their supper should I step down?"

The man emitted a deep belly laugh before spitting a stream of tobacco juice from between his brown-stained teeth. "You're safe so long as I'm nearby. Get on down," he commanded, his smile widening as he met Jasmine's wary gaze.

"Got ya a good-lookin' woman. Too bad I didn't see her afore ya, or I'd have fought ya for her hand," he said, his gaze going up and down the full length of Jasmine's form.

"Don't tell him I'm a widow," Jasmine whispered when Nolan came alongside her. "I don't want him making unseemly advances toward me."

"I was jest getting ready to ride off when you got here. What can I do fer ya?"

"Quite the host," Jasmine murmured.

Nolan grinned at her disdainful rejoinder. "Be careful," he whispered while bending down and scooping Spencer into the crook of his arm. "He may hear you, and we need to remain on good terms if we're to find Obadiah."

The man wiped one hand on his dirty pant leg before reaching to shake Nolan's hand. "Jacob Harshaw. I'm the owner of Harwood," he said, waving his arm in an expansive motion.

"Nolan Houston," he said. "And this young man is Spencer Houston, along with his mother, Mrs. Houston."

"Pleased ta make yer acquaintance." His leering gaze came to rest upon Jasmine's bodice. "What brings ya to Harwood?"

"Slaves," Nolan said.

"Well, I got me plenty of them, but ain't particularly set on sellin' any," he said while massaging his ample belly. The front door opened and a dour-looking woman with a tightly wound knot atop her head strode forward to take her place beside Mr. Harshaw.

"Appears we got company. How come ya didn't let me know?" the woman asked with a modicum of irritation lacing the question. Before her husband could reply, the woman turned her attention toward Jasmine and Nolan. "I'm Rosemary Harshaw, mistress of Harwood." Her seeming annoyance turned to obvious pride as she made the announcement.

"Pleased to make your acquaintance," Jasmine and Nolan replied in unison and then grinned at each other.

"You want to bring the boy inside?"

Jasmine glanced toward Nolan, hoping he would give her an indication of what he considered most helpful.

"We were telling your husband we're wanting to purchase some slaves and heard that Harwood had some fine specimens. I'm particularly interested in a good buck or two. We'd like to look at any you think might meet our needs."

Harshaw narrowed his eyes and ejected another stream of spittle. "Don't know as I'd be willing to turn loose any of my best breedin' stock, but I can have my overseer bring them for you to inspect. Never know—we might be able to come to some sort of agreement."

Mrs. Harshaw hissed an inaudible remark to her husband and then turned toward Jasmine and Nolan. "I can offer ya a cup of tea while we wait. It'll take the mister some time to get the slaves up here. You can best review 'em from the upstairs portico. That's where we go to watch when he whips the runaways."

"You watch when they're punished?" Jasmine gave the other woman an incredulous look.

" 'Course! Outside of going to town once in a while, it's the only entertainment around this place," she stated harshly. "Besides, we gotta keep our darkies under control. We're not like you folks that buy only a few slaves to help operate your small farms. We own nearly a hundred, and they gotta know who's in charge. Otherwise, they'll run at the first opportunity. Can't let that happen. We got too much money tied up in our slaves."

"Perhaps kindness would cause them to stay of their own volition," Jasmine commented.

Mrs. Harshaw cast a disdainful look in Jasmine's direction. "It's obvious you haven't had many dealings with slaves. Come along. We'll go up and have us a look from upstairs while your husband examines 'em close up. I'll educate you on how to deal with slaves, and you'll have little trouble after that . . . if you follow my ways."

Jasmine followed along behind the woman, hoping she wouldn't be quizzed any further about why they were in the area. She certainly didn't want to divulge the fact that Malcolm Wainwright was her father. Jacob Harshaw might not remember selling Mammy some twenty-one years ago, but there was always the possibility he would recollect past events if he realized she was a Wainwright.

A stoop-shouldered black woman appeared in the hallway as they entered the front door. "You can serve us tea on the upstairs portico, Hessie. And be quick about it." Mrs. Harshaw turned to Jasmine. "You want the boy to come with us or you want Hessie to look after him?"

Jasmine tightened her hold on Spencer's hand. "He had best stay with me. I'm certain Hessie already has more than enough chores to keep her busy, and Spencer is quite a handful."

"Got him spoilt, have ya? Slaves and children—they both need to be treated with a strong hand." Her stern glare caused Spencer to immediately tuck himself behind Jasmine's skirts.

Had circumstances been different, Jasmine would have told Rosemary Harshaw exactly what she thought of her malevolent advice. Instead, she remained silent and lifted Spencer up into her arms and followed the older woman. Mrs. Harshaw escorted Jasmine upstairs and then to the outer gallery, where she took a seat in one of the willow chairs along the east end of the gallery. Spencer sat near her side until the old slave emerged a short time later, bearing a sizeable silver tea tray. Obviously the sight of flaky pastries, fruit-topped cakes, and berry tarts was enough to fortify her son's bravery. Spencer rushed forward the moment Hessie placed the tray on a small table near Mrs. Harshaw, with his chubby fingers aimed toward one of the tasty-appearing delicacies.

"Don't touch!" Mrs. Harshaw barked. Her eyes had suddenly narrowed to mere slits, and she leveled a formidable gaze that sent the child scurrying back to his mother.

Jasmine pulled her son into a protective embrace before she removed a lace-edged handkerchief from her dress pocket and wiped away his tears. "He is but a young child unaccustomed to such harsh words, Mrs. Harshaw."

"Youth is no excuse for ill manners."

Jasmine bit her lower lip for several seconds before responding.

"I believe we likely disagree about what constitutes proper behavior. However, if my child has offended your sensibilities, please accept my apology."

Mrs. Harshaw's shoulders squared as she drew herself up straighter in the chair and looked down her bulbous nose at Spencer. "Apology accepted," she said and then placed one of the tarts on a napkin and offered it to the boy.

Instead of accepting the treat, Spencer buried his face in Jasmine's bodice. "Perhaps later," Jasmine said on the boy's behalf.

"Here they come," Mrs. Harshaw announced, pointing a finger toward the dirt road leading up to the mansion. "Finest-looking bucks you'll find this side of the Mississippi."

Jasmine watched as the overseer herded fifteen sturdy male slaves into two lines at the east end of the house. The overseer cracked his whip, and the first slave stepped forward as Mr. Harshaw called out a name and methodically recited the man's pedigree to Nolan. The procedure followed for each of the men in the front line before continuing to the second row.

"Obadiah," Mr. Harshaw called out as the first man in the second group stepped forward. "This here boy is a strong one, and I can vouch for his bloodline. A good, strong buck from over at the Elmhouse Plantation sired him. I paid a hefty fee to have this one sired, and I'd be willing to let him go at a fair price."

They went through the entire line like this. Harshaw calling out names, suggesting each man's strong points, even commenting on the scars, pointing out that each man had been given very few beatings and hence was well behaved.

Jasmine watched as Nolan pretended to take each man under great scrutiny. The minutes seemed to tick by like hours until he and Mr. Harshaw were once again standing in front of the man called Obadiah. Nolan appeared to be saying something, although Jasmine couldn't hear the words.

Mr. Harshaw poked and prodded at Obadiah as though he were pointing out the attributes of a prized bull. Jasmine leaned forward and peered over the railing a little more closely. Mr. Harshaw said something indistinguishable, and Nolan appeared to nod in agreement. "Go fetch the woman and boy," Mr. Harshaw called out to the overseer.

"You strike a bargain on Obadiah?" Mrs. Harshaw called down to her husband.

"Quit your hollering, woman. I'll talk to ya later."

"You'll talk to me now!" she said, jumping up from her chair.

Jasmine stared after the woman as she stomped into the house and appeared downstairs beside her husband a few moments later. Mr. Harshaw pulled her aside, and the two of them moved away from Nolan and engaged in what appeared to be a less than amicable conversation.

Nolan glanced up to the gallery and motioned for Jasmine to join him. When she and Spencer came alongside Nolan, Mr. and Mrs. Harshaw were still occupied with their private conversation. "Has he agreed to sell Obadiah?"

"Yes, but he insists we purchase Obadiah's wife, Naomi, and their child."

"Seems a strange request from a man such as Mr. Harshaw. While my father would never separate slave families, I have difficulty believing the Harshaws are concerned about preserving the sanctity of a slave's family."

"I don't think this has anything to do with pleasing the slaves. Mr. Harshaw is anxious to be rid of Obadiah's wife, Naomi. Seems Mrs. Harshaw has an intense dislike for the female slave. Harshaw says it has to do with his wife's persistent and unfounded jealousy."

Jasmine cupped her hand across her mouth and suppressed a giggle. "I'm sorry, but I can't imagine Mrs. Harshaw as a woman concerned about losing her husband's attentions."

Nolan smiled. "Nor can I, but let's not question our good fortune. I doubt whether Obadiah will consider us his benefactors if he's forced to leave his wife and child with the Harshaws. I'll strike a bargain for the three of them, and unless you're inclined to accept the hospitality of the Harshaws, I suggest we go back to town and stay at the hotel. I'll ask Harshaw to have one of his men deliver Obadiah and his family to us in the morning."

Jasmine focused on the perimeter of the grounds and watched

as a young woman carrying a child approached. "If Mr. Harshaw is giving special attention to Obadiah's wife, I can now understand Mrs. Harshaw's jealous reaction," Jasmine whispered as the woman drew nearer. "She is a beautiful woman."

The stark contrast of color among the small family was disquieting. While Obadiah bore the rich chocolate brown skin and onyx eyes of his mother, Naomi's complexion was a soft, tawny shade and her eyes a golden brown. And the child—Jasmine couldn't withhold her stare. The child's limbs were skeletal and pasty—so pale, in fact, that had Jasmine not known better, she would have believed the boy to be white.

The next morning Jasmine and Spencer joined Nolan in the small restaurant adjacent to their hotel. Once they had completed their breakfast, Spencer began fidgeting, obviously anxious to leave the table. "If you want to stroll around outdoors with Spencer, I'll go to the loading dock and ascertain our departure time. Since we were detained an extra day, I'm hopeful your family's cotton has been loaded and we can soon be on our way. Mr. Harshaw or his overseer should deliver Obadiah at any moment."

"I'll watch for their arrival," Jasmine said as they exited the small restaurant.

Spencer toddled after a small frog he spied hopping in the roadway, giggling each time the creature would croak and jump. Enjoying the sight, Jasmine followed along behind him until she saw Mr. Harshaw jump down from his wagon in front of the hotel. She lifted Spencer into her arms and hurried forward, waving to gain his attention.

"Mr. Houston has gone to the docks, but you may leave the slaves in my care," she said as they approached.

Giving her a look of disdain, Mr. Harshaw shook his head. "No chance you can control Obadiah if he decides to run. You gonna buy the shackles?"

Jasmine looked into the rear of the wagon. Iron hinges lined both sides of the wagon bed, with Obadiah secured to one of the hinges by a shackle encircling his leg. His other leg was shackled to Naomi. Jasmine recoiled at the sight. "Remove the irons. We're not concerned that either of them will run. After all, exactly where would they go?" She leaned forward a few inches, as though preparing to include the man in some dark conspiracy. "To be completely honest, Mr. Harshaw, we don't believe human beings should be restrained in any manner."

Mr. Harshaw spit a long stream of tobacco juice and tugged at the unraveling hem of his silk vest. "Human beings? These here darkies are *property*—same as livestock, but I s'pose you can call 'em whatever you want—they're yours. Mark my words, though, you're gonna be sorry. First opportunity that comes along, they'll run. Just don't come back to me expecting your money back. You been warned," he growled while unlocking the heavy irons that secured Obadiah and Naomi.

"Thank you for enlightening me," Jasmine replied.

Two perpendicular creases formed between Mr. Harshaw's eyebrows. "If I didn't know you were a lady with proper manners, I'd think you were mocking me."

"Why, Mr. Harshaw, why on earth would anyone consider scoffing at you—a man of obvious worth and distinction," she said, her voice taking on a heavy Southern drawl.

Loosening the final leg iron, Harshaw motioned the three slaves out of the wagon and then leveled a heated gaze at Jasmine. "Your husband needs to gain control over you, Mrs. Houston."

"My husband is deceased, Mr. Harshaw. Nolan Houston is my late husband's brother, *not* my husband."

"With your lack of respect, it's unlikely you'll ever attract another," he crossly rebutted. "I believe our dealings are complete." He hoisted himself onto the seat of the wagon.

Jasmine graced him with a demure smile. "Good day, Mr. Harshaw."

Several passersby had stopped to listen to the exchange and now stared at the strange-looking group. Obadiah's strong arm now embraced Naomi, who held the emaciated child close to her breast, the two of them staring wide-eyed at Jasmine. Meanwhile,

Spencer was tugging at Naomi's tattered dress, obviously hoping to gain a better view of her child.

"We need to talk," she said to the slaves. "Let's go over to those trees and sit down."

She strode away, unsure whether they would follow, yet hoping her act would exhibit a level of trust. There was no indication they had moved along behind her, so she sat down, carefully arranging Spencer beside her before turning her gaze toward the street. They stood transfixed where she had left them. Jasmine smiled, motioned them forward, and then patted the grass beside her, hopeful they would take her cue.

When Obadiah took Naomi's hand and began walking toward her, Jasmine's smile widened. "Please, sit down," she encouraged as they grew nearer. "There are many things I want to share with you before we board the ship."

Naomi's lower lip trembled. "Where you takin' us?"

"That's what we need to discuss. Won't you sit down?" Jasmine waited until they had arranged themselves beside her on the grassy mound. Immediately, Spencer got up and began tottering across the uneven terrain, obviously intent upon reaching Naomi and the child she held in her arms. "Spencer, come back and sit down."

"I don' mind. He's jes curious," she said, reaching out to take Spencer's hand in her own when the boy stumbled. "You wanna see my little Moses, don' ya?" she asked, her gaze fixed on Spencer.

"Moses? That's your little boy's name?"

"Yessum," Obadiah replied. "We's all three got names from the Bible. When dis here youngun was borned, I tol' Naomi he should be like his mammy and pappy—have a name from da Good Book." His eyes shone with pride while taking in the sight of his wife and child.

"That's an inspired decision. Choosing a name from the Bible would have pleased your mother."

"Don' know nothin' 'bout what would have pleased my mammy—never knowed her, but I do know Moses was a man used by God. If my boy lives, I'd like for him to be a man of God too. Maybe help free our people."

Jasmine nodded. "I know that idea would have pleased your mother also. You see, Obadiah, your mother was my mammy from the time I was an infant. My father purchased her from Mr. Harshaw when you were only a year old. My mother was ill and my father was looking for a wet nurse, but he didn't believe in dividing families. Had he known you were alive, he would have insisted on purchasing you, but Mr. Harshaw told him Mammy's child had died only days earlier and he was willing to sell her."

Obadiah's gaze filled with suspicion. "If dat be the truth, how come she didn't tell your pappy once they left Harwood Plantation? And how come you know all dis now, but nobody knowed nothin' afore?"

"Mammy never told anyone because Mr. Harshaw threatened to kill you. Even though she knew she couldn't see you again, there was comfort in knowing you weren't going to die. Your mother didn't divulge your existence until just before she died. It was her final request that I find you and purchase your freedom."

"*Dat's* what dis is all about? So now we's yours. Where you takin' us dat we gotta get on a ship?"

Jasmine brushed a leaf from her blue plaid wool dress. "You aren't required to go with us. Mr. Houston has your papers, and we plan to sign them, showing you've been freed. However, the last thing I want is to give you your freedom without helping you plan for a future. Otherwise, you'll not survive. Remaining in the South would be far too risky. You'd be picked up and, papers or not, you'd be sold back into slavery. You know that's true, don't you?"

He lowered his gaze. "Yessum. So what you plannin' for us?"

"Although I grew up in Mississippi and my family still owns cotton plantations, I no longer live here. When I married, I moved to Massachusetts."

"Dat up north?" Obadiah asked, his eyes shifting to Naomi.

"Yes. And although there are few Negroes living near my home, there are many people who are committed to aiding runaways and who are anxious to see slavery abolished. I thought perhaps you would want to come and live at my farm and work for me. It's a horse farm, not a plantation, although I do have a vegetable garden," she said with a smile. "There's a small stone outbuilding where the three of you could live. If you decide to remain, we could build something more suitable."

His brow furrowed. "Where else you think I might be wantin' to go?"

"Most of the runaways we help don't remain in the United States. They go farther north to Canada."

"Um hum, I heard tell o' dat place. Been three or four of Massa Harshaw's slaves run off tryin' to get north to dat place." He wagged his head back and forth. "Dey never made it. Massa brung 'em back and whipped 'em till dey was near dead." He massaged his forehead as though he could somehow erase the memory.

"If you like, you could work for me until you decide. You would always be free to leave, Obadiah. There will be no shackles, no restrictions on your coming and going—you are all free to make a choice about where you will live and how you will earn a living."

"Don' think I'd be much use to ya, Missus. I don' know much 'bout horses," he said soulfully. "Massa was 'fraid we'd steal a horse and run off, so we didn't do no tendin' of the horses."

"You can learn, Obadiah," she said before turning her attention to Naomi. "If you'd like to earn money of your own, Naomi, I can always use help in the house and with Spencer. I'm hopeful Spencer and Moses will become good friends."

"Moses be a sickly kind o' chile. He don' play much."

"He does appear very thin. We'll have the doctor see to him once we arrive home." She took in the child's sad eyes. "Does he eat well?"

"Massa force all the younguns to stay in the nursery, and dat fat ole woman he got watchin' after dem chillens don' care if dey eat or not. She lick their plates clean afore dey get much chance to eat. I tried complainin' to Massa, but den dat ole woman in the nursery begun to hittin' on Moses, so I was afeared to say no mo'."

Jasmine gave her an encouraging smile. "We're going to fatten him up in no time. Why, I'm certain he'll be as big as Spencer within a few months."

Naomi's eyes sparkled and she leaned toward Jasmine. "Fo' sure? You think dat's possible?"

"I certainly do. Ah, here comes Mr. Houston," she said, motioning toward Nolan as he walked toward them. "I'll go visit with him while the two of you decide what you'd like to do."

"No need, Missus. We's gonna come with you. We ain't willin' to take our chances in dis here part of the country."

Jasmine smiled. "I'm glad, Obadiah. Why don't we go and join Mr. Houston? Once we're on board ship, I want to spend some time telling you about your mother. She was a wonderful woman. I only wish she could have lived long enough to be reunited with you. I know she would be proud of you and pleased to know you are now a free man."

"Dat would be nice," Obadiah said.

"Your mother came to Massachusetts and lived with me for a while," Jasmine said as they approached Nolan.

"Did she like it dere?"

Jasmine laughed. "She said the winters were too cold for her old bones. When we returned to Mississippi, she was ready to remain in the warmer climate. I was sorry to leave her behind when I returned home, but I saw her on each of my visits to The Willows. She was a wonderful woman who taught me many things. She loved to talk about Jesus. I was home when she died." Jasmine looked up into the onyx-colored eyes that reminded her of Mammy. "I had returned to Mississippi due to my mother's illness. It seems both of our mothers contracted yellow fever and never fully recovered. They died within only a few days of each other, and I know my life will never be the same without them. I'm so very thankful we were able to find you and I could do at least this much for your mother. I loved her very much."

Obadiah hesitated, shuffling back and forth for a moment. "If you loved her so much, Missus, den how come you never did set *her* free?"

CHAPTER · 7

SPENCER TOOK Jasmine's hand, and together they walked the newly formed path between the main house and the brick and stone outbuilding now occupied by Obadiah and his family. Jasmine smiled down at her son. His sturdy legs appeared to lag behind his body, unable to keep pace and deliver him to his desired destination. He had struggled from Jasmine's arms, determined to make the trek under his own power. Jasmine pulled her cloak more tightly around her body and shivered as a gust of wind stung her face. Spencer's cheeks were a ruddy red by the time she knocked on the heavy wooden door.

Naomi pulled open the door with Moses by her side. Both boys squealed in delight at the sight of each other and rushed forward as though they'd been separated for weeks. "You don' need to never knock on the door, Missus. Jes' come on in."

"This is *your* home, Naomi. I would never consider entering without knocking, but thank you for your kind offer."

"Here, let me hang up dat coat and get you warm by da fire."

Jasmine handed Naomi her cloak and showed her a length of fabric she'd been carrying beneath it. "I brought you some material I had at the house. I thought you might want to use this for a dress, and this piece would make some fine new curtains."

TRACIE PETERSON / JUDITH MILLER

Naomi pressed her hand back and forth across the cloth, the flecks of gold in her brown eyes glistening. "Oh, Missus, I can't afford to be buyin' all this. Obadiah says we got to be careful with our money till we figure how to spend it proper."

"This is a gift, Naomi. Please tell Obadiah I insisted you accept it. Or I'll tell him, if you prefer."

Once again, Naomi gently touched the fabric, stroking it as though it were the finest silk. "I can tell him, but iffen he says I gotta return it, I hope you won' be gettin' angry with me. He already thinks you done too much for us. He says it ain't natural for white folk to be so kind."

"I wish I could argue that point, but I fear what Obadiah says is true. However, there are many white people who are working very hard with the Underground Railroad and are adamantly opposed to slavery in any form."

Naomi glanced at the two boys as they sat playing side by side. "I don' know nothin' 'bout that, but I do know you been merciful to us. Jes' look at Moses and how he's growed since we come here to live."

Jasmine turned her attention to the children, who were busily stacking small pieces of wood Obadiah had carved into various shapes and sizes. So light-skinned was Moses that when the boys' hands were intermingled, it was difficult to tell them apart. "He's grown nearly as big as Spencer. Why, by this summer, they'll likely be the exact same size. I can't tell you how much Spencer looks forward to his playtime with Moses."

"Yessum. They sho' do play good together. Obadiah says it was God's plan for us to come here. He tol' me 'bout how you wanted to free his mammy but you couldn't 'cause o' your husband."

"It's true that Bradley forced Mammy's return to The Willows, but she was never my slave; I didn't own her so I was unable to free her. She belonged to my father, who has never freed a slave. Even if I could have gained Mammy's freedom, Bradley was insistent she return to Mississippi. To free her and leave her in the South with no means of support would have . . ."

Naomi nodded her head up and down. "Jes' like me and Obadiah. Somebody's hounds woulda chased her down and put her in shackles. But she free now, ain't she, Missus? Up there in glory, reapin' her reward."

"Precisely. You know, even as she lay dying, she was thinking of others—wanting to assure Obadiah could live as a free man."

"Don' surprise me none. Ain't no way I could ever forget Moses. Can't be forgettin' a chile after carryin' him in your belly and birthin' him, now can ya? It's like they's a part of you forever. I don' know what I'd do if somebody took my chile. I don' think I could go on livin' if that happened."

"But if she hadn't gone on living, Obadiah wouldn't be a freed man today," Jasmine whispered.

Naomi's eyes widened and her lips curved into a faint smile. "I reckon dat's the truth. Ain't no way to know what God's got in mind for us, is dere?"

"I don't think so," Jasmine replied, mirroring Naomi's smile. "I'm going to have to return to the house and complete some tasks. You tell Obadiah I want him to give you permission to accept the fabric."

"I'll tell 'im, but can't make no promises on what he'll do."

Jasmine took her cloak from a wooden peg near the door. "Come along, Spencer. It's time to go home."

Both boys began howling the moment Jasmine gave the command, and Naomi shook her head back and forth. "Listen to dat wailin'. You'd think somebody took a hickory switch to 'em. It's fine wib me if Spencer stays here. I'll have Obadiah bring him home once he gets done in da barn."

"If you're certain he won't be—"

Naomi bent her elbows and placed a hand on each hip, her arms fanned open like two chicken wings. "He won' be no trouble. He'll keep Moses busy. You go on now and leave him to me."

The boys' tearful protests ceased once they realized their separation had been postponed—at least for the present. "Come give me a kiss," Jasmine said, opening her arms. Both boys hurried to her, each placing a wet kiss on her cheek before returning to their play. "You're certain bringing Spencer home won't be a burden?"

" 'Course not—you don't need to be worryin' at all 'bout such a thing as that youngun bein' a burden."

Careful to fasten her cloak before opening the door, Jasmine gave Naomi a warm smile and then directed her attention to Spencer. "You be a good boy," she cautioned before hurrying out into the bitter cold.

The shortened winter day had already faded into nightfall when Obadiah came to the door with her sleeping child in his arms. "He's tuckered out from playin' all day. Moses be sleepin' too. Naomi fed 'em supper, and afore she knowed it, they was fast asleep. You want me to carry 'im up to his bed?"

"Yes, thank you," Jasmine replied while leading the way. She stepped aside when they neared Spencer's room and watched as Obadiah tenderly placed her son on his bed.

"Naomi says jes' leave him wrapped in dat blanket so's he don' wake up," he whispered as he stepped back and looked down on Spencer's sleeping form.

"You can tell her I'll return the quilt tomorrow," Jasmine said softly. "I was having a cup of tea when you came in. I'd like to visit with you for a few moments; would you join me?"

Obadiah's eyes opened wide, and his eyebrows raised high on his forehead. "You want *me* to have tea—wib you?" He moved back several steps and stared down at her before emitting a loud guffaw. "Can you jes' 'magine what ole Massa Harshaw woulda thunk of me sittin' down to tea with a lady like yo'self?"

Jasmine joined him in his laughter and then pointed to the dining room chair. "Please. Sit down, Obadiah. I truly do want to talk to you."

He gingerly lowered himself onto the chair and sat poised at an angle as though ready to jump and run at a moment's notice. "Don' want no tea, Missus. I ain't never took a likin' to it."

"Very well. Now that you and Naomi have had time to settle into your new home, I was wondering how you like working with the horses. I know you had fears about adapting to the animals, but Paddy and Mr. Fisher indicate you've done very well."

"I's likin' dem pretty good—some better den others. Dat Paddy, he's good with *all* dem horses. He sure do love 'em, and he's been showin' me how to handle 'em. Paddy says horses is like people, takes 'em a while to get used to ya," Obadiah said with a wide, toothy grin.

His smile was a duplicate of the giant beams of approval Mammy had bestowed upon her as a child, unleashing a torrent of memories. Jasmine steadied her hand before pouring a cup of steaming tea. "I'm pleased you're beginning to feel more at ease with the animals and that Paddy is helping you. I'm hopeful you and Naomi are beginning to make plans to remain on the farm. Once spring arrives, I'd like to begin construction of a more acceptable home for your family."

Obadiah sat back in the chair and began shaking his head from side to side. "Oh, no, Missus, we be jes' fine in the place we're livin'. Naomi got it fixed up good, and she's set herself to makin' curtains out of dat cloth you gave her. And I'm thankin' ya for that—I was gonna say somethin' when I first got here and den fergot."

"You're quite welcome. Aside from the fact that the place you are living in is no more than an outbuilding for storage, I *want* to construct a more suitable home for your family, Obadiah. Building a home for your family would give me great pleasure."

"Don' know how to put dis into proper words, Missus, but all you's doin' for us, well, it's hard to understan'. I keeps thinkin' I'm in a dream and gonna wake up to Massa's whip any minute."

Jasmine's stomach lurched at the mention of a whip. "This is no dream, Obadiah. You have the papers showing all of you are free, and it would give me much joy to have you agree to remain here on the farm. However, if you think your family would be more content elsewhere, I'll not attempt to force you to remain in Massachusetts."

"Don' see how there could be anyplace we'd be treated better, Missus. This here has been a blessin' straight from God. When we was livin' with Massa, I spent mos' all my time worryin' 'bout Naomi and Moses. Didn' matter none if he beat me, but I didn't want him hurting Naomi."

Deep ridges creased Jasmine's forehead. "Why on earth would anyone whip Naomi? I can't imagine her ever causing a problem. She's so gentle and sweet-spirited."

Obadiah paused a moment before speaking, his voice almost a whisper. "Ol' Massa didn't whip her. He used her body for his own pleasure. Knowin' what he did to her, dere was times when I wanted to kill dat man with my bare hands. 'Specially what with her bein' his own flesh and blood and all. You'd think that woulda stopped him. But weren't nothin' got in Massa Harshaw's way when he was drinkin' and wantin' him a woman."

Jasmine sought to hide her incredulity, but her jaw had gone slack at the revelation and she couldn't seem to regain her senses. "Naomi is Mr. Harshaw's *daughter*?" she asked in a hoarse whisper.

Obadiah gazed down at the patterned wool carpet and nodded his head. "Never made her life no easier, neither. The missus hated Naomi from the day she was born. When Naomi got older and the massa begun having his way wib her, there was no help for Naomi. She was abused at night by the massa, and the next day his missus would be taking a whip to her, acting like it was Naomi's fault."

"He didn't *bother* her after you became her husband, did he?"

Obadiah released a deep growl. "Only reason he let us get married in a slave ceremony was to make his missus think dere was nothin' more goin' on with Naomi. When he'd come to our cabin at night, he said Naomi weren't my wife 'cause slaves ain' got no right to get married. First time he come, I tried to stop him, and he went and got the overseer. Overseer near beat me to death while ol' Massa stayed in da cabin with Naomi. After dat, Naomi said she was gonna leave me if I didn't let the massa have his way with her. Naomi said he'd kill me nex' time, and she wasn't going to be responsible if dat happened." Obadiah buried his face in his large callused hands. "I didn' want her to leave me."

"You ought not feel ashamed. You did the only thing you

could—you gave her comfort and loved her."

"Sometimes dat ain't enough," he lamented. "Tell you the truth, we don' know *who* be Moses' father. I knows one thing fer sure. Miz Harshaw thought Moses was sired by da massa. She did everythin' she could to get da massa to kill the boy. I don' know why, but he didn' give in to her."

Jasmine could hear the pain in Obadiah's voice as he recounted their past. "Probably because he feared killing Moses would be an admission to his wife that he had been continuing in his reprehensible behavior with Naomi after she was married to you."

"I never thought 'bout dat. You's prob'ly right. But dat ole mistress forced Naomi back to the fields and made her leave Moses in da nursery. Naomi even begged to carry da baby with her to the fields. We knew dat ole slave in the nursery was gettin' extra rations fer treatin' Moses poorly and not feedin' him, but there wasn't nothin' we could do. For sho' Moses would be dead if you hadn't come and saved us from dat place. I tol' Naomi it was da hand of God dat worked through you and saved us."

Jasmine stared at him, taken aback by his pronouncement. "I was merely doing what your mother asked of me, Obadiah."

"Well, we all is God's instruments, if we jes' listen and do what He asks. I'm sho' glad you took it upon yo'self to be obedient." Obadiah got to his feet. "'Less der's somethin' else you need to talk 'bout, I bes' be gettin' back home. Naomi's gonna be wonderin' if I got myself lost between here and dere." He chuckled loudly at his own humor.

"No, nothing else. I merely wanted to tell you about my hope that you and your family would remain here on the farm and my desire to build a house for the three of you come spring."

"Like I said, dat place we got now is plenty fine, Missus. We ain't plannin' on goin' nowhere."

"I'm pleased to hear that," she said while escorting Obadiah to the door. "Tell Naomi thank-you for looking after Spencer this afternoon," she called after him. She could see the outline of his muscular arm as he waved.

"Glad to have him." His deep voice resonated though the cold night air like a vibrating tuning fork.

Long after she closed the door, Jasmine weighed the revelations spoken this night. She believed every word of what she'd been told. There was little doubt Naomi's bloodline was mixed, but Jasmine had never considered the possibility that Jacob Harshaw might be her father. The thought sickened her. Yet that same repulsive man had likely fathered sweet little Moses. Moses with his pale, buttery skin. Moses, more white than Negro. Moses, sired by his own grandfather! A chill ran through her being. Obscene!

––––––––

Jasmine stood inside the front door of her home and welcomed each member of the Ladies' Aid Society. This marked the first time she would be acting as hostess since her return to Lowell, and she was pleased to see the group was continuing to increase in numbers. Thankfully Kiara had helped with preparations and would assist with serving while Naomi maintained a mindful watch over Spencer for the afternoon.

"Don't stray too far," she whispered to Daughtie Donohue. "I'm not certain I remember the names of some of the ladies."

"I'll be right by your side as soon as I hang my cloak," Daughtie replied.

"Never ya mind. I'll be takin' that for ya," Kiara said, grasping the cloak before Daughtie could object.

"Kiara insisted there was nothing that needed to be done in the kitchen until later, and she might as well impress the ladies with her ability to act as my maid," Jasmine said. "She is a dear friend."

"She isn't still working for you, is she? I'm certain Rogan's wages are sufficient, although I know there are days when Liam hasn't enough work to keep him busy."

"On those days when Liam can't keep Rogan busy, I do. He helps out with the horses at every opportunity. Paddy and Mr. Fisher do a fine job, but there's always plenty of work around here. Now that I'm certain Obadiah is planning to stay, I may buy some additional land and increase our stock."

Daughtie raised her eyebrows. "So he's decided to remain in Massachusetts? I thought they might feel safer if they went on to Canada."

"They're safe right here. He has his papers showing he's free, and he lives on my property."

"We both know that even papers are sometimes not enough to keep a freed man out of shackles. For their sake, don't ever involve them in helping the runaways, Jasmine. There's little doubt that their house is the first place where bounty hunters are going to look. Eventually, they'll come to realize that they're not involved, but you should prepare Obadiah for his house being searched and possible ill treatment."

Jasmine arched and straightened her shoulders until she looked like a soldier standing at attention. "Not while he lives on my property!"

Daughtie motioned toward a group of women entering the house and then whispered to Jasmine, "Anyone in this group you don't know?"

"No. I remember all of them," Jasmine whispered in return before turning her attention to the clustered visitors. "Welcome, ladies. Kiara will take your wraps, and then you may go into the parlor."

After all the expected members had arrived, Jasmine welcomed the group before requesting Daughtie come forward to direct the meeting.

Appearing younger than her thirty and five years in a golden taupe silk dress, Daughtie gracefully moved forward to face the assembled group. "I'm pleased to see so many in attendance and want to first tell you that your good works have helped many on their journey to freedom. However, we cannot rest upon our past good deeds. There is much work that remains before us, and I hope each of you will prove equal to the task. We've received word that arrangements are being made for the movement of another large group of runaways. They will assemble together for their journey northward."

"How many and exactly when are they arriving?" Nettie Harper inquired.

"I can only tell you early spring, Nettie. Quite frankly, the less information we have, the better it is. A slip of the tongue can prove dangerous," she said with a pleasant smile.

"I merely wondered how much time we would have to acquire goods for them. There isn't much left on hand."

"Exactly," Daughtie said. "We are in dire need of replenishing supplies, and that is why I asked Jasmine to hostess this meeting. None of us realized there would be so many provisions required for the last large group that passed through. And, of course, there have been several smaller groups since then. At this particular point, we couldn't be of substantial assistance to even a small number of runaways."

"Except to hide them and escort them onward. I'd say that's substantial," Elinor stated.

"Well, of course, Elinor," Daughtie agreed. "Our highest priority is to provide safe haven, but my prayer is that we will concentrate our efforts and do much more than that."

Elinor moved to the edge of her chair and leaned forward to gaze upon the assembled women. "I suppose you are all aware that the South is not going to continue tolerating Northern assistance to runaways. Is there some plan how the Society is going to handle that matter?"

Jasmine glanced back and forth between Daughtie and Elinor. "Having recently been in the South, I don't think we have major concerns at this point. Let's not borrow trouble."

"My thought also. You're always expecting the worst instead of celebrating our successes," Nettie Harper snapped.

Elinor glared at the older woman. "Perhaps life has taught me to proceed with caution, Nettie. Unlike you, I've encountered more tragedy than success in my years."

"If we could get back to the reason why we've gathered," Daughtie interjected, "I'd like to focus our energies upon collecting necessities. I've given thought to having each of you take charge of one specific type of goods."

Nettie waved her handkerchief in Daughtie's direction. "I'd like to be in charge of quilts and blankets."

"I've assigned quilts and blankets to Hannah," Daughtie replied. "With your exceptional needlework, I hoped you would agree to take charge of clothing for babies and children."

"Well, 'tis true my stitching is finer than most," she said, pursing her lips into a tight knot. "I suppose I *am* better suited for something more difficult than blankets and quilts."

"Might be good for you to check the Scriptures addressing the issue of pride," Elinor muttered.

"Speak up, Elinor. You're mumbling," Nettie snapped.

Jasmine noted the flash of anger in Elinor's eyes and interrupted before an argument could ensue. "What about *other* articles of clothing, Daughtie? Have those been assigned?"

Daughtie glanced at the list she was now holding in her hand. "Elinor, I wondered if you would take charge of shoes. Is that acceptable?"

Elinor looked around the room, obviously expecting someone to challenge her assignment. When there was no objection, she nodded her head. "I'm certain many of the mill girls can be persuaded to donate their old shoes. We need only tell them we're collecting for the needy. I'll ask the other keepers to spread the word."

"That's a wonderful idea," Jasmine commented. Finally, Elinor was exhibiting some enthusiasm!

Elinor gave her a modest smile. "Do you think so?"

"Absolutely," Jasmine replied.

Nettie tapped on the walnut table beside her chair until she gained the group's attention. "That may well work for ladies and even the older children, but how do you propose getting shoes for the men? Now there's a task you'll not resolve quite so easily."

"Rest assured I'll find a solution," Elinor curtly assured.

CHAPTER · 8

June

ELINOR BRUSHED a damp curl from her cheek and absently tucked the strand of loose hair behind one ear. Momentarily gazing into the cloudless sky, she continued walking. The scorching sun had slipped beneath the horizon, yet the penetrating afternoon heat lingered. Days of abnormally high temperatures had passed without any sign of intruding rain, and now strained tempers and harsh words had begun to gain a stronghold among members of the community. Elinor had not been immune to the scourge. Standing over a hot stove and cooking three meals a day while performing the myriad of other chores required of her to keep her boardinghouse had taken its toll.

The stir of a faint breeze cooled the beads of perspiration forming along her upper lip and forehead and provided a momentary respite from the heat. Clouds of dust billowed from the roadway as horse-drawn wagons and carriages passed by. Elinor angrily brushed the mounting layers of grimy film from within the folds of her foam green gown.

"I should have remained at the boardinghouse. I'll have to beat the dust out of this dress before I can wear it again," she muttered.

"Talking to yourself?"

Elinor whirled around and was met by a smiling Oliver

Maxwell. "Mr. Maxwell! I didn't realize you were walking behind me."

"Actually, I was running. For such a little lady, you have quite a stride. Might I ask why you find it necessary to maintain such a rapid pace—if you don't think me overly bold for inquiring," he hastily added.

"I'm on my way to the antislavery meeting at the Baptist church, and if I stand here much longer, I'm going to be late. There won't be a seat remaining. Do forgive me for hurrying off, but I'm already weary and I don't want to stand throughout the meeting."

"Well, isn't *this* a fortunate coincidence? I'm on my way to the very same meeting. I would be most pleased to accompany you," he offered while brandishing his black hat in a grand sweeping motion and bowing from the waist.

The wind whipped at Elinor's skirts, twisting the chambray fabric around her legs. She gave a tug to her skirt and then pushed her teetering hat back into place. Her lips formed a diminutive frown. "Strange, but in all the visits you've made to the boardinghouse, I don't believe I've ever heard you make mention of being involved in the antislavery movement," she said as she placed a firm hold on her chapeau.

"During my travels I've learned to keep my personal feelings and beliefs to myself." His gaze shifted and he glanced over his shoulder. "One never knows who can be trusted. As I'm certain you're aware, even the various residents of a boardinghouse may have differing opinions when it comes to the slavery issue."

" 'Tis true there are a few girls in my own boardinghouse who disagree with the antislavery movement. However, those girls have no ulterior motive. They are merely self-involved youth with seemingly little compassion for anyone. I wonder, however, if you fear that your shoe sales will be affected should you divulge your opposition to slavery?"

Oliver tilted his head to one side and scrunched his eyebrows. "My intentions are sincere—I remain silent only to protect those connected with the cause. I consider myself much like you: I simply want to help where needed."

Elinor's cheeks flamed with embarrassment. "I apologize, Mr. Maxwell. I'm certain you think me rather suspicious, but it seems I come in contact with many who have ulterior motives. While I believe there are those who need help as much as the slaves, I do not think it appropriate to become attached to a cause merely to benefit oneself. Wouldn't you agree?" she asked as they continued onward toward the meeting.

"Certainly I concur with your opinion. The country would be in far better condition if we would all place others before ourselves. Those poor slaves are suffering beyond what any of us can imagine."

Elinor merely nodded her agreement. However, she wanted to tell him that she, too, had suffered beyond what anyone could imagine—not at the hands of a cruel plantation owner, but her suffering was every bit as painful. She had buried two husbands and been left in poverty—forced to support herself by keeping house for unappreciative mill girls. Yet, she remained silent. Voicing the afflictions she had been forced to tolerate would make her seem trivial and self-indulgent—the very traits for which she had berated others only moments earlier before being reminded by a nagging, clawing guilt that she had attended her first antislavery meeting simply because she feared isolation. She then joined the small group aiding the Underground Railroad, for she knew the meetings would provide her with much-needed social contact— not because she genuinely believed in the cause. She continued attending more from a need to escape the boardinghouse than a genuine desire to free the slaves from their bondage. However, being a part of the effort had begun to alter her beliefs. She now took pleasure in reaching the goals assigned by the small group. The days of believing life intolerable were fewer, and she even indulged herself with a small glimmer of hope from time to time. She also enjoyed the larger gatherings, where they heard orators proclaiming the good being accomplished by Northern activists.

"We'd best take these seats. Doesn't appear there's anything closer," Oliver remarked.

Elinor agreed with his advice and, after gathering her skirts, edged past several couples already seated in the row. "This will be fine. I don't think we'll have any difficulty hearing the speakers," she said as Oliver situated himself beside her.

"I see several of the keepers are in attendance," he said, nodding toward Mrs. Ebert and Mrs. Wynn.

"Yes, they generally attend," Elinor absently remarked. "Oh, it appears they're ready to begin. We got here none too early."

In a show of unity for the cause, ministers from several churches were seated on the dais, and each took a moment at the lectern to expound upon the good deeds accomplished by their individual congregations on behalf of the antislavery movement. After listening to the preachers ramble on for nearly an hour, the sound of shuffling feet and agitated murmurs began to permeate the room.

The minister of the Freewill Baptist Church finally stepped forward. "I'm sorry to announce that our speaker for the evening has not yet arrived." The balding pastor glanced over his shoulder toward the preachers seated behind him and then turned back toward the gathered crowd. "We had hoped that Mr. Alderson might appear during our introductory remarks. However, it's obvious he's been detained, and it now seems quite doubtful he will arrive in time to present his scheduled lecture. Since the evening is warm—especially in this overfilled room, I think it best if we dismiss—unless you absolutely insist upon staying to hear about the good deeds of *my* congregation."

A smattering of laughter could be heard as the crowd rose to its feet and began inching their way out of the room. Silently chastising herself for having left home without a fan, Elinor flapped her limp handkerchief back and forth, hoping to create a breeze. Turning sideways, Elinor continued moving forward, irritated at those who blocked the passageway as they stopped to visit with one another.

"Finally! I thought we would never get through that group."

Oliver smiled down at her, revealing a small dimple in his right cheek. "Just appeared as though folks wanted to stop and exchange pleasantries for a few minutes," he remarked.

"Boorish behavior," Elinor snapped. "Those who wish to visit should step out of the aisle. It's much too warm to be held captive in that narrow passageway by a swarm of people. For a moment I thought I might faint."

"Rest assured I would have caught you before you neared the floor," Oliver nobly stated.

Elinor fanned her hanky a bit more rapidly. "Why, thank you, Mr. Maxwell. I take comfort knowing you were looking after my welfare."

"I am hoping you'll grant me the opportunity to look after your welfare a bit longer. If you don't object, I'd be honored to escort you home," he said as he offered his arm.

"I suppose that would be acceptable." Elinor surveyed the crowd before taking his arm.

"Afraid someone might see us together?" he inquired, his grin returning.

"No. Well, yes, I suppose I am," she admitted. "The girls who board with me take pleasure in gossiping. I'm certain they would find great delight in discussing the fact that I am in your company."

"Is *that* all? Well, let them talk! They can whisper and giggle and make up any story they so desire. If they derive pleasure from seeing us together, let them have their enjoyment."

"They don't enjoy *observing* us, Mr. Maxwell. They enjoy *gossiping*. If one of them sees us, she'll spread the word. By week's end, everyone at the Appleton Mill will have us betrothed."

He tipped his hat at a passerby and then turned back to Elinor. "They could say much worse. In fact, I'd be flattered if folks believed a lady as lovely as you would consider marrying an itinerant shoe peddler."

She gave him a demure smile. "You flatter me, Mr. Maxwell."

"Not so, Mrs. Brighton. I speak the truth," he said as they continued down the street. "I admire a lady who has proven she can not only support herself, but also keep her beauty and charm intact while doing so."

"Thank you for your kind words. Now tell me, where do you call home, Mr. Maxwell?"

"Wherever I put my head down for the night," he cheerfully replied.

"Surely you have someplace you consider your home," she pressed.

"Baltimore is where I was born and reared and where my mother and sister continue to reside. However, I much prefer New England. My shoe business has flourished in this area. Of course, the cold weather means folks need good warm shoes and boots."

"From the number of shoes you sell in my boardinghouse alone, it would appear you could permanently remain in Lowell. Seems the girls always have money to spend on themselves. Why, I believe some of them have at least three pairs of shoes—and the money they spend on jewelry and fabric . . . why, it's almost sinful. They could put their money and energies to better use, if you ask me. While girls in the other boardinghouses show a genuine interest in helping with the antislavery cause and expanding their minds at the lyceums or writing for the *Lowell Offering,* none of the girls in my house appears interested in anything other than spending money on herself and finding a husband."

"They're young and will likely expand their horizons in a year or two. However, I do understand your exasperation with their behavior. Especially when more help is always needed for good causes such as the antislavery movement and the Underground Railroad."

Elinor stopped and turned toward him. "You know of the Underground Railroad movement in Lowell?"

"Of course. I likely shouldn't tell you this, but I know you can be trusted. There are hundreds of runaways who have benefited from the simple maps I've drawn for their use. With my constant travels throughout New England, I'm aware of new roads and houses—you know, changes taking place along the route into Canada. I update the maps as needed. I like to think I'm providing a useful service to those operating the Underground Railroad as well as the runaways."

Elinor's brows furrowed and creases lined her forehead. "I didn't realize." She hesitated and stared up into his cobalt blue eyes. "I've never heard anyone speak of your connection with the Underground."

"I'm pleased to know my involvement astonished you. That alone verifies the fact that my participation in the Underground hasn't been widely exposed."

She nodded her agreement. After all, anonymity was vital to the cause. There were likely hundreds involved whose identities were unknown to her. "How long have you been helping?" she ventured as they walked down Merrimack Street.

"Many years. I find the work gratifying, don't you?"

"Oh, yes. However, there are times I worry about difficulties that might arise. I certainly can't afford to lose my position with the Corporation."

"Oh, I don't think you need worry in that regard," he said. "I'm certain they have much more important matters worrying them than a few employees aiding the Underground Railroad. Besides, it's my understanding that the mill owners are publicly supportive of the abolitionist movement."

"You're probably correct on that account, but one can never be too careful." They reached the front door of the boardinghouse. "Would you care to come in for a glass of lemonade?"

"Something cool to drink would be most welcome," he replied.

Elinor entered the hallway and carefully removed her hat. "Why don't you have a seat in the parlor and I'll fetch our lemonade."

She hurried off to the kitchen, pleased to see none of her boarders were in the parlor. Had any of the girls known Mr. Maxwell would make an appearance this evening, they would surely have been present. All of the girls made it a point to be at home when Mr. Maxwell came to sell his shoes. He was, after all, a handsome bachelor who had a way with words. Elinor poured the lemonade into two tall glasses and placed them on a wooden tray, along with a plate of sugar cookies she'd baked early that morning.

"Here we are," Elinor announced as she returned to the room. She centered the tray on a small table in front of the sofa and then offered Oliver one of the glasses of cool lemonade. His hand, warm and firm, wrapped around her fingers. The liquid sloshed toward the lip of the glass as she hastily tugged away from his grasp. "*Whatever* are you *doing*?" Her fingers splayed and she placed one hand to her chest. Perhaps the pressure of her clammy palm would still the erratic pounding of her heart.

Oliver's eyes widened as she retreated to the other side of the room. "I'm sorry. I didn't mean to offend you. Please accept my apology. I thought . . ."

Retrieving her handkerchief from the pocket of her gown, she delicately wiped her brow. "I know *exactly* what you thought, Mr. Maxwell. You believe I'm quite like the fawning mill girls who scurry to the parlor and vie for your attention the moment you enter the boardinghouse. You've decided I am a lonely widow in need of companionship who will compromise her behavior and morals. Well, I am *not*! I offered you a glass of lemonade, nothing more."

"Dear lady, please forgive me. You extended your hospitality and friendship, and I behaved boorishly. I meant no harm. I find your conversation refreshing after endless hours of listening to the prattle of mill girls who insist upon having me call on them two or three times before placing an order for their shoes."

"Is that what they do? There is no doubt such behavior would soon become incommodious."

Oliver nodded and took a sip of his lemonade. "I don't want to strain our friendship further. If you prefer I leave immediately, I will abide by your decision. However, it is my fervent desire to remain in your company and become better acquainted."

Elinor loosened her grip on the wadded handkerchief in her hand. "I suppose it would be acceptable since we now understand each other."

"Thank you for your kindness. Now, won't you please sit

down? I know you must be weary."

Pleased by the obvious concern in his voice, Elinor sat down opposite him and picked up her glass of lemonade. "Do tell me more of your association with the antislavery movement. How did you become involved?"

Oliver rubbed his forehead. "I hope you won't be offended, but I'm not at liberty to discuss any further details of my involvement. I've likely already told you too much. What with my travels, I've become acquainted with many people like yourself who are helping with the cause. I've made it a practice never to divulge names or relate facts that might jeopardize those who are a part of the movement. I would never want it said that Oliver Maxwell was the cause of a failed escape."

"An admirable quality, Mr. Maxwell. How could I possibly be offended? I realize the need for secrecy. Even our small group of women who help with the Underground Railroad must remain cautious. We've learned that attendance at antislavery meetings doesn't necessarily mean one favors the cause."

"Exactly my point," he agreed. "Of course, there is no doubt in my mind that you are trustworthy, or I wouldn't have even told you about my work preparing maps. On second thought, I don't believe it would be imprudent for me to share more of my background with you."

"No, no—I wouldn't consider encouraging you to do such a thing," she replied hastily.

"Then if it wouldn't pain you to discuss your past, I would be honored if you would tell me more about yourself."

Elinor hesitated. Revealing private information with someone who was practically a stranger was foreign to her. Aside from her brother, she lived in a town filled with strangers. How could she expect to form friendships if she remained unwilling to disclose even a part of herself?

"My childhood was quite pleasant. I came to America when I was nine years of age. My brother, Taylor Manning, and my uncle, John Farnsworth, had come to America to work for the Corporation. Taylor had recently married, and he and his new bride,

Bella, came to England on their wedding trip. I returned with them and have been in America since that time."

"Your parents?"

"Deceased. Taylor and Bella were good to me, and living in their home made me desire the pleasure of a good marriage such as theirs. When I was seventeen I met Wilbur Stewart, and we were married when I was eighteen. He was a kind young man and I loved him very much," she said, pausing momentarily.

"I trust you were happy in your marriage to Mr. Stewart."

Her eyes clouded briefly. "He drowned only weeks after our marriage. I thought I would never love another and yet, two years later I met and married Daniel Brighton. We moved to Philadelphia, where Daniel worked for the newspaper. He contracted yellow fever and was dead six months after our wedding day."

Oliver hunched forward, his hands folded together as he met her gaze. "My dear, dear Mrs. Brighton. How you have suffered. Having buried two husbands, I understand your fear of ever again giving your heart to another. Yet I would be honored if you would count me among your friends."

Elinor tugged at the lace edging of her handkerchief before glancing up at Oliver and sending him the ghost of a smile. She wondered at her own willingness to share such private information with this stranger. Yet he seemed to sense her fragile condition. "Thank you, Mr. Maxwell," she whispered. "Your kindness has touched my heart."

CHAPTER · 9

JASMINE HURRIED down the stairway at the sound of her grand-mother's voice. "Grandmother, what a pleasant surprise!"

"I was anxious for a visit with my great-grandson. I suppose you're going to tell me he's napping or some other nonsense," Alice Wainwright said while offering her cheek for a perfunctory kiss.

Jasmine bent and kissed her grandmother's rouged cheek. "Of course not. However, he is with Naomi and Moses. They can't seem to escape the house without him. Naomi comes over to help with chores or ask a question, and Spencer insists upon returning home with them."

"I hope you're not giving in to the boy's every whim, Jasmine. You don't want him to grow up thinking he can always have his way. Discipline! That's the key to excellent child rearing."

Jasmine looped arms with her grandmother and led her into the parlor. "He doesn't always get his way, Grandmother, but I do encourage Moses and Spencer to play together. The boys learn from each other—each of them needs a sibling. They fill a void for each other, and I've grown to love Moses. He's a sweet child."

"I agree that Moses is a fine little boy, but Spencer needs a brother or sister of his own. You need to cease this foolishness of being a contented widow and agree to marry Nolan. And I don't mean a year or two from now. As far as I'm concerned, you should be planning your marriage to Nolan at this very moment."

"I'm not certain Nolan would agree, Grandmother."

"I don't know why not. Men never want to be included in making wedding arrangements. And if you're concerned a large wedding is inappropriate for a widow, plan something simple—yet elegant, of course."

Jasmine sat down beside her grandmother. "Since Nolan has not asked me to be his wife, I think he would be somewhat surprised to hear I'm planning the details of our wedding."

"What?" Alice's pale lips formed a large oval, and she clasped a hand to her chest.

Stifling a giggle, Jasmine grasped her grandmother's hand. "I know you believe the rumor that Nolan had asked for my hand shortly after Bradley's death, but it isn't so, Grandmother. You seem to forget that even though Bradley was not a loving brother—"

"Or husband," Alice interjected.

Jasmine nodded. "Or husband—there is still a need for honor and respect. Nolan has been a true friend and I care deeply for him. . . ."

"Oh, pshaw! The two of you need to stop this nonsense. It's obvious you love each other. Why hasn't he declared himself? Must I travel to Boston, grab him by the ear, and personally escort him to Lowell in order to force his proposal?"

"Grandmother! I can't believe you would even entertain such a notion. If and when Nolan asks me to become his wife, I want it to be his idea—*not* yours. Please promise me you will not interfere."

"When he finally asks, you'll agree to marry him? You do love him, don't you?"

Jasmine lowered her eyes. "Yes, I love him, and I would be pleased to marry him."

"Well, then, that's settled. Now, when do I get to see my great-grandson?"

"If you like we could walk over and you could see the progress being made on the new house for Naomi and Obadiah."

"That sounds like an excellent idea. I know you feel an obligation to Obadiah, but I want you to remember the concern that arose when Mammy was here in Lowell—folks upset that a slave was living under your roof. Since you have Obadiah's family living on your property, there are those who will assume they are slaves."

"There is a vast difference between the two situations. After all, Mammy *was* a slave. That fact aside, if there were concerns, I think I would have heard some rumors by now, don't you?"

"It's difficult to know. The mills give rise to a more transient populace, and there's always the chance someone will arrive in town, pleased to cast aspersions."

"Both Obadiah and Naomi carry their papers showing they are free, and all of the local merchants know them as freed. Should any question arise, I think there are many who would vouch that they came here as freed slaves and live on my property by their own choice. They come and go at their own pleasure and are paid a wage the same as the others who work for me. If they were white, no one would question the arrangement."

"You need not defend yourself to me, Jasmine. *I* realize they are free. I merely ask that you remain alert. Ah, I see my great-grandson is not afraid of becoming dirty," she said, pointing toward the boys.

"They seem to think that mound of dirt is their personal playground. It takes quite a dousing to get Spencer clean after he's been hard at play."

"From all appearances, I can only imagine," Alice agreed. "It looks like Obadiah has made good progress on the new house. Have you hired any additional help, or is he doing all the work himself?"

"I've hired several men to assist with the labor. I've recently purchased additional horses—breeding stock. Paddy and Mr. Fisher need Obadiah's assistance in the barns. I don't expect Obadiah to spend his days working with the horses and helping with farm chores and then build a house by himself."

"You're much too defensive, Jasmine. I was merely inquiring, not preparing to condemn you. It's of no concern to me if you have the entire house constructed for him."

"I'm sorry, Grandmother. After your earlier comments regarding the slavery issue, I suppose I felt a need to defend all of my decisions regarding Obadiah." Jasmine turned her attention back toward the two little boys. "Spencer! Look who's come to see you," she called.

The boys glanced toward the two women, and both came running on wobbly legs. Naomi stood in the doorway of the house, wiping her hands on a frayed calico apron. "Moses! You stay here. That ain't your granny."

Moses stopped momentarily, his gaze shifting between his mother and his little friend, who continued running toward the women.

"It's all right," Jasmine called to Naomi. "I'll look after him."

"But I gotta take food over to da Marlows. You want me to tell Obadiah to come fetch Moses when he be done working in da barn?"

"That will be fine. You go ahead," Jasmine said.

"Naomi is cooking for another family?" Alice asked as Spencer bounded into her skirts, his chubby fingers clinging to the deep folds of fabric.

"Yes. Nancy Marlow has been ill for several weeks. Henry asked Naomi if she would prepare meals for them. He has no family nearby, and with three strapping young boys, he needed help. I told Naomi she didn't need to feel obligated to take on the additional work, but she said she wanted to earn the extra coins. I think she's hoping to earn enough to purchase some new items for the house," Jasmine explained. "I fear your gown will need a cleaning," Jasmine continued while pointing to the smudges of dirt on Alice's rose and paisley print skirt.

"Seeing this happy little fellow is worth the trouble." Alice grasped Spencer by the hand. "Come along, young man. Let's go back to the house and have some cookies, shall we?"

"Tookie," Moses mimicked.

"Yes, Moses. We'll get you a cookie," Jasmine replied, taking him by the hand. "If you'd like to fix a plate of cookies and some lemonade for the boys, I'll see if I can wipe some of this grime from their faces and hands."

Once the boys were settled with their cookies, Alice gave Jasmine a thoughtful look. "I believe Spencer is getting old enough to come home with me from time to time. What do you think?"

"I don't think he'd be happy to make an overnight visit without me."

"No, of course not. But he could spend the afternoon occasionally, don't you agree?"

"Yes, but you must remember that he's become accustomed to having Moses nearby. I doubt you could handle both of them for an afternoon. They can become quite rowdy."

Alice chuckled and nodded in agreement. "Yes, I can well remember having three boys of my own years ago. Your father was always antagonizing one of his brothers."

"And I'm certain Uncle Franklin and Uncle Harry caused their share of problems also."

"Indeed, the three of them were quite a handful. I do miss those days. Don't let this time slip away from you, Jasmine. I wish I had spent more time with my children when they were young. Back then I thought it more important to attend social functions than be with my children. Now I have all the time in the world to attend teas and parties, but what I desire is having family near me."

Jasmine noted the tears clouding her grandmother's hazel eyes. "If it's that important to you, Grandmother, we can decide upon an afternoon and I'll bring Spencer each week. Would you like that?"

"Yes," she said, the gleam returning to her gaze. "What about Wednesdays?"

Jasmine nodded. "We'll begin next week and see how both you and Spencer make it through the afternoon."

"Good. I'll go home and begin making plans for our first afternoon together. You need not see me to the door. You stay here with the boys," Alice said before kissing Spencer's cheek and hugging Moses good-bye.

Alice called out a final farewell as she departed the front door. "We'll see you on Wednesday," Jasmine called in return.

Moments later, Jasmine spun around at the sound of the front door closing, which was immediately followed by footsteps and chattering. "Look who was arriving as I was leaving the house," Alice chortled, pulling Kiara forward. "I couldn't leave. I wanted to see your face when she tells you her news."

Kiara was beaming, her cheeks flush and her dark brown eyes shining. "I'm goin' to have a baby," she said. "I was goin' to wait to tell, but Rogan is announcin' the news to every stranger he meets," she said. "He can't seem to keep the matter to 'imself."

"I'm so happy for you, Kiara. I know how much this means to you and Rogan. When do you expect the baby?"

"Not until the end of January. That's why I told Rogan 'twas foolish to be spreadin' the word so soon."

"I don't blame him. He's happy and proud, and I'm happy for both of you," Jasmine said, embracing Kiara. "And what does young Paddy think of all this? Is he anxious to become an uncle?"

"Aye. Between Rogan and Paddy, there seems to be nothin' else to talk about. I told them by the time the baby finally arrives, they'll be weary of the idea."

"I don't think so," Alice said. "They'll have him out riding horses before he turns a year old!"

Kiara tilted her head to the side and laughed. "I told Rogan and Paddy I'd have their hide if they told ya before I had the chance, Jasmine. They said if I didn't come over and tell ya soon, they'd not be held responsible. I wish I had time to stay for a visit, but I must get back and fix supper."

"Promise you'll come back tomorrow when you have more time."

"I promise I'll come if ya do na mind me workin' on my lace while we visit. I've orders I can na keep up with."

"Bring your lace and whatever else you must, but please come and visit with me."

"It's agreed, then. If ya're leavin', Mrs. Wainwright, I'll walk out with ya," Kiara said.

Jasmine followed along behind the two women, with Moses and Spencer each clasping one of her hands. The three of them watched from the wraparound front porch as their guests departed and then remained outdoors, with the boys playing on the porch while Jasmine sat embroidering an intricate pattern on a pair of silk stockings.

"This is certainly our day for unexpected company," Jasmine said to the boys as a horse-drawn wagon turned into the driveway and came to a stop in front of the house.

"Good day, ma'am. Oliver Maxwell's the name," the man said while jumping down from the wagon and removing his hat with a flair.

"Good day."

"I'm a shoe peddler well acquainted with the residents of Lowell but decided I would begin including some of the surrounding community when I come to call upon the boardinghouses and other residents in town. Would you be interested in the purchase of a pair of new kid slippers for yourself or perhaps some new riding boots for your husband?" Oliver glanced toward the two boys. "Or some fine new shoes for your sons?"

"Shoes," Spencer said, pointing toward his feet.

Moses giggled and pulled at his shoe. "Shoes."

"Yes, you both have shoes," Jasmine said with a smile. "But they are certainly worn, and you could both use a new pair. In fact, I imagine everyone in the household would benefit from some new shoes. Why don't you measure the boys' feet, and then we'll go out to the barn. I have several men working for me, and you can measure them also."

Jasmine watched as the salesman removed Spencer's shoes and carefully made drawings of her son's feet. The peddler had a way with the children, making them laugh as he traced around their small bare feet.

"What names should I place on the drawings?" he asked.

"Spencer on the larger size and Moses on the smaller," she replied.

"There's a size difference in the boys' shoes, but your sons appear to be about the same age. Are they twins?" Mr. Maxwell asked.

Jasmine smiled at the question. "No, they're close friends. But you're correct about their ages. They were born within nine weeks of each other."

He gave a triumphant nod. "Are you certain they're not related—cousins, maybe? They sure favor one another with that dark wavy hair and those big brown eyes."

It was difficult for Jasmine to keep from laughing aloud. She'd often thought the same thing when the boys were toddling about the house or playing in the yard together. Grandmother Wainwright called their resemblance uncanny, and Jasmine agreed. No one, including Mr. Maxwell, would ever guess one of the boys was a Negro. Jasmine waited while the salesman returned his tools to the buggy and then mounted the box of his small wagon. "If you'll follow the driveway to the back, it will lead you to the barn. I'll meet you there."

"Thank you, ma'am," he said, once again tipping his hat and giving her a broad smile.

By the time Jasmine had corralled the two boys back through the house and out to the barn, Mr. Maxwell, Paddy, Obadiah, and her old groomsman, Richard Fisher, were all gathered together.

"Papa!" Moses cried as he scurried with outstretched arms toward Obadiah.

Mr. Maxwell looked in all directions and then watched with widened eyes as Moses buried his tiny cherub face in Obadiah's pant legs. The peddler's fingers tightened around the leather reins until his knuckles were void of color. His mouth was compressed into a thin, hard line. She should have told him, for he was obviously embarrassed by his earlier remarks.

"Why don't you measure Paddy first, and then he can water your horse, if you like," Jasmine suggested.

Mr. Maxwell jumped down from the wagon seat and turned toward Padraig. "I'm sure the horse would appreciate it, and I know I'd be pleased," he said to the boy. "I've quite a ways to travel yet today."

Paddy rubbed one hand down the horse's withers and gave the strawberry roan a firm pat before leaning down to pull off his boots. "Sure and that's a fine-lookin' mare ya got. I'll be pleased ta water her for ya," he said, pushing a tousled mass of black curls off his forehead.

"I'm certain she doesn't compare to the horseflesh you're accustomed to taking care of around here, but she serves me well," Mr. Maxwell said, placing a piece of paper atop a wooden board.

Paddy placed his foot on the paper and watched as Mr. Maxwell carefully traced around it. "I'm learnin' horses are a lot like people. Can't be judgin' 'em only by appearance or ya'll be disappointed. Sometimes the ugly ones turn out to be much better than the beauties. Kinda like they need to be provin' themselves because they do na have their beauty to depend upon."

"You're wise for your years, young man. Beauty is only skin deep, but there are those of us that will never completely learn that lesson. We like a woman that is easy on the eyes," Mr. Maxwell commented as he finished the drawings.

Paddy pulled on his boots. "I'll na be denying a pretty lass is hard to overlook, but it's the plain ones that cook up a tasty stew and keep yar house in order."

"Well, I think there are many exceptions to that observation," Jasmine said with a grin. "Your sister, Kiara, being the first one that comes to mind."

"Aye, and for sure ya're right about Kiara as well as yarself, ma'am," he hastily added. "But most times the pretty lasses depend upon their looks rather than their skills ta carry them through life. Do ya na think that's so?"

Mr. Maxwell gave Paddy a hearty laugh. "Sometimes it's best to cease defending yourself. I believe this may be one of those instances. Why don't you go ahead and care for my horse," he said, giving the boy a quick wink.

Paddy left the others and approached the horse. "Top of the day to ya," Paddy said as he reached up to stroke the animal's mane. "For sure ya're a lovely one. I don't suppose yar owner would be havin' time for me to unhitch ya and treat ya proper, but we'll be doin' our best."

Paddy walked back to the wagon, released the brake, and then came alongside the mare once again. "We'll just be headin' over yonder for somethin' to drink." The animal seemed completely at ease with him. Kiara often told him he had a gift from God. A sort of ability to know what the horses were thinking, and because of this the animals would work for him in ways they would not for other people. Paddy didn't know if that was exactly the truth, but he knew he loved the beasts.

As the horse drank her fill, Paddy studied the pattern of her coat. He hadn't seen but one other strawberry roan in all his life. The mottling color was a wonder, to be sure. The undercoat was basically that of a chestnut, but the body was covered with white hair, giving it a pinkish tint against the reddish brown. Paddy thought it quite lovely.

He ran his hand down the muscular shoulder and forearm, immediately noticing the clubbed right foot. The inward turn wasn't overstated, but it was enough of one that a trained eye could easily spot the trouble.

"Ya're a fine one," Paddy said, running his hand up the mare's leg. "For sure ya don't let your infirmities stop ya."

The mare turned her head ever so slightly and bobbed it up and down as if agreeing. Paddy gave a hearty laugh. "Ya'll do just fine, I'm thinkin'. I wouldn't mind havin' ya meself." He walked the mare back to the barn and resecured the brake. "I'll be findin' yar master and lettin' him know ya're ready to go." Paddy glanced over his shoulder conspiratorially and added, "But first a wee treat." He pulled out a piece of dried apple and offered it to the mare. She gobbled the treat quickly, then nuzzled his hand for more.

"Now don't be greedy, lass. Come back and see me again, and thar'll be more of that."

Paddy walked away whistling a tune. He loved his life here in America. He sometimes remembered the bad days in Ireland. The pain of losing his da and ma had been like nothing he'd ever known, but Kiara had always been good to him—always watching out for him. Even when there'd been no food, his sister had found ways to see that he ate—even when she went hungry. The memories sometimes turned him to great anger and sorrow, but then like a fog lifting from those emerald shores, he'd remember those days were gone and could no longer hurt him.

"Like Kiara says, they can only be hurtin' me if I let them."

"Who you talkin' to?" Obadiah asked as Paddy entered the barn.

"Meself. I'm the only one who'll be listenin' to such foolery," Paddy replied with a grin.

Obadiah laughed. "And what you be tellin' yo'self?"

"That the bad things of the past can't be hurtin' me unless I let them." Paddy's serious tone had a sobering effect on the broad-shouldered man.

Obadiah nodded slowly. "Dat be da truth—no foolery there. I think that most of da time. Bad times come to mind, but they be in da past and need to stay dere."

"Aye, 'tis true," Paddy answered, knowing that the black man had much more to fear from his past than did Paddy. " 'Tis true."

———

Elinor hurried to the front door as the persistent knocking grew louder with each passing moment. She pulled on the door-knob and looked down into the watery blue eyes of a young boy dressed in a ragged shirt and breeches. Elinor stared at the child's crusty fingers surrounding the soft, supple beauty of a small bouquet of roses, momentarily taken aback by the contrast.

"Mrs. Brighton?"

His voice brought her back to the present. "Yes. Are these for one of my boarders?" she inquired.

"No, ma'am. I was told they're for you." The child thrust the bouquet toward her hand.

Elinor reached to take the offering. "Who sent you?"

"Don't know. There's a note in the flowers," he said before racing back down the street.

She held the mixture of greenery and pink roses to her face, inhaling a fragrant whiff and permitting herself to be transported back to another time, happier days when she was married to Daniel and life was filled with joy and excitement. Removing her cut-glass vase from the uppermost shelf of the china closet, Elinor remembered how she would scold Daniel for picking the neighbors' flowers as he came home from work on a summer's evening and how his deep laughter would fill the room while he placed the flowers in water.

"Stop this reminiscing or you'll soon be weeping," she chided herself while discarding the damp paper surrounding the bouquet. The boy had been correct. There was a note tucked deep among the flowers. The words were written in a strong masculine script:

Dear Mrs. Brighton,
I realize my behavior earlier this week was far too bold. Please accept my apology. It is my fervent desire you will accept my offer of friendship. I ask nothing more.
Your humble servant,
Oliver Maxwell

"Oliver! I never expected such gallantry," she murmured.

The sound of the front door closing echoed through the house and was soon followed by the chattering girls returning home for supper. Elinor automatically checked the clock sitting on the mantel. It appeared she was on schedule and the meal would be ready on time.

"Are those flowers for Jane?" Nancy Engle inquired while walking into the parlor.

Elinor glanced over her shoulder. "No, they're for me."

"For you?" Nancy turned toward the other girls, who were now entering the room behind her. "Why would *you* receive flowers?"

"Yes, do tell us," Jane concurred. "I'm especially interested since we have no way of knowing if the flowers were actually sent to you or meant for one of us."

Elinor's jaw tightened. "Have I ever lied to any of you? These flowers were sent to me, but if you believe otherwise, please take them," she said, yanking the flowers from the vase. She thrust the dripping bouquet at Jane, who was staring at her in open-mouthed surprise. "If they're so important to you, by all means take them," she commanded through clenched teeth.

Jane stepped back, her gaze fixed on the dripping stems. "You're getting water on the rug." She pointed toward the floor while taking another step away from Elinor.

"I don't care about the water or the carpet. If you girls think these flowers belong to one of you, please take them." Her words were low and measured as she once again propelled the flowers toward the group. "I am *not* a liar or a thief, and I *certainly* am not so anxious for a bouquet that I would claim flowers sent for one of you."

Jane nudged Nancy's arm. "I didn't mean to imply you were lying," Nancy said. "It was an honest mistake. Harry Lorimer said he was going to send Jane flowers. Didn't he, Jane?" Nancy turned a pleading gaze toward the girl.

"He did say he was going to send flowers, but we believe what you've told us, Mrs. Brighton," Jane said. "Please don't be angry. We meant no harm."

Elinor turned on her heel and placed the flowers back in the water-filled vase. "Instead of boarders who are intent upon educating themselves and doing good works, the Corporation sends me the ill-mannered, unpleasant workers. All of the fine, upstanding girls are sent to board with the other keepers. I have yet to have one girl who thinks about anyone except herself," she muttered as she returned to the kitchen.

An abnormal silence pervaded the supper table that evening. The girls filled their plates without the usual chatter, occasionally glancing toward Elinor with uncertainty. There was no diatribe about disliking the food she had prepared, nor was any comment made when the evening meal was served a half hour late. In fact, Elinor decided afterward, the evening had been the epitome of civility.

CHAPTER · 10

MALCOLM GAVE his youngest son a sidelong glance. The little boy had disappeared and was now a man of twenty and four years. McKinley's youth had evaporated as quickly as fog rising off the bayou, and the realization caused a twinge of sadness to seep into Malcolm's heart. Too late, he had acknowledged a lack of involvement with his children during their youth. Back in the days of their childhood he had eased his conscience by telling himself rearing children was a mother's responsibility. After all, he had the plantation to run and little time for anything else. It wasn't until after Madelaine's death that he'd given serious consideration to the fact that his wife might have fared better with her bouts of melancholy had he helped more with the children—or at least had given *her* more attention. But it was impossible to change the past—one could only hope to do better in the future.

McKinley brushed aside a golden-brown wave of hair that was creeping downward onto his forehead. "You're particularly quiet this morning, Father. Are you reconsidering our visit to President Taylor?"

Malcolm jerked out of his reverie and met McKinley's puzzled gaze. "No, of course not. In fact, Zachary would be irate if he discovered we were in Washington but failed to call upon him.

That fact aside, I'm anxious to hear how he has been doing since we saw him last fall. After reading newspaper accounts for the past several months, I'd like to hear Zachary's version of what's been happening in Congress. I'm certain we'll receive a colorful recitation."

McKinley drank a final sip of coffee and placed his cup on the matching white china saucer. "Did you send word we'd be visiting? There's always the possibility he's away from the city. As I understand it, folks in these parts often escape the heat and dangers of the city. I believe they have trouble with fever, just as we do in the South."

"I sent a letter back in May telling him we planned to visit in late June or early July. I did pen a note after our arrival last night and left it with the hotel clerk. He promised to have it immediately delivered to the president. Besides, I doubt Zachary would depart the capital with Fourth of July activities in the offing. Have you finished your breakfast?" Malcolm asked while surveying McKinley's empty plate.

McKinley nodded and patted his flat stomach. "I've gorged myself as much as I dare. If I eat any more, I'll need to have my buttons set over at least an inch."

"Then we'd best leave—I don't want to be party to such a calamity," Malcolm said with a wide grin on his face as he pushed away from the table.

McKinley touched his father's arm and nodded toward the front desk of the hotel. "The clerk is signaling for you, Father."

Malcolm's gaze shifted to the portly clerk, who was waving a folded missive above his head. Malcolm advanced with quick strides, arriving at the desk in record time. "May I assume that message is for me?"

Thick fleshy folds settled over the clerk's collar as he lowered his head and thrust the letter toward Malcolm. "From the White House," he proudly announced while glancing about the lobby.

As Malcolm began to unfold the envelope's contents, he noted the clerk's beefy torso extended across the counter. "I'm certain you're not attempting to read my personal mail," he said as he met the man's inquisitive eyes.

The clerk jumped away from the counter. "Oh no, sir," he said, shaking his head like a wet dog attempting to dry itself.

Malcolm scanned the contents of the letter and told his son, "Zachary will be expecting us for the noonday meal. We have ample time to do a bit of exploring about the city before then. Why don't you hail a carriage, McKinley?"

The clerk was once again leaning across the counter. Eager anticipation filled his face. "You're joining the *president* for dinner?"

"You appear to have a penchant for prying into the business of the hotel guests, don't you?"

"I apologize, sir. It's just that I've never met anyone personally acquainted with the president."

The excitement in the man's voice lessened Malcolm's irritation. "Truly? Well, Zachary Taylor is a mere mortal made of flesh and bone. No different from the rest of us."

"My children will be agog when they hear I've met someone who dined with the president."

Malcolm's looked deep into the clerk's eyes and was taken aback by the awe reflected in the man's gaze. "Here—take this to your children." Malcolm handed him the missive emblazoned with Taylor's strong signature and strode off toward the front door.

———

Zachary entered the room, his twinkling eyes and wide smile momentarily erasing the worry lines from his craggy face. "Malcolm—and McKinley! I can't tell you what pleasure it brings having the two of you come for a visit. Peggy has made me promise we'll dine upstairs in her sitting room. She's anxious for news about you and the children. And she needs to see for herself that you've been taking care of yourself since Madelaine's death."

Malcolm clasped the president's outstretched hand. "If you're certain she's feeling up to our visit."

"I think it will improve her spirits greatly," Zachary replied.

"But first, would you care for a little tour of these rooms?"

"I most certainly would. I cannot imagine coming all this way and not seeing the people's house."

"The people's house is right," Zachary said. "The people are here morning, noon, and night. That's one of the reasons my poor Peggy seeks the confines of her room. There is never a moment when this place isn't overrun. You've come at a good time, however. Some of my staff have taken a large assembly of do-gooders and congressmen to one of the local eating establishments. They should be gone long enough to give us some liberty." He motioned them to follow.

The house was as grand and glorious as Malcolm had often heard said. He was impressed with the variety of furnishings, some which went back to the original orders of James Monroe.

"This is a lovely room," Malcolm stated as he followed his friend.

"We call it the blue room. Van Buren painted it in such a manner and it's seemed a natural color to maintain. I like its oval nature."

"As do I. It seems an entertaining room. Very unusual," Malcolm mused.

McKinley joined in pointing out the chandelier. "I believe this style would suit us well in our dining room back home. I know you've talked often of replacing the one there now."

Malcolm studied the wood and cut glass encircled with acanthus leaves. "Yes. Yes. I believe you're right."

"I can put you in touch with a workman who might be able to replicate this piece," Taylor told them.

They continued touring, enjoying many fine parlors and receiving rooms, and even a grand dining room. Malcolm was notably impressed with all of it. "I'm glad for this opportunity, Zachary. I truly would have hated to pass from this life without seeing this wondrous house."

"I agree," McKinley added. "I shall cherish this memory."

"Now, are you quite certain Peggy will be up to this visit? I certainly wouldn't want to overstay our welcome or overtax her."

"To be honest, I think Peggy's overall health improved once Betty accepted the official role as my hostess. Peggy never did enjoy public life. She prefers the company of close friends and family. And I believe the two of you fit into both categories. But we dare not remain down here discussing anything of a personal nature or Peggy will force us to repeat our entire conversation. She made me promise to bring you directly upstairs."

"Then we had best do as instructed. Lead the way and we'll follow along," McKinley said.

Malcolm gave a hearty chuckle as they walked up the stairway. "You know, Zachary, the clerk at our hotel would be incredulous if I were to tell him you do your wife's bidding."

Zachary looked over his shoulder, his smile returning. "How so? Isn't that the first rule we husbands are taught?"

"I suppose you're right, but the hotel clerk was quite impressed that I know you. In fact, I believe I've made a lifelong friend. I took a few moments to tell him you're quite common—even told him he might see you walking about the city unobserved from time to time."

"It's one of the few things that helps me maintain my sanity while attempting to deal with those bullies who call themselves representatives of the people. There's nothing I enjoy more than making my way about this town without anyone taking notice. Amazing the things you can see and hear when folks have no idea you're the president," he said with a grin.

"I'm certain that's true," Malcolm said.

An insistent tapping could be heard as they approached an open door. "Is that Malcolm Wainwright's voice I hear in the hallway?"

"Indeed it is, my dear," the president replied as the three men walked into Peggy's sitting room.

Zachary's words were true. Peggy sat in a dark blue brocade chair, with her feet clad in silk slippers that were propped on a matching footstool. At first glance, the ornate ivory cane she held in her hand gave the appearance of a royal scepter. Attired in a dress of peach fabric with her thick white hair perfectly coifed in the latest fashion, Peggy appeared healthier than Malcolm had seen her in years. There was now a pink tinge to her cheeks, and her piercing blue eyes held a spark of vitality. Only when she stood to take Zachary's arm and walk to the dining table did her frail health become evident. She leaned heavily upon her carved cane with one hand and held tightly to her husband's arm with the other, the tap of her cane slow and labored, unlike the insistent knocking he'd earlier heard.

Malcolm watched as Peggy slowly settled herself at the table and then turned her gaze toward him. "I want to hear how your family is managing, Malcolm. I can see that McKinley has turned into a handsome young fellow. I can't imagine how you've managed to escape all those Southern belles, young man."

McKinley grinned at the older woman. "I've not yet met the young lady to whom I'm ready to commit the rest of my life. And who knows—I may decide to leave the comfort of The Willows one day, and most Southern women prefer to remain among their families."

Peggy nodded her affirmation. "I'd say you've a sound head on your shoulders, McKinley. Marriage is not a commitment to be taken lightly. The vows you make are not only to the one you love, but also to God. You'll know when the time is right. And how is Jasmine? Has she decided to return home to Mississippi and care for the Wainwright men?"

Malcolm's gaze remained fixed on McKinley, for he was still not completely certain he'd understood his youngest son's reply. McKinley had never before indicated a desire to leave Mississippi.

Peggy gave an insistent tap of her cane. "I was asking about Jasmine's returning home, Malcolm."

Malcolm rubbed his jaw as though he were suddenly plagued by an aching tooth. "No, I don't believe any of us gave that idea much consideration—including Jasmine. She is quite happy living in the North, and I doubt she could be convinced to leave. In fact, we're on our way north on business and will be staying for a visit with Jasmine and my mother."

"I'm certain it would ease your loss if she would return to The Willows," Peggy said.

"I wouldn't consider asking her to do so. She would be eternally unhappy. In addition, I fear my mother has turned Jasmine into a Northern sympathizer."

Peggy leaned forward, her fork in midair. "How so?"

"I believe she's become an antislavery activist and forgotten her true Southern heritage."

McKinley shifted and edged forward on his chair. "Just because Jasmine opposes slavery doesn't mean she's forgotten her heritage."

There was a spark of anger in McKinley's gaze, and Malcolm knew he'd offended his son. He no longer knew with certainty what McKinley was thinking, but he didn't want his comment to escalate into a family argument. "No, of course not. Tell me, Zachary, how are you progressing with issues before the Congress?"

With a hand on either side of his plate, Zachary used the table for leverage and leaned back against the chair's hard wood. "I suppose you've already heard about my stormy conference with the Southern leadership back in February—I managed to anger most of them."

Malcolm smoothed the fringe of hair that circled his bald head. "I think it could be more appropriately stated that you angered *all* of them, Zachary. I wonder if that whole ordeal couldn't have been handled more diplomatically."

"They're hardheaded when it comes to the issue of slavery, Malcolm. You know that better than most. There's no reasoning with them. They all believed I would bow to their whims because I own slaves. You know as well as the next man that I respect slaveholders' rights in the fifteen states where the institution is legal. I adamantly oppose the extension of slavery. I am not going to jeopardize the Union because of the extension issue. My position was clear, but I sat quietly and permitted them the courtesy of expressing their views. Yet, after they saw that I would not be swayed, they began talking of secession. It was at that point I told them that if they rose up against the laws of this land and the

Union, I would personally lead the army against them."

"If memory serves me, you also told your Southern brothers you wouldn't hesitate to hang them just as you had done to deserters and spies during the Mexican War," Malcolm added.

"More than that, I told them that if they were taken in rebellion against the Union, I would hang them with *less* reluctance than I'd shown toward the traitors in Mexico—and I meant every word I uttered."

Malcolm stared at Zachary, unwilling to believe the words his friend and kinsman had spoken. "Surely you don't fault the men who are willing to fight in order to protect their very livelihood."

"I'm doing nothing to change how they live and support themselves; I'm not proposing an end to slavery in any of the states where it presently exists. I'm merely standing in opposition to extension. You would think they'd be willing to accept the fact that their lives will not change a jot if they'll simply leave well enough alone. I had hoped to assuage their concerns by purchasing a sugar plantation and another sixty slaves several months ago. Wouldn't you think my actions should have made a strong statement to the Southern elite?"

"But you're sending mixed messages to the entire nation. The North thinks they'll sway you into their antislavery camp while the South hopes you'll return to where your true allegiance should rest. Your loyalties are divided."

"They are *not* divided, Malcolm. My loyalty is with the Union," Zachary refuted between clenched teeth.

"Enough of this talk, gentlemen," Peggy said. "You can discuss the state of the nation once you've departed the dinner table. For now, I'd like to hear about the rest of your family, Malcolm. How is David? Any prospects for marriage?"

"As a matter of fact, I believe David will soon wed. He's been keeping company with a fine young lady for over a year now, and I think he's soon going to declare himself. I know the girl's father is anxious for the union—he owns several cotton plantations in Mississippi and I think he sees the marriage of his daughter as a way to expand his own holdings."

Zachary emitted a loud guffaw. "Then her father doesn't know you very well, does he?"

"She is a good match for David, and I believe they may elect to live at The Willows," Malcolm replied.

Peggy clapped her hands together. "What an excellent arrangement! Now that's the type of news I enjoy hearing. Tell me more about this young lady. Do we know the family?"

"The Burnhams—father's name is Winstead Burnham. He inherited the plantation from a great-uncle and they've been in Mississippi for only the last two years. Prior to that, they lived in Georgia. Winstead was happy to receive the inheritance—he's the second son, and the family holdings in Georgia were destined for his brother."

Peggy appeared to be deep in thought. "Would his current holdings be the Twin Oaks Plantation owned by John Hepple?"

"Indeed, that's the one. Winstead's made a number of improvements to the home, and I think he had a fair crop this year, but I don't believe he has the financial means needed to get the place back in top-notch condition. John's health was bad for many years, and his overseer did a poor job of keeping the place running properly."

"Be certain to tell David that we will expect an invitation to the wedding. I don't know if my health will permit the journey, but if Zachary is able, he'll attend. Won't you, dear?"

"I'd count it a pleasure," the president assured. "I do have some meetings this afternoon, Malcolm, but I insist the two of you join me for some sightseeing tomorrow. Perhaps I can sneak about town unrecognized before we return back here to the White House. Peggy and Betty have been planning some special festivities for the family's Independence Day celebration. We're hoping you can join us."

The loud thwack of Peggy's cane against the marble overlay surrounding the fireplace brought all three men to attention. "Of course they'll be here. A hearty yes is the only answer I'll accept," she stated in her sweetest voice.

Malcolm's lips turned up to form a broad grin. "Having

observed your ability to wield your cane with such absolute power, we dare not refuse."

———————

The president stepped out of the black horse-drawn carriage, pushed his stovepipe hat onto his head, and instructed the driver to wait for their return. Striding into the hotel, the president paused. "Is that him?" he asked Malcolm as he nodded in the direction of the hotel's front desk.

"It is. And he's likely to be rendered speechless when he realizes who you are."

Zachary's eyes danced with mischief. "That's what makes this such fun. People don't expect the president to walk up and introduce himself."

Malcolm and McKinley stood back and watched the scene unfold. Zachary approached the clerk as though he were any guest seeking accommodations for a night or two in the nation's capital. Although the Wainwright men could not hear the conversation, the clerk laughed as Zachary obviously entertained the man with some tall tale. Moments later Zachary appeared to introduce himself and then reached to shake the clerk's hand. The middle-aged clerk pushed away from the counter with his gaze fixed on the president in a trancelike stare.

With a spirited grin, Zachary turned and waved Malcolm and McKinley forward. "You'd best confirm what I've told the clerk, or I don't believe he's going to regain his power of speech."

Malcolm approached the clerk. "Sir, when I met with the president yesterday, I mentioned your admiration of him both as our president and as a formidable adversary during his military service in Mexico. President Taylor insisted upon meeting you."

"Then this is—this is—truly the—the—president?" he stammered.

"Indeed. And he came here specifically to meet you," Malcolm reiterated.

The clerk reached across the desk and grasped Zachary's hand, propelling the president's arm up and down with the enthusiasm of a dehydrated man priming a pump for a taste of water. "Oh, thank you, sir, thank you," the clerk said, his words synchronized with each pump of Zachary's arm.

Malcolm covered his mouth with one hand lest he laugh aloud. The clerk had captured Zachary's hand in a stranglehold and continued to maintain his grasp while the president wiggled his fingers in an obvious attempt to extricate himself.

McKinley finally moved forward and stood beside Zachary. "We really must be going, don't you think, President Taylor?"

Zachary wrested his arm free and gave McKinley an appreciative smile. "Yes, absolutely. I told the driver we would be only a few minutes." He turned back to the clerk, now careful to keep his hands clasped behind his back. "Pleased to meet you. And my regards to your family."

"I see what you mean about deriving pleasure from going about the city, Zachary. That little meeting was extremely entertaining," Malcolm said as they exited the hotel.

"Poor man appeared as besotted as a lovesick debutante. And you, Malcolm, could have at least attempted to hide your enjoyment of my predicament. I had begun to wonder if I would ever disentangle myself from the good fellow's hand."

"What we needed was Peggy's cane," Malcolm said, emitting a boisterous guffaw.

"On a more serious note, don't you believe your behavior somewhat dangerous?" McKinley inquired.

"I don't normally introduce myself, McKinley, and I have yet to have one person step forward and ask if I am the president. I'll notice an occasional congressman assessing me, but he doesn't approach. Of course, I never give them any sign of recognition. I think they fear being made the fool should they be incorrect. Those pompous men fail to remember they continually make ninnies of themselves in Congress."

"No one who truly knows you would deny the fact that you are a man of simplicity, Zachary. A quality I richly admire, I might add."

Zachary swiped the perspiration from his forehead. "Thank

you, Malcolm. This heat is overbearing, is it not? Let's make our way over to the Washington Monument. I'm expected there for special festivities, and I want you and McKinley at my side."

Malcolm's eyebrows arched high on his forehead. "Seems an odd place to host a celebration. From what I've seen, they don't even have a good start on the monument."

"True, but ever since the Masonic ceremonies and huge celebration when the cornerstone was laid two years ago, folks seem to think it's the place to host the celebration. However, once the official ceremonies are completed, we'll join the family for our personal Independence Day celebration. We can hope the weather will become more bearable once the sun goes down."

The captain's chest swelled like a bloated fish as he announced to the passengers they would arrive in Boston the next afternoon—virtually a full day ahead of schedule.

"He acts as though he played some large part in our early arrival. The fair weather is the only reason we've made good time on this journey," Malcolm muttered.

"The man is an excellent seafarer," McKinley replied.

"It's the weather, not his seafaring ability he's got to thank for our early arrival. He's portentous and immodest—acting as though he's accomplished some great feat through his own proficiency."

"Why are you angry, Father? The captain was merely informing us we'd be arriving early. You've been irritable since we departed Washington. Did you and President Taylor argue?"

"No, of course not. I know where Zachary stands. I don't agree with him, but I know he'll not change his mind. Frankly, it's your behavior that has occupied my thoughts since our departure."

McKinley started at the retort. "*Me?* Whatever for?"

With his chin thrust forward and hands tightly clasped behind his back, Malcolm stood against the ship's railing as though prepared to do battle. "I was taken aback by your agreement with Zachary on the slavery issues. Every time the topic arose, you either sided with Zachary or argued beyond what either of us believes. To be honest, you sounded more like Grandmother Wainwright's protégé than my son."

"And do my oppositional views make me any less your son?" McKinley's words burned with the same defiance that filled his angry eyes.

Malcolm rubbed his jaw and stared at McKinley. When had he lost his son to these irrational beliefs? First Jasmine and now McKinley! Yet it seemed impossible to believe McKinley had been swayed. He wasn't around people who could influence him with absurd antislavery sentiment—or was he?

"You've obviously been consorting with those who hold views that are in direct opposition to everything our family believes. May I inquire whom you've been meeting with?"

"I can't imagine why you find it difficult to comprehend that my beliefs are independent of yours. We have little in common, Father. You're eager to take charge of the physical operation of the plantation while my involvement has remained in the accounting and finances."

A stiff breeze crossed the deck and Malcolm bent his head against the wind, his nostrils filling with the odor of fish and salt water. "I've maintained close supervision on the accounts throughout the years, and had you shown any interest in anything else—"

"Anything so long as it lent itself to raising cotton. If you'll think back to the time when I was ready to choose a vocation, I talked to you about my desire to become a doctor."

"Oh yes—something about becoming a physician so you could provide the slaves with improved medical care."

"Exactly. As I recall, you laughed and told me you needed someone to manage your finances and you would continue to look after the medical care for the slaves."

Malcolm turned his gaze toward the ocean. "Surely you weren't serious about such a pursuit. We're a family of cotton growers. I need my sons actively involved in the business of raising cotton, especially now that Samuel is acting as an agent for the Southern growers. Moving Samuel into Bradley Houston's old position with the Corporation in Lowell was excellent for this entire area of the South—The Willows included. However, it left me without his talent and physical presence. Hence my need to move David into his position and rely more heavily upon you to ensure the accounts and business matters are in proper order."

"The fact remains that each of us is required to perform the work *you* designate advantageous, whether we agree or not."

"I don't recall your ever being unwilling to accept your wages or other benefits derived from your occupation. However, since you find your life at The Willows repugnant, perhaps you should support yourself in someone else's employ." Malcolm enunciated each word with a clarity that bit the air like glassy shards.

"I'll give that further thought, Father," McKinley replied tersely as he strode away from the railing.

"Further thought? What does he mean, 'further thought'?" Malcolm muttered, balling his hand into a tight fist and pounding against the ship's balustrade.

Slowly the realization that his son was already weighing the possibility of moving away from The Willows began to seep into Malcolm's consciousness, and a fierce anger began to build from deep within.

Malcolm turned and faced directly into the wind, with the damp air stinging his face. "I'll *not* lose another child to the North," he vowed.

CHAPTER · 11

ALICE WAINWRIGHT beckoned to her grandson, who was descending the stairway. "Good morning, McKinley. Why don't you escort me out into the garden? I've taken the liberty of asking Martha to serve us breakfast outdoors. I hope you can tolerate the foolish whims of an old woman. I enjoy spending a few hours in the garden before the heat of the day sets in, when the world still seems fresh and untouched."

McKinley's gaze turned toward the door leading to the garden, where Martha was giving the table her final touch. McKinley smiled at the sight of Martha wearing a wide-brimmed bonnet while arranging the garden breakfast table. Obviously, his grandmother's hired servant was intent upon protecting her fair complexion even at this early morning hour. "I would be pleased to accompany you, Grandmother. The heat of the day up here seems mild compared to home. Even Washington seemed more stifling. Is Father planning to join us?"

"No. He had an early meeting with Matthew Cheever and some other gentlemen. He said he would return midmorning. However, he asked me to tell you that the family has been invited to dine with the Cheever family this evening and he expects you to attend and be on your best behavior. I'm not certain what that last remark meant. I told your father I'd never seen you anywhere that you weren't on your best behavior."

Alice took McKinley's arm and walked alongside as he escorted her to the small table Martha had prepared with a linen cloth and china. "I doubt Father would agree with your evaluation of my conduct," McKinley replied as he assisted his grandmother into her chair and then seated himself across the table.

"It's obvious something is amiss between you and your father. But when I inquired, he quickly changed the topic. Tell me, McKinley, what has occurred to cause this breach? Is this something related to your mother's death?" Alice clasped a hand to her chest. "Has Malcolm been courting someone? He's come here to tell me he plans to remarry, hasn't he?"

"No, of course not, Grandmother. I doubt Father will ever marry again." He leaned back and allowed Martha to set a plate heaped with scrambled eggs, sausage, and fluffy biscuits in front of him.

Alice sipped her tea and studied her grandson. "Then what is the problem causing the two of you to scarcely acknowledge one another?"

"As you know, we spent time with President and Mrs. Taylor in Washington."

"Yes, of course. Your father went into detail regarding your activities. Of course, I was primarily interested in hearing about Peggy, but I listened to his lengthy report with as much concentration as I could muster," she said with a sheepish grin.

"Did he mention our conversations with President Taylor regarding slavery?"

A guarded smile crossed Alice's lips. "Your father and I ceased discussing the topic of slavery a number of years ago. What began as a conversation would soon develop into an argument; therefore, we decided if we were going to maintain family civility, the issue would not be discussed. I do know Zachary's position has angered your father—along with most of the Southern plantation owners, but what has that to do with the two of you?"

"I sided with the president. Actually, I went beyond siding

with him and told Father I oppose slavery."

Lifting her napkin, Alice dabbed her lips. She didn't want McKinley to suspect the alarm elicited by his statement. "Sometimes there is wisdom in weighing our beliefs against timing and consequences, McKinley. Don't misinterpret what I'm saying: I believe we must have the courage to take a stand for our principles. However, it's wise to evaluate when to take such a stand. Exactly what did you say?"

Alice listened as McKinley related the conversations that had taken place, both in Washington and on board the ship. When McKinley completed the recitation, she remained silent for several minutes, staring at her roses and praying God would give her the perfect solution, some ideal method to heal the discord. "You know your father is prone to speak in anger and then regret his words, don't you?"

"I realize we all speak out of turn from time to time, Grandmother. However, Father said what is truly in his heart. If I return to The Willows, he will expect me to embrace his beliefs, but I can't do that. From the time I was very young, I couldn't understand why we owned other human beings—and nobody ever gave me a proper explanation. Consequently, I've tolerated plantation life but have not had the courage to speak my mind until now. I don't take any pleasure in causing Father pain, but I cannot continue acting as though I find slavery acceptable. I'm hoping you will agree to take me on as a temporary houseguest."

Alice clutched at her chest. "Oh, dear! It would be a treat to have you remain in Lowell. And having you live with me would prove a genuine delight. However, I'm not certain your father would ever forgive me. He already holds me accountable for influencing Jasmine in her stand against slavery."

"He can't blame you for my beliefs, Grandmother. And as I said, he's told me that if I disagree with slavery, perhaps I should find some other way to support myself."

She began fanning herself with her limp cloth napkin. "I do believe the temperature has dramatically risen since we first came outdoors."

"I've made you uncomfortable. I'm sorry, Grandmother. Forget we had this conversation. Let's return indoors." McKinley stood and then assisted Alice from her chair.

Grasping McKinley's arm, Alice met his gaze with an encouraging smile. "Don't give up on me so soon, my boy. I need only a bit of time to think this matter through. I don't want to see the family thrown into chaos, nor do I want to see you unhappy. I need some time for preparation so that we may present a firm plan to your father. Our actions will merely serve to provoke him if we have no definitive plan."

"Then you *will* help?"

"Yes, of course. How could I turn down such a request? However, you must remember we do not want to cause your father undue pain. For the present, put aside your differences and attempt to reconcile with him. Do you think you can do that?"

"I promise to make every attempt, but I don't believe Father will do the same."

"You do your part and leave the rest to me," she said as they walked into the house.

The trio sat in silence as their carriage moved through the streets of Lowell. Finally Alice turned her focus to her son. "You've not told me how your meetings progressed today, Malcolm. I trust all went well?"

"Everything went well, Mother."

"Can you say no more than those few words? Surely you have more to report—you were gone all day."

Malcolm shifted his weight and turned toward Alice. "I doubt my business meetings are of interest to either of you. Suffice it to say our discussions were fruitful, and I'm certain the agreements we reach will prove beneficial to all concerned."

McKinley's eyebrows arched. "I thought Samuel was overseeing all contractual negotiations for the Southern cotton growers."

Malcolm directed an icy look at McKinley. "Your brother negotiates the contracts regarding prices and quantities for the growers. These meetings deal with issues more intricate and far-reaching than next year's prices—matters I don't believe we should discuss."

Alice grasped her son's arm with a gloved hand. "Forgive me, Malcolm. I shouldn't have been prying into business matters. Especially after a difficult day of meetings when I'm certain you're looking forward to relaxing and forgetting your worries. McKinley and I were simply interested in your day. We'll save our idle chatter for the Cheevers' dining table."

Thankfully McKinley took her cue and nodded his agreement. "Are you a regular visitor at the Cheever home, Grandmother?"

"I visit Lilly on occasion, and she frequently acts as hostess for some of the groups to which I belong. She's a fine lady. In fact, she worked in one of the mills before marrying Matthew Cheever. And this is their home," Alice said as their carriage slowly came to a halt.

McKinley looked out the window and then back at his grandmother, his brows furrowed. "I expected something more . . ."

"Pretentious?" she inquired.

"At least more spacious."

"You grew up on a plantation and equate real estate with power and wealth," Malcolm told his son. "Make no mistake: Matthew Cheever wields plenty of power, and he could live much more splendidly if he so desired. Shall we go in?"

"He takes umbrage at everything I say," McKinley whispered to his grandmother.

"Trust me—your father will soften as the evening wears on and he's around other people."

Lilly Cheever awaited them at the front door, poised in a pale blue dress edged with fine ivory lace, while Matthew stood on the front porch engrossed in conversation with several other men.

"Come join us, Malcolm," Matthew called. "We decided the parlor was much too warm."

Malcolm cast a glance toward the men. "If you'll excuse me, Mother, I believe I will accept Matthew's invitation."

"By all means—I have McKinley to escort me," she replied

with a warm smile before turning her attention to Lilly. "Lilly, I'd like to introduce my grandson, McKinley Wainwright."

"A pleasure," Lilly greeted warmly. "And this is our daughter, Violet, and son, Michael. Violet, perhaps you would like to accompany Mr. Wainwright and introduce him to some of the other younger guests."

The flounces of Violet's white organdy dress gave a gentle swish as she stepped forward and clasped McKinley's arm. "I would be delighted."

"Thank you for your kindness, Miss Cheever. Grandmother?"

Alice remained beside Lilly Cheever and waved the young couple forward. "You two go along. I can manage on my own."

"Your grandson is a handsome young man. Is this his first visit to Lowell?" Lilly inquired.

"Yes, it is, and I know he'll have a much better time this evening now that he's with Violet. I don't think he'd enjoy hearing the Lowell matrons discuss their flower gardens or latest ailments."

Lilly's soft laughter filled the warm evening breeze. " 'Tis true young people have little patience when it comes to flower gardens or illness. How long will your family be visiting?"

"I'm uncertain. As you know, Malcolm has been involved in business meetings with your husband and other members of the Boston Associates. It's my understanding he'll book passage once they've concluded their meetings."

"Then we'll have to hope they are slow in concluding their business. Your grandson would make a nice addition to the few eligible men in Lowell. Ah, and here is your granddaughter."

Jasmine leaned down and gave her grandmother a warm embrace. "What's this I hear about eligible young men coming to Lowell?"

Alice pointed a finger in Jasmine's direction, her face crinkling as she smiled at Jasmine. "Now you see? That's how gossip gets started. Folks hear part of a conversation and the next thing you know, a false rumor has begun."

"I *know* I heard talk of eligible men," Jasmine insisted.

"I was telling your grandmother that your brother would make a fine addition to the few eligible men we have in Lowell. He's a handsome young man."

"Speaking of eligible men, where is Nolan? I thought he was going to accompany you this evening," Alice interjected.

"He sent word he would meet me here. Perhaps we should go inside and permit Mrs. Cheever the opportunity to greet her guests," Jasmine suggested, gently guiding her grandmother through the front door. "And where is McKinley? I noticed Father when I arrived, but McKinley wasn't with him."

Alice glanced about and then took Jasmine's hand. "McKinley is with Violet Cheever. Let's sit in the alcove near the stairway, where we can talk without our conversation being overheard. I have much to tell you. Your father and McKinley are at odds with each other."

———

Malcolm wiped his brow and continued pacing back and forth across the burgundy and gold wool carpet that adorned the floor of his mother's parlor. Life as he knew it continued to change, and he didn't like it one bit. "I can't believe it!" Malcolm exclaimed, his face ashen and drawn.

Alice motioned toward the settee. "Do sit down, Malcolm. The fact is, whether you choose to believe it or not, the president is dead."

Malcolm ceased his pacing and wheeled around. "Zachary was more than the president; he was my friend. Even though we weren't related by blood, I considered him kin."

"I understand, Malcolm. However, there is nothing you can do to change things. It's a shock to all of us. I cared for Zachary also. And dear Peggy. We must pray she'll find the fortitude to withstand Zachary's death."

Malcolm dropped onto the settee and once again began rubbing his forehead. "To think we were with Zachary when he was eating cherries and milk on the Fourth of July. In fact, I joined him and ate some of the same. The doctors conclude that's what caused his death. Seems strange that would be the source of his ailment since I was completely unaffected, don't you think?"

"The newspaper said something about the heat also. I'm surmising that as the day wore on, he became extremely overheated. I do recall you mentioned the extreme heat during the time you visited Peggy and Zachary."

"True. It was unbearably hot in Washington, particularly on the Fourth. However, I find it difficult to believe it was cherries and milk that killed the president—more likely his heart. I can't believe Peggy is willing to accept such an outlandish explanation. Are you?"

Alice tucked a wisp of white hair behind one ear. "The shock has likely caused Peggy to take to her bed, and I doubt she's intent upon discovering the cause of Zachary's death. After all, knowing the cause is not going to bring him back to her. Are you thinking you should go to Washington?"

"Matters here in Lowell will not permit me to leave at the moment. And by the time I would arrive, I doubt there would be a member of the Taylor family remaining in Washington. There's little doubt Peggy will at least be pleased to be out of the political turmoil that surrounded the family."

The sight of McKinley descending the staircase caused a faint smile to appear upon Alice's lips. "Are you leaving the house?"

Twirling his straw hat on one finger, McKinley stepped into the doorway of the parlor. "I'm calling on Violet Cheever. She's agreed to give me a complete tour of Lowell and the surrounding countryside." Her grandson's wide grin was infectious.

"Splendid! And will you be returning for the noonday meal?"

"No. Miss Cheever suggested a picnic. Fortunately the weather has cooperated and there's not a sign of rain."

"What fun!" Alice exclaimed, giving a resounding clap of her hands. "Picnics always remind me of your grandfather. He loved finding a grassy place beneath the trees, close to a river or stream, where he could relax and watch the water. He said the water had a calming effect upon him."

"Some of us must work in order to earn our keep. Instead of lazing about some grassy meadow, I'll be attending meetings this afternoon. You may want to give some thought to the difficulties of earning a living while you're staring out into the Merrimack River," Malcolm asserted.

Malcolm didn't wait for his son's reply before exiting through the parlor doors leading out into his mother's small flower garden. With a determined stride, he walked across the slate stepping-stones that curved away from the garden until he reached an old elm. The giant branches provided a leafy canopy over a weather-worn wrought-iron bench. He dropped onto the cool metal and rested his arms across his thighs, staring at the ground as a crushing weariness permeated his bones.

"Zachary, Zachary—what is your death going to mean to this country? I fear none of us can even fathom what lies in wait for us," he muttered.

"Has life become so difficult that you've begun talking to yourself, Father?"

Malcolm started and quickly turned toward the sound of Jasmine's voice. "I didn't know you were paying a visit today. Had I known, I wouldn't have scheduled a meeting for this afternoon."

Jasmine smiled and sat down, the flounces of her yellow morning dress spreading across the bench in waves of fabric and ribbon. "I needed to make some purchases at the mercantile. It is my practice to stop and visit with Grandmother whenever I'm in Lowell. I'm sorry you have a meeting, but we can share this time together, and Grandmother has invited me to remain for supper also. I won't return home until evening. You appear troubled. Are you regretting your visit to Lowell?"

"In some respects, I suppose I am. I thought this journey would be good for both McKinley and me—help us grow closer. Instead, it's had the opposite result. I believe he intends to remain here in Lowell. And now with Zachary's death, the country is bound to be in an upheaval, and I don't know what to expect from Millard Fillmore. Of course, he may be more of an asset to the South than Zachary was. It's difficult to know what a man will do once he's in a powerful position."

"Your words are filled with sadness and disappointment,

Father. I know you worry about The Willows, but you must try to remember that your life will not be measured solely by what is accomplished on that cotton plantation."

"You think like a woman, Jasmine. Men know from an early age that they are measured by their ability to gain wealth and power. Yet, at this moment in my life, I realize I've lost my children to those endeavors."

She reached for her father's hand. "Whatever do you mean? You haven't lost any of us. I know I can safely say that all of your children love you."

He brushed the back of her hand with a fleeting kiss. "Love? Perhaps. But do any of my children like me or desire to live in the home I created for them? I think not."

"David is going to remain at The Willows. I'm certain he intends to live there once he marries. And Samuel will return eventually, Father. Remember it was your suggestion for Samuel to replace Bradley. You knew his work would require him to spend a great deal of time away from The Willows, and McKinley . . ."

"Yes, McKinley. I've lost him to the North, just as I lost you. Did your grandmother tell you he hopes to remain in Lowell?"

"Grandmother said the two of you had a disagreement regarding the antislavery movement and you told McKinley he should seek other employment if he was unhappy with your beliefs."

"He condemns my way of life, yet he has never refused the benefits. My words were spoken in anger—my feeble attempt to bring him to his senses."

"Instead of anger, perhaps he needs your affirmation," Alice said as she neared the bench.

"Please sit down, Grandmother. I must go inside and check on Spencer—I'm certain he's a handful for Martha."

Malcolm watched as Jasmine made her way toward the house before he turned to meet his mother's gaze. "So you think my son needs affirmation? Of what? His belief in the antislavery movement? I'm sorry, Mother, but you know I will never side with you and your Northern allies on this subject, nor will I give McKinley my blessing to embrace such principles. I don't want him to remain in Lowell. He needs to return to The Willows with me. Once he's back in Mississippi, he will see things more clearly."

"Surely you don't think his beliefs suddenly materialized on your voyage to Boston. It's obvious to me that McKinley has harbored antislavery sentiments all of his life. Can't you see that he has feared losing his relationship with you if he truly declared his views? He's a grown man, Malcolm. Permit him the privilege of making his own decisions."

"You argue on his behalf because he has embraced your views. Have you swayed Samuel to your side also?"

Alice jerked away. "I've not attempted to influence my grandchildren. I have always answered their questions truthfully, nothing more. And as for Samuel, I see him rarely and have no idea whether his views regarding slavery have changed since he's been working closely with the Associates. However, I seriously doubt you'll lose his alliance. Samuel has always been pro-slavery. Had you taken note as the children were growing into adulthood, I think you would have seen evidence that neither Jasmine nor McKinley ever held to your sentiments."

"And David?"

"You won't lose David—he hopes to permanently win Samuel's former position at The Willows. From the time he was a little boy, David was insecure in his rank as the second son. With Samuel's departure, David views himself as your rightful heir. You can be certain he will remain firmly aligned with any opinion you adopt. And now that he is considering marriage, his sights will be firmly set upon The Willows."

Malcolm sat up and looked deep into his mother's eyes. "You judge David harshly."

"I don't judge him at all. David holds values and opinions that differ from those of McKinley and Jasmine. You and I have differing views, but that fact doesn't change my love for you, and I hope your love for Jasmine and McKinley won't change. I know you have made great strides toward healing your relationship with Jasmine after forcing an abominable marriage upon her. I do not see that she holds that against you any longer. So I have to believe that the love between you has also given you the power to heal the hurts. It's my prayer you'll continue down that path with McKinley. Your harsh words have caused him great pain."

"And what of *his* remarks? They were harsh as well."

Alice held his eyes with a slight smile tugging at her lips.

"Oh, I know I should be the one to make the first gesture toward forgiveness, but it seems all I hold sacred is slipping away. First Jasmine, then Madelaine, and now McKinley. I'll apologize to McKinley, but I'll let him know I expect him to return home with me."

His mother's face was filled with a profound sadness he hadn't seen since the day they'd buried his father. "Have you heard *nothing* I've said to you?"

"Yes, Mother, but—"

"Malcolm, I've not forced my beliefs upon any member of this family, and perhaps you should consider doing the same. Your children are now adults, quite capable of forming their own opinions, and you should permit them to do so. You and Madelaine gave your children a solid foundation; now permit them to put their training to use. They can, and *should,* make their own decisions."

"They still need my guidance and influence."

"That may be true, but the final decision is theirs, and you should honor their right to choose. Free choice, Malcolm—let them apply it in their daily lives and trust you've taught them well. Of course, continued prayer is helpful also," she concluded with a sweet smile.

He managed a sheepish smile. "I don't believe I'm as confident they'll make the choices I'd prefer."

Alice's laughter rose upward and mingled with the soft afternoon breeze. "Your decisions didn't always concur with my preferences, but it didn't change my love for you. We can dislike choices that are made, but our love must always remain constant—wouldn't you agree?"

Malcolm rose from the bench and helped Alice to her feet.

"It's impossible to disagree with anything you've said, but that doesn't change the fact that I'll still be doing everything in my power to influence McKinley to return to The Willows."

"You seem rather sad today," Violet Cheever said as McKinley smoothed out their picnic blanket.

"Perhaps introspective is a better word," he said as he picked up the picnic basket. "Where do want this?"

She sank gracefully to the blanket and patted the center. "Right here. This shall give us easy access to all of Cook's culinary delights."

McKinley smiled, but his heart wasn't in it. Joining Violet on the blanket, he let out a heavy sigh.

"Perhaps such heavy introspection would be more easily borne if shared with a friend?"

"Perhaps, but I would hate to burden such a new and generous friend as you."

"Pshaw, as Mother would say." She laughed, and the sound caused McKinley to relax.

"Grandmother would agree," he said, smiling.

Violet began pulling food from the basket. She never looked up but asked in a very serious tone, "Does this have something to do with your father?"

He startled. "Why do you ask that?"

"I recognized some tension between the two of you last night. Forgive me, but I asked Jasmine if something was amiss. She, of course, refused to betray any details but said I should pray for you. So I did."

McKinley eased back on one elbow and stretched his legs out across the blanket. "Father and I have grown distant—perhaps we were never all that close to begin with. We don't share the same ideals."

Violet worked to fix a plate of food for each of them. "Regarding your future? Most fathers seem quite set upon the path their sons should take, while it's been my experience that most sons have entirely different ideas."

He laughed. "Your experience, eh? You are all of what, sixteen?"

Violet looked up in absolute astonishment. "I beg your pardon!"

McKinley shot to his feet and took several paces back. He waved his hands in protest. "I was only joking. I know you're much older."

"You think I'm old?" she said, her voice changing from astonishment to irritation.

McKinley suddenly realized this wasn't at all going the way he wanted it to. "I do not think you're old. You are just the right age."

Violet lowered her face for a moment, then lifted it to reveal her huge smile. "The right age for what?"

McKinley suddenly realized she wasn't at all upset with him, she'd merely been giving him back some of his own medicine.

He dropped back down by her side and grabbed a cookie from one of the plates before she could stop him. He took a bite and grinned. "Why, the right age for a picnic by the river. What else could I mean?"

"Hmm, I cannot imagine, Mr. Wainwright, but I shall endeavor to thoroughly explore the possibilities." She gave him a most alluring simper before turning back to the food.

"Why, Miss Cheever," he said, trying not to sound too surprised, when in truth he was quite taken aback. "I do believe you're flirting with me."

Violet handed him a plate. "I believe you are correct, Mr. Wainwright. How very astute."

CHAPTER · 12

Late August

ROGAN SHEEHAN and Liam Donohue propped themselves against the log-hewn railing that surrounded Jasmine Houston's neatly manicured lawn and separated it from the remainder of her acreage. Rogan lifted the cap from his head and waved it high in the air until Obadiah noticed him and waved in return.

"Can ya spare us a minute of yar time?" Rogan called out before tucking his black curls back beneath the flat, billed cap.

Rogan watched as Obadiah hesitated just long enough to wipe the sweat from his walnut brown face before heading in their direction. Taking giant strides, he made crossing the distance appear nearly effortless. "Fine-lookin' vegetable garden ya've got for yarself," Rogan said. "I admire a man that can make the land produce."

"Dirt, rain, and sunshine is all provided by the good Lord. I jes' add da toil. We had us some fine eatin' outta dat garden, and what we couldn't eat, Naomi got stored for da winter. I was jes' hoeing down some weeds. What can I do fer ya?"

"We're needin' yar help, if ya're willin'. Rogan got word there's a movement of slaves headed our way, and we're gonna need to take three wagons to get 'em back to the farm."

Obadiah's lips tightened and deep creases formed along his jaw.

"Three full loads comin' at one time? Hard to believe a group dat size could make it dis far north wibout being spotted. You sho' you ain' got some bad information? Sounds to me like maybe dis could be a trap. You don' think someone's gotten wind of what's goin' on and dey's baitin' us, do you?"

"Well, now, anything is possible, but Rogan misspoke a wee bit," Liam said. "Fer sure we need to be usin' three wagons, but they'll be loaded with stone ta make it appear like it's a normal day of work fer me. I'm thinkin' we can get far fewer in each wagon, but doin' it this way will permit us to work in the daylight, which is somethin' no one will be expectin'. The only dangerous time will be loadin' 'em in and out of the wagons. With three of us to keep watch, I'm thinkin' we'll 'ave no problem. Can we count on ya to help us?"

"I done tol' you I'd help any time you needed me. When you thinkin' dis is gonna take place?"

"In the mornin'," Liam replied.

"Tomorrow mornin'? That sho' ain' much time to be makin' my excuses for being gone."

Liam dug the toe of his boot into the dirt. "Wiser to keep people in the dark until there's a reason for passin' on the information. Less chance of word slippin' out to the wrong ears. Might be best to just tell the mistress ya're helpin' us with the runaways. She's always been willin' to aid in the cause."

"It ain't the mistress I got a problem with—I know Miz Jasmine wouldn't hesitate for a minute. It's my wife, Naomi. She's afeared somethin' bad's gonna happen to me. That woman do worry all da time. She says she don' want me helpin' no more. I tol' her dat ain' right, but she's scared."

"I find thar's times it's better to remain silent about what I might be doin'. Kiara can na worry about what she does na know."

"Naomi asks lots of questions. If I start ta sidesteppin', she's gonna know for sho' I'm hidin' somepin'."

"If ya're sure ya want to help, I'll go to Mrs. Houston and tell her I need yar help with the runaways. I do na think she'll turn me down. I'll tell her ya do na want your wife ta worry and ask that she na say anything. Ya can tell yar wife ya're going to help me haul rock and, best of all, ya'll na be telling a lie. Do ya think that would solve the problem ya're havin'?"

"If it be alright with Miz Jasmine, I think we got us a plan," Obadiah said, shaking hands with Liam.

"I'll be goin' to talk to the missus right now, and unless thar's a problem, one of us will come by to fetch ya in the mornin'. Are ya comin' with me, Rogan, or are ya planning to grow old leanin' on that fence railin'?" Liam asked with a glint in his eye.

Rogan gave a hearty laugh and pushed away from the railing. "Just catchin' me rest where I can."

"Then let's be on our way. It's gettin' dark, and I do na want to be late for supper," Liam said.

Giving Liam a hearty slap on the back, Rogan called back to Obadiah, "Ya can see that his woman has 'im well in hand also!"

" 'Tis na me woman that worries me but me stomach," Liam corrected in a loud voice as they walked toward the Houston home.

Rogan waited until he was certain Obadiah could no longer hear their voices. "Do ya think he'll have a change of heart afore mornin'?"

"He's a good man—a man of his word. If he was na goin' ta help, he would have told us. Obadiah would na want to take a chance on havin' runaways captured on his account."

"Ya're right. I hope he's able to keep his senses about him this evenin'. Otherwise his wife will get the idea somethin' is wrong and keep at 'im until he tells her. If that happens, ya can be sure we'll be needin' someone else to help us come mornin'."

"Ya worry too much, Rogan. Do ya want to be the one to talk to the missus, or do ya want me ta speak ta her?"

"I'll talk to her, but if she begins askin' a lot of details, ya'll have to fill her in," Rogan said as he rapped on the front door.

Moments later the front door swung open, and the two Irishmen were rendered temporarily speechless.

"May I help you?" McKinley Wainwright inquired.

Rogan strained on tiptoe, hoping to see Jasmine Houston

approaching. "We was hopin' to have a word with Missus Houston."

McKinley's eyes narrowed. "Was she expecting you?"

"We're na the type to be makin' appointments nor havin' callin' cards, but the lady of the house knows us," Rogan replied. "If ya'd tell her Rogan Sheehan and Liam Donohue would like a word with her, I think ya'll find she's willin' to see us. We'll wait here on the porch while ya fetch her."

McKinley nodded and closed the door. "I'm hopin' that means he's gone to fetch her," Rogan said. "Do ya know who he is?"

"I've never seen him before in me life," Liam said. "And here I been thinkin' the missus was goin' to marry Mr. Houston's brother. Looks as though she's found herself another suitor."

"I do na think he's a suitor. Fer sure I'm thinkin' she's goin' to marry Nolan Houston. Kiara has told me as much, but I do na think they've set a date."

"Kiara might be assumin' too much. Maybe he hasn't even proposed and the lass has grown weary of waitin' on him and found her someone else."

Before Rogan could reply, the door reopened, and Rogan quickly pulled the flat cap from his head. Jasmine Houston stood in the doorway with the gentleman at her side. "Rogan! Liam! Do come in," she said, stepping aside to permit them entry. "I'd like you both to meet my brother, McKinley Wainwright," she continued as they walked into the foyer.

Rogan grinned. "Yar brother, is he? Liam here was thinkin' perhaps you'd found a new suitor."

A hint of crimson darkened Jasmine's pale cheeks. "And you corrected his ill-conceived notion?"

"Aye—quick as a wink I told him ya had yar cap set fer Mr. Houston's brother."

McKinley burst into laughter. "Now will you believe me when I tell you that you wear your feelings on your sleeve, dear sister?"

"Oh, shush! Come sit down and tell me what's on your mind."

The men followed Jasmine into the library that also served as her business office.

"It's a private matter we need to be discussin' with ya," Rogan said, his gaze shifting toward her brother.

"If you would excuse us, McKinley? I'm certain we won't be long." There was a ring of authority in her voice that would not be denied.

McKinley nodded. "Nice to have made your acquaintance."

"Please close the door," Jasmine requested as McKinley made his exit. The moment the latch clicked, she turned her attention to Rogan. "Runaways?" she asked, keeping her voice low.

"Aye. And we need yar help."

She listened carefully to his request. "If Obadiah has given his consent to help you, then I have no objection. Paddy and Mr. Fisher can handle the horses without him for one morning. Is there nothing more I can do to help?"

"Ya can keep this information to yarself," Rogan told her.

She jumped up from her chair, her back rigid. "What do you mean? If it's my brother that concerns you, he's sympathetic to the cause. In fact, McKinley stood against my father and has remained in Massachusetts because of his opposition to slavery. He was will-ing to alienate himself from our father and lose any chance of an inheritance for his beliefs. He can be trusted. And I sincerely hope you do not question my loyalty."

"Sorry I am to have offended ya, ma'am," Rogan said. "I did na mean ya could na be trusted, but we do na want Obadiah's wife ta know he'll be helpin' with the runaways. He said she does na want him puttin' himself in danger, and he does na want to tell her a lie. He'll be tellin' her nothin' but that he's helping haul rock. So if ya could find it in yar heart to tell her nothin' more, we'd be obliged."

Jasmine's face softened, and she lowered herself onto the settee. "You may be certain I'll divulge nothing to Naomi—or anyone else. I only wish there were more I could do."

"We know we can always be dependin' on ya fer aid, ma'am,"

Rogan said. "'Tis thankful we are, knowin' that when there's a need ya're always willin' to help."

Before the sun had ascended the next day, Jasmine hurried down the back stairway into the kitchen. She tightened her silk robe and strained to peek out the window for any sign of Liam's wagon. For nearly half an hour she raised herself on tiptoe and braced her body against the coarse wood shelving beneath the window. Her legs trembled from the strain until she thought the ache in her legs would become unbearable. Moving to adjust her position, a barbed splinter broke loose from the wood shelving and penetrated the slick, silky fabric of her nightclothes. With a jerk, she pulled away from the window and paced the room until the plodding of horses' hooves and rumble of the wagons could be heard in the distance. Pulling the door closed behind her, Jasmine crept outside into the diffused shadows of daybreak and watched as Obadiah clambered up into one of the wagons.

Long after the wagons were out of sight, she continued her vigil, wishing she could join the men. Instead, she returned to her bedroom and prepared for the day. Nolan would be arriving this morning, and there was much to accomplish before his visit. She had promised Spencer they would have a picnic, and she didn't want to burden Naomi with the preparations. Perhaps she should ask Naomi and Moses to join them. Peeking into Spencer's adjoining bedroom, she stared at the boy with his rosy cheeks and bow-shaped smile.

Leaning down, she placed a kiss upon her son's warm cheek. He wriggled and his eyelids fluttered before finally opening to reveal his deep brown eyes. "Mama," he said sleepily, extending his arms for a hug.

Jasmine lifted him into her arms and kissed him soundly. "Are you ready to begin a new day?"

Spencer giggled and squirmed until she placed him on the woven rug beside his bed. "I wanna play now!" he commanded.

"First you must get dressed and eat your breakfast. Then we'll talk about playing," she said as she unbuttoned his nightshirt and tugged it over his head. "Such a big boy," she cooed. He was growing up so fast. Almost overnight his speech had taken on a decided improvement toward clarity. "I can't believe you have grown so much in just the last few months."

In a blink, he was running toward the door, off to discover the pleasures of a new day. "Not without your clothes," Jasmine admonished, quickly grasping his arm and shaking her reflective thoughts away. With Spencer around, there were only rare occasions that could be given to introspection.

When she had finally cajoled him into a shirt and tiny breeches, she took his hand and led him to the stairs, carrying his shoes and stockings in her hand. She would struggle through that battle while her son ate his breakfast. Spencer hurried through his breakfast and was wriggling from his chair when a knock sounded at the front door.

"Hurry, Spencer. Let's see who has come to visit," she said, following her son as he ran down the hallway.

He stretched until one chubby hand was on the doorknob before looking up to his mother. "Open, Mama."

Heeding his request, Jasmine turned the knob and pulled back. "Look who has come to visit," she said while gazing into Nolan Houston's sparkling blue eyes.

"Good morning to my two favorite people," he greeted them.

"Unca Nolan," Spencer screeched, throwing himself into Nolan's legs.

"Now there's a welcome that makes a man happy to be alive," Nolan said while scooping Spencer into his arms. "And what of you, Jasmine? Are you as happy to see me as my nephew?"

Above Spencer's brown curls, their eyes locked. "I believe that would be a true statement," she said. "Why don't you join us in the parlor?"

After only a short time of being contained in the parlor, Spencer began tugging at his uncle's hand. "Play with me," he said, pointing toward the door.

"You want to go outside? I agree. It's much too beautiful to remain indoors. Why don't we all go outdoors?"

"If you're willing to oversee him for a short time, I'll go into the kitchen and begin preparations for our picnic."

Nolan took Spencer by the hand. "I think I should be able to handle him for a while. Any objections if he should want to play with Moses?"

"Of course not. In fact, I'm certain your job will be much more manageable with Moses to keep him company. The two boys have become accustomed to spending most of their waking hours together," Jasmine said as the three of them walked down the hallway and into the kitchen.

Jasmine watched Spencer and Nolan as they laughed and ran across the yard, Nolan pretending he was unable to keep pace with the small boy. The sight caused a smile to cross her lips, and she watched until the two of them crossed through the gated fence and stood in front of the small cottage that had been constructed for Obadiah and Naomi. Seeing Naomi's thin form as she walked into the yard with Moses in tow caused Jasmine's thoughts to quickly change direction. Were Obadiah, Rogan, and Liam encountering any difficulty on this day?

"Keep them safe, Father God, both those who lend their help and the runaways who need them," she whispered. Danger remained at the forefront of her mind as Jasmine absently retrieved a basket from the pantry and lined it with a white linen cloth.

Moving about the kitchen with her thoughts focused upon the three men and their mission, she started at the sound of Naomi's voice. "Mister Nolan said you was busy fixing a picnic. Why don' you let me finish up in here? Seems if a man come all dis way to visit, you should be spendin' some time wib him. I know he likes da chile, but it's you he's wantin' to see. 'Sides, I don' know when Obadiah gonna be home. He tol' me not to be plannin' on him for noonday meal 'cause he was helpin' cut stone—said you tol' him it was alright. How come you havin' him help with dat work, Missus? Ain't as though dere's nothing needin' done 'round this place."

Jasmine tightened her hold on the silverware she was placing in the basket and hesitated briefly as she met Naomi's questioning gaze. "Mr. Donohue and Mr. Sheehan came to the house last night and asked if they could hire Obadiah to help them for the day. Obadiah is strong and can handle the heavy rock more easily than either of them."

"Seems odd they ain' never needed no help from Obadiah afore. They say who been movin' dat heavy rock in da past?"

"No, I didn't inquire," Jasmine said, moving around Naomi. "I believe I will take you up on your offer and join Mr. Houston—if you're certain it won't be an imposition."

"'Course not. You go on out there, and if dem boys start to givin' you trouble, tell 'em you'll make 'em come in da kitchen with me if they don' behave."

Jasmine gathered her skirts in one hand as she crossed the threshold. "Please pack enough for you and Moses too. I want you to join us."

"Yessum."

The sound of Naomi's soulful tune followed Jasmine through the open door, the words muted as the early afternoon breeze lifted them off toward heaven. Jasmine slowed her pace and listened, hoping she would hear the returning rumble of Liam Donohue's wagons. Yet she knew it was much too early to expect the men. After all, Obadiah had told his wife he wouldn't be home for the noonday meal. But if the runaways had already arrived and had been waiting, they could already be loaded and on their way.

"Enough!" she muttered while continuing across the lawn, knowing she must cease her incessant worrying. After all, weren't they all entrusted into God's tender care? Would He not protect them?

"Mama!" Spencer shouted as he came running toward her and buried his face in her skirts.

Jasmine ruffled his dark brown curls with her fingers. "Are you having fun?" she asked, taking his small hand in her own and walking back to where Moses sat on the grass playing with some wooden figures Obadiah had carved for him. "You boys play nicely," she said before sitting down on the woolen blanket Nolan had spread under one of the leafy oak trees.

"Where's Naomi?" Nolan inquired.

"She insisted I come and spend time with you while she completed the lunch preparations on her own," Jasmine explained.

"She's a thoughtful woman. Do remind me to thank her," he said with a grin.

Jasmine smiled in return while she arranged her skirt. "Have the boys been behaving?"

"Absolutely. In fact, I find it amazing how well they get on together," Nolan commented, glancing toward Spencer and Moses. "There were so many years between Bradley and me, we both grew up as though we were only children. You likely experienced the same feelings having been the only girl in your family."

"Not exactly. I don't recall experiencing feelings of loneliness, but then, I was always privileged to have a tutor who filled her time by either teaching or entertaining me."

Nolan smiled and nodded before continuing to regale her with tales of his childhood.

Jasmine endeavored to listen, but her mind soon wandered back to the runaways and the three men who were attempting to provide them with food and safe haven before directing them farther north into Canada. She longed to know if the runaways had arrived, how many there were, and if the trackers had followed them into Massachusetts or given up the chase farther south. She hoped for the sake of the poor runaways the pursuers had given up long ago.

"Jasmine! Will you not answer me?"

"What? Oh yes, whatever you think will be fine with me," she absently replied.

Nolan's face filled with amusement. "That is likely the most offhanded reply to a marriage proposal in the annals of history."

"What?" Jasmine cried, now giving Nolan her undivided attention.

"Now I understand how this works. Once you've actually heard the word *marriage,* you're interested," he said with a wide grin. "Several minutes ago, I poured out my heart—telling you of my love and adoration. I don't want to take the chance of once again losing you to your own reflections, so I will merely repeat that I would consider myself the most fortunate man alive if you would consent to become my wife. Will you marry me, Jasmine?"

"Oh, Nolan," she whispered, her body melting into his embrace while she momentarily enjoyed the warmth of his strong arms. Finally, she was able to experience the complete love she had never had with Bradley. "Of course I'll marry you. I was beginning to think you would never ask," she said with a soft laugh.

"I didn't want to give anyone a reason to question the propriety of our union. I had intended to wait until three years after Bradley's death, but I now know I can wait no longer to take you as my wife," he said, lowering his head and covering her lips with a gentle kiss that slowly grew more urgent. "Tell me we can soon wed," he whispered, his gaze filled with passion.

"I am in complete agreement. However, Grandmother Wainwright may not be so easily convinced."

"She'll object to our marriage?" A note of panic laced his words.

Jasmine laughed and shook her head. "No, not to the marriage itself. In fact, she was so anxious for you to propose she'd begun harassing *me*. She thought I should help you along and said perhaps you were too shy to propose. However, knowing Grandmother, she'll want to have parties and plan a large wedding."

"And is that what you desire?"

"I had all of those things when I married Bradley. I have no desire for a long engagement, but Grandmother can be unrelenting."

"We'll remain steadfast. I believe six weeks is more than enough time, and October would be a lovely time of year for a wedding, don't you think?"

"Absolutely," Jasmine replied, tilting her head to accept another kiss.

———

The fresh air and hearty picnic lunch caused Spencer to finally succumb. He crawled onto Nolan's lap and was asleep within minutes of nestling himself into his uncle's strong arms. Jasmine watched the two of them for a moment, obviously enjoying the picture of serenity they created.

"Shall I carry him inside?" Nolan asked.

She gave him a grateful smile. "Please. Once he's down for his nap, perhaps we can discuss our wedding plans."

"I'd like that very much."

Nolan felt an overwhelming rush of pride. She had said yes to his proposal. Not that he had truly been worried that she would refuse him. Well, perhaps there had been some concern. He chuckled as he carried his nephew to bed. Truth be told, he had done a great deal of fretting, practicing his lines over and over the night before . . . wanting to ask in just the right way.

"And then she didn't even hear me."

Spender stirred in his arms. Nolan bent to place a kiss on the boy's forehead. "Soon you'll be my son—as I've always felt you should be."

———

The early evening sun had begun its descent, and Nolan was enjoying a final cup of coffee when Jasmine stood and began pacing in front of the fireplace. Spencer had long since risen from his nap and was happily playing at Nolan's feet. Yet Jasmine couldn't contain her growing concern about the runaways.

"Why don't we return to the back lawn for a little longer?" she suggested.

Nolan swallowed a final sip of coffee and returned the cup to its matching gold-rimmed saucer. "Why so restless, my dear? Have you not had enough fresh air for one day?"

Warmed by his playful grin and sparkling eyes, Jasmine stood and grasped his hand. "If we are very fortunate, there may be a few fireflies on the prowl that we can capture for Spencer."

He laughed and pushed his chair away from the table with his free hand. "I think it's a little early in the evening to see any fireflies, much less capture them!"

"Play! Outside!" Spencer chimed. "I go now, Mama," he said, tugging at Jasmine's fingers.

"You're outnumbered," she said, giggling.

Much to Spencer's amusement, Nolan paraded about the yard, pretending to seek out fireflies. The young boy followed his every move while Jasmine delightedly enjoyed their antics. Bradley would never have considered such playfulness appropriate; perhaps that fact alone made their liveliness today all the more precious.

"How is your brother faring since your father's departure? I'm certain McKinley would have preferred staying with you rather than your grandmother," Nolan said as he inspected the leaves of a rosebush for possible fireflies.

"Such would have been my preference also. However, Father was quite serious about their agreement. He will expect McKinley to honor his word and return to The Willows if he doesn't find a suitable position, and that task will be more easily accomplished if McKinley is living in Lowell rather than out here on the farm."

Nolan continued to examine the thorny rosebush. "Once he begins his search in earnest, McKinley will have no problem. With the variety of businesses in Lowell and the number of men leaving for California in search of gold, there are a multitude of opportunities."

"Still, he must avail himself of such opportunities, and he can't do that if he's busy escorting Grandmother around town. He tells me she expects him to act as her escort to all of her social functions. And you know what a full calendar she keeps!"

Nolan laughed and turned in her direction. "You, my dear, are not your brother's keeper. I'm certain McKinley can hold his own with your grandmother. If he has an appointment, I know that he'll ask her to make other arrangements for an escort to her soirees," he said before cupping one hand to shade his eyes and peering into the distance. "Wonder who that could be?"

Jasmine moved to where he stood, though the sun blinded her vision. "Is it wagons?" she asked, still unable to identify anything nearing the farm.

Nolan moved to the left. "Yes. In fact, there appear to be

three," he said while squinting and drawing nearer to the fence line. "Looks like Obadiah is driving one, but I can't make out the other two men."

"Liam and Rogan?"

He lowered his hand and looked at her suspiciously. "I believe you're correct. How did you know?"

"Liam and Rogan asked if Obadiah could accompany them today and help quarry stone."

"Truly? Why would they suddenly need Obadiah's assistance?"

"They said they would need to use three wagons, and since there are only the two of them available to drive the wagons . . ." Her voice trailed off as she watched the billowing clouds of dust rising from beneath the wagon wheels.

"Odd they'd ask for Obadiah's help. You'd think they'd hire one of the Irishmen from down in the Acre. There are always Irish laborers hoping to find work."

Was Nolan looking askance at her explanation, or was it her own guilt that caused her to think he didn't entirely believe her weak explanation? Certainly Nolan could be trusted with such information—he'd supported the antislavery movement long before she had. Yet she had given Liam and Rogan her word she'd say nothing. She didn't want to break her promise, so she walked away and stood by the fence.

Obadiah waved as the wagons drew closer. "Evenin', suh, Miz Jasmine."

"Good evenin' to ya," Rogan called, waving his hat at the welcoming committee before pulling back on the reins. "Good it is ta be seein' ya, Mr. Houston."

Nolan approached Jasmine and stood beside her. "It's good to see you also. I trust you had a profitable day?"

"Aye. Sure and it was more of a success than even we could 'ave imagined," Liam replied. "Without Obadiah's fine help, we might have lost some of the runaways. Some of 'em shied away, thinkin' we might be bounty hunters until Obadiah put their minds to rest and told 'em we could be trusted."

"I promised I wouldn't tell anyone," Jasmine said to Nolan's unspoken question.

"You didn't think you could trust *me?*"

"Now, don' be blamin' the lass," Liam said. "I was pretty hard on her last night, and I'm the one that caused her to keep her lips sealed. 'Course, I was na thinkin' she'd be afraid to take someone such as yarself into her confidence. Mostly we did na want Obadiah's wife findin' out he was helpin'."

"I'll explain later. Naomi doesn't want Obadiah helping with the runaways," Jasmine whispered. "We're pleased all went well, but you'd better get Obadiah home or Naomi will soon be joining us. She's likely heard the wagons and will be expecting him."

"Right ya are, ma'am. It's off we are," he said, giving a slap of the reins.

CHAPTER · *13*

ALICE WAINWRIGHT fluttered into the kitchen, where Kiara and Naomi were assisting Alice's housekeeper, Martha. Leaning over, Alice inspected the trays of petit fours and raspberry tarts. "I presume the cakes are frosted with lemon icing."

"For sure some are. Others have a wondrous rosehips glaze that Naomi taught us to make. Here, why don't ya be tryin' one?" Kiara offered Alice one of the cakes. She smiled and took the treat.

"I don't believe Martha and I would have been prepared for this engagement party if you two hadn't offered your assistance," Alice said. "Isn't that right, Martha?"

"Yes, ma'am. We're both getting much too old for these large gatherings."

Alice pursed her lips. "Tut, tut. Being around lots of people makes one feel vibrant and alive. Besides, Martha, you're only as old as you feel."

Martha sighed and looked at the two younger women. "Then I must be at least a hundred. And I think my poor feet are even older."

Alice took a bite of the cake. "Oh, but that is a delightful flavor. You'll have to leave Martha the recipe. I would very much like to serve this again."

"I'd be pleased to, ma'am," Naomi said, her gaze never quite reaching Mrs. Wainwright's.

"I do hope we'll have enough food," Alice said, gazing around the room at the trays of prepared delicacies. "It would never do to run out."

"I'm na one to be judgin' what ya're doin', Mrs. Wainwright, but I was thinkin' Miss Jasmine said she was wantin' just a small gatherin' of folks fer this engagement party ya're hostin'."

"Exactly!" Martha agreed enthusiastically.

"Jasmine is insistent her *wedding* be understated. I completely disagree with her thinking. However, I know I did *not* agree to a small engagement party. She may have assumed I would adhere to her wedding guidelines, but that would be purely supposition on her part."

"Um hum. She should know better than to think you'd do things her way," Martha retorted.

"No need to take that sassy tone with me, Martha. You've known me long enough to know it will serve no purpose."

"True enough—besides, it's too late to change things now. People will soon arrive. Let's just hope the guests of honor appear before there are too many carriages lining the street. Otherwise, they may turn and go home without even stopping," Martha said with a chuckle.

"That's not funny, Martha. I'm going to make certain Martin is at the front door. You may need to come and assist."

"Martin can announce the guests without my assistance. Besides, I'm needed here in the kitchen. Especially if it starts to look as though we'll run out of food," Martha said with a wink at Kiara and Naomi.

"'Tis true, Mrs. Wainwright. There's more to get done than me and Naomi can handle on our own. Me mind is willin' but me body will na cooperate—the babe seems ta sap me energy," Kiara said, patting her enlarged belly.

"Fine, fine," Alice said absently. In truth, she hadn't even heard Kiara's response. Her mind was too cluttered with the many details requiring her immediate attention. "But make certain the food is promptly served. And Naomi, if you'll see to keeping the punch bowl filled?" she added.

"Yessum, I'll make certain it's full to da brim—most of da time anyway."

Alice retreated from the kitchen, uncertain whether any of the three women understood the finer nuances of handling a large party. "This entire evening may turn into a disaster," she muttered while walking down the hallway. She paused long enough to check her appearance in the gilded mirror. The blue and silver brocade gown was one of her favorites. And although it was a heavy material and the weather had been sufficiently warm, Alice still felt a bit of a chill. *I've grown very old.* She sighed and gave her upswept hair a reassuring pat. "But not too old to enjoy seeing my Jasmine happily married." She smiled and noticed that it took years off her appearance. It gave her hope that she might yet live out many long years to enjoy her grandchildren and even great-grandchildren.

Martin was standing guard over the door like a sentry guarding the king's castle. Alice warmed at the sight. At least someone was handling their responsibility in a serious manner. A knock sounded at the door, and with great bravado, Martin opened the door and permitted Nolan and Jasmine entrance. He turned toward Alice and with grand enthusiasm announced, "Mrs. Bradley Houston and Mr. Nolan Houston."

"Oh, forevermore, Martin! I know who *they* are."

Martin's face was filled with puzzlement. "But you know everyone attending the party, ma'am. I thought you said I was to announce *all* of the guests."

"Jasmine and Nolan are the guests of honor, Martin. There is no need to announce my own granddaughter."

"I see. Well, am I to announce Master McKinley or Master Samuel?"

"If the other guests have begun arriving, then you need to announce them."

"But if Master McKinley comes downstairs before they arrive, it's not necessary—even though Miss Jasmine and her betrothed are here?"

Alice sighed and gave the older man a look of exasperation. "Never mind. Just announce *everyone,* Martin."

"That's exactly what I was trying to do when you said I wasn't doing things proper," he muttered.

Nolan chuckled but tried hard to mask his amusement when Martin looked his way.

Jasmine patted Martin's arm. "This shouldn't be such a problem, Martin. There won't be very many guests."

"That's what *you* think, ma'am," he whispered.

Jasmine followed her grandmother into the parlor. The rooms were festooned with fall foliage, candles were glowing in every corner, and chairs were arranged to accommodate guests throughout the rooms and spreading out into the garden.

"How many guests have you invited, Grandmother?"

"My, don't you look pretty," Alice said, pretending to fawn over Jasmine's dark burgundy creation. "Did you have this made in town? I don't remember seeing it before, so it must be new."

Jasmine raised a dark brow. "You know very well I ordered this dress from Boston. We discussed it on more than one occasion. Now answer me. How many guests have you invited?"

With a coy smile, Alice walked toward the garden. "Come see how I've arranged the garden, my dear. I think you'll find it quite ingenious." If she could stall long enough, the guests would arrive and eliminate—for the time—further questions from her granddaughter.

"Grandmother, you are playing a game of cat and mouse," Jasmine declared.

"Mr. and Mrs. Matthew Cheever, Miss Violet Cheever, and Master Michael Cheever," Martin announced vociferously.

Jasmine looked very seriously at her grandmother, but Alice only smiled. "I suppose," Jasmine began, "you should have made this a surprise party, for I'm sure to be very surprised as the night goes on."

"We had best go inside, for our guests are arriving." Alice scurried through the door, pleased she'd been able to avoid further inquisition.

A brief time later, the rooms overflowed with laughter and conversation while the many guests circulated throughout the house.

"Come along, McKinley. I have several people I'd like you to meet," Alice said, grasping McKinley's arm and maneuvering through the crowd until she reached the garden. She stopped beside Elinor Brighton only long enough for introductions and brief conversation before moving along toward several other guests.

Alice finally came to a halt beside the Cheever family. "Matthew and Lilly, you've already met my grandson, McKinley. I don't know if McKinley has told you—or perhaps Violet—that he has aspirations of utilizing his education and skills for one of the many industrial enterprises here in Lowell. Isn't that correct, McKinley?"

McKinley grinned at his grandmother before turning his attention back to Matthew Cheever. "I certainly am interested in locating employment. Father has given me an ultimatum—if I don't find a suitable position within three months, I must return to The Willows," he replied.

"Violet did mention your father departed and agreed you could remain in Lowell," Matthew said. "However, she didn't say you were seeking employment. I assumed you were merely remaining for an extended visit with your family. What type of work are you seeking?"

"So your grandmother has outfoxed you again," Nolan said as he stole a moment alone with his intended.

"It would seem so," Jasmine replied. "Although I have to admit, I'm having a wonderful time. These guests are mostly dear friends. I suppose I cannot be cross about celebrating the happiest moment of my life with them."

Nolan smiled down at her and Jasmine felt her heart skip a

beat. "I hope you know how happy you've made me," he said, his voice husky.

"If it's only a portion of the happiness you've given me, then you must be a contented man indeed."

Nolan scanned the room. They'd slipped into a smaller parlor, one Grandmother seldom used. "Dare I steal a kiss?"

"Absolutely not," Jasmine said with a smile. "For I shall willingly give you all that you desire. There's no need to steal."

With that, he pulled her into his arms and with a tantalizingly leisurely pace, kissed her long and passionately. Jasmine felt her knees grow weak. How marvelous the way this man affected her. It was all that she had wished for in her marriage to Bradley—wished for, but never knew.

"I suppose," Nolan said, pulling back, "we should rejoin the others."

She nodded, unable to speak.

He grinned. "Or we could just elope."

Again Jasmine nodded, only to have Nolan laugh uproariously at her. Jasmine could only relish the moment. He pulled her back to the party, and she clung to his arm as they circulated around the room.

"I'll procure us each a glass of punch," Nolan said, maneuvering Jasmine to a nearby chair.

She watched him as he strode through the well-wishers. The fact that he would soon be hers was still a marvel Jasmine could not quite grasp.

"You look so happy," Violet Cheever said as she joined Jasmine. "I just know your wedding will be very beautiful." She sighed. "I can only hope to have such things for myself one day."

Jasmine laughed. "And of course you will, for you are quite lovely, and rumor has it that many a young man has been intrigued by your beauty."

"Most of them are dowdy bores," Violet said, surprising Jasmine.

"I hope you do not consider my brother to be among their numbers."

Violet shook her head, and her expression almost took on a frightened look. "McKinley is certainly not in their number. McKinley is . . . well . . . he's in a place all by himself."

"Not dowdy or boring?" Jasmine grinned, enjoying Violet's comments. It was very evident the young woman was more than a little interested in McKinley. And Jasmine knew from her brother's continual questions regarding the Cheevers, particularly Violet, that he, too, was interested.

"Your brother could never be boring. I find everything he says to be quite fascinating."

"I'm sure he feels the same about you," Jasmine said, leaning closer to the young woman. "In fact, I've noticed that he hasn't taken his gaze from you all evening."

"I worry that he'll think me too forward. I'm just not myself when I'm around him. I become so extroverted and . . . well . . . I'm even given to flirting."

Jasmine laughed heartily at this as Nolan rejoined them.

"And whatever is so funny?" he asked as he handed Jasmine a glass of punch.

Violet turned red and lowered her face immediately, while Jasmine simply shook her head. "You wouldn't understand—the talk of young women, you see."

"Ah." He took a sip of his punch before adding, "Which of course always involves young men."

The next morning Jasmine hastened to the front door with Spencer in tow. "McKinley—and Violet! Do come in. What a pleasant surprise. I wasn't expecting to see you again so soon. To what do I owe the pleasure of this visit?" she asked as she led the couple into the parlor.

A broad smile spread across McKinley's face. "I wanted to share my good news with you first." Jasmine put her hand to her throat. Had McKinley proposed? Surely not. She looked to Violet as if for some sign or proof of the topic, but Violet simply smiled. "There's nothing I love more than good news. Do tell me," she said as

Spencer climbed onto McKinley's lap.

"I am now an employee of the Boston Associates—hired to work as Mr. Cheever's assistant."

Jasmine gaped at her brother, astonished he had so quickly secured the impressive position. At the same time, she was very glad she hadn't blurted out some comment about a betrothal. "I'm astonished—not that I don't believe you're capable. But I'd think there would have been someone already working for the mills with more experience, someone they would have promoted into such an opportunity."

"That's what I thought when Mr. Cheever told me about the job. However, he explained he preferred someone who would come into the position without any preconceived ideas—someone who would bring a fresh perspective to the business aspects of the mills—just as he had when Mr. Boott took him on. With my knowledge of the cotton business and education in accounting, Mr. Cheever thought me the perfect choice. Needless to say, Grandmother was elated with the news."

"No doubt," Jasmine said. "She's likely penning a letter to Father as we speak. When do you assume your new duties?"

"Monday morning. I mentioned I would immediately begin my search for another place to live."

Jasmine laughed and waved her hand. "Let me guess! Grandmother became indignant that you would even consider living anywhere else."

"Exactly!" he said. "I thought she would prefer to return to the peaceful existence of living alone. Instead, she acted as though I had intentionally insulted her."

"I wouldn't consider broaching that subject again—leastwise not until you're planning to wed and purchasing a home of your own." Jasmine glanced toward Violet as she completed her comment. Violet blushed, but McKinley ignored the reference.

"I doubt Father will be nearly as pleased with the news as you and Grandmother," McKinley said. "I honestly believe he thought me incapable. A complete buffoon, unable to make my way in the world without benefit of my father's assistance."

Jasmine could see the concern in McKinley's expression and knew he didn't want to remain at odds with their father. Yet he was correct: Malcolm Wainwright would not be pleased with the news.

Violet edged closer to McKinley. "I heard my father say to Mother that he thought hiring you would be pleasing to the Wainwright family."

"What else did he say, Violet?" Jasmine inquired.

"Just that Mr. Wainwright had been anxious to have your brother Samuel working to secure cotton for the mills and that hiring McKinley would surely reinforce the Southern cotton growers' relationship with the Lowell mills." She hesitated a moment and frowned, her forehead creased into deep wrinkles. "I'm not certain I heard all he was saying. I truly don't listen very well when Father begins talking about business matters."

McKinley patted her hand. "Don't concern yourself, Violet. At this juncture, the comments would be of little consequence. Isn't that correct, Jasmine?"

Obviously McKinley wanted her to assist in easing Violet's noticeable anxiety. "McKinley is correct—the conversation changes nothing. However, I find Mr. Cheever's reasoning quite interesting," she replied.

———————

Oliver Maxwell stepped off the train and entered the bustling Baltimore depot, pleased his journey was over. He detested traveling—which was somewhat of a troublesome matter for a man employed as a traveling salesman. However, he'd never enjoyed sharing space and being forced into conversation with total strangers, especially those who believed they had a right to pry into his personal affairs. And there had been a number of them on this journey: women making coy remarks and proud men boasting about themselves as they attempted to delve into his personal life. The remembrance caused an involuntary shiver to course through him.

Tightly gripping his satchel, Oliver made his way through the station. Stretching his stiff, tired muscles, he walked with long strides toward his mother's boardinghouse, thankful the old house was nearby and he'd not be required to ride in another coach. He pulled out his pocket watch and clicked open the case. There wouldn't be time to linger at his mother's residence. He'd drop off his satchel with a promise to return for supper.

Taking the front steps two at a time, Oliver opened the front door of the house. A small brass bell over the door jingled to announce his entry.

"Read the sign. I got no openings," his mother said as she bustled from the rear of the house.

"Well, that's good news," Oliver replied. "I'm pleased to hear you've a full house and can easily make the mortgage payments."

Edna Maxwell wagged her head back and forth. "When I heard the bell, I said there were no vacancies, but I do have empty rooms."

Oliver's eyebrows arched. "Why would you lie, Mother?"

"It's not a lie. I've filled as many rooms as I can handle at one time. I'm an old woman, Oliver. I grow weary of cleaning rooms and cooking meals for ungrateful boarders who have nothing but complaints to give me in return. Look at these hands," she said, shoving them forward to ensure they were in his direct line of vision. "They're gnarled and crippled from age and years of hard work."

Oliver dropped his satchel and walked to the open ledger lying on the desk. Using his finger as a guide, he traced the entries for the last two months. He was incredulous as he shot a look at his mother and then back to the pages, flipping through them in rapid succession. "You're renting only three rooms? I'm sending you money to meet the mortgage when you've intentionally permitted rooms to stand empty?" He clenched his jaw in an attempt to keep his temper in check.

"I told you it's all I can do," she defended.

"And what of Gertrude? She may be lame, but surely she can help with some of the chores. Gertrude! Come to the parlor!" he yelled.

He fell onto the frayed settee, his anger mounting while he waited. "Gertrude! I haven't all day to wait on you."

His sister's uneven steps could be heard as she neared the parlor. With as much grace as her crippled body would permit, Gertrude entered the room. "Oliver, what a wonderful surprise. I'm sorry to keep you waiting. I was peeling potatoes—it takes me longer than it should," she apologized.

Truth be told, he didn't know how she could even peel a potato with her crippled arm and clawlike hand. The entire left side of her body, save her face, was disfigured. A freak of nature, their father said; punishment for their father's drunkenness, her mother said. But as far as Oliver was concerned, it was the plague of being poor and unable to have a doctor at his sister's birthing. The reason no longer mattered. He was left with the unwanted responsibility of a mother who no longer wanted to work and a sister who was physically unable to be of much assistance.

"Your limp appears to be growing worse," he commented as his sister neared his side.

She leaned down and placed a fleeting kiss upon his cheek. "It's no worse than when you last visited. The left side of my body grows weary quite rapidly, and when I'm overly tired, the limp appears more pronounced. Do not worry yourself, brother. I'm quite healthy otherwise."

He couldn't remain angry with Gertrude. Through all her years of pain and the added torment of enduring cruel remarks by family and strangers alike, her sweet nature prevailed. "I'm concerned over the fact that only three rooms in the house are being rented out."

"I try to help all I can," Gertrude said, "but Mother ails and is unable to do much anymore. She says it's all we can handle. Isn't that right, Mother?"

Edna shifted in her chair. "I could possibly take on one more."

"I've been taking in laundry and doing a bit of sewing to earn extra money," Gertrude said while giving her brother a sweet smile. "The money helps with groceries."

Oliver's gaze settled on his sister's lame hand. "How can you do laundry and sewing with that hand?"

"I manage. It takes me longer, but my customers seem pleased with my work."

Oliver cradled his sister's face in his palm. She was the only woman in whom he'd ever discovered virtue—the rest always wanted something from him, including his mother. "You're a fine girl, Gertrude, and I'm sorry I hollered at you earlier. I was weary from traveling and overwrought when I discovered how the rentals were being handled. It's not your fault. Please forgive me."

"Of course, Oliver. Mother and I are very thankful for all you do. I know how difficult it must be traveling about the country selling shoes. I know you'd likely prefer to remain in one place."

Edna narrowed her eyes. Oliver could feel her studying him. "I know that look. What is it you want to say, Mother?"

"We can talk later, when we're alone. You can put your satchel in room eight."

He returned his mother's steely glare. "I've a business meeting I must attend, but I'll return this evening. I won't take supper with you, as I'm certain you weren't planning on another mouth to feed," he said in an acerbic tone.

"And what business is it that needs the immediate attention of a shoe peddler?" his mother rebutted.

"I'll not always be a shoe peddler, Mother. In the meantime, I haven't noticed you hesitating to line your purse with the coins I earn selling shoes."

"You're always ready with a bit of sass and disrespect."

"And you're always quick to find fault with me, so I'd say you're reaping what you've sown, old woman. The fact that you've a kindhearted daughter who can bear living with you day after day is nothing short of unbelievable. I'll take my satchel upstairs when I return."

He strode out of the house, unwilling to be detained by her outbursts, before their argument could escalate any further. Gertrude's faint good-bye echoed in his ears as he hurried down the street. If all went well over the next year, he would buy a small house for Gertrude and send her a monthly stipend. Let his mother fight to meet the monthly bank note on her own. Maybe then she'd realize how much she relied upon him and come groveling for his help. Oliver reveled in the thought of finally forcing his mother to acknowledge her dependency on him. She withheld her love like a miser clinging to golden coins, never willing to share affection with others.

"Likely why Father found warmth in the arms of other women," he muttered as he entered a small tavern not far from the train depot.

Oliver edged his way through the tavern, skimming the sea of faces in an effort to find his new business partners. Spotting Enoch Garon near the rear of the room, he worked his way toward the tall, muscular man. Enoch wasn't bright, but he followed instructions and his brute strength was an asset.

"Enoch! You're looking well," Oliver greeted while pulling a chair away from the table and sitting down. "Where's Joseph?" He scanned the place for the third member of his business association.

"He'll be here. Told me yesterday he might be a little late." Enoch turned toward the front of the tavern. "Here he comes now."

The men greeted each other, ordered their ale, and waited until it had been served before commencing their discussion in earnest. "I take it you both have been hearing about the Fugitive Slave Act being signed by President Fillmore," Oliver said after taking a swig of his ale.

"'Course we heard. Probably long afore you folks up in Massachusetts," Enoch replied. "Wondered if you was ever gonna get down here and get things going. There's been lots of opportunities, but me and Joseph wanted to keep our word to you. The time is now to begin hunting down them slaves that's running north. With this new policy, we're gonna be able to make some fine money."

Joseph nodded his head. "Especially since the authorities are required to help us round up any runaways if we ask. Can't ask for nothin' better than that."

"Problem is there's more and more men seeing this as a golden opportunity. The competition is going to increase, and I'm guessing more of the slaves are going to be afraid to run off, knowing they won't have safe sanctuary up north anymore. That means fewer runaways and more people out there trying to find 'em."

"Hadn't thought of that," Enoch said. "So we're really not much better off, are we?"

"Only if you're using your head to develop a plan beyond the obvious. And that's exactly what I've done," Oliver said.

The two men leaned in further, anxious to hear what Oliver had to say. "Tell us what you've been planning. You know you can trust the two of us," Enoch urged.

"I keep my eyes and ears open while I'm traveling about the countryside, and I'm certain I'll be able to pry loose information from time to time about runaways. But we need to do more if we're to make a dependable income from this new law. I'm thinking we should consider capturing some of the freed Negroes that have moved north. We can take them back down south and sell them at auction. Lots easier than actually hunting for runaways."

Enoch rubbed his hands together. "Or we can take 'em to most any plantation. Those owners won't care where they come from or if they claim to be free. You got you one good idea, Oliver. And I'll wager you know where there's some fine specimens up north that we can get our hands on."

"Around Lowell, I think I can find a number of fine-looking freed Negroes. More than either one of you can imagine," he said while beginning to formulate a list in his mind. Obadiah, the strong buck over at the Houston horse farm, made the top of his list.

CHAPTER · *14*

ALICE FANNED HERSELF with a vengeance. "I did *not* agree to a small, intimate wedding, Jasmine. You took my silence as agreement, just as you did with your engagement party. If you won't consider your old grandmother and the pleasure a lovely wedding would bring to me, then think of your friends and other relatives. Give them the enjoyment of such festivities."

"A grand weddin' would be enjoyable," Kiara agreed as she sat down beside Jasmine while holding a piece of lace in one hand.

Alice gave Kiara an engaging smile. "You see? Your friends want to attend a nice affair as much as I do."

"Grandmother! Will you stop at nothing to have your way in this matter? I do not want a large wedding, nor does Nolan. We've decided upon a small garden wedding in October. I think you should be ashamed of yourself for attempting to manipulate me with your emotion-filled statements."

"To tell ya the truth, I could use some extra time to complete the lace I'm makin' fer yar weddin' veil. It's ta be my weddin' gift to ya," Kiara said.

Jasmine sighed and gave her friend a feeble smile. "You don't need to go to all that trouble, Kiara. I had a large wedding when I married Bradley. Nolan and I truly do not desire a large affair.

Besides, you need to spend this time making special clothing for your baby."

Kiara's eyes clouded as she dropped the lace onto her swollen belly. "Ya do na want me ta make yar weddin' lace?"

"That's not what I meant, Kiara. The lace is beautiful and I truly appreciate your kindness, but I wasn't planning to wear a veil. Couldn't we use the lace on my dress?"

"If that's what ya're wantin'," she replied, though her dejection was obvious.

Alice poured a glass of lemonade from a cut glass pitcher and took a sip of the sweetened drink before speaking. "Now you see what you've done? You've hurt Kiara's feelings, and you're attempting to shame me for wanting something as simple as an appropriate wedding for you. I'm an old woman, and I'll likely die before I have an opportunity to see another of my grandchildren wed. I would think that instead of considering only yourselves, you and Nolan would think of bringing others pleasure also. And before you mention David's possible wedding, let me say that I doubt my health will permit me to ever travel to The Willows again. We both know David will not come to Massachusetts to wed his Southern wife, and there's no possibility McKinley will wed in the near future."

Jasmine clasped a hand to her breast and could feel her heartbeat begin to accelerate beneath her fingers. "What health problems would prohibit your travel? Is there something regarding your well-being you've kept secret from me?"

Alice took another sip of her lemonade. "Would such information change your mind?"

"No, I don't believe it would. However, if you're ill, you should confide in me so that we can find proper medical treatment. Besides, if you're truly ailing, I do not want to subject you to the rigors of planning a large wedding."

A frown pinched Alice's fine features. "I'm certain my health would improve if I could occupy my thoughts with something exciting—such as a wedding. I've been told you can trick the mind into thinking you're well if you concentrate on other matters and don't dwell on your illness."

Kiara moved to Alice's side and gave the older woman's hand a gentle pat. "I did na know ya was ailing, and ya can always look ta me to help ya, ma'am. Good I am at takin' care of those that are sick. Just ask Paddy—I could always nurse 'im back ta health."

"How sweet you are, Kiara. And I'm sure *you* wouldn't deprive *your* grandmother of something so simple as a wedding, would you?"

Kiara wagged her head back and forth. "Oh, no—I'm only wishin' me ma could 'ave been here when I married Rogan. What a blessin' that would 'ave been. And even more 'appy I'd be ta 'ave me mother see this wee babe when it's born."

Jasmine closely watched the exchange between Kiara and her grandmother. "I believe you're as fit as the day I arrived in Lowell and this whole discussion is nothing more than a charade so that I'll give in to your whims."

"Such accusations!" Alice retorted. "Do you desire a written statement from the doctor?"

Hesitating momentarily, Jasmine watched her grandmother shift uncomfortably in her chair. "Yes. I believe that would be acceptable."

Alice wilted at the challenge, yet remained unrelenting. "If you loved me, you wouldn't require proof of what I say."

Neither woman noticed Nolan enter the room. "What's going on in here? I could hear the ruckus before I entered the house. I believe I've heard fewer angry voices in the local tavern."

Jasmine's cheeks flushed. She should never have engaged in such uncomely behavior—especially with her grandmother. She grasped Alice's hand. "I apologize for my argumentative conduct."

Alice sighed contentedly. "Apology accepted, my dear. Now, shall we begin planning the wedding? I've a list of things we must accomplish before week's end, and Kiara must return to working on the lace for your wedding veil."

Nolan cleared his throat. "Ladies! The wedding plans have already been settled. The ceremony will be small and take place on the twelfth of October. We will be married in the garden, weather permitting, and a reception will follow indoors. There will be *no* changes to our plans and absolutely *no* delays."

Jasmine and the two other women stared at him, all three rendered momentarily speechless by his unyielding declaration.

Completely composed, he walked to the divan and sat down beside Jasmine. "Now that we've settled the wedding issue, I believe I would enjoy a glass of that lemonade."

Elinor Brighton sat in the last row of chairs, ready to hear a lecture on South American butterflies. She wasn't sure why she'd even come. Butterflies were of no interest to her, and her free time was so scarce that it seemed quite wasteful. Still, here she was—picking lint from her coarse brown skirt and wondering where life was taking her.

Sometimes the memories of Daniel and Wilbur were so painful that they threatened to steal away her will to live. Other times, like now, they were bittersweet, almost reassuring reminders that at one point—at one time—she had been loved.

Why were they gone? Why had they died so young? Her best memories of her life with Daniel were their times together before they'd even married. Oh, it wasn't that their intimacy as husband and wife hadn't been joyous, wondrous . . . but rather it was the time spent in conversation, walks in the park, or simple moments in each other's company that touched her most deeply.

How she missed the conversation of a man. She longed for something more than inane chatter of the mill girls. Their idea of exciting discourse ran along the lines of what new dress so-and-so had bought, and which young gentleman they were seeing at the time. They were silly and young . . . much younger than Elinor could ever remember being.

I'm only twenty-six, she thought. Not so very old. But much too old for conversations centering on hairstyles and parties. The loss of her youth to widowhood often made Elinor angry, but this time it just made her feel defeated. The reassurance of being loved faded in light of the loss.

The lecturer took his place and began to speak of his studies and eventual trips to South America. He spoke with a great booming voice that promised much authority on the matter. Elinor sighed. Jasmine Houston was remarrying in a few days. She was one of the only other young widows Elinor had ever known. Jasmine was very much in love—of that Elinor was certain, so it only seemed right that she should marry.

But I was in love too, and look where that took me.

The lecturer held up a specimen of some type of butterfly, the name of which escaped Elinor. Instead of pretending to listen any longer, she quietly got up and excused herself from the row of rapt listeners. Perhaps butterflies were meant to be a part of their world, but they certainly had no place in hers.

The streetlights shone a path for Elinor to follow home. All along the way she watched other people . . . couples . . . families. Everyone had someone. The lights that shone from the houses promised happy homes where people gathered in love. Through one of the massive widows trimmed in gauzy lace curtains, Elinor caught a glimpse of a young man lifting a small child in the air. She turned away quickly, the pain encircling her heart like a band, threatening to stop its beating.

"I wish it would stop," she murmured, picking up her pace. "I wish I could just cease to be—to hurt."

———

Jasmine drew her grandmother into a warm embrace. "You'll have to admit that our wedding was a nice affair, even if it didn't meet your original expectations," Jasmine whispered.

"I would agree that the wedding was nice," Alice answered. "It certainly was neither elegant nor the social event of the year, but it was a nice little gathering."

Jasmine laughed and tightened her embrace. "Nolan and I are truly pleased your illness did not keep you from attending."

"All right, young lady, you got your way. No need to harass

me about my earlier tactics. Truth be told, my health isn't that good, nor will it remain stable forever. I am an old woman."

"Grandmother, are you trying to worry me?"

Alice's features softened. "No. I'm simply remembering how devastated you were to lose your mother. I won't live forever, Jasmine, and you must be prepared. Perhaps I did play at exaggerating it when trying to convince you to change your wedding plans, but you must see the truth. Each winter I grow a little weaker."

Jasmine hugged her grandmother close. "I couldn't bear to lose you."

Grandmother stroked Jasmine's hair. "But we will see each other again—in heaven. You must never fear my passing. Death is a part of life and shouldn't be feared. God has said He will never leave us nor forsake us. Never . . . not even in death."

Jasmine pulled away and looked into her grandmother's eyes. "I love you, Grandmother. So very much. I know we'll have all eternity, but I'd like a little longer here on earth."

Alice Wainwright smiled. "I'll do what I can to ensure that, but don't fret over it if God has other plans." Jasmine nodded soberly and Alice added, "You had best go upstairs and change into your traveling gown. I daresay Nolan is not going to be detained at this reception much longer."

"Do come help me, won't you?" Jasmine asked as she grasped her grandmother's hand.

"*Now* you want my help," she said with a chuckle as she happily followed Jasmine to her room.

Alice unfastened Jasmine's fawn gown that had been elegantly embellished around the neckline with Kiara's ivory handmade lace. "I do think you should have agreed to something longer than a few days in Boston for your wedding trip. I'm sure Nolan isn't pleased with your decision."

"Nolan is fine with my decision. Neither of us wanted to leave Spencer for any longer. Besides, we're imposing upon Kiara and Naomi to care for him. I wouldn't expect them to tend to him any longer than a few days—especially with Kiara's baby due in only a few months."

"I told you I would come and stay here at the farm and look after him."

"Really, Grandmother—an hour or two tending a young boy is one thing, but any longer and you would have to take to your bed. And we've just talked about your health and keeping you around for a while. I've told both Kiara and Naomi to call upon you if they need your help," she added.

A rumble of thunder sounded overhead as Alice helped Jasmine into her traveling dress of periwinkle blue silk. "As usual, you look lovely, my dear. Permit an old woman to tell you that I am very happy you and Nolan found each other. You deserve the joy of a good marriage, and I know Nolan is going to make you very happy."

"Thank you, Grandmother. I'm certain he will also." She placed a kiss on the older woman's cheek.

Alice glanced out the bedroom window. "Those clouds appear ominous. We had best get you downstairs to your groom so that you may leave before the rain begins."

———

Oliver Maxwell hunkered beside a large oak tree, securing what shelter could be found while permitting him a partial view of the small cottage occupied by the three Negroes. Oliver's horse was tethered in a nearby clump of trees to remain hidden from view until he was prepared to make his move. He shivered as the cool fall air pressed his damp garments against his body. The sound of an approaching wagon caused him to shrink out of sight.

"Are ya ready ta get ta work on those fences, Obadiah?" one of the men called out from the wagon with a strong Irish brogue.

Oliver edged out from behind the tree and watched in dismay as the wagon came to a halt near the cottage. Obadiah exited the house and climbed into the wagon. Leaning against the tree, Oliver slid down into a squat and tilted his head against the tree's rough bark. He'd suffered through this rain and cold for naught! Making a tight fist, Oliver slammed it into the open palm of his other hand. He had counted upon making some quick money and assured Enoch and Joseph his plan for kidnapping and selling freed slaves would prove effective.

Oliver didn't know how long he'd been sitting at the base of the tree when he heard the voices of a woman and small child coming from the opened door of the cottage. Obadiah's wife and child! If he captured them, he could use them as bait to lure Obadiah into his clutches. Naomi walked out of the door carrying a basket of clothing and moved toward the cauldron of water hanging over an open fire. The child remained close to her side. Moving quietly, Oliver made his way to the clump of bushes and then untied and mounted his horse. With two quick jabs, he dug his heels into the horse's shanks and sped off toward the woman and child. Moving with lightning speed, he entered the yard and dismounted.

"Nooo!" Naomi screamed as he grabbed her around the waist.

Slapping his hand across the struggling woman's mouth, Oliver wrestled her to the ground. With a knee wedged into her back, he moved to quickly gag her with a dirty handkerchief before securing both hands behind her with a piece of rope. He lifted her feather-light body onto the horse and then grabbed the screaming child under his arm. With greater ease than he could have hoped for, Oliver hoisted himself up and slapped the reins.

Balancing a basket of dirty clothes under one arm and holding Moses with her other hand, Kiara ambled toward Obadiah and Naomi's nearby cottage. "Come on with ya, Moses. Let's go and see yar little friend Spencer. The two of ya can play while yar mama and me do our washin'," she said, suddenly distracted by the sight of a horse speeding away from the cottage.

She stopped and squinted into the sun. "Stop! Stop!" she screamed, dropping the basket and scooping Moses into her arms. Running as fast as her burgeoning body would permit, she finally came to a halt and dropped to her knees, gasping for breath. The horse was now out of sight.

Clutching Moses close to her side, Kiara was uncertain what to do. Her mind raced.

"Wet go," Moses said, wiggling against her arms.

Hands trembling, Kiara loosened her hold on the child. "Don't be runnin' off—we must go find your papa."

But Liam, Rogan, and Obadiah were mending fences, and Paddy and Mr. Fisher had taken one of the horses to the farrier in Lowell. There was no one close at hand to help, no one to go after Naomi and Spencer.

"Settle yarself, Kiara. We can na understand a word ya're sayin'," Rogan admonished as he pulled her close.

Moses toddled toward Obadiah. "Papa!"

"What you doin' here, chile?" Obadiah lifted the boy into his arms and in several long strides was beside Rogan and Kiara. "What's goin' on? How come you got Moses out here?"

"She's been tryin' to tell me," Rogan said. "Take a deep breath, lass, and try ta talk."

Kiara swallowed hard, knowing she must relay the information. "Naomi came over to visit with me after the three of ya left this morning. Moses fell asleep, and I told her ta be leavin' him with me and I'd join her after he woke up. We was gonna do our washin' together. Naomi took Spencer home with her. When Moses woke up from his nap, I gathered my washin' and headed out to the cottage. The sun was blindin' me, but I heard a scream and then I saw a man ridin' off with Naomi and Spencer."

Obadiah was shaking his head forcefully. "No! Dat can't be true."

"'Tis true. I ran as fast as I could, but I was carryin' Moses and with me in my condition, I could na run fast enough. They was down the road and out of sight before I could even make it ta the cottage."

"Come on! We gotta go get her!" Obadiah hollered.

"Settle yarself, Obadiah," Liam admonished. "If we're gonna find yar wife and little Spencer, we've gotta be thinkin'. Ain'

191

nobody gonna listen to a couple Irishmen and a Negro. We need ta get us some help. I'm thinkin' maybe Mr. Cheever could lend a hand. I'll take the horse Kiara rode out here and go and tell him what's happened. The rest of ya go back to the farm and wait for me there. See if ya can be findin' anything that's gonna give us some idea of what happened. Look far any clue the culprit may've left behind. We're gonna need all the help we can get if we're gonna find them."

Kiara began to sob as Rogan helped her into the wagon. "We've got ta find them, Rogan. Miss Jasmine's gonna be home in a few days. She'll never fargive us for lettin' this happen ta little Spencer—and poor Naomi, what's gonna happen ta her?"

"We'll find dem—ain' gonna rest until we find both of dem," Obadiah said, his back rigid and jaw clenched tight.

A short time later, Rogan pulled back on the reins, and the horses came to a halt in front of the barn. Obadiah jumped down with Moses in his arms while Rogan lifted Kiara to the ground. "Ya're still tremblin', lass. Ya need to keep yar faith. We're gonna find them, and I'm thinkin' the best way to help is go back over to the house and see what's in the area. Looks like the fire's still goin'," he said as they grew closer.

The woven basket was overturned near the fire, and dirty clothes and linens lay scattered on the ground. Kiara grabbed the basket and began picking up the garments. "We were goin' ta wash together," she said, glancing toward Obadiah. "I already told ya that, didn't I?"

Obadiah nodded. "Try to remember everything from da time you left da house with Moses," he encouraged.

Kiara looked at her husband, who gave her an encouraging smile. "Naomi brought both of the boys ta the house, and we had a cup of tea and visited. She said she thought Moses might be takin' a cold and that he hadn't been sleepin' well the last couple nights."

"Tha's true. He been mighty hard to please da last few days."

"For sure he was fussin', and I began rockin' him on me lap. He fell asleep, and I told Naomi to just leave him until he woke up. She said she'd be takin' Spencer back to the cottage so he wouldn't wake up Moses. We agreed to do the washin' when Moses woke up."

Rogan patted her shoulder. "Ya're doin' fine, lass. What happened next?"

"Moses woke up, I picked up my basket of dirty clothes, and we left the house. All of a sudden, I heard a scream and looked toward the cottage. The sun was shinin' bright, and I moved enough to block the sun from me eyes so I could be seein'. By that time, all I saw was the back of a man. He had Naomi sprawled across the horse and Spencer tucked under 'is arm. The boy was kickin' and cryin' as they rode away."

"And what kind of horse was he ridin', lass? Can ya be tellin' us about the horse?"

Kiara looked at the road, trying to visualize it. "The horse was na unusual—nothin' like the Arabians. It was just a horse."

"What color?" Obadiah insisted.

"A light sorrel. I'm sorry, but the sun was in me eyes," she said with a tremble in her voice. "I'm thinking it might be a mottled red."

Rogan drew her close and wrapped her in his arms. "Stop yar tears, lass. If ya're to help, ya must remain calm. Think of the boy," he whispered. "Ya'll have him upset all over again."

Kiara turned and took in Moses' tear-stained face puckered into an image of gloom. "Come here, Moses. Come sit with me." She sat on the step of the cabin and spread her arms to welcome him.

He rushed to Kiara and wiggled onto the bit of lap remaining unoccupied by the child growing inside her. Kiara began to rock back and forth as the child shoved his thumb into his mouth and rested his curly head on her breast while Rogan and Obadiah continued to search for some sign of the man.

"We's wastin' time. While we's standin' 'round doin' nothin', he's gettin' farther on down da road with Naomi and Spencer. We should take a couple of dem fine horses and go after dem—ain' nothin' to be gained standin' here. We done seen all dere is to see—which turns out to be nothin'."

"Liam said to wait, and I ain't one ta be goin' against Liam Donohue. Besides, if anyone saw us on those Arabians, they'd far sure hang us high. Sure and I can see it now—an Irishman and a Negro tryin' to explain how they happen ta be ridin' a couple of expensive Arabian steeds."

The sound of approaching horses caused both men to cease their arguing and turn their attention toward the road.

"Looks like Liam found Mr. Cheever," Rogan said as he waved at the men. They all rushed to the horses—even Kiara, still holding Moses.

Liam pulled back hard on the reins as he and Matthew neared the cottage. "Have ya anything more ta tell us?"

Rogan shook his head. "There's na a scrap of a clue ta be found around the place."

"Can you think of any reason someone would kidnap Naomi and Spencer?" Matthew asked as he dismounted. "Have you had any threats against you, Obadiah?"

"No, suh, ain' had nothin' like dat. Ain' nobody woulda even knowed Spencer was at da house and ain' no reason for no one ta be takin' Naomi. She ain' never done nothin' to nobody."

Matthew removed his straw hat and wiped the beads of perspiration from his forehead. "What about your former owner, Obadiah? I know Mrs. Houston purchased your freedom, but I wonder if he might have something to do with this."

"No, suh, I don' think so. Miss Jasmine paid him what he was askin' fer us. Fact is, she paid Massa Harshaw more than what anyone else woulda paid. Mean as dat man was, I don' think he'd be tryin' such a thing as kidnappin' Naomi. Don' make no sense."

"I'm merely trying to think of any reason there might be for someone to specifically take Naomi and Spencer," Matthew said. "I asked my wife to go and speak to Alice Wainwright. I thought she should know Spencer is missing."

Kiara pointed down the road, where an approaching horse and rider could be seen in the distance. "Here comes Paddy."

The group stood watching the young man as he approached

on one of the beautiful Arabians, the horse prancing toward them with the elegant beauty of a trained dancer.

"I was na expectin' such a welcome," Paddy said, a bright smile curling his lips. Kiara watched as her brother scanned their faces and then turned his attention to her. "What's the matter? Ya all look as though someone has died."

"Naomi and Spencer 'ave been kidnapped," Kiara told him. "I saw a man ride off with the two of them as I was leavin' the house with Moses."

"Surely ya're jokin'. Why would anyone want to be kidnappin' Naomi and Spencer?" Paddy asked. "When did they disappear?"

Once again Kiara recounted the activity leading up to the kidnapping, and though the details were few, she attempted to recall every one for her brother.

"I think we should take one more look outside the house; then Liam and I will see if we can follow their trail," Matthew said. "Obadiah, I think it's best if you remain here with Moses."

"Ya're not gonna find nothin' by lookin' again," Rogan remarked. "Me and Obadiah already done that two times."

"Then it shouldn't take long. We'll give the area a fresh look. You and Obadiah can stay with the horses, Rogan," Matthew said as he led the others closer to the cottage.

Paddy stooped down and settled on his haunches, scanning the damp ground before glancing up at his sister. "Did the kidnappin' happen before or after Mr. Maxwell came to the cottage?"

"Mr. Maxwell did na come today, Paddy," she said.

"Look at those muddy prints." He pointed to the ground as Matthew and Liam returned. "Mr. Maxwell's horse has a clubfoot. I noticed it when I watered the animal, but I do na see any wagon marks. He must 'ave been riding the horse. Did ya na say the horse was red, Kiara? Do ya think it might've been a strawberry roan?"

"May 'ave been. The sun was in me eyes, Paddy, but I thought there was a reddish color to the animal. They disappeared afore I could see very good."

"Seems we need to talk to Mr. Maxwell. Any idea where he

stays when he's in Lowell?" Matthew asked, glancing around at the others.

"I heard him tell Miss Jasmine he'd be deliverin' our shoes in a month, or she could check at the Merrimack House if she was in town." Paddy replied, his chest puffing as he shared the information. "He said he'd made arrangements with the owner of the Merrimack since he always took a room there when he was in town."

Matthew patted him on the back. "You've got a sharp eye and good listening skills as well, my boy. Let's go see what Mr. Maxwell has to say about where he's been today."

———————

"If you'll excuse me for a moment, I'll answer the door," Elinor said. "No doubt it's someone calling on one of my boarders, but none of them seems able to answer the door."

Oliver nodded and smiled before relaxing his posture and watching Elinor leave the parlor. He enjoyed the gentle sway of her hips and imagined her brown tresses loosed from the tight knot and swinging softly around her shoulders. Perhaps one day she would remove the hairpins and grant him the pleasure of such a sight. Yes, Elinor had some fine characteristics, though he could barely tolerate her when she began her wearisome complaints about the mill girls or droned on about her sad lot in life.

"We want to see him *now!*"

The sound of angry voices and clattering shoes drawing closer caused Oliver to stiffen and turn his attention to the hallway. A sundry group filled the doorway, and their anger was evident.

"Gentlemen," he greeted, standing and moving to shake hands with Matthew Cheever. "What can I do for you?"

Matthew didn't extend his hand to accept Oliver's greeting. Instead, he met the shoe peddler's smile with a steely glare. "I didn't notice a horse outside the house. Did you walk here from the Merrimack House, Mr. Maxwell?"

"As a matter of fact, I did. I've been making deliveries in Lowell all day, and when I don't have far to travel, I prefer to walk.

Encourage my customers to do the same—wears out the shoes more rapidly," he said with a false bravado.

Liam edged through the doorway. "And where might we be findin' yar horse, Mr. Maxwell, 'cause it ain't at the livery stable."

"You must be mistaken. I left the animal there last night after making deliveries. What's this about, anyway?" he asked.

"We'll tell you once we've located your horse," Matthew replied.

"I'll be more than pleased to accompany you to the livery and prove there's been a mistake."

"Excellent suggestion. Why don't you lead the way," Matthew said, moving out of the doorway.

Elinor hastened to Oliver's side and directed a glare at Mr. Cheever. "You need to tell Mr. Maxwell why you're detaining him."

"We're not detaining him, Mrs. Brighton. We're asking for his cooperation. He's freely agreed to assist us, so if you'll step aside, we'll be on our way."

"I'll visit with you tomorrow, Elinor," Oliver said as he departed the house.

The group traversed the streets of Lowell, garnering the attention of both storekeepers and shoppers until the men finally reached the livery, all of them squinting as they entered the dim stall-lined structure.

"Right over here," he said, leading them toward a stall near the end of the row. His eyes widened, and he hoped he appeared surprised when he encountered the empty stall. "I don't know where she is. Maybe she's been moved to another stall," he said. "Did you happen to ask Mr. Kittredge when you were here earlier?"

"There was na anyone here—still isn't. Are ya sayin' you do na know where yar own horse is?" Liam asked.

"I told you that I left the horse here last night and I've not been back since then. I have no idea where the animal might be—I fear it may have been stolen. I've a mother and sister to support, and I don't know how I can afford to replace my horse. Needless to say, I want to locate the animal as much as you do," Oliver said.

"Are you now going to tell me what has happened?"

"I think he's lyin'," Rogan whispered to Liam while glowering at Oliver.

Matthew nodded. "Obadiah's wife, Naomi, has been taken, as well as young Spencer Houston. Whisked off on horseback earlier today."

The blood drained from Oliver's face, and his legs grew weak. "Did you say Spencer Houston?"

"Da boy was at my place when it happened. You measured him and my boy, Moses, for shoes a while back," Obadiah reminded him.

Oliver's hands were shaking as he walked from the stable, the group of men following close behind. "I'll talk to Mr. Kittredge and ask if anyone was around the livery today."

"No need. We'll talk to him ourselves," Matthew said.

Oliver leaned against the rough-hewn door, watching the group depart. Fortunately the screaming woman had alerted him he'd been seen leaving the cottage, and he'd had the foresight to hide the strawberry roan. Better still was the fact that no one had seen him leave the stables with the horse, as he'd left before first light.

Surely they'd been mistaken about Spencer Houston. He was certain he'd taken Obadiah's boy. The city marshal and constabulary force would no doubt be drawn into the disappearance of a white child—especially the white child of a wealthy family. Matters had quickly taken an unfortunate turn. He needed time to think!

CHAPTER · 15

KIARA HELD MOSES snugly on her lap, rocking back and forth as the child sucked his thumb. The young boy had wandered about Obadiah's cottage and yard crying for his mother until he'd grown exhausted. After using all of her feminine skills, Kiara had finally convinced him to go home with her and eat supper. With his belly full, he'd grown weary and his eyelids now fluttered, heavy with sleep.

Rogan sat opposite her, his gaze fixed upon the child. "I'm wonderin' how anyone's gonna be able to explain little Spencer's disappearance to Miss Jasmine and Mr. Nolan when they return."

"I still think it was a mistake na sending word to them. I'm thankin' the good Lord I was na the one charged with that decision. I do na think Miss Jasmine's gonna look kindly upon Mr. Cheever for his decision."

"Aye, yet I'm hopin' she'll see his aim was to keep her from sufferin'. He truly thought we'd 'ave the child back afore they returned home."

Kiara carried Moses to bed and then returned to her rocking chair. Pulling her thread from a basket near the chair, Kiara began creating a new piece of lace. "I'll tell ya, Rogan, this whole matter is another reminder of how quickly life can be changin'. One moment everything is fine as can be and the next, yar whole life is turned upside down."

"Ya're right about that, lass," Rogan said as a long shadow fell across the floor.

Kiara turned and saw Obadiah standing in the doorway. "Come in, Obadiah. Moses fell asleep and I put 'im in bed. Sit yarself down and I'll dish ya up some stew."

Obadiah rubbed his stomach and sat down. "Thank you, but I don' think I can eat. My belly's been hurtin' all day. I been thinkin' Miz Jasmine's gonna be comin' home tomorrow and dere's still no sign of Naomi or little Spencer." He leaned his elbows on his knees, resting his forehead against his open palms. "She ain' gonna be able to bear it."

Kiara rocked her chair more fervently, her heart aching for the pain he must bear. She longed to offer him help, yet there was nothing anyone could say to ease his pain.

"Don' know what I'll do iffen anything's happened to Naomi. I can't live wibout dat woman," he said without lifting his head.

"It's times like this, when we're feelin' alone and helpless, we need ta remember God's with us," Kiara said. "And He's with Naomi and Spencer too. We need ta all be prayin' instead of thinkin' there's nothin' remainin' ta be done."

"Ya're right about that, lass," Rogan said. "I'm always figurin' I can handle things, and then when they don't work out, I get down on me knees. Ya'd think I'd learn it should always be the other way around."

"Me an' da boy been doin' our share of prayin', but I ain' so sure da Lord's hearing us. Iffen He is, He sure ain' let me know. It sho' do shake a man's faith when somethin' like dis happens. I been tryin' hard to hang on, telling the youngun da Lord's gonna bring his mama home, but as da hours keeps a passin' by and nothin' happens, I ain' so sure no more."

"I know what ya're sayin' is true enough," Kiara said. "'Tis hard to be maintainin' faith in times of trouble, but ya must na give up hope, Obadiah. Sure as I'm sittin' here, God's gonna see ya through this."

Jasmine clung to Nolan's arm, feeling strangely giddy as their carriage approached the driveway. "I can barely contain my excitement. I know it's been only a few days, yet I feel as though I haven't seen Spencer for weeks. Do you think he'll be angry with us for leaving him?"

"His anger will quickly subside when he sees all the gifts you've bought him. I'd even venture to say he'll likely encourage us to leave again," Nolan said with a hearty laugh.

The carriage had barely come to a halt when Jasmine attempted to exit. Laughing at her excitement, Nolan took her hand and then helped her down. "Hurry! The baggage can wait," she said, rushing up the front steps.

Nolan followed close behind as she rushed into the foyer, but he was forced to an abrupt halt when his wife stopped short in the doorway of the parlor. Alice sat facing them with her hands folded and back straightened into a rigid posture that seemed to emanate a foreboding message.

"What is it, Grandmother? Something has happened, hasn't it? Something dreadful. Tell me!"

"Now, now, my dear. Sit down and we'll talk," Alice said in a soothing voice.

"I prefer to stand and I want to know. Father hasn't taken ill, has he?"

"No, your father is fine." She paused, her expression betraying her discomfort. "It's Spencer, dear."

"Oh no. Is he sick? Where is he? Did he take the measles? I heard measles were going around." Jasmine started toward the stairs.

"He's not sick. At least not that I know." Alice drew a deep breath. "This will be difficult to comprehend, but Jasmine . . . he's been kidnapped."

The room began to spin and Jasmine felt her knees buckle. She attempted to move toward the divan. For some reason, her feet would not move, yet she could feel her body sinking deeper and deeper into a swirling eddy from which there was no escape. Nolan's name was on her lips, but no sound would emerge. Spencer's smiling face flitted through her memory as she slipped into the deep abyss.

"Miss Jasmine! Can ya hear me?"

Kiara was leaning over her, their noses nearly touching.

Fogginess blurred Jasmine's thoughts as she stared back into Kiara's chocolate brown eyes. She blinked and tried to recall why she was lying on the divan in the middle of the day.

"Do na worry yarself. The lad is gonna be found. I can feel it here," Kiara said, patting her palm on her chest.

Spencer! That's why she was lying on the settee. She had fainted. Her son was gone. A lump settled in her throat, squelching the scream she desired to release into the noticeably hushed room. An overwhelming grief settled upon her like the mantle of sorrow she'd experienced when her mother had died.

"Noooo," she moaned, shaking her head from side to side. This couldn't be happening. Who would take her son? Why would they take him? Money? She'd gladly give them whatever they asked for. She merely needed to know what they were after.

"Has there been any note—any letter to explain why they've taken him?"

Kiara shook her head. "None. They've taken Naomi too. We can't imagine why unless the man was afraid she'd be able to identify him."

Jasmine sat up with a jerk and immediately felt the blood rush from her head. "We must develop a plan," she insisted.

"Lay yar head back and rest. We're doin' all that's possible ta find them."

Nolan moved to her side and knelt down. "Liam has filled me in on the details of the search, Jasmine. There's little doubt they've done everything possible to find Naomi and Spencer. The constables as well as many residents of Lowell and the surrounding countryside have been searching in earnest. I believe the best thing we can do is remain calm and pray."

"Oh, Nolan, this is more than I can bear. It hurts so much to think of him scared and alone. And all the while, I was making merry in Boston."

"We didn't know what had happened, Jasmine. We were making merry because God brought us together in love. We aren't being punished for something, so stop fretting. You've done nothing to cause this."

She let Nolan cradle her in his arms, feeling the warmth, knowing the love. "He's just a little boy, so undeserving of this. What manner of man performs such cruelties?"

"An evil one ta be sure," Kiara said, standing over Nolan. "But evil can na be standin' against our Lord. Ya must be havin' faith that God will care for Spencer and see 'im home safely."

Jasmine nodded, but her heart was so heavy. "If it be His will," she murmured. But of course she wasn't all that convinced. After all, it should have been well within God's will that a small boy be protected from kidnapping.

Oliver stroked the dapple gray Mr. Kittredge offered. "Are you certain you won't need the horse today? I don't want to inconvenience you."

"It's the least I can do," he said. "I feel responsible that your horse was stolen. After all, if the door had been locked or I'd had the stable boy looking after things while I was gone, maybe you'd still have that strawberry roan. I keep thinking someone will find it. Too uncommon a horse to go unnoticed."

Oliver reveled in the comment, pleased his deceit had been received as truth. He waited until Kittredge was out of sight before hanging a bag of oats across the horse's back. After loading his saddlebags with additional supplies, he quickly made his way out of town.

He traveled at a steady pace, keeping to the road for several miles before veering off to the east. Moving across the hilly farmland that spread before them, he remembered the first time he'd crossed this terrain—when he'd discovered the abandoned farmhouse. It had been on one of those tiresome journeys when he'd grown weary of traveling the same route. Thinking to save time and break the monotony of his journey, he'd grown bold, never thinking of the ramifications of a broken wheel or injured horse at a remote location. But fortune had been with him, and the only thing that had occurred was a treacherous thunderstorm.

It was then, in his search for shelter, he'd located the deserted farmhouse and outbuildings. Weeds had overgrown what had once been a family garden, and the house was ravaged by years of neglect and offered little sanctuary. But he'd found the root cellar and there, beneath the ground, he'd found safety from the storm and a secret place where he could occasionally stop and lose himself in dreams of a better life. A perverse smile crossed his lips, knowing he'd outsmarted the locals. None of those men had searched anywhere near the secluded farm.

"Fools!" he muttered as he dismounted and tied the horse to a nearby tree. With the sack of grain over his shoulder, he made his way to the stall, deciding to exercise the strawberry roan after checking on the woman and child.

Oliver stopped to catch his breath after removing the pile of branches and rocks he'd placed over the entry to the root cellar. He was certain the drugs he'd forced into the woman and child had kept them sedated, yet he'd blocked the door as an added precaution. He didn't want the woman escaping before he returned. Although he hadn't planned to revisit the site until tomorrow, he now knew he must positively establish the identity of the child he'd placed in the dank hole in the ground. His heart pounded as he pulled back the heavy door.

The woman and child were exactly as he left them, sleeping soundly on the blankets he'd placed on the ground. After all, he didn't want them getting ill. The price of a sickly Negro decreased considerably—especially for a small-framed woman and child. Pulling the drawing of Moses' foot from his pocket, he placed it against the sole of the boy's foot and then rocked back on his heels. This boy's foot was much larger than the drawing. Angrily, he thrust the drawing to the dirt floor and rubbed his forehead. He'd taken Spencer Houston. Not a black child, but a wealthy white woman's son.

"I need a plan," Oliver said between clenched teeth. He walked back up the steps, deciding a short ride on his horse would give the animal some needed exercise and would also permit him time to think. He saddled the horse and rode for nearly an hour before stopping near a stream. Sitting under a tree and watching as the horse drank deeply from the flowing water, Oliver formulated his strategy.

By the time he had returned to the barn, he knew the woman must die. He could bury her in the root cellar and then pretend to find Spencer Houston. He'd be a hero and certainly entitled to a reward. Yet the thought gave him little consolation. He doubted the Houstons would give him anywhere near what he had expected to receive when he sold the woman and child into slavery. And the thought of actually killing a woman gave him pause—he'd have to think on the matter tonight. The two of them should sleep until morning. He'd return and do what was required. He had no choice.

Naomi felt the cold in her bones before even fully awakening to the darkness around her. She had dreamed of working in the fields, only these fields weren't in the South, they were cold and unyielding. Pushing the dream away, she struggled to sit up. Her head ached something fierce, and a dizziness overcame her that seemed to settle only when she put her head back down.

After a few minutes she tried again to sit up. This time it wasn't quite as bad. She felt around her, trying to figure out her location. It seemed to be some sort of cellar. The floor was dirt, hard-packed and cold. She had a blanket but nothing else.

Reaching her hand out timidly, she was startled to feel the warm flesh of a human arm. A very small arm. Spencer! The memories of their kidnapping came flooding back. It was the shoe peddler. She couldn't even remember his name. But why had he taken them?

"Spencer?" She whispered the boy's name in case their assailant should be close enough to hear. The boy stirred but didn't awaken. Naomi pulled him into her arms and cradled him to keep him warm.

"Po' boy. Your mama's gonna be worried sumptin' fierce."

Outside there was a noise as if someone or something was digging at the door. Unable to see in the dark, Naomi could only rely on sound. But it didn't sound good. The noise continued until the unmistakable sound of a door being opened gave her mixed hope and trepidation. Either someone had found them . . . or their kidnapper was returning.

Lantern light blinded Naomi as she clutched more tightly to Spencer. "Who's dere?"

"So you're awake." The shoe peddler came down the wooden stairs, and Naomi struggled to fix her gaze on the man. What she saw, however, terrified her. The man carried a shovel and there was a revolver in his waistband, barely visible as the man's coat pulled away when he set the lantern on one of the steps.

"I've come to take care of business."

"What be yo' business with me and da boy?" Naomi asked, her voice quivering.

"Well," the man said, leaning on the shovel, "I thought I knew well enough what that was, but I was mistaken. I'm afraid I've come to put an end to your miserable life and to take the boy back to his grieving mother."

Naomi felt her breath quicken. The man was going to kill her. But why? Most of the white folks in the North had been kind to her. Why would this one want to end her life? "Why ya wanna kill a Negro woman like me?"

The man laughed, chilling Naomi to the bone. Spencer stirred but still did not awaken as the man replied, "I took you because you were a Negro woman. There's good money down south for the likes of you. But I didn't intend to take the boy. I thought he was your boy. Thought I'd entice his pappy to follow after us if I took his family. But that's not going to be the case. I took a white woman's child, and while society would most likely not lift a finger to search for a black baby, they'll move heaven and earth to locate a wealthy man's son."

Naomi knew her life depended on coming up with some reason for him to keep her alive. "I'm beggin' you, suh," she began. "Think 'bout what you're fixin' ta do. If you keep me alive, I'll take care of the chile for you. The longer he goes missin', the more thankful his mama's gonna be. I promise I won' give you no trouble. I'm thinkin' you could tell 'em you found da both of us, and I'll tell Miz Jasmine she should pay you a handsome sum of money. Ya need ta remember dis here boy is smart. He's gonna tell his mama you's da one what took us away. I can tell her he's mistaken. Ya should spend some more time thinkin' 'bout what you's gonna do."

The peddler stared at Naomi, looking confused about what he should do with her. "Surely the child isn't old enough to tell his mother much."

"Suh, he be a smart boy. Smarter'n most his age."

The man growled, then tossed the shovel to the side. "Nothing in my life is ever simple. Nothing."

Naomi gently stroked Spencer's head, more for the comfort it offered her than for any it might allow him. She would just remain silent and pray. Pray for God to see her and Spencer and to have mercy on them . . . pray for the peddler to have mercy on them too.

CHAPTER · 16

ELINOR PLACED a heaping bowl of green beans seasoned with bacon drippings and minced onions in front of one of the girls and then surveyed the table.

"The bread-and-butter pickles," she muttered before hurrying back to the kitchen. Without fail, Lucinda Pritchett would remind her if she didn't immediately see pickles on the table.

Placing the crock directly in front of Lucinda with a firm thud, Elinor said, "You may ask God's blessing on our supper, Lucinda."

"It's Mary's turn," Lucinda replied while opening the pickles.

Elinor sighed and looked heavenward. "Mary, would you please pray for us?"

Mary uttered a quick, unintelligible prayer, followed by a loud amen. The clatter of metal utensils against china dishes began in earnest.

"Cecilia Broadhurst told me this afternoon they think the little Houston boy that was kidnapped is dead," Sarah Warren remarked while heaping a mountain of creamed potatoes onto her plate.

"I don't know how you have time to talk to Cecilia without causing yourself injury on the machines," Lucinda said tersely. "At the speed they've got the machinery operating, it's a wonder we aren't all maimed."

"You do have a way of adding charm to dinner conversations," Sarah said with a giggle.

"I'm not the one who mentioned the dead boy." A loud clank sounded as Lucinda dropped her fork onto the china plate. "Speeding up the machinery is *not* a laughing matter. Do you realize how many mill workers have been injured this year alone? I think what they've done is sinful. It's no wonder they're permitting the Irish to work alongside us. If it weren't from pure necessity, I'd quit working for those cruel taskmasters tomorrow."

"Now you've done it," Mary whispered to Sarah. "You've gone and got her started on a tirade."

Fire burned in Lucinda's cheeks. "I heard you whispering, Mary. When it's *your* hair or fingers that're caught in one of those evil machines, you'll be singing a different song."

There were several gasps, and Lucinda's lips curled in a smug grin before loading a forkful of potatoes into her mouth.

"I believe that's enough talk about accidents and injuries," Elinor said. "Perhaps we can find another topic to discuss."

"Do you think it's true about that little boy?" Mary asked while glancing around the table at her dinner partners.

"I think Cecilia's right," Sarah replied. "I truly doubt he could live this long without his mama to care for him."

Lucinda pointed her fork in Sarah's direction. "Exactly where did Cecilia get her information? Likely her remarks are pure supposition, the same as anyone else's."

"Don't point your fork, Lucinda—I expect proper etiquette from you girls," Elinor corrected.

Lucinda directed a look of irritation toward Elinor before lowering her fork and spearing several green beans. "Well, what do you think, Mrs. Brighton? Surely you don't think a simple girl working in the mills knows what's happened to the Houston boy, do you?"

"I have no idea. The only thing I truly know is that what happened is a tragedy, and I pray both the boy and woman have survived and will soon reappear."

Lucinda wagged her head back and forth. "That's about as

likely to happen as the mill owners deciding to slow down the machinery or give us a raise in pay."

Sarah glared at Lucinda. "Do you *never* tire of your negative outlook?"

"And why should I? I've never had any reason to do so. Unlike you, Sarah, my life has been filled with responsibilities and disappointment—even here in Lowell. Am I assigned to one of the floors with a kind supervisor like you? Of course not. Do the girls in my room afford me quiet time to read or meditate? Of course not. Am I able to spend my pay on fabric and jewelry like most of you? Of course not. When my life more closely resembles yours, perhaps I'll have reason to become less negative, Sarah."

"Someone from the Tremont Mill told me they found that black woman by the mill pond," Janet Wilson remarked.

"Another rumor," Lucinda said.

"She's probably correct," Mary commented. "If they'd found either of them, I believe word would rapidly spread around town."

While the girls continued their spirited discussion, Elinor thought of Oliver and the pain he'd endured knowing his horse had been used in the kidnapping. He'd suffered through the questioning by Matthew Cheever as well as the city marshal while enduring the gossip of the locals until the marshal concluded he'd not been involved. She'd personally witnessed the toll the entire incident had taken upon him, making him anxious and in ill humor, which was exactly the reason she'd taken time to bake a special apple cobbler. He'd be delivering shoes to the house this evening, and perhaps her baked goods would cheer him when everything else failed.

"Don't forget Mr. Maxwell will be distributing shoes this evening," Elinor said as she began clearing plates from the table.

Janet frowned and pushed away from the table, her chair scraping on the wood floor. "That means we'll have to wait to go shopping."

"Instead of worrying about going to the mercantile and spending more of your wages on frivolities, you should be pleased you had sufficient funds to purchase new shoes," Lucinda retorted.

Janet scowled at Lucinda before turning her attention to Elinor. "I'll be upstairs if Mr. Maxwell should arrive early."

Elinor nodded and continued into the kitchen. By the time
she'd emerged from the kitchen after washing the dishes and making final preparations for the morning meal, Oliver had arrived
and unpacked the last shoe.

Shadows of concern seemed to surround Oliver as he closed
his case. He moved the container to one side and then met Elinor's
gaze. "I believe I've finally finished for the night. I had planned
only on making my deliveries but after seeing Janet's new slippers,
two of the other girls wanted to be measured."

"I hope you're pleased to have the additional business," she
said.

"Yes, of course. However, I had hoped to have time to visit
with you, and now it's getting late."

"It's only nine o'clock. I can't lock the door and retire until
ten, so we have at least an hour," she said sweetly. "I've made an
apple cobbler if you'd like a piece."

He smiled broadly. "You're too kind," he said. "May I help?"

"Why don't you have a seat in the dining room," she suggested.

Moments later they sat opposite each other, Oliver devouring
his cobbler while Elinor sipped a cup of tea.

"Your cobbler is quite tasty. You do have a knack for baking,"
he complimented as he picked up a napkin and wiped his mouth.

"Thank you, Oliver. I've been concerned about you. How
have you been faring?"

"As well as can be expected under the circumstances. I feel as
though a cloak of suspicion surrounds me, and my thoughts constantly return to that poor boy's mother and stepfather. This must
be a terrible burden for them to bear—the ongoing worry about
the child's welfare, not knowing whether he's alive or dead."

Elinor nodded her agreement. "It must be equally hard on the
Negro woman's husband and child. I understand she has a small
child about the same age as Spencer Houston. They must be suffering terribly also."

Oliver ignored her remarks regarding Obadiah and Moses. "I think the search might be more successful if Mrs. Houston offered a reward. There's nothing that makes people become more involved than the possibility of a reward. You might mention that fact to her or one of her many friends who attend the Ladies' Aid meetings."

Elinor's brow puckered into deep creases. "Several of the girls mentioned at supper tonight that there have been rumors the boy is dead. And another girl mentioned the Negro woman was found by the mill pond. Have you heard anything further regarding their whereabouts?"

"No. Although I'm certain they haven't been found. Otherwise, there would be more than a few idle rumors. The marshal and his constables would make certain everyone in town knew if they'd been successful locating the Houston boy. I still believe a reward would help. Will you be visiting with Mrs. Houston anytime soon?"

"Under the circumstances, I don't imagine she'll be at the next Ladies' Aid meeting. If you think a reward would be helpful, perhaps you should mention it to the marshal. I would feel quite uncomfortable broaching the topic with Mrs. Houston if I should see her."

"And I would feel equally uncomfortable approaching the marshal. I've given them enough of my time. I wonder what punishment will be levied against the kidnapper. Likely there would be little, if any, retribution if only the Negro had been taken, but having that Houston boy changes things, don't you agree?"

Elinor gave him a puzzled gaze. "The woman is as important as the boy, Oliver."

"Maybe in your eyes," he said, but then met her eyes. "Of course, the woman is important, but the boy, the boy is, I mean his parents are . . ."

"Wealthy? White? Does that make their loss greater than that of the Negro woman's husband? It's that attitude that makes me even more committed to helping the runaways. People must begin to realize that the color of a person's skin does not increase or decrease one's value."

"No, of course not," he muttered. "So you're continuing to assist with runaways and enjoying your Ladies' Aid meetings?"

"Indeed. I've finally found something in which I find value, and I enjoy the thought that I'm helping others begin a new life," she said, surprised at her own anger. "I can't imagine how terrible it must be to live in some of the conditions I've heard the slaves tell about. Helping them gives me a sense of hope," she said, giving him a wistful smile.

"I do admire your willingness to aid those who are seeking to find a better life. We are, after all, commissioned to tell others of Christ and to do good works in His name."

Elinor leaned forward and rested her forearms on the table, for the first time feeling that Oliver actually understood her conviction. "I didn't realize you were so strong in your beliefs."

"Ah, dear lady, you underestimate me. I was reared by a mother who made certain I knew the Bible. If nothing else, she wanted her children to know how to read and how to write, and to believe what she believed. I memorized my Bible verses or was beaten until I did."

"While I don't agree with your mother's methods, I do wish I'd memorized more verses during my formative years. I've just recently found that the recollection of Scriptures can be a genuine blessing in times of difficulty," Elinor said.

"That may be true for many, but I find reliance upon my own inner strength a greater asset."

"Do you? I think that's one of the many differences between men and women. Men want to rely upon themselves, while women tend to find it more comforting to rely upon others. I've wondered if that's why fewer men are able to completely give themselves over to God's authority. Girls are taught at an early age they are to be subject to the authority of their fathers and husbands. On the other hand, boys are taught they are to grow into roles of authority."

Oliver stroked his narrow mustache as though the act somehow helped him recall his memories. "My mother assumed authority without any difficulty whatsoever. I believe she enjoys control—which is likely what drove my father to drinking and an early death."

"Life tends to take unexpected twists that we'll never understand in this world. However, I'm beginning to learn I can use those experiences, whether good or bad, to assist me with my current dilemmas."

Oliver squared his shoulders and gave her a confident smile. "And what dilemmas would you be facing? Perhaps I can be of some assistance."

For a brief moment Elinor faltered, but when Oliver leaned forward and earnestly gazed into her eyes, she returned his smile. Deep within, she believed he could be trusted. "The Ladies' Aid group has entrusted me with the task of securing shoes for the runaways. During the summer months, shoes are not nearly so important, but winter will soon be approaching, and although I've had success in securing footwear for women and even children, it has been difficult finding shoes for men and older boys. I've met with limited success by placing containers at the churches and boardinghouses asking people to leave their old shoes for the needy. However, there have been very few donations of men's shoes."

"You're correct in thinking that sturdy shoes will be a necessity. Even now, though the weather is warm, shoes would aid the runaways as they traverse the rough terrain." He tapped his fingernails on the table. "I think I can be of assistance to you."

Elinor's eyes sparkled with anticipation. "You can? Oh, Oliver, now I wish I'd spoken to you sooner. When I think of the number of runaways who could have benefited from a pair of shoes had I only taken you into my confidence."

He patted her hand. "What's done is done. We can't change the past. However, we have the future. Starting tomorrow, I'll ask my customers to donate their old shoes for the needy and will deliver them to you each time I'm in Lowell. In addition, I'm certain that I can aid you with some new shoes and boots from time to time. Occasionally someone will order a pair of shoes but fail to have the funds when I deliver, and I can also talk to the cobblers who make my shoes. They may be willing to help."

Elinor savored the taste of victory, the sweet aroma of success tingling her senses. At the next Ladies' Aid meeting, she would give an excellent report. "What a kind man you are. I look forward to your assistance. I only wish it could come sooner."

"Do you have an immediate need?"

"Yes. In fact, there's a group heading toward Lowell as we speak. I've agreed to help, yet I have only four pairs of shoes."

Oliver moved to the edge of his chair. "Truly? If you would care to confide more particulars, I will do all in my power to secure additional shoes before their arrival."

"You are much too kind, Oliver."

He stroked his mustache and smiled. "It's my pleasure to help the cause."

CHAPTER · 17

BEFORE NOLAN REACHED the top of the stairs, he heard Jasmine's sobs. This had become an all too familiar sound since their return from Boston. He tapped lightly on the bedroom door before entering, without expecting an answer. When Jasmine took to her bed in these bouts of tears, she heard nothing but her own out-pouring of sorrow.

"My dear," he said gently, perching on the edge of the bed and rubbing her back. "Is there nothing I can do to console you?"

"Find Spencer and Naomi."

Her reply was always the same. "We're doing all we can, Jas-mine. If it were some simple matter, they would already be home. I know your concern is great—as is my own. However, you do no one any good when you become incapacitated by your fears."

"I can't help myself," she sobbed. "Have you talked to Mat-thew Cheever? Is there any word at all?"

"I assumed he would send word if there were anything to report, but I will go and talk to him if it will make you feel better."

"Please," she whispered, wiping her swollen eyes with a corner of the bedsheet.

"If you're certain you'll be all right, I'll leave immediately."

"I'll be fine," she whispered, her fingers wrapped tightly

around the cotton lace that edged the white sheets.

Despite the early afternoon warmth, Nolan left her ensconced in layers of bed linens and blankets. He knew she would fight any attempt he made to remove them, just as he knew she would remain silent when he bid her good-bye.

The Cheevers would likely be enjoying their Sunday dinner when he arrived, yet he felt no remorse about interrupting them. Too frequently of late he found himself recalling Madelaine Wainwright's bouts with melancholy. And although Jasmine's grief over Spencer was well founded, he didn't want to see her following in Madelaine's footsteps under any circumstances. He wanted to see her rise up and fight rather than give way to defeat.

He knocked on the Cheevers' door. His mind overflowed with thoughts of the kidnapping, and he wondered when all of this would possibly cease. Would they ever find Naomi and Spencer? Were they still alive? Surely if they were still in the area they would have been found by now.

"Nolan! What a pleasant surprise," Matthew greeted. "Come join us. We're just getting ready to enjoy dinner."

"Thank you, but I can't stay. I promised Jasmine I would come by the house and see if there had been any word about Spencer and Naomi. I assured her you would have sent word, but she has taken to her bed and isn't easily consoled."

"Jasmine is ill?" McKinley asked as he approached the other two men.

"Sick of being without her child. I fear she's permitting her distress to control her life. I can't get her to leave the confines of her bedroom for even a few hours," Nolan explained.

"Visions of our mother," McKinley said quietly.

"My thoughts exactly. Yet I can't seem to find any way to shake her from her despair. I hoped you might give me some word of encouragement that I can take to her."

"I wish that I could," Matthew said. "However, we've found nothing—not a sign. In my heart I still believe that shoe peddler is involved, yet there's no further evidence of his complicity. Outside of continuing the search, I can think of nothing further to do."

"I'm giving consideration to offering a reward. What do you think of such an idea?" Nolan asked.

Matthew glanced at the floor and stroked his chin before turning his gaze back to Nolan. "I'd like to think that if anyone has information, he'd come forward without the offer of money. What makes you think a reward will help?"

"Elinor Brighton came by to pay Jasmine a visit the other day, and although Jasmine wasn't up to receiving her, Elinor left a note. I read her short missive just this morning. She made the suggestion that a reward might prove beneficial. Seems that an itinerant salesman had posed the possibility that money sometimes loosens tongues, and she wanted to pass along the idea."

"Interesting. It's true there are any number of transients passing through Lowell who might have a piece of information and yet feel no moral obligation to come forward," Matthew said.

"And a few gold coins may be all the incentive that is needed," McKinley enthusiastically agreed. "You could place an ad in the newspaper, where it will gain enough attention that the reward will soon be discussed all over town."

Violet came forward and stood beside McKinley. "Why don't you stay for dinner, Mr. Houston? We can discuss this further; and then McKinley and I can return home with you. Perhaps if we can enthusiastically present your plan to Mrs. Houston, she'll regain hope."

"How kind of you," Nolan replied. "I think you've an excellent idea."

Oliver greeted Enoch and Joseph with energetic handshakes before sitting down. He'd given them directions to a small inn located ten miles south of Lowell, where he'd not be recognized by any locals. "It's good to see both of you. I trust you had no difficulty getting here?"

"Only a lack of funds that caused us to sleep outdoors on our way up from Baltimore," Enoch replied.

Oliver ignored the remark but ordered food for all of them, hoping they'd be willing to remain compliant on a full stomach. "I've brought you here in order to help line your pockets with gold," he said. "You should be thankful, for I could have found any number of good men willing to help with my plan for much less than what I've offered the two of you."

"We are thankful," Enoch said, wiping his mouth across his sleeve. "We never doubted you was going to be loyal to us."

With a decisive nod of his head, Oliver carefully explained that a large group of runaways was expected. "With the Fugitive Slave Act in place, the marshal is required to help anyone attempting to return runaways. Once I've confirmed the information, you two go and talk to the marshal—repeat exactly what I tell you. He'll have no choice but to help with the capture and then turn the slaves over to you."

"What about you, Oliver? Ain't you gonna help?" Joseph asked.

Oliver shook his head and gazed heavenward. "You're as dumb as a fencepost, Joseph. If the law finds out I'm involved, I'll never be able to gain further information about runaways. Don't you remember how this is supposed to work? I find out when and where the runaways come through, while you and Enoch help with the capture and return them down South."

"I remember," Joseph said. "It just seems as though you're getting the easy part of the deal."

With a quick jab, Enoch poked Joseph in the ribs. "Shut up, Joseph. There wouldn't be no slaves for us to take back and sell if Oliver didn't get the information and pass it along to us."

"If you want out, I can find others who'd be more than happy to take your share of the money," Oliver threatened.

With an embarrassed grin, Joseph said, "Naw, I was just sporting with ya."

"I'll be meeting tonight to make certain the runaways are still coming through as planned. Unless you hear from me, go to the marshal tomorrow afternoon and tell them you've word of runaways coming through the next night. I won't be there helping you, but rest assured I'll be watching from nearby," he said before slapping several coins on the table. "Sleep here tonight. I want you where I can easily find you if there's a change in plans."

———

The two days passed slowly. Now, waiting in a clump of bushes only a short distance from Enoch, Joseph, and several constables, Oliver clenched his jaw and listened for the sound of the runaways approaching. Elinor had confirmed they would be taking this path tonight and, for the moment, he had nothing to do but wait, hidden from both the runaways and their hopeful captors.

Suddenly he heard the hushed whispers. He held his breath, hoping the others had heard the sounds. Slowly and quietly, he exhaled. The sounds were growing closer, nearing the place where Enoch and Joseph were hidden with their weapons. He watched as several runaways made their way past the men and then signaled for the others to move forward. As the group reconnected, Enoch and the other men made their move. Completely off guard and unable to respond to the threat, most of the group immediately capitulated to the men.

Only one of the large bucks attempted to run away, and he was quickly stopped when Joseph held out a branch and tripped him. The runaway tumbled forward, striking his head on an adjacent tree, rendering the man unconscious. Had he not witnessed the event, Oliver would have disbelieved the ease with which the slaves were detained. They were unarmed and offered little resistance, and none could produce papers proving they had been freed—so all were subject to the Fugitive Slave Act.

Oliver longed to applaud the efforts of his partners but forced himself to remain quiet. Their plans would quickly unravel should the marshal learn of his connection to Enoch and Joseph. Once the group had departed, he mounted his horse and headed back to his room at the Merrimack House.

"At least something went right," he murmured. He was still wrestling with thoughts of what to do about the Houston boy and the Negro woman. The woman had convinced him that leaving her alive, at least for the moment, was the better plan. He would only need to go back to the abandoned farm on rare occasion with Naomi caring for the child. He simply would drop off supplies and resecure the prison he'd formed for them.

"I'll know if you've so much as climbed the stairs," he'd told Naomi after sprinkling flour on each step. He'd promised to kill her swiftly if she attempted any type of escape—even hunt her down should she somehow be successful. The woman seemed amply convinced by his threats, and so far he'd not noticed any attempt on her part to flee her confinement. Of course, putting laudanum in the soup and tea he brought had only helped his effort.

"Still, I must do something soon. The weather is sure to turn any day." Oliver was still muttering to himself when the lights of Lowell welcomed him back. And then, as if the lights stimulated his mind's own brilliance, a plan began to form in his mind. A plan that just might work.

The following afternoon, after delivering additional food and assuring himself Naomi and Spencer remained secure, Oliver knocked on the door of Elinor's boardinghouse and waited several minutes until the door swung open.

"Oliver! I wasn't expecting you."

"I had deliveries nearby and thought perhaps you might be ready to relax a moment and have a cup of tea," he said. "You appear distressed. Is something amiss?"

Elinor tucked a straggling piece of hair behind one ear and gave him a bewildered look. "The runaways were due at their safe house last night. But they never arrived. I'm fearful they've been captured. Oh, where are my manners? I've left you standing in the doorway. Do come in and have a cup of tea."

Oliver followed her through the house and into the kitchen and watched as she deftly prepared a pot of tea and then poured two steaming cups. "Shall we remain here in the kitchen, or would you prefer to sit in the parlor?" he asked.

"The parlor. I spend far too much of my time in the kitchen."

"Let me carry those," he said, placing the cups on a nearby tray.

Elinor wearily settled on the divan and took a sip of tea. "I am terribly worried about those poor runaways. I haven't been able to keep my thoughts straight all day. Have you heard any word in your travels this morning?"

"Truthfully, that's why I stopped to see you. However, I didn't believe it prudent to discuss the matter on your doorstep. I wanted to assure myself we could talk in private."

Elinor placed her cup on the tray and focused her undivided attention upon him. "Please tell me what you've heard."

"The constables were called in to assist with capturing the runaways under the provisions of the Fugitive Slave Act. I believe all of the runaways were detained and are possibly being returned to their owners as we speak. It grieves me to bring such devastating news, but the moment I heard, my primary concern was for you. I knew if you'd received word of the capture, you would be distraught. I wanted to lend my comfort and assure you of my willingness to help in any way possible."

"You are so very kind to put aside your own business interests to come and offer your assistance. Do you believe your information is reliable?"

"Unfortunately, I believe it is. I'm certain word will soon begin to spread about town once the constables begin discussing the incident. They'll likely find the matter a topic of interest since I believe this is the first time they've been called into service under the Fugitive Slave Act," he added.

"A terrible law! However, for those of us committed to seeing slavery come to an end, it only heightens our resolve. Don't you agree?"

"Absolutely. And I'm pleased to see this entire debacle is only one setback. I'm certain our successes in gaining freedom for the runaways will far outnumber instances such as this one."

The clock in the hallway chimed, and Elinor jumped to her

feet as though the house were afire. "I must begin supper or the girls will return to an empty table."

"Already? It's but four o'clock. The girls will be working until seven, will they not?"

"You men have absolutely no idea how long it takes to prepare a decent meal. And believe me, these girls eat as much as any farmhand while expecting the food to far surpass the fare they had at home."

Oliver reluctantly followed her to the door. He had hoped to engage her in further conversation, yet he dared not push. He'd return in a few days when she had more information to share.

Elinor waited until she was certain Oliver had departed the vicinity before tying her bonnet into place and leaving the house. With a purposeful step, she quickly walked to town and marched onward until she reached the city hall.

"I'd like to speak to the city marshal. It's very important," she told the clerk who was sitting at an oversized wooden desk.

The man nodded and rose, walking into a room off to the left. He soon returned with a tall man whom Elinor immediately recognized from a number of antislavery meetings. She walked toward him.

"I am Elinor Brighton. May I speak with you privately?"

"Of course. Why don't you come into my office," Emil Baxter replied.

Elinor followed him until they reached his office, where he offered her a chair and then sat down at his desk. "Now, how may I be of assistance to you?"

"I've been told you are an active participant in the Underground Railroad. I know I've seen you at antislavery meetings in the past, but of course there are many who attend those meetings yet do not assist with the Underground," she said, her words tumbling out like bubbling water in a brook.

"And if I am?" he inquired evenly.

"There was a group of runaways due through Lowell last night.

They've not appeared at their station. I've been told by a reliable source that you were involved in their capture under the requirements of the Fugitive Slave Act. Is that information correct?"

Mr. Baxter stood and placed his palms on the desk, leaning forward across the wooden expanse until they were nearly nose to nose. His face had turned a deep shade of red. "Did your informant say where he received such information?"

"No. Why does it concern you where the information came from?"

"Because no one was told of the incident; the runaways were apprehended and left immediately with their civilian captors. Those of us who were required to assist vowed to remain silent regarding the entire matter. Consequently, I'm wondering how your friend acquired the information—unless he was somehow involved."

Elinor's mouth dropped open, dumbfounded by the announcement.

CHAPTER · *18*

ONCE AGAIN BORROWING Mr. Kittredge's horse, Oliver loaded his wagon and headed eagerly toward the outskirts of Lowell. He kept to the road until he was well out of town. Maintaining a watchful eye, he made certain no one was in sight when he turned off the dirt road and headed toward the abandoned farmhouse. His excitement continued to build as he neared the dilapidated barn. He jumped down and led the horse and wagon into the structure.

Enoch stepped out of the shadows, the shuffling sound of his feet causing Oliver to hesitate. "It's me, Oliver. I thought you was never gonna get here. Do you know how hard it's been keeping all these runaways quiet?"

"You won't be complaining when you get all that money we're going to make off of them. Just be thankful I told you to bring along shackles, or the two of you wouldn't have gotten any sleep last night. I've brought some supplies, and I have one more run-away for you to take along," he said. "I'll go and get her while you transfer the supplies to your wagon."

A short time later, Oliver returned. He held Naomi firmly by the arm as they neared Enoch. "You need to get her in shackles right away. She'll run if given any opportunity," he warned.

"She's sure enough a beauty, but she don't look like she could

227

run ten feet. She sickly?" Enoch asked.

"Once the laudanum fully wears off, you'll have your hands full. I've been keeping her drugged until I could get her back down South. She fought me every step here, so be warned. She's easy to look at but full of lies, so don't believe a word she says and don't trust her for a second."

"This one will be worth the trouble," Joseph said. "She'll fetch a handsome price."

Naomi glared at Oliver. "What you gonna do with da boy? His mama'll have ya strung up fo' what you done." She spat at his feet. "You ain' nothin' but trash."

Oliver raised his hand, but Enoch swiftly grabbed his wrist, halting the blow he had intended for the rebellious woman. "Don't mark her!" Enoch hollered.

Wresting his arm from Enoch's hold, Oliver stormed to the wagon. "Get this wagon loaded and get moving. The sooner you're out of here, the better!" he shouted in return.

"What ya gonna do with da boy?" Naomi screamed over and over again as the wagon rolled out of the barn.

"Gag her!" Oliver called out to Joseph and then relaxed when he could no longer hear Naomi's haunting voice.

He turned the horse back toward town, knowing the boy would sleep. He'd given him a dose of laudanum, but he must soon find a way to return young Spencer Houston. No telling what ill effects the ongoing medicine might be having on the boy.

———

Oliver slapped the reins, forcing his horse into a trot while straining forward in an attempt to see the group gathered outside the livery.

"What's going on?" he inquired as he jumped down from the wagon.

"We're organizing another search party. Some of the men have already departed. They'll be searching north and west of town. This group will divide and head south and east."

"I'd like to assist. Which group is heading south?" he asked.

The man nodded toward a group at the rear of the livery. Oliver made his way through the crowd and approached a constable standing with the group. "I'd like to help," he said.

"That group could use an extra hand," the constable said, pointing toward a smaller cluster of men.

Oliver hesitated, glancing toward the group. "I'm a shoe peddler and know more of the area to the south. I think I could be of greater assistance if I remain with this group."

The constable shrugged. "Whatever you want. Prager, why don't you go with that other group? Let's get going. We're wasting daylight."

Oliver silently rejoiced at his good fortune. These men had solved his problem. He couldn't have planned a more opportune solution to his dilemma. The men rode off toward the south, as Oliver followed behind with the wagon, obeying the constable's orders when he directed them to dismount and search one area and then the next.

When they finally neared the area where the abandoned farm was located, Oliver called out to the constable.

"What is it?" the constable asked as he rode back to the wagon.

"Long ago when I first came to Lowell, I got off the road hoping to travel cross-country and save some time. Instead, I managed to get lost. I remember coming upon an old abandoned farmhouse somewhere off in this area. I'm wondering if anyone has searched that old place."

The constable removed his hat and scratched his head. "I don't know, but it's worth looking at. Think you can find it again?"

"I'm not certain, but surely one of these men may recall the place," he replied evasively.

Using his stirrups for leverage, the chief constable lifted himself up off his saddle and surveyed the group. "Anyone remember seeing an old vacant farmhouse around these parts?"

Oliver listened to the murmurs among the men. Surely one of these men knew of it. He didn't want to be the one to direct the group to the farmstead.

"I think the old Ross place is about three miles off the road and maybe another two miles west," one of the men called out.

The lawman directed the group to fan out in the direction of the old farm. Oliver aligned himself with several other men who were moving in a direct line toward the house. He hoped they would have enough sense to check the root cellar without prompting. Although he wanted to assure himself the child was found, he didn't want to be overly involved in the rescue, lest he arouse suspicion.

When the group dismounted, Oliver remained in close proximity as the search began in earnest. He followed along, encouraging his group to begin at the house rather than the barn since the other men were nearing the outbuildings.

"You two go upstairs and check things out," the constable directed. "You two look around down here, and I'll go with Martin and see if there's a cellar anywhere nearby." The man pointed at Oliver. "If you get done down here before we do, check for a well or a springhouse. No telling how many places there might be to hide a child around here."

They'd barely begun their cursory search of the downstairs rooms when they heard a loud whoop. "We found him! We found him!" a male voice hollered before firing a shot into the air.

Oliver remained in the distance, permitting the others to gather around the child. "He looks dead. You sure he's still breathing?" one of the men asked.

"He's breathing, but it's shallow," Martin Simmons replied. "Best we get him to the doctor right away. Don't appear to be no broken bones. I ain't never seen the boy afore, so I don't know if he looks okay or not, but to my mind, I'd say he's mighty pale."

"Take him to his home. Someone with a fast horse ride for the doctor and have him meet us at the Houston place," the constable ordered. "The boy will do better with his mother close at hand."

———

Jasmine heard the commotion outside and jumped from the bed. Her heart raced as she went to the sill and threw open the window. "What's happened?" she called down.

The collection of men, which her husband was now joining, stopped in midsentence and looked up at her. She watched with wide eyes as one of the man placed a child in Nolan's arms. What she couldn't see was whether the child was still alive.

Without waiting for their reply, she pulled on her shawl and ran for the stairs. She reached the bottom step just as Nolan entered the room. "He's alive, but . . ."

"But what?" Jasmine cried, coming to the limp form of her child. "What's wrong with him?"

"He's been drugged. I can't rouse him."

"Oh, dear Lord, help us," she moaned, pushing back Spencer's hair. The child was filthy, but his shallow breathing reassured her. "Has someone sent for the doctor?"

Nolan nodded, meeting her eyes. "He should be here any time now."

"Let's get him cleaned up. The doctor might have a better time of caring for him."

"I'll take him to the kitchen," Nolan suggested. "We'll have plenty of hot water and such." He paused and leaned down to Jasmine. "It might be wise to see to yourself first. I can begin to clean Spencer, but I'd much rather my wife be gowned properly before all of Lowell ends up in our house."

Jasmine looked down at the nightgown and shawl she'd worn for several days. She was reluctant to leave Spencer's side. "But what if something—"

"He's home now, sweetheart. He's home."

Jasmine drank in Nolan's loving gaze. "Yes," she murmured. "He is home."

Hours later, Jasmine rocked a less lethargic Spencer in her arms, still unable to believe her son had been delivered safely to her care. Dr. Hartzfeld had quickly determined the boy had been drugged with laudanum or some other similar tonic in order to keep him asleep. He prescribed rest, nourishment, and fresh air, but with the steady stream of visitors during the first hours after his return, rest had been impossible. Realizing the celebration was taking too great a toll on the boy, Jasmine had taken him upstairs and remained secluded, permitting only Moses in the room. Their delightful reunion had brought tears to her eyes. She took pleasure in seeing their joy, yet the pain of knowing Naomi remained missing made their happiness a bittersweet sight.

Once most of the visitors had departed, Jasmine returned downstairs, with Moses on one side and Spencer on the other. She could hear Nolan's and Obadiah's voices and walked down the hallway toward the kitchen.

"Papa, Papa," Moses chanted. "See Spencie," he said, pointing toward his friend. "Spencie come home."

Jasmine could see the tears forming in Obadiah's eyes. "I'm so sorry, Obadiah," she said. "I was certain they would be found together."

He nodded. "Yessum. You know I's happy as can be dey found Spencer. Jes' hard," he said, his voice fading.

"You go rest. Moses is fine here with us. The boys don't want to be separated right now, anyway," she said.

"Thank you, ma'am. You be a good boy, Moses. I'll be back ta fetch ya after a bit," he said while walking out the back door.

Jasmine glanced at her husband. "I feel terrible. I wish there were something more we could do. The search party promised to go back again tomorrow and search for further clues, but the constable indicated there was nothing more to be found."

"All we can do is offer our encouragement. The marshal said no one is entitled to the reward we offered since the authorities were involved in finding Spencer. But I've told Obadiah I'm going to continue the offer in the hope that someone will come forward with information regarding Naomi." He pulled her close and kissed her forehead. "I believe Violet and McKinley are waiting to see you in the parlor, if you feel up to more visitors."

"I'm always happy to see my brother and Violet. Come along, boys. Uncle McKinley is here."

The boys walked down the hallway, their small feet clattering on the hardwood floors. "Unca Mac!" Spencer hollered, flinging himself into McKinley's arms. Moses followed, and the two boys soon were clamoring for McKinley's undivided attention.

Violet grinned and shook her head. "McKinley, why don't you and the boys go to the other room so Jasmine, Nolan, and I can visit for a few minutes."

"Better yet, why don't we go upstairs to your playroom? Uncle McKinley wants to find a special toy to play with," McKinley said, hoisting Moses under one arm and Spencer under the other.

Jasmine watched as the giggling boys ascended the steps, tucked under her brother's arms like two sacks of flour. "McKinley is so good with children," she said, returning her attention to Violet.

"He does have a way with them," Violet agreed. "I know how relieved you must be to have Spencer home with you again. You've been forced to bear a terrible burden. I'd wager you're ready to celebrate."

"No," she said with a faint smile, "I'd hardly say I want to celebrate. Don't misunderstand—I'm forever grateful for Spencer's return. Yet my heart breaks that we've not yet found Naomi. I never suspected that when we found Spencer we'd not find Naomi too. Poor Obadiah is grief-stricken. And Naomi was much like the sister I never had. We'd become very close since they came to live here. And with the boys being so near the same age, we had much in common."

Violet gasped, her eyes wide. "Jasmine Houston! How can you even think such things, much less say them aloud? Referring to Naomi as a sister—Naomi is a *Negro*. You best not talk like this around anyone else. People won't accept or understand such remarks. Working to free the slaves is one thing, but you must remember that even here, Negroes have their place."

"And what place is that, Violet? Naomi, Obadiah, and Moses are like family to me. I see them more often than I see most members of my family. Naomi has been a faithful friend to me and to Spencer. I owe her family more than anyone can imagine. Obadiah's mother cared for me all of my life—our roots are deep. I'll not compromise my love and concern for their family merely because it may offend someone else."

Violet stiffened slightly and cleared her throat. "Well, of course. I understand you are upset. You've been through trying circumstances," she said. "I'll go upstairs and see if McKinley is ready to return to Lowell. We're expected at my parents' home for supper."

"It was good to see my sister so happy," McKinley said as he climbed into the buggy and joined Violet.

"Beware she has some peculiar ideas."

McKinley put the horse in motion. "Such as?"

"She told me Naomi was like a sister to her. That the entire family had become quite important to her—that their roots ran deep."

McKinley frowned. "I'm not sure I understand."

"It seems odd that she would attach herself so completely to a Negro family. As I told her, it's one thing to free the slaves but an entirely different matter to embrace them into our society. They certainly won't be accepted there."

"No, I suppose not. I'm sure you misunderstood her intent, however. Jasmine's nurse was Obadiah's mother. I'm sure it causes Jasmine to hold special feelings for his family. That's probably all it is."

"But why?"

"Well, you must understand the role Mammy played in her life. In mine. We were raised by her—she provided for our every need. We seldom saw our parents during the day, except for meals when we were old enough to join the adults in the dining room."

"Truly?" Violet seemed completely amazed.

"We were raised in the nursery until we were old enough for school. Even then, it was Mammy who continued our care. Jasmine was even more sheltered and nurtured. Father sent us boys away to school for a time. Jasmine remained home and was tutored. Mammy couldn't read or write, but she would spend hours telling Jasmine stories from the Bible and talking about the life Jasmine would have when she grew up."

"How is it you know so much about what Jasmine discussed?"

McKinley smiled. "She told me. I guess I was one of the only ones who was still around to listen. We're only two years apart. David is five years older than Jasmine, and Samuel is eight. That's a long span of time when you're children. Jasmine and I have always listened to one another."

"Then perhaps you should arrange to have a talk with her about her attachment to the former slaves. The Northern states are sympathetic to the Negro plight, but the people of Lowell and Boston will hardly allow for them to intersperse themselves in our social circles."

"Unless, of course, they're holding a tray of refreshments," McKinley said under his breath.

"What was that?" Violet questioned.

He shook his head. It wasn't an easy topic no matter how they looked at it. "Nothing. Nothing of import." Abolitionists would press to see the slaves freed, but he wondered seriously how faithful they would be to concern themselves with housing, jobs, churches, and social interaction. Freeing them seemed a wondrous first step, McKinley thought, but it hardly constituted a resolution to the problems they would face afterward.

Nolan and Jasmine had just finished supper when Obadiah returned to the house, his eyes swollen and his gaze filled with a painful sadness.

"Come sit down," Nolan offered. "Have you eaten?"

Obadiah nodded. "I fixed me some supper a while ago."

The boys came into the dining room, hand in hand, and Moses climbed into his father's lap and planted a kiss on his cheek. Obadiah squeezed his son and then put Moses on the floor when he started twisting and squirming.

"Why don't you boys go play in the playroom while we adults talk in here," Jasmine suggested. They watched until the boys disappeared from sight.

"I spent all afternoon thinkin' 'bout Naomi and what I gotta do."

Nolan leaned over and patted Obadiah on the back. "Nothing has changed, Obadiah. We're going to continue searching for Naomi. She's bound to be found soon."

"Nossuh, I don' think so. I think Naomi's in da hands of slave traders who done took her back down South to sell her at auction or to any plantation owner who'd pay a good price. I gots to go after her. I don' know how or why any o' dis happened, but my insides are tellin' me she's gone. Spencer ain' said nothin', has he?"

"We haven't attempted to question him at all, and he's offered nothing," Nolan replied. "The doctor thought he was drugged to some extent the entire time they were gone. So even if he was awake, I doubt his thoughts would be clear."

"He's barely three years old, Obadiah. I don't think we could rely on anything he said," Jasmine added.

"Yo're right 'bout dat. 'Sides, I don' wanna upset him none, and that's fer sure, but I gotta go and find Naomi."

Nolan sat down opposite Obadiah and leaned forward, resting his forearms across his thighs. "Surely you realize that if you go south, you put yourself in extreme danger. Even if you have your papers with you, there are those who would disregard them—even take them from you and declare you a runaway."

"I understand all 'bout what could happen ta me. But I know I can' live with myself if I don' go lookin' for Naomi. Tell ya da truth, I don' know if I can live without her. I come here ta ask if you would look after Moses fer me. I can't take him wib me, and I don' know if I'll ever make it back. I'd like to leave knowin' Moses ain' never gonna end up like me and Naomi."

"Won't you wait at least another week?" Jasmine asked. "Give the constables additional time to search the area and then make your decision. If they don't find her in a week, then you go and we'll keep Moses for you."

Obadiah shook his head. "Dem constables ain' gonna spend any time lookin' for Naomi. Only reason they kept lookin dis long is 'cause of Spencer. Don' nobody care 'bout findin' no colored woman. I done made up my mind, Miz Jasmine. I got to leave now. Will ya see after Moses fer me?"

Jasmine glanced at Nolan, who gave an affirmative nod. "Of course we will, Obadiah. We'll make certain he's well cared for."

"I lef' all his clothes and toys at da house. Figured you could get 'em tomorrow. If I don' make it back, ya tell him 'bout his mama and papa and how much dey loved him," he said as he rose from his chair.

"You know we will, but I believe you'll both be back." Her voice caught in her throat. She dared say nothing further for fear she would break down in front of him.

He gave her a weary smile. She knew what he was thinking, but neither of them spoke as they bid each other good-bye.

Two hours later, Jasmine helped the boys into their nightshirts and tucked them into bed side by side. She helped the boys say their bedtime prayers and then turned to her son. "Good night, Spencer. I love you," she said, placing a kiss on his forehead.

"I wuv you, Mama."

She kissed Moses and said, "Good night, Moses. I love you."

"I luff you, Mama," Moses parroted.

She didn't correct him.

CHAPTER · *19*

Late February 1851

JASMINE BUTTONED her wool coat and pulled on her black kid gloves. "Are you certain you want to watch after Moses and Spencer? I fear it's too much for you now that you have that sweet baby of your own."

"The boys will na be a problem, and ya can report anything of interest when ya return. Ta be honest, I find the meetin's a wee bit dry and borin'," Kiara said with a smile. "The only reason I attend is ta lend any help I can regardin' the runaways. The rest of the idle chatter and talkin' does na hold my attention. Besides, it's terrible cold ta be takin' the wee babe outdoors for so long."

"You're right on both accounts. I don't think little Nevan should be subjected to this merciless weather, and much of the time, the meetings do turn into visiting fests more than anything else. But I do want to remain abreast of what's being accomplished with the runaways. Since we've had no success finding Naomi, I feel this work is the least I can do."

"Do na give up hope. Obadiah is a strong, determined man. He'll find Naomi."

"Or die trying. That's my greatest fear—that we'll never hear from either of them again and poor little Moses will be left without both of his parents. I feel I should have done more to convince Obadiah to remain here with us."

"There woulda been no convincin' him. We both know that, so ya just as well quit blamin' yarself for somethin' ya could na control. Ya best be goin' on ta the meetin' or ya'll be late."

"The boys should be asleep for at least another half hour. Moses usually awakens from his nap first. . . ."

Kiara waved, as though shooing a fly away from the table. "Go on with ya. I been tendin' these boys often enough I do na need ya tellin' me when they might be wakin' up from a nap."

Jasmine laughed. "I know! By now you're as accustomed to caring for them as I am. And I'm truly thankful Rogan hasn't objected to the time you spend helping me—especially since Naomi's disappearance."

"Rogan does na feel neglected in the least. Now be off with ya."

Waving a quick good-bye, Jasmine hurried down the front steps. "Hello, Paddy," she greeted. "I'm sorry to keep you waiting."

"Do na worry yarself, ma'am. It's pleased I am ta be takin' ya to yar meetin'," he said as she stepped into the awaiting carriage.

As the carriage rumbled toward town, Jasmine settled back into the cushioned leather seat and pulled her fur collar high around her neck. Tucking a wool blanket across her lap, she mused, "I'll never become accustomed to these cold Massachusetts winters."

Her teeth were chattering when the carriage came to a halt in front of the Cheever home. A gust of wind entered the carriage as Paddy pulled the door open, and she shivered as he assisted her down.

"Thank you, Paddy," she said.

"If ya do na mind, I was thinkin' to go and visit with Mr. Kittredge for a wee bit. He's been wantin' to hear more about the Shagyas," he said with pride. "I told him ya would na be opposed if he was wantin' to come and 'ave a look at them."

Jasmine smiled warmly at him. "You go and visit. I'll be at least two hours, perhaps longer. And you tell Mr. Kittredge we're proud of our Arabians, particularly our new Shagyas, and to come have a look whenever he'd like."

A strong north wind caused Paddy to pull his cap farther down onto his head. "Thank ya, ma'am. I'll be back and waitin' fer ya within two hours."

Jasmine bowed her head against the persistent wind and hurried up the front steps of the Cheever house. Before she could knock, the front door opened and a smiling Violet Cheever greeted her. "I'm so glad you've joined us, Jasmine. We've missed you at the last several meetings."

Jasmine stiffened slightly. She was still feeling a bit uncomfortable from Violet's upbraiding regarding her love of Naomi. "I was otherwise preoccupied during those meetings. You'll recall Spencer and Naomi were still missing."

"Of course. I wasn't passing judgment. I merely wanted you to know you'd been missed," Violet replied.

Jasmine relaxed as she felt a wave of heat emanating from the parlor fireplace. "I know you weren't being critical, Violet, but I do feel a tinge of guilt when I miss a meeting."

Violet squeezed Jasmine's hand and smiled. "Well, you certainly need not feel one smidgen of remorse. If anyone had reason for being absent, it was you."

Jasmine glanced about the room, with her gaze settling on Elinor Brighton. "I see Elinor is here. I'm glad she's continued to attend," Jasmine said as she slipped out of her fur-trimmed coat and hat. "I think I'll go and visit with her before the meeting begins."

Elinor was sitting alone on the settee, while the assembling women seemed to cluster into small groups that excluded her. "Elinor! How good to see you. May I sit with you, or is this seat spoken for?"

"I'd be most pleased to have you sit with me." Her eyes appeared to glimmer with expectancy as she pulled her skirts aside to make additional room on the divan.

Jasmine smiled and nodded to several ladies as she sat down. "How have you been, Elinor?"

"Very well, thank you. I've not had an opportunity to tell you how pleased I am that your son was returned unharmed. I know you must have suffered terribly while he was missing. Has there been any word about the woman who disappeared with him?"

Jasmine felt a lump rise in her throat. Elinor was the only person to have inquired about Naomi since her disappearance. There had been numerous questions and offers of assistance during Spencer's absence, but now it seemed as if Naomi had been forgotten. "How kind of you to ask. I wish I could report we've had some word. Unfortunately, that's not the case. In fact, her husband, Obadiah, has gone south in search of her. He believes her kidnapper has sold her into slavery. And as time goes on, I fear he is correct."

Elinor leaned closer. "We can pray he found her and they've attached themselves to the latest group of runaways scheduled to arrive in the next week."

"We also need to pray that things go more smoothly than with the last group coming through. How sad that after reaching Massachusetts, they would be apprehended and returned. With the passage of the Fugitive Slave Act, it appears there has been an increased interest in capturing the runaways. After all, with the local constables required now to assist in the detainment of escaped slaves, the lure of making money from the capture of fugitives has become appealing to a wider faction."

"I couldn't agree more," Violet said as she settled between them. "We must be particularly careful that there are no mishaps with this group of runaways while they're staying with Liam and Daughtie. Word has been received that they cannot be moved farther north for at least a week, perhaps longer."

"You mean they'll need to remain at the Donohues' for an extended period of time? That's very dangerous," Jasmine said.

Violet nodded vigorously, her carefully arranged curls wobbling back and forth. Jasmine stared in wonder, amazed the hairdo had remained intact. "Exactly! That's why there are only a limited number of people at our meeting today. The fewer people knowing details, the better—only those in charge of coordinating clothing, food, and shelter have been invited. We're certain those who are here can be trusted completely."

Elinor walked toward home, keeping a brisk pace. Mrs. Houston had offered her a carriage ride, but she'd declined. After all, the Houston home was in the opposite direction from the boardinghouse, and she didn't want to impose. That fact aside, she was accustomed to walking and, unlike most of her counterparts, found the cold air invigorating.

Her cheeks were ruddy and her fingers growing numb by the time she entered the boardinghouse. The sound of chattering girls wafted from the parlor into the hallway as Elinor untied her bonnet before removing her heavy wool cloak. Peeking into the vestibule mirror, she checked her hair and tucked a loose blond curl behind her ear before walking to the parlor door.

Luminous shadows of a man on one knee in front of several young ladies danced off the walls of the candlelit room. "Oliver! I didn't realize you were here."

Oliver swiveled, losing his balance and sprawling in a heap before the three girls seated on the divan. "Elinor! You startled me," he said while attempting to stand. By the time he had regained his composure, Oliver's complexion had turned nearly as ruddy as her own wind-stung cheeks.

The three girls continued to giggle, obviously enjoying the spectacle. Elinor bit her bottom lip and attempted to erase the picture of Oliver collapsed on the floor. Otherwise, she knew she would join the girls in their unmitigated amusement at the spectacle. "I apologize for surprising you. However, I didn't realize you were making deliveries this evening."

"I received my order earlier than expected and thought the girls would be pleased to receive their shoes," he said.

"And I'm certain they are."

"Oh yes," they said in unison. "Aren't mine lovely, Mrs. Brighton?" Abigail Morley lifted her skirt a few inches and revealed a pair of black calfskin slippers.

"Indeed, although they won't serve you well standing at the looms."

"They're not intended for work," Abigail replied. "I'll wear them when I attend the theater or a symposium."

"Or to church, when we can get her out of bed," Ardith Fordham added with a giggle.

"I go to church on the Sundays when I'm not feeling ill," Abigail defended.

Sarah giggled. "Strange how you feel fine every other day, but you always seem ill on Sunday mornings—and then have a rapid recovery when we arrive home."

Abigail glared at the other two girls. "I'm going up to my room."

"Aren't you coming to town with us? There's ample time before the shops close, and there was a sign at Whidden's Mercantile that a new shipment of gloves and lace arrived today."

Abigail hesitated on the stairway. "I'll change into my old shoes and be back down in a moment. Don't leave without me!"

Elinor watched as Oliver remained focused upon packing his wares, apparently ignoring the girls' repartee. Elinor neared his side. "Would you care for a cup of tea, or do you have other deliveries you must make?"

"A cup of tea would be very nice." He smiled broadly as he locked down the lid of his leather and wood case.

"The girls tell me you were gone to a meeting," Oliver commented as he followed her into the kitchen.

"Yes. The Ladies' Aid group was meeting at the Cheever home this evening."

Oliver watched quietly as she deftly prepared the tea and arranged a small plate of lemon cookies on a tray. "May I carry that into the parlor for you?"

She gave him a demure smile and nodded.

"I trust you had a fruitful meeting and there was a good attendance," he said while following her into the parlor with the tray.

"Oh yes. Thank you for inquiring. I was extremely pleased that Mrs. Houston was once again in attendance. What with the disappearance of Spencer and Naomi, she had been required to miss several of our meetings."

"You speak as though you know the family quite well," he mused.

"No, of course not, but the upheaval surrounding the disap-pearance of the woman and boy made most of us feel almost as if we knew them, don't you think?"

"Perhaps that's true. The entire issue was well discussed about town, and with so many people involved in searching for the boy, they likely developed a sense of association with the family."

"Precisely. At least I know that's how I was affected," Elinor said as she poured tea into his cup. "Mrs. Houston tells me her son appears to be doing quite well, although she worries some-what over the boy having nightmares since he returned home."

"I suppose that's to be expected. Did she tell you about them?"

"His nightmares?"

"Yes. Does he remember anything about them?"

She gave him a quizzical look. "I don't know—she didn't say. Why do you ask?"

He hesitated. "I've heard it helps to talk about bad dreams and nightmares if you can recall them. Personally, I never remember my dreams."

The front door opened, and noisy chatter was followed by sev-eral girls calling out their good-nights as they ran up the steps. "I did inquire about the black woman, Naomi, and whether there had been any further word regarding her whereabouts. Poor Mrs. Houston remains quite distraught over the woman's disappear-ance."

"Did she say if they had any new information?"

"No. Although Mrs. Houston now believes Naomi has been resold into slavery. Isn't that a sad thought? After suffering all those years as a slave and being set free—but then to be once again forced back into the misery of slavery! It seems more than a person ought to bear in one lifetime."

"Surely Mrs. Houston must have set aside talk of the woman and expressed joy over having her son returned. I would think she'd find her son's safety of greater importance than that of a col-ored woman."

Elinor felt compelled to defend Mrs. Houston—perhaps because of the harshness of Oliver's statement. "Well, of course, she is thrilled beyond words to have Spencer home, but the burden of such a loss lies heavy upon her heart. She tells me that Naomi's husband has gone in search of her. He left his son behind with Mr. and Mrs. Houston. I find the entire situation very sad."

"But having the Houston boy returned was of the greatest import," Oliver stressed.

"To Naomi's husband, I doubt that's correct, but I'm certain the Houstons would agree."

He sat up straighter and squared his shoulders. "Did Mrs. Houston happen to mention the important role I played in unearthing her son's whereabouts—the fact that I was the one who thought of the abandoned farm as a possible hiding place?"

Elinor stared at him for a moment. "No. At least she didn't mention it to me."

"I find it rather strange that with all her money, she didn't even offer me a pittance of a reward. After all, I doubt whether any of these locals would have ever thought of that old farmstead. The boy would still be missing if it weren't for me."

"Frankly I'm surprised you would expect a reward for doing a good deed. I believe the Houstons have continued to offer the reward for Naomi's safe return. I do hope she's able to be reunited with her child. That little boy must certainly be frightened and confused with both of his parents now gone from home."

"Seems they ought to be able to find her, what with her light color and beauty. She's one of the prettiest women, colored or white, I ever saw. She'd sure stand out in a crowd."

The hair bristled on the back of her neck. "And how would *you* know about Naomi?"

Oliver shrugged his shoulders. "I measured her for shoes when I was at the Houston horse farm. Mrs. Houston had me measure everyone for new shoes. Hard to believe, but she was buying expensive shoes for everyone on the place—even the coloreds."

Elinor sipped her tea and stared across the brim of her cup into Oliver Maxwell's eyes. An increasing sense of suspicion and uncertainty had begun to settle in her heart.

CHAPTER · 20

MCKINLEY WAINWRIGHT stood at the bottom of the stairs await-ing his sister and her husband. "Do hurry, Jasmine, or we'll be late," he called up the stairs.

"We'll be down as soon as we tell the boys good-night," she replied. "Have Paddy bring the carriage around."

McKinley shook his head in exasperation. "Paddy brought the carriage around fifteen minutes ago. He, too, is waiting."

A short time later, Jasmine descended the steps in a pale green gown that trailed the steps in small billowing waves resembling the morning tide lapping at the shoreline.

"As usual, you look lovely," McKinley said.

"She's always worth the wait, isn't she?" Nolan agreed while following her down the stairway.

McKinley nodded. "However, it's Violet who is to be the cen-ter of attention tonight. Let's hope your beauty this evening doesn't diminish her introduction into society."

Jasmine giggled. "Between the two of you, I could become quite vain. And I'm certain that if I were wearing jewels from head to toe, I couldn't surpass Violet's beauty in your eyes, McKinley."

Her brother winked and gave her a bright smile. "I do think she's quite captivating. Now that her parents are finally introducing her into society, I plan to ask Mr. Cheever's permission to court her."

Nolan gave his brother-in-law a fond slap on the back. "And what do you call these occasional rides in the country and visits to her home, if not courting?"

"Our outings have been simply as friends. I now wish to seek proper permission to come calling. My hope is that there won't be others standing in line to vie for her attention. I do worry that Mr. Cheever may have preconceived ideas about whom he would like his daughter to marry."

Jasmine worked her fingers into a pair of lace gloves before moving toward the door. "Arranged marriages seem to be considered rather old-fashioned here in the North. Although I have heard of one or two, most families do not seem to be inclined to marry their children off in such a fashion as we did in the South."

"I see nothing wrong in arranging marriages for the benefit of the family," McKinley admitted, then quickly added, "but only if true love can be found at the same time."

"Well, Mr. and Mrs. Cheever seem to be of an open mind— less than traditional I would think. I'd be surprised if he forced his daughter into a loveless marriage. After all, he married a woman for whom he had deep affection. Certainly he should understand the value of that concept."

"Let's hope you're correct," McKinley replied.

"And let's hope Spencer and Moses go to sleep and don't give Kiara a difficult time," Jasmine remarked. "I worry she may have her hands full with both of them as well as little Nevan." She looked back up the stairs and hesitated.

Nolan reached out and touched her arm. "I know you're still nervous about leaving the house and the boys, but Rogan will soon be here, and the other servants won't allow a soul to cross the threshold unless they are friend or family."

McKinley nodded. " 'Twould be unlikely for such an episode to happen more than once in a person's lifetime. I believe your troubles are behind you, sister."

"I pray you are right."

Nolan assisted his wife into the carriage and then sat down beside her. "Now stop fretting. Kiara won't be alone for long. Rogan was to be done with his work early today and told me he'd promised to come over to the house and lend her a hand with the children. To be honest, I doubt she needs any help. The boys both follow her instructions more quickly than they do ours."

"Unfortunately, I believe you may be right on that account."

McKinley laughed. "But then didn't we always obey Mammy better than Mother or Father?"

Jasmine looked at him oddly. "I never thought of it, actually. It's true that Kiara has been instrumental in helping me to raise Spencer, and she's spent a good deal of time with Moses. But certainly she hasn't been with them as closely as Mammy was with us. Especially with me."

"I was telling Violet about our childhood a time back. She finds it all fascinating."

"She no doubt struggles to understand our ways. Or perhaps I should say, our parents' ways," Jasmine admitted. "She was none too keen on my friendship and love for Naomi."

"But why?" Nolan asked.

"She thought it inappropriate. She said she could firmly get behind the cause of freeing the slaves, but not of associating with them," Jasmine recalled.

"I have to admit, sister, such thoughts reflect my own. Not because I think the black man or woman to be less than valuable. But what would we have in common? People in social classes come together as such because they value the same things, they work or live in similar fashion. Can you possibly see a former field hand wearing tails and sipping champagne?"

"But we were taught how to conduct ourselves in such situations. In the nursery, I was shown the proper etiquette for holding teas. I learned to dance because someone took the time to teach me the steps," Jasmine said, her tone intense.

McKinley recognized something in her manner that suggested he move cautiously. "I'm uncertain whom you would find with a willing heart to teach such things. The Negro isn't going to be allowed in regular schools. Their mannerisms are frightening to most white people."

"It's fear born out of ignorance and nothing more," Jasmine protested. "If people would learn to look beyond their fears, they might find their views drastically changed."

Elinor hesitated before entering the walkway to the Cheever home. She felt strangely out of place attending Violet Cheever's coming-out party. Yet Lilly Cheever had insisted, citing the fact that she and Mr. Cheever did not stand upon social traditions— along with the fact that much of her husband's success in the mills had depended upon Elinor's uncle's and brother's abilities making calicos and implementing new technology and patterns for the mills. And so Elinor had diffidently agreed to attend, though now she wondered why she had done so. Had her brother Taylor and his wife, Bella, not been in Scotland, they would have accompanied her. But when word of the unexpected death of their eldest sister, Beatrice, had arrived, Taylor and Bella immediately sailed for Scotland in order to lend their assistance to the family.

The Houston carriage came to a halt a short distance beyond where Elinor stood outside the house. "Good evening, Elinor," Jasmine greeted as she stepped down from the carriage. "Won't you join us?"

Elinor issued a silent prayer of thanks. At least she'd not have to enter the party alone. "Yes, thank you. I feel a bit awkward without Taylor and Bella. I usually attend social functions with them."

"I understand they're visiting in Scotland," Jasmine said.

"Yes, with my sister's family. I don't expect them back for another six weeks."

"Then you must permit us the pleasure of escorting you this evening," Nolan said.

"Thank you. The party promises to be quite an event, don't you think?"

McKinley's lips turned up in a wide grin. "I heartily agree."

Jasmine took Elinor by the arm and leaned close. "He's hoping Miss Cheever will grant him exclusive courting privileges."

Elinor smiled at McKinley as they walked up the steps. "I wish you good fortune with Miss Cheever. She appears to be a fine young lady."

"Thank you, Mrs. Brighton," McKinley said while opening the door.

The music from the small orchestra floated into the entryway as Matthew and Lilly Cheever stood greeting their guests. Once properly introduced, Elinor made her way into the room and was planning to find a corner in which to quietly watch the festivities. Jasmine, however, remained close by her side, taking her by the hand as she and Nolan moved among the guests.

"I don't believe we've met these folks," Jasmine said to her husband as they approached a small cluster of men and women gathered near the double doors that led into the garden.

One of the gentlemen turned in their direction, and Nolan drew closer, extending his hand. "Nolan Houston and my wife, Jasmine, and Mrs. Elinor Brighton," he said.

"John and Jenny Riddell and my sons, Charles and Luther. Mr. Cheever graciously extended an invitation to our family. We're in Lowell planning several investment opportunities."

"Lowell is an excellent community in which to place your trust—and your money," Nolan said with a grin.

"Are you planning to invest in the mills?" Jasmine inquired.

"Possibly. However, my sons are more interested in the patent medicine business. They believe they'll encounter fewer problems dealing in a smaller enterprise rather than working through the layers of organization developed by the Boston Associates in their conglomerate."

"I'm not certain I agree with your thinking," Nolan said. "I believe you'll find James Ayer rather unwilling to permit you entry into his growing pharmaceutical venture."

Luther moved to Nolan's side and tilted his head closer. "If he doesn't desire a partner, then we may be inclined to compete with him."

"I do hope you have a new and inventive product in mind, as I don't believe you'll be able to compete with his Cherry Pectoral or Cathartic Pills. I believe he has captured the market."

"If my research serves me, Ayer began an apprenticeship with a gentleman by the name of Robbins not so many years ago," Luther said. "I'm certain he didn't know much about the pharmaceutical business at the time he began his apprenticeship. Ayer had seen a need for specific medicinal products and then developed a product to fill that particular void. He is obviously an astute businessman, but so are we."

"Then why not discover another need within society and fill that void, rather than merely choosing to expand upon the pharmaceutical business?" Jasmine inquired.

Elinor glanced toward Nolan, who was giving his wife a look of obvious admiration.

"As you've possibly surmised, my wife is an astute businesswoman, as well as an astonishing wife and mother," Nolan praised.

"Truly? And what void did *you* fill in the business world, Mrs. Houston?" Luther asked with a smirk.

"Are you familiar with Arabian horses, Mr. Riddell?"

"I've seen one or two. They're fine-looking animals, but quite expensive."

"Indeed! However, there is an exclusive market for Arabians in this country. I fill that void with my Arabians, and now we've expanded and are raising Shagyas, an even more exclusive breed of Arabian."

Luther Riddell gave a hearty laugh. "Pray tell, what is a Shagya?"

"It's an Arabian breed that was developed at the military stud farms of the Austro-Hungarian monarchy. The Shagya combines the advantages of a Bedouin Arabian with the requirements of a modern riding or carriage horse. This breed has inborn friendliness toward humans. President Taylor was quite interested in the Shagyas and had planned to visit our horse farm. His untimely death prevented the visit, but he had a true love for Arabians and was very enthusiastic about the breed."

"I must say that if you had the interest of a horseman such as President Taylor, you most certainly must be raising some exceptional horseflesh," John said.

"Thank you, Mr. Riddell. If you'll excuse us, I believe my brother desires to speak with me."

As they made their way across the room, Jasmine waved at Daughtie and Liam Donohue, then turned toward Elinor. "You did receive word the group of runaways we're awaiting won't be arriving as expected, didn't you?"

"No, I wasn't notified. Are you certain?"

Jasmine nodded. "Violet said she'd send word to everyone, but I fear with all of the preparations for her party, she may have forgotten any number of people. Now that I realize she failed to send word to you, I believe I'll check with the others, but first I must talk to McKinley."

"If you'll excuse me, I believe I'll go out to the garden for some fresh air," Elinor said.

"Outdoors? I fear you may be a little chilly," Jasmine said.

"I'll be fine."

Being careful to avoid the couples moving toward the portion of the room designated for dancing, Elinor wended her way through the crowd. She walked out the doors into the cool night air and immediately began briskly rubbing her arms. The garden appeared eerily forsaken. Swiping dead leaves from a nearby bench, Elinor sat down and contemplated the information Jasmine had just divulged, wondering what had occurred to cause the runaways' delay. Likely there had been a fear their plans had been compromised.

"Probably some unsuspecting person making idle conversation. Someone exactly like me," Elinor whispered, thinking of Oliver Maxwell and his suspicious behavior. She fervently hoped he would disprove her growing concerns.

A breeze cut through the leafless branches. She shivered and rose to her feet, pacing back and forth in front of the bench, hoping that the movement would warm her. Oliver's recent remarks had given her pause, especially his harsh statements regarding

Naomi and the description of her appearance. Oh yes, he'd given her an explanation, yet she increasingly doubted Oliver's word. Even if he'd spoken the truth about measuring Naomi for shoes, how had he known about the capture of the last group of runaways? Even though she'd felt an urging to be honest with the marshal, she'd instead given him ambiguous replies to his many questions. Now she needed to know exactly what role Oliver Maxwell may have played in all of these incidents.

"And there's only one way to be certain. Prepare yourself to be tested, Oliver," she murmured, hoping that he would soon return from New Hampshire.

The girls gathered around the dining table, their hunger evident as they forked thick slices of ham onto their plates and ladled creamy gravy over heaping mounds of boiled potatoes. "Pass the apple butter," Abigail requested.

Mary handed the apple butter to Sarah, who passed it down the line of girls until it reached Abigail. "I heard one of the girls say that McKinley Wainwright received permission to court Violet Cheever at her coming-out party last night. Looks like he's going to marry himself right into a permanent position with the mills."

"There are going to be a lot of girls sorry to hear your news," Sarah said. "More than a few had their hopes set upon winning the heart of Mr. Wainwright."

"Obviously he has his sights set upon someone who can ensure him a place within the hierarchy of the wondrous Boston Associates," Abigail said.

Elinor refilled a bowl of green beans and placed them on the table with a thud. "I believe you girls are being unfair. You're judging a person and a situation about which you have no personal knowledge."

"Mrs. Brighton is correct on that account: we really don't have reliable information. Perhaps you'd be willing to share *your* personal knowledge with us since you had the privilege of attending the party last evening," Abigail replied with a smug grin.

"I'll respond by saying only that McKinley Wainwright is an upstanding young man who doesn't need to rely upon anyone else in order to succeed in life. From all that I have observed, his interest in Violet Cheever is based upon genuine affection, nothing else. But I certainly do not consider myself an authority on the topic."

"But he has asked and received permission to court her, hasn't he?" Abigail insisted.

"Yes. And they do make a striking couple," Elinor replied before turning on her heel and returning to the kitchen.

Once she'd completed the supper dishes and satisfied herself the kitchen was in order, Elinor retrieved her needlework and joined several of the girls in the parlor. She knew they'd soon leave for an evening stroll into town or go up to their rooms to write letters and visit. She'd just begun her stitching when a knock sounded at the front door. Moments later, Sarah escorted Oliver into the parlor.

"Since Mr. Maxwell isn't carrying his case, it appears as if he's come to call on you, Mrs. Brighton," Sarah announced.

Elinor felt the heat rise in her cheeks. "Do come in and join us, Oliver."

Oliver sauntered into the room but remained standing. "I thought perhaps we could take a stroll, where we could be afforded a bit more privacy."

Several of the girls covered their mouths and snickered while they exchanged gleeful glances, as though they'd been privy to a valuable tidbit of gossip.

Tucking her needlework into the sewing basket beside her chair, Elinor smiled. "Yes, of course. A walk sounds delightful, but I need to speak to you in private before we leave."

Oliver dutifully followed her into the dining room. "Why all the secrecy?"

"I didn't want any of the girls to overhear, but I received word only a short time ago that the runaways we weren't expecting until next week will be arriving by midnight tonight. I was asked to

255

gather additional supplies from town since we weren't entirely prepared for them just yet."

Grasping her arm, Oliver looked straight into her eyes. "Are
you saying they will be here tonight?"

"Yes! That's why I was delighted when you mentioned going
for a walk. I can use your help carrying my purchases. I was concerned about how I would get the items home and then, thankfully, you arrived."

"But I won't be able to assist you," he said beginning to edge
away from her.

"Why not? You asked me to go for a walk . . . I don't understand."

"I've just remembered something that requires my immediate
attention."

"Surely it can wait," she said, taking hold of his arm.

He pulled away from her and turned toward the door. "I must
go now."

Elinor watched as he all but ran from the house. She leaned
against the dining room table, weak from the realization that Oliver Maxwell was her enemy. He stood for everything she despised,
yet she had helped him succeed. Her loose tongue had given him
enough information to capture the last group of escaped slaves.
Cupping a trembling hand over her mouth, Elinor collapsed onto
the wooden chair and sobbed.

CHAPTER · *21*

WITHOUT TAKING TIME to apologize for his rude behavior, Oliver pushed his way through the small groups of mill girls and evening shoppers that unwittingly blocked his path. He must get to the livery immediately. Gone were the days when he had his strawberry roan at his immediate disposal. Instead, he now relied upon the use of Mr. Kittredge's livery horses while he continued to maintain his horse had been stolen when Spencer Houston and Naomi were abducted.

He had hoped the Houstons would give him a reward or, at the very least, a fine horse to replace his roan. They'd done neither, but after selling the group of runaways Enoch and Joseph would capture this night, he promised himself the ownership of a well-bred horse.

"Since they didn't appreciate my information enough to give me one of their horses, perhaps I can convince them at least to give me a good deal on one of those fine Arabians," he mused.

"You talking to me? 'Cause if you are, I didn't hear what you were saying."

Jumping back a step, Oliver turned and saw Mr. Kittredge bent forward, examining the hoof of a fine-looking sorrel. "You startled me."

"Did I now? I'd think you'd be expecting to see me in this place since I own it," Kittredge said with a hearty laugh. "You needing a horse?"

"Yes. I won't be taking my wagon."

Kittredge nodded. "Want to take this sorrel out and give him some exercise? I'm boarding him for a few weeks. Thought I'd get him out earlier today, but I got too busy. Won't charge you for the use if you give him a good run."

"Be glad to help you out," Oliver replied. He smiled at his good fortune and waited as Kittredge deftly saddled the animal.

He mounted the horse and kept the animal at a trot until they reached the outskirts of town. With more force than he'd intended, Oliver dug his heels into the horse's flesh and sent the animal into a gallop. He didn't slow the horse until they neared the overgrown path leading to the abandoned farm, where he hoped Enoch and Joseph were merely doing as he said—remaining well hidden. However, if the two of them hadn't yet returned, all would be lost—at least with this group of runaways. The thought of such a monetary loss was something Oliver didn't want to consider.

To the untrained eye, the farmstead appeared deserted. Oliver squinted and gazed toward the barn. Stars twinkled, and a sliver of moonlight shone brightly from the cloudless sky to reveal an unhitched wagon alongside the barn. His horse neighed, and Oliver drew back on the reins as Joseph lifted himself from the wagon bed and aimed his weapon directly at Oliver.

"Put that thing down before you kill me, Joseph!" Oliver called. "What's that wagon doing outside the barn?"

Joseph jumped down from the wagon as Oliver approached on horseback. "I'm using it to keep watch. Appears it worked, 'cause I got the drop on you."

Annoyed by his smug attitude, Oliver ignored his comment and rode into the barn. "Where's Enoch?" he hollered.

"Behind you," Enoch replied. "Whadda'ya think of our setup to stop intruders?"

Oliver dismounted and handed the reins of the horse to

Joseph. "I think you'd be much wiser to do as I told you—remain hidden, and if anyone approaches, stay out of sight until you're certain they're gone. Instead, you put that wagon out there in plain sight, and Joseph draws his weapon on anyone riding onto the property. Don't you two see how that might cause suspicion? Sometimes I wonder why I ever brought the two of you in on this deal."

Enoch lit the stub of a candle, which illuminated the small area of the barn where they stood. "You needed us, that's why," he said simply. "You can rant and rave at us all you want, but you know we've done a good job. We got all them darkies sold at a good price and got back up here in less time than you ever figured."

"Besides, *we're* the ones taking all the risk and doing the hard part of this job. Ain't no reason for *you* to be complaining about nothin'," Joseph remarked as he pulled a small knife from his pocket and began using the blade to clean his fingernails.

"You two had best remember that the information about the runaways comes from *me*. Without me, you've got nothing but an empty wagon. Speaking of the good price you got for that bunch, how about turning over my share right now."

Enoch walked across the barn while holding the stubby candle in one hand. Oliver watched as he entered one of the ramshackle stalls and pulled a leather pouch from his saddlebag.

"Your share," Enoch growled, tossing the bag at Oliver.

Oliver dumped the contents onto the dirt floor and began counting. "Doesn't appear you got such a good price if this is my half."

"Half?" Joseph yelled, jumping to his feet. "You're lucky we're giving you a third. What makes you think you're entitled to half?"

Oliver turned to Enoch. "We agreed I'd get half and the two of you would split the other half, didn't we, Enoch?"

Enoch nodded. "We did. But our agreement was unfair and you know it. I guess you can take what we're offering or nothing at all."

"And what if I turned the two of you in to the marshal?"

"You ain't gonna do that—we know it and so do you. Greed

ain't a pretty thing, Oliver. You need to remember there's two of us, and we plan to stick together," Joseph said in a menacing tone.

Oliver gathered the money and shoved it back into the pouch. "Fine. We'll go with an equal split, but you two had best not cheat me. And remember, without my information, there's no more money for either of you. Now get the horses hitched. There's another group coming through tonight."

"Tonight? I thought they wasn't due for three more days," Joseph said.

"The plans changed. I got word they're coming through tonight."

"When and where?" Enoch asked.

"About five miles down the road. They should come through around midnight, but we need to get hidden well before they arrive."

"You shoulda told us when you first got here instead of wasting time talking and worrying about your money," Joseph said.

"Is that my roan you're using?" Oliver asked Enoch while ignoring Joseph's condemnation.

"Yep. Sure is."

Oliver bristled at his casual reply. "I told you to board him down south and purchase another horse. Plenty of folks around here recognize that horse."

"We ain't got time to argue about it now," Joseph snarled. "We best head out or them darkies are gonna be long gone 'fore we get there."

———

Once Oliver departed, Elinor donned her bonnet and woolen cape. She truly couldn't afford the expense of a carriage but walking to the Donohues' was out of the question. She hurried toward town. If good fortune was with her, she'd locate a carriage for hire near the train depot. She drew closer to the Merrimack House and watched as several passengers stepped out of a carriage and entered the hotel. Boldly, she approached the driver as he unloaded a satchel.

"I need to hire a carriage immediately," she said.

"Soon as I unload one more trunk, I can take ya."

Elinor watched, pacing back and forth as the driver wielded the trunk onto his shoulder and carried it inside the hotel.

"Where to?" he asked as he returned moments later.

"The Liam Donohue residence."

The driver scratched his head and gazed heavenward. "Donohue," he muttered.

"The property adjoining the Houston horse farm."

"Oh! Right you are. I'll have you there in no time." The driver slapped the reins and urged the horses into a gallop that jolted Elinor's head against the back of the seat.

The driver was good to his word. He drew the team to a halt in front of the Donohue residence. After handing her down from the buggy, she rushed up the steps and rapped on the door several times before banging the metal door knocker.

"I'm comin'! I'm comin'!" Liam shouted before pulling open the door.

"Mr. Donohue, I must talk to you!" Elinor exclaimed.

"Ya need na shout, lass. I'm right here in front of ya," he said with a grin. "Come on in and sit ya down in the parlor. I'll fetch me wife."

Daughtie was already midway down the hall. "What is it, Liam?" she asked while wiping her hands on a checked cotton dishtowel.

"Mrs. Brighton's needin' to have a word with us."

The couple sat down and gave her their full attention, Liam leaning forward like a cat ready to pounce.

"I've something terrible to tell you," Elinor said, her tears already beginning to flow.

"Ya do na need ta be weepin', lass. Hard it is to be understandin' a cryin' woman."

Daughtie poked him in the side and then offered Elinor a handkerchief. "Take your time, Elinor. Breathe deeply. I'm certain nothing has happened that can't be set aright."

Her tone was soft and kind, and Elinor responded with a

feeble smile. "You're wrong on that account. You see, I'm responsible for the capture of the last group of escaped slaves coming through."

Liam gave her a patronizing smile. "I do na think a wee lass like yarself was able to accomplish that feat."

"No, but I gave information to the man who was responsible."

"Ya *what*?" Liam shouted. "Why would ya do such a thing?"

Elinor shrank back in her chair. "It wasn't intentional. I thought he could be trusted—that he was working for the cause, but I'm now certain he's the one responsible for their abduction. I, however, am equally at fault, for had I not told him, those poor runaways would now be free."

"Are ya willin' to tell us the name of this man?"

"Oliver Maxwell," she whispered.

"The shoe peddler?" Daughtie asked.

Elinor nodded and then explained how she had unwittingly taken Oliver into her confidence, watching Liam's and Daughtie's changing expressions as they listened intently. "Because I wasn't certain of his involvement, I set a trap for Oliver this evening," she said as she finished her sad confession.

"Wha' kind of trap?" Liam asked.

"I told him another group of runaways was expected tonight, that they would be passing through the same route as the first group. If he's guilty as I suspect, he's already out there waiting for them."

"Yet he may very well be at home snug in his bed," Daughtie remarked.

"Aye. I can see there's some coincidences tha' make ya wonder if the man is true, but we need ta be findin' out if he's the black heart ya believe him ta be," Liam said. "If this shoe peddler is the culprit, then 'tis true ya've made a terrible error in judgment."

Daughtie gave Elinor an encouraging smile. "Let's hope he's not the guilty party."

"But I'm certain he is! Can't you see the depth of my transgressions?"

" 'Tis true that if ya're right, many a person has suffered fer yar error—and will suffer for a long time ta come. But ya can na change things. Ya've done right by comin' ta me and tryin' to set things aright. Thar's no doubt we all make mistakes in judgment."

"But my mistake is greater than those made by others. All those slaves who were tasting freedom are now back in captivity, likely suffering from an overseer's whip—all on my account," Elinor moaned.

"If we find that what ya've told us is true, it's the shoe peddler that's ta blame," Liam said. "I'm na discountin' the fact that ya had a loose tongue, but yar heart was right. Ya were tryin' ta get shoes for the runaways, and that was an admirable thing."

"I fear the depth of my transgression is as deep as Oliver's," Elinor said as she pulled a handkerchief from her pocket.

"Ya judge yarself too harshly, lass. Thar's nothing tha' can na be forgiven by God."

"Liam's right. There's no doubt you made a mistake, Elinor, but you didn't intentionally set out to harm the runaways or aid in their capture. Oliver preyed upon you, realizing you were a member of the antislavery movement who might divulge important information. Unfortunately, he was correct. But God will forgive you if you'll but ask."

"I don't know if I can forgive myself," Elinor said, tears beginning to once again roll down her cheeks.

Liam jumped to his feet. "I'm goin' for Rogan. We'll ride out to the narrows and see if thar's any sign of Oliver."

Daughtie stood and grasped her husband's arm. "Promise me you'll be careful. If there's anyone out there, I doubt they'll give in without a fight."

Elinor watched as Liam bid his wife good-bye, now wondering if coming to Liam with the information was prudent. If anything happened to Liam Donohue or Rogan Sheehan, she'd never be able to live with herself.

"I should go," Elinor said. "I paid the driver to wait, and I need to be back to the house before ten."

Daughtie walked with her to the carriage. "Pray, Elinor. Pray hard."

Elinor nodded. It seemed their only hope.

Liam saddled his horse and rode the short distance to the Houston farm, entering through the second set of gates leading directly to the house Jasmine Houston had had built as a wedding gift for Rogan and Kiara. Before he could dismount, the front door opened and Rogan stood in the doorway, holding a lamp in one hand and a shotgun in the other.

"Who's there?" he called out.

"It's Liam. I do na have time to explain. I need ya ta come with me. Bring your weapon and saddle your horse as quickly as ya can. Do na permit Paddy ta come along."

Kiara stepped forward and took the lamp from Rogan. "What is it, Liam?"

"Do na worry, lass. We should be back afore mornin'. A few problems with some runaways. Keep Paddy with ya. I do na want him followin' after us like he's done afore."

"Ya're riding inta danger, are ya?"

"Nothin' we can na handle."

Kiara gave Liam a faint smile. "Do na let anything happen to me 'usband."

"Ya have me word, lass."

Rogan clearly trusted Liam's instincts and followed his friend's lead as they rode in earnest through the countryside. Liam slowed his horse as they drew closer to the narrows and then signaled for Rogan to dismount.

"We'll leave the horses here and walk the rest of the way," Liam said, keeping his voice low.

"Are ya goin' ta tell me what's goin' on?" Rogan asked as they settled in a clump of bushes near the narrow path that cut between two hills.

"I'm na certain it's going ta work, but Elinor Brighton has laid a trap. She thinks the shoe peddler and some others are involved in capturing the runaways. She told him thar's a group moving through tonight. She believes we'll find him out here waitin' on 'em," Liam whispered.

They sat waiting, hoping they'd hear something—anything. Liam's legs began to cramp, and Rogan suggested they leave.

Liam grasped Rogan's arm and strained forward. "Listen!"

The voices grew louder and the two men sat quietly, eavesdropping on the conversation taking place nearby.

"We've moved places three times now, Oliver. Looks to me like you got a bad piece of information."

"Keep your voice down," Oliver warned in a hoarse whisper.

"Ain't no need. If them runaways was coming, they'd already be through here by now," Joseph snarled. "The last ones was here by eleven o'clock. It's way after midnight by now. I'm cold and tired. Let's get outta here."

"I was right last time, wasn't I? And you ended up with plenty of money, didn't you? The two of you need to be patient. Maybe something happened along the way to slow them down."

"Yeah. And maybe they already been captured—if there were any headed this way to begin with. Just because you was right last time, that don't mean you got good information this time. Come on, Enoch. Let's go. You know they ain't coming tonight."

"He's right, Oliver. We're leaving. You wait if you want, but we're heading back to the barn."

Oliver refused to relent, remaining in place while Enoch and Joseph rode off. He didn't intend to wait long—there would be little he could do by himself to stop the group of runaways if they did happen along. However, he wasn't going to concede to Joseph's idea. They'd been gone only a short time when Oliver heard the brush rustling behind him.

"Who's there? You decide maybe I was right and come back, Enoch? Joseph?"

"Yar friends are gone, Mr. Maxwell. But Rogan and me, we been sittin' nearby, and we heard every word the three of ya was sayin'. Seems ya got yarself involved in capturin' runaways," Liam said.

"You can't prove a thing. Besides, *you're* the ones operating outside the law—helping runaways. What *I'm* doing is perfectly within the law. I even have the right to request the marshal's assistance if need be. Something called the Fugitive Slave Act. Surely you don't dispute I'm in the right."

"You're not returning those slaves to their rightful owners," Rogan countered. "You're selling them to the highest bidder, and that's not legal."

Oliver gave him a brash grin. "Again, you have no proof of your allegations. You overheard my conversation. Do you believe the word of two Irishmen is going to be taken over my word and that of my two men when we insist every attempt was made to find the rightful owners before offering the slaves at market?"

Liam hesitated. "You weren't operatin' under the Fugitive Slave Act when ya rode off with Spencer Houston and Naomi."

"Maybe I wasn't, but nothing that's been said here tonight frightens me, nor do the two of you. There's no way you can prove anything we've talked about."

"So I don't frighten ya?" Liam asked, grabbing Oliver by the collar and slamming him against a tree. "When ya're countin' off the things that can na be proved, ya might remember thar's no way ya can prove it was *me* that beat that smugness outta ya on this night, is thar?"

Oliver knew he must appear in control or all would be lost. "Put me down. You need to remember that if you ever want to see that darky again, you best not lay a hand on me."

"Yar word is worthless. We do na believe a thing ya say, and I figure I may as well have myself a little satisfaction. If takin' it out of yar hide is the only thing I can get, then so be it," Liam seethed, balling his fist.

"Wait!" Oliver shouted, attempting to stave off a blow by thrusting his arm forward. "If you'll let me leave and go about my business, I'll send word to have Naomi released and sent back home." He hurried on when Liam's arm cocked even higher. "I'll even pay to have her transported—and I'll leave Lowell and give you my word I'll not return. You know there's no choice—let's do what's best for all of us."

"Ya best remember the promises ya've made here this night.

Be a man and keep yar word, or ya'll find out what fightin' Irishmen look like," Liam warned.

Without a moment's hesitation, Oliver mounted his horse and rode off. He glanced over his shoulder and breathed a sigh of relief. Apparently, he could now consider himself a capable actor, for those simple-minded Irishmen had actually believed he was going to return Naomi. The fools!

"I can na believe you let him ride off," Rogan said as Oliver disappeared into the darkness. "We should follow 'im. Naomi might still be hidden in these parts."

"We have a group of runaways comin' through in a few days, and they're going to need us. I think he was tellin' the truth—I figure she's down South, and we can na risk the lives of the group coming through in a few days by leavin' and followin' Maxwell."

Rogan leaned against the trunk of a large birch and shook his head. "I know what ya're saying is right, but I do na like it. What if that man knows where Naomi is and we let 'im walk away?"

"I do na like it either. Thar's one thing that's certain, Rogan. We can na tell the women what 'appened here tonight."

CHAPTER · 22

THE EARLY SPRING mix of snow and rain subsided during the nighttime hours, and by ten o'clock the next morning, the sun shone brightly through the stained-glass windows of St. Anne's Episcopal Church. Colored prisms cast their hues across the devout worshipers awaiting the beginning of the morning service.

After escorting his grandmother to her seat, McKinley Wainwright stood beside the Cheever pew near the front of the church. "Good morning," he greeted in a hushed voice.

Violet looked upward and gave him a bright smile. "Good morning." She scooped aside her lavender and green striped skirt and shifted closer to her mother. "It's going to be a beautiful day after all," she whispered to McKinley as he sat down beside her.

He nodded, enjoying the floral scent of her perfume. "I'm looking forward to spending the day with you."

Her smile and the glimmer of delight in her sparkling blue eyes warmed his heart on this chilly March morning. He settled as comfortably as possible on the hard straight-backed pew and silently prayed the sermon would not be excessively long or un-inspiring.

However, as the morning progressed, McKinley realized he would be disappointed on both accounts. The visiting pastor appeared to be enjoying his return to the pulpit following a year of retirement, and after a forty-five-minute sermon, the good man didn't seem to be winding down. McKinley watched Mr. Ross, the organist, who had returned to the keyboard, his hands perched in obvious anticipation.

"As I draw to a conclusion . . ."

The remaining words were drowned out by the chords of the pipe organ bleating out the beginning strains of the finale. Before the preacher could say another word, the members of the congregation had risen and were making their way out of the pews and down the aisles.

"I believe I owe the organist a word of thanks," Matthew Cheever said as they exited the church.

"Matthew!" Lilly chided.

"You must admit that he could have ended that sermon after fifteen minutes," Mr. Cheever said with a chuckle. "The remainder was pure repetition. You agree with me, don't you, McKinley?"

Violet's parents turned their scrutinizing gazes upon him. "Perhaps it would be best if I withheld my opinion."

Mrs. Cheever smiled at McKinley and nodded her agreement. "You obviously learned at an early age that it's wise to remain neutral in marital disagreements."

"I didn't realize we were having a marital disagreement," Mr. Cheever retorted. "I thought we merely had differing opinions."

"We're married and we disagree. Thus, we are having a marital disagreement, Matthew."

"I stand corrected," Mr. Cheever replied before turning toward McKinley. "I understand you and Violet are going to your sister's home for a visit."

"Yes. And I promise to have Violet safely home by eight o'clock, if that's acceptable," McKinley said.

"I see you haven't left for Jasmine's just yet," Alice Wainwright said as she bustled her way through the crowd and neared the small group. "I was thinking perhaps I should join the two of you."

McKinley gave her a feeble smile. "Of course. Although I

don't think we'll be returning until eight o'clock."

"Your answer makes it sound as though you don't actually want me to come along," Alice said with a shrewd glint in her eyes.

Violet stepped closer to McKinley's grandmother. "We would be honored to have your company."

"Why, thank you, my dear," Grandmother Wainwright said while giving McKinley a smug grin.

"I'm certain you're eager to see Jasmine," Lilly Cheever commented. "I haven't seen her or Nolan in church for some time now. I hope there's not some problem keeping them away."

"No problem except keeping them all healthy enough to attend, I suppose," Alice replied.

"I do hope they'll soon be able to return. I miss seeing Jasmine," Lilly said.

"I miss seeing her also," Alice said, "which is why I asked to intrude today."

Mrs. Cheever smiled gently at Violet and McKinley. "I'm certain the children are delighted to have your company. And we best be getting along so the three of you may be on your way."

They bid their good-byes, and Violet stopped to brush a kiss upon her mother's cheek. McKinley frowned as he watched his grandmother take her place next to the carriage. Obviously she planned on sitting between Violet and him. He had spent the entire week anticipating time alone with Violet as they journeyed to Jasmine and Nolan's home, but now his grandmother was determined to intrude. Well, she might accompany them, but she was *not* going to insert herself between them.

"If you'll excuse me, Grandmother, I'll help you into the carriage once Violet has been seated," he said with as much decorum as possible.

"I thought she'd have a better view of the scenery from the outer seat," his grandmother said.

McKinley smiled down at the older woman. "Oh, she's quite familiar with the scenery. We prefer to visit on the journey, which is a feat much more easily accomplished if she sits beside me."

"I suppose you're correct," his grandmother replied before taking several steps away from the carriage and waiting until Violet was seated. "I wanted to see how assertive you'd be about the young woman. I do believe you care for her, McKinley. On second thought, why don't you just drive me home? I believe I'm a bit overtired for a trip to Jasmine's today." She gave him a fond smile as she settled onto the seat.

McKinley returned her smile. Women! He would never understand their thinking.

———

Jasmine walked out the door, relieved to see McKinley's carriage moving up the driveway. She waved and smiled as they drew nearer, pulling her shawl a bit closer against the breeze. "I was beginning to fear you had forgotten my invitation," she said as her brother assisted Violet out of the carriage.

"Of course not. How could we forget something we've been anticipating all week? Unfortunately, the church service was longer than usual this morning."

"And then your grandmother couldn't decide if she was going to come along with us or remain in Lowell," Violet added.

Jasmine peeked down toward the carriage. "It appears as if she decided to remain behind."

McKinley held the front door for the two women, then followed them inside. "Only after deciding she was overly tired and we should instead take her home."

Jasmine giggled. "Sounds exactly like Grandmother's antics. I hope you won't be disappointed, but as the hour grew late for dinner, I went ahead and fed the boys. They've already gone upstairs for their naps. However, they should be full of vim and vigor by the time we finish our meal."

"It's good you had the foresight to give them their meal. I imagine they would be quite cross if they had been required to wait for our arrival," McKinley agreed.

Nolan stepped forward to shake hands with McKinley and grinned. "Glad to see you've arrived. Jasmine wouldn't permit me to eat with the boys, although I protested."

"Tell the *entire* story. You wanted to eat with the boys and then *again* when Violet and McKinley arrived. I told him he'd soon not fit through the door if he began that sort of behavior," she said while patting her husband's arm. "And it appears you've survived the extra hour's wait in fine order."

"So I have, yet I fear I may soon suffer severe repercussions if we don't eat now," Nolan said, pulling her close to his side.

"Then we best get you into the dining room," she said, enjoying her husband's banter. "Why don't you and McKinley sit across from each other? I had Nolan remove the extra boards from the dining table so we could have a more intimate visit."

"How thoughtful," Violet said as she sat down.

Nolan immediately signaled for a girl to begin serving. The young woman moved quickly to offer a platter of baked chicken. Nolan held up two fingers. Jasmine chuckled at his excessive indulgence.

"It's a good thing I asked Cook to fix extra," she murmured as McKinley also asked for two pieces.

Violet turned her attention to Jasmine as the serving girl continued making her rounds. "I haven't seen you since my coming-out party, but my father tells me that you have acquired some admirers."

"You must be referring to Mr. Riddell and his sons, Charles and Luther," Jasmine replied.

"Father said they'd made a visit to see your Arabians and couldn't say enough good things about the farm. You obviously charmed all three of them."

"She is quite a charmer," Nolan said, "but I think their admiration went well beyond Jasmine's alluring personality. The Riddells were astonished both by the horses and Jasmine's business acumen—and rightfully so," he boasted.

"The proud husband," McKinley said with a wink.

"Absolutely! I'm blessed to have a wife with so many virtues. If she continues in this manner, she'll soon be equal to the woman of Proverbs thirty-one."

"Oh, I think we can cease the accolades," Jasmine said. "The truth is, the gentlemen are looking for investment opportunities, and after touring the farm, asked if I might be interested in partnering with them."

McKinley leaned back in his chair. "Truly? They're interested in a partnership? What did you tell them?"

Jasmine wiped the corner of her mouth. "Neither Nolan nor I have any interest in taking on *investment* partners."

McKinley gave her a quizzical look. "You make it sound as though you're interested in some other type of partners."

"As a matter of fact, we currently have two partners," Nolan reported.

"What? Whom have you partnered with?" McKinley asked.

"Rogan and Paddy," Jasmine said simply.

"Truly? I'm amazed." McKinley stared at her and gnawed on his bottom lip.

"Of course, Padraig is not yet a man," Jasmine said. "However, both Rogan and Paddy are buying an interest in the business with a portion of their wages. There's no better employee than one who owns a portion of the business."

"I disagree. The best investor is the one who has knowledge and money," McKinley said.

"I believe a person need be invested with more than their purse strings," Jasmine stated. "A worker who has reason to care what happens to his position and livelihood responds in a much more attentive and devoted manner than does one who does not."

"People can be given reason to care, beyond owning a part of the business," McKinley protested.

Nolan took a sip of water and cleared his throat. "I think this may be a topic on which we will not agree. Perhaps we best move on to another subject. How are you enjoying your work for the mills?"

"Father says that McKinley is a natural born leader," Violet answered before McKinley could offer a reply. "He has a great deal of business sense, and my father values that above most everything else."

"My brothers are all intelligent men and good hearted as well," Jasmine agreed. "Although they were rather given to pranks when we were growing up. I remember more than one good scaring."

Violet cast a side glance at McKinley. "You purposefully tried to frighten your sister?"

McKinley grinned. "Only in fun. She gave as good as she received. Don't let her innocent look fool you."

"I cannot imagine my wife ever causing you so much as a moment of discomfort."

McKinley laughed out loud. "You, sir, do not know your wife if you say such a thing. Why, she loved nothing more than seeing us in discomfort."

"Enough of such talk," Jasmine declared. "We simply had great fun growing up."

"I can't imagine what it must have been like to have slaves," Violet said, surprising them all.

"Little different than having servants, as you grew up with," McKinley told her. "They worked around the house and took their orders from the master and mistress. Is that not the same as even here in Jasmine and Nolan's home?"

"Yes, but our servants may cease their employment whenever they desire," Jasmine threw out.

"But your servants cannot go far without a letter of recommendation," McKinley pointed out. "And employment is not always that available. So in some ways, it is no better."

"Are you backing away from your desire to see the slaves freed?" Jasmine asked in surprise.

"No, but neither do I believe freedom resolves the issue. They may indeed be set free, but I believe what comes afterward will be difficult to contend with."

"So, McKinley, what are the Boston Associates' plans for Lowell?" Nolan asked as he waved off the serving girl as she offered him more bread.

Jasmine gave her husband an appreciative smile as McKinley launched into a discussion of the decision of the Boston Associates to open yet another mill. "I know Samuel will be pleased to hear the news. After all, another mill means an ever-increasing need for more cotton and—"

McKinley's statement was cut short as Spencer and Moses came running into the room, both of them rushing toward Jasmine and burying their faces in her lap.

"If you've all completed your meal, perhaps we should adjourn to the parlor," Jasmine said with a laugh.

McKinley and Violet led the way, situating themselves side by side on the settee. "I believe Spencer has grown a full two inches since I last saw him," McKinley commented. "Come see Uncle McKinley," he said, holding out his arms to the boy.

Jasmine watched as Spencer ran into his uncle's arms. McKinley and Violet showered her son with attention while completely ignoring young Moses, who now appeared near the point of tears.

"Come here, Moses," Jasmine said with a bright smile.

He ran to her, his smile matching Jasmine's. "Mama," he said, crawling onto her lap. Jasmine embraced the boy in a giant hug and kissed his plump cheek. Her gaze settled on Violet, and she was surprised to note the girl's patent aversion to the sight of Moses on her lap.

"You need to put a stop to that," McKinley said.

"To stop *what*?" Jasmine asked.

"Letting that boy call you Mama. It's unseemly, Jasmine."

"He's a little boy who has lost both his parents—he needs compassion, not condemnation. He hears Spencer call me Mama. It's only natural Moses would follow suit. There's no need to make an issue over such normal behavior. It's obvious you're lacking in Christian love. Did you leave it in church this morning?"

"Don't give me platitudes about Christian love, Jasmine. As I said before, I'm happy to see the coloreds freed. However, you carry matters too far with your behavior. Can you imagine what your friends in Mississippi would think?"

"I have few friends in Mississippi and care little what Southerners think—which is one of the reasons I chose to live in Massachusetts," she retorted.

Violet moved to the edge of the settee. "But surely you realize you're doing the boy no favors by rearing him as though he's white. To continue such a charade will only hurt him in the future."

"Perhaps now you realize why we haven't been in church of late. It's because I feared this type of repercussion from some members of the congregation. However, I didn't expect this type of reaction from either of you. I thought you were both strong in your stand against slavery and for freedom for the Negroes. Obviously I was incorrect."

McKinley's jaw tightened. "I've already said I stand for abolition—and so does Violet. However, abolition is an entirely different issue from what's going on in your house, Jasmine. Continuing down this path of reckless behavior will only lead to disaster for both your family as well as Moses. Did you not hear anything I said earlier?"

"Indeed I did. I tried to ignore and forgive it," Jasmine replied angrily.

Nolan stood and moved to stand by Jasmine. "I think we should all calm ourselves a bit. Let's not permit our emotions to rule. I wouldn't want any of us to say something we'd later regret."

Stroking Moses' cheek, Jasmine continued to rock back and forth. "I believe McKinley and Violet have already spoken their true feelings—as have I. When I gave my word to Mammy to help Obadiah, my promise was unqualified."

"You're a fool, Jasmine. You know that even a single drop of Negro blood is enough to categorize a person as colored," McKinley argued. "That boy may appear as white as you or me, but by law, he's a Negro. The entire country is dividing itself over issues such as these."

Jasmine clenched her fists. "I believe the Southern ways are morally flawed. Moses shouldn't be penalized because of his heritage. Truth be told, there's more white blood running through his veins than Negro blood. And you, McKinley! I can't believe we're having this conversation. It's obvious I don't know you. You increasingly appear as much a bigot as the Southern plantation owners."

Violet clasped a hand to her chest. "I do believe you've become overwrought, Jasmine. You know McKinley and I both support the abolition movement. We both oppose slavery, but you go too far. Raising a colored child as though he's white goes beyond the pale. You may think you're doing an admirable thing, but Moses is the one who will suffer for it."

Jasmine stood with Moses in her arms. "Before another word is said against this child, I want both of you to leave our home."

CHAPTER · 23

BASKING IN THE ADULATION of the evening's festivities, Malcolm Wainwright leaned back in the padded dining chair and smiled as his eldest son stood to speak to the gathered members of the Boston Associates. All agreed Samuel Wainwright had proven to be a wise choice as Bradley Houston's replacement several years prior. Although some members of the Associates had initially voiced their misgivings regarding Samuel's abilities, they soon withdrew their criticism. Moreover, Samuel had far exceeded the expectations of even the most hardened opponents, securing prices and suppliers that pleased both the Associates and the cotton growers.

"I thank you for your vote of support and the fact that you've been accommodating when circumstances required. Such willingness to negotiate has won the confidence of the Southern growers with whom I deal. Consequently, they have become our greatest champions when securing new growers. They are vocal in their praise, and I now have growers contacting me."

Nathan Appleton raised his glass of port. "You've become one of our greatest assets, young man."

"Thank you, Mr. Appleton. I consider it a privilege and an honor to work for the Associates. And you may rest assured there will be no shortage of cotton for the new mill you plan to open this year. In fact, I may be required to turn away growers in the future."

"Such an event is difficult to believe. However, I, too, applaud the great strides you've made," James Morgan said. "I wonder if it would be prudent to begin accumulating and storing the cotton while the prices are good. If abundant supplies are now available, I think we should take advantage of them. After all, who knows what the future holds."

"Good point. However, before we begin stockpiling, we need to assure ourselves there's adequate space and ability to maintain the quality of the cotton. Let's remember, we're now producing fifty thousand miles of cloth annually. Matthew, could you or McKinley assess the viability of such a feat?"

"Of course," Matthew said. "We'd be pleased to take on the project and report to you at our next meeting, unless you want an answer prior to then."

Nathan glanced around the room. "I think the next meeting would be acceptable. After all, you'll need some time to survey the possibilities and formulate your report. Don't you agree, gentlemen?"

Murmurs of assent circled the room, and after the men had discussed a few remaining routine issues, the meeting adjourned. Malcolm watched as McKinley spoke briefly to Matthew Cheever before crossing the room. "Good to see you, Father. I knew you'd been invited to the dinner meeting but didn't know if you'd make the journey north. I'm pleased you chose to attend."

Malcolm grasped his son's hand and pulled him forward into a brief embrace. "Good to see you also, my boy. Appears as if things are going well between you and Mr. Cheever."

"Yes, quite well. I was hoping to accompany you and Samuel on the train—if you're returning to Lowell in the morning. Mr. Cheever is required to remain in Boston for several more days."

"Of course we're returning to Lowell. Your grandmother would have my head on a plate if I failed to visit, and your sister would never forgive me if I didn't spend time with her and the family." Malcolm's brows furrowed, his brown eyes filled with curiosity. "I'm surprised Jasmine didn't mention my arrangements. I sent an updated schedule for my visit in my latest missive to your sister and asked that she share the information with you and your grandmother. Have you not seen Jasmine of late?"

"Not for nearly three weeks. I'd prefer to wait and explain the circumstances as we travel to Lowell. I have another meeting with Mr. Cheever before I return to the hotel," McKinley said as he glanced toward several of the Associates standing nearby.

The next morning the trio boarded the train and once they had settled into their seats, Malcolm turned his attention to McKinley. "Now do tell me why you haven't been to visit your sister. I can't believe your work keeps you so busy you can't spend an occasional Sunday afternoon with her. Although our family is now scattered about the country, those of us who are near one another should be mindful to maintain strong familial ties."

"You're lecturing the wrong person, Father. Jasmine expelled both Violet Cheever and me from her home."

His father and brother looked like they didn't believe him.

"What nonsense is this you're speaking?" Malcolm said. "Do you truly expect me to believe your sister would bar you from her house?"

McKinley raked his fingers through his disheveled hair. "Believe what you will, but when you visit her, she and Nolan will both confirm the truth of my statement."

Malcolm frowned while lowering his spectacles farther down on his nose. "And what did you say or do to cause such an edict?"

"You immediately assume it is *my* impropriety that caused the breach between us. But you have been away from Jasmine too long and forget her behavior can sometimes become unruly when she doesn't get her way. Believe me, even Violet Cheever was appalled by Jasmine's conduct."

Certain he now had both his father's and Samuel's attention, McKinley launched into an explicit reenactment of the Sunday afternoon debacle, leaving no detail to the imagination.

Malcolm's jaw went slack as he listened to McKinley's words. "So she actually plans to rear that boy alongside Spencer as though they're equal—like brothers?" He choked on the last two words.

"Yes. She's gone completely daft over the notion that she promised Mammy she'd help Obadiah. Pure nonsense. Mammy would never have expected such inappropriate behavior. Quite frankly, I'm certain Mammy would have preferred her grandson to be raised as he is—a Negro," McKinley said.

Malcolm frowned. "What are you talking about? Mammy had no grandchild. She had no children."

McKinley froze. He'd been certain that Jasmine had told their father the truth about Obadiah, yet it was clear that Malcolm had no idea what he was talking about. McKinley drew a deep breath. "I suppose I'd better explain."

"I suppose you'd better," his father agreed.

"Before Mammy died, she called Jasmine to her side and told her that she'd given birth to a son many years earlier. I can't remember what happened to her husband, but he was gone. Her master, Mr. Harshaw, threatened to kill the child if she ever said so much as a word to you about him, because Harshaw knew your desire to keep families together."

"But why not just sell the boy with his mother?" his father questioned.

"I don't know. I presume because he figured to raise the boy to be a strong field hand. Obadiah was his name, and he did indeed grow up to be a strong man. After Mammy told Jasmine about it, she asked Jasmine to try to set Obadiah free."

"That seems so unlike Mammy." Malcolm looked at Samuel. "Did you know anything about this?"

"Nothing."

"I am sorry," McKinley began again. "I presumed that by this time you knew."

"I knew there were former slaves living on Jasmine's land," Malcolm admitted. "I just didn't realize why they were living there or the connection to Mammy."

"Jasmine felt honor bound," McKinley stated. "As I suppose

she feels now with Obadiah's son, Moses."

"This is the boy she's raising as an equal with my grandson?"

McKinley nodded. "She'll hear nothing of protest against this. That's why I've long been absent from her company."

Malcolm balled his fists against his thigh. "She's insane to believe such a thing will produce anything but grief. She knows about the slave laws."

"Indeed, but she cares little for that or what people think. She merely sees her treatment of Moses as an extension of her abolitionist work. But it's not, and this will no doubt lead to trouble in the future."

Samuel nodded his agreement. "It's all this freethinking that's led to Jasmine's irrational actions. First she came up here and got herself involved in the antislavery movement, then she became an outspoken advocate, willing to set aside her Southern roots, and now she's breaking ties with her own family. What else will she do?"

"She's already done more. I failed to tell you she's permitted those two Irish workers to purchase an interest in the horse farm— and the young one, Paddy, not even a man yet," McKinley added, his anger building as he told the tale.

"It appears there's much at stake here," Malcolm said, "but I think the issue of Jasmine raising that colored boy as her own flesh and blood is my first priority. I sincerely doubt that Nolan will overrule Jasmine concerning the child. Years ago he expressed a deep belief in the right to equality for all Negroes. Consequently, it will be difficult to persuade either of them that their decision regarding the colored boy is flawed. Especially given her promise to Mammy. I must think on this matter."

The train car swayed and gently rocked back and forth over the tracks as they continued on toward Lowell. Malcolm leaned back, his thoughts filled with the information McKinley had shared. Frightful news for a journey he had hoped would be filled with pleasure. The only positive aspect of the entire conversation had been McKinley's comments regarding coloreds. Perhaps his youngest son was finally realizing that abolition was not the answer to the country's unrest regarding the slavery issue.

Malcolm thought about Mammy and the baby she'd been forced to leave behind. It grieved him, as he had always prided himself on keeping slave families together. It had been one way that he told himself he had risen above the rest. Slavery was a necessary evil, but a master needn't be cruel.

But I was cruel and I didn't even know it, he thought, closing his eyes against the world.

———

With Spencer on one side and Moses on the other, Jasmine knocked on the front door of her grandmother's house. "Good morning, Martha."

"Good morning, Miss Jasmine. Come in. Your grandmother's upstairs, but I'll tell her you're here," the aging housekeeper replied.

Martha stepped aside and moved toward the stairs. Glancing briefly over her shoulder as she ascended the steps, Martha said, "I'm certain your grandmother will be pleased to see you. It's been too long since you've visited."

"Thank you, Martha," Jasmine replied before leading the boys into the parlor. "Now sit nicely," she instructed them, seating the boys on either side of her.

"Jasmine! What a wonderful surprise," Alice Wainwright said as she entered the room and gave her granddaughter a hug.

"I should have sent word I was going to call. However, I discovered only yesterday that McKinley was out of town, and I wanted to be certain and tell you I had a letter from Father. He said you were aware he was coming for a visit but to advise you he'd likely arrive tomorrow."

Alice pursed her lips and frowned. "I wish I would have had a bit more time for preparation."

"I apologize, but I didn't want an encounter with McKinley. He's likely told you I've banned him from our home. I have no interest in being around him."

"And since he lives with me, I'm forced into the middle of your dispute."

Jasmine frowned. "If you've been placed in an uncomfortable position, that's McKinley's doing. After all, I've not even seen you for over three weeks."

"Exactly my point. In the past, you would stop whenever you were in town, and I could always depend upon having some time with you and your family on Sundays. Now all of that has changed. And from what McKinley tells me, your decision to stay away is due only in part to your argument with him."

"Why? What did he say?"

"He mentioned your lack of attendance at church is due to your feared reaction from church members—regarding Moses."

Moses immediately pointed to himself. "Moses," he said.

Jasmine smiled at the child. "Yes, you're Moses. Grandmother, if we're to have this discussion, perhaps the boys could join Martha in the kitchen for cookies."

Alice rang a small bell that sat near her chair, and within moments, the housekeeper appeared at the parlor door. "Would you have some cookies or fruit that might keep the boys occupied in the kitchen for a time, Martha?"

Martha smiled. "I have some gingerbread I'm certain they'll enjoy. Come along, boys. I have a treat for you in the kitchen."

Spencer and Moses wriggled down from the settee and trailed after the housekeeper like goslings following a mother goose.

"Thank you, Martha," Jasmine called after the older woman before turning back toward her grandmother. "I do have concerns about attending church with Moses. There are many judgmental and self-righteous members at St. Anne's."

"There are judgmental, self-righteous people everywhere, child. The church is filled with imperfection. After all, this world is populated with sinners. I would like to say that from the time I became a believer, I no longer sinned, but that would be a lie, and one more transgression," Alice said with a chuckle.

"However, it appears those who profess their belief in the Lord are sometimes the worst offenders—always looking for reasons to find fault with others," Jasmine said.

"I learned long ago I can't change others and the way they act, but I can attempt to live in a way that I hope is pleasing to God. If others see a glimmer of Christ in me, perhaps they will have changed hearts and attitudes. If you believe rearing Moses as your own is what you should do, then have the courage of your convictions. You can't hide at the farm for the remainder of his life. Besides, you'd be doing both Spencer and Moses an injustice."

"Then you believe people will eventually accept the boy?"

"Accept? No. Tolerate? Possibly. Oh, there will be some who will be cruel and never attempt to understand, and there will be a very few who will accept what you're doing. However, you cannot base your decisions on what others think. If you believe this is what God is leading you to do, then take heart and have courage."

Pulling a handkerchief from her pocket, Jasmine wiped away the tears that had begun to form in her glistening brown eyes. "I'm not certain what God would have me do, Grandmother. None of this was planned. Obadiah made his decision to go and find Naomi, and the situation simply evolved after that."

"So this is more a matter of happenstance than planned behavior?"

The muted sound of the boys' carefree laughter could be heard in the distance and a faint smile curved Jasmine's lips. "Yes. My hope is that Obadiah and Naomi will return, but I promised Obadiah I would make certain Moses knew about his parents if neither of them came back to Lowell. I intend to keep my word. However, the first night Moses stayed with us after Obadiah's departure, I was putting the boys to bed and Moses mimicked Spencer and referred to me as Mama. I didn't have the heart to tell him no. I still don't. Such behavior seems cruel and could cause him irreparable harm. I love Moses very much and I won't hurt him."

Alice rose from her chair and walked to the doors leading to the garden. "You should make this situation a matter of prayer, Jasmine. I will do the same. I am sympathetic to your decision and want what is best for all concerned. Please remember you are always welcome in my home—and this is *my* home, not McKinley's. I do hope you will give careful thought to what I've told you. I believe you must continue to live your life as you always have in spite of the criticism you will surely receive."

"Thank you, Grandmother. Knowing I can depend upon your support gives me courage."

The metal latch on the front door squeaked. Before either of the women could say anything further, the three Wainwright men stood in the parlor doorway.

"Father! Your missive said you'd be arriving *tomorrow,*" Jasmine said as she hurried toward him.

Malcolm gathered her into a warm embrace. "You must have misread my letter. I'm certain I said we'd be arriving in Lowell today. But no matter. We're here and all is well. Now let me give your grandmother a much-deserved hug."

Careful to avoid McKinley, Jasmine turned her attention to Samuel. "It's good to see you, Samuel. We don't see you often enough."

Samuel gave her a measured look. "I'm generally too busy for social visits when I'm in Lowell."

"I'm surprised to see you here," McKinley said to his sister.

Jasmine ignored his remark and turned toward the noise in the hallway. The boys were running into the room, obviously determined to investigate.

"Look at how you've grown," Samuel said while giving his nephew a brief hug. "You're quite a fine young man, Spencer Houston."

Spencer giggled as he escaped Samuel's hold, immediately running toward Jasmine with Moses following close behind. "I trust you had a pleasant voyage, Father," Jasmine said.

"A fine voyage—on one of the Houston ships. Come here, Spencer. I haven't had an opportunity to say hello to my grandson."

Jasmine tugged Spencer out from behind her skirt. "Spencer, don't pretend to be bashful. Go and give your grandpa a proper hello."

Her son's eyes grew large when his grandfather pulled a piece of candy from his pocket to entice him away from his mother. Jasmine gave the boy a gentle nudge.

Propelled by the lure, Spencer moved to his grandfather. "Hello, Grappa," Spencer said with a sweet smile.

Moses edged from behind Jasmine and then quickly darted toward the older man. Pointing to his tiny chest, Moses said, "Me candy, Grappa."

"He is *not* your grandpa," Samuel barked.

His eyes wide and filled with obvious fear, Moses rushed to Jasmine's arms. "You're fine—don't cry," she said, cradling the boy and rocking him back and forth.

"Disgusting!" Samuel said through clenched teeth.

"*You're* the one who is disgusting, Samuel. How *dare* you bring your prejudice to bear on a tiny child—especially one who has been welcomed into this home. I find your behavior abhorrent. I'm sorry to leave abruptly, Grandmother, but I fear that if I remain, I will be forced to tell my brothers exactly what I think of their behavior. Father, I trust you will come to the farm and spend several days with us."

Her father appeared perplexed and merely nodded before Jasmine escorted the boys from the house.

Malcolm remained silent, watching his daughter while she assisted the boys with their wraps and hastily exited the house. Jasmine's departure created a deafening silence that hung in the parlor for several minutes.

When Malcolm could no longer bear the quiet, he turned toward his mother. "What happened to my gentle-spirited daughter?"

Alice laughed. "Jasmine is the same compassionate girl she's always been, Malcolm. In this instance, her gentle spirit, as you so aptly refer to it, is directed toward Moses and not toward her brothers. Therein lies the difference. I believe she has chosen to protect the boy at all costs, including the loss of her family. Yet I do pray that none of us will permit *that* to occur."

Malcolm rubbed his throbbing neck, hoping to release the tension. "Why don't we go down to the mills? I understand our final cotton shipment of the season sailed for Boston two days before we left New Orleans. Surely it's been delivered to the mills by now. Right now I think I'd prefer a discussion of cotton and the manufacturing business."

"What about dinner?" Alice inquired.

"If we're hungry, we can find our way to the restaurant in the Merrimack House, Mother. Don't worry yourself on that account," Malcolm replied. "I'll be back by midafternoon, and we can have a peaceful visit."

The three men departed without further discussion. "If you don't object," McKinley said, "I'd prefer we stop first at the Appleton. With Mr. Cheever still out of town, I want to assure myself all is well. Besides, the major portion of the cotton shipment was destined for the Appleton."

With the agreement of Malcolm and Samuel, the three men disembarked the carriage at the Appleton Mill a short time later.

"I'll stop in the office and the two of you can go—"

"Mr. Wainwright! I'm relieved to see you," the accountant called out while rushing toward McKinley. "You need to go down to the unloading area. The shipment of cotton we've been waiting on has arrived, but all the bales are terribly flawed. There's total confusion what with you and Mr. Cheever both gone. Seems one of the men signed for the delivery and he's now fearful he'll be held accountable. No one wants to make a decision. The men are standing around arguing about whether to unload the remainder of the shipment or let it sit."

The Wainwright men hurried off to see for themselves, each one hoping the information they'd received would prove incorrect. However, it took only one glance to see the words of the accountant were true.

Chaos reigned.

CHAPTER · 24

ELINOR HEAPED the fried potatoes into a large china bowl, thrust a large serving spoon deep into the dish, and carried it to the sideboard. After filling her plate, she took her place at the end of the table and joined the girls, who were already eating their supper. While in the kitchen, she had managed to hear bits and pieces of the girls' excited conversation but hoped she'd misconstrued their discussion. After offering a silent prayer for her supper, Elinor speared a forkful of the savory bread-and-butter pickles she'd preserved and momentarily enjoyed the results of her accomplishment.

"I fear this incident is going to have far-reaching effects upon all of us, at least temporarily," Cecilia said.

"There's little doubt there will be girls who will lose their positions for a time," Sarah agreed.

"Excuse me for interrupting your conversation, but exactly what is the problem at the mills?" Elinor inquired.

"There was a vast shipment of cotton delivered to the Appleton today," Janet Wilson explained. "It appears the entire shipment is of such inferior quality and full of debris the management has declared it unsuitable for use by any of the Lowell mills. The cotton was intended for use by several of the mills, but the Appleton will be most deeply affected since our supply of cotton is nearly depleted."

"Mr. Cheever came out to the mill yard and spoke to us at quitting time this evening," Sarah added. "He said they are still hopeful they'll find some resolution for the problem, but he didn't appear convinced. He said some of us should be prepared for layoffs, as the work force may need to be reduced if there is insufficient cotton to operate the mills."

Elinor listened carefully to the explanation. "Did they indicate how many workers may be laid off?"

"No, but I fear they may close down the Appleton until they receive new shipments," Sarah said, "which would likely mean waiting for the delivery of the first crop next year before they'd reopen. Mr. Cheever talked as though this had been the last shipment expected until the next harvest. In fact, this cotton had been held in storage in New Orleans awaiting shipment to Lowell until it was needed."

"Oh, surely they wouldn't need to close down until next year," Elinor objected.

"From what Mr. Cheever said, if they must wait for the next picking, they'll supply all the other mills with cotton before proceeding to reopen the Appleton," Janet said. "It's a terrible situation."

"And the layoffs will be determined by length of employment, which means some of us will likely be going home," Mary commented.

Elinor winced at Mary's statement. She had a full house and didn't want to lose any of her boarders. Although the mills closed from time to time due to accidents, an unexpected repair, or a spring freshet, those closings were seldom and brief. In contrast, this sudden depletion of cotton would affect many more employees and for a longer period of time.

Sarah glanced down the table at Elinor. "Do you think they'll close any of the boardinghouses?"

Elinor's fork slipped from her fingers and clanked on the white china plate before sliding off the table, to her lap, and down to the floor. Why hadn't she immediately thought of the consequences the mill closing might have upon her boardinghouse? Her thoughts began to race wildly. She couldn't remember if the contract she had signed included a clause regarding the closure of a house. And even if it did, where had she placed her contract?

"Do any of you know if the Corporation has ever closed a boardinghouse?" Elinor asked.

"I've never known of them to close one," Sarah replied. "But they've never closed down a mill for any length of time either."

"They'll likely close a number of houses if they close the Appleton mill," Elinor mused.

"Oh, I hope they don't close this house. I don't want to move to another house. I'd have to get accustomed to new roommates and take whatever bed is left," Janet said, her voice growing shrill and whiney. "We'd be the new girls all over again with no choice, forced to accept any open space."

"Don't be selfish, Janet. There are girls who will lose their positions, and perhaps even Mrs. Brighton will be without her position as a keeper." Cecilia's face was filled with compassion.

"Please don't worry overmuch, Mrs. Brighton," she continued. "My mother says we fret most about those things that never actually happen."

Elinor tried to smile, but her attempt was in vain. With each passing year, it seemed as if her life became even more catastrophic than the last—a vicious, unending whirlpool of misery sucking her downward and now threatening to dissolve her very livelihood. The chatter of the girls grew faint as a parade of dismal events marched through her mind: memories of the husbands she had buried; the towheaded, laughing children she had never conceived; the house and worldly possessions she had been required to sell in order to pay off encumbrances; and a life of drudgery in this boardinghouse that scantily supported her. And now it appeared even that meager crumb would be taken from her. Was she destined to remain in penury for the remainder of her life?

Why her? What had she done to deserve losing even this pitiable existence?

Retribution! The thought crystallized like the thin layer of ice on a freezing winter morn. Losing her position at the boarding-house was surely God's reckoning for the part she'd played in the recapture of the slaves. It had been her loose tongue to blame, and now she must suffer, just as those poor enslaved Negroes were surely suffering.

"Mrs. Brighton! Mrs. Brighton!"

Somewhere in the distance, Elinor heard the faint sound of her name. She startled at the touch of a hand upon her own. "What? Oh, I'm sorry, Cecilia. I was caught up in my thoughts. Is there something you needed?"

"No, but I wanted to be certain you were all right before I went upstairs."

Elinor glanced around the room. She and Cecilia were the only ones remaining in the dining room. "The girls finished their supper?" she asked.

"Yes," Cecilia whispered.

Cecilia was staring at her as though she'd taken leave of her senses. "I'm quite fine, Cecilia, but thank you for your concern. Please feel free to go to your room. I'll get busy with these dishes."

"If you're certain," Cecilia replied hesitantly.

Hoping to reassure the girl, Elinor stood and began removing the supper dishes. She exhaled deeply when Cecilia finally departed the room, relieved to be alone with her work. Remind-ing herself that busy hands and a tiresome routine would surely prove advantageous, Elinor returned to the kitchen and began washing the dishes. Perhaps the mundane task would help clear her mind. The idea, however, proved futile. A myriad of thoughts continued to skitter through her mind like the mice rushing to and fro behind the plastered walls.

Lowering a stack of plates into the steaming water, Elinor shuddered as she remembered Oliver's deception and her own foolishness. She had permitted him to exploit her! The dishcloth dripped over the basin as she relived the humiliation of confessing to Liam and Daughtie she had been responsible for disclosing information regarding the runaways. The Donohues had been kind and supportive, declaring Oliver the true villain. Daughtie had even come to visit with her, praying and directing her to the story of Joseph and his brothers in the Old Testament. But Elinor had turned a deaf ear, unwilling to be assuaged. She hadn't wanted to be reminded of Bible stories that showed how God used evil for good. For there was no way the evil she'd done could become right with the Lord—or with those poor slaves. Throughout the entire ordeal Daughtie remained kind and compassionate, asking only that she go back and read the account of Joseph and meditate over the Scriptures. However, Elinor had never done so.

She had confessed her offense to both God and man; she had asked forgiveness as the Bible instructed. Yet obviously her compliant behavior was not enough. For if God had actually forgiven her transgression, her position with the Corporation would not now be in jeopardy.

———

Since hearing the news of the possible mill closing, the girls had been in a constant state of unrest, their behavior rapidly changing from giddy laughter to overflowing tears. Elinor had neither laughed nor cried—she was too angry and fearful to do either. A loud knock sounded at the front door, and she ceased clearing the table and wiped her hands on the frayed apron that covered her faded blue calico dress.

With a heavy step, she trudged down the hallway and pulled open the front door. "Mr. Cheever!"

Matthew Cheever stood in the doorway, his gray felt hat in his hands and a hesitant look on his face. "Good morning, Mrs. Brighton. May I have a word with you?"

"Yes, of course. Do come in, Mr. Cheever." Her fingers trembled on the doorknob as she permitted him entry and then closed the heavy wooden door. She hung his hat and coat in the hallway before leading him into the parlor as though she'd expected his visit.

Mr. Cheever sat down in one of the overstuffed chairs, his gaze finally settling upon her. "I've come as the bearer of news that will likely result in difficult circumstances for you, Mrs. Brighton. Because of my close business association and friendship with your brother Taylor, I wanted to bring this news to you personally, especially since Taylor and Bella are currently so far from home. As I'm sure you're aware, we've been required to lay off a number of workers at the Appleton."

Elinor nodded. The cottony taste in her mouth made speech impossible. She clutched the arms of the wooden rocking chair, her eyes fixed upon Matthew as she waited for the completion of his discourse.

"There is a very strong possibility we will be forced to close one of the boardinghouses. Should that occur, you would be the keeper who would lose her position—the other keepers have been with the Corporation much longer," he quickly added.

"I expected it would come to this," she replied.

"Then you've already begun to make plans? For that is why I've come in advance—to encourage you to formulate some ideas for your future."

Elinor's lips formed a wry smile. "I've made no plans, Mr. Cheever. I've never wished to decide to whom I shall be obliged. I'd rather delay my decision until I know it's a certainty."

"I do wish your Uncle John were still alive," he mused.

"Or that he'd left me a portion of his inheritance—but neither fact is a reality. I have but one living relative in this country, Mr. Cheever, and he is currently in Scotland."

"Do you know when Taylor and Bella will return?"

"At the time of their departure, they were hoping to return by April, but Taylor did not book their return passage. He was uncertain of the situation in Scotland and said they would make their decision after he had an opportunity to assess the situation. I'm surmising he may bring some of Beatrice's family back to America."

"There's little doubt Taylor will want you to come and live with him. I'll do everything in my power to keep you in your current position until his return," Matthew said. He stood, obviously convinced there was nothing more to be discussed.

"I'll retrieve your coat," Elinor said. She jumped to her feet and hurried into the hallway, remaining silent while he donned his coat and hat.

"I'm sure you are most grateful to have a brother in this time of need," Matthew said as he departed the house.

Elinor closed the door and then leaned the full weight of her body against the hard wood. "Glad to have a brother in this time of need? Is that what Mr. Cheever really thinks? That I should be thankful because I must now grovel and beg my brother for a pittance of charity?"

She balled her hands into tight fists and banged them hard against the door—once, twice, and then repeatedly until her hands ached with pain. "How dare he treat me like some pitiable creature? And how dare God place me in this wretched circumstance? I held myself accountable for what I did, asked for forgiveness— yet that is not enough, is it? What is it you want from me? Have I not suffered enough? Is my sin so much more than others' that you cannot forgive me?" she screamed toward heaven.

Elinor dropped to the floor, her body wracked by uncontrollable sobbing until she was totally spent. When she finally stood up, a swollen red face surrounded by unkempt hair greeted her in the hallway mirror. She held both hands to her temples, hoping somehow to diminish the searing pain that threatened to incapacitate her.

"Tell me what I am to do, God," she whispered, dropping to sit upon the hallway stairs.

In the distance, she heard a whisper in return. *Trust me.*

Startled, she turned to look up the stairway, but no one was with her. No one . . . but God.

CHAPTER · 25

MALCOLM PROPPED his feet upon the footstool in his mother's parlor and swallowed a gulp of hot tea. His eyes watered, and he covered his mouth for a moment. "I wish you would have warned me the tea was hot."

Alice glanced at her son and chuckled. "The tea is *supposed* to be hot, Malcolm. That's why I place a cozy on the pot—to keep the contents hot."

He grinned and nodded. "Yes, Mother. I had forgotten your penchant for scalding beverages."

Before Alice could rebut Malcolm's comment, Samuel entered the front hallway and, with a loud whack, slammed the front door. Without taking time to clean his boots, he strode into the parlor and thrust a folded missive into his father's hand. "Look at this," he said in a commanding tone.

"And you look at *that*," Alice ordered while pointing her index finger at the mud her grandson had tracked across the floor and onto her carpet.

Samuel scanned the damage and then lifted his boot to check for mud. "I'm sorry, Grandmother, but this is urgent business."

Her lips tightened into a pucker. "I doubt taking a moment to wipe your feet would cause insufferable damage to your existing problems, although it *does* damage my new carpet."

Samuel gave his grandmother an exasperated sigh. "If Martha is unable to remedy the destruction I've caused, I'll purchase you a new rug."

"So they're summoning us to a meeting!" Malcolm slapped the piece of paper onto the marble-topped table, his hand hitting the saucer and causing his teacup and its contents to fly helter-skelter across the carpet, the cup shattering into several pieces.

Alice grabbed her small brass bell and began to violently shake it back and forth. The ringing didn't cease until Martha's footsteps could be heard skittering down the hallway. The housekeeper came to a screeching halt as she entered the room, her unsettled gaze flitting from one catastrophic sight to the next.

"Oh, madam!" she gasped with one hand clasping the bodice of her dress.

"I fear we've created quite a mess for you, Martha. My apologies," Malcolm said. "Samuel and I must be off to this meeting, Mother. I don't know when we shall return."

Alice flicked her wrist, shooing the men from the room as if they were two naughty puppies. "Off with you both. I fear I'd be unable to pay for the damages should the two of you remain in the house much longer."

"Do you have your grandmother's carriage?" Malcolm asked as he strode to the hallway and donned his hat and coat.

"Yes, and I asked Martin to wait for us."

"Good. I'm in hopes we'll have at least a short time to confer with McKinley before the meeting begins. Hopefully, he can give us some insight as to the best way to approach these men. From the tone of their note, they're going to be completely unreasonable. What if I hadn't been available at their beck and call? Since several of the Boston Associates are in town for the discussion, it's obvious they planned this meeting in advance."

"I couldn't agree with you more fully," Samuel said as their carriage rolled toward the mill.

Malcolm stared out the carriage window, his brow furrowed. "McKinley acted completely normal at supper last night. In fact, when I asked if there had been any further developments regarding the shipment, he said there had been none. Do you suppose he was aware of this meeting yet withheld the information from us?"

"I doubt he would be privy to much information. The Corporation wouldn't want him forced to compromise his loyalty. And even if he did know, his first obligation is to his employer, not the cotton growers in Mississippi," Samuel replied.

"His first loyalty is to his family—or at least it should be," Malcolm contradicted.

"Father, let's not get caught up in a discussion regarding McKinley's obligations to the family. We need to remain focused upon the meeting."

Malcolm nodded. "You're right. Do let me take the lead if they become antagonistic."

"Thank you for your concern, but you're not the one responsible for resolving this problem. I'm the one who was selected as the buyer for the Lowell mills."

"I am, however, the one who recommended you for the position, and the end result of this issue will affect the entire family as well as our friends and neighbors in Mississippi. However, I will acquiesce if that's what you prefer."

"It is," Samuel stated with a decisive nod.

They disembarked the carriage outside the Appleton Mill. After a brief glance toward the interior of the mill yard, Malcolm followed Samuel inside. On their previous visit, they had been confronted with the defective bales of cotton; today's meeting would likely prove every bit as taxing. Samuel led them directly into Matthew Cheever's office, where Wilson Harper, Nathan Appleton, and Leonard Montrose had already gathered. McKinley was seated behind a table piled with ledgers, directly to Matthew's left.

"Gentlemen," Samuel greeted. "Good to see all of you."

"I wish I could say the same," Leonard muttered.

Matthew glowered at Leonard. "Please take a seat and we'll get started. I know all of you are busy, and we want to make this meeting as productive as possible."

"Don't see how that can be done," Leonard murmured.

"Leonard, would you please cease your comments. They're distracting and unnecessary," Nathan said before turning his bespectacled gaze upon Samuel. "On behalf of the Boston Associates, I am requesting a full report of what has occurred regarding the latest shipment of cotton, Mr. Wainwright. We will expect your explanation, remedy, and plan for guaranteeing we will not undergo a repetition of this ruinous episode *if* we decide to continue using you as our buyer. For now, I would at least appreciate some form of oral explanation I can share with the other members. Needless to say, they are more than a little unhappy."

Malcolm's gaze had shifted back and forth between his two sons during the course of Nathan's reproach. Samuel had turned pale. Behind the pile of books and ledgers, McKinley's complexion shone bright red. Malcolm wanted to rescue his sons—the eldest obviously overwrought with fear, the youngest appearing completely embarrassed or angry, he wasn't certain which.

Samuel sat with his hands tightly wrapped around the arms of his chair, his fingers turning the whitish-purple hue of a corpse. "You may assure all of the Associates I will be filing a detailed written report," he said. "However, it is impossible to give you information until I've had time to investigate. After a cursory examination several days ago, I've been unable to probe into this matter any further. May I have freedom to examine the entire shipment? Depending upon what I find, I'll know the next step that must be taken."

"What do you need to examine? The product is unacceptable, and we're left to develop a plan for the operation of the mills without adequate cotton," Leonard snarled.

Nathan signaled Leonard to silence himself. "As I'm sure you surmised before arriving here today, tempers are short and nerves are stretched taut. We've been placed in the precarious position of closing down at least one mill. That means telling employees they no longer have positions with the Corporation. Obviously the Associates want answers, and they are looking to you, Samuel. We will give you freedom to examine the shipment, but I'd appreciate something to report back as soon as possible."

Samuel massaged his forehead for a moment. "I want to more closely examine the markings on the bales to assure myself they all carry the stamp designated for the shipments to Lowell and satisfy myself that the entire shipment is flawed."

"Even so, we remain without the necessary cotton to continue production," Nathan reiterated.

"Is there no way we can use the cotton we received?" Leonard asked while scratching his beard.

Nathan slapped his palm on the desk. "Absolutely not! Doing so would be worse than closing down the mill. We've worked for years to build our reputation. I'll not jeopardize it by using inferior product."

Wilson Harper, who had been unusually silent, addressed Samuel. "Does anybody use cotton of that substandard quality?"

"A few of the smaller mills here and the mills in England will take whatever they can get from us," he replied.

Nathan cleared his throat. "I'm sorry to say that the majority of the Associates have lost their trust in your ability to act as buyer, Samuel. It brings me no pleasure to tell you that your position with us is tenuous at best."

McKinley gasped at Mr. Appleton's statement and Malcolm jumped to his feet, no longer able to remain silent. "Tenuous? Perhaps you need to explain to the remainder of your Boston Associates that they have benefited greatly by Samuel's representation among the Southern cotton growers. Do you so quickly forget the plaudits all of you heaped upon Samuel at your dinner meeting in Boston? Should Samuel lose his position, your Corporation will lose all of the Wainwright cotton as well as every other grower we've brought to you. It is the Wainwright power that has caused you to significantly prosper these last few years, and that influence can be withdrawn at any moment."

"Is that a threat?" Nathan asked.

"That, sir, is a promise," Malcolm replied, his voice low and menacing.

"Father . . ." Samuel started.

Malcolm shook his head. "I'll not be silenced. If these men want to intimidate you by saying your position is *tenuous,* after one mistake—a mistake that most likely was not of your doing, then let them know the truth: their cotton supply depends upon the Wainwrights. When you return to Boston," he said, setting his eyes on each man in turn, "do take a moment or two and tell your Associates that I can produce a myriad of letters from mills all over England that are willing to go to any length in order to have our cotton. It is not the Wainwrights or the cotton producers who will suffer by your actions; it is your own corporation. You will close more than one mill if you continue down this path."

Matthew motioned Malcolm to take his seat. "No need to become overwrought. We must all work together to resolve this situation. There are, after all, many who are going to be laid off and possibly lose their jobs. I heartily believe that Samuel did not intentionally send us a bad shipment of cotton. However, the fact remains, a bad shipment is what we received. Neither side will accomplish anything with idle threats. We need to work toward finding a resolution."

"Then if we're agreed to that fact, may I go and examine the bales?" Samuel asked.

"Absolutely," Matthew replied. "I believe everything has been said for now. We'll look forward to your report."

Malcolm donned his hat and fell in step with Samuel as they departed, both equally determined to uncover what had gone amiss with this latest shipment. Not only was Samuel's position at stake, but the Wainwright family name also hung in the balance. And Malcolm would not see their reputation tarnished—particularly by a group of Northern businessmen.

"Father, wait!"

The sound of clattering footsteps and McKinley's urgent plea caused Malcolm to stop and turn. His brows arched in surprise. "Yes?"

"I told Mr. Cheever I could not sit idly by while Samuel was taken to task for an error over which he'd had no control. You've performed exceptionally for the Corporation, Samuel, and I'm appalled by their ability to forget your record of accomplishments when one error occurs. Mr. Cheever needs to realize that my family is important to me also."

"Thank you, McKinley. I appreciate your loyalty," Samuel said. "However, if this issue cannot be quickly resolved, you may decide your loyalty has been misplaced. The Associates may decide they want neither of us."

Malcolm tugged at his collar. "And what difference? We were doing well with the English before Bradley Houston convinced us to change our loyalties to the American mills. My statement to those men was no idle threat—they'll go begging for cotton if they continue down this arbitrary path of intimidation." His words shot through the air like tiny darts bearing lethal venom.

With a wry grin upon his lips, Samuel said, "But aren't you behaving in the same manner, Father? That's why I asked you to let me speak at the meeting."

"Too late now. We've placed our cards on the table. At least they know we're not frightened."

McKinley nodded. "Of that fact, there's little doubt."

Malcolm clapped Samuel on the back. "Aha! You see? A strong offense is exactly what was needed."

"No, Father," Samuel said. "What is needed is a truthful explanation of exactly what occurred. If I don't find the answer, neither the Associates nor I will ever again feel comfortable in our working relationship."

"You may not feel comfortable, but you'll be their buyer until *you* decide to terminate your position. And therein lies the difference," Malcolm retorted in an austere tone he seldom used with his family.

"McKinley, I want you to return to work," Samuel directed. "You've expressed your feelings to both Mr. Cheever and to me, and I appreciate that fact. However, there's nothing more you can do, and I would prefer you went back to your office."

McKinley looked back and forth between Samuel and his father, his gaze finally settling upon Malcolm. "Do as your brother has requested. Who knows? You may garner information that will be helpful to us," Malcolm instructed.

"If you believe that's what's best, I'll do so, but know that if you need my assistance, I will make myself available to you," McKinley promised.

———

Malcolm settled beside Samuel as the train departed the Lowell station. "I'm certain your grandmother is going to be unhappy when Martin delivers the message we've departed for Boston without so much as a good-bye."

Samuel grinned. "While the Boston Associates cause you little fear and trembling, it appears Grandmother has maintained her touch."

Malcolm laughed aloud for the first time in several days. "Your grandmother is a woman to be reckoned with, and it's best none of us forgets it!"

"I believe Jasmine's the only one who of us who has developed the ability to influence Grandmother, rather than the other way around."

"You may be correct on that account. Curiously, they do seem to get on rather well—perhaps because they have much the same temperament."

They fell silent, and Malcolm stared out the window, his thoughts flitting about like pebbles skipping across a vast expanse of water. What if they couldn't resolve this issue with the cotton? He'd blustered about the English and their desire for his cotton, yet he had little desire to realign with the overseas market. Not that he wouldn't do so, but he much preferred the current arrangement. And Jasmine! What was he to do in order to heal the widening breach among his children? He wanted to die knowing they could always rely upon each other. They were family, and family needed to remain intact, even if disagreements occurred.

"Father. . . . Father!"

Malcolm startled to attention and gave Samuel a sheepish grin when he realized the train was pulling into the Boston station. "Sorry. I wasn't very good company. I'm afraid I became absorbed in my own thoughts. What is it?"

"I assume we'll go straight to the docks?"

"Yes. I'll talk to the agent and examine the company's ledgers. If the *Americus* has not yet set sail, see if you can locate the captain and gather any information from him."

The docks were teeming with passengers wielding their cumbersome baggage and surrounded by families who had come to bid them farewell. The beefy dock workers paid the intruders little heed while loading goods onto the ships lining the harbor. Malcolm grasped Samuel by the arm as they neared the Eastern America Shipping Company's office. "I'm sure the agent can tell us if the ship has already sailed."

Samuel hurried into the shipping office and leaned across the counter. "Has the *Americus* set sail for New Orleans?" he called to the agent.

The agent strode toward them and glanced at the clock. "Not due to cast off for at least another hour."

Malcolm shook hands with the agent. "Malcolm Wainwright and my son Samuel."

"Pleased to make your acquaintance. Jacob Hodde," the agent replied, pointing to the inscription of his name above the counter.

"Any chance they'd depart ahead of schedule?" Malcolm inquired.

The agent gave a hearty laugh. "Unless the captain chained his crew on board the ship last night, I doubt they'll cast off for at least another three hours. They'll all be nursing the effects of too much rum and ale—probably take the better part of that time for the crew to stagger on board."

"You see if you can locate the captain, and I'll remain and visit with Mr. Hodde," Malcolm said.

"It's Captain Whitlow," the agent called after Samuel.

Samuel waved and continued moving toward the door.

The agent shook his head. "Young folks—they're always in a hurry."

"Indeed," Malcolm agreed, giving the agent a friendly smile. "I wonder if you might allow me to examine the records you maintain for the *Americus*—only those concerning our shipment, of course."

"Is there a problem?" he inquired.

"Yes. However, we're not yet certain who's responsible. The cotton destined for Lowell did not arrive."

The agent traced his finger down the open page and began running it alongside the entries. "What? You didn't receive your shipment? But my ledger reflects it arrived and was shipped to Lowell." The agent peered over the top of his spectacles at Malcolm while tapping his finger alongside an entry.

"I misspoke, Mr. Hodde. A shipment arrived in Lowell—a shipment of cotton, defective cotton. Certainly not the cotton purchased and baled for shipment to Lowell."

"Take a look," the agent said as he turned the ledger toward Malcolm.

———————

Samuel thanked the captain and disembarked the *Americus*. With his head bowed against the ocean breeze, he began to slowly wend his way through the crowds.

"Samuel! Samuel Wainwright!"

Shading his eyes against the sun with his hand, Samuel turned toward the sound. A short distance away, Taylor and Bella Manning were smiling broadly and waving him forward. John, the youngest of the Manning children, stood on tiptoe while brandishing his hat high in the air. Samuel hastened his step and smiled in return.

"What a surprise. I didn't realize you were due back from Scotland," Samuel greeted while shaking hands with Taylor.

"I would have preferred to remain a few more weeks. However, Bella was growing homesick, and we'd accomplished everything we set out to complete on the journey. I believe my sister's family is well in hand for the present. I take it things are going well in Lowell or you wouldn't be down here on the docks. Shipment due in?" Taylor inquired.

"No. I was checking on my last shipment. There are problems."

Taylor's forehead creased beneath the wave of dark blond hair that crossed his brow. "At the mills or with the shipment?"

"Both," Samuel said. "I'm on my way back to the agent's office to meet my father, and then we'll be returning to Lowell."

"We're hoping to board the last train," Taylor said. "We'll meet you at the station. You can explain everything during our return to Lowell."

CHAPTER · *26*

ELINOR GAVE ONE final pat to the dough before setting it to rise in a large crock. With a swipe of her hand, she gave the dough a light coating of lard and then covered the bowl with a clean linen cloth before checking the beans with pork she had begun cooking earlier in the morning. Her decision to serve half of the baked beans at supper that evening and the remainder with corn bread for dinner the next day had stretched her food budget for the week. And she had been able to purchase enough plums for two of the moist, fruity cakes the girls had requested for supper. Dipping a cup into the flour sack, she began to measure the required six cups as a knock sounded at the front door. "Who could that be?"

Before she could reach the door, a voice called out, "It's me, Elinor. We've arrived home from Scotland, and I couldn't wait any longer before coming to call."

"Taylor! What a fine surprise."

He took in her flour-smudged apron. "It appears I've come at an inconvenient time. Shall I return later?"

"If you don't mind joining me in the kitchen, I'd be pleased to have you remain and keep me company. I'm most anxious to hear about your journey to Scotland. How did you find Beatrice's family? I thought you might bring several of her children home with you," she said as they walked down the hallway and into the kitchen. "Pull up a chair and sit down. I'll fix you a cup of tea. When did you and Bella return?"

"Thank you," he said, tugging a chair from under the wooden table. "We arrived on the final train from Boston last night. Had it not been so late and both of us weary from our travels, I would have stopped to see you then. I must say I'm surprised by your demeanor. I rather expected to be greeted with anger rather than hospitality."

Elinor placed the teacup in front of him. "Why is that?"

"I understand the boardinghouse may soon be closed."

"Word does travel quickly in Lowell. How did you receive the information so soon?"

Taylor took a swallow of his tea and placed the cup on its saucer. "We happened upon Samuel and Malcolm Wainwright at the docks in Boston. The five of us traveled from Boston to Lowell."

"I see. Then it's likely you know more than I. Mr. Cheever paid me a visit and explained my boardinghouse would close if they didn't receive the anticipated cotton shipment. A few of my girls will be sent home—others will move to another boardinghouse if they're needed in any of the other mills. I'll miss this place and I'll miss them if the boardinghouse closes."

Her brother was staring at her as though she were a stranger. "You'll *miss* the girls?"

"Strange, isn't it? After all my complaints about their selfish behavior and my station in life, I find myself longing to remain in my position."

"You've changed, Elinor. You appear to have lost your . . ."

"Anger? Not completely. But I have come to the realization I hold no sway over the situation at the mills. And there is nothing I can do to alter my circumstances here at the boardinghouse. However, I *can* control my attitude. So I've decided to trust God and see what He has in mind for me."

"May I say I heartily approve of the change?"

"Thank you," she whispered, her cheeks growing warm at his praise.

"I came to tell you that Bella and I talked after we arrived home last night. Should the boardinghouse close down, we want you to come and live with us. I know it's not ideal, but we would truly like to have you join our family."

"Two women under the same roof is never a good thing, Taylor," she said.

He met her gaze. "You find Bella difficult to abide?"

"Oh, no, not at all. I love Bella and I appreciate your kindness. I worry having me about would make your lives more complicated. I could help with the house and young John, but I would worry for fear I'd overstep my boundaries."

"Don't be silly. You're creating problems where none exists. Say you'll agree," he insisted.

Elinor poured the cake batter into two large pans and set the bowl on the table. "If the boardinghouse closes and there is no other position available for me, I will come and live with you. However, I want you to know that I would leave as soon as I could find other work to support myself," she added.

"Agreed." Taylor stood and kissed her cheek. "Now I must be off to attend to a few matters or Bella will be unhappy with me."

McKinley entered the office of the Appleton Mill and situated himself behind his small desk. There were accounts and ledgers that required updating, but he'd found concentration difficult of late.

"Glad to see you've come in early," Matthew Cheever said as he entered the front door. "I was looking at the ledgers last night. I don't want you falling any further behind on those accounts— makes calculations much too difficult. Have I assigned you too much work?"

"No," he replied while watching Matthew hang his coat and hat on the ornately carved coatrack that had been a birthday gift from Mrs. Cheever the preceding year.

"Then enlighten me, my boy. What's the difficulty?"

"My level of concentration isn't what it should be, I suppose," McKinley said, "what with the problems regarding the cotton shipment."

Matthew nodded. "Ah—so it's your family's troubles with the cotton shipment that's to blame for your inability to maintain the ledgers."

McKinley's grip tightened on his pen. "You're putting words in my mouth, Mr. Cheever. The ledgers will be brought to date."

"From all appearances, those ledgers won't soon be reflecting any payments to your family for cotton," Matthew said, his comment followed by an exasperated sigh. "I understand your father talked briefly to Nathan after examining the shipment, but he has yet to give me any explanation. Consequently, I'm assuming the entire debacle remains unresolved. I don't believe the Corporation has ever experienced a blunder that has the probability of causing so much damage. As you know, we stand to suffer significantly due to this mismanagement."

The hair along McKinley's collar bristled. "I believe you are unjustly blaming my family members, Mr. Cheever. Human error is something one must expect from time to time. The cotton had been properly stored awaiting shipment, and Samuel's paper work is faultless. He did everything possible to ensure your shipment would arrive in a timely fashion."

"And it did. Time is not the concern, McKinley. Unsuitability of the product we received is the problem. As buyer for the Corporation, Samuel is responsible for guaranteeing our product is received on time and as specified. You say he did everything possible to ensure the shipment arrived properly. But did he? If so, it seems we would not be faced with this problem. Obviously he didn't watch as the shipment was loaded, or he would have known of the problem, don't you agree? What has occurred affects many lives. If he's not accountable, then who?"

McKinley combed his fingers through his hair. "Samuel can't be expected to oversee loading every bale of cotton placed on a ship. This error is not his doing. It appears that although Samuel has performed his duties with excellence in the past, that fact is now forgotten. Gone are thoughts of those beautiful shipments of perfect cotton; gone are the memories of those new suppliers he signed on one after another; gone is the praise Samuel received for bartering reduced cotton prices on behalf of the Corporation. The Associates forget too quickly what they have gained from the Wainwright family—particularly Samuel. He has been a good and loyal employee who is now being treated as a leper."

Matthew rested his palms on McKinley's desk and leaned forward until their faces nearly touched. "I must remind you that you, too, are an employee of the Corporation. If you wish to work as my assistant, your loyalty must remain with me and with the Corporation, McKinley. If I do not believe I can trust you, then I do not want you as an employee of the Corporation."

"As I've told you in the past, Mr. Cheever, my family is of great importance to me. I do not always agree with them, but in this instance I know they are correct. Would you respect a man who did not remain loyal to his family?"

"I've told you what I expect, and if you plan to continue in my employ, you'll think long and hard about where you place your loyalty. Be a man and think for yourself, especially if you have intentions of ever becoming a part of *my* family."

Matthew grabbed his coat and hat from the rack, slamming the door behind him on his way out.

McKinley rubbed his forehead. "So much for bringing the ledgers up to date," he muttered.

Strolling down Dutton Street, Violet breathed deeply, enjoying the feel of springtime in the air. She stopped to view the merchandise displayed in several store windows along the way but came to an abrupt halt in front of Hatch and Taisey, surprised to see McKinley inside the shop. She entered the door and quietly approached him. "Whatever are you doing in here? Purchasing some tripe or pigs' feet? Perhaps placing an order for a butchered hog?" she asked with a grin.

His gaze was clouded, almost as though he didn't recognize her. "What?" he asked, suddenly coming to his senses and looking about. "I believe I entered the wrong door," he finally said.

"You don't seem yourself, McKinley. Is something wrong?"

"Yes. I promised Grandmother I would stop at Paxton's on my way home and purchase some soap—'fancy soap,' as she so fondly calls it. I dare not forget or she'll send me back to retrieve it."

"You're just now leaving the mill?" Violet asked as McKinley guided her out the door and into the neighboring establishment.

He nodded. "The ledgers required updating. My work had fallen behind. All this upheaval over the cotton shipment makes it difficult to concentrate."

"No doubt. How terrible this entire ordeal has been for your brother and father, but I'm confident it will soon be resolved. I'm certain Father and the Associates will aid them in remedying the situation. After all, there surely is some credible explanation," Violet said while leading him toward a section of shelving containing the toilet and fancy soaps.

McKinley gave a sardonic laugh. "Your father and the Associates have expressed nothing but disparagement and anger throughout this ordeal. Only this morning I attempted to explain that Samuel and my father had gone to Boston and talked with the shipping agent and captain in an effort to determine what happened."

"Father wouldn't listen to you?" she asked with a hint of incredulity in her voice.

McKinley picked up several pieces of soap. "Oh, he listened, but he doesn't believe there is any acceptable excuse for what occurred. He says only that Samuel is to blame, no matter what the cause."

Violet placed her hand atop McKinley's. "Truly? Father generally listens to reason. It's difficult for me to hear that he would be so callous."

"Indeed. He further said that if I intended to continue in his employ or ever become a part of his family, I should determine exactly where I place my loyalties. His warning was clear. If I side

with my family, my position with the Corporation will be jeopardized and, more importantly, he may withdraw his approval of
our relationship."

Violet's knees buckled and she grasped McKinley's arm, feeling
as though she might actually faint. "How could he behave in such
a manner? I've never known my father to be so ruthless."

"I must admit his behavior has seemed out of character ever
since this mishap. I realize he's in charge of daily operations, but
it's the Associates who hired Samuel, not your father. When Samuel and Father went to Boston they discovered there may have
been an error in the shipment. Although they hold no evidence,
they believe the stamps were wrongly affixed to the bales, causing
the error in shipment. But your father and the Associates aren't
willing to listen."

"Why not?"

He shrugged. "Your father said he doesn't want excuses. The
delivery of high-quality cotton is what he requires, and nothing
else will suffice."

Violet accompanied him to the counter and waited while
McKinley paid Mrs. Paxton for the soap. "Any word on the cotton
shipment?" the store owner inquired while wrapping McKinley's
purchase in brown paper.

"Nothing that I care to speak of," he replied.

"This is going to mean a loss of business for all of us if they
close down the Appleton," she remarked.

"Yes, so I've been told—numerous times," McKinley said as he
and Violet exited the store.

"I would enjoy nothing more than to keep company with you,
but I fear any further tardiness will cause Grandmother distress.
She tends to forget I am a grown man."

The apologetic tone of his voice made McKinley even more
endearing, and Violet smiled at him as she released her gentle
grasp on his arm. "I understand."

He brushed her fingertips with a kiss, whispered a soft good-
bye, and departed. Violet watched until he was no longer in sight
and then turned on her heel and marched toward home. Gone was

her tender emotion. In its place, her anger began to simmer slowly, like a kettle of water with tiny bubbles circling the edge, waiting for the heat to escalate before bursting into a churning boil.

She lifted her skirts, ran up the front steps of the house, and burst through the front door. Her father sat reading in the parlor while her mother stitched a piece of decorative needlepoint.

Her father glanced up from his book. "Back so soon?"

Without taking time to remove her cape, she firmly planted herself directly in front of her father. "What has come over you?"

"I beg your pardon? Whatever are you talking about?"

"McKinley! How dare you say he must choose between his family and me? Your attitude is appalling. What were you thinking? Or were you?"

Her father rose from his chair, a tinge of scarlet inching upward from beneath his white-collared shirt. "Whom do you think you are speaking to, young lady? Have *you* forgotten proper behavior?"

Tears threatened and Violet bit her lower lip, hoping she could maintain control of her emotions. "I'm no longer an impudent child. Nor am I a chattel you can withhold as a bartering tool in order to maintain control over McKinley's actions."

"Although you're no longer a child, your actions *are* impudent. You cannot begin to fathom what is at stake in this matter."

"So you're telling me manipulation is acceptable if the stakes are high? That is not a principle you taught me when I was growing up. You told me I should live my life in a manner that would be pleasing to God—and I listened. Although I haven't always been successful, I do attempt to mend my mistakes when I realize I'm incorrect. Will you not do likewise, Father?"

Moving in front of the fireplace, her father crossed his arms. His eyes grew dark and somber. "My responsibilities reach far beyond this family. I'm forced to make decisions at work that impact *many* lives. Jobs are being jeopardized, and much money will be lost because of Samuel Wainwright's inattention. I cannot condone such behavior, nor can I tolerate people working for me who do not properly place their priorities."

"I pray you will rethink your decision, Father. You're forcing me to choose between the two men whom I love the most in this world. Please realize there is much at stake here at home also."

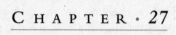

CHAPTER · 27

WITH SPENCER AND MOSES at her side, Jasmine read from the Brothers Grimm volume of fairy tales while the three of them enjoyed the warm springtime weather. "Grappa!" Spencer shouted, pointing toward the horse-drawn buggy that had turned toward the house and now drew near.

Jasmine shaded her eyes against the bright sun and looked toward the carriage. Surely Spencer was mistaken. "It's Grandmother I'm expecting," she murmured, but it was her father who was now stepping down from the buggy. Shifting forward, Jasmine returned his wave before rising. Grasping the boys' hands, she walked to meet him.

Her father's steps grew hesitant as they neared one another. "Father," she said, opening her arms to embrace him.

"Jasmine—how I've longed to visit with you."

She heard the tremble in his voice. "No need to be nervous, Father. I'm surprised by your visit but pleased beyond belief that you have come. I must admit it was Grandmother I was expecting, but Spencer spied you in the carriage as you came up the driveway."

He winked at his grandson. "I'm pleased to see you're happy to see Grandpa." He stooped down and pulled the boy into the crook of his arm. "And you come here for a hug too." He extended his other arm toward Moses, and the child rushed forward giving a delightful giggle.

"Thank you," she whispered.

"No need for thanks, my dear. Come along, boys. Let's see if we can find some cake and lemonade in the house."

"You'll spoil their dinner," Jasmine cautioned.

"That's what childhood is for—special treats to spoil our dinners as well as the pleasure of enjoying each day," he said with a chuckle.

"I don't believe that was your attitude when *your* children were growing up," she said, giving him a broad smile as they walked arm in arm toward the house.

He nodded. "But that is the special pleasure of being a grandparent. Besides, if the boys are busy with their cake, we can have some time to ourselves for a visit."

For the first time since his arrival, Jasmine became uneasy. "I hope that doesn't mean we are going to argue. I want this rift between us to heal."

"As do I. However, my hope is that we will arrive at a solution that will heal our family while doing what is best for Moses—not necessarily what is most agreeable to *you,* but what will best serve the child. Do you have someone helping with the boys since Naomi's . . ." He hesitated, obviously unsure how to broach the topic of Naomi's disappearance.

"We are rather short on help. We had a young girl who helped in the kitchen and another who helped with the upstairs. Both have quit to move to Boston. Kiara comes each day, but as her baby grows older, I'm certain she'll be unable to help as much as she has in the past. With Rogan working here at the farm and also assisting Liam with his business, they have become self-sufficient. And Kiara continues to receive more orders for her lace than she can fill. I know she would never refuse to assist me, but my hope has always been they would become independent. She's here today, however, so perhaps she wouldn't mind caring for the boys while we work on your *solution.*"

"Oh and fer sure here are a couple of hungry boys," Kiara said as she looked up from peeling potatoes. She smiled at Jasmine and then gave a brief nod toward her father.

"We thought perhaps some treat would occupy them so that I might have a talk with my father."

"But of course. Just be sittin' 'em down. I'll fetch some milk and a wee bit of cake."

After settling Spencer and Moses at the small kitchen table, Jasmine smoothed the folds from her skirt. "You're certain they won't disturb you?" she asked Kiara.

A bright smile curved Kiara's lips as she sliced pieces of cake for the boys. "O' course na'. Nevan's sleepin' sound as can be," she said, nodding toward the baby's cradle in one corner of the kitchen. "Besides, Cook will be back shortly. She had Paddy take her to town for a few supplies. I'm expectin' her any time."

"You boys be good while I visit with Grandpa, and we'll go back outdoors this afternoon," she promised as she turned to leave the room.

Her father appeared weary—or was age to blame for the new lines creasing his face and the additional gray hair fringing his balding pate? With each visit to Lowell, he appeared more fatigued and a little older. His mortality entered her thoughts more frequently than she would like nowadays. "Have you been resting well, Father?"

His smile was warm and familiar as he patted the seat cushion next to him. "As well as one can expect when away from home. Come sit beside me."

She leaned close and embraced his arm. "You're anxious to return home?"

"Only because I'm weary of the many trials and tribulations that have occurred during my visit. The difficulty with the cotton shipment has been extremely distressing, coupled with the rift that's occurred within our family."

Jasmine sighed. "In some measure, *that* portion of your concern was brought about by my quick temper, and I apologize for the part I've played in causing strife. I know your visit has been fraught with turmoil. However, I must add that I believe Samuel, McKinley, and Violet overstepped the boundaries of suitable behavior. Their condemnation of me and lack of sympathy for Moses and his plight are quite distressing—and you didn't come to my defense either. I want resolution for our family's disagreement, but my primary concern is Moses. I made a promise to rear him as if he were my own. I won't go back on my word."

"Not even if it's in the boy's best interests?"

Jasmine scooted on the cushion, quickly distancing herself from her father. "I know what you're thinking! You believe I should send him to The Willows. Are you so attuned to Southern ways that you can't see the harm he would suffer? Not only would he be living in an unfamiliar home, he would also be surrounded by strangers. I won't send him to become a slave on the family plantation. Out of the question!"

"Do settle yourself, Jasmine. You've rushed to incorrect conclusions. Taking Moses to the plantation never entered my mind. I agree such a decision would be harmful to the child."

Her rigid shoulders relaxed at his words. "Then you're on my side in this matter?"

"I'm on the boy's side," Malcolm hastened to reply.

Her forehead crinkled and she tilted her head to the side. "What does that mean? I'm also on his side."

Patting her hand, her father leaned toward her with a judicious look in his eyes. "Let's see if that's true. I have a proposal to make. And I believe the plan I've developed is best for Moses. Will you listen?"

Jasmine gave him a begrudging nod.

"First, let me tell you what I see for Moses if he remains a member of your household," he began.

She leaned farther into the deep cushions of the settee, not wanting to hear his predictions for Moses' life. She had her own thoughts about the boy's future should Obadiah and Naomi not return. However, she had agreed to hear her father out. "I'm listening," she said.

"Your compassion is admirable, Jasmine. I know you want only the best for Moses, but think about what you will do if you raise him to know only what it is to live as a white child. You're denying the boy his own roots. What if Obadiah and Naomi return in two or three years? I know you doubt they will ever be able to come back. But what if they should? Their son will believe he is white and that you and Nolan are his parents. How would you correct that damage? And it's not as though people in this area don't know the boy is colored. One day someone will take great pleasure in telling him the truth. He'll be devastated and possibly turn against you for withholding that information."

"I *do* plan to tell him about Obadiah and Naomi—when he's old enough to understand," she defended.

"Don't you see, Jasmine? You'll put off telling him for one reason or another until you've buried the past deep inside and begin to believe he *is* your child. You'll cause him great pain if you continue down this path."

She wilted, nodding her head. "Late at night, I'm plagued with these thoughts. I don't want to do anything to hurt Moses, yet I cannot send him away from here."

"I have a young slave couple at the plantation. . . ."

Immediately Jasmine came upright, her eyes flashing. "I've already told you, I will *not* send Moses to The Willows or anyplace else, for that matter."

"Please! Let me finish."

"I'm sorry. Continue."

"I have a young slave couple I would be willing to set free and send to you. Nolan could make arrangements for them to sail into Boston on one of your ships. They could remain here on the farm and raise Moses. The boy would return to the house where he lived with his mother and father, and you would be keeping your promise."

She was silent for several minutes, allowing the idea to take hold in her mind. "Such a plan would likely return our lives to a semblance of what they had once been. But what if this couple doesn't want to come—or if Naomi and Obadiah should return?"

"Why wouldn't they want to come, Jasmine? I'd be offering

them their freedom, an opportunity to live in the North with a place to live and receive wages—a new life. If Obadiah and Naomi return, they would be reunited with Moses. Simon and Maisie could stay on if you had sufficient work for them, or they could seek employment somewhere else. I'll explain the possibility that Obadiah and Naomi might return, if that makes you feel easier."

"It's only fair they know the complete circumstances under which they'd be coming. Do they have children of their own— Maisie and Simon?" she asked.

"No—not yet. If memory serves me right, she lost a baby in childbirth a year ago."

"But she likes children?"

Malcolm shrugged and gave his daughter a grin. "I have no idea—I thought *all* women loved children. I think you'd find her very acceptable, and Simon puts me in mind of Obadiah. Strong, hardworking, big smile. I know this isn't what you planned, but I believe it truly is the best for Moses. He'll still have your family close at hand, and you can aid him financially in the future, if you desire. Send him to school, do whatever you like in that regard, but don't raise him believing he's your son or Spencer's brother. In the end, you'll harm Moses as well as your own son."

As tears began to trickle down Jasmine's face, her father quickly retrieved a folded cotton square from his pocket and wiped her cheeks. With a gentle motion, he pulled her into a warm embrace.

"No need for tears, my dear. I know that together we're going to do what is truly best for Moses."

Taking a deep breath, Jasmine attempted to contain her sobbing. "In my heart, I know this is the right thing to do, but I truly don't want to give him up."

"But you're *not* giving him up. You're merely returning him to his own home. He'll still be here playing with Spencer, enjoying the very life he would have had with his own parents. Don't you see how attached you've already become?"

"Yes, and it seems inequitable that things cannot continue as they were."

"But God has a plan even in this, is that not right, daughter?"

She nodded. "I'm afraid I've not been speaking regularly with the Lord. I . . . well . . . I suppose without the fellowship of other people, it's been easy to let myself slide away."

"And you've not been going to church because of Moses?"

"I've been afraid of how they might receive him."

Her father rubbed his chin. "That hardly seems like something the Lord would approve of, now does it?"

She sighed. "No. Even Nolan said as much."

"We want to do right by the boy. He deserves that much."

Jasmine looked at her father. "Please do not think me harsh, but why do you care what happens to him? Why do you care when you own slaves and treat them as property?"

Malcolm lowered his gaze. "Mammy." He blew out a heavy sigh and looked up. "I care because he's Mammy's grandson."

Jasmine realized then that someone had told her father the entire story. She reached out to pat his hand. Tears poured down her cheeks.

Kiara walked into the parlor with Nevan in her arms. "The lads are near done with their cake and are wantin' ta go outdoors. I'm going to take Nevan and join . . . Forevermore, why are ya cryin'? Yar eyes are puffed as big as hen's eggs."

The comment brought a tiny smile to Jasmine's lips. "We've been discussing Moses," she whispered.

Lifting Nevan to her shoulder, Kiara turned to glare at the older man. "I see ya've been a success in causin' her more heartache."

"No, not at all, Kiara. I believe Father has helped me to resolve Moses' future," Jasmine said.

Kiara bobbed her head up and down. "And I see his plan has made ya mighty happy too."

"Sit down and let me explain. The boys will be fine in the kitchen for a few moments."

Kiara sat down with the baby cradled on her lap and appeared to listen attentively while Jasmine explained her father's plan. "Well, what do you think?"

"Is it the truth ya're wantin' ta hear?"

"Of course," she replied.

Kiara glanced back and forth between the Wainwrights and gave a brief nod of her head. "Then I'll tell ya. No offense, but under the same set of circumstances, I'd be wantin' Nevan raised by someone that was Irish. I'd want him growin' up knowin' about Ireland and who we were. Even though Nevan is white, I'd still want 'im raised by his own people. Have I insulted ya?"

"No. You've been honest, and your answer affirms what Father has been attempting to tell me. I'd like to believe that one day people will be more accepting and issues of race and color won't need to be the determining factor in matters such as this. But for now we can only continue to work toward that end."

———

McKinley looked up from his desk as Matthew Cheever rushed into the office at the Appleton and excitedly grasped McKinley by the arm. "Put the ledgers aside and come with me, McKinley."

"Has there been an accident in the mill?" he asked, immediately jumping up from his desk and hurrying to keep pace with Mr. Cheever.

"No accident—this is good news. Come see what's in the mill yard," he hollered over his shoulder, by now nearly running.

McKinley increased his speed as a group of boxcars entered his line of vision. Men had already unloaded several bales of cotton. "What's this?" McKinley panted, doubling over from the waist until his breathing slowed.

"Cotton—the excellent grade we've come to expect from Samuel," Matthew said.

"How can that be?"

"I don't know—I sent word for your father and Samuel to meet us here before I fetched you. They should be arriving soon."

McKinley watched in amazement as the cotton was unloaded. "Have you spot-checked it to assure yourself it's of good quality?"

"Yes. That's the first thing we did. I've told the men to hold up before unloading any more of the shipment until I talk to Samuel. I must make certain this cotton was destined for Lowell. He didn't tell me he was expecting another shipment. Did he mention anything to you?"

"No, of course not. I would have promptly told you—as would Samuel. I know Samuel apprised you of his plan to return to New Orleans on the next Houston ship leaving Boston. He is determined to further investigate what occurred there," McKinley said before moving closer to check a few bales of cotton. "These bales appear to carry the proper stamp."

"As did the others," the older man mentioned.

Mr. Cheever pointed toward the front gate of the mill. "That may be your grandmother's carriage arriving now."

McKinley shaded his eyes against the sun and stared toward the front gates. He waited until the men disembarked the carriage. "Yes, it is Samuel—and Father has accompanied him. Shall I go and escort them?"

"Why don't we both go?" There was obvious excitement in Mr. Cheever's voice and a noticeable spring in his step as he accompanied McKinley up the sloping grade toward the carriage.

McKinley waved them onward. When they drew near, he clasped his father's hand as Samuel shook hands with Mr. Cheever. "Come down to the mill yard."

"I realize it has taken longer than expected to remove the unusable bales, but I have now made final arrangements for their return to New Orleans," Samuel said.

"That's fine, but this is another matter entirely," Matthew told him as they made their way to the boxcars.

Samuel stopped and stared, obviously overwhelmed by the sight. Hurrying forward, he checked one of the opened bales and then rushed forward to inspect the stamps. "These bales also contain the special stamp we developed for the Lowell shipments. I don't understand what has occurred. Both the last shipment as well as this one bear our stamp."

"The overseer brought this letter," Matthew said. "He said it accompanied the shipment and is addressed to you."

Samuel tore open the missive and began to scan the contents of the letter. McKinley and the others stood silently waiting, all of them obviously anxious to know what information the letter contained. After several restless minutes, Samuel folded the letter and tucked it into his jacket. "It seems our mysterious shipment has been explained," he told them.

"Is this cotton ours? May I let the men continue unloading?" Matthew inquired jubilantly.

"Absolutely!" Samuel exclaimed.

Resounding yelps of enthusiasm filled the mill yard as the men began calling out the good news. Quickly, they scattered throughout the area, calling the rest of the men to assist them in the yard.

"I'd like to know what the contents of your letter revealed," Matthew said, raising his voice so that he could be heard over the clamoring noise.

"Why don't we go back to the office and I'll tell you," Samuel suggested.

Once the men had departed the mill yard and settled themselves in Matthew's office, Samuel withdrew the letter from his pocket. "This letter is from my good friend and associate, Walter Rochester. He sends his deepest apologies. His letter states that the shipment we first received was one destined for England. It was instead routed to Boston. When Walter realized the error, he immediately set out to correct the problem by shipping the original bales to Boston. He has agreed to waive all fees for our shipment and pay any damages caused by his carelessness."

"Does he give further explanation?"

Samuel nodded. "It seems he sent a new employee, a young fellow with no prior experience, to stamp the bales with our Lowell imprint. The boy misunderstood and stamped all of the bales in the warehouse with the imprint. When it came time to load the ship, the dock workers had a bill of lading in their possession detailing only the number of pounds they were to load and that the bales should bear the Lowell imprint. Unfortunately, the bales near the front of the warehouse were the ones of poor quality but they bore our imprint."

"And of course the dock workers wouldn't know the difference," Malcolm said. "They'd merely look for our imprint and load the weight listed on their paper work."

"Exactly," Samuel said. "The next day Walter went into the warehouse and discovered what had occurred. He immediately placed our bales on the next ship departing for Boston."

"And what of the first shipment? Did Walter say what's to be done with it?" Malcolm inquired.

"He's asked that I reroute it to Manchester, England—at his expense, of course."

"Quite a mistake," Matthew said as he leaned back in his leather-upholstered desk chair.

"Yes," Samuel agreed, "but Walter is a good man, and I don't intend to push aside the years of excellent service he's rendered to my family for one mistake. He tells me in his letter that he has put safeguards in place to prevent another such occurrence in the future. If the Associates decide I should remain on their payroll, it could be only with the understanding I'd continue to use Walter's services."

"There's little doubt the Associates will want you to continue as their buyer. That said, I believe I owe several apologies. Samuel, I hope you'll forgive me. Given your excellent performance in the past, I should have come to your defense instead of going along with whatever the Associates decided. I'm sorry for my behavior." Matthew paused and inhaled very slowly. "I was blinded by the worry and concern for so many lives. I should have trusted God to have an answer, but I did not seek Him. I pray for His forgiveness as well as yours." He looked to Malcolm Wainwright. "I know my lack of support for you and Samuel came as a painful blow to you. Please accept my apology."

Samuel and Malcolm alternately shook hands with Matthew. "Apology accepted," Malcolm said.

"But please remember to caution the Associates," Samuel said. "I will not continue to work for them if they insist I contract work with anyone other than Walter."

"Point taken. I don't believe there will be a problem," Matthew replied.

"Then I think we had best be on our way." Malcolm stood and Samuel followed suit. "I'll want to share the good news with Mother, and Samuel needs to modify the arrangements for shipping the original load of cotton to Manchester. We'll see you at supper, McKinley?"

Before he could answer, Matthew interceded. "Once I've had a chat with McKinley, I'm hoping he'll join *our* family for supper tonight. If that won't interfere with your plans."

Malcolm tilted his head and smiled. "Not at all. Samuel will be boarding the train for Boston. Perhaps Mother will agree to supper at the Merrimack House. If not, I think the two of us can enjoy a quiet supper at home."

McKinley bid Samuel and his father good-bye and then turned a questioning look toward his employer.

"A moment of your time, please," Mr. Cheever requested.

"Of course," McKinley replied.

"I also owe *you* an apology, McKinley. I am ashamed of my behavior and ask your forgiveness. Ordering you to choose between your family and your employment as well as my comment in regard to becoming a member of our family constituted shameful behavior on my part. I fear I acted in haste and desperation, more concerned about my position than my own family. In short, I'm ashamed of myself. If it helps at all, please know that Violet or Lilly would have forced me to my senses before permitting me to stand in the way of love. That aside, I was wrong and hope we can begin afresh."

The sun suddenly appeared more radiant as it shone through the office window. "I believe I would like that very much," McKinley said with a broad smile.

———

The sound of the girls' enthusiastic chatter drifted toward the kitchen, where Elinor was ladling boiled corned beef, potatoes, and turnips into several large serving bowls. She heard the scraping of chairs in the dining room and quickly checked the bread pudding. It would need another few minutes in the oven.

"You have time to wash up before supper," she called to the girls.

"Do hurry! We have exciting news," Lucinda told her.

The comment was almost enough for Elinor to break her rule and permit the girls in the kitchen during meal preparation. Almost as quickly, one of her grandmother's old adages rang in her ears. *Once permission is given to break a rule, it's never again taken seriously.*

"I can wait to hear the news," Elinor muttered aloud as she gave the pan of bread pudding a firm shake. Done enough, she decided, placing it on the cabinet to cool before filling small china bowls with the horseradish sauce the girls enjoyed with their corned beef. With an agility that surprised even her, she deftly sliced two loaves of rye bread and carried them to the table.

"Please tell the others supper is ready," she asked Lucinda, who was sitting at the table with her hands folded, obviously anxious to be there when the important news was announced.

Lucinda nodded. "But please let me tell you," she whispered.

"I will," Elinor replied, giving the girl a pleasant smile.

By the time they had all gathered around the table, filled their plates, and offered the blessing, Lucinda was wiggling like a vigorous newborn babe.

Elinor carefully tucked a frayed napkin onto her lap. "I believe you had some news you wanted to share with me, Lucinda."

The girl immediately perked to attention. "None of us is going to have to leave, and you're not going to lose your position as our keeper. The house will remain open," she spurted, her cheeks aglow with excitement.

Elinor sat back in her chair and gazed around the table. All of the girls appeared to be nodding affirmation of what Lucinda had told her. "How can that be?" she asked. Her heart pounded intensely beneath the bodice of her calico dress.

"A new shipment of cotton arrived at the mill. There was a mix-up of some kind in the shipments, and now that the mill has received the proper cotton, none of us will lose her job or be required to move! Mr. Cheever made the announcement as we left work this evening. Isn't that marvelous news?"

"Answered prayer," Elinor whispered.

"What?" Lucinda asked.

"I said this is an answer to my prayers," she said aloud. "Even though my brother and his family generously offered me a home, it has never been my desire to be an added member of another family. I've come to think of you girls as my family. And now we'll be able to remain together," she said with a bright smile.

Steam spiraled upward and hovered over the pan of hot dishwater awaiting the supper dishes. Elinor gingerly dipped her hands into the heated water and enjoyed the relaxing warmth before beginning the dreary chore. But unlike evenings in the past, she issued a silent prayer of thanksgiving for the soiled dinner plates and grimy cooking pots that needed her attention. And tonight she thanked God that her position as a boardinghouse keeper was once again secure.

A hesitant smile made its way across her face. "Once I turned loose my anger and believed you would keep me safe, you wrapped me in your arms and protected me. Now I pray I will remember always to place my trust in you," she murmured.

That night when the house was quiet and the girls were asleep, Elinor took up her Bible and opened it. Without looking upon the pages, she began to pray. "I know I'm a terrible sinner, Lord. My faith has been so weak that it was hardly in existence. Thin threads that barely held together. It's not been easy, but then, I suppose you already know that, because you know everything."

She paused and leaned back against her simple headboard. "I'm lonely, Father. Lonely for the company of my family. Lonely for friends. Lonely for the lost love of my husbands. I want to believe that you will fill that lonely place—that emptiness. You've asked me to trust you, and I am trying. But I know too that I'm weak. I know I will fail you. But it is my heart's desire that my faith should grow strong. That the strands of faith would thicken into cords bound by your love. Please help me, Father."

She sat in the silence a moment longer, then read the words of Isaiah fifty-four. *"Fear not; for thou shalt not be ashamed: neither be thou confounded; for thou shalt not be put to shame: for thou shalt forget the shame of thy youth, and shalt not remember the reproach of thy widowhood any more. For thy Maker is thine husband; the Lord of hosts is his name; and thy Redeemer the Holy One of Israel; The God of the whole earth shall he be called."*

Elinor wiped her tears with the cuff of her dress and continued. *"For the Lord hath called thee as a woman forsaken and grieved in spirit, and a wife of youth, when thou wast refused, saith thy God. For a small moment have I forsaken thee; but with great mercies will I gather thee. In a little wrath I hid my face from thee for a moment; but with everlasting kindness will I have mercy on thee, saith the Lord thy Redeemer."*

Elinor let the Bible fall to her lap, sobbing freely into her hands. The Lord had spoken to her heart as though He sat by her side. The words of this declaration felt as if they'd been penned just for her.

"I am redeemed," she declared. "I am not forsaken."

CHAPTER · *28*

August

VIOLET LOOKED ACROSS the elegantly dressed table and smiled at McKinley. She knew he was nervous, anxious about something. He wouldn't tell her what it was, but Violet had ideas of her own. For weeks McKinley had hinted at asking for her hand, but so far as she knew, he'd failed to move forward on this.

She toyed with her half-filled goblet as her father droned on about warehousing cotton and shortening the length of time by ship. She hated to say she was bored, but the business of the mills had always put her to sleep. Perhaps it was wrong to feel this way; after all, the mills were responsible for her fine social standing and wealth. Still, it was the business of men, and she could hardly be expected to care about profits and losses and schedules.

Violet knew it was expected she would marry and produce a family, and to her that was quite acceptable. However, it was the wait that wearied her mind. Men would take forever to resolve such matters if not prodded by women.

"I disagree with your approach," Violet heard her mother exclaim.

"But you're a woman, and you would no doubt have the entire mill designed with lovely cushioned French furnishings and a tea stand in every corner," Violet's father teased. She had no idea what the conversation was about, but she took the opportunity to lean toward McKinley just as her brother, Michael, boisterously entered the conversation and took the attention of both of her parents.

"McKinley, I just want to know something," Violet began softly.

He looked up from his plum pudding with a questioning expression.

Michael had raised his voice to what was generally an unacceptable level as he protested his mother's comments. Violet smiled and leaned closer.

"Do you plan to marry me or not?"

The entire table went silent as everyone turned. Violet hadn't meant for the words to come out so loud. She felt her cheeks grow hot as she caught the stunned expressions. Then without warning, everyone, McKinley included, burst into laughter.

Violet shrank into her chair, wishing the earth would simply open up and swallow her whole.

"I think you'd better answer the girl," her father declared.

McKinley recovered and straightened his shoulders. "I had intended to ask you properly, later tonight. Of course, now that you've clearly made the room our audience, perhaps I should simply proceed." He got up from his chair and came around the table to where Violet sat. Pulling her to her feet, he gazed tenderly into her eyes.

Violet thought she might well swoon, although she had never been given to such things. She forced her knees together to keep her legs from trembling.

"I have fallen in love with the most beautiful woman in all of Lowell," McKinley began. "A Northern girl with a heart of gold. It is my desire that you would accept me as your husband—that we might marry and live here for the rest of our lives. To answer your question, I do plan to marry you, Miss Cheever . . . if you'll have me."

Violet grinned, no longer caring about the embarrassment she'd caused herself. "I will happily take you as my husband, Mr. Wainwright."

Violet's family began to applaud, but she only had eyes for McKinley. Her dreams had all just come true. What did a little embarrassment matter?

The sound of an approaching carriage drifting through the open parlor window captured Jasmine's attention. She moved to the front door, fanning herself against the onslaught of yet another warm spell. Clouds of dust plumed from under the horses' hooves as the carriage neared the house. Pushing open the door, she walked onto the porch and immediately gained an improved view of the conveyance. Violet Cheever waved from the window of the carriage, her face illuminated by a bright smile.

"This is a surprise," Jasmine said as Violet made her way up the front steps.

The two women briefly embraced. "Mother chided me for calling on you without proper notice. In fact, she followed me to the carriage in order to upbraid me for my rude behavior. Obviously she was distraught that I failed to heed her warnings over breakfast this morning." Violet cleared her throat. "But I couldn't let matters remain unresolved between us. I acted in a poor fashion . . . making an undue judgment against you. I have come to seek your forgiveness."

Jasmine smiled. "It is my harsh words that need to be forgiven. You sought only to share your concerns. I pray you might forgive me as well."

They embraced again, only this time there was much more feeling. It was as if a dam had burst open to free a flood of emotion.

"I'm so sorry," Violet said, tears forming in her eyes. "I never meant to hurt you or Moses."

"And I am sorry for my sharp tongue," Jasmine said as they pulled away. She wiped her tears with the tips of her fingers. "Please know how much I love you. You are as dear to me as a sister. Indeed, soon to be my sister."

"Yes, sisters. I've always wanted a sister."

"Come," Jasmine instructed. "Come and sit. Tell me all about my brother's proposal."

Violet laughed. "You mean you haven't heard the embarrassing truth of that day?"

Jasmine shook her head. "No, I suppose I had no idea of there being any reason for embarrassment. Pray tell, what did my brother do?"

"It wasn't him at all," Violet protested. " 'Twas I. I'm afraid I grew weary of waiting for his proposal. As my family argued at the dinner table, I leaned to ask him . . . quite boldly . . . if he intended to marry me or not."

Jasmine grinned, then put her hand to her mouth as a giggle escaped.

Violet shrugged. "I'm afraid McKinley will always tell our children of their mother's bossy nature and how she pressed him to propose."

"Oh, it will be a dear story," Jasmine assured. "Now come and tell me all about the wedding plans." She pulled Violet into the house.

Violet removed her pink silk bonnet that had been fashionably trimmed with an ivory feather and matching ribbons. "That's one of the reasons I've come. I've been busy making plans for the wedding, and I'm hoping you'll agree to aid me with your insight."

"I would be delighted. Kiara made a fresh pitcher of lemonade only a short time ago. Why don't you sit down while I fetch a glass for each of us?"

"A cool drink would be most enjoyable. I'll come along and help you. The heat this summer has been most agonizing. I don't recall an August quite this warm."

"Yes, it almost makes me think I've returned to Mississippi," Jasmine said as they walked to the kitchen. "One must feel sympathy for all those Southerners who have come north to escape the scourge of summer's unbearable temperatures, only to be greeted by much the same discomfort when they arrive."

"Yes, indeed. Although McKinley mentioned that many of them come here not only to escape the heat, but also to escape the possibility of contracting malaria or yellow fever."

"True. Many a planter's family has been stricken by one of those dreadful diseases, and God alone knows how many slaves have succumbed to one of those maladies. My own mother and beloved mammy might be alive had they not taken the fever," Jasmine said, sorrow thick in her voice. She sighed and reached for the pitcher. "There are always griefs to bear." She poured lemonade into two glasses, each one etched with a beautifully scripted *H.* "Let us speak of happier things."

Violet nodded and picked up one of the glasses and ran her finger over the engraving. "Wedding gift?" she inquired.

"Yes—received when Bradley and I married." She put the sorrow behind her and smiled.

Violet giggled. "Works out nicely that you may continue to use them."

Memories of her marriage to Bradley momentarily clouded Jasmine's visage. These thoughts weren't the happier things she would have pondered, but her marriage had been an important part of her young life. The experience had taught her many things, but best of all, it had given her Spencer. She smiled. "Yes, it worked out quite nicely. Especially since I'm now able to use them in much happier circumstances."

"I do hope my marriage to McKinley will prove joyous," Violet said softly.

Jasmine forced her thoughts back to the present. "Why, of *course* it will. McKinley is a wonderful man, and I know he loves you very much. I wish you the happiness Nolan and I have enjoyed since our union. Treat him with respect and he will love you beyond your expectations. Now come sit and tell me of your plans. McKinley mentioned the two of you have set a September date. I must admit that will put a rush to things. I cannot imagine you bringing such a large wedding together in less than a month's time."

"Mother has been planning my wedding since I was twelve," Violet said with a laugh. "Fear not. She has more things already arranged than either of us could imagine. However, she cannot arrange my witness in the ceremony. I came today particularly to ask if you would be willing to stand with me. McKinley has asked Samuel, but since I have no sister, I would be most pleased if you would agree."

"I'm honored you would ask. I would be delighted. Now, do tell me what plans you've made thus far."

"Several months ago, Mother purchased the finest bolt of satin, and unbeknownst to me, has had Kiara fashioning the lace since last December. Naturally, Mrs. Hepple will be making the gown. Mother says her work far surpasses that of any Boston seamstress, although I'm not certain that's true."

Jasmine took a sip of her lemonade and wiped the sweating glass with a napkin before placing it on the table. "I believe your mother is correct. Mrs. Hepple does fine work, and I'm pleased to hear Kiara will be making your lace—a treasure for certain. Your mother was prudent to put her to work so long ago. Making lace is tedious work."

Violet nodded. "Mrs. Hepple has been working on a sample of the pattern using my measurements. I'm having a fitting this afternoon."

"And what of the wedding location?"

"We'll be married at St. Anne's, of course, and Mother insists upon a gathering at the house afterward. I believe McKinley would prefer to leave immediately on our wedding journey."

"Yes, I'm certain his preference would be to have you to himself as quickly as possible, but I know your mother to be a woman of great determination."

"Indeed," Violet said, taking another sip of the lemonade. "Mother has plans for an orchestra to serenade us as we receive our friends and family. She's reserved every flower in Lowell, and probably those in Boston as well. I think it will be a great ordeal. The more I hear of her plans, the more overwhelmed I become."

"With all of that, there seems little I can add." Jasmine smiled and offered to pour Violet another glass of refreshment.

The girl shook her head. "You can help me with the invitations. Mother says I must tend to them, but I have no idea what to say, and my penmanship is quite bad. I've seen your script and it is so very lovely."

"I'd be happy to help."

"I think men get the better part of the arrangement in marriage. They have nothing to do but show up for the wedding."

"Is my brother not planning a lovely wedding trip?"

"I suppose, but that hardly seems as taxing."

"Have you determined where you'll be going? Please say you're not taking an extended voyage. You'd be gone much too long for my liking if you did that."

"I suggested we travel to The Willows since I've never visited there, but McKinley said there was time for us to make that journey at a later date. He would like to show me Washington. He enjoyed his time there with your father—particularly his tour of the president's house. Most of all, he insists we visit White Sulphur Springs in Virginia. He mentioned having fond memories of going there when you were young."

"Indeed, we did visit and had a lovely time—back when Mother could be coaxed into occasionally leaving the house. I'm certain you'll have a most enjoyable time at the Springs and Washington. And what of your other plans? Housekeeping and such?"

"Did McKinley tell you Father and Mother purchased us a house as our wedding gift?"

Jasmine nodded enthusiastically. "He did, and I know he was exceedingly astonished by their generosity. I understand the house is quite lovely and not overly far from the mill, which certainly pleased him."

"I believe that was Father's doing. He doesn't admit to it, but I think he's come to rely more and more upon McKinley and has begun to enjoy having extra time to spend at home with Mother. They've even begun talking of a voyage to England next year."

"Well, the house sounds lovely."

"That's the other thing I have to ask of you," Violet admitted. "I do not care for Mother's ideas on decorating, but I'm enchanted by the way you've arranged things here. I'm hoping you will help me with my house."

"I'm flattered." And truly she was. Jasmine had never honestly considered that her home was anything special in a physical sense. Rather it was her family's enjoyment of it that made it valuable to her.

The chattering sounds of Moses and Spencer drifted into the parlor, and Jasmine turned her attention toward the doors leading to the small flower garden. She spied one of the boys running toward the rosebushes and quickly jumped to her feet and rushed toward the door.

"Spencer! Don't run near the bushes or you'll scratch yourself on the thorns," she warned as Kiara rounded the corner with Nevan on her hip and Moses following close behind.

"It appears they've become a bit unruly. Why don't we go outdoors and lend Kiara a hand. Do you mind, Violet?"

"No, of course not."

Jasmine moved toward a small bench situated under a cluster of trees as Violet walked along beside her. "Come over here, boys," Jasmine called.

The two boys immediately did as she ordered. "I'm going to make a large circle around this bench, and if either of you goes outside the circle, you must go inside and take a nap. Is that understood?"

Spencer eyed her for a moment. "Where's the circle?"

"In just a moment, I'm going to show you. Wait here."

A few minutes later, Jasmine returned with a large ball of twine. She began unraveling the numerous pieces and tying them together. "Pieces I've accumulated from my purchases in town," she explained to Violet.

Once she'd tied the bits of twine together, Jasmine circled the bench in a wide loop, dropping the string as she walked. "You must remain inside the twine," she cautioned.

The boys smiled, obviously entranced by this new constraint. There was little doubt they immediately considered it a game, going as close to the twine as they dared without stepping over. Jasmine smiled and shook her head. "I hope one of them doesn't err in judgment, for I dare not go back on my word."

Kiara smiled as she shifted Nevan to her other hip. "Aye, but fer the time, they seem to think it great fun."

"I'll watch after them, Kiara. I understand you have a new order for Violet's lace, and I'm certain you have many chores of your own to accomplish."

"Aye, that I do. If ya're certain ya won't be needin' me. It's fer sure Nevan could stand to be put down for a nap."

"Then off with you," Jasmine said. "The boys will be fine. Besides, I'm expecting Nolan within the hour."

"Things are ready at the cottage, and I'm sure the new folks will be pleased as punch ta see what all ya've done ta make them feel welcome. Will ya send someone ta fetch me when they arrive? I'd like ta welcome them."

"Of course," Jasmine replied.

"You have guests arriving?" Violet inquired.

"Not guests. The slave couple Father agreed to free and send north to care for Moses. Nolan went to Boston to meet their ship and accompany them to Lowell. He thought they might feel more welcomed if someone met the ship and escorted them for the remainder of their journey. I'm certain that they're frightened and unsure about what awaits them."

"I do admire your willingness to heed your father's lead in this matter. I know you thought McKinley and I had turned on you and were unduly harsh when we sided with your father and Samuel. And, in retrospect, perhaps we were. But I believe what you are now doing is best for all concerned."

Jasmine gazed toward the two boys, who were busily playing with the small hand-carved wagons Obadiah had whittled for them. "So do I. However, I must admit that when you and McKinley took your stand against me, I wondered if either of you were truly dedicated to the antislavery movement. For a time I thought perhaps you were merely paying lip service to the cause. However, through Father's counseling, I've come to realize we all spoke in the heat of the moment. Although we all felt justified in our stand, none of us was completely correct."

"You're right. I fear that when you moved too far in one

direction, the rest of us immediately attempted to pull you back into alignment. However, we yanked a bit too hard in the process. I can now see how you would question our integrity."

"In any case, there's no doubt that God has been faithful throughout. He has given us the wisdom to find a path that will restore our family as well as provide a good and loving home for Moses. I cling to the thought that Obadiah and Naomi may one day return and their family be completely restored again. But if not, I'm trusting these new parents God has provided will supply a supportive and loving home."

Violet smiled as Moses dumped a pile of dirt into Spencer's wagon. "And the boys will continue to have the company of one another."

"Yes. And of this new babe I now am carrying."

"What? You're expecting another child? Jasmine, how simply wonderful! You and Nolan must be delighted beyond compare."

"Indeed. Of course, I'm hoping for a healthy little girl, but we'll also be most pleased to have a little brother for Spencer."

"Oh, but when will the baby come? The wedding is next month. Will that be too taxing on you?"

"Not at all," Jasmine assured. "I am told the baby will come in spring."

"What a wonder. I'm so happy for you." Clicking open the small watch pinned to her bodice, Violet's face lined with disappointment. "Oh, I fear I must be returning home. Mrs. Hepple is due shortly for my fitting. I wish I could stay and visit with Nolan upon his return."

"You mustn't be late or your mother will be concerned. Come back tomorrow if you like, and you can meet our new arrivals— Simon and Maisie."

"I'll plan to do just that. You remain with the boys. I can see myself to my carriage."

"No, we'll accompany you. Come along, boys," Jasmine instructed, extending her arms to take them by the hand.

The three of them stood on the front porch and watched until Violet's carriage pulled away from the house. "All right, my little men," Jasmine said as she turned them toward the front door. They'd not yet entered the house when Spencer tugged his hand free and pointed at the driveway.

"Daddy! Daddy!"

Jasmine glanced over her shoulder. "You're right; it is. No need to go inside," she said as they stood waiting on the front steps.

"What's this? A welcoming committee come to meet us?" Nolan asked as he jumped down from the buggy. He kissed Jasmine and then swooped the boys into his arms. "And how are my fine fellows?"

Moses immediately began to wiggle in his arms, apparently anxious to get back on the ground. Jasmine watched as the child's eyes filled with recognition of someone from his past as Simon heaved his large-framed body from inside the buggy. Hesitating for only a moment, Moses ran to Simon and held open his arms, appearing to sense a connection to his own father.

Simon leaned down and raised the boy high in the air. "You's a nice big boy. Is you Moses?"

Moses bobbed his head up and down and gave Simon a toothy smile. "You knowed me. I be Moses."

"Well, so you is. We's gonna have us some good times," he said, giving a hearty chuckle.

"Mama?" Moses looked beyond Simon to the woman behind him. The look on his face told Jasmine he was confused. She wondered if she should intercede, but Simon had it all under control.

"I be Papa Simon, and this here be Mama Maisie. We be heppin' you mama and papa."

"Papa Simon," Moses said, slapping his hands twice on the big man's shoulders. Simon laughed and tossed him in the air.

"That be right. Now come see Mama Maisie."

"Let me help you down," Nolan said, extending a hand to Maisie.

The woman was obviously stunned by Nolan's kindness but accepted his hand nonetheless. "Thank you," she whispered.

Maisie came to her husband and smiled up at Moses. "Moses, I be Mama Maisie."

"Mama May-see," Moses repeated. He looked hesitant, as if he were trying to understand the situation. "You help me—help my mama. My mama went away."

Maisie gently stroked the boy's cheek. "You be a right fine boy."

Moses reached up and touched Simon's face and then leaned down to touch Maisie's face in turn. "You be like me."

Jasmine felt her breath catch in the back of her throat. The boy clearly saw unity in Simon and Maisie because they were black. Black like him. Only his skin was so pale that Jasmine could hardly believe he understood they were the same race. Could everyone have been right in believing that even at this tender age, Moses knew that he was not white?

Nolan seemed to understand the discomfort of the moment. He cleared his throat. "This is my wife and my son, Jasmine and Spencer Houston. Why don't we go and see your new home," he offered. "We can see to your belongings in a bit." He motioned them toward the path that led to the house.

Moses wiggled in Simon's arms. "Come on. Come wif me. I show you my house."

"That'd be mighty fine," Simon said, putting the boy down. Moses reached for his hand and then Maisie's. The two exchanged a smile with the boy and allowed themselves to be led.

"You've done a good thing here, my love," Nolan said as he lifted Spencer. They followed behind the trio in slow steps to give them time together.

"Do you think they'll be happy?" Jasmine whispered as Moses led them into the house. He hadn't stopped talking since pulling the couple along with him.

"They are a wonderful young couple, and I think Moses will be most content with them. Did you see how he rushed to Simon?"

"There's such a striking resemblance to Obadiah that it nearly took my breath away when Simon stepped out of the buggy."

"I thought the same thing when I met them in Boston. For the briefest of moments, I thought Obadiah had returned."

"It's as if God's hand has guided them to us and He's restoring us to bearable circumstances. Surely the future will hold good tidings for all of us."

"I wanna go too," Spencer said, growing weary of being held back by Nolan.

Putting his son to the ground, Nolan gave his permission. "Go ahead then. Join your friend."

Spencer laughed. "Moses is my friend. I love him." He ran off to the house, leaving Jasmine and Nolan to stare after him.

Jasmine breathed in deeply. "It's so hard to let Moses go with Simon and Maisie, even though I know it's for the best. You see, I love him too."

Nolan lifted her face to meet his. He tenderly stroked her jaw. "As do I. The boy will no doubt need all of our love as the future plays itself out. Perhaps in time, Maisie and Simon will give him a brother or sister to play with."

Jasmine smiled, knowing the time had come to share her secret. "As we will give Spencer . . . come spring."

His eyes widened in surprise. "A baby?"

She laughed, feeling freer and happier than she'd ever been before. "Yes. A baby."

Nolan lifted her in the air and twirled her around until Jasmine was quite dizzy. The strands of faith that had once threatened to break under the strains of an unhappy union, the kidnapping of her son, and the threat of her family ties dissolving had thickened into a solid cord of hope. Grandmother had once said that faith had to grow, just like a fine tapestry being woven line after line. It didn't look like much when there were only a few rows, but with time and effort . . . and love, the beauty and strength of the piece was soon discovered in the whole.

Jasmine nuzzled the neck of her husband and sighed. *And that is what I am,* she thought. *I am whole.*

A Midwestern Plains Series That Delights and Inspires

Beginning with the opening pages, Lauraine Snelling's newest historical fiction series will put a smile on your face. From the Torvald sisters' cross-country trek to receive a most unusual inheritance to the lassoing of a cowgirl's heart by an unexpected suitor, these historical novels overflow with humor, faith, and joy.

Ruby
Pearl
Opal

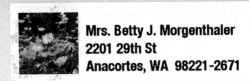
A TAPESTRY
OF HOPE

Books by Tracie Peterson

www.traciepeterson.com

The Long-Awaited Child • *Silent Star*
A Slender Thread • *Tidings of Peace*

BELLS OF LOWELL*
Daughter of the Loom • *A Fragile Design*
These Tangled Threads

LIGHTS OF LOWELL*
A Tapestry of Hope

DESERT ROSES
Shadows of the Canyon • *Across the Years*
Beneath a Harvest Sky

HEIRS OF MONTANA
Land of My Heart • *The Coming Storm*

WESTWARD CHRONICLES
A Shelter of Hope • *Hidden in a Whisper*
A Veiled Reflection

RIBBONS OF STEEL†
Distant Dreams • *A Hope Beyond*
A Promise for Tomorrow

RIBBONS WEST†
Westward the Dream • *Separate Roads*
Ties That Bind

SHANNON SAGA‡
City of Angels • *Angels Flight*
Angel of Mercy

YUKON QUEST
Treasures of the North • *Ashes and Ice*
Rivers of Gold

NONFICTION
The Eyes of the Heart

*with Judith Miller   †with Judith Pella   ‡with James Scott Bell

TRACIE PETERSON
AND
JUDITH MILLER

A TAPESTRY
OF HOPE

BETHANYHOUSE
PUBLISHERS
MINNEAPOLIS, MINNESOTA

Published by Bethany House Publishers
11400 Hampshire Avenue South
Bloomington, Minnesota 55438
www.bethanyhouse.com

Bethany House Publishers is a Division of
Baker Book House Company, Grand Rapids, Michigan.

Printed in the United States of America

ISBN 0-7642-2894-3 (Trade Paper)
ISBN 0-7642-2910-9 (Large Print)

Library of Congress Cataloging-in-Publication Data

Peterson, Tracie.
    A tapestry of hope / by Tracie Peterson and Judith Miller.
       p.   cm. — (Lights of Lowell ; 1)
    ISBN 0-7642-2894-3 (pbk.) —ISBN 0-7642-2910-9 (large-print pbk.)
    1. Irish American women—Fiction. 2. Indentured servants—Fiction. 3. Textile industry—Fiction. 4. Lowell (Mass.)—Fiction. 5. Married women—Fiction.
I. McCoy-Miller, Judith. II. Title III. Series: Peterson, Tracie. Lights of Lowell ; 1.
    PS3566.E7717T37   2004
    813'.54—dc22   2004001022

To Ann Dunn—
my dear Proverbs 17:17 friend.
Thanks for your love and prayers.
Judy

Proverbs 17:17
A friend loves at all times. . . .

Special Thanks
To Retired Colonel and Mrs. Walt Hylander
of Rosewood Plantation, *Lorman, Mississippi,*
for their insight and hospitality.

TRACIE PETERSON is a popular speaker and bestselling author who has written over fifty books, both historical and contemporary fiction. Tracie and her family make their home in Montana.

Visit Tracie's Web site at: *www.traciepeterson.com*.

JUDITH MILLER is an award-winning author whose avid research and love for history are reflected in her novels, many of which have appeared on the CBA bestseller lists. Judy and her husband make their home in Topeka, Kansas.

Visit Judy's Web site at: *www.judithmccoymiller.com*.

CHAPTER · 1

May 1846, Lorman, Mississippi

THE TEMPERATURE was unseasonably hot, insufferably repressive. By all accounts, springtime had scarcely arrived in Mississippi, but nature's cruel trick was going unnoticed by no one, including the residents of The Willows plantation.

Jasmine Wainwright flattened herself against the bedroom wall, her right arm wedged against the red oak window frame. She wriggled in protest when a tickling bead of perspiration inched its way down her narrowed shoulders. Taking great care, she lifted the lace curtain between two fingers and peeked below. "I see a carriage arriving, Mammy. It must be Papa's houseguests. I'm tempted to pretend I have a headache and remain in my room. I know he plans to show me off like prize cotton from the season's first picking."

Mammy stood by Jasmine's dressing table with her arms folded across her ample bosom. "Um hum. Well, you don't know fer sure what your papa got in mind, but iffen you don't set yourself down, supper's gonna be over and dem visitors be gone afore I get a chance to fix your curls."

Jasmine glanced at the plump servant who had been her caregiver since birth and knew she could remain a few more moments before provoking Mammy. The old woman's gaze had not yet grown stern. "Just let me get a glimpse of them first. I'd like an idea of who will greet me when I descend the stairs. Oh, look, Mammy! One of them is nearly as old as Papa, but the other appears much younger—and more handsome."

"I thought you weren't lookin' fer no husband."

"I'm *not*! But Papa seems determined to marry me off." She pulled the curtain back a bit farther and continued spying on the two men. "The younger one has a kind face."

The familiar sound of Mammy slapping the hairbrush on her open palm captured Jasmine's attention. "Oh, all right. I only wanted one more look," she said while scurrying back to the dressing table. "The older man looks rather austere and rigid. Perhaps he's the younger man's father."

She plopped down and stared into the oval mirror as Mammy plunged her thick fingers in and out of Jasmine's heavy golden-brown hair, coaxing the strands into perfectly formed ringlets. Perspiration trickled down the sides of the black woman's face and dripped onto her bodice, leaving her cotton dress dotted with wet spots.

"Chile, I ain't never gonna get these curls fixed proper if you don't quit flutterin' that fan back and forth. Jest when I think I got one curl fixed all nice an' proper, you go whipping that fan around and stirring up a whirlwind. And quit that frowning. Them creases you's making in your forehead is gonna turn into wrinkles. You gonna look like your grandma afore you turn twenty if you don' stop making dem faces."

Jasmine giggled.

"Ain't funny, chile. When you's gone and got yourself all wrinkled and can't find no man to marry you, what you gonna do then? Come runnin' to Mammy, 'spectin' me to make you look young and purty?"

Jasmine met Mammy's stern gaze in the mirror's reflection. "I'm sorry," she said while grasping the servant's roughened hand and drawing it against her own soft, powdered cheek. "But since I don't want a man, I don't suppose it matters very much if I wrinkle my face," she added with another giggle.

"You bes' get that out o' your mind. 'Sides, I's hoping to see you bring some little babes into this house one day. Maybe I'll be takin' care o' them too."

Jasmine flushed at the remark. "Whatever would I do without you, Mammy?"

"Don't know, chile, but ain't no need to worry 'bout that. I ain't made plans to meet my Maker jes' yet. 'Course, He may have some different ideas. But if so, He ain't told your ole Mammy. And since I ain't never plannin' to be parted from you any other way, I's thinkin' we'll be together for a spell o' time." The servant gave a hearty chuckle, her ample figure jiggling up and down in tempo as she laughed. "We better hurry or you gonna be late to supper for sure. Then we both be in trouble. Anyways, that's as good as them curls is gonna get for now. This hot, damp weather makin' everything limp, including your hair."

Jasmine checked her appearance in the mirror one last time, patted the ringlets, and rose from the cushioned chair. "You won't get in trouble, Mammy. I'm here to protect you." She pulled the woman into a tight hug, her slender arms barely spanning the old servant's broad waist. "Besides, after all these years, you know Papa is all bluster and bristle. He'd never lay a hand on anyone."

"Um hum, you jes' go on thinkin' that, child."

Jasmine loosened her hold and leaned back. She looked deep into the old woman's eyes. "Whatever do you mean?"

"You never know. Your pappy might jes' decide you're still young enough to turn over his knee." The words were followed by another deep-throated laugh. "Now get on downstairs and be nice to your papa's visitors."

"You know they'll bore me. Papa's visitors always want to talk about business matters instead of entertaining topics."

"Well, hot as it is this evenin', you know your pappy's bound to be in bad humor. He don't like this heat—never has."

"He complains about the heat every summer. I don't under-stand why Papa doesn't move us north with Grandmother."

"How he gonna do that? Can't move this cotton plantation up there where it's cold. 'Sides, your papa stays here 'cause this here is his home. He wouldn't live nowhere else. Even if he could, can't nobody get your mama out o' this house anymore."

Jasmine's brown eyes momentarily clouded. "I convinced her to go to White Sulphur Springs two years ago."

The old servant's head bobbed up and down. "Um hum. And she convinced all of you to return home only three days after you got there. Your mama doin' some better this past year, though."

"It's her headaches," Jasmine commented.

"It's her fears," Mammy corrected. "I don' know—maybe that's what causes her headaches. But your mama's been full of fears ever since I knowed her. Yes, sir. Being afraid, that's her real problem. Don' know what she thinks is gonna happen outside this here house." The old woman shook her head back and forth. Her forehead creased and formed a deep V between her wide-set eyes. "Um, um, it's a terrible thing to be so afraid of life."

Jasmine knew her father wouldn't care for Mammy's forth-rightness, especially in regard to the mistress of the plantation. But Jasmine wouldn't forbid Mammy to address the matter. At least Mammy was honest with her, saying the things that others thought but refused to confide.

Jasmine shook her head at the frustrating situation. "But she's been doing much better managing the household this past year. I've not been required to help her nearly so much."

Mammy patted Jasmine's narrow shoulder. "You's right, chile. She is doin' better." Mammy seemed to realize Jasmine needed encouragement. " 'Sides, the Good Lord, He done give us His promise to never leave us or forsake us. He won't be desertin' us now."

Jasmine smiled. Kindness shone in the devoted servant's eyes as their gazes locked. "What about you, Mammy? Wouldn't you like to live somewhere besides Mississippi?"

"Don't reckon I need to be givin' much thought to such a notion. The Willows is where I been livin' most all my life, and it's where I'll die. Don't know why we're even talkin' 'bout such a thing, 'specially when you need to go get yourself downstairs. You's jes' tryin' to avoid going down to supper."

Jasmine flashed a smile that brightened her whole face. "You never know where God might take you, Mammy. You're always singing that song about meeting Jesus." Her words grew distant as she raced down the stairs with her blue silk gown swaying in quickstep rhythm while she descended the spiral staircase. However, one stern look from Madelaine Wainwright slowed Jasmine's pace.

All eyes were focused upon her as she entered the parlor. She looked at her father. His normal pleasant demeanor appeared to have escaped him this evening. He pulled on his fob and removed the gold watch from his vest pocket, giving the timepiece a fleeting look. "I was beginning to wonder if you were going to join us."

"I apologize for rushing down the stairs—and for my tardiness. I hurried only because I didn't want to further delay dinner."

Her lips curved into what she hoped was an apologetic smile before her gaze settled on one of her father's guests. He was grinning back at her.

"Jasmine, I'd like to introduce you to Bradley and Nolan Houston. They've come from Massachusetts."

The words brought a broad smile to her lips. "Massachusetts? Oh, but this is wonderful. Do you live in Lowell? My grandmother lives in Lowell. Perhaps you know her? Alice Wainwright?"

Malcolm Wainwright cleared his throat and moved to his daughter's side. "I believe we would like to go in for supper, Jasmine. You can interrogate our guests once they've had something to eat. You'll recall that we've been awaiting your arrival."

Jasmine's three brothers were all smirking at their father's riposte when Bradley Houston stepped forward and drew near to her side. He didn't appear quite so old as she had first thought when she spied him from the upstairs window, and when he smiled, the sternness temporarily disappeared from his expression. "Miss Wainwright, I'd be happy to await my supper every evening if it afforded me the opportunity to keep company with someone of your beauty and charm."

11

"Why, thank you, Mr. Houston. You are absolutely too kind." Jasmine grasped Bradley's arm, graced him with an endearing smile, and permitted him to escort her into the dining room. The moment he glanced in the other direction, Jasmine turned toward her three older brothers and, with a great deal of satisfaction, stuck out her tongue.

"You must be careful if you ever visit up north where the weather is cold, Miss Wainwright. You wouldn't want your lovely face to freeze in such a position," Nolan Houston whispered as he took his seat next to her at the table.

Jasmine looked up in surprise, then leaned slightly closer and grinned. "Thank you. I shall make note of your kind advice, sir."

Nolan laughed aloud at the reply.

Bradley furrowed his brow and turned his attention to Jasmine. "Pray tell, what advice has my brother given you?"

"Cold weather. I was merely explaining how easily one can freeze when the weather turns frigid," Nolan replied.

Jasmine gave a quick nod of agreement to Nolan's reply before whispering a brief thank-you to him. Although she knew her brothers would have enjoyed listening while she attempted to wiggle out of such inappropriate behavior, it appeared Nolan Houston had been amused rather than offended.

Malcolm Wainwright pulled a freshly pressed white handkerchief from his pocket and mopped the beads of perspiration from his forehead. "I could do with some frigid weather right now. This heat is stifling, and it's barely the end of May. I don't know how I'm going to make it through another summer in Mississippi. Once the cotton crop has been laid by, I'm hoping to convince Madelaine we should make a return visit to White Sulphur Springs in Virginia or perhaps journey to Niagara Falls."

Jasmine's mother flinched at the suggestion but nevertheless remained the epitome of genteel womanhood. "I don't think we need to weary our guests with such a topic just now," she said and smiled. "After all, they've known nothing but travel these past weeks. They must be anxious to settle in for a time."

"I wasn't asking them to make further journey, my dear,"

Jasmine's father stated evenly, the tension evident in his tone.

Jasmine listened with interest to her parents' exchanged remarks. Perhaps over the next two months she could influence her mother to travel east. Certainly such an excursion would do them all good.

A wisp from a large feather plume floated downward, interrupting her thoughts, and she glanced up at Tobias. The young slave was perched on his small swing secured to the ceiling above the dining table. Tobias gave her a toothy grin as he swung back and forth above them while brandishing his oversized plume to deflect any flies that might enter through the open windows and hover over the dining table.

"If you don't stop distracting Tobias, he's going to fall off that swing one of these days," Samuel said.

"And a fine mess that would make. I don't believe Father would be quick to forgive you if Tobias dropped into the middle of the dining table," David agreed.

Malcolm glanced back and forth between his two older sons. "Gentlemen, please forgive the behavior of my children. It appears as if we're having a jousting match rather than dinner conversation."

"I believe McKinley should be applauded for his behavior. He hasn't said a word all evening," Jasmine commented while giving her youngest brother a bright smile.

Her father shook his head. "I'm going to hire someone to teach all of you proper etiquette if this sparring doesn't cease immediately. Ring that bell, Madelaine, and let's get this meal underway."

The jingling bell signaled two servants into immediate action. They entered the room carrying heaping platters of ham, biscuits, and roasted potatoes. Jasmine daintily helped herself to a biscuit before turning her attention to Nolan. "I'm still anxious to discover where you live in Massachusetts and if you might possibly know my grandmother. She lives in Lowell," Jasmine eagerly explained.

"Although I've visited Lowell on several occasions, I continue to make my home in Boston. Were I ever to move, I believe it would be to Cambridge rather than Lowell. I have far more friends located in Boston and Cambridge," Nolan replied. "Bradley, however, has numerous contacts in Lowell. In fact, he recently relocated from Boston to Lowell in order to expand his business ventures."

"Truly, how interesting. I thought Boston was a much larger city than Lowell. How is it your business will expand by moving to a *smaller* city, Mr. Houston?" Samuel Wainwright inquired.

Bradley straightened in his chair, obviously pleased by the question. "I'm a member of a prestigious group of men known as the Boston Associates. Perhaps you've heard of them?"

Jasmine's father gave a brief nod. "I've heard some vague references to the group. Seems I've been told they're intent upon monopolizing the entire textile industry in this country."

Bradley shifted in his chair and faced Malcolm. "Actually, the Boston Associates *are* the textile industry in this country," Bradley said with authority. "There are others, of course, but they are inconsequential. However, the Associates are anxious to see this country achieve industrial independence from England rather than attempting to monopolize trade for themselves. By basing our own textile industry in America, we reap the benefit of creating jobs that utilize products raised in this country and are then sold both here and abroad. It also lessens our dependence upon England for manufactured goods. Additionally, it gives cotton producers an excellent market for their crop."

Malcolm finished chewing a piece of ham and then lifted his glass and took a drink of water. "We already have an excellent market for our cotton. The Wainwrights have exported their cotton to the same English mills for as long as I care to remember. Don't expect we'll be changing business partners at this juncture."

"I hope while I'm here you'll permit me to at least point out the possibilities for business growth and higher income by considering another market. Doubtless you want to receive the best price for your efforts. Am I correct?"

"I want a good return, but profit isn't my only consideration when forming a business alliance. Trust and reliability are key factors I insist upon from my business partners, and I give them the same in return. I owe loyalty to my English customers. They were understanding during the drought that hit us back in 1834. While many cotton growers determined it was best to leave this area and move west, my family was able to sustain with advances on future crops paid to us by our English buyers."

Samuel nodded his head in agreement. "There were many cotton growers who posted signs on their property reading 'GTT'—Gone to Texas."

"Then you were indeed fortunate to have aligned yourself with such loyal buyers. However, one must constantly be looking toward the future. I believe you will find the Boston Associates can meet your every expectation in areas of trust and loyalty, plus provide a higher profit margin," Bradley said.

Jasmine listened intently, although she was rather bored by the conversation. Her mother had always taught her that a woman's place was to be supportive of her menfolk. She should appear interested, but not in a mannish fashion that would lead to asking questions. But her brothers certainly could ask their questions, and they did so with an amazing like-mindedness to her own thoughts.

As if reading her mind, McKinley turned toward their father as a wry smile curved his lips. "Perhaps you don't concern yourself with the profit factor, Father, because you no longer worry over the accounts. I would like to see The Willows receive a higher price for its cotton. Certainly the cost of shipping cotton to Massachusetts would be somewhat less than shipping it to England. Isn't this true, Mr. Houston?"

"What difference? The buyer pays the shipping costs," David retorted.

McKinley tapped the side of his forehead with his index finger. "Ah, but if the shipping costs are less, we can demand a higher price for the cotton based upon that very issue. Could we not?"

"Exactly!" Bradley replied. "And the higher the volume you can deliver, the higher the price the Associates will offer."

Jasmine couldn't help but find herself caught up in the

moment. Bradley's enthusiasm was contagious. Samuel leaned forward and gazed down the table toward his father. "Perhaps we should talk to our uncles about the possibility of a joint venture in which we could *all* obtain the higher price."

Jasmine's father waved his hand back and forth as if shooing flies away from his plate. "Now hold on! You boys are moving much too quickly with this idea. Making business decisions is not something done over the course of only one evening. My brothers are cautious men—steeped in tradition and fiercely loyal, just as I am."

Samuel would not be put off. "But how many times have you admonished us to be considerate of change and the development of products that will improve our abilities? I'm merely suggesting that this might well be one of those times."

Jasmine could read in her father's expression that he was more than a little annoyed to find his son brazenly sharing information that had at one time passed for private family business issues. She bit her lip to keep from saying something that might further upset her father. She caught Bradley Houston's expression even as her father began to counter Samuel.

"We in the South have always prided ourselves on moving ahead—not in speed and haste, but rather in determined, well-planned movements. We aren't talking of popping pieces back and forth atop a checkerboard. Rather, we prefer something more like a game of chess, where each move will have consequence for the moves to come." Their father toyed with his glass before taking a long, steady drink. Jasmine thought it a nice touch, an emphasis of his previous words.

Putting down the glass, her father continued. "I could never risk the well-being of my family—my beloved wife and daughter, our home, and all of the people who live here—without a great deal of prayerful consideration."

Bradley nodded in agreement. "Nor without evaluating additional reports and information upon which to base your decision. However, I can assure you that the Associates would be pleased to count you among their suppliers. It would appear to even a casual observer that your home and grounds are evidence of how well you've managed your plantation—especially in light of the depression you suffered only twelve years ago."

"We haven't always lived so well, but this house was Madelaine's dream. Wasn't it, my dear?" Malcolm's gaze settled upon his wife.

"I will admit that after visiting several other plantations, I was somewhat obsessed with having a Greek Revival home in which to rear our children," she replied.

"And it reflects the charm of the two ladies who grace its interior," Bradley added.

"Why, thank you," Madelaine replied, a tinge of pink coloring her cheeks. "I was determined to find the exact pieces of rococo furniture to accentuate the beauty of our home. I had given up all hope of finding a reviving-game sofa that met my expectations when I discovered one of our slaves is an extremely talented woodcarver. He carved and fashioned the woodwork and frame, leaving only the upholstering to be completed."

"I find all of your furnishings exceptional," Bradley said, his gaze scanning the immediate area.

Madelaine appeared to bask in Bradley's flattering remarks. "I don't think my husband shares your enthusiasm for household furnishings, although he has been very generous in permitting me my fancy," she modestly replied.

"Ah, but your husband realizes that a finely furnished home increases his social standing. It's a visible sign of his wealth and status," Bradley said.

"I thought the South's most desirable social status was that of slaveholder, not of home or property owner," Nolan interjected.

"That's true," Malcolm responded with a modicum of pride. "And here at The Willows, I have nearly a hundred slaves. Why, some of my prime hands are worth fifteen hundred dollars, and I could easily get two thousand for that woodcarver Madelaine mentioned—not that I plan to sell him."

"Of course not," Nolan replied quietly.

Jasmine heard the reproach in Mr. Houston's tone. She eyed

him curiously. What was it he meant to interject? She suddenly felt uncomfortable, but she had no idea why. This was her own home, her family table where conversations of productivity and the land often took place, but Mr. Nolan Houston did not seem impressed or approving.

Bradley cleared his throat and appeared to frown at his brother. "How much land do you own?" he inquired, shifting his attention back to Malcolm.

"Two thousand acres—some planted with corn, but the vast majority is cotton. It's as much as we can handle unless I purchase additional slaves, and we're making a nice profit at this juncture. No need to be greedy."

Before Bradley could reply, Jasmine pushed aside her discomfort and flashed a charming smile in his direction. "I wonder if we might discuss something other than cotton and slaves." She looked to her father as if asking permission for such a transition. She saw her mother nod in agreement.

"Our women are of such a delicate nature," Jasmine's father began. "They are strong, don't get me wrong. But such matters are well beyond them, and I have come to realize that it wearies them if we remain upon such topics overlong."

Bradley wiped his mouth with one of the monogrammed linen napkins and gave Jasmine his full attention. "I'm sorry. I have monopolized the conversation, haven't I? What topic would be of interest to you?"

She straightened in her chair and met his gaze. "I'd like to return to my original question regarding my grandmother."

"Ah yes. I never did respond, did I? Well, I'm sorry to say I have not met your grandmother. However, it is because of your grandmother that I've come here."

"How so?" Jasmine asked.

"I'm told your grandmother visits frequently with the wife of Matthew Cheever. Mr. Cheever holds a position of importance with the mills in Lowell. During their conversations, your grandmother mentioned the fact that her family was involved in raising cotton. Since our mills are always in need of cotton, I decided a visit to The Willows might prove beneficial to all of us."

"I see." She twisted in her chair to face Nolan. "And *you*, Mr. Houston? What brings you to The Willows?"

"I'm a poet and writer, Miss Wainwright. I've accompanied my brother in the hope of capturing the tangible essence of the South in some of my writings. I find it difficult to adequately describe places or people in my writings without actual observation. Since I want my readers to authentically experience the words I write, I thought this visit would prove fruitful."

Bradley raised one brow and gave a sardonic grin. "Nolan is quite the romantic, much like all of his writer friends."

Jasmine's attention remained focused upon Nolan. "I keep a journal and find writing to be a liberating experience. Of course, my writings are merely musings over my daily routine, whereas your writing influences and impacts upon the lives of others."

"At least that's my hope. Of course, one must have a somewhat extensive following in order to effectuate the type of change you speak of," Nolan remarked.

"My brother tends to conceal the success he's accomplished with his writing. Many who attend his readings proclaim his writing excels that of his contemporaries." Bradley took a sip of his coffee before settling back in his chair, meeting Mr. Wainwright's stern expression. "Nolan makes an excellent traveling companion. Our observations are completely opposite. Obviously our interests differ greatly, but we are both hoping you will favor us with a tour of your plantation."

"And perhaps your brothers' and neighbors' plantations as well," Nolan added, looking overhead. "A genuine representation of Southern living is what I'm seeking."

Jasmine thought his words sincere enough in his interest, but there was something almost mocking in his tone. She followed his gaze up to the small wiry-haired boy swinging above the table. The child had fallen asleep, still clutching the feathered plume in his hand. For a moment, she actually wondered if this tiny event in their evening might well appear on the pages of some Nolan Houston work. She smiled to herself and lowered her gaze, only to realize Nolan was grinning at her.

CHAPTER · 2

THE NEXT MORNING Bradley and Nolan walked out the vast front door of the white frame mansion, passing through the Doric colonnade that stood sentry over the upper and lower galleries of the home. Mr. Wainwright and Samuel led the way, with Jasmine close on their heels.

"Please say I may go with you," she begged. "I promise I won't say a word."

"Absolutely not," Malcolm Wainwright replied. "Go back inside. Your mother needs assistance with her household duties."

Bradley watched the young woman's expression. There was a desire to defy but also a respect that kept her from making too much of a scene. He saw her lower her gaze, as if rethinking her plan, as her father continued to speak.

"We'll be stopping in the fields before we go on to visit your uncle Franklin's plantation," Wainwright said. "That's no place for proper young ladies to be seen."

Jasmine looped arms with her father, lifted her face, and batted her eyelashes. "Would it be so difficult to go directly to Uncle Franklin's? I haven't seen Lydia since the dance two weeks ago."

"I can make arrangements for you to go visiting next week. I've already determined our route for today. Besides, we'll be discussing business. You'll be bored."

"I would be pleased to escort you to your uncle's home tomorrow, if your father agrees," Bradley offered.

Jasmine brightened at the offer just as he'd hoped she might. "Perhaps all three of us can go. You could recite poetry for us, Mr. Houston," she said, turning her attention to Nolan.

Nolan exchanged a glance with his brother. "We'll see what occurs. I may be so overwhelmed with my memories of today's observations that I'll want to spend tomorrow committing my thoughts to paper."

"It would hardly be proper for you to gallivant across the land unescorted," Jasmine's father reminded the trio. "However, perhaps I can spare Samuel to accompany you. If not, then Mammy will surely enjoy the time away."

"Oh, Father, you are very generous," Jasmine declared, looking quite pleased.

Bradley's suggestion appeared to appease Jasmine more quickly than her father's vague proposal—a concept which gave him pause for momentary reflection. Apparently Southern women were no more difficult to handle than those he'd encountered in the North. Females were females, and controlling them was merely a matter of utilizing proper management skill, he determined. Pleased with his incisive observation, he settled into the carriage opposite Malcolm and Samuel Wainwright. The carriage pulled away from the mansion and down the circular driveway before turning onto the dusty road. They traveled a short distance with Wainwright giving a brief commentary on the flora and fauna along the way.

He carefully pointed out the Spanish moss that draped itself like a gray veil from the trees that dotted the landscape. "Northerners are always intrigued by our Spanish moss," he commented. "Jasmine calls it Southern lace, although I don't think most would share her romantic notion."

The older man became more energized as they neared the first sighting of his planted acreage. "I thought I'd begin by having you view the fields," Wainwright said, pointing toward the sprouting cotton crop. The fields were lined with slaves who were chopping at the young shoots.

Bradley leaned forward and peered from the carriage. "It appears they're hacking up your new crop."

"They know better than to ruin my crop," his host said before giving a hearty laugh. "The crop would be strangled if the sprouts were to remain this thick. The slaves use their hoes to thin out the plants and create a stand."

"Might we stop so that I may examine the plants more closely?" Bradley inquired.

Wainwright beamed at the request, obviously pleased by Bradley's interest. "Pull over," Malcolm ordered the driver, who immediately pulled the horses to a halt alongside the dusty road.

The foursome exited the carriage, and Wainwright led them out into the fields with a determined step. He stopped and waved his arm in an encompassing gesture. "All this land you see belongs to my family. We've been cultivating cotton on it for many years. There've been many a good year, and many a bad one to follow."

"I want to learn everything I can about the difficulties you endure to produce your crop," Bradley said. "Although we Northerners are well acquainted with what it takes to get cotton from bale to bolt, we have no idea about the seed-to-bale process. I realize that without cotton, our mills are useless. And, quite frankly, it's you cotton growers who are the true heroes in the industrialization process."

Wainwright's chest puffed in obvious delight. "It's good to hear someone finally acknowledge the South is needed in order to make the industrialization process a success in this country. I will be most happy to show you the trials and tribulations we are forced to endure yearly in raising our cotton. We are, of course, dependent upon the weather, which is an issue of great importance to growers—while of little consequence to mill owners who operate their business indoors."

Bradley pulled his hat down to block the sun, his gaze resting upon the dark-skinned men, women, and children in the fields. They moved up and down the rows like an army of ants, their backs bent forward from the waist as they swung their hoes and chopped at the growing crop in hypnotic rhythm. He wondered at the efficiency ratio in light of other factors such as sickness and expenses.

Nolan pointed toward the slaves. "And *these* people? Are they also heroes?"

The other men turned and looked at Nolan as though he were speaking a foreign language. Samuel seemed confused, while Mr. Wainwright appeared to at least try to understand why Nolan would suggest such a thing. He once again pointed toward the fields. "Heroes? No, sir, those slaves are my overhead, an enormous expense that is ignored by anyone not involved in operating a plantation. As I told you at supper last night, there are few slaves on this plantation that didn't cost me nearly a thousand dollars."

"Of course you breed them, and there's no expense as the years go by," Nolan remarked.

Wainwright tugged on his vest and stepped closer. "No expense? Who do you think feeds, clothes, and houses them? Who cares for them when they're sick? These slaves are a constant financial drain on our income, yet we can't operate without them. And I do take issue with your remark about breeding. I permit my slaves to marry and bear children. I don't breed them, and I don't separate them from their families by selling them off, though there are many slave owners who think me lenient, even disruptive to our way of life for my kindness. Until you've operated a plantation of this enormity, you can't begin to fathom the financial obligation of caring for over a hundred slaves."

"One of life's necessary evils?" Nolan asked. "At least when one engages in this peculiar little institution, eh?"

Their host actually sputtered "P-peculiar? Evil? There's nothing peculiar or evil about raising cotton."

Bradley grasped his brother's arm. "My brother didn't mean to offend you, Mr. Wainwright. We admire the abilities and strength of our Southern brothers, and we're thankful you've agreed to educate us on plantation life. Don't you agree, Nolan?"

Nolan looked up from his notebook, his brow creased. "Actually, as a writer and poet, my interest in the South is quite different from yours, Bradley. I'd prefer to move freely on the land rather than hear the facts and figures of cotton production. No offense, Mr. Wainwright."

Wainwright nodded in a stern but gracious manner. "I'll have my overseer bring you a horse if you like."

"That would be most agreeable. I'll ride about the countryside and return to the house later in the day."

"Strange man, your brother," Wainwright remarked a short time later when they had once again proceeded on their way.

Bradley glanced over his shoulder and watched as Nolan mounted the horse and began following the overseer into a field. "I find most writers and artists are much like Nolan. They're all dreamers, out of touch with the realities of life."

"I'm certain your father is pleased to at least have one son with a sound head on his shoulders," Wainwright said.

"I believe he was quite proud of me. Our parents are both deceased, which is one of the reasons I've taken Nolan under my wing. As the older son, I was expected to assume the reins of the family business and gladly did so. Nolan's artistic bent was accepted by my parents, even cultivated by my mother, who was overjoyed to have a poet in the family. An emphasis on culture in an age of industrialization, to be sure. However, as you are well aware, philosophies and thinking vary greatly from North to South. The country is a veritable selection of thoughts and opinions that may very well do more to see us divided and at each other's throats than any foreign enemy could hope to accomplish."

Wainwright eyed him quite seriously for a moment, and Bradley couldn't help but wonder if his comment would meet with affirmation or condemnation. Finally Wainwright nodded ever so slightly. "It is difficult to understand the heart of another man when sitting at your own table. I must at least credit your brother for wanting to know more."

Bradley smiled. "Then credit me as well, for I am here for no other purpose than to better understand how your family business operates and how my family business might benefit yours in the future."

The carriage continued onward, the fields spread along either side of the roadway covered with sprouting green plants for as far as the eye could see. "What is your family business?" Samuel inquired.

"My father was primarily in the shipping business. However, I've sold a portion of the business, which, as I told your father in my letter, I've recently invested in the textile industry. My investment is why I'm visiting the South. I believe a man must learn all aspects of a business in order to excel as a manager of his holdings."

"Absolutely. I couldn't agree more," the elder Wainwright replied. "And although we sell our cotton to England, we're pleased to help you in your endeavor. This is my brother Franklin's home."

The men stepped out of the carriage in front of a house that appeared to be a duplicate of Malcolm Wainwright's balconied Greek Revival home. "Who knows? One day I may be able to convince you to sell your cotton to me." Bradley concluded the statement with a confident smile and was pleased neither man issued a negative response.

Wainwright led them up the steps to the house and knocked at the front door. A tall black woman escorted them into the library, where Malcolm and Samuel made themselves comfortable. Bradley stood by the fireplace and immediately stepped forward when Franklin Wainwright entered the room. Malcolm rose from his chair. "Franklin, I'd like to introduce Bradley Houston from Massachusetts. Bradley, my brother Franklin Wainwright."

"Pleased to make your acquaintance, Mr. Wainwright," Bradley said while firmly grasping Franklin's hand.

"Thank you, Mr. Houston," Franklin replied before shaking hands with Malcolm and Samuel.

"Bring us something cool to drink," he ordered the servant before turning his attention back toward Bradley. "Malcolm told me you would be visiting, and I must say I am impressed and pleased that you've chosen to familiarize yourself with the production of cotton. Tell me, Mr. Houston, what do you think of our cotton kingdom thus far?"

Bradley took the glass of lemonade a young girl had just offered. "I'm impressed. Your brother has given me a brief overview of the entire process, although it's difficult to imagine what these fields must look like when harvest time arrives."

"Likely they appear much like your New England countryside after a winter snow," Samuel submittted. "It's a virtual sea of white in every direction."

"Exactly," Franklin agreed. "You should return in the fall or early winter to see for yourself. It's truly a sight to behold."

"I may decide to do just that," Bradley replied. "And your acreage is comparable to Malcolm's?"

The two Mr. Wainwrights exchanged an expression that suggested Bradley had done something out of line. He revisited his words even as Franklin cleared his throat to answer.

"A gentleman seldom discusses the size of his property in comparison to another. Perhaps in the North that type of thing is no longer considered intrusive, but in the South it is akin to my asking you what your profit ledgers revealed from last year."

Bradley realized he was well out of his knowledge when it came to Southern manners and etiquette. "I do apologize. Please forgive me. I never meant to be offensive."

Franklin nodded, appearing appeased. He waved his hand and went on, much to Bradley's surprise, to answer his question. "I merely choose to apprise you of the matter. As for the Wainwright family, Malcolm owns slightly more land than either Harry or I. His inheritance was larger—oldest son," he said with a laugh.

"And a more frugal way of life that has afforded me the ability to continue purchasing additional acreage," Malcolm added.

"True. However, I believe Harry and I have outproduced you the last two years."

"But only because we haven't cleared and planted our additional land." Samuel gave a hearty laugh and nudged his uncle. "Just wait and see what we do next year."

His uncle didn't appear in the leastwise offended that the

younger man had joined in to challenge his elder. Bradley's own father would have boxed his ears for such an intrusion.

A short time later the youngest Wainwright brother, Harry, arrived and joined them for the noonday meal. Bradley listened and watched the men, gleaning information in an unassuming, congenial manner throughout the afternoon. He liked the Wainwright men. They were ambitious but didn't appear overly greedy, determined to continue with their plantations, yet open to modernization and change—men he could possibly influence.

———

Bradley was in his room relaxing before supper when Nolan finally returned to The Willows. "I was beginning to grow concerned. I thought perhaps you'd lost your bearings and couldn't find your way back to the house."

"I apologize. I didn't mean to worry you, but you know how I am when caught up in a project. I become unaware of anything but what I'm working on at the moment."

Bradley finger-combed his thinning brown hair and patted it into place. "So your writing went well? I was somewhat concerned when we parted this morning. You appeared rather distressed, and I regretted letting you go off on your own. I think you would have found Malcolm's brothers to be quite entertaining."

"I'm certain they are fine men. However, I'm pleased Malcolm allowed me to see the countryside on my own. I spent most of the day with the slaves, watching them work, visiting their quarters, talking to them. Did you visit the slave quarters at any of the plantations?"

"No. Malcolm did give me a few additional facts and figures concerning the costs involved in caring for the slaves. He owns more than I anticipated, but of course, some are household help—and there are also the elderly and the children."

"But most of them work in the fields. It's a miserable existence—nearly indescribable."

Bradley jerked to attention. "Then there is no reason to make any attempt to illustrate anything other than the beauty of the countryside. After all, that's why you're here, to encapsulate the beauty of the South."

"Yes, of course, and that's exactly what I plan to do. Give Northerners a word picture of genteel Southern living."

"Good, good," Bradley replied earnestly. "In fact, I'm giving some consideration to returning in the fall or early winter when the crops are ready for harvest. Samuel tells me the entire countryside turns almost as white as New England after a winter snow. You may want to consider coming with me. The sight of all that ripe cotton would surely lend itself to poetic beauty."

Nolan sat down beside his brother. "If not poetry, I'm certain it would be worthy of at least a lengthy essay."

"Then you might come along?"

"Absolutely. I wouldn't consider remaining in Massachusetts if you return."

CHAPTER · 3

WEEKS LATER, Jasmine raced down the spiral staircase and bounded toward her father as he walked in the front door. "Papa, I need to talk with you."

"Honestly, Jasmine! You must cease running about the house like a child," Malcolm admonished as he continued through the foyer and into the parlor. "Good afternoon, Madelaine. I trust you've had a pleasant day."

Madelaine Wainwright sat on the velvet-upholstered settee while fanning herself with a vengeance. Her latest needlepoint project was lying on the couch beside her. "No mishaps of importance, thank you. And you?"

"Quite a few of the slaves are sick. I sent Luther to fetch the doctor. I don't want an outbreak of some kind right before picking time."

"It's only the end of June, dear. If there's sickness, they'll be fine by the harvest. You worry overmuch about their health. This heat is stifling, isn't it?"

"It's not too late to consider a trip to White Sulphur Springs," Malcolm suggested.

"You know I'm not able to travel, Malcolm," she replied.

"Besides, traveling to Virginia will not ensure or aid the health of our workers."

Jasmine remained near the doorway, pacing back and forth. "Do stop that pacing, Jasmine!" Her father turned toward her, beads of perspiration dotting his forehead.

His command brought her to an immediate halt. "I'm sorry, Father. I'll talk to you after supper."

"Oh, do come in and sit down. It's this unrelenting heat—it has me on edge. What do you want to discuss?"

Jasmine walked farther into the room and held up a folded sheet of paper. "I received this missive from Grandmother Wainwright. She asked that I come for a visit. You know how much I miss her, and I was thinking we could go to Massachusetts for a visit—where the weather is much cooler this time of year. An excellent solution to avoid the summer heat, don't you think?"

Malcolm alighted beside his wife on the yellow silk sofa. "I don't think a visit to Massachusetts is in the offing for any of us— at least not now. Didn't you hear your mother say she can't travel at present? Why don't you write and invite your grandmother to The Willows for a visit? That would at least alleviate your longing to see her."

"I invited her in my last letter. But she says she hasn't been feeling well enough to make such a tiring journey. That's why she requested we come visit her. Please take time and reconsider, Papa."

"What's this? Grandmother's ill?" McKinley, Jasmine's youngest brother, asked as he walked into the room and joined them. "I don't recall Grandmother ever ailing when she lived at The Willows. It must be something she's contracted by living in those crowded conditions in the North."

"What does she say is ailing her? Let me see the letter," Malcolm said. Wrinkles began to line his brow as he examined the contents of the missive.

"Nothing serious, I hope," Madelaine said, her gray eyes bright with concern.

Malcolm pulled out his handkerchief and swiped away the

perspiration that had formed across his forehead. "The letter is rather vague. She says she hasn't been feeling quite herself and finds it impossible to make the journey south. I do wish she'd been more explicit. She goes on to say that seeing Jasmine once again would fulfill her deepest desires."

By now Samuel and David had returned home and joined the family in the parlor. "Why is everyone looking so somber?" Samuel questioned, striding across the room to his usual perch. Jasmine noted Samuel and David were dressed almost identically in fawn-colored trousers, navy blue jackets, and knee boots. They'd apparently been riding.

"Did somebody die?" David chuckled as he scanned around the room.

Madelaine raised her hand to the neckline of her lavender and white striped dress and gasped. "Do you think *that's* why Mother Wainwright has asked to see Jasmine? Do you think she's—*dying?*"

David immediately moved to his mother's side. "What's this about Grandmother?"

"She's written Jasmine," their father announced. "She asks that Jasmine visit her in the North."

"I'm a dolt. Forgive me," David said, meeting Jasmine's steady gaze even as he patted his mother's hand. He quickly turned his full attention to their mother. "I shouldn't have said such a thing. Forgive me for upsetting you. Grandmother has always been fond of Jasmine and likely misses her very much."

"Yet she could be in dire circumstances and not want to worry us," their mother countered anxiously.

Jasmine watched as they all seemed to forget she was in the room. It was often that way. The men in her family were generally compelled to decide her fate regarding every issue of her life. Her mother accepted this graciously, with exception, of course, to traveling. Upon this issue, Jasmine's mother had made it very clear: There was to be no travel unless absolutely necessary. Perhaps Mammy was right. Fear of the unknown—or possibly the known—kept Jasmine's mother a homebound prisoner. Still, as easily as her mother accepted direction from her husband in most every other area, Jasmine was hard-pressed to be as congenial. As the only daughter in the family, she was generally doted upon and she tried not to abuse this privileged position. However, at times like this, she found it hard not to press to have her own way.

"It's difficult to determine the exact scenario from the meager contents of this letter," Jasmine's father was saying. "However, knowing my mother, I'm guessing supplying such scant information is her way of forcing me to heed to her beck and call. She's likely enjoying life to the fullest while suffering from occasional loneliness for Jasmine. I *knew* this would happen. I warned her when she returned north that she would miss being with family."

Jasmine could see her possibilities for a trip slip away with each turn of her father's reasoning. "She may truly be ill, Papa. Mr. Houston mentioned the fact that he hasn't seen her at any of the recent social functions he's attended in Lowell."

Malcolm turned toward Jasmine, his eyebrows arched into twin mountain peaks. "Mr. Houston? You're corresponding with him also?"

Her father's scrutiny caused her cheeks to grow even warmer. "I've merely replied to his letter. I didn't think you would disapprove. Before Mr. Houston departed The Willows, he begged me to reply if he should write to me. I finally agreed, although I had little interest in corresponding with him. I've received only one letter."

"It's not that I disapprove. I'm merely surprised. He didn't mention your grandmother's illness when he wrote me. What exactly did Bradley say? Bradley is the Mr. Houston you're referring to, is he not?"

"Yes, Papa. He merely said what I've already told you. He said he had made it a priority to make Grandmother's acquaintance upon his return home. In fact, he called on her only three days after returning to Lowell. He went on to mention that she hasn't been present at recent social functions."

"I don't think his comment is indicative of anything worrisome. They simply may not be invited to the same social events," Samuel concluded.

"But what if she *is* dying and you ignore her plea? How could you ever live with such a decision?" Madelaine argued, much to Jasmine's surprise.

"So you think I should immediately heed to her bidding?" Malcolm asked.

"I think you should give serious consideration to making the journey," Madelaine replied. "I could hardly live with myself if something were to happen and you missed being in her attendance because of my poor constitution."

Malcolm rose from the sofa and prowled about the room like a cat searching for the perfect place to curl and rest. "And who would run The Willows during such a long absence? Leaving at this time of year isn't wise. What if we couldn't return in time for the first picking? I've never been gone from the plantation during any part of picking season."

"Really, Malcolm! Only a few minutes ago you were attempting to persuade me to travel to White Sulphur Springs."

"That is not even close to the same thing. We could certainly return home from there before first picking. A journey to Massachusetts will take much longer. And it's already late June."

"What about the three of us?" Samuel asked. "Do we not assist in the management of the plantation? Surely we could tend to matters while you're gone."

"Absolutely," McKinley said while David nodded his agreement.

Madelaine graced her husband with a winsome smile. "You see, you have already resolved that issue. And if a problem of consequence should arise during your absence, your brothers would be close at hand to lend assistance. After all, with adjoining plantations—Harry on one side and Franklin on the other—there would be scant possibility of the boys needing any further support."

"Could it be that you would consider making the journey with us?" Malcolm inquired, a hint of expectation lacing his question.

"You know my affliction makes travel impossible. I'm merely

35

pointing out that I would not be averse to you and Jasmine making the journey. After all, there are few plantation owners who would find themselves in such excellent circumstances if they needed to be away for a substantial period of time. We both know that many of the plantation owners leave for the entire summer with no one other than an overseer in charge."

"Well, they can manage their businesses as they see fit, but I'll not leave my plantation to the hands of an overseer for months on end. Even with my sons and brothers to take charge, I've no intent on being gone for a *substantial* period of time. If I agree to travel north, I will make every effort to return prior to harvest. It's difficult enough to consider leaving the boys in charge at this time; much more so during picking season."

"I understand your concerns, Malcolm, but you will give the journey consideration, won't you? It causes me great distress to think of your mother alone and ailing."

"I'll give the matter thought. If you would agree to accompany us, I would be willing to make immediate preparations. You know I'd go to almost any length to get you away from The Willows for a short time. It distresses me that you continue to seek refuge within the walls of this house, my dear. It's not healthy."

Jasmine immediately took up her father's argument. "Oh, do say you'll come, Mother."

Madelaine dropped her gaze toward her lap and began picking at the lace edging on her linen handkerchief. "I couldn't possibly travel to Massachusetts. And I do go outdoors—every day. I love tending the flowers in my gardens. Truly, my desire to remain at The Willows is not harmful to my well-being in the least. Please don't make my unwillingness to accompany you a factor in your decision. And if you want to be back in time for harvest, you must leave immediately."

Malcolm nodded. "I'll ride over and talk to Harry and Franklin tomorrow. Hopefully they'll be able to shed some light on Mother's possible ailments—or at least add their thoughts as to the obvious ambiguity of her letter."

"And you'll ask if they'll assist with the plantation should you decide to journey to Massachusetts?"

"Yes, dear. I'll discuss that matter also, but Jasmine need not begin packing her trunks just yet," he warned.

"Of course not, Papa," Jasmine agreed. She was barely able to repress the delighted giggle bubbling in her throat. Though difficult to believe, it certainly appeared as if her father would relent. If Uncle Harry were reasonably convinced Papa should make the journey, there was no doubt Uncle Franklin would agree also.

Samuel folded his arms and took a serious stance. "Should you decide to go visit Grandmother, I hope you will give me the opportunity to actually manage the plantation. It truly isn't necessary for Uncle Harry or Uncle Franklin to spend time at The Willows. David and I can manage the slaves, and McKinley already maintains the books and accounts for you. Should there be any sort of trouble, you know I would immediately send for one of them."

"I'm sure you would, Samuel. However, I want to speak with my brothers before making a final decision about any of this," Malcolm replied.

"May I please be excused?" Jasmine inquired softly. "This heat has caused me to feel faint, and I'd like to go to my room and lie down." It wasn't exactly a lie, but truth be told, she wanted to think out her plans for the upcoming trip. Despite what her father said about not packing her trunks, Jasmine felt confident the journey would take place.

"By all means," her mother replied. "I'll send Tobias to fetch you when supper's ready."

Mammy was busy mending a cotton chemise when Jasmine reached her bedroom. "What you doin' back up here so soon, chile? You feelin' poorly?"

Jasmine twirled around the room and finally fell upon the bed. "Oh, Mammy, I think I'm going to get to go to Massachusetts and see Grandmother!" she exclaimed. Rising up to a sitting position, she clasped her hands together. "Won't that be *wonderful*?"

"Um hum. It surely would be fine. I knows how much yo' grandma loves you."

"And how much I love her," Jasmine added. "It's been so lonely since she left The Willows."

Mammy nodded her head up and down as she continued jabbing her needle in and out of the white fabric. "Now tell me, when your pappy gonna take you north?"

"Well, it's not absolutely positive yet, but he said he was going to talk to Uncle Franklin and Uncle Harry tomorrow. If they agree that it would be wise for Papa to go and check on Grandmother's health *and* say they'll help supervise the work here at The Willows, I think we will leave very soon."

The old woman smiled, and her white teeth shone like a fine row of ivory piano keys. "What your mama think 'bout all this?"

"She encouraged us to make the journey. All I did was show Papa the letter, and Mama immediately took up the case. It was *so* perfect, Mammy."

"Well, I surely will miss you, chile," Mammy replied.

"And I'll miss you too, but I'm certain it's going to be a grand adventure, Mammy."

Chapter · 4

Bradley carried the letter into his library, seated himself, and carefully opened the missive, excited to read the contents. He had anxiously checked the mail each day, eager to see if Jasmine would reply. He had begun his letter to her while he and Nolan were still on board ship returning home from their visit to The Willows, but he waited to mail it. He knew the girl would want to hear word of her grandmother. He hoped to woo her in a slow yet deliberate fashion. She was young for him, a closer match in age for Nolan, but she would fit perfectly into his own plans. Besides, women were more easily controlled if they married at a young age—before they developed a mind of their own. The fact that Jasmine was beautiful had been a pleasant surprise, but he also realized her beauty might prove an additional challenge in winning her hand. With that thought at the forefront of his mind, he had also been corresponding with Malcolm Wainwright. Once he had Malcolm as an ally, achieving his plan to marry Jasmine should prove uncomplicated.

A knock sounded, and the front door opened as Bradley finished reading the letter. "Bradley?"

"Nolan! I wasn't expecting you in Lowell. What brings you here?"

"Nathan Appleton convinced Henry and Fanny to accompany him to Lowell for a meeting of the Associates this evening. Since Nathan plans to stay in Lowell for several days, Henry thought I should join them and we could take a canal boat and reminisce about the leisurely summers that have long since passed."

"Henry Longfellow remains the constant romantic. I can't imagine how Nathan, the ever-vigilant businessman, abides a son-in-law with no business acumen whatsoever," Bradley said.

"He seems quite fond of Henry—perhaps because his daughter is so obviously happy in her marriage to him. I thought we might have supper together before your meeting with the Associates."

"I'd like that. We'll have sufficient time to dine at the Merrimack House if we leave now. I can go on to my meeting from there."

Once they were seated at a small table in the Merrimack House restaurant, Nolan said, "Nathan mentioned you're planning to buy the Hinch estate. Is that true?"

"Word does travel quickly, doesn't it? I've made an offer to Hinch's widow. She's anxious to rid herself of the place, and I'd like a home that has some acreage surrounding it. It's become more and more difficult to find such a place, and even though it's a short distance from Lowell, I believe it would serve my needs very well."

"Serve your needs? That place is *huge,* Bradley. Why would a man with only one servant want to live—" Nolan stopped midsentence and stared at his brother. "Are you planning to wed in the near future?"

Bradley cleared his throat and tugged at his collar. "It is my hope, but I don't know if my proposal will actually be accepted. I hesitate even to discuss the matter for fear she'll reject me and the whole of Massachusetts will know I've been turned away."

"You can confide in me, brother. Ever since Nathan made mention of the matter, I've been attempting to determine if a woman might well be involved, and if so, who the woman might be. I'm thinking she's likely someone I haven't met. I promise I'll not breathe a word to any of the local gossips," Nolan said with a genial laugh.

"Actually, you *have* met her. When the time is right, I'm planning to ask for the hand of Jasmine Wainwright."

Nolan's brows furrowed as he placed his coffee cup on the white china saucer. "You jest!"

"No. I found her appealing."

Nolan leaned back in his chair and gazed at his brother, his eyes narrowed to thin slits. "Was it Jasmine you found appealing or her father's cotton plantation?"

"You believe me to have an ulterior motive?"

"Have you ever done anything in your life without an ulterior motive?" Nolan asked wryly. "I observed your enthusiastic efforts to impress the Wainwright family. You utilized every available moment to your advantage, plying them with the benefits of selling their cotton to you rather than shipping their crops to England."

Bradley fingered his thinning hair and met his brother's accusations with an unwavering gaze. "A marriage that combines both love and business is a match most men long for, Nolan. At least those of us who aren't enmeshed in your world of poetry and literature and must actually perform productive work."

"Ah, Bradley, you know that power and control are your aspirations in life. You would never choose to live in the literary world. Competition and power are your aphrodisiacs, not music and poetry. However, I, too, was drawn to Jasmine. She seemed a sweet girl—sheltered from the outside by her family. How do you propose to win her hand? Better still, how do you plan to fit her into your ambitious world?"

"Truly you can be a bother," Bradley said, shaking his head. "How often does the average wife fit into the ambitions of her husband's world? Women are necessary for the procreation of the race. A man wants a son to carry his name—to take the helm of the empire he builds as a legacy."

"Have you talked with her father?"

"I've been communicating with both Jasmine and her father.

In fact, I had a letter from Jasmine today telling me that she and her father are coming to Lowell for a visit with her grandmother. From the content of her letter, I doubt it was mailed much before they sailed. I'm guessing they'll arrive any day. I plan to speak with her father while they're in Lowell. If things go well, the marriage could take place when we go south for the harvest."

Nolan shook his head back and forth. "I can't believe you've plotted out this entire scheme. Have you considered her youth and the fact that she'd prefer a marriage based upon affection? Doubtless, in the beginning, she'll mistake your attention for love and later be disappointed. Surely you can barter an arrangement for the cotton without compromising the future of a young girl."

"Just like your friends, you think there are idyllic solutions to all of life's situations. Well, dear brother, that occurs only in your make-believe world of poetry and prose. Should Malcolm agree to the marriage, and I think he will, rest assured that I will treat Jasmine well."

"You'll treat her well so long as she adheres to your parameters," Nolan said.

Bradley arched his eyebrows. "Rules are made to be followed. As you've pointed out, she's young and will need guidance in what is expected of a proper wife. However, I'm confident that her mother has probably already seen to much of her training. You have to understand that in the South, especially among genteel families such as the Wainwrights, daughters are brought into the world with no other purpose but to make a prosperous match. Marriage to me would prosper that family in more ways than I can illuminate for you at this moment. Once she realizes how this match will benefit her, Jasmine Wainwright will be happy and content." Bradley pulled his watch from his vest pocket and glanced at the time. "Though I'm completely enjoying our conversation, I really must be on my way. The meeting tonight is important and I dare not be tardy. The Associates are considering me as their primary buyer. I'll present my proposal for expansion this evening. We can discuss this matter further tomorrow and perhaps have supper at that time as well."

Bradley leaned against the stone fireplace and surveyed the room, hoping to exude an air of confidence. He nodded to James Morgan and Leonard Montrose when they entered the doorway and then shifted his full attention to Nathan Appleton and Matthew Cheever. His fingers tapped nervously along the highly polished wood of the mahogany mantel as he waited for the meeting to commence. There was little doubt the members of the Boston Associates would follow the lead of Appleton and Cheever this evening. Consequently, Bradley knew he must impress them above all the others.

Leonard Montrose approached, blocking Bradley's view of the two men. "For someone who's hoping for a prestigious appointment this evening, you're looking rather grim, Bradley."

Bradley repositioned himself alongside Leonard, now able to once again observe Nathan Appleton. "I'm not certain the matter will come to a vote tonight, but if it does, I hope I can count on your support."

"I'll go along with them." Leonard tipped his head toward Matthew and Nathan. "If they want you, so do the rest of us. It's the way of things around here these days. With Tracy Jackson ailing, Matthew and Nathan seem to carry most of the control. I trust them to know what's best for the Corporation."

Bradley took a deep draw on his cigar and blew a funnel of gray smoke toward the ceiling. "Then once I lay out my proposal, let's hope they think I'm what's best for the Associates."

Leonard took a sip of port and looked around the room. "Thought maybe Tracy would be here tonight, but perhaps he's unable to tolerate the late-night air. These business meetings always take longer than necessary," he mused.

Before Bradley could comment, Leonard waved to several men across the room. "Good luck on the proposal," he absently remarked as he sauntered off.

Bradley didn't reply. Instead, he watched Nathan and Matthew as they continued their private conversation. Perhaps they were discussing him. He had yet to achieve the level of acceptance into the Associates that he so desperately desired. There was no doubt it was his substantial investment in the mills that had swayed the Associates to permit him entrance into their ranks. Selling his father's shipping business had been risky, yet Bradley yearned for the esteem his alignment with these powerful men would surely produce.

"Prepared for your presentation?" James Morgan asked jovially. The man's bulbous nose was the color of a cardinal. Bradley hoped James hadn't imbibed too much—he needed all the support he could garner, and none of the Associates would pay heed to a man who was in his cups. Perhaps it was merely the heat.

"I'm anxious to begin," Bradley told him, "and it appears that will soon occur." He nodded toward Nathan and Matthew, who were moving to the front of the room.

Nathan seated himself nearby, but it was Matthew Cheever who took immediate control of the meeting. Bradley maneuvered through the crowd, angling for a better view of the proceedings. Upon Kirk Boott's death nine years ago, Matthew had easily transitioned into the older man's powerful position, and that conversion had been a matter of intense interest to Bradley. The entire process reinforced his own desire to eventually be elevated into a position of leadership among the Associates. He hoped he would make that first step tonight.

"Now, I know you're all aware that as our textile industry has grown, so has the need for cotton. We have discussed the possibility of appointing a liaison to expand our acquisition of cotton from the Southern plantations. Demand is high for all of the textile products we can produce. However, I think you would all agree that unless we can purchase sufficient raw cotton, there is no need for further expansion or development."

Matthew waited until the murmuring ceased and then motioned to Bradley. "Move on over here, Bradley. All of you know our good friend and loyal investor, Bradley Houston."

"Indeed, and we're pleased to have his allegiance," Leonard Montrose called out.

"And his *money*," some unseen member added from the back of the room.

A smattering of laughter followed the latter remark. Matthew smiled and waited patiently until the noise diminished. "Bradley has indicated a strong desire to help the Corporation convince our Southern cotton growers to refrain from exporting their products to England and begin looking to the North as their primary buyer. This won't be an easy task. As we all know, most of the Southern plantation owners are comfortable with the English markets they've developed and see no reason to change their habits. We've convinced a few of the growers, but not nearly enough."

"We'll have to give them reason to make those changes," Bradley said.

"They should be loyal to their own country, if nothing else," James put in, "but I imagine additional money is what they'll ultimately insist upon. However, if anyone can convince them they owe allegiance to this country, it's Bradley Houston."

Bradley gave him a grateful nod and then looked at the remainder of the gathered men. "I hope the rest of you will agree."

Wilson Harper, one of the more recent members to join the Associates, stepped forward. "Is this a *paid* position? Seems to me there might be others who need a job more than you, Bradley."

"I've told Nathan and Matthew I'd be willing to accept the position on a commission basis. You'll pay for nothing unless I'm successful—which will equate to your success also. Now, I know there will be stumbling blocks. I've heard reports some Southerners resent the growth and industrialization taking place in the North while the South is relegated to raising the cotton."

Robert Woolsey, another new member of the group, leaned forward and set his eyes on Bradley. "Those plantation owners don't realize how easy they've got it. Their slaves do the work while they live a life of leisure."

"I don't think we can approach negotiations with that kind of attitude, Robert." Bradley continued, "Our Southern brothers have a significant investment, in both their land and slaves. I've recently traveled south to learn more about cotton production, and while we face difficulties and expenses with our mills, they, too, face adversity. They're dependent upon the elements, whereas we have few concerns in that regard, and I believe we'll need to be sympathetic to their situation if we're to develop good relations. The Southerners resent their reliance upon Northern factories for the majority of their purchases while they are forced to depend upon agriculture for their economic well-being. I believe that's why many of them continue to ship their cotton to overseas markets. They'd much prefer to develop their own textile mills and avoid the tariffs placed on our products. And while you decry the fact that they have slaves performing their labor, the Southerners would likely argue that the mill girls and Irish work for *us* while *we* lead lives of leisure."

Robert's face knit into a tight frown. "The difference is, we pay wages."

Bradley shifted in his chair. He didn't want to beleaguer the point, but Robert's condescending attitude annoyed him. "And the Southerners have constant costs associated with their slaves, including food, housing, clothing, and medical needs, all of which I believe the mill girls are charged for. Slaves do not pay for these amenities; they are provided for by the plantation owner. In order to attract additional Southern suppliers, we need to refrain from imposing our values and harsh judgments upon them. After all, they might just as easily judge you."

Matthew cleared his throat. "I'm sure we all agree that we need each other if the country is going to prosper. Right now we need to embrace, rather than alienate, the Southern growers. Far too many of them still prefer to sell their cotton to England for the very reasons Bradley has so eloquently stated. They see no reason to practice any extended allegiance to the North because as far as they're concerned, they are a country unto themselves. Consider the current state of affairs. We have complications with Mexico and the southern territories they claim. We have individual states that prefer being left to decide for themselves how their particular regions will be operated—and no taste for Northern interference."

"I don't understand their separatist mindset," Wilson Harper threw in.

"Exactly," Matthew said, looking around the room. "Who here understands that fierce drive to isolate and serve the desires and means of the state, rather than the country as a whole?"

Mutters filled the air, but no one offered a concise thought. Bradley smiled. "I understand it—probably better than most Americans. My years in the shipping industry, traveling with my father to various southern ports, learning to deal with the businessmen and their aspirations—all that has afforded me a better understanding of the Southern mind."

"Pray include us in this understanding," Woolsey requested in a sarcastic manner that suggested he disbelieved Bradley's ability.

Bradley toyed with his watch fob. "I am a businessman and I offer you a business proposition. The risk to yourselves and this Association is very limited." He very nearly suggested that if the Associates weren't interested in his abilities, there would no doubt be others who would, but he held his tongue.

Leonard Montrose lifted his cigar in the air, with the ash glowing orange as a breeze wafted through the open window. "Since Bradley has agreed to take this position on a commission basis, I see no reason not to move forward with his election tonight."

With only minor exception, the men exhibited their faith in Bradley. At the same time, they had been quick to express the necessity for results. If expansion were to continue at the rate the Associates desired, the growth of their cotton markets must keep pace. They were placing their confidence in him to find a supplier. And he would prove their confidence was well placed. No matter the cost, no matter the effort—he would exceed their wildest expectations.

CHAPTER · 5

ALICE WAINWRIGHT quickly thumbed through the mail that had been delivered by her servant on the hand-painted breakfast tray only moments earlier. Breakfast in the private sitting room adjoining her bedroom was one luxury Alice afforded herself each morning. Not that she was a spoiled or pampered woman. On the contrary, she considered herself rather self-sufficient. However, she coveted this quiet time when she could gaze out her bedroom window and reflect upon God's creation while planning her day, for she knew that once she descended the staircase, interruptions would greet her at every turn.

As was her custom, she seated herself in the small alcove overlooking the tidy flower garden below her bedroom window and picked up Jasmine's letter. She couldn't deny the surge of anticipation and delight she felt each time one of her granddaughter's frequent letters arrived. She momentarily held the envelope in her hands while contemplating what tidbits of information the contents might divulge. Jasmine's letters were always filled with the daily happenings at The Willows. Somehow the child could make the most mundane occurrences seem exciting. Her imagination seemed endless, and Alice had encouraged Jasmine's interest in writing. In fact, she'd given her granddaughter a thick leather-covered diary before moving to Lowell, suggesting Jasmine try her hand at journaling or poetry.

As she edged the blade of her silver letter opener under the envelope's seal, Alice wondered if Jasmine had been writing any poetry. She'd be certain to ask when next she wrote. Removing the pages from their snug paper cocoon, Alice lovingly pressed out the deep creases with her hand.

Page by page, she read the letter before leaning back in her steam-bent, cushioned chair and staring out at the flowering trees. She remained motionless for several minutes, enjoying the shades of pink and ivory that peeked through the green foliage. Then, with a quiet determination, she picked up the small gold bell beside her chair and gave one sharp ring.

Moments later, Martha hurried in as though she expected to see the room engulfed in flames. "Yes, ma'am? Is something wrong with your breakfast?"

Alice waved the letter back and forth like a flag at half-mast. "No, my breakfast is fine, thank you. It's this letter from my grand-daughter. She says she and my son Malcolm will be arriving—possibly within the next few days. There's much to do, Martha. The guest rooms will need airing and we'll need fresh linens for the beds—and food, we'll need to discuss menus. Let me see—perhaps I should begin a list."

"A list is a fine idea, Miss Alice, but at the moment you need to prepare for your visit to the Cheever home."

Alice glanced at the mantel clock. "You're absolutely correct. We'll begin preparations as soon as I return home. For now, you can take my breakfast tray, and if you would ask Martin to bring the carriage around, I'd be most appreciative."

Alice was hard-pressed to believe her good fortune. If she'd known Malcolm could be so easily convinced to come visiting, she would have hinted she was ailing long ago. She smiled into the mirror while adjusting the lavender feathers that were quivering above the wide brim of her champagne-colored bonnet.

She then descended the stairs, barely able to contain her delight. By this time next week Jasmine no doubt would be here.

They would have such fun exploring Lowell, and perhaps Malcolm would escort them to Boston. She hoped Jasmine would find the house to her liking. It was, after all, very different from The Willows. Instead of a sprawling, pillared mansion, Alice had purchased a house much like herself: sturdy and dependable. She enjoyed its every nuance, and the fact that the home was situated on a small plot of land within the town of Lowell had been an added bonus.

Tall and rigid, Martha stood at the front door, resembling a soldier guarding the castle gate as Alice approached. "We'll begin our list when I return, Martha," she instructed before leaving the house.

Outside, Martin offered his hand and assisted Alice into the leather-clad interior of her small carriage. Alice was sprightly for her seventy years, and they both realized she was capable of lifting herself into the cab without help. But, of course, civility required a woman of her social standing to exercise decorum in such matters. Once she was ensconced in the carriage, Alice's thoughts immediately returned to Jasmine's letter. What perfect timing! If there were no problems on their voyage, Malcolm and Jasmine should arrive in time for the Cheevers' summer social. Once Malcolm visited Lowell and accepted the fact that refined people did reside in Massachusetts, she hoped to convince him that Jasmine should remain with her there—at least for the remainder of the summer and early fall. The matriarch of the Wainwright family crossed her arms and leaned back in the carriage. At this moment, Alice Wainwright was the personification of smug satisfaction. She had a plan!

Lilly Cheever stood at her front door in a daffodil-yellow morning dress embroidered with tiny white flowers bordering the scalloped flounces.

"Yellow becomes you, my dear. You should wear it more often. I adore yellow but, alas, it causes me to appear sallow," Alice

51

said. She followed Lilly into the parlor, admiring the younger woman's graceful carriage.

"It is always a pleasure to have you visit, Mrs. Wainwright. I was delighted when you agreed to help with the charity ball. There's never a shortage of requests for the funds we amass but always a shortage of workers for the actual event. Do sit down."

Alice chose one of the overstuffed blue-and-gold brocade chairs where she had an unobstructed view of the rose garden. "Personally, I enjoy keeping busy, preferably with those of you who are youthful—it keeps me young at heart."

Lilly laughed and settled into a matching chair opposite Alice and began pouring tea. "I wouldn't call myself youthful. My two children think of me as old and decrepit."

"Tut, tut. What do children know of old age? They think anyone a few years their senior is ancient. Why, I remember a time when I thought twenty and five to be positively doddering. Time has a way of altering your perspective."

Lilly's lips curved into a winsome smile as she nodded in agreement. "You're certainly correct on that account." She handed a cup of tea on a saucer to Alice.

"And speaking of young people, I received word earlier today that my son and granddaughter will be arriving in Lowell for a visit."

"That's wonderful news. Will they arrive in time for my summer social?"

Alice smiled. "Indeed, they will. In fact, when I opened Jasmine's letter and discovered she was coming to visit, your social was one of the first items that crossed my mind. It will be a perfect opportunity for her to meet a few people her own age. And I'm certain she'll enjoy Violet, even if she is a few years younger."

"Where does Jasmine attend finishing school?"

"Jasmine has received her entire education at home. Madelaine, that's my daughter-in-law, insisted on having a tutor rather than sending Jasmine to a finishing school. In my opinion, the isolation has stilted Jasmine's level of maturity. She's a dear girl, very sweet, but I fear she's rather naïve for a young lady of eighteen years. However, having her at home all those years permitted me the opportunity to develop a closer relationship with her while I was living at the plantation. I must admit I've missed her terribly. In fact, I'm hoping to convince my son to allow her to remain with me until the Christmas holidays, or at least until fall. I'd like Jasmine to experience life away from her mother and the confines of The Willows."

"The Willows?"

Alice nodded and took a sip of tea. "Yes, The Willows is a cotton plantation that has been in the Wainwright family for generations. But certainly not an enterprise that was ever near or dear to *my* heart. However, from all appearances, my sons and grandsons will follow in their ancestral footsteps. Having been reared in Massachusetts and not having lived in the South until after my marriage, I never really embraced plantation life. Of course, my sons thought me daft. When I decided to move back North after my beloved husband's death, my entire family opposed my decision. They thought me completely foolish." She leaned forward and lowered her voice to a whisper. "I'm certain my sons don't believe it, but I've been more content since my return to Massachusetts than any time since my husband's death."

Lilly patted Alice's hand. "I'm pleased to hear you're satisfied, and I'm looking forward to meeting Jasmine. Perhaps we can journey to Boston for a day of shopping while she's here. I'm certain Violet would enjoy the diversion. And Matthew has mentioned the possibility of spending some time near the ocean in August— perhaps Rhode Island. You might want to give that idea consideration."

"I have to admit I had similar ideas in mind. At least with thoughts of Boston and shopping," Alice said, smiling.

"I only wish Elinor were here," Lilly said absentmindedly.

"Elinor who? Have I met her?"

"She's Taylor Manning's younger sister. She's . . . well . . . I believe she's twenty-two. A smart woman, with a head for bookwork, believe it or not." Lilly smiled. "She's been married twice and unfortunately widowed twice. Poor girl. Taylor's wife, Bella, tells me she believes herself cursed with misfortune."

"She does seem quite young to have endured so much sorrow. Where is she now?"

"Philadelphia. Taylor and Bella have gone to fetch her home. Her husband died from a bout of yellow fever."

Alice nodded knowingly. "I had heard that many areas suffered horribly with the fever this year. Did Elinor take the sickness?"

"No, amazingly enough, she didn't. But it only served to deepen her sorrow."

"When she returns, she would probably benefit from spending time with others," Alice said. "Perhaps the shopping trip to Boston would be a bit taxing, but we could promise her time in her own interests."

"I think it would definitely do her good," Lilly said, finishing her tea. "When she lost her first husband at eighteen, I know she thought she would never love again. Poor man drowned in an accident at the mill," Lilly added, as though it were important.

"Then when she met Daniel Brighton at church, I know she was quite apprehensive about giving her heart. They seemed such a good match. He was the nephew of dear friends and had a good business in Philadelphia. He courted Elinor fervently, coming to Lowell whenever he could spare the time. I think he finally wore her down." Lilly smiled. "But don't take that to mean Elinor didn't love him. She did. I was so happy to see her find true love a second time . . . and now this."

"God alone knows why these things happen," Alice commented in a motherly tone. "We must trust that He knows better than we do."

Lilly nodded. "And that He has better things ahead for Elinor."

"Exactly!" Alice agreed. "Hopefully between the two of us, we can take Elinor under our wing and see her heart mended in time. Meanwhile, I do suppose we should turn our efforts toward planning the charity events for the upcoming year."

Laughing, Lilly rose to her feet. "This is probably why I suffer through with limited assistance from others. I am easily distracted. Come, I'll show you my list of tasks."

Jasmine swirled into her grandmother's bedroom and made an exaggerated pirouette. Her silk gown cascaded in a sea of pink ripples as she seated herself on the brocade fainting couch and waited for her grandmother's assessment.

"You look absolutely beautiful, my dear. However, I do believe my diamond-and-pearl necklace would add the perfect touch to your ensemble." Alice opened her jewelry case and lifted a velvet pouch from the depths of the box. With a practiced ease, she placed the necklace around Jasmine's neck and fastened the clasp. Alice stepped back to appraise the effect. "Stunning! There won't be another young lady who will compare."

Jasmine smiled in return, wishing the aura of self-confidence she'd exhibited for her grandmother moments earlier were genuine. "Will attendance be sizable, do you think?"

Alice stared into the mirror, her attention focused upon the cameo pin she was clipping to a wide ribbon she'd fastened around her neck only moments earlier. "I'm not certain. Do you like the cameo on this ribbon? Or shall I wear my topaz necklace?"

"The cameo." Jasmine blotted her face with a lace-edged handkerchief. "Will there be more guests than attend the balls at Hampton House or The Willows?"

"Why are you so curious about the number of guests?" Alice turned to face Jasmine. "Oh, child! You're white as a sheet. Are you ill?" Without a moment's hesitation, Alice moved to her granddaughter's side and placed a hand alongside her cheek. "No fever."

"I'm not ill, at least not in the way you're talking about."

"In what way, then?"

"Attending a party where I won't know anyone except you and Father makes me extremely uncomfortable. You won't leave my side, will you?"

Alice patted Jasmine's hand. "You might have difficulty dancing if I remain by your side throughout the evening. But I promise to stay with you as long as you need me if that will help conquer your anxiety."

Jasmine's lips curved into a timid smile as she nodded her agreement. "You think I'm acting like my mother, don't you?"

"Absolutely not! And don't you worry yourself with such thoughts. I want you to attend this party and enjoy yourself. There's an exciting world outside of The Willows, and I want you to experience a portion of it—beginning this evening." Alice wrapped a silk shawl around Jasmine's shoulders and pulled her into a warm embrace. "Now, set aside your fears, and let's be on our way. You're going to meet some fascinating people. By the end of the evening, you'll look back on this moment and wonder why you ever harbored the slightest concern."

Jasmine hoped she was right. She had the utmost respect for her grandmother's opinions. Still, this was possibly the most frightening event of her life. Jasmine followed her grandmother from the room, wondering what the evening might hold in store. So many of her friends back home had met their mates at just such events. Most had married within the last year.

Will I meet the man of my dreams? she pondered. *I've never concerned myself with such things before, but what if . . .*

Malcolm hurried forward to meet the women as they descended the staircase. "Look at the two of you! I'll be escorting the prettiest ladies to the party."

"Thank you, Papa," Jasmine said, her thoughts interrupted by her father's enthusiasm. She forced a smile. "Grandmother has loaned me her necklace. Isn't it beautiful?"

Jasmine's father nodded and glanced toward the tolling clock in the hallway. "Indeed, it is. We'd best be on our way, or I'd venture to say that we'll be more than fashionably late to the Cheevers'. I do wish I'd had time to inform Bradley Houston of our arrival. He knew we were making the journey, but he didn't know exactly when we planned to arrive. He wrote that he'd made a point of meeting you, Mother. What did you think of him?"

Alice donned her white lace stole and took hold of her son's arm. "He seemed nice enough, I suppose, but he was more interested in discussing cotton and textiles than any matters that were of interest to me. He probably believed my years of living at The

Willows made me an excellent partner with whom to discuss cotton markets. Little did he realize how I abhor the topic." She gave her son a fleeting apologetic look. "Now, his brother, Nolan, is another matter entirely. Nolan enjoys theatre, poetry, and literature and can discuss them all quite eloquently. He's a man after my heart. In fact, I shared one of Jasmine's poems with him. He confided she hadn't mentioned her literary abilities when he visited The Willows. Bradley didn't appear to show much interest, but Nolan was quite impressed. I wouldn't worry about business this evening. You'll have ample time for discussions of cotton and textiles later in the week if Mr. Houston isn't present tonight."

"Since it's obvious your health has greatly improved, Mother, I'm certain we won't be in Lowell for an extended period."

Jasmine stifled a protest. She might fear the events of the evening, but she longed to spend more time in her grandmother's company. Surely Papa wouldn't rush her back to The Willows without time for a good long visit.

A playful smile tugged at Alice's lips. "You're not hiding your agitation very well, Malcolm. Why don't we spend this evening enjoying each other's company and the fact that we have a lovely party to attend?"

Jasmine watched her father's expression soften. "I am enjoying your company, in spite of the false pretenses upon which you forced my arrival."

"Tut, tut. Tonight is for fun—not admonitions. I am determined to show my granddaughter, and perhaps my son, that the Northern states are just as fond of parties and revelry as is the South."

"Then let us go among your Northern neighbors," Jasmine's father said, smiling.

Jasmine relaxed a bit. Her father was clearly not nearly as annoyed with his mother as he let on. She followed her elders to the carriage, watching as her grandmother lovingly placed her gloved hand against her son's face. Jasmine couldn't hear what she said, but the look on her grandmother's face was one of pure love.

The exchange warmed Jasmine and made her forget her fears. At least momentarily.

By the time they arrived at the Cheevers', Jasmine's father appeared to relish the idea of a party, hurrying them out of the carriage and up to the porch with a swiftness that caused Jasmine's grandmother to tug on his sleeve.

"Do slow down, Malcolm. This isn't a footrace, and I'm an old woman."

Papa winked at Jasmine before turning back toward his mother. "Since when do you consider yourself old?"

"When such a comment suits my fancy, of course." She gave her son a smug grin and looped arms with Jasmine. "Come along, my dear. I'm going to introduce you to some of the most eligible bachelors to be found north of Mississippi."

Malcolm immediately sobered. "Don't get any ideas, Mother. As I said on our way here, with your improved health, we'll be returning to Mississippi very soon. I much prefer to be home in time for picking season."

"Don't discount my medical ailments so quickly, Malcolm. You assume because I'm able to navigate the streets of Lowell, I am completely well. However, my health hangs in the balance, changing from day to day, much like the weather."

"Or to suit your circumstances?" he inquired as they reached the front door.

Alice ignored his question, stepping forward to greet Lilly Cheever. "Lilly, Matthew. May I introduce my son Malcolm Wainwright and my dear granddaughter Jasmine?"

Matthew grasped Malcolm's hand in a warm handshake. "I believe Bradley Houston mentioned your name to me only this morning. He said he had visited your plantation and that you and your brothers have some of the finest cotton fields to be found in the South."

Malcolm nodded. "I'm pleased to hear he was so favorably impressed with our cotton. Bradley appears to be quite a shrewd businessman. In fact, we've corresponded since his departure."

"We're pleased to welcome you to our home. I believe Bradley is expected tonight, isn't he, my dear?"

Lilly nodded. "Yes. Actually, Bradley's already here, though Nolan hasn't yet arrived. He's coming from Cambridge with Henry Longfellow." She lowered her voice and leaned close as though she were sharing some privileged piece of information. "They've both agreed to read poetry for us later this evening."

Alice clapped her hands together in obvious delight. "How enchanting! I know we'll all enjoy hearing them," Alice said before stepping aside to permit the other guests entry.

The three Wainwrights walked down the hallway toward the drawing room, and Malcolm gave his mother a smug grin. "It sounds as though Mrs. Cheever's entertainment will provide me with ample opportunity to talk to Bradley Houston this evening."

"Listening to something other than the price of cotton would expand your mind," Alice gently chided.

When her father gave no retort, Jasmine looked upward and followed his gaze. Bradley Houston was wending his way through the crowd. He plainly stared at her as he approached where they now stood. He looked quite dashing dressed in gray and black. His rigid features gave him a hard but handsome appearance.

"I didn't know you had arrived in Lowell. I thought you would send word," he said. She couldn't discern if he was angry or merely surprised by her appearance. He took hold of her gloved hand and bent over it, refraining from touching his lips to the cloth. When he looked back up to meet her face, Jasmine thought his expression suggested that he expected some sort of explanation.

"There wasn't sufficient time, what with preparations for the evening and visiting with Grandmother," she replied. "I'm sorry."

"You're young." He straightened, his gaze boring past any facades of bravery Jasmine might have put in place. "You are forgiven. In time you'll learn where to direct your time and attention."

He then smiled with the warmth of a summer day. Yet something in his voice caused her to shiver.

CHAPTER · 6

JASMINE KNOCKED on her grandmother's bedroom door and then stepped inside when Alice bid her enter. "Good morning, Grandmother. I trust last evening's dinner at the Merrimack House didn't tire you overly much."

She smiled and motioned Jasmine forward. "On the contrary, I'm fine."

"I'm so glad. I thought perhaps the activities of the last week might have wearied you."

"You mustn't fret about me. I'm aging to be sure, but I'm still very capable. I've been meaning to ask if you enjoyed the Cheevers' party last week. We've scarcely had a chance to speak of it."

Jasmine considered that evening, and Bradley Houston immediately came to mind. "I'm not sure what to think about that night. I thought the party itself was lovely. Mrs. Cheever is very gracious. Mother would say she has the grace and manners of a perfect Southern lady. Although as I understand, she's very much of New England background."

"That she is. She was born and reared right here in Lowell," Grandmother replied. "But let us speak about you, my dear. What seems to trouble you about that evening?"

Jasmine shrugged. "I'm not sure I would say that the evening troubles me; rather, I'm not sure what it all meant."

Grandmother tilted her head to one side as if to study her for a moment. Jasmine felt silly for having even brought up the matter. "I suppose it was nothing," she murmured, looking away from her grandmother's prying gaze.

"Nonsense. You seemed completely perplexed. Tell me what this is about."

Jasmine turned, trying hard to put her thoughts into words. "Mr. Houston said several things to me—things that confused me."

"Did he try to take liberties with you, child?"

"Oh no," Jasmine assured. "It's just that he spoke to me in a very familiar way, as if he'd known me for a long time. It confused me."

"Did he speak of love?"

Jasmine grew warm around the lace of her collar. "No, not exactly. He spoke of obedience and helpfulness. He talked of my learning where best to direct my attention. I'm not at all certain what he wanted me to understand, but he seemed quite intent with his words."

"Well, child, you are of a marriageable age, and you're quite beautiful. The man probably fancies thoughts of you for his wife."

Jasmine shook her head. "Bradley Houston is too old for me, and he's a Northerner, after all. He would never understand our ways, and no doubt Papa would never consider him as a suitor for me."

"Yes, but what of you, Jasmine? Would you consider him?"

Jasmine couldn't give her grandmother an answer. Truth be told, she hadn't really considered anything so farfetched as a marriage proposal from Bradley Houston.

As if understanding Jasmine's bewilderment, her grandmother motioned to the chair. "Sharing these last few days with you has been wonderful. Sit down and have breakfast with me. Martha tells me your father is meeting with Mr. Houston again this morning, so perhaps the mysteries will be explained." She smiled with reassurance. "But even better, we shall have the day to ourselves. I thought perhaps we might go to some of the shops and see about a small gift for your mother, something your father could take home that might cheer her."

"Perhaps a book of poetry," Jasmine suggested, pushing aside her troubled thoughts.

"An excellent idea. Nolan Houston is quite eloquent, is he not? His reading was impeccable the other night."

Jasmine placed a linen napkin across her lap. "It's a shame he doesn't have a published book of poems we could purchase for Mother. It would be great fun to give her a book written by someone she's actually entertained in her home, even if he didn't read any of his writings for us."

"I doubt your father would have encouraged him. And Bradley doesn't appear to lend much support either. I was rather horrified when the two of them got up and went outdoors during Mr. Longfellow's reading at the Cheevers', although I suppose I shouldn't have been. Your father told me he planned to utilize the time to discuss business. He's convinced my health doesn't require his presence in Lowell, and I'm certain he'll soon book passage for your return to The Willows. He thinks the first picking won't occur without him."

"Oh, Grandmother, do try to convince him we should remain awhile longer. We've only just arrived, and I don't think I could bear to leave you so quickly."

Grandmother Wainwright's face seemed to suddenly come alive with excitement. "What if I could convince him to allow you to remain until the end of November? I could then accompany you home and spend the holidays with all of the family." The animation in her tone confirmed she was quite delighted with her new idea.

Jasmine pulled her grandmother into a tight embrace. "What a *perfect* plan! Surely Papa will agree, especially if it means you'll be at The Willows for Christmas."

"I doubt he'll be quite as enthusiastic as you. He'll immediately worry about your mother's reaction to your absence. She'll be distraught when you don't come home and will surely take to her bed."

Jasmine pulled back, carefully contemplating her words before she spoke. "I do want to stay, Grandmother, but Mama's health is fragile at times. I wouldn't want to cause her distress. However, she was most supportive of our journey, even telling Father he had an obligation to come north and personally check on you. And she encouraged him to bring me along to see you."

Alice patted Jasmine on the cheek. "Then we'll leave it to your father and abide by his decision. In the meantime, let's get ready for our shopping trip. I saw some of the loveliest velvet at Paxton's Mercantile in town. I think it might make a very fetching Christmas gown."

Jasmine smiled and turned her attention back to the breakfast tea. "I'm certain to be impressed if it caught your attention." Jasmine pushed aside her anxieties and the pending question of whether her father would allow her to remain in Lowell and concentrated on the joy of the moment. Tomorrow would surely see her troubles smoothed over and her mind at peace.

Bradley stepped out of his carriage in front of the Merrimack House. He'd agreed to meet Malcolm Wainwright for breakfast and then escort him on a tour of the textile mills. Settling at his table with a steaming cup of coffee, Bradley contemplated the events of the past few days. He didn't believe Wainwright was ready to sign a contract, but he appeared somewhat receptive to the possibility of shifting his cotton sales away from the English markets. With a bit more time and persuasion, Bradley hoped to convince him such a decision would be beneficial for his entire family, as well as all of the Mississippi and Louisiana cotton growers. The Wainwright family was renowned in the South, and Malcolm Wainwright could be a strong ally.

The Associates were anxious for Bradley to move forward with a speed that defied developing the type of associations needed for long-term business relationships. Business was done much more quickly in the North, whereas Southern deals were struck over mint juleps and lazy summer afternoons.

Bradley had learned long ago that pushing a cause too strenuously often resulted in adverse outcomes—in all aspects of life. But nowhere was this truer than with Southern gentlemen, and Malcolm Wainwright seemed no exception to this rule. Bradley was willing to move at a more respectable pace if it meant accomplishing his goal in the end. After all, he didn't want to frighten off the patriarch of the Wainwright family before their business relationship had even commenced.

And then there was the matter of Jasmine. He would be extremely cautious in that regard. The girl was young and likely to object to any advances from him. What little he had tried to coax from her in conversation seemed completely void of depth and understanding. But he reminded himself that she had led a very sheltered life and that someone of his worldly knowledge was no doubt a threat to genteel sensibilities. Still, she had been quite spirited while associating with Nolan and his literary friends during the evening, which he found somewhat disquieting. Especially since she had been as frightened as a church mouse when he escorted her home from the Cheevers, careful to keep a safe distance between them and running into the house the moment he helped her out of the carriage.

You aren't a handsome man, Bradley chided himself between sips of coffee. He knew his features were considered by some to be quite stern, even imposing. He wasn't a very tall man, standing only five and eight, but his square jaw and penetrating gray eyes had managed to cower many an adversary. There was, as some said, a look of determination, even unto seeing the last man fall before giving up. Bradley rather liked that people considered this of him. It made them cautious in saying no to him. Of course, Malcolm Wainwright was not as naïve as some. He was the type of man, in fact, that was sure to smell a bad deal before it ever reached the table.

A shadow passed across the window in front of him, and Bradley glanced up to see Wainwright enter the building. "I didn't notice your carriage," Bradley remarked as the man seated himself.

"I walked. It's a lovely morning, and everything is close at hand here in Lowell. As a matter of fact, I find it rather refreshing that I can leave Mother's front door and walk downtown in such short order. The town is quite compactly organized."

"Indeed it is. In fact, that very concept is what the Associates envisioned when planning this community. I believe they were very successful in most aspects."

"I'm looking forward to touring the mills and seeing the remainder of the town. Of course, a man like myself could never live in these close surroundings, but I can certainly admire the thought and effort that was required for an endeavor such as this."

The men paused as a waiter placed a cup of coffee in front of Malcolm.

"Before you leave, I hope you'll have opportunity to meet with many of the gentlemen responsible for the achievement of their vision," Bradley commented. "Kirk Boott was the man who was originally in charge of managing construction of the mills, boardinghouses, and canals, and then the Associates determined he was the best man to remain in Lowell and direct the day-to-day operations as well. Until his death nine years ago, Kirk remained a viable leader, although he had begun grooming Matthew Cheever many years earlier. At the time of Kirk's death, Matthew was well positioned to take his mentor's place."

"Sounds as though Boott handpicked him, so it would be my guess he's well suited to the job. His interest in the Wainwright cotton is flattering. It's always encouraging to know that others value your work."

"I think you'd find that all of the Boston Associates value the commitment and hard work of cotton producers. While we realize the textile industry is dependent upon cotton, I doubt you'd find any one of us willing to assume the daily rigors or risks associated with planting and harvesting a huge cotton crop each year."

A satisfied smile spread across Wainwright's lips. He appeared pleased by Bradley's accolades, so Bradley determined to use the situation to best advantage. "If I might change the subject for a moment, I might say that I find Jasmine to be an engaging young woman." He paused as the waiter put a plate of food in front of each of them. "I'd like your permission to call upon her while you're visiting in Lowell."

Wainwright's eyes narrowed slightly at the request. "We won't be here long, and I specifically brought her to visit with her grandmother. Don't misunderstand, Bradley. I have no objection to you as a suitor, although I always presumed my only daughter would marry one of our Southern boys. Still, it's a matter of timing. You do understand?"

"Yes, of course, but I had hoped you would remain in Lowell until the end of summer."

"My mother's health is much better than I had anticipated. Consequently, I'd like to return to the plantation before the first picking. Perhaps there will be another opportunity in the future that will prove mutually acceptable."

Bradley nodded in agreement and they made small talk as they finished their breakfast. Bradley placed his napkin on the table. "If you're still interested in a tour, I think we should be on our way."

By carriage, their trip to the Appleton Mill took only a matter of minutes, during which time Bradley pointed out the numerous mills and boardinghouses as they passed by.

Matthew Cheever stood near the front gate awaiting their arrival. "Gentlemen. Good to see you," he greeted. "I'm anxious to show you at least one of our mills, Mr. Wainwright. Why don't we begin in the counting building," he said, leading the way toward the one-story brick structure. "The girls working in this area trim, fold, and prepare our cloth for shipment," he explained, pointing across the room. "We maintain the time cards, pay records, and accounts of the Corporation in our office adjacent to the counting room."

As they walked into the yard area, Bradley noticed Wainwright move toward the huge loads of baled cotton. "Appears you've got yourselves quite a bit of cotton to turn into cloth," he said with a smile.

"Absolutely. Once a bale is opened, the cotton is picked and cleaned on the large machinery over on that side of the room," Matthew said as they walked into a larger building. "From there it goes to those monstrous carding machines."

"That's quite a leap from the handheld carding tools we still use at the plantation. My wife has always enjoyed spinning her own yarn," Wainwright added.

"If you'd like to see our spinning and weaving machines, they're in these other buildings. We'll have to climb several flights of stairs," Matthew warned.

"I had best see it all so I can explain it to my brothers. And I'm sure my wife would be interested to hear about that carding machine too."

Matthew led them back across the mill yard and up the enclosed stairway until they stood in front of the door to the third floor. "We have drawing and spinning machines in separate areas on this floor. As you can already hear, it's very noisy. The long slivers from the carding machines are stretched until the cotton ropes are about two inches thick on the drawing machines. Those fragile ropes go to the roving machine, where they are drawn out and lengthened still further and given a slight twist," he explained before escorting them inside.

The men jumped aside as two young bobbin girls came scurrying through, pushing their carts of bobbins in opposite directions. Once the aisle cleared, they made their way slowly through the machinery before returning to the stairwell.

"An entire floor is given over to the weaving looms," Matthew said. "We'll go and see those if you're up to the noise."

Malcolm Wainwright gave an enthusiastic nod, and Bradley relaxed a modicum. The older man appeared to be impressed with what he had seen thus far. Once he actually realized the vastness of the Associates' holdings and the fact that this was but one mill among their myriad of brick buildings daily converting raw cotton into cloth, he surely would want to align himself with their empire.

"Have you traveled to England?" Bradley inquired after they bid Matthew good-bye and were traveling down a street that fronted the most advantageous view of the mills.

"No, I can't say that I have—although my father made two trips during his lifetime. I must admit, the sights of Lowell are not what he described having seen in England. He spoke harshly of both the working and living conditions. It appears that having farm girls work in the mills and constructing this paternalistic community around your business was a stroke of genius."

"Certainly not *my* stroke of genius. However, I take great pride in being associated with these men and their ability to take a giant step in the industrialization of this country. Do you think your brothers might be persuaded to come and see exactly what we're doing here in Lowell? That it might help convince them that the Wainwright cotton could be put to better use among Americans rather than Englishmen?"

"My brothers are reasonable men, and we've always been willing to support this country in her expansion so long as we didn't place our family's financial growth at risk in the process."

Bradley tightened his hand on the reins and carefully measured his words. "After seeing the amount of capital invested in this community, do you think you and your brothers might consider making Lowell the primary market for your cotton?"

Wainwright turned, his visage serious. "I couldn't speak for my brothers, but when I return home, I would be willing to tell them what I've seen here. They would be pleased to hear they could get a better price in Massachusetts than England, but that doesn't mean they'll want to cease doing business in England."

Bradley rubbed his forehead. "Then what will it take?"

"Guarantees. We've been doing business in England for many years. Accordingly, there's a level of trust and comfort in our relationship. Even though you can promise us higher prices *this* year, they may plummet by *next* season."

"That could happen in England also," Bradley argued.

"Not to the extent you might think. My father was able to barter an agreement whereby our prices could fall only by a given percentage if market prices dropped. We never experienced the huge losses suffered by other growers when prices deflated. With you, we have no guarantees and no trust."

Bradley was ill prepared for Wainwright's revelation and struggled briefly to gain his momentum. "I can't promise you percentage guarantees without the approval of the Associates any more than you can promise me all of the Wainwright cotton without your brothers' consent. But if you will give me percentage guidelines, I will speak to the Associates about such an arrangement on your behalf, just as you have agreed to speak to your brothers about changing their market to Lowell. Regarding the trust issue, I hadn't planned to discuss this with you so soon, but I now feel compelled to do so. As I mentioned earlier today, I hoped you would favor me with permission to call upon your daughter. My hope had been that one day you might consider me a suitable husband for Jasmine. I believe our marriage would seal the future with a level of trust and commitment that even your English associates cannot provide." Bradley cleared his throat, uncertain whether the words he would next offer would be impressive to the older man or completely irrelevant. "And lest you think me without feeling, I must say that I have been smitten with your daughter since our first meeting. She would not be without love and affection."

Wainwright leaned back against the carriage seat, rubbed his jowl several times, and then nodded his head up and down. "I believe this might work. We've not made any promises other than to do our best toward reaching a mutually satisfactory arrangement that will prove financially beneficial to all concerned."

"Except the English," Bradley said with a wry grin. "What of Jasmine? Do you think she will object? After all, she barely knows me."

"Most Southern women think they have a hand in choosing their marriage partners, but truth be known, few of them do. As I mentioned, it's all a question of timing, but perhaps these matters can be helped along. It might bode well for Jasmine to remain in Lowell when I return to Mississippi. I'll tell her I think her grandmother may still be ailing and also stress to her that a season in the North might better round out her education. Jasmine won't object to remaining with my mother. While she's in Lowell, you can call upon her, letting her believe this is a matter of romance. If I know my mother, she'll have Jasmine at every social event given in a twenty-mile radius.

"If our business arrangements are successful, you can move forward with the marriage, and Jasmine will be none the wiser. If our business arrangements go sour, you can cease calling upon her and declare you've lost interest due to her youth."

Bradley viewed Malcolm Wainwright with a new admiration. He had misjudged him—thought him weak where his only daughter was concerned. This man was much more cunning than even Bradley would have imagined. Definitely not a man to be taken lightly in business negotiations.

"Look, Grandmother. Papa and Mr. Houston are getting out of a carriage just up the street." Jasmine waved her closed parasol overhead until her father finally caught sight of them.

"What an unexpected pleasure," Bradley said as they approached, his gaze riveted upon Jasmine.

"Have you ladies been having any success with your shopping expedition?" Malcolm pleasantly inquired.

"As a matter of fact, we have. However, we were going to stop for a cup of tea. Would you gentlemen care to join us?" Alice asked.

"Of course," Bradley replied before Jasmine's father could object.

Bradley beamed her a smile that instantly set Jasmine's heart pounding. What was it about this man?

"I want to show you the wonderful gift I've found for Mother," Jasmine said as soon as they'd been seated. She carefully unwrapped the brown paper and pulled out a leather-bound volume. "Look! It's *Lays of My Home and Other Poems* by John Greenleaf Whittier. I decided Mother would adore the volume since she admires Mr. Whittier's writings. The bookstore had a copy of *Legends of New-England in Prose and Verse,* but I remembered you gave her that volume for Christmas several years ago. I think she will adore it, don't you?"

Her father took the book and leafed through the pages. "I'm certain she will be most pleased, especially since you chose it for her."

"Grandmother and I decided it was an absolute necessity to find Mother's gift today. We've been scouring the shops all morning, but our efforts were finally rewarded."

"Why the urgency to purchase your gift *today*?" Bradley asked. "The shops are open every day except Sunday."

"Papa is threatening to leave for Mississippi very soon, and I was afraid he would come home this afternoon with our passage secured on the next vessel leaving Boston."

"I've been giving that matter some additional thought, Jasmine, and perhaps I was a bit hasty in declaring the restoration of your grandmother's health. After all, I'm not a physician."

Jasmine gave a single clap of her hands. "We're going to extend our visit?"

"No. As you predicted, I'm going to sail on the next ship. You, however, are going to remain here in Lowell with your grandmother."

Jasmine and her grandmother exchanged looks of pure delight. "Truly? It's almost as though you were listening to our conversation this morning. Were you eavesdropping on us, Papa?" Jasmine teased in her lilting Southern drawl.

"No, but I'd be interested to hear what the two of you were planning."

"Grandmother suggested you might permit me to remain with her until the end of November, and then the two of us would travel to The Willows and she would stay with us throughout the holidays. Wouldn't that be grand fun? All of us together again?"

"Indeed. I think your grandmother has struck upon a very suitable plan—so long as her health permits the voyage."

Grandmother Wainwright gave her son a rather sheepish grin and took a sip of her tea. "I think my health will be much improved by the holidays."

"I'm pleased to hear that bit of news, Mother. I shared my plans with Mr. Houston earlier today and he has asked for exclusive permission to call upon Jasmine during her extended visit in Lowell. I have given my hearty consent."

Jasmine paled at her father's remark. Call upon her? The very idea brought back a rush of panicked and bewildered thoughts. Bradley Houston was no Southern gentleman. If he were to become serious-minded in matters of matrimony, he would never give any thought to living in Mississippi. What could her father possibly be thinking?

"My dear, are you quite all right?" her father asked.

Jasmine fanned herself with a lace handkerchief. "I'm sure I am. However, I am quite surprised by this turn of events. I must say, I never thought the journey north to be such adventure."

Bradley gave a deep, emotionless laugh at this, his beady gray-eyed gaze making her most uncomfortable. "You may find the North full of surprises and adventure, Miss Wainwright. And I will personally be honored to reveal them all to you in due time."

Stifling a shudder, Jasmine could only smile and look demurely to her shaking hands. Clenching the hanky between her fingers, Jasmine tried to imagine what the future might hold in the company of Bradley Houston. Somehow, the thoughts were not all that comforting—nor desirous. There was something about this man that made her uneasy—not at all like his brother, Nolan. Perhaps it was his more serious nature—his lack of genuine warmth and joy. Perhaps it was the fact that Bradley Houston seemed to be a man very much used to getting his own way. And this time, that might very well include taking Jasmine for his wife.

CHAPTER · 7

SUMMER LINGERED in the air, even as a decided chill announced the coming of autumn. The days had not been as pleasant for Jasmine as she had imagined them when she and her grandmother had planned for her extended visit in Lowell. Bradley Houston had made a positive nuisance of himself, and today was no exception.

Jasmine stiffened as Bradley pulled his chair closer and cupped her cheek in his palm. It seemed he was always touching her—something that would never have been tolerated at The Willows. Why, Samuel alone would have called out the first man to lay a finger to his beloved sister. But Samuel wasn't here to stand guard. Neither was McKinley or David or her father.

"Tell me, my dear, what is it that has been keeping you so busy of late? It seems that every time I send word I'd like to call upon you, your grandmother returns a message that you've already made plans or you're not available."

Grandmother padded into the room with the stillness of a soft breeze and placed a vase of flowers on the table beside him. "I prefer having her close at hand when I'm ailing, Bradley. It gives me comfort to have her read aloud or visit with me when I must take to my bed. Having Jasmine here to aid me during my times of illness is, after all, why my son had her remain in Lowell."

"Yes, I understand Mr. Wainwright's reasoning," Bradley replied cautiously. "But I've noticed her in town with Violet Cheever on several occasions and—"

"Taking care of some shopping for me," Jasmine's grandmother interrupted. "But I'm certain you find Matthew Cheever's daughter acceptable company for my granddaughter."

"Why, of course," Bradley said defensively. "I've merely been concerned."

"There's no need for worry, Mr. Houston. In the event there's a problem, rest assured I will immediately send word. However, it is heartening to know of your concern," the old woman decorously replied.

Bradley turned toward Alice Wainwright and placed his folded hands in his lap. He looked like a schoolboy preparing to recite his daily lessons. "I had hoped to escort Jasmine on a picnic after church tomorrow afternoon. With your permission, of course."

"I think a picnic would be very nice. In fact, the fresh air would likely do me good. Will you escort us to church also?" Jasmine's grandmother asked while fussing with the floral arrangement.

Jasmine held her breath, wondering what his reply might be. Bradley didn't seem the type overly concerned with spiritual matters. Then again, her own parents had been rather remiss in church attendance these past few years. It was, of course, due to Mama's affliction, but they were always faithful to at least read the Scriptures on Sunday morning.

Bradley hesitated only for a moment. "Yes, of course. I would be pleased to escort you to church."

"Why don't I have Martha pack our dinner? After church we can return to the house and pick up the basket. Oh, and I have a delightful idea. Why don't we invite the Cheever family to join us? Jasmine and I are going to visit with them later this afternoon, and I'll see if they're available. I know how much you enjoy Matthew's company. Yes! I think we'll have a grand time, don't you, Jasmine?"

Jasmine flashed a grateful smile at her grandmother. "Yes, and

I'm certain Violet will be pleased to join us. She told me only the other day she had been longing to go on a picnic."

Bradley stood and looked down at Jasmine. "Well, then, I suppose the picnic is arranged. Not exactly what I had planned. Nonetheless, I look forward to our time together. I hope you will make time for a walk with me. There are several things I would enjoy discussing with you."

Jasmine heard the determination in his voice and it took all of her resolve to keep from cringing. "Perhaps," she whispered, hoping it would be enough of an answer to satisfy him.

After Bradley made his departure, Jasmine sighed and leaned against the front door for a moment. "Thank you, Grandmother," she said as she walked back into the parlor. "I know Mr. Houston is likely a fine man, but his overbearing character disturbs me. Besides, I've written Papa that he is much too old for me. I'd prefer a gentleman caller who is more to my liking—and closer to my own age," she added.

"Don't discount the role your father has played in Mr. Houston's behavior. He gave Bradley exclusive permission to call upon you. There may be little you can do except begin looking for Bradley's finer qualities."

Jasmine plopped down on the settee beside her grandmother. "What do you mean? Surely you don't think Papa is arranging a marriage between Bradley Houston and me? Why, that's preposterous." She turned and looked deep into her grandmother's steely hazel eyes. "Isn't it?" Up until now, the entire matter of courting Bradley Houston had seemed simply a game, a sort of cat-and-mouse venture where Jasmine would find ways to escape being snatched up by Mr. Houston's sharp claws.

"No, Jasmine. In fact, the idea is quite believable. You seem to forget that you've reached a suitable age for marriage."

Jasmine detected the sad resignation in her grandmother's voice. What was she saying? Was she keeping something from Jasmine? "You truly believe Papa has chosen Bradley Houston as a possible husband for me?" She gasped the words, as though Mammy had just cinched her corset too tight. "I don't want to marry a man I don't love. I'd rather remain a spinster."

Alice chuckled and tucked a stray curl behind Jasmine's ear. "Sometimes we must accept the fact that we aren't the ones who make the choices affecting our lives. If your father chooses Bradley, you must accept him as your husband and work toward creating a happy home. This may come as a surprise to you, but I didn't love your grandfather when I married him. Our marriage was arranged. I thought I would never survive leaving Boston to live on a cotton plantation. Those first years at The Willows were very difficult. However, in time I learned to love your grandfather, I had my children, and we were very happy."

Jasmine grimaced and shook her head back and forth. "I could *never* learn to love Bradley Houston. We have nothing in common. Unlike Grandfather and Father, he's interested only in textile and cotton production. I don't believe he is educated enough to discuss anything intellectual or cultural."

"I, too, have noticed he expresses little interest in cultural topics, although I know he is well educated. Perhaps it will take some of your Southern charm to draw out his latent qualities. Even your father is difficult to dissuade from talk of business from time to time. However, once Bradley realizes a variety of conversational topics will serve him well both in private and in the business world, I'm certain he will make every effort to expand his realm of dialogue."

"Whether he does so or not will be of little consequence—I have no intention of changing my feelings toward Bradley Houston."

"I fear your mother's insistence upon sheltering you at home all these years has left you naïve concerning matters of marriage, my dear."

"You may be correct. However, I've always been able to somewhat influence Papa's decisions regarding my future. After all, he didn't force my introduction to society with a coming-out ball."

Alice gave her granddaughter a sidelong glance. "I believe your mother's fear of hosting such an event may have played a larger part in your father's decision than any argument you posed."

Jasmine moved to the marble-topped mahogany side table and idly rearranged the colorful zinnias her grandmother had placed in a vase only a short time ago. Unbidden, she looked into the gilded mirror across the room and met her grandmother's troubled gaze. Would her father force her to marry someone she didn't love? Could he do such a thing to her? Surely not.

That night Jasmine's sleep was restless, her dreams fraught with worrisome visions of her future. She saw herself as a bride, walking down the aisle to a masked man. She knew the man was Bradley Houston, but he refused to allow her to see his face. Once the ceremony was over and she was pronounced to be his wife, he lifted the mask, much as a bride would lift her veil. Beneath his coverings, Bradley's face contorted and turned monstrous.

Jasmine awoke screaming softly into her pillow. She sat up with a start, her heart pounding relentlessly.

What was it Grandmother had said earlier? *"I fear your mother's insistence upon sheltering you at home all these years has left you naïve concerning matters of marriage."* What did she mean? Was it something more than merely the thought that her father might marry her off to a man Jasmine didn't and couldn't love?

"Oh, I'm so frightened," she whispered to the darkened room. Jasmine thought momentarily of praying, but she had never been very good at such things. She always pictured God as a distant king upon His throne, a solemn-faced judge who tried each case with stoic indifference. Grandmother had other ideas, however. She spoke of God's tender compassion—His mercies.

"I pray you take mercy on me, dear God," Jasmine murmured, pulling her covers tight against her neck. "I pray you intercede on my behalf and remove this notion of marriage between me and Bradley Houston from my father's mind."

Bradley rested his back against a large elm and watched the unfolding scene. His plan for a quiet picnic with Jasmine had turned into an afternoon of frivolity attended by a myriad of people—some of whom he didn't even know. Bradley wasn't certain who had given Violet Cheever free rein to invite guests, but he suspected Jasmine may have had a hand in the situation. She'd been avoiding him since their arrival, and now that his brother had arrived with Henry and Fanny Longfellow, she was involved in an animated discussion about some literary nonsense. He motioned her to join him and grew increasingly irritated when she chose to ignore him. Unwilling to tolerate her behavior any longer, he stood and walked to her side.

He leaned down until his lips nearly touched her ear. "Please join me," he whispered forcefully.

His words were a command, not a request, yet she smiled demurely and said, "I prefer to remain here, thank you."

He grasped her elbow and squeezed more tightly than he'd intended. "I expect you to join me—now," he hissed.

"Please release my arm. You're hurting me," she said when they were a short distance away from the crowd.

"Perhaps you should have come when I motioned to you," he replied. "I invited you because *I* want the privilege of enjoying your company."

Jasmine sat down beside him. "You could come and join the rest of us. Perhaps I would take more pleasure in being with you if you would discuss something other than the textile mills."

"Ah, so you find me rather boring and would prefer to delve into the works of Shakespeare or Keats—perhaps Scott? You may be surprised to learn that I far outranked my brother while studying the classics in college. Merely because I do not stand around professing literary knowledge does not mean I have none. However, some of us have moved beyond such puffery, realizing what is truly important in life. And just look at Henry in his flowered waistcoat and yellow kid gloves. Wherever does he find those clothes?"

"There is more to life than work, and it appears there are many who find Mr. Longfellow—and his attire—quite interesting."

"I'm surprised Fanny isn't embarrassed to be seen with him in public. After all, her people are of some quality in Boston."

"She appears quite devoted to him," Jasmine replied, glancing toward the couple sitting side by side on a patchwork quilt. "I believe them to be very much in love—something I very much value."

"Well, I think he enjoys making a spectacle of himself. It's much easier than working for a living."

"You judge him rather harshly, Mr. Houston."

"When Longfellow married Fanny Appleton, Nathan gifted him with over one hundred thousand dollars worth of stock in the mills. Nathan's generosity has permitted Henry to enjoy the life of a wealthy man while he earns nothing more than a professor's salary at Harvard. For all intents and purposes, he lives off of his father-in-law rather than working to support himself."

"His writing is his work," she protested.

"It will never come to anything," Bradley asserted dryly. "He'll no doubt disappear into oblivion when his father-in-law's fortune and good intentions are gone."

"I think not," Jasmine declared. "Obviously Mr. Appleton can appreciate the fact that something other than textile production is of value to the world."

Bradley stroked his fingers down her arm softly. "There are one or two things I value more than textile production also."

Jasmine recoiled from his touch. "You forget yourself, sir," she said, her drawl quite pronounced.

Bradley shook his head. "I'm well aware of what I'm suggesting. I just wonder if you understand it as well."

CHAPTER · 8

ALICE TAPPED her fingers on the table beside her chair and contemplated the wisdom of her decision. If Malcolm should find out, he would be upset. No—he would be furious. She had given her consent to Jasmine in haste, and now she couldn't go back on her word. "And what of Bradley?" she muttered.

"Excuse me, ma'am?" Martha drew closer. "I didn't hear your question." The tall, stern-faced woman watched her employer with some interest.

"Oh, Martha, I didn't know you had come into the room. I'm talking to myself. I fear I've made a muddle of things," she confided.

Martha began arranging an armful of flowers from the garden. "I've never known you to possess anything but the soundest of judgments. How could you have possibly muddled any matter?"

"When Jasmine and I were at the library yesterday, we happened to see Lilly Cheever. She reminded me of the antislavery meeting that's taking place on Wednesday. Of course, Jasmine heard the conversation and immediately asked if she could attend."

Martha put her hand to her neck in surprise. "Oh, Mrs. Wainwright! You didn't agree?"

"Yes, I'm afraid I did."

"Whatever will her father think?"

Alice appreciated her housekeeper's frankness. They had always shared more of a friendship than a relationship of employee and employer. "That's my concern. I know Malcolm will be angry and likely never permit Jasmine to visit again. My only hope is that he won't find out. After all, it's only one meeting, and if I tell Jasmine never to discuss her attendance with anyone, perhaps Malcolm will remain unaware. Quite frankly, I'm more concerned with the possibility of someone mentioning her attendance to Bradley Houston. Should he find out, there is little doubt he'd tell Malcolm."

Martha trimmed the stems on several crimson roses before placing them in the vase. "I thought Mr. Houston was active in the antislavery movement."

"Nolan Houston is active, but I've never seen Bradley at any of the meetings or heard him profess his beliefs one way or the other. However, with his involvement in the textile mills, I think he would frown upon any active participation in the antislavery movement. And now that he's professed a romantic interest in Jasmine, I'm certain he won't want her exposed to the ever-growing antislavery sentiments."

"Have you considered telling the child you've reconsidered and believe your decision was ill-advised?"

"I could, but a part of me believes Jasmine needs to hear the truth about slavery. She's never given any thought to the fact that the Wainwrights actually own human beings."

Martha gave her mistress a shrewd grin while pushing a scarlet-red rose deep into the vase. "Well, if you change your mind, you could always be forced to remain at home due to a stomach ailment—or perhaps a headache."

Alice returned the smile. "I'll keep your suggestion in mind, but I'm thinking that if the need arises, I can always tell Malcolm and Bradley the truth: that hearing both sides of any issue is important to sound decision-making. Although I'm certain Bradley thinks a woman should embrace the same beliefs as her husband, *I* certainly don't adhere to such a viewpoint."

Martha nodded. "Whatever you think is best."

Bradley donned his black silk hat and checked his pocket watch one last time. Tardiness, he had decided many years ago, was a habit of ill-bred individuals who would never succeed in life. That resolve in mind, Bradley knew he would be on time for his meeting today, no matter the cost or inconvenience. His image with the Associates was of paramount importance, and today's meeting would likely prove decisive. He tucked Malcolm Wainwright's letter into his pocket, stepped up into his carriage, and arrived at Matthew Cheever's office within fifteen minutes. The number of carriages already present startled him, and he once again looked at his watch. The meeting wasn't due to begin for another ten minutes.

He hurried through the iron gate and across the mill yard toward Matthew's office. All of the other Associates who had been summoned to the meeting were already assembled in the room when he entered. All eyes turned in his direction. He hadn't felt this level of discomfort since his primary school days when the instructor would sometimes call upon him unexpectedly.

He took a brief moment to gain his composure before removing his hat. "Good day, gentlemen. Was the schedule for our meeting changed without my knowledge?"

"Welcome, Bradley," Matthew greeted. "No, the time wasn't changed. I asked the other members to come a half hour early."

Bradley waited, but Matthew offered no further explanation, which left him to wonder what the group might have wanted to discuss in his absence. "I trust I gave you sufficient time to conclude your conversation."

"Indeed," Nathan Appleton said. "What news can you share regarding our friends in the South? Are you making any headway with your negotiations?"

Bradley reached into his jacket and extracted Wainwright's recent letter. "As a matter of fact, I received this letter from Malcolm Wainwright only two days ago. He and his brothers are close to reaching an agreement with us. They sent a refusal to Mr.

Haggarty, their English buyer, with notice they'll negotiate terms no further. They requested Haggarty's signature on a refusal to contract. Once they receive the endorsed refusal, they will be prepared to contract with us. The tone of the letter is extremely positive."

"That's excellent news," Nathan commented. "I don't think I could be more pleased."

Bradley took a moment to bask in Appleton's accolades before continuing. "I believe the balance of the letter may prove you wrong on that account. There is even more good news," he said. "With my strong encouragement, Mr. Wainwright has taken it upon himself to tell other growers about our strong desire to do business with Southern plantation owners throughout Louisiana and Mississippi. There are a number of them who are looking favorably toward conducting business with us if it would prove more lucrative than continuing their current contracts with England. Of course, none of them would yield the amount of cotton that the Wainwrights' harvest will, but if we can gain control of the area one grower at a time, I'm certain we'll soon have all the cotton needed to keep our mills operating at maximum capacity. Perhaps it will even signal a time for expansion."

Nathan Appleton's tremendous enthusiasm was beyond expectations. He bounded from his chair and pumped Bradley's arm in an exaggerated handshake while encouraging the other members to offer their congratulations. "You see? I told you our earlier meeting was unnecessary. Bradley is worthy of the confidence Matthew and I placed in him."

Wilson Harper shifted in his chair. "I never said he wasn't worthy of our confidence. I said the reports thus far had not been favorable and I feared the Wainwrights would remain with the English markets. I'm pleased now that Bradley has been able to prove me wrong."

"That's good to hear," Bradley put in. He knew Harper had never been one of his strong supporters, which made his comment even more pleasurable.

"For planning purposes, does Mr. Wainwright say when we

may expect to have a signed contract in our hands? Or, for that matter, when do you expect to secure a signed contract with any of these men?" Wilson Harper asked with a sanctimonious grin curving his lips.

"I'll be returning to Mississippi in mid-November and expect we will already be receiving cotton from the Wainwrights by the time I sail. As for the other producers, I believe we'll have contracts from some of them in the very near future. Others may wait until the Wainwrights have actually begun doing business with us. However, we will benefit from their contracts even if they sign late in the year. Many of the producers are still harvesting in December and January."

"If you've secured an agreement with the Wainwrights, why do you find it necessary to return to Mississippi in November?" Wilson asked.

Several members turned their attention to Bradley, and he knew he must respond now. Otherwise, the powerful momentum he had gained during the meeting might be lost. "I'm going to escort Miss Wainwright back to The Willows, where we will be married during the Christmas holidays. I hope that news will put to rest any further concerns you might have, Mr. Harper."

There were several surprised gasps, followed by what seemed an interminable silence. Nathan was the first to speak. "Let me offer my hearty congratulations, Bradley. Miss Wainwright is a beautiful young woman, and I'm certain she'll make you a fine wife."

Eyes sharpened, Robert Woolsey gave Bradley a slow smile. "And seal his business transactions as well."

Bradley wasn't certain if Woolsey's remark was filled with scorn or jealousy, but he decided to let the retort pass when Matthew slapped Woolsey on the shoulder and said, "Sounds as though you're sorry you didn't have the wherewithal to win Miss Wainwright's hand for yourself."

Woolsey flushed. "No offense intended, Bradley. After all, your success swells all of our coffers. Accept my best wishes for your happiness with Miss Wainwright."

By the time the meeting ended, Bradley was receiving enthusiastic best wishes from every one of the men in attendance. He departed the meeting with a sense of elation he hadn't experienced since receiving his father's business assets, but by the time he arrived home his emotions were as mixed as when he'd been told Nolan would receive his mother's valuable paintings as his inheritance. Telling the assembled group of Associates that he planned to marry Jasmine Wainwright before advising Jasmine of his intentions and actually having the betrothal approved and announced by her father might prove to be a frivolous mistake. However, if luck remained with him, neither Malcolm Wainwright nor his daughter would ever become aware of his boastful—and premature—announcement.

CHAPTER · 9

ALICE SETTLED into the church pew with Jasmine at her side. Her granddaughter was busy looking over the crowd assembling in the old Pawtucket church, where antislavery meetings had been conducted for more than fifteen years. The church soon filled to capacity, and many of the attendees were forced to stand in the aisles or out in the churchyard.

There were two speakers, both freed slaves who spoke to the gathering of their work with Frederick Douglass and William Lloyd Garrison. When they finished their short speeches, it was Nolan Houston who called out from the back of the room and asked them to tell the crowd how they had gained freedom.

The slave who called himself George moved forward on the small stage. "It was de hand of God what moved in a mighty way to give us our freedom, for our master was cruel and so was his missus. We's got de scars to show for his mean streak. One day some Quakers come through Virginia, and dey stopped and asked if the master could spare a cool drink. Dem Quakers stayed and talked and talked to the master and his missus.

"Dey stayed for three days, talking and praying until they finally convinced our owner it was de right thing to emancipate his slaves. So de master and his missus, dey decided dey was gonna sell their place and move off to Ohio and earn dem a living by working with they own hands. Dey told us all we was free to go on our way. We thought it was a trick until de Quakers told us about de praying they'd been doin' for days. Even so, we 'spected de dogs to come huntin' us down. But dey never did. Don' know what happened to any of dem white folk. Ain't never see'd 'em since den. I ain't never looked back, but I'm mighty thankful for dem Quaker folk."

The two former slaves talked awhile longer, answering questions and removing their shirts to reveal the angry scars of abuse—scars that spoke louder than any words they might utter. The entire crowd seemed to groan in unison as the men told of iron shackles, bullpens, and stocks being used to punish slaves.

Jasmine nudged her grandmother. "I know all these people are abolitionists, but do they not realize there are many slaves who are well treated and happy?"

Alice arched her eyebrows. "And where would that be?"

Jasmine stared at her grandmother in disbelief. "Why, at *any* Wainwright plantation."

"Do you believe the slaves at The Willows are content with their lot in life, Jasmine?"

"Of course they are. They are well cared for. Happy. Content. They love us."

"You need not continue to defend your opinion. I'm not going to argue with you, dear, but why did you want to come to this meeting if you disagree with abolition?"

Jasmine fidgeted with her gloves. "I wanted to hear their views, but I didn't expect the speeches to be inflammatory. I think they should temper such talk by explaining there are slave owners who treat their people exceedingly well."

Alice smiled at her granddaughter but said nothing. She'd not enter into a disagreement that might cause Jasmine to discuss this gathering with her father at a later date. She sighed, knowing Jasmine had been sheltered from the realities of life on the plantation. Alice tried not to fret about the matter, but an uneasiness hung over her like a foreboding of tragedy to come. Now she was certain she'd made a mistake. She should have followed Martha's advice and remained at home.

The meeting broke up a short time later. Had Alice been there alone, she might have lingered to revisit some of the evening's discussion with her friends. Now all she wanted to do was depart before Jasmine managed to get drawn into some of the more heated arguments. With an authoritative, no-nonsense air, Alice moved Jasmine to the door.

"Why are we leaving so quickly, Grandmother? Is something wrong?" Jasmine questioned as they descended the stairs.

"The night air can cause us both to take sick," Alice replied, linking her arm with her granddaughter's. "Besides, Martha has promised to have fresh cinnamon scones ready for our evening tea. You haven't yet tasted her special recipe. They are quite delightful."

Jasmine seemed easily placated with this response. Alice almost felt sorry for the girl. Her innocence made it simpler for Alice to explain away their departure, but her ignorance of the truth was distressful.

They were but a short distance from the church when Alice noticed Nolan Houston walking toward them with a quizzical look on his face. "Good evening, ladies. I must say I was surprised to see you in attendance, Miss Wainwright. What brings a Southern belle to an antislavery meeting?"

"I was curious, anxious to expand my knowledge."

"And does my brother know you were in attendance this evening?" He flashed her a broad smile as if already knowing the answer.

Alice stepped forward and took Nolan's arm. "No, he doesn't, Nolan. And I would be most appreciative if you didn't mention seeing us. I fear I took it upon myself to bring Jasmine without seeking her father's approval. I beg your indulgence in this matter."

Nolan's smile faded. "Of course, Mrs. Wainwright. I would never betray your confidence."

Alice breathed a sigh of relief. The handsome young man seemed to easily understand her plight without forcing her to give further explanation. "Thank you. And if I may be of assistance to you in the future, you have only to ask."

He nodded. "I understand the delicacy of the situation." Turning his attention to Jasmine, he said, "I hope you found the meeting informative, Miss Wainwright."

"I thought the presentation rather one-sided. As I was telling my grandmother, there are many slaves who are happy and well cared for. In fact, we have such slaves on the Wainwright plantations."

"That's good to hear. For when I toured your plantation, I failed to ask the slaves I saw whether they were happy. Of course, most of them were out in the fields laboring in the relentless heat, but when I again visit The Willows, I'll make it a point to inquire."

Jasmine frowned at his seemingly flippant reply. "You need only ask Mammy. She'll tell you how happy she's been living with us."

Alice cleared her throat. "We really must be going home. We have a full day tomorrow. The Ladies' Society from the church is meeting at my house."

"Certainly," Nolan said graciously while tipping his hat.

Once they were settled in the carriage and Martin flicked the reins, Alice took Jasmine's hand in her own. "The meeting tonight is *not* something you should mention publicly, my dear, even with those who were in attendance. Caution is the best practice."

Jasmine arched her thin, perfectly shaped eyebrows. "So tomorrow I'm not to speak of having been at tonight's meeting? Is that what you want me to understand, Grandmother?"

"No need to take umbrage. I make this request of anyone I take to the meetings. Those who attend the antislavery meetings have an expectation their confidentiality will not be breached. I'm asking no more of you than I request from any of my other guests."

Jasmine bowed her head. "I'm sorry. I'm acting like a spoiled child after you were kind enough to take me to the meeting. My lips are sealed. You have my word."

"Thank you, dear. I knew I could count on you."

But even with her granddaughter's promise, Alice Wainwright could not settle her discomfort. She could hardly explain her situation to Jasmine. How could she hope for her granddaughter to understand that the very institution that put jewels around her throat and silks on her back was the very nightmare Alice had turned her back on when she returned to live in the North? No, there would be no easy way to explain the matter. To Jasmine, life on the plantation was leisurely afternoons reading and sewing—it was tender care by Mammy, who had raised the girl since infancy—it was a facade of a utopia that didn't exist.

But I won't be the one to open her eyes to the truth, Alice thought uncomfortably. *She'll see it for herself soon enough. She's an adult now, and while protected, Jasmine is no dolt. She'll learn the truth.*

"And the truth shall make you free," a voice whispered deep in her heart.

"But the truth is often very hard to take," she responded quietly.

Jasmine looked up and smiled. "What did you say, Grandmother?"

Alice shook her head and patted her granddaughter's hand. "Just the mutterings of an old woman. Nothing of import." But in her heart, Alice knew better. It was possibly the most important lesson Jasmine would ever learn.

Jasmine stood beside her grandmother while affably greeting their guests the next afternoon. The ladies flocked into the house in their plumed hats and silk carriage dresses as though they were attending the social event of the season rather than a meeting of the Ladies' Society.

Violet grasped Jasmine by the arm and pulled her away from the crowd. "Did you enjoy the meeting last night?"

Jasmine cocked her head and met Violet's intense gaze. "What meeting?"

"The antislavery meeting, silly. I saw you there with your grandmother."

"I have no idea what you're talking about," Jasmine insisted.

Violet placed her fingertips to her lips. "Oh, I understand. You're holding fast to the privacy rules. But it doesn't matter if you talk to me—after all, I was in attendance too. However, I must admit that I was quite surprised to see you at the meeting. What did you think after hearing those poor slaves talk about how they were mistreated? And those dreadful scars on their backs—did you *look* at them?"

Jasmine chewed on her lip and strengthened her resolve. She would keep her word. "Would you like a cup of punch? It's really quite good. I tasted it earlier."

Violet sighed and folded her arms across her chest. "Well, then, let's talk about your wedding. I'm surprised you've remained in Massachusetts. Is your mother making all the plans for your nuptials without you? I would much prefer to plan my own wedding when I get married."

Jasmine's soft laughter floated through the room. "Nuptials? I'm not getting married. Wherever did you get such a preposterous idea?"

"My father told us at breakfast this morning. If you don't believe me, ask my mother."

Jasmine clamped on to Violet's arm and pulled her out the stained-glass doors leading into the garden. "Exactly *what* did your father say?" Dread rushed over her like a cold, damp breeze.

Violet's gaze was riveted upon the fingers digging into her flesh. "You're hurting my arm."

Jasmine loosened her hold but didn't turn the girl free. "Tell me what your father said about marriage plans. I don't even have a suitor."

"Of course you do," Violet retorted, shaking free. "Bradley Houston! He's been your constant escort since you arrived in Lowell. Although, personally, I find his brother much more appealing. He has the loveliest eyes—don't you think?"

"Is *Bradley* who you're talking about?" Jasmine placed her hand on her chest and sighed in relief. "Bradley's not my beau. He escorts me as a matter of convenience and safety—at my father's request."

"Really?" the fourteen-year-old questioned. "Well, my father said that Mr. Houston would be escorting you back to Mississippi in mid-November and the two of you would be married during the Christmas holidays. Perhaps your father has requested more of Mr. Houston than you realize."

A flash of anger stabbed at her like a red-hot poker. "Mr. Houston has never asked me to marry him, and I'm certain he hasn't asked for my father's consent. In addition, my mother would have written me."

"I can't imagine he'd announce your wedding plans to all of his business associates if he didn't have your father's permission," Violet countered.

Jasmine was uncertain how to respond. She had more questions than answers, and right now she wanted only to awaken from this nightmare. The warm afternoon heat closed in like a suffocating shroud. "He made a public announcement?" She shook her head and looked around. "I must sit down. I feel as though I'm going to faint."

Violet helped her to the bench and then sat down beside her. "I'm sorry I was so unkind, but it never entered my mind you didn't know. I just thought you were being coy. When Father told us, I did express my surprise that you would agree to marry Mr. Houston since you've told me in the past you did not enjoy his company."

"His behavior makes me extremely uncomfortable," Jasmine confided. "Besides, he's too old for me. I'm but ten and eight and he's . . . well . . . he's much older."

"What will you do?"

"As soon as the meeting is over, I'll talk to Grandmother and see what she knows of these arrangements. If she, too, is uninformed, we'll need to talk with Bradley Houston. Until then, I'm going to pray this is all a misunderstanding."

So great was her sense of humiliation that she wanted to disappear from sight, and Violet's wan smile was doing nothing to help buoy her spirits. There was nothing to do but return to the parlor and act as though all was right with the world.

"I suppose we should join the others," Jasmine said, finally staying her nerves. "But please, Violet, say nothing about this."

"I promise I won't," the girl said, jumping to her feet. "I cannot vouch, however, for what my mother might say or do. She loves weddings and babies. I think she always longed to have more daughters to plan events for, but alas, she has to suffer with me. Of course, my brother, Michael, keeps her very busy. Mother often says that twelve-year-old boys are much more difficult to contain than fourteen-year-old girls."

Jasmine listened only half-heartedly to Violet's girlish chatter. Inside her head, a million questions were spilling over one another. How could Bradley Houston have made a public announcement of marriage? It was unheard of. The embarrassment he would face when she rejected him would be a hard matter to face among his peers. Why would he put this burden upon himself? Unless . . . Jasmine couldn't even bear to let the words form in her thoughts. It couldn't be true. Her father and mother would have said something.

"Oh, I'm so glad you've joined us," Lilly Cheever said as Jasmine and Violet came into the room. "I have someone I want you to meet."

Jasmine forced a smile, meeting the dark-eyed gaze of the woman. Lilly Cheever wasted little time pulling Jasmine along beside her.

"Elinor, this is the young woman I was telling you about. Jasmine Wainwright, I'd like you to meet Elinor Brighton. She's the younger sister of Taylor Manning. His wife, Bella, is that lovely woman speaking with your grandmother."

Jasmine met the face of Elinor Brighton and knew immediately that the woman was in no more mood to be at this gathering than was Jasmine. "I'm pleased to meet you," Jasmine said, struggling with her composure.

Elinor nodded. "As am I."

The brown-haired woman looked immediately past Jasmine as

though expecting someone to come through the door. Jasmine had heard from her grandmother that this woman had been recently widowed. In the South she wouldn't be allowed to join in a public gathering.

In the South a man would never speak out of turn about marrying a woman he hardly knew.

But we aren't in the South, Jasmine reminded herself.

Bradley had planned to take the train to Boston, but Alice Wainwright's message summoning him to her home had required him to postpone the journey. The old woman's note had been vague and somewhat terse, and he had momentarily considered ignoring her request. But caution prevailed—he dare not upset Malcolm Wainwright's mother at this juncture. Even though his meeting in Boston wasn't urgent, Bradley detested the interruption nonetheless.

After all, he'd made arrangements to meet with Mr. Sheppard first thing in the morning to go over the shipping business accounts, and now he'd had to send his apologies and ask to reschedule their appointment. Although Bradley had sold the majority of the family shipping business upon his father's death, he still retained ownership of two of the newer vessels and a moderate share of the stock. And while he didn't look after daily maritime operations, Bradley was an astute businessman who knew the wisdom of making an occasional visit to inspect Mr. Sheppard's books.

Attempting to squelch his irritation as he walked up the steps, Bradley took a deep breath and knocked on Alice Wainwright's front door. He nodded at Martha as he handed her his silk-banded hat. "I trust the ladies are expecting me," he commented brusquely.

Martha returned his aloof gaze, her chiseled features void of emotion. "They're in the parlor, sir."

Although he was none too happy about Mrs. Wainwright's request for him to make an immediate appearance, he was determined to maintain his composure. Losing his temper with the old woman would not be wise.

Bradley entered the elegant yet simple sitting room. To one side of the room Jasmine stood near a large floor-to-ceiling window. Her gown of pale pink hugged her figure, stirring Bradley's interest. She might well be the factor that clinched the deal in his business relationship with Malcolm Wainwright, but it certainly was beneficial that she was slender and beautiful.

He flashed her a smile just as she turned to meet his gaze. She said nothing and turned away quickly to take a seat, a frown lining her otherwise worried expression. Bradley turned to greet Mrs. Wainwright, who sat stock-still in a high-back padded chair.

"I'm pleased to see that you both appear to be in good health. The vagueness of your message left me wondering what mayhem might greet me when I arrived," he stated.

"Sit down, Bradley."

The chill in Mrs. Wainwright's words sent icy fingers racing down his spine. He glanced toward Jasmine, whose cold stare held the same chill as did her grandmother's words. Perhaps this matter was more serious than he had contemplated. Bradley startled when Mrs. Wainwright rang for Martha and then instructed her to bring tea. He wanted to forego the ritual. Instead, they sat quietly, saturated by an ominous silence that hovered over the room like a vaporous fog. Waiting. Staring first at some indistinguishable spot on the floor and then the ceiling. Listening as the mantel clock ticked off the minutes. Finally, when he thought he would surely break his resolve and speak out, Martha reappeared with their refreshments, and Mrs. Wainwright ceremoniously poured their afternoon repast.

The old woman took a sip of her tea, leaned back into the soft cushion of her chair, and met Bradley's stare. "I summoned you here because I have heard what I hope is only idle gossip."

His teacup hit the saucer with a loud clink, the amber liquid splashing over the edge of the cup and spilling onto the carpet. He ignored it. "You summoned me here to discuss gossip? Do you realize I cancelled a business meeting in Boston? I care little about the nonsensical chitchat of women who have too little to occupy their time or their minds, Mrs. Wainwright."

The silver-haired woman stiffened. "Your condescending tone will not serve you well today, Mr. Houston, for I have heard from a most reliable source you have announced in public that you plan to marry my granddaughter this winter. What say you, Mr. Houston? Idle gossip or truth?"

The blood drained from Bradley's face. How had word spread to the old woman so quickly? He'd been certain he would have time to correspond with Mr. Wainwright before she found out. Apparently members of the Associates gossiped as much as their wives. The very thought provoked him. There was nothing to do but own up to his words. If he lied, he'd surely be made the fool.

"What you've heard is a true expression of exactly what I *hope* will occur this winter. I admit my folly in speaking as though I've already received Mr. Wainwright's permission. I will tell you, however, that the marriage proposal is under consideration, and Mr. Wainwright has given tentative approval to our marriage."

"*Our* marriage? *My* marriage? To *you?*" Jasmine wagged her finger back and forth between them as she spoke. "Preposterous! I simply don't believe you. Papa has never said one word in his letters. Nor has my mother. And she would have written about wedding plans, wouldn't she, Grandmother?"

Mrs. Wainwright didn't answer. Bradley watched the shrewd look of awareness slowly creep into her countenance, and he knew she understood. He was careful not to smirk. After all, he didn't want to alienate her. He doubted Jasmine's father would be pleased by his social blunder, and Bradley certainly didn't want his business acumen judged by this one mistake.

"So, then, this is to be a *business* arrangement," Alice finally replied.

"If all goes according to plan."

Jasmine rushed to her grandmother's side. "Grandmother, what are you saying? Don't take his side against me in this."

Alice turned to face her granddaughter. "I'm not taking his side, my dear. I have no say-so in this matter. But you may trust I will make every attempt to dissuade your father. I doubt Malcolm will be pleased to hear of your conduct, Mr. Houston. There is little doubt in my mind that you've overstepped the boundaries of your gentlemen's agreement with my son."

The blood rushed to his head, throbbing in his temples like a pounding drum. He must remain calm or all would be lost. This wretched old woman could ruin everything. He longed to retaliate with venom-filled words, but instead he smiled graciously. "I hope I can convince you that this is more than a business arrangement, Mrs. Wainwright. I care deeply for Jasmine and I will do my utmost to make her happy."

Tears were now streaming down Jasmine's face. "If you want to make me happy, you'll tell my father you don't wish to marry me."

Her disgust at the possibility of their union was evident, causing Bradley's anger to grow. He was determined to hold his tongue, however. It would be to his benefit to show contrition for his actions, even sorrow at her rejection.

"I am sorry for having spoken out of line. I'm afraid the spirit of the moment was upon me and I erred in judgment. However, I believe that in time you will grow to love me. And once we have children, you'll be content with this union."

Jasmine shivered. "Children? I'll *never* have your children." Her look of repulsion deepened, offending Bradley in such a way that he put down his cup and saucer and got to his feet.

He knew he must leave or he would explode in anger. How dare Jasmine assess his plans with such distaste? She could do much worse than to marry a wealthy Northern businessman. He'd held his temper in check as long as humanly possible. "I think we are all distraught with this surprising turn of events. I'll come back tomorrow morning when all of us have had time to gain our composure and think rationally."

Before either of them could say anything further, Bradley turned and exited the room. "I'll see myself out," he said as he hurried into the entrance hall.

CHAPTER · *10*

BRADLEY BOUNDED into the room as though he hadn't a care in the world. Jasmine watched his animated behavior, amazed at the change in demeanor since his hasty departure only yesterday.

She had spent a restless night reliving the moment when Bradley had not only admitted to his loose tongue but also announced his plans to marry her as a means to further his business. Her heart ached at the very thought, and she felt she had aged overnight. Her girlish naïveté had altered in the wake of conversations with her grandmother. She could still hear the older woman say, *"Arranged marriages for the sake of bettering the family coffers are nothing new, Jasmine. It has been done this way for centuries."* But how could her beloved papa allow it to happen to his only daughter? *Wouldn't he want me to marry for love?*

"You're looking quite lovely, my dear," Bradley announced. The return of his confidence was apparent. "Perhaps reflection has caused you to feel more favorable toward the idea of matrimony."

"You appear to be feeling rather brash," Jasmine remarked dryly.

He glanced about the room and into the garden. "Indeed. Where is your grandmother?"

"She'll be down shortly. She spends the first few hours of the morning studying her Bible and praying."

"Asking forgiveness for her sinful nature, I suppose."

"What?" His rude remark caught her off guard. "My grandmother is an honest, gentle lady."

"Your grandmother is willing to bend the rules to suit herself when necessary."

Alice Wainwright descended the stairs wearing a green-and-gold print morning dress that accentuated the golden flecks in her hazel eyes. "If you care to defame me, please wait until I'm present, Mr. Houston."

He held out a letter that had been neatly addressed to Malcolm Wainwright. "I took the liberty of removing this from the tray in the entrance hall. After we've completed our conversation, I doubt you'll want to post your missive."

Jasmine's surprise at his boldness bordered on hysteria as she turned to her grandmother. "I cannot believe such behavior."

Her grandmother took the letter and placed it on the table beside her. "I'm certainly pleased I took ample time for prayer this morning, Mr. Houston, as you are already trying my patience. I must say, this is a side of you that I have not yet been burdened to witness."

Bradley seemed to enjoy watching her irritation rise. In fact, Jasmine thought he seemed quite pleased with himself.

"Before you say anything you might regret, let me advise you that when I left here yesterday, I stopped at the Merrimack House. There was quite a crowd, and I was seated near a table of people who were discussing the merits of abolition." Jasmine noticed her grandmother startle when he mentioned abolition.

"That's of little interest to us, Bradley. I thought you came to discuss the improper announcement of our impending marriage," Jasmine interjected.

"If you'll not interrupt, you will see how this all comes together, my dear. Just sit down and listen."

Bradley relished the moment as Jasmine appeared stunned by his command and immediately dropped onto the brocade-upholstered bustle chair. Watching as she followed his commands gave him a heady feeling of power.

"As I was saying, the people sitting adjacent to me were discussing abolition. In the course of their discussion, they mentioned an antislavery meeting that was held at the old Pawtucket church several days ago. Apparently there were a couple of former slaves who spoke about their life on a plantation. But then, you two already know what they talked about, don't you?"

"Excuse me? What *are* you talking about?" Jasmine asked.

"There's no need to feign ignorance. I know that both of you attended the meeting. I'm certain your son would be appalled to discover you took Jasmine to an antislavery meeting, aren't you, Mrs. Wainwright? After all, how would it look for a man of his status and reputation—an owner of over a hundred slaves—to have his daughter and mother notably involved with such a movement? Why, it might mean their neighbors would condemn the family. It could mean a great loss for everyone."

He paused, watching both women carefully. Jasmine paled considerably, but her grandmother held her head upright, waiting for him to continue.

"Not only that, but it could see the family fortune in ruin."

"Our family is very successful," Jasmine protested. "It would take more than something this trivial to ruin us."

Bradley raised a brow. "Trivial? You think this trivial?" He shook his head. "The Boston Associates are heavily dependent upon cotton for their mills. Your father and uncles are vast producers of this cotton. However, the Associates are not fools. They won't brook nonsense or a threat to their well-being. Your father and his brothers have already cut many of their ties with English markets. They are counting on the Associates to purchase their cotton crops. A single word from me could put an end to that."

"But what purpose would that serve?" Jasmine questioned, her voice breaking slightly. "How would it help your case?"

"It might not necessarily help my case, but it would devastate your family. If I choose to tell the Associates that your family is less than reliable—that there are problems with the dependency of the product—your father and uncles will sit with tons of cotton on the docks and no buyer. England won't have them now, not even if they agreed to take a huge loss of profit. No, my dear ladies, the Wainwright family has burned several bridges over these past few days. Wouldn't you say so, Mrs. Wainwright?"

Alice Wainwright remained silent, staring at the rose bushes in her flower garden, obviously unwilling to make a rushed admission.

Bradley rubbed his hands together in satisfaction. "Let me see, what were your words to me yesterday, Mrs. Wainwright—'idle gossip or truth'?"

Alice glared at him. "Truth. And now, Mr. Houston, what is it you want from me?"

Bradley gave her a self-satisfied grin. "I'd say this piece of information puts us on equal footing, Mrs. Wainwright. I'll not mention to your son the fact that you escorted Jasmine to an anti-slavery meeting if you'll refrain from divulging my overzealous declaration of our impending marriage. I won't suggest to the Associates that the Wainwright family is anything other than solid, and you, my dear Jasmine, will happily agree to our union. Think of it, my dear. You will be saving generations of Wainwrights from disgrace and financial ruin."

"This can't be our only recourse," Jasmine said, looking to her grandmother.

The old woman shifted in her chair and gave Jasmine a look of defeat. "I won't send the letter, Mr. Houston."

"And there will never be any mention of this to Mr. Wainwright from either of you. Is that agreed?"

Jasmine and her grandmother locked gazes and then nodded their heads. "Agreed," they stated in unison.

Bradley stood. "I believe you'll both begin to see the wisdom of this in time. For now, I simply require that you keep your unhappy thoughts to yourself." He gave a brief bow. "Now, you ladies finish your tea." He started to go, then turned and fixed his gaze on Jasmine.

"Oh yes, I nearly forgot. There's a social at the Harper home next Friday evening. I'll expect to escort you, Jasmine. Be ready at eight o'clock."

The two women sat in stunned silence after Bradley Houston departed. For Jasmine, it was the moment she realized that she had very little say over her life and future. Men would make choices for her, and she would be nothing more than a pawn in their game.

How could this be happening? What had started out as a lovely trip north to spend time with her grandmother had turned into a nightmare.

"Father will agree to this marriage, won't he?" she whispered.

Her grandmother shrugged. "It is very possible, but there is no way of knowing the full truth of the matter without discussing it with your father. And of course, we've just agreed not to do that."

"Surely Papa doesn't want to see me married to the likes of Bradley Houston? He's much older and not at all pleasant company. He's pompous and overly confident in his abilities."

"Some would say those are the perfect qualities for a leader— a man of great means. Bradley Houston is, unfortunately, the very kind of man your father would look for."

Jasmine shook her head, still unable to believe that her world was tumbling so chaotically out of order.

———

Jasmine examined herself in the mirror. Grandmother had insisted she wear her peach silk gown to the Harpers' party. Jasmine's preference was to remain at home or, in the alternative, wear her old green plaid. She had no desire to impress Bradley Houston with the lovely new gown. But her grandmother was already distraught, so she deferred.

Alice came into the bedroom as Jasmine was clasping her grandmother's pearl necklace around her neck. "You look absolutely beautiful. The color of your dress accentuates the blush of your cheeks."

"Thank you, Grandmother. I do wish you were going along

this evening. I dislike being alone with Bradley. He makes me uncomfortable."

"He's never acted in an ungentlemanly fashion, has he?"

"I consider his threat regarding our attendance at the antislavery meeting ungentlemanly. Especially since I merely wanted to expand my education. If I didn't fear the whole issue would cause harm to Father, I would have told him to leave the house and never return."

"I appreciate your willingness to join with me in accepting his terms, dear. This will all work out for the best, I'm sure."

A knock sounded at the front door, and Jasmine checked her reflection one last time. "There he is. I'd best go down."

Jasmine lifted the skirt of her gown ever so slightly before descending the stairs, followed by her grandmother. She could feel Bradley's gaze upon her as she approached, but she purposefully ignored him. Instead, she turned to Martha, who was holding her shawl, lace gloves, and beaded miser purse. Moving in slow motion, she pulled on one glove and then the other in leisurely fashion. She then took the purse from Martha and methodically reviewed its contents.

When her shawl had finally draped to her satisfaction, she turned around and faced Bradley. "I believe I'm ready to leave when you are, Mr. Houston."

If her actions annoyed him, he didn't reveal his dissatisfaction. Instead, he smiled and offered his arm. "We can leave immediately," he said.

She leaned down and kissed her grandmother's cheek before taking Bradley's arm.

"You look quite lovely this evening, Jasmine. Orange becomes you," Bradley emoted.

"Peach."

"Excuse me?"

"The color is peach, not orange."

"Oh, I see. In that case, peach becomes you, as does the style of the dress. I was pleased to see you had taken such pains to look your most beautiful tonight. I feared you might come down in sackcloth and ashes."

"That would have been my preference. However, Grandmother insisted I dress appropriately."

He emitted a deep belly laugh that completely surprised her. "I realize your youth is responsible in large part for your audacity. However, you'll learn that I will tolerate only occasional impudence. Fortunately for you, this evening happens to be one of those instances." He helped her into the closed carriage, then with great audacity, sat close beside her.

Jasmine hugged her side of the carriage, desperate to avoid even the aroma of his cologne. "Since you are being so tolerant, I suppose I should move forward with great boldness. I've hesitated to ask previously, but I would like to know your age. I'm certain you won't mind sharing such private information with your future wife."

"I am pleased to hear you've accepted your role as my future wife, albeit I may have detected a caustic ring to the words. As for my age, I'm thirty-nine. Old enough to channel your zealous behavior in the proper direction, yet young enough to father your children."

"Mr. Houston!"

"If you ask cheeky questions, you should expect answers in kind."

"I expect nothing but the worst from you," she replied.

He appeared to consider this for a moment before continuing. "Jasmine, you can make this very easy or very difficult. I cannot deny I have goals and ambitions in taking you as my wife; however, I am prepared to forget our rather rocky beginning and work toward a smooth path. You may find the aspect of our union to be completely abominable, but I assure you it will not change my mind on the matter. I intend to be your husband. The sooner you get used to the idea and accept it, the better for all concerned."

"Hardly that," Jasmine retorted. She tried hard to keep from allowing tears to come to her eyes. "I do not think it better to marry a man I do not love—cannot abide—rather than return to my father's house and remain a spinster. Does it not bother you in the least that I do not love you—that I will never love you?"

Bradley surprised her by laughing. "You are such a child. If only the choices were that simple. This has nothing to do with love."

"Exactly my point," Jasmine declared. She determined to ignore him rather than partake in his verbal sparring, and for the remainder of their carriage ride, she turned a deaf ear to his questions. But he seemed not to care, eventually growing silent himself. The carriage came to a halt in front of a gambrel-roofed frame home, banked by an abundance of birches and pines. It was, Jasmine decided, a cozy-appearing house that seemed to beckon visitors enter and stay for a while.

A servant took their wraps and then directed them toward Mr. and Mrs. Harper. Their hosts stood below the two steps leading into the drawing room, and after proper introductions had been made, Bradley escorted Jasmine into the large candlelit room. The rug had been rolled back and couples danced in the center of the room while others congregated in small groups around the perimeter, the muted light causing their shadows to flutter upon the walls. They appeared to go unnoticed until Josiah Baines called out Bradley's name and waved in their direction.

"Come join us. We've plenty of questions, don't we, Thomas?" Josiah said, drawing Thomas Clayborn into the conversation as Bradley and Jasmine neared the men.

"Ah, so this is the future Mrs. Bradley Houston, I take it," Josiah remarked. "I'm pleased to make your acquaintance, Miss Wainwright." He leaned toward Jasmine in a conspiratorial fashion. "We already know your name since the Boston Associates are quite impressed with your father's cotton empire."

"And because Bradley shared your wedding plans with us at our last meeting," Wilson Harper added as he joined the group. He slapped Bradley on the shoulder. "I can see why he was anxious to announce his betrothal."

Jasmine blushed at the remark, but her presence was soon forgotten as the men's conversation shifted to talk of the mills and reduced productivity. Her attention soon shifted to the laughing couples swirling around the room.

"Would you care to dance?"

She startled and turned at the voice, for her thoughts were distant. "Why, yes, Nolan. I would be pleased to dance with you." She began to walk toward the dance floor, and he touched her arm.

"Let me ask Bradley's permission. We don't want to offend him." He gave her a lopsided grin. "It would serve no useful purpose."

Jasmine nodded and waited. Bradley looked at her before returning his attention to Nolan. She waited, wondering if Bradley was denying the request, but Nolan returned, took her hand, and led her onto the dance floor.

"He didn't object?"

"Why should he? Bradley's hoping to impress the Associates, and he can't do that if he's on the dance floor. If you're otherwise occupied, he won't be required to leave his discussion."

Jasmine shrugged. "He won't leave his conversation on my account. Bradley knows I have no desire to dance with him."

Nolan moved back an arm's length and arched his eyebrows into twin peaks. "You told him that?"

"No. There was no need. He knows exactly how I feel about him."

"But he just now told me the two of you are to be wed."

"Since we will soon be related, I don't think your brother will mind if I share with you the actual reason *why* we will be married."

"It's really not my business, Miss Wainwright. As you likely noticed upon first meeting us at your plantation, both our age and our interests divide Bradley and me. We live, if you will, in different worlds. Bradley enjoys amassing wealth and influence. However, I find my pleasure in seeking the beauty of God's hand in nature and creativity. Of course, I attempt to find God's beauty in mankind also, but it becomes increasingly difficult," he said and then smiled at her.

She tilted her head to one side and looked into his eyes. "Your smile is filled with sadness."

"Perhaps because I feel so inadequate to make changes in the evils of mankind. My labors seem fruitless and my prayers continue to go unanswered."

"Mammy says no prayer goes unanswered," Jasmine said gently. "She says God responds to every request with either a 'yes,' a 'no,' or 'not right now.'"

Nolan nodded. "And I'm certain Mammy and the rest of the Negroes living down South are quite used to hearing God's 'not right now' response to their prayers."

"Well, I certainly hope God isn't going to deny my prayers regarding marriage to your brother. This wedding will be nothing more than a charade. The entire idea is nothing more than a proposed business arrangement. I've not yet discussed the bargain with my father, and consequently, I'm not privy to all of the details. In fact, my father hasn't even formally agreed to the marriage."

"Possibly you won't be forced into the marriage after all," he said uneasily.

"I fear all chance of such an escape has been ruined."

He led her from the dance floor and retrieved two cups of punch from a nearby table. They walked out the wide door leading into a small garden off the drawing room. The rosebushes were in full bloom, filling the summer night with an intoxicating fragrance.

"Will your father not listen to your protest? Surely he'll be offended that Bradley has announced your engagement without gaining his consent."

"I can't tell him what Bradley has done." She surprised herself by explaining the requirement exacted by Bradley after his discovery she'd attended the antislavery meeting.

Nolan rubbed his palm across his forehead as though he were trying to erase what Jasmine had told him. "I wish I could tell you I'm surprised by his deed, but I can't. My brother mentioned his intentions some time ago. However, I shall pray that having you in his life will soften and change him so that one day he will realize what is truly important."

"No doubt he had formulated his plans from the moment he set foot in our home. How is it that two brothers who were reared in the same household could be so dissimilar?"

Nolan glanced over his shoulder toward where his brother stood in the drawing room. "Bradley was fifteen years old when I was born. He was being groomed to take over my father's business. Quite frankly, another child was quite unexpected so late in my parents' lives. My father took little interest in a second son. After all, he had already set in motion the plan to ensure his shipping business would survive. Consequently, I spent much more time with my mother, who was an artist. From an early age, I would sit and read the book of Psalms to her while she created lovely pastoral settings with her oil paints."

"And were you jealous of Bradley and his close connection to your father and his business?"

Nolan smoothed down the lapel of his wool coat. "No. Quite the contrary. I thought my life wonderful—I still do. I never wanted to trade places with Bradley. When our father died, Bradley inherited the entire business. A year later our mother died. I inherited her paintings, as well as her small art collection, and the family home."

"Did you not feel a twinge of jealousy when Bradley inherited the business?"

Nolan laughed. "No. Bradley had worked for years with my father. He loved the business and deserved to receive it. Besides, I had always known Bradley would inherit the business, and I knew I would receive Mother's artwork. However, I would much prefer her company to her art collection. I still miss her."

"I can't imagine what it must have been like to lose both your parents in such a short period of time. Of course, you and Bradley had each other, but I do hope you had other family to help you through your time of loss."

"We have no other family in this country. Both of my parents emigrated from England at an early age. At the time of my mother's death, my grandparents were all deceased, except my maternal grandmother, who had returned to England several years earlier. Bradley wasn't around much. He was involved in negotiations to sell the business shortly after Mother's death."

"I don't understand why he would sell the family business, especially since it was profitable and he claimed to enjoy it."

"He had become acquainted with Nathan Appleton through the shipping business. Nathan was already heavily invested in the textile industry and was looking to expand his horizons by investing in a small shipping firm. It was through Nathan my brother learned about the Boston Associates and their powerful influence throughout New England. He became obsessed with the idea of becoming a member of their elite group."

"Couldn't he have entered into their numbers with his shipping firm?"

"Nathan was building his own shipping empire and didn't want the competition. Even though Bradley assured him there was more than enough business for both of them, Nathan rejected the idea. The Associates required a sizable cash investment, more than Bradley had available without selling a substantial portion of the business. He wanted a more powerful position in the business world more than he wanted to retain the business, although I'm not certain the shipping firm wouldn't have made him wealthier had he retained full interest in it."

Jasmine's head was swirling with all the information Nolan had conveyed during the past half hour. The glimpse into Bradley's life was even more unattractive than what she had conjured up in her own mind. It appeared his only goal in life was to achieve money and power.

"How did you and Bradley happen to visit The Willows?"

"He wanted to find cotton growers in the South who would be willing to consider changing their markets from England to Boston. Through contacts in the shipping business, Bradley gained access to manifests with names of growers who shipped large quantities of cotton to England. Your family was his first choice to visit. However, he truly didn't go to The Willows with marriage in mind. The availability of a prospective bride was an added bonus."

Jasmine pressed her fingertips to her temples. "And now I find myself unwittingly drawn into this quagmire. What little respect I might have had for Bradley has disappeared."

Engrossed in their conversation, they failed to hear the approaching footsteps. "People are going to begin gossiping if you two remain secluded out here much longer."

Even in the darkness Jasmine could detect the disapproval in his eyes. She wondered how long Bradley had been listening.

CHAPTER · 11

JASMINE'S ENGAGEMENT to Bradley Houston was soon spoken of in all the social circles. Jasmine found it laborious to accept congratulations for a marriage she hoped might never take place, and she avoided discussing the event whenever possible. Her grandmother tried to encourage Jasmine at times when the thought of marriage to Bradley left her particularly discouraged. Still, there was nothing she could do about it. This was, as her grandmother told her in no uncertain terms, the way things were done.

Adjusting the lace collar on her pale yellow gown, Jasmine tried to think of another way to word her request in such a manner that her grandmother would yield. She'd been cajoling the Wainwright matriarch in the rose garden for well over half an hour, but there was no indication she would budge from her position.

Grandmother concentrated on her stitching as though the piece of embroidery required unremitting attention. "You will not change my mind upon this matter," she said as if reading Jasmine's mind. "I insist upon acquiring Bradley's permission. If you'll recall, the last time I hastily agreed to one of your requests, we suffered dire consequences."

Jasmine thought to stomp her foot but stopped short of the act. She knew such childlike behavior wouldn't serve her cause.

"There's nothing further Bradley can do to me—to us. He's already imposed himself on me with this ridiculous engagement."

Alice Wainwright looked up and shook her head. "You know better, Jasmine. There are many ways Bradley could punish us both. However, he's been civil and even kind. It was very generous of him to send us that gift of exotic fruit."

"I don't care how many gifts he sends. I have no desire to be his wife."

Grandmother caught her eye and was silent a moment before saying, "This truly isn't an issue about whether you want to marry him or not. Your father has arranged an advantageous union. It is your duty to put your family ahead of yourself. Women have done this for generations and will go on doing it for generations to come."

"Not if I can help it," Jasmine replied bitterly. "I would want my children to marry for love."

"But emotions are greatly overrated. There is much to be said for making a good marriage—knowing you and yours will be provided for, that you will always have shelter and food. It was thus with my father, and I learned to be happy, even grateful, that he had made such a choice on my behalf."

"Well, I'll never be grateful for Bradley Houston," Jasmine said, folding her arms against the ruching of her bodice. For several minutes she paced back and forth before trying to turn the conversation back to her original request.

"I can't see the harm in this outing. Besides, I truly want to go, Grandmother. You'll be with us, and we could ask Violet and Mrs. Cheever to attend."

"No need to extend an invitation until you've received Bradley's permission. You're now betrothed to him, Jasmine. It is improper to go on an outing with another man without Bradley's express permission."

"Nolan isn't another man; he's Bradley's brother. And I need no further reminders I am betrothed. That distasteful news constantly haunts me."

Grandmother looked over the top of her reading glasses with a raised brow. "I don't believe Bradley would appreciate your appraisal of the situation." Her expression softened into sympathetic concern. "My dear, you must try to accept your fate and make it work so that you'll be happy. I would not have chosen this man for you, but your father has."

Jasmine plopped down on a cushioned garden chair. "Yes, I know." There was resignation in her voice. The issue of her marriage to Bradley Houston was no longer something to be discussed or deliberated. Her father had agreed to their betrothal, and her mother was already making arrangements for the wedding. Perhaps that was why it seemed so important to insist on this one simple outing. "So there is nothing I can say that will convince you?" she finally asked.

"Nothing short of Bradley's consent." The old woman continued stitching. Jasmine wondered how she could possibly be so at ease. Without looking up, her grandmother asked, "Shall I send word to Bradley?"

Jasmine shook her head and folded her hands in her lap. "No need. I didn't expect you would relent. He should be here any moment."

Alice stopped stitching and gazed at her granddaughter. "Had I yielded, what would you have asked him when he appeared?"

Jasmine shrugged. "Something would have come to mind. However, I hadn't prepared. I was certain you wouldn't acquiesce."

Alice shook her head and pursed her lips. "I dare say—"

"Excuse me, ma'am. Mr. Bradley is here to call on Miss Jasmine," Martha said quietly.

Bradley came up behind Martha in long, determined strides and brushed past her. "I told her I didn't need to be announced, but she insisted. I'm in a bit of a rush, Jasmine. What is so important?" He gave a slight bow in the direction of each woman, then waited for an explanation.

Jasmine looked up in distaste. She didn't always abhor his presence, but his forceful nature irritated her. Even now, he was in a hurry to be somewhere else, tending to business far more important than the needs of his fiancée. Getting to her feet, Jasmine held his gaze. "I'd like to attend a gathering in Cambridge on Tuesday, and Grandmother insisted I obtain your permission before accepting the invitation."

He smiled in that self-satisfying way that Jasmine had come to hate. "I can't escort you on Tuesday. I have business that needs my attention."

He spoke slowly, enunciating each utterance as though she couldn't possibly understand anything more complex than a two-syllable word.

Jasmine barely held her temper. "I'm not asking you to escort me. Nolan is attending and has agreed to act as an escort for Grandmother and me. I understand Lilly and Violet Cheever will be attending also. Fanny Longfellow has invited all of us to be guests at her home."

Bradley sat down on one of the benches and gave a wry grin. "Henry and Fanny are hosting another one of those literary gatherings, aren't they?"

Jasmine came to stand directly in front of him. "I believe that's what Nolan said. I understand there will be various discussion groups. Nolan tells me that Nathaniel Hawthorne, Horace Greeley, and many others will all be in attendance." She couldn't contain her excitement.

"And I'm sure Henry Longfellow will be in his glory with his erudite cronies surrounding him. As much as I don't understand why you would want to make a tedious journey to hear pompous men profess their intellectual and philosophical beliefs, I don't suppose it will do you any great harm." He got to his feet. "Now, I really must get back to my business. You may walk me to the door, Jasmine."

She knew his words were a command, and under other circumstances she would have balked. However, he had granted her the permission she earnestly sought, so she submissively followed him to the entrance hall. After collecting his hat, Bradley turned and tenderly caressed her cheek. Instinctively, she moved back a step and hovered in the doorway.

Bradley's eyes narrowed into an icy stare. "You should be

favoring me with accolades. Instead, you withdraw from my touch. I'll remember your thankful nature the next time you seek my agreement."

The slamming door shuddered in the wake of his anger. She'd made a mistake, but permitting him to stroke her cheek had been insufferable. His very touch repulsed her.

———

Nolan offered an arm to Jasmine and Alice Wainwright and escorted them to the carriage, one of them on either side of him. "I must say I was surprised to hear of Bradley's accord. I expected him to recite the many arguments against your attendance. Did he not attempt to dissuade you at all?" Nolan asked. After helping the older woman into the carriage, he took Jasmine's hand and assisted her up.

"No. At first he thought I expected *him* to escort us, but once he realized his presence would not be required, he was most amenable to our attending."

Jasmine hadn't informed her grandmother of the encounter with Bradley prior to his departure, and telling Nolan about it would certainly be reckless. Although she believed she could trust Nolan, there was no need taking undue risk. She'd already alienated Bradley with her behavior.

"And what of Violet and Lilly Cheever? Have they decided to join us?"

"No. They had a conflict and send their regrets. I had tea with Violet yesterday and she said her father isn't fond of the transcendentalist views espoused by those who frequent the gatherings at the Longfellows' home. I'm afraid I appeared quite the fool as I didn't realize you adhered to such beliefs."

"I'm not a transcendentalist, and I certainly don't count myself among those who believe God is immanent in man and that individual intuition is the highest source of knowledge. That kind of thinking has led such believers to place an optimistic emphasis on individualism and self-reliance. I believe in God and His ultimate authority. My faith and trust are in God, not myself. However, I do occasionally enter into debate with them. For I believe if I'm going to associate with these men, I have an obligation to speak God's truth."

"Good for you, Nolan," Mrs. Wainwright said. "I'm glad you have the courage to express your beliefs."

"Thank you, ma'am. However, I must admit that many times I would prefer to remain silent. Doing battle with that group of learned men makes me realize how David must have felt when he confronted Goliath."

Jasmine's grandmother chuckled at his reply. "I'm sure you can hold your own with any of them."

"I'd like to think so, but Bradley has always been much stronger in the skill of debate. He could certainly make some of them appear foolish if he had a mind to do so."

"Are his Christian beliefs well-founded enough that he would challenge such men?" Jasmine inquired. She'd seen no evidence that her future husband esteemed any faith except that which he placed in himself.

Nolan's gaze remained fixed upon the roadway. "He attends church regularly."

Jasmine gave him a sidelong glance. "Simply attending church doesn't mean he's a Christian. Is he truly a believer?"

"That's a question you'll need to ask Bradley. I don't feel qualified to answer for another man's salvation, even if he is my brother."

"If I were to ask Bradley if *you* were a Christian, how would *he* answer?" Jasmine persisted, now certain he was avoiding her question.

Nolan gave her a lopsided grin. "I'd like to think he would speak in the affirmative, but then, I hope that is true of anyone who knows me. Although I'm not always successful, my goal is to make Christianity my life pattern. I want other people to see Christ in me rather than merely hear me advocate some vague philosophy."

"And is that what your brother does? Practice religiosity?"

He chuckled and shook his head. "I never said such a thing.

You're putting words in my mouth, Miss Wainwright. If you truly want to find out who Bradley is and what he believes, you've merely to ask him. In fact, now that the two of you are betrothed, it would seem prudent for the two of you to discuss these matters."

Jasmine smelled the heavy scent of pines as the carriage moved into the countryside. "I haven't asked him because I fear his answers. Unfortunately, I know that no matter what he believes, I'll be forced to marry him. Remaining ignorant somehow seems easier."

"You must do what you believe best, but lack of preparation can sometimes prove fatal."

Jasmine leaned back and stared out the window of the coach, but the beauty of the passing countryside wouldn't erase the ominous warning in Nolan's earnest words.

―――――――

Nolan motioned Jasmine from the circle of older women gathered in one corner of the room. "Come meet a few of these people," he said, taking her by the arm.

They moved through the crowd, stopping in front of a wingbacked chair. "Jasmine, I'd like to introduce you to Horace Greeley," Nolan said. "And, of course, you know Fanny Longfellow."

Jasmine dipped in a small curtsy. "It is a genuine pleasure to meet you, Mr. Greeley," she said while attempting to hide her excitement.

"My pleasure," Horace replied. Before he could say anything further, Henry Longfellow grasped him by the elbow and pulled him off in another direction.

Jasmine turned her attention back to Mrs. Longfellow. "I do want to thank you, Mrs. Longfellow, for the gracious hospitality you've extended to Grandmother and me."

"It's my pleasure, Jasmine. And please, call me Fanny. Only Father refers to me as Frances and only *very* young children address me as Mrs. Longfellow. Now come sit with me and let's get better acquainted." She patted the cushion of a nearby chair.

Jasmine glanced toward Nolan. He said, "I'll leave you ladies

TRACIE PETERSON / JUDITH MILLER

to become better acquainted while I join Henry and the other men for some stimulating conversation."

"Isn't Nolan quite a wonderful man? I've attempted to play cupid on several occasions but to no avail. He always tells me my choices have not been women that adhere to his beliefs. Probably because most of the people whom Henry and I befriend have become transcendentalists. Poor Nolan finds himself quite outnumbered in these gatherings. Unfortunately, there are few Episcopalians, Baptists, or Methodists who care to discuss topics that interest the rest of us—including Nolan. However, I'm pleased to see he has found a young lady who meets his requirements."

A warm blush colored Jasmine's cheeks. "Nolan is my escort this evening. However, I am betrothed to his brother."

Fanny's eyebrows arched. "Bradley?"

"Yes. Do you know him?"

A vague smile played at the corner of Fanny's lips. "Don't think me impolite, but you'll soon come to learn that all of us who attend these gatherings speak quite frankly to one another. I know Bradley better than I care to, and I must say that you seem more suited to Nolan than to his brother—both in age and disposition. How did you and Bradley become acquainted?"

"Our marriage is a business arrangement between my father and Bradley. He is certainly not the man I would choose to wed."

Fanny nodded earnestly. "I thought not. Bradley has little in common with any of us, and he wouldn't abide Henry or me were it not for my father's position among the Boston Associates. I think Nolan is drawn to us as much because of our antislavery beliefs as our literary discussions. Bradley, however, aspires to be in the hierarchy of the Associates, but I'm certain you already know that. Now, do tell me about yourself. You have an odd accent. Where do you call home, Jasmine?"

"The Willows. It's a cotton plantation near Lorman, Mississippi."

"Oh? I may have misjudged you, Miss Wainwright. You may have more in common with Bradley than I thought."

"Whatever do you mean? Because I'm from the South you

believe me interested in power and money rather than kindness?"

"I'm certain your views on slavery would be vastly different from the views of everyone else in this room, but they would likely coincide with Bradley Houston's. Of course, when he's in our company he professes merely to tolerate slavery and, like many of his contemporaries, advocates no further expansion of the practice—an opportunistic attitude at best. Would you agree?"

"I realize there are few among you who will believe me, but there are slaves who are content and even happy with their owners. I believe generalities are an unfair way to judge people, especially when you've not investigated for yourself. Not all slaves are mistreated, and not all owners are ogres."

Fanny turned her attention to Nolan, who had returned to stand quietly behind Jasmine's chair. "Would you agree with Miss Wainwright's statement, Nolan?"

"Having investigated for myself, I can say with authority that I never found a slave who was happy to be held captive, but I can't speak as authoritatively about their owners. I didn't spend much time with them."

"Have your slaves expressed to you that they are happy with their lot in life, Miss Wainwright?" Fanny asked.

"I've never asked them," Jasmine admitted. "As I told Nolan, our slaves are treated very well. He visited our plantation with his brother earlier in the year, and I'm certain he can confirm that fact."

Nolan moved from behind the chair and offered his hand. "They're beginning a reading in the other room. You won't want to miss hearing Mr. Greeley."

Jasmine took his hand and nodded at Fanny. "A pleasure visiting with you. I look forward to further discussion while we're here."

"I'm glad you found our time together enjoyable," she replied with a wry grin.

"Thank you for saving me," Jasmine whispered to Nolan as they walked away. "I fear she intensely dislikes me. Perhaps Grandmother and I should plan to stay at an inn here in Cambridge."

Nolan laughed. "She may disagree with some of your beliefs, but you're much too sweet-tempered to dislike. And you would certainly affront Fanny by leaving to find accommodations elsewhere."

"I imagine my father would find your remark quite amusing, for he finds my temper quite disagreeable. And what have you been off discussing?"

"Unfortunately, several of our group got themselves caught up in talk of the war with Mexico. You've probably heard General Taylor and his men inflicted over a thousand casualties before moving south out of Palo Alto last May, while our navy has more recently seized Monterey and Los Angeles. Killing and mayhem based upon the concept of Manifest Destiny is an idea I certainly don't embrace."

"Our family and General Taylor's are quite close. Believe me when I say he is quite a gentle soul. Still, it sounds as though we both were drawn into uncomfortable discussions. Perhaps we should remain together."

With his eyes twinkling and a smile tugging at his lips, he said, "I certainly wouldn't object, but I believe Bradley might lodge a complaint."

CHAPTER · *12*

JASMINE SAT waiting in the parlor with her parasol firmly balanced against the deep-cushioned chair, her trunk packed and stationed beside the front door. Everything was in readiness for the future—everything except her heart. She tapped her foot and pulled at the lace edging on her handkerchief until she could no longer sit still. Jumping to her feet, she began pacing back and forth in front of the carved marble fireplace, her steps short and frantic. "I pray Bradley has changed his mind. And if he hasn't, then I pray something has happened to prevent him from making the journey."

Grandmother frowned her disapproval. "You need to resign yourself to this marriage, Jasmine. Bradley is not going to change his mind, and you'll be much happier once you accept the fact that you are going to be his wife. Gladly I must admit, I've seen changes in him over these past months. I honestly believe he has grown to care for you."

Jasmine knew her eyes revealed the unremitting resentment that festered in her heart. She saw it there every time she looked in the mirror. "I care little whether he's grown to care for me. I don't love him, and I don't want to be his wife. We are unsuited. I pray daily Bradley will decide against the marriage."

Before Alice could reply, a knock sounded at the front door.

"Perhaps Nolan has come to tell us Bradley was struck down by a runaway carriage and died a quick and painless death," Jasmine said in a sardonic manner. She hated her own cynicism but felt there was no reason to change it. It wouldn't win her freedom from this farce of a marriage.

"Jasmine Wainwright! What shameful things you are saying. You need to ask God's forgiveness for having such thoughts about your future husband."

"Did I hear someone mention a future husband?" Bradley asked as he took long strides into the parlor.

Grandmother quickly interceded. "Jasmine had just mentioned that you were in her prayers each day."

"Surely you know I don't put much stock in prayer—hard work and determination benefit a man more."

Jasmine looked at her grandmother with her eyebrows arched. The older woman immediately turned away, obviously unwilling to acknowledge what Jasmine already knew: Bradley Houston placed his faith in himself—not in God.

"I've had your man load the trunks, and we should be on our way," Nolan called out from the foyer. "If we don't hurry, the train will leave for Boston and we'll miss our voyage." He came into the room and immediately went to Jasmine's grandmother. "May I escort you to the carriage?"

"Certainly." She took up a wool cloak and Nolan quickly moved to help her don it. "There's a chill in the air," she said as if explaining her actions as they walked out of the room.

"There certainly is a chill," Bradley said dryly as Jasmine moved to take up her own cloak and parasol. "I do hope you will warm to the idea of this trip and of the celebration to come," he continued as Jasmine swung the voluminous cloak around her shoulders. "Surely you are anxious to see your family."

"Being reunited with my family and Mammy are of utmost importance to me. If my future included plans to remain with them, you would hear pure delight in my voice." She walked from the room, not even bothering to look back.

Bradley lengthened his stride and came alongside her as they approached the carriage. He leaned down close to her ear. "Perhaps if you could show more enthusiasm toward our marriage, I would be willing to make arrangements for Mammy's return with us."

So that's how Bradley viewed their future marriage, Jasmine realized—as a bartering system. If she behaved in a fashion he found acceptable, he would reward her efforts. There was little doubt he planned to train her like a pet. Be good, follow orders, and you'll get the scraps from the table. She didn't reply. After all, she didn't need Bradley Houston making arrangements for Mammy's future . . . or anything else, for that matter.

The carriage came to a halt on Merrimack Street, where the four passengers disembarked. Nolan took charge of their trunks and baggage while Bradley escorted Alice and Jasmine into the train station. Excitement filled the air. Passengers scurried about, anxious to ensure their tickets and baggage were in proper order; small children clung to their mothers' skirts, obviously frightened by the huge iron monster billowing and puffing like a giant demon; and the remainder sat waiting, their anticipation reaching new heights when the conductor finally called for them to board.

The four of them were alone in the finely appointed coach belonging to the Boston Associates. Jasmine sat down near the center of one of the supple leather-cushioned seats. Her hope had been to sit alone, but Bradley immediately wedged himself into the narrow space beside her. She scooted close to the window and turned her attention away from him. The train jerked and hissed into motion, and Jasmine leaned back and stared at the passing countryside, contemplating her future with this man sitting next to her.

After several curt responses, she was relieved when Bradley finally turned his attention to her grandmother and Nolan. The three of them conversed continually until they arrived in Boston an hour later. Jasmine longed to shout she would go no farther until she was released from this contemptuous engagement. Instead, she boarded the private carriage awaiting them at the station and rode in silence to the docks, where Captain Harmon greeted them. The jovial bewhiskered captain personally escorted the entourage onboard the *Mary Benjamin,* one of the few vessels remaining in Bradley's trimmed-down shipping business. The captain's dutiful attention left little doubt he understood the primary reason for sailing down the coast to New Orleans. The important cargo on this ship was his four passengers, not the partial shipment of goods loaded on board earlier in the day.

"I believe I'd like to retire to my cabin," Jasmine said.

Bradley offered his arm but instead of leading her to the cabin, held tightly to her hand and moved toward the ship's railing. "I think we should remain at the rail. It's always exhilarating to watch as a ship sets sail. Rather romantic—slowly moving away from land on the rising waves, watching the city finally grow dim on the horizon."

Jasmine knew he was toying with her, attempting to play the role of a besotted lover. Had it been anyone but Bradley, she would have found the effort amusing. But everything he did served only to annoy her. If it meant she must stand arm in arm with Bradley, she didn't want to watch Boston disappear from sight. In fact, she didn't want to be in Bradley's company at all. Hurling herself into the depths of the sea seemed a much more appealing alternative.

Alice Wainwright came alongside her granddaughter and patted Jasmine's shoulder. "Jasmine didn't sleep well last night, Bradley. I fear she may become ill if she doesn't get her proper rest. Perhaps if she could lie down and take a short nap, the voyage would go more smoothly."

"I don't see how remaining on deck for an hour is going to cause her enough distress to ruin the remainder of our voyage. I can bring a chair for her."

"Sitting in a chair isn't the same as actually resting. Jasmine is prone to excruciating headaches when she doesn't sleep well."

Jasmine stood sandwiched between the two of them, listening while they discussed her until she could abide no more. She pulled away from Bradley. "Why don't you two remain at the rail and watch the city 'grow dim on the horizon' as Bradley suggested? I, on the other hand, will go to my cabin and rest." She hurried off across the deck, motioning to a deckhand who had carried their trunks on board. "Take me to the cabin where you placed the large black trunk with engraved hasps."

She expected to hear Bradley's footsteps and feel his fingers clutch her arm. Instead, he let her escape to the safety of her cabin, where she bolted the door and fell upon the bed. Her tears flowed freely. How could she possibly survive a loveless marriage? There must be a way to convince her father this plan was doomed for failure.

Surely Papa will listen to reason. He loves me and wouldn't want me unhappy. If I simply tell him the truth, then things could be different, she reasoned. For the first time Jasmine gathered hope from her thoughts. She sat up and dried her eyes.

"I haven't told Papa of my feelings. We haven't discussed the marriage," she murmured. "He has always spoiled me. . . . Perhaps I can convince him to give me my way just one more time."

The thought intrigued her. If her father understood the misery she felt, he might very well relent and break his agreement with Bradley. After all, surely her father would rather see his only daughter happy than expand the family fortune.

Wouldn't he?

"I just need you to keep Bradley occupied while I speak to my father," Jasmine told Nolan. "If you can draw Bradley's interest long enough for me to talk in private, perhaps I can convince my father to reconsider this entire situation."

Nolan seemed less than convinced. He rubbed his chin and looked past Jasmine. She turned and followed his gaze to where Bradley reprimanded the stevedores who were handling their luggage. "I suppose I could seek a delay by suggesting the need to stop by the bank. That would keep us here overnight, but Bradley would never allow you to journey to The Willows by yourself."

Jasmine returned her gaze to Nolan. "Leave that to me. You suggest the delay to Bradley, and I'll speak to my grandmother. Perhaps I can convince her to request a delay as well. She could explain how much the trip has tired her and that she'd like to rest before we continue to The Willows."

"That would seem very reasonable. It's a good day's journey from this point to the plantation," Nolan said thoughtfully. "Bradley surely can't protest an older woman's request for rest, while he might very well deny the delay for something as insignificant as bank business."

"I'll speak to my grandmother," Jasmine told him. "Can you manage to keep Bradley away from us for a few minutes?"

Nolan nodded solemnly. "I'll do what I can. I just hope you know what you're doing."

Jasmine drew a deep breath. "I hope so too."

She went quickly to her grandmother as Nolan ambled down the dock. "Grandmother," Jasmine said, rather breathlessly, "we need to talk."

Alice Wainwright looked up from where she sat patiently waiting for the next portion of their journey.

"Whatever is wrong?"

Jasmine sat down. "I need to talk to Papa without Bradley anywhere around. I've had an idea, and I need your help."

Her grandmother raised her brows. "What are you saying?"

"I'd like you to ask Bradley to delay our trip to The Willows. Just ask him to allow us to spend the night here—tell him the journey has taxed you overmuch."

"Well, that would be no lie," Alice Wainwright admitted. "But, Jasmine, I don't know what you hope to gain with this delay."

Jasmine squared her shoulders. "I'd rather not divulge my plan, otherwise you might face Bradley's wrath. The less you know, the better."

"This isn't like you," Jasmine's grandmother stated in a worried tone.

"I'm afraid," Jasmine said, feeling somewhat strengthened by her own revelation, "that I'm not the same girl I used to be." She patted her grandmother's hand. "Truly, this is very important. I hope it might even mean changing Papa's mind regarding the wedding."

"I cannot do something that would place you in harm's way."

"I won't be in harm's way. This is where I grew up. I know most everyone here in Lorman and in the surrounding countryside. You mustn't worry. I'll be as safe here as in Mammy's arms. Just trust me on this—please."

It took some convincing, but Bradley finally relented and the foursome checked into the nearest hotel. Jasmine and her grandmother pleaded to be left to rest for the remainder of the day, while Nolan suggested that Bradley could use the time to speak to other cotton growers in the area.

Jasmine waited until her grandmother went into the adjoining room for an afternoon nap before hastily exchanging her traveling suit for a riding habit. She would borrow a horse from the Bordens. Dr. Borden was a good friend of the family and had tended most every Wainwright member for one illness or another. He and his wife were also much more liberal in their beliefs than some of their Southern contemporaries. They wouldn't think anything amiss or in the leastwise troubling when Jasmine made her request known.

Jasmine knew she would have to hurry if she were to make it home before dark, however. Her father would not be at all sympathetic to her cause if he thought she'd risked her well-being by traveling in the darkness—unescorted. *He won't approve of this,* she knew in her heart. But on the other hand, once he saw what she was willing to do in order to plead her case, Jasmine felt confident her father would at least delay the wedding, if not cancel it altogether.

Dr. Borden was gone on rounds when Jasmine arrived at the house, but his wife, Virginia, was more than happy to accommodate her.

"You will hurry back for a long visit, won't you?" Virginia

questioned as the groomsman came forward with a fast-looking bay.

Jasmine touched the horse's dark mane, stroking him gently as a means of introduction. "I will do my best to see that we have a nice long talk very soon." Jasmine allowed the groom to help her into the sidesaddle. "Thank you again for the loan," she said. Then without further ceremony, she yanked the reins to the right and quickly headed out.

Her biggest fear was the possibility of running into Bradley as he moved among the folk of Lorman seeking yet someone else to devour. Jasmine thought momentarily that perhaps it wasn't fair to equate her fiancé with the devil, but it didn't overly bother her conscience.

The road home was in good condition, much to Jasmine's relief. The old sights and sounds of her beloved Southern home reached out to embrace her, welcoming her back to that which she loved. Urging the horse to a canter, Jasmine passed from town into the rural areas, where cotton fields were dotted with dark-skinned workers. She slowed the horse momentarily and watched with interest as she remembered the words of the abolitionist speakers back in Lowell. She saw no signs of rough treatment, no proof that these slaves were unhappy or ill-treated.

Picking up her pace again, Jasmine smiled to herself. Surely the things spoken of in Lowell were extreme circumstances and not the normal events of Southern life.

The hours passed as Jasmine urged the horse to his limits. The sun had long since set and the skies were pitch black when Jasmine rounded the final bend for home. Her skin tingled from the exertion of the ride, as well as the overwhelming knowledge that her father would be greatly displeased with her actions. Still, she had seen no other recourse. She had to be allowed to speak her mind and explain her feelings on the matter.

A groomsman approached as Jasmine brought the bay to a stop at the porch stairs. "Miz Jasmine?" the man asked in disbelief. "Is dat you?"

"It is indeed," she replied, happy to be home at last. "I need to speak to my father. Is he here?"

"Shore 'nuf. He was over to Master Franks, but he comed home nearly half an hour back."

Jasmine smoothed her dirty habit and bounded up the steps in an unladylike fashion. She didn't bother to knock but rather pushed back the ornate oak door and stepped into the sanctuary that had been her home for eighteen years.

"Hello?" she called out as she moved through the foyer and into the front sitting room. The room was empty. Jasmine sighed. She knew in her heart that she'd most likely find her father in his study, but she had hoped that she might encounter him first in the presence of others. That way, she presumed, the shock would be less and his anger would abate more quickly.

Giving up on that hope, however, she made her way to her father's office and took a deep breath before knocking loudly on the door.

"Come in."

Jasmine opened the door and peeked in. "Hello, Papa."

"Jasmine!" Her father got to his feet from behind his austere mahogany desk. "I didn't realize you were arriving tonight. We'd had no word and had intended to send someone to check on you tomorrow." He came forward and embraced her.

Jasmine enjoyed the moment, knowing that once her father learned the truth there'd be no pleasantries. "I missed you so much. I just couldn't wait another moment." She pulled away and eyed her father seriously. With any luck at all, she'd get their conversation started before he realized the situation for what it was.

"We must talk, Papa. I'm not at all happy about this marriage."

He looked at her oddly. "But Bradley assured me . . . well . . . that is to say, he implied you were content with the arrangement."

"But I am not. I do not love Bradley Houston. I have no intention of ever loving him. Please reconsider this marriage, Papa. I am most desperate to be freed from this responsibility."

Her father backed away as if she'd struck him. "I'm afraid I don't know what to say."

Jasmine nodded and tried her best to sound sympathetic. "I

know arrangements have been made and that people are counting on those arrangements. But, Papa, I long to marry for love—not because it suits the family business. Would you deny your only daughter this one request?"

"Have you discussed this with Bradley?"

Jasmine wondered how best to answer. "He knows of my feelings, if that's what you're asking. But, Papa, I'd rather all of this conversation stay between you and me. I would rather not worry Mama, and I certainly don't wish to anger my brothers or bring any further shame down on the family. I wanted to write you and discuss the matter sooner, but then before I realized what was happening, we were on our way back here. That's why I had to come to you alone—why I had to talk to you before Bradley or Grandmother or anyone else."

"Truly we cannot continue to discuss it now," her father said. "It's very poor manners that we should leave them alone. Where are they? Did you at least situate them with refreshments?" Her father began to pull on his jacket.

Jasmine looked down. "They are in Lorman."

Her father stopped even as he was buttoning up the coat. "What did you say?"

"I said they remained behind in Lorman. I rode out alone. No one knows I'm gone." Jasmine watched her father's face contort. "Before you get angry, please hear me, Papa." She went to him, tugging on his arm like a little child. "I had to talk to you about this marriage without Bradley hanging on my every word. I cannot marry him. He's abominable to me."

Her father stared in disbelief. "You risked your life—your reputation—to ride all the way from Lorman unescorted, for this?"

"I thought if we had some time to talk, for me to explain how I feel . . ."

He jerked away from her and began to pace. "Jasmine, this has nothing to do with feelings. This is a business arrangement that will benefit generations of Wainwrights to come. It will see our family secure, as well as the families of your uncles and cousins. How dare you come here as a spoiled and frightened child and declare that the entire arrangement be dissolved in order to suit your feelings?"

Jasmine felt as though she'd been slapped. Her father had always been gentle and protective of her. This was the first time she'd ever faced his wrath.

"I only pray that Mr. Houston doesn't change his mind. If that were to happen, this family would face extreme consequences."

Jasmine shook her head, forcing back the tears that threatened to spill. "But, Papa—"

He held up his hand. "No. No more. I won't hear another word." He came to stand directly in front of her. "You are too young to understand the importance of this matter, and because of that, I can and will overlook your foolhardy behavior of this evening. I am uncertain as to how we will explain the matter to Mr. Houston or whether he'll be as sympathetic, but you will not speak of this again."

Jasmine felt the truth tighten around her neck like a noose. "So it doesn't matter to you that I not only do not love Mr. Houston, but I cannot bear to be in his presence?"

"Time will change that," her father assured. "Few women can honestly say they marry for such luxuries as love and attraction. This is a good match. It benefits the greater good of our family."

Jasmine saw the determination in her father's eyes and in that moment felt herself age a decade. "So my heart is to be sacrificed for the greater good, is that it?" How foolish she had been to imagine that her desires were important to anyone other than herself. Somehow she had been confident that she could come home, speak to her father in private, and persuade him to put an end to her engagement. She realized her foolishness.

"You may not understand my decision at this moment, but in time you will."

Jasmine shook her head. "I understand that I am nothing more to you than a possession to be bartered. I might as well be one of your slaves, up on the block, sold to the highest bidder."

Jasmine hadn't expected the hard slap across her face. From the look of her father's expression, the move took him by surprise as

TRACIE PETERSON / JUDITH MILLER

well. It was the first time he had ever struck her. Jasmine touched her gloved hand to her cheek, staring in disbelief at the man she thought she knew so well.

Embarrassed, her father went back to his desk. Toying with some papers there, he said, "We will speak of this no more. Your wedding will take place as planned. One day you will understand, but until that time, I demand that you keep your childish notions to yourself. I cannot have you ruining this arrangement for nothing more serious than little-girl fears. This is an excellent arrangement. You will never want for anything, and despite your feelings, Bradley assures me that he has come to love you quite ardently. Your love for him will come in time. You'll see."

Jasmine stared at her father for several minutes, then backed away as if it were impossible to grasp the meaning of his words. For the first time in her life, she felt very much alone.

———

Jasmine sat alone in the music room when Bradley approached her. "I believe we should talk," he said rather dryly. He closed the door behind him and, to Jasmine's surprise, slid the lock into place. "I'd rather we not be disturbed."

Jasmine trembled at Bradley's tone. No doubt he meant to berate her for her actions. "I presume you wish to discuss last night."

"Among other things," he said, pushing out his coat tails before taking a seat. "Your actions were imprudent—dangerous."

"I thought you would see it that way," Jasmine replied, trying hard to show no fear. "I do not regret my choice, however. I was very homesick."

Bradley nodded. "I'm sure you were. But you could have met with grave harm. It was inconsiderate of you to risk your life in such a manner."

"I didn't know you cared," she said sarcastically. "Unless, of course, you're speaking merely out of concern for your business arrangement."

"You do me injustice," Bradley said softly.

136

Jasmine hated his calm, determined manner more than the times when he was forceful and mean-tempered. "You are the one forcing me to marry you. I'd say that's a bigger injustice."

"You feel that way now because you're young. In a few years, you'll see this as a completely different matter. You'll have children and a new home . . . you will be happy."

"Or else?"

Bradley's expression altered and a hint of anger tinged his voice. "Why do you insist on making this difficult?"

Jasmine got to her feet and began to pace. Her burgundy gown swirled around her heels as she turned abruptly. "If you were the one being forced against your will to marry someone you don't love, perhaps then you would understand my difficulty."

"I am sorry that you cannot conjure up some kind of affection for me. I have tried to win your heart. I've tried to show you that I am worthy of your love—that I will make a good provider and protector. Still you refuse to yield any ground to me whatsoever."

Jasmine looked at him hard. "You speak as though it's some kind of war—a battle for territory. I speak of the heart and a desire to be in love with the man whom I marry. Why is that to be considered such a terrible fault on my part?"

Bradley got up and came to her. To Jasmine's surprise he didn't sound in the leastwise angry. "It's not a fault, my dear. It's simply unrealistic. Do you honestly mean to tell me that your friends have married purely for love—that their feelings were considered first and foremost?"

Jasmine thought of her three closest friends. One had been matched to a man nearly twenty years her senior because his land holdings adjoined her family's property. Another friend had been pledged to her cousin since birth, while the third was also a victim of an arranged marriage to a local politician.

"I can see you realize the truth of my words." He reached out and took hold of her. "I'm not asking you to lie and say you love me. I know that you do not. I am, however, demanding the respect I am due. If you want to be happy in this union, you will respect me and honor my wishes."

Jasmine knew there was little to be gained by agitating Bradley. She would marry him no matter her desires. "Very well. I will do as I am bid."

Bradley seemed surprised by her response. He stared at her for several moments before saying, "But?"

Jasmine shook her head. "But nothing. I have no say in this. My father has arranged for the marriage. My husband doesn't care that I feel nothing for him. My life has been decided for me and I am resigned to acquiesce." The girlish dreams of her childhood faded into oblivion with the realization that nothing she longed for would ever be realized.

Bradley stepped back, dropping his hold. Jasmine thought he almost looked shocked—perhaps stunned by her declaration. But why? Why should he find this surprising? Then again, maybe it bothered him to realize that she was resigned to their union—not happy but no longer angry, merely reconciled. What a horrible revelation. Especially for one with Bradley's passion for life.

Composing himself once again, Bradley asked, "And you will no longer put your life at risk for foolish notions?"

"It wouldn't really serve any purpose, would it?" Jasmine said softly.

———

A tear trickled down Jasmine's cheek as Mammy arranged the Honiton lace wedding veil onto her soft, honey-brown curls before carefully fastening it into place. She circled Jasmine, straightening the lace to accentuate the turkey-tail edging and delicate florets. "You jes' as well quit that boo-hooin'. You know them tears ain't gonna change nothing 'cept to make your face all splotchy."

Jasmine took the handkerchief Mammy offered and blotted her cheeks. "None of this is fair." She was trying so hard to remain calm and resigned to her lot, but as the moment of her nuptials came closer, Jasmine found it more difficult. It was as if her heart were rising up in one last charge of emotion—one last moment of hope before her feelings were forever buried deep within.

"Lots of things in life ain't fair—don't mean they gonna change. 'Sides, you gonna have Miss Alice livin' nearby, and that's a blessin'. She'll make sure you okay."

"Having Grandmother close at hand didn't stop this wedding," Jasmine curtly replied before patting Mammy's hand. "I'm still hoping to take you with me, Mammy. Father hasn't given me his final answer."

"I don' know iffen I'd be likin' it up north. People says it's mighty cold up der. 'Course, it might not be so bad, but I'd still miss da other slaves. Best you don' be pushin' at your pappy to send me along, or Mr. Bradley be gettin' mad."

"If Bradley said he had no objection to your coming, you wouldn't be unhappy or complain, would you?"

"Complainin' don' do no more good than dem tears you was crying a few minutes ago. Jes' a waste of time and words. Now stand up and let me see you afore I go and tend to your mama." The old slave pressed a palm to her forehead and wiped away the beads of perspiration. "I'll likely never get your mama dressed. Last night she tol' me she was takin' to her bed and never gettin' back out." Mammy moved her finger in a circular motion, and Jasmine slowly turned around for inspection. "You look mighty fine. Now sit down while I go and check on your mama and Miss Alice."

The bedroom door opened and Alice Wainwright stepped inside. Her attire was impeccable. A sapphire blue ruching bordered her silk gown and perfectly matched the beaded reticule she carried. "You take care of Madelaine. I'm ready," she announced. Her face was painstakingly powdered and rouged. A strand of iridescent pearls dangled from one finger. "For you, my dear. A wedding gift. Actually, I have another gift awaiting you in Lowell, but the pearls must suffice for now."

"They are beautiful, Grandmother. Thank you so much."

Alice ran her fingers over the lace veil. "Not so beautiful as this wedding veil. When Bradley told me his mother's veil could not be equaled, I questioned his words. But I've never seen such beautiful lace—or such a beautiful bride."

"I wanted to wear *my* mother's veil. I didn't force him to wear clothing that belonged to a member of my family, so why should I be forced to wear *his* mother's veil?"

"Bradley's mother is dead. This is one way he can include her in his marriage. If the veil were unsightly, I would understand your feelings. However, it is stunning. You should be honored and delighted to wear it, Jasmine."

Jasmine sat quietly while her grandmother reached under the veil and arranged the pearls around her neck.

"You don't appear pleased. Perhaps I should have purchased an emerald. Would you have preferred an emerald? Or perhaps a diamond?"

"No, Grandmother, the pearls are perfect. Your gift is too generous, especially under these circumstances."

"What do you mean, *these* circumstances?"

"You know this wedding is a farce. I don't love Bradley Houston, and even though he seems to have convinced you and Father he cares for me, I believe he loves only his money. A man doesn't barter for a wife and then avow he loves her."

"Now, now, my dear. I've told you, it's best you begin to think of your marriage in positive terms. When you wanted a chance to speak to your father on the matter, I completely understood. However, you gave it your very best and the time for questioning the event is past. In time, I'm certain you'll learn to care for Bradley. Perhaps you'll never love him, but these arranged marriages are not so bad as they sometimes seem at first."

"Easy enough for you to say. You're not the one being bartered off to seal a business relationship. And that's all I am, you know: a commodity they're using for their own purpose. Why is it my brothers are permitted to choose any young woman they desire, while I am forced into a loveless marriage?"

"You know your statements aren't completely true, my dear. Your brothers will also be expected to make marriages that benefit the family. And even though you don't want to believe it, I think Bradley is quite smitten with you. He keeps you in his sights like a man who is totally besotted."

"Or a man intent upon keeping his prey within striking distance. I want a marriage like you had, one that is based upon love instead of financial gain."

Alice's lips curved into a wry grin. "As I told you before, Jasmine, my marriage to your grandfather was arranged. Some would say it was almost barbaric. We met only once before our marriage, and our parents monitored the entire conversation during that meeting."

"But you appeared to be blissfully happy. Was it all a charade?"

"Of course not! I *was* happy—though not at first, I admit. In those first months, I was too frightened to be anything but gloomy and depressed. However, as time passed, your grandfather and I fell deeply in love. We became devoted to each other. Ironically, years later, your grandfather confided that he, too, had been terrified when we married. So you see, you may be misjudging Bradley."

"Bradley isn't afraid of anything. He's a consummate businessman who is used to having his own way."

"He may excel in business, my dear, but affairs of the heart tend to intimidate even the most stalwart of men."

Jasmine wanted to hear no defense of Bradley Houston. "Still, my marriage is different. Bradley schemed with Father to arrange our marriage, while Grandfather was innocent of such behavior. I'd truly like to believe you're correct, but I've found nothing to like in either Bradley's beliefs or his behavior. I know you consider Father a good judge of character, but he's missed the mark this time. Unfortunately, I'll be the one to pay for his mistake."

Alice cupped Jasmine's quivering chin in her hand. "Have faith, Jasmine. Faith that even if your father has made a mistake, your heavenly Father will sustain you. Your mother is distraught over this entire turn of events and blames me. And I suppose she's right. If you hadn't come north to visit me . . ."

Her grandmother's voice trailed off into a deafening silence. Jasmine reached up and took her grandmother's hand tenderly in her own. "Don't blame yourself, Grandmother. I don't regret coming to visit you. We had a wonderful time together. My father could have denied Bradley's request. If Mother wishes to place blame, she has only to look at her husband—he's the one holding the ultimate power."

"I do regret the role I've played in creating your unhappiness, but now there's nothing we can do to change things except maintain our faith. We best go and see how your mother is faring. It will soon be time for the nuptials to begin."

The two women walked hand in hand down the hallway. Jasmine could hear her mother's soulful weeping mingled with Mammy's soothing voice as they neared the bedroom door. She glanced at her grandmother.

Alice gave her a reassuring smile. "Your mother will be fine. She doesn't think so right now, but she will. If only she would release herself from her self-imposed confinement here at the plantation, her life would be more enjoyable."

"I think it's too late for her to change her ways, Grandmother. She's become so emotionally frail, I fear that one day she won't rebound from her depression. Her condition seems to worsen as she grows older."

"I'll speak to your father. Perhaps if he encouraged her to invite some of the ladies for tea or to attend a few social functions, it would help. And with both of us living in Lowell, we'll work toward having her come and visit us."

Jasmine brightened. "Yes, that's a wonderful idea. If need be, I'll come back and escort her. We just will not permit her to refuse our invitation."

Alice pulled Jasmine into an embrace. "Exactly! Now chin up and take courage in the Lord. You are not facing this alone. Remember what the first chapter of Joshua says: 'Have I not commanded thee? Be strong and of a good courage; be not afraid, neither be thou dismayed: for the Lord thy God is with thee whithersoever thou goest.'"

The words touched Jasmine deeply. *I am not alone . . . God is with me.* "I'm not alone," she whispered.

———

Bradley Houston straightened his cravat, tucked his watch into the pocket of his vest, and walked to the gallery. He surveyed the willow-lined road that led in and out of the Wainwright plantation, certain fate had delivered him to this point in his life. He was destined for greatness—he knew it. Indeed, these past months had been heady. His new position with the Boston Associates, coupled with his engagement to a beautiful Southern belle, had placed him in an enviable situation. His ability to align himself as the only buyer of Wainwright cotton was hailed as a major coup by the Boston Associates. They'd promised a bonus with each delivery of raw cotton that exceeded projections, which was something he was anxious to discuss with his future father-in-law.

"Ah, Bradley, there you are."

He turned to see Malcolm Wainwright walking toward him and reached forward to grasp his future father-in-law's hand in a hearty handshake. "Not much longer until I'm a married man," Bradley said victoriously.

Malcolm patted him on the shoulder and gave a deep chuckle. "I trust you're not reconsidering your decision."

"That thought hasn't once crossed my mind, Mr. Wainwright."

"I believe it's time you called me Malcolm," the older man declared.

Bradley smiled. "If that's your wish, Malcolm. I was anxious to meet with you before we leave for the church."

"Sounds serious."

"I met with Matthew Cheever and Nathan Appleton the day before departing Lowell. As you know, they are pleased with your agreement to supply the mills with your cotton crop. They wanted me to inform you that they were delighted when you convinced your brother Franklin to market his cotton with us as well. Should you convince your other brother, Harry, to join us, they will reward you. In fact, they said that any shipments above what was previously agreed upon will entitle you to a substantial bonus."

"That's quite generous, isn't it?"

"Indeed. I thought you would be in high spirits. Their offer gives you ample reason to move your production to maximum levels."

"We're already at maximum production."

"You can't tell me that a heavy hand on the whip won't cause those slaves to increase your production."

"I've found the whip to be a hindrance—except for runaways. It creates resentment."

"Perhaps you might find some innovative measures that could be taken. Isn't Samuel in charge of production? Surely he could think of some method to increase production."

Wainwright's lips tightened and his brows furrowed into wiry lines of disapproval. "Samuel does a fine job on production."

Bradley knew he'd overstepped his bounds by inadvertently insulting Malcolm's eldest son. He pulled out his watch and clicked open the silver casing. "I suppose we should be leaving soon. I'm certain Jasmine won't forgive me if we're late."

Malcolm's eyebrows arched. "Then she's finally content with the marital arrangement?"

The question startled Bradley. "Has she expressed dissatisfaction regarding the marriage since our arrival in Mississippi?"

"Yes, of course. I've listened to a myriad of complaints, but women have no idea what they want or need when they're young, especially those like Jasmine, who have led protected and sheltered lives," Wainwright replied. He gave his future son-in-law a shrewd wink. "I'm certain she'll come around."

Bradley's face flushed with the humiliation of knowing Jasmine had continued to express dissatisfaction over their marriage to her father. Although Bradley had exerted time and energy on their relationship, it was apparent Jasmine had not intended to yield, even with their wedding close at hand. It seemed as if his kindness and indulgence would pass without reward. If she continued down this path, his attempts to win her over would cease. When Jasmine had cajoled and wept, he had begrudgingly conceded to a church wedding, although he would have much preferred the ceremony be held at The Willows. But he would no longer tolerate her childish behavior. He had neither the time nor the need to cater to her whims once she was his wife.

"Here's our carriage now."

Bradley hoisted himself up alongside Malcolm and glanced back toward the doorway. "Your sons aren't riding with us to the church?"

"No, I sent them on ahead to escort the women." He directed the servant to move on and turned his attention back to Bradley.

"That bonus you mentioned earlier. Was there an exact figure agreed upon?"

Bradley hesitated a moment. "Five percent above the regular price. How does that sound?" He watched Malcolm's reaction closely.

"Considering the fact that they've already agreed to pay me more than I can receive in the English markets, the additional five percent seems fair. Of course, I don't foresee much excess, at least not this year."

Bradley didn't exhibit his jubilation. Wainwright had imparted a subtle message in his reply: it was obvious his future father-in-law would take advantage of the bonus next year. This tidbit helped remove the sting of embarrassment from his future wife's complaints regarding their marriage. He would train her in short order that there would be repercussions for such inappropriate behavior.

CHAPTER · *13*

March 1847

JASMINE SAT opposite Bradley at the breakfast table, her gaze fixed upon the pristine white china plate. She traced her finger around the gold edging while contemplating the most effective way to approach her husband. She peeked at him from under hooded eyelids to see if he was looking in her direction. But Bradley's attention was focused upon serving himself hearty portions of scrambled eggs, sausage, biscuits, and gravy.

She continued to secretly watch him, her emotions muddled with uncertainty. Bradley's behavior remained perplexing. One day he was kind and generous, while the next he was angry and overbearing. Throughout the past three months she had attempted to be a good wife, hoping her grandmother was correct—that in time she would learn to love Bradley. But thus far she had not developed any feelings of love. Sometimes she intensely disliked him; sometimes she merely tolerated him; yet, on some occasions, when he was kind, she took pleasure in his company. However, she was never certain of his mood, and this morning was no exception.

While spreading one last spoonful of jam onto his biscuit, Bradley glanced in her direction. "I'm certain you'll be pleased to know I have business in Boston. I'll be leaving tomorrow and will be gone for several days. Please have one of the servants see to my baggage."

"Of course. Business for the mills or with your shipping business?"

He dipped his fork into the sausage and gravy before looking up from his plate. "How unusual. You sound genuinely interested." Sarcasm dripped from his voice like the gravy dribbling off his fork.

"I do take interest in your work, Bradley. I've tried my very best to assist in every way possible. In fact, I'm hosting a group of your Associates' wives this afternoon, just as I have on several previous occasions. I'm doing my best to become acquainted and entertain on your behalf. However, it seems as if you inevitably find fault with all my efforts."

"Your tea parties seem to garner me little aid. I asked you to entertain these women and learn about the mills. Thus far they've shared nothing but recipes and needlepoint designs. Tell them you have an interest in hearing what goes on in the mills so that you may intelligently converse with your husband about his work."

"When I broached the subject of the mills at our previous socials, the ladies quickly turned the conversation to other topics. Since I want to represent myself as a suitable hostess, I granted them the courtesy of discussing issues they found of interest. However, I will do as you suggest. I'm sure it will prove successful, and when you return this evening, I'll have much to tell you."

He stared across the table as though memorizing her features. "We'll see."

She twirled a ringlet of hair around her index finger and smiled. "If I am successful, will it please you very much?"

"Yes, it will please me."

"Enough that I might ask a special favor?"

He motioned to the servant and pointed to his coffee cup. "You are always free to ask, my dear."

"But will you grant my request?"

"We'll wait and see how successful you are—and just what it is you want."

She pushed her food around her plate for several moments. "Would you like me to tell you now?"

He pushed away from the table, wiped his mouth, and placed the linen napkin on his plate. "No. It can wait until I return this evening."

He moved to where she sat, pecked her on the cheek, and left the house. She sighed. Her hopes now rested on the success of the women who would visit this afternoon, and success she would have. If necessary, she would break the rules of etiquette.

"Mammy," she called out while scurrying up the stairs. "Please pack Master Bradley's bags—he'll be gone for several days." She thought for a moment and added, "Better pack for a week. He'll be leaving for Boston in the morning. Take special care that everything is in order. I want to keep him very happy."

The old slave's ample body filled the bedroom doorway. "Keepin' dat man happy is harder than tryin' to shoot a rabbit dat keep poppin' in and out of its hole."

Jasmine giggled at the remark. "Well, difficult or not, we must try. I'm hoping he will agree to a visit from Mother. I plan to ask him tonight."

A broad toothy grin lit up Mammy's face. "Miss Madelaine gonna come see us? Oh, dat be very nice. I be sure to pack extra careful so Massa Bradley say he gonna let her come. You think your mama gonna be willin' to make dat boat ride?"

"No. I would have to go and get her. I thought Grandmother and I could travel to The Willows, remain a few weeks, and then return with Mother. If Bradley doesn't want her to stay with us, she can stay with Grandmother for a portion of her visit. I'm hoping Father will come and visit and then accompany her home."

Mammy placed her hands on her broad hips, her elbows sticking out like plump chicken wings. "Um, um. Don' know if Massa Bradley gonna agree to all dat."

"I'm hoping that he'll be in an extraordinarily good mood this evening. The ladies are coming for tea, and if I do as he's told me, I'm certain things will go according to plan."

"Ain' nothing gone accordin' to no plan since you been in dis house," Mammy muttered.

Jasmine ignored the comment. "I'm going downstairs to make certain things are on schedule in the kitchen. I want everything to be perfect this afternoon."

The cook and her helper were hard at work; Sarah, the maid, was ensuring the house was in proper order; and Mammy was busy packing Bradley's bag. Jasmine took her Bible into the small sitting room and spent the remainder of her morning reading. Grandmother always took such comfort from her quiet time with God that Jasmine had tried hard to emulate the practice. She had to admit there was a certain amount of comfort, although some of what she read confused her.

After lunch, Jasmine carefully dressed for the gathering, all the while contemplating the proper way to maneuver the afternoon of tea and conversation.

"You gots to sit still iffen I'm gonna finish your hair," Mammy said as she struggled to twist a handful of golden hair into a stylish coiffure.

"I just want everything to be perfect," Jasmine protested. She wiggled on the chair, trying to reach the pearls her grandmother had given her. "If things go well this afternoon, we shouldn't have any trouble convincing Bradley."

Mammy *harrumph*ed, obviously unconvinced. She pinned the last of Jasmine's hair in place, then took up the pearls to secure them around her young mistress's neck. No sooner were the pearls secured than Jasmine jumped to her feet to survey her image in the mirror.

She loved the powder blue color of the gown and turned quickly to watch the skirt fall into place. "Do you think this gown smart enough?" she asked Mammy.

"I think it be fine."

Jasmine nodded. "It needs to be perfect."

One by one, the ladies arrived, all impeccably attired and obviously looking forward to an afternoon away from home. A buzz of conversation filled the room until Lilly Cheever raised her voice just a bit and gained their attention. "Ladies, I don't know if you've been advised, but Tracy Jackson's health continues to decline. Matthew has been most concerned about his health. I told Matthew I would be certain to inform you and ask that you pray for Tracy and his wife. This is a very trying time for them, and I know they would be most appreciative. And you all know how Tracy is: he wants to be in the midst of all that's happening with the Associates, which makes it doubly hard for him to follow the doctor's orders and remain abed."

Nettie Harper nodded in agreement. "Especially with all the problems in the mills right now. Wilson has been most difficult to live with over the past few months. It seems as if there is one problem after another to deal with."

"What kinds of problems?" Jasmine asked. All of them looked at her as though she had lost her senses. "My husband is gone much of the time, what with purchasing cotton and overseeing shipments and deliveries. He doesn't have opportunity to keep abreast of the inner workings of the mills."

"Well, of course, my dear. I tend to forget there's more to the operation than the mills and canals," Nettie said. "After all, we can't operate without cotton, can we?"

Rose Montrose patted Jasmine's hand. "Absolutely. Your husband's position is extremely important. Because of his hard work, I'm sure our husbands are relieved of many headaches. In fact, Leonard has told me your husband is a very shrewd businessman."

"Indeed," Wilma Morgan agreed. "James mentioned just the other day that your husband had been very successful in contracting with several plantation owners since he became chief buyer. I know from what he's told me that those additional suppliers have eased many concerns."

"Coming from the South, I know little of the mills and would be most interested in learning more. As you know, Bradley and I have been married only a few months. I long to talk with him about matters that are of interest to him."

"Well, of course you do," Rose Montrose put in. "I think that's an admirable attribute. Currently Leonard expresses dismay over the workers. Since they've begun using more Irish women in the mills, he says there appears to be more discontent."

"Really? Does your husband believe the problems are because the Yankee and Irish girls dislike working together?" Lilly Cheever asked.

"Well, the Irish girls obviously don't believe the Yankee girls should be paid higher wages for the same work," Rose replied. "And, of course, there are the ongoing complaints about the speedup and premium methods, but if the companies are to retain a profit margin, they must be innovative."

"What is that? A premium and a speedup?" Jasmine inquired.

"It's merely a method of keeping the mills operating at top production in order to make the best profits," Rose said.

"Not quite," Lilly Cheever corrected. "The speedup method is exactly what it implies. The machines are set to operate at a faster production level, which means the workers are forced to work at a higher rate of speed all day. However, the machinery is dangerous, and speeding up the machines heightens the likelihood of accidents. There are already many accidents in the mills, and I'm certain the additional speed worries all of the girls. The premium method means the girls are paid according to how much they produce rather than the hourly wage that they've always been promised."

"I forgot you were once a mill girl, Lilly. Your sympathy for the workers certainly seems to outweigh your loyalty to the Associates," Wilma Morgan observed.

"This isn't a matter of loyalty, Wilma. It is a matter of right and wrong. I believe the Associates made certain promises to the workers, and if they are going to change those promises, they need to go about it in a proper manner rather than merely forcing their new methodology on the workers without any concern for their welfare.

"I know what it's like to work in those mills. Speeding up the machinery is not safe, and I don't agree with the premium method. The workers have always been hired for hourly wages, and those have decreased rather than increased. It's little wonder there's strife among the workers. And the attitude that wages should be adjusted because of where you were born doesn't sit well with me. Who has control over her place of birth? Only God, I believe. Does an Irish girl not work as hard as a Yankee girl?"

"The Yankee girls have been in the mills longer and have more experience," Rose defended.

"Some, but not all. I don't disagree with paying higher wages to the more experienced girls, but I do disagree with paying different wages to employees with equal experience," Nettie remarked. "My husband says the girls complain more about having the windows nailed down than about the nationality of the girl standing at the next loom." She looked at Jasmine and said, "They nail down the windows to keep the rooms humid. That way, the threads don't break as easily. The girls, of course, would prefer to have the windows open. In fact, they say the steam and lint fibers are making them ill."

"You mark my words: unless these issues are addressed, the girls will begin talking of another strike," Lilly advised. "And I don't think our husbands want to see that occur."

"Nor do I. There would truly be no living with my husband if a strike became imminent," Nettie Harper put in.

Wilma Morgan turned her attention back to Jasmine. "And what do you and yours think of the growing antislavery movement?"

The women stared in her direction, obviously awaiting a response. The room was silent—like a cold winter night after a fresh snow. "I attended an antislavery meeting at the Pawtucket church before my marriage to Bradley. Two former slaves spoke at that meeting. I was as shocked at their revelations as anyone else in attendance. But you must remember that not all slave owners are cruel and treacherous. My father is certainly not that kind of man."

"Surely you realize that we who live in the North abhor the very idea of slavery," Wilma submitted.

"Yes, I've been told. But those of you who live in the North need the cotton the South supplies. Who will raise your cotton if there are no slaves?"

"You could free them and pay a fair wage for their labor," Rose argued.

"And if the price of cotton rises and you must finally pay the mill workers higher wages in order to keep them from striking, your profits decrease. Will you remain staunchly against slavery when that occurs?"

"Of course we will," Rose insisted. "It's only because you've been indoctrinated with these beliefs that you can rationalize these matters in your own mind. One human owning another is wrong."

"Perhaps you are correct, Mrs. Montrose. I'm no more an authority on slavery than on the issues between the Irish and Yankees. There appears to be injustice at every turn, doesn't there?" Jasmine replied. "May I pour you some more tea?"

Rose covered the cup with her hand. "No, not right now."

Lilly Cheever picked up her teacup. "I would like some more tea, please. You know, given our differing opinions, I think we should each pray and see how God directs us. I'm sure there are more than enough injustices in this world that need correction, and there are too few willing to be used in God's service. If we each seek where we can best serve, I believe we'll find our perfect place to do God's will without causing divisiveness among our little group. We want to remain friends and still serve our fellow man. If there is conflict among us, we'll be of no use to God or others."

"You're right," Rose agreed. "I apologize, Jasmine. I spoke out of turn. And while we're praying, let's pray that there's not another strike and the conflicts in the mills are settled in an amicable manner."

"I do wish the girls hadn't formed that labor group. I think it has only made matters worse," Wilma said.

"If someone would have taken their complaints seriously when they were seeking a ten-hour workday, I doubt whether they would have thought a union necessary," Lilly observed. "Establishing the Labor Reform Association seemed the only answer at the time. That's why I believe all of these issues should be a matter of prayer."

The ladies nodded in agreement as Rose picked up her reticule and dug deep inside. "I almost forgot—I have a recipe I want to share with the rest of you."

A smile tugged at Jasmine's lips. If Rose discussed recipes and sewing designs for the remainder of the afternoon, Jasmine would be fine. Surely she had garnered enough information to satisfy Bradley. He should be in excellent humor after hearing the details of today's discussion.

Bradley gazed out the carriage window and spied Jasmine standing by the open front door. He had been gone a full week, and she was obviously anxious to see him. At least, he surmised, she was anxious to hear his decision. She had been completely deflated when he announced he would wait until his return from Boston to answer her request.

Granted, she had gathered a good deal of information regarding the mills and had done exactly as he'd instructed. However, he hadn't been prepared for her question. He had thought she wanted merely to purchase some fancy bauble or new dress fabric; he hadn't anticipated she would request permission for her mother to make a lengthy visit in their home. Having Madelaine Wainwright in the house would not be comfortable. He would need to be on guard with everything he said and did in his own house, which he found foreign and distasteful. Jasmine's suggestion that her mother spend a portion of her time with Grandmother Wainwright made the idea somewhat palatable but not enough so that he wanted to render an immediate decision.

After his meetings in Boston, he was glad he had waited. He silently congratulated himself on his choice as he walked up the front steps of the house and greeted his wife. "How pleasant to have you dutifully waiting to greet your husband."

She smiled and turned her cheek to receive his kiss. "Let me take your bag."

"No. I'll take it upstairs. Why don't you join me and we can talk."

Her excitement was evident as she hurried up the stairs while chattering about events that had transpired throughout the past week. She watched as he placed his baggage in his room, obviously fearful to ask if he'd arrived at a decision yet. They were playing a game of cat and mouse, and he enjoyed watching her attempt to bait him. However, if he was going to complete his accounting work before supper, he must cut short this diversion.

"I've decided your mother's visit is acceptable. However . . ."

Before he could say anything further, she flung herself into his arms. "Oh, thank you, Bradley. Thank you, thank you, thank you." She turned her face to kiss him.

He met her lips with a passionate kiss before taking her by the arms and holding her a short distance away from him. "You didn't permit me to complete my statement. Your mother may come to visit. You and your grandmother will go to fetch her, and she will spend half her time in our home and half her time in your grand-mother's home. Is that acceptable?"

"Oh yes! Completely acceptable." Her face was alight with pleasure.

"There is one other condition. One that will likely displease you."

Her smile began to fade. "And what is that?"

"You must take Mammy with you."

Her smile once again brightened. "Is that all? Why would I be unhappy to have Mammy join me?"

"You misunderstand what I'm telling you, Jasmine. Mammy will *not* return to Lowell with you. She must remain at The Willows."

The happiness evaporated from her face like a morning fog rising off the lake. "Why? What have I done that you're punishing me?"

"This has nothing to do with punishing you. I've been berated all week because we have a slave in our household. Slavery is a topic frowned upon by the Associates—at least as it pertains to the *Northern* states."

"What does *that* mean? The prestigious Boston Associates find slavery acceptable so long as it remains in the South?"

"Exactly. It's the general consensus that slavery may continue in states where it is already in effect; however, they do not believe it should spread to other states. Nor do they believe anyone living in the North should own slaves, especially one of their members."

"You don't own Mammy. She belongs to my father."

"It doesn't matter, Jasmine. Another person owns her. She's a slave. I'll find you another maid to take her place—someone to help with your hair and other personal needs."

He stepped toward her, but she quickly turned and pulled away from his embrace. "What the Boston Associates want is more important than your wife's comfort? You tell me you want a child. Well, I can't imagine having a baby without Mammy here in Lowell to help me."

He clenched his jaw and fought to keep his anger in check. "Is that a threat? Are you telling me you'll refuse me my marital rights over the loss of that old slave?"

She obviously knew she'd overstepped her bounds. He could see her resistance had now been replaced by fear.

"I'm saying I don't want her to leave me."

"There is no choice. She must go." He walked toward the bedroom door. "I must get to my bookwork or I'll not complete it before supper." He stopped and turned as he reached the doorway. "I saw Nolan while I was in Boston. He will escort you and your grandmother."

"Why? We don't need an escort to make our journey to Mississippi."

"Nolan was particularly fond of The Willows. He thought this trip an excellent opportunity for another visit. Besides, my dear, it will give me comfort knowing there is a man along to look after you should any difficult circumstances arise—and it assures me of your return to Lowell," he added. "You sail at week's end. I'll send word to your grandmother so that she may prepare for the voyage."

CHAPTER · *14*

The Willows, Lorman, Mississippi

"NOLAN, WAIT!" Her voice was a raspy whisper in the night air, and she prayed he would hear. He slowed but then picked up his pace. "Nolan!" He stopped. "Nolan! It's Jasmine. Wait for me."

The tall shadow of a figure remained still, waiting, poised—as if ready to take flight and hide under cover of darkness. She ran hard, with her chest heaving, lungs begging for air as she forced herself onward. A piece of dead wood rose up to greet her. Without warning, she sprawled pell-mell into Nolan's arms. They fell to the ground, his arms cradling her while she gasped for breath. Several minutes passed before her ragged breathing returned to a steady cadence.

"What are you doing out here?"

He was still holding her close; she could hear the beat of his heart, and the sound was reassuring, comforting. She remained very still, not wanting to move away from the warmth of his chest. "I heard you ask one of the kitchen servants if you could deliver food to the quarters for her tonight," she said. "I also heard her agree."

He shifted and pulled himself to his feet, then gazed down at her. "Your plan was to follow me to the slave quarters?"

"Yes," she said as she stood and brushed debris from her skirt.

"Why?"

"For many reasons. Some of them date back to conversations with you and with Mrs. Longfellow at Cambridge, as well as that first antislavery meeting I attended before my marriage to Bradley," she explained. "Since then, there have been discussions that made me realize I didn't truly know anything about the slaves here. I've never been to their quarters, never talked to any of them except the ones who work in the big house. In fact, I've seen the other slaves only from a distance. Father never permitted me to go near the field slaves or anyplace where they work. So I decided it was time I found out for myself what it is like to be a slave at The Willows."

"If Bradley or your father finds out, there will be a terrible row. I fear there's already too much dissension between you and Bradley. You need to work toward smoothing the troubles in your relationship. Going to the slave quarters will only make matters worse."

"Bradley will never find out unless you tell him when we return to Massachusetts. Father is going over his accounts and will soon go to bed, and I've sworn Mammy to secrecy. I've already kissed both my mother and grandmother good-night. By the time we return, everyone in the house will be asleep, save Mammy. She promised she would be waiting to let us in the door."

"You've thought of everything, haven't you?"

"I hope so," she whispered.

He didn't argue further. Instead, he grabbed her by the hand and pulled her along. With only the sliver of a moon and a smattering of stars to provide light, they neared the quarters. Nolan yanked her to a halt. "We'll need to circle around or we'll pass the overseer's house. He has dogs that will catch our scent. If that happens, we'll be spotted. There will be no escaping those hounds. Stay close and don't talk."

For the first time since deciding to follow Nolan to the quarters, a fleeting tremble shuddered through her body. As a child she'd watched from the gallery when the overseer brought the baying hounds to the big house for her papa's review. She'd seen those hounds straining at their leashes with foam dripping from their jowls and hunger in their eyes. They were a fearsome sight and one she didn't want to personally encounter.

She did as she was told, following Nolan in a wide circle and then inward, where her gaze settled upon four long rows of dilapidated wooden cabins that lined either side of two narrow dirt roads. "This is it? This is where the slaves live?" she whispered in hushed wonder. The sight held her spellbound. "But we have over a hundred slaves. Surely there are other quarters."

Nolan was already on his feet, carefully moving forward when he turned and waved her onward. "Come on," he hissed into the balmy darkness.

She crouched low and followed him in a zigzagging pattern toward one of the cabins. "How do you know where you're going?" she asked.

"I was in the quarters more than one time on my first visit to The Willows with Bradley. Once your father granted me permission to explore the property, I came out here at least once a day, at varying times. I also came back to visit with the slaves when I was here for your wedding in December."

"If the overseer knows you, then why are we hiding?"

He stopped and looked down at her, the whites of his eyes barely visible in the thin sickle of moonlight. "Because I'm smuggling in food from the main house. And even if I could slip these provisions past the overseer, it would be difficult to hide *you*. There's little doubt in my mind that Mr. Sloan's first priority would be your safe return home. I don't think you want him waking the household to announce he's rescued you from the slave quarters."

"No, of course not. I wasn't thinking clearly. Please lead the way."

They inched forward until they were in front of a sagging door hanging on worn leather hinges. The plank swayed on its hinges as Nolan tapped. "Carter! It's Nolan Houston from Massachusetts."

The door opened a crack, and Carter peeked out at them. His

eyes grew wide and shone like ebony marbles set in bolls of snowy cotton. "Yes, suh?"

"I brought you some food from Tempie. She's worried you and the children aren't getting enough to eat."

"We's doin' fine." His voice was unconvincing, his gaze veering off toward Jasmine as he spoke. "You tell Tempie we's doin' good and we hopin' to see her come Sunday. We don' need no extra food. Massa feed us jes' fine."

Jasmine was certain her presence was contributing to the slave's standoffish behavior. She touched his hand and he jumped back as though he'd been scalded. "I'm not going to tell anyone that Tempie sent food. Please take it. You can trust me."

Carter's gaze swerved toward Nolan and then he nodded toward Jasmine.

"She won't tell," Nolan said.

" 'Den I guess we'll be takin' dat food you brung." He reached out and took the cloth-wrapped bundle and was soon surrounded by a throng of smaller black faces and a rush of grabbing hands.

Only meager slices of moonlight sifted through the chinked log walls, but Jasmine's eyes had now adapted to the darkness, and she viewed the unsightly conditions within. There was a small fireplace at the end of the room, and a few cots had been fashioned from saplings. A shabby hand-hewn table sat near the fireplace along with two worn stools. And, although she couldn't be certain, she determined there were likely twelve or thirteen people living in this cramped cabin.

Her gaze settled on Carter and she pointed toward the end of the room. "You cook in that fireplace?"

His white teeth gleamed in the darkness. "No, ma'am. Dis ole slave don' know how ta cook," he said and then gave a hearty laugh. "I leaves da cookin' fer da womenfolk. But dey do mos' da cookin' outdoors 'cause dat chimney gets too hot. When dat happen, it catches on fire and we hafta push dat chimney away from da house. And dat ain' no good time."

Jasmine frowned, not understanding how a chimney would

catch on fire. "How do you keep warm in the winter if you can't use the fireplace?"

"Oh, we lights da wood in der, but sometimes we haftta get up in da middle o' da night and push da chimney away from da house. Dat chimney can catch fire purty easy 'cause it be made o' sticks and clay and moss—ain' like dem brick chimneys in da big house," he explained.

Even though the room was warm, Jasmine shivered. "So you must wear warmer clothes and pile under heavy blankets at night when the weather turns cold?"

Carter slowly wagged his head back and forth. "You don' understan' much 'bout life here in the quartah, ma'am, and best it stay dat way," he said before turning toward Nolan. "You need ta get her outta here afore the massa finds out. But I do thank ya fer bringin' da food."

"They don't receive ample food or clothing, do they? Does my father know this?"

Carter turned, his eyes alight with fear. "Don' say nothin' to your pappy, girl. Iffen you do dat, the overseer gonna think us'n been complainin' and he whup us fer sho'."

"Whip you? Surely not," Jasmine replied in disbelief.

It took only a fleeting glance around the room to observe young and old alike in tattered clothes and bare feet. The truth slowly sank in. She realized something substantial needed to be done. "I want to try and help if you're not getting enough food—or clothing."

"Can't nobody help us 'less you got some way o' convincin' your pappy to set us free."

Jasmine met Nolan's gaze. He didn't smirk. His eyes weren't filled with recrimination. He didn't say a word. His body appeared weighed down by the overwhelming helplessness that surrounded them.

"Surely there must be something we can do," she whispered to Nolan.

"If you want to help Carter and these others, do what he's asked. Say nothing. If you want to see an end to all of this suffering, work against slavery now that you're married and living away from this place. Time will tell if the sights you've seen tonight will fade from your memory or if they will burn more vividly each day and spur you onward to greater good."

CHAPTER · 15

ALICE DIPPED a linen cloth into a basin of cool water, wrung out the excess, and placed it across her granddaughter's forehead. "Jasmine, I am concerned. You are much too pale, and your inability to hold down any food over the past few days worries me. Never in your life have I seen you in this condition while at sea. I hope you haven't taken yellow fever."

Jasmine gave her grandmother a bleak smile. "I'm sure it's nothing so dramatic. I can't imagine why I'm ill. The waters have been calm throughout our voyage."

"At first I thought the illness was caused by something you'd eaten. But you've eaten the same meals as the rest of us. As far as I can determine, no one else appears to be suffering from this malady. Try a sip of water," Alice fussed. "You need to have some liquid in your body. I'll see if the ship's cook has some broth you might be able to tolerate."

The mention of broth caused Jasmine to think of food, but the thought of eating caused her to once again begin retching. When the unwelcome gagging finally ceased, she fell back upon the damp, flattened pillow, her forehead beaded with perspiration. Her stomach and ribs ached from previous days filled with sporadic heaving followed by constant painful headaches.

"I suppose this is a fitting conclusion to our trip. The entire journey has been nothing but one disaster after another."

"Now, now, no need to exaggerate, my dear. You'll only upset yourself and feel worse. Moreover, we had many relaxing days visiting with your dear mother."

"If you recall, Mother was supposed to return with us. That was the entire reason we made this voyage. As for visiting with her, I don't think she even knew we were there most of the time. I fear she's completely escaped into a world of her own making and hasn't any idea what's going on around her." Jasmine shifted and turned on her side, resting her head on one arm. "It breaks my heart to see her in this condition. I wish I were close at hand to help care for her, but I doubt there's any chance Bradley would consider moving south."

Her grandmother's waning smile confirmed what Jasmine already knew. Bradley would never consider leaving his position with the Boston Associates.

"If we look at the positive outcomes of our journey, I think you'd have to agree it was a good thing Mammy returned with us and is remaining at The Willows."

Jasmine gave a weak nod. "That's true. Leaving Mother didn't seem quite so terrible with Mammy there to care for her. But being without both of them is a greater personal loss to me. The house will seem quite empty with only the hired help. Mammy had become my confidante—I trusted her." She swallowed hard, not wanting to once again begin the violent retching. The wave of nausea momentarily passed and she squeezed Alice's vein-lined hand. "At least Bradley should be pleased."

"Whatever do you mean?"

Jasmine knew she shouldn't speak objectionably about her husband to her grandmother. And since her marriage to Bradley, she'd attempted to refrain from doing so. But she wondered if her reticence to criticize Bradley's behavior caused her grandmother to believe he had evolved into a genuine saint rather than remaining the difficult, demanding man Jasmine had married. "I had to bargain with Bradley in order to gain his permission for Mother's visit."

Alice grew wide-eyed at the remark. "In what way? Or dare I ask?"

"Mother's visit was contingent upon Mammy's permanent return to The Willows."

"I wondered why you weren't overly upset about Mammy leaving. But I thought perhaps she had asked to return because she missed the warmer climate."

"There's no doubt Mammy prefers the South, but she would have remained in Lowell had it not been for Bradley's edict that she leave. Apparently he received severe criticism from many of the Boston Associates because a slave was living in his household." She wrinkled her nose and pursed her lips together. "And, of course, we must manage our households as ordained by the Boston Associates."

"You shouldn't be surprised by their disdain. You know slavery is abhorred by most in the North, Jasmine."

"And I now see the merits of abolition also. However, the Northerners speak from both sides of their mouth. They speak against slavery except as it relates to making them wealthy; then they turn their heads the other way. It's pure hypocrisy. The slaves are necessary to produce cotton, and the cotton is necessary to operate their mills. I don't see any of them refusing to buy cotton from Southern plantations. In fact, that's precisely why Bradley was hired—to convince Southern growers to sell up north instead of shipping their crops to England."

"You have a valid argument, child. Of that, there is no doubt. This very issue has been argued at antislavery meetings. However, you must remember that Bradley's position hinges upon doing what his superiors request. And having Mammy with your mother is for the best." Alice gave her a bright smile and plumped Jasmine's flattened pillow. "I know you and Bradley are eventually going to look back upon these early days of your marriage with amusement. You'll wonder how you ever thought it impossible to love him," she said in an obvious attempt to buoy Jasmine's spirits.

Jasmine glanced up at her grandmother. "Bradley is *not* the man you think he's become, Grandmother, and I doubt I will ever grow to love him. I try to be a good wife and I will continue to do so. However, his distasteful actions make it difficult to like him, much less consider feelings of love."

"Don't let this particular matter divide you. There are many Northerners who decry slavery when what they actually believe is slavery should not spread into other states. I think this one issue may eventually split the antislavery movement—at least politically. I pray it doesn't fracture the movement so badly that we lose our impetus. I'm for complete abolition, but if we can't have abolition, I don't want to see any more proslavery states coming into the Union."

"My disagreement with Bradley wasn't over the slavery issue. Bradley insisted that I give Mammy up, and he also insisted that Mother spend half her visit with you. As for Mammy, I said we could request her papers from Father and free her. We could hire her as a servant like the other maids. But he denied my request."

"You've not been married long. He likely requested your mother spend time with me because he wants more time alone with you. And even if you freed Mammy, folks know she came to your household as a slave and would always think of her in that capacity. It has all worked out for the best, Jasmine. Your mother needs Mammy, and Mammy is much happier at The Willows. Think about how pleased she was to see the other slaves when we arrived at the house. Overall, I think we had a good visit."

Jasmine dipped her fingers in the cup of water and moistened her lips. "Have you ever been to the slave quarters, Grandmother?"

"Only once. I never went again." Alice peered at her for a long moment. "Have you, Jasmine?"

"Yes. I had to go and see for myself what it was like. You know that I have declared the Wainwright slaves are well treated. However, I decided if I was going to continue making such statements, I needed to assure I was speaking the truth."

"And what did you find?"

"I find I have spoken falsely. I saw and heard things that made me weep." She paused and looked toward the wall. "Does Papa advocate whipping the slaves?"

Her grandmother said nothing for a moment, so Jasmine looked back and saw her expression take on a look of discomfort. "He believes in discipline."

"And discipline is meted out at the end of a whip, correct?"

"I suppose you could say that. Although your father generally leaves such matters to the overseers."

"I suppose that assuages his conscience," Jasmine said, shaking her head. "And no doubt the overseers rid themselves of guilt by saying they are only following orders."

"You are probably right."

"But what good does it do me to be right, when such injustice is going on? I thought our slaves were happy and well kept. I thought things were different because we were good, honest people."

"But in learning otherwise, what can you do?" her grandmother asked softly.

"I learned slavery should be abolished. I can work toward that end."

Alice leaned forward and placed a soft kiss on her cheek. "Then this journey was not a disaster—this journey was designed by God."

"And this illness? Is it a part of the design also?"

"With God, who can tell? You try to rest. I'm going to finish one more row on my needlepoint, and then I'll see about that—"

Jasmine put a finger to her lips. "Don't mention food, Grandmother. My stomach has finally settled."

Alice smiled. "Try to sleep. We'll soon be home."

CHAPTER · 16

County Kerry, Ireland

KIARA O'NEILL grasped her legs tight and pulled them to her chest, her gaze fastened upon the young boy lying before her. She leaned forward, resting her dimpled chin upon bent knees while she listened to her brother's labored breathing. Padraig turned onto his side and curled his body into a half-moon. Instinctively, she reached out and brushed the shock of black curls away from his damp forehead. The fever must be breaking. She drew closer to his side. His thin body was drenched in perspiration. As if she held a fine wool coverlet, Kiara wrapped a filthy piece of blanket tightly around the boy and then mopped his face with the hem of her ragged skirt.

Through the open door of the hovel, a thin shaft of golden light could be seen on the horizon. "Ya ain't answered many o' me prayers, God, but I'm takin' this as a sign that ya'll be savin' Paddy from the grave. And I'll be tellin' ya I think it's the least ya could do under the circumstances."

"Who ya talkin' to, girl?"

Kiara startled and turned. Mrs. Brennan was peering in the door of the cottage with a misshapen basket hooked on one arm. "I'm talkin' to God. Nobody else around here to listen to me complaints."

Mrs. Brennan jumped away from the door as though struck by a bolt of lightning. "Ya best keep that sass to yarself. I doubt the Almighty needs ya tellin' Him what He should or shouldn't be doin'."

Kiara gave a snort and wheeled around to face the woman. "Outside o' killing Padraig, there's not much else He can do to hurt me."

"He could take *yar* life too if ya're not careful."

"And I'd be considerin' that a blessin', so I doubt He'll favor me with such a decision."

"Ya're not the only one sufferin', Kiara O'Neill. All of us have endured loss."

"Right you are—and the Almighty could'a saved the potato crop instead of sending this awful curse upon us. Does na seem it would be so difficult for Him to look upon us with a bit o' favor. We already got the hatred of the English to contend with . . . seems as though that ought to be enough for one group of people. Unless, o' course, He's planning to rid the world of us Irish. Then it would seem He's doing a mighty fine job."

"That smart mouth is gonna be your downfall, lass. If I told yar mother once, I told her a hundred times, ya—"

"Well, me ma and me pa are dead along with all me brothers and sisters, exceptin' for Padraig. So whatever ya told me ma is of little consequence now. All I'm carin' about right now is keepin' this lad alive, and if I'm to do that, I'm gonna need food for 'im."

"Well, ya'll not find anyone around here to help ya, and that's a fact. I been to every hovel this side of Dingle, and there's not a potato or a cup of buttermilk to be shared. We're all goin' to starve to death if we don't soon find some help. Ya may have pulled the lad back from the brink only to watch 'im die of hunger."

Her eyes burning with an undeniable fury, Kiara jumped up from Paddy's side, and in one giant stride she was in front of the woman. "Don't ya be placin' yar wicked curse upon me brother." Kiara's command hissed out from between her clenched teeth and caused Mrs. Brennan to back out of the doorway. The sun cast a bluish sheen on Kiara's greasy black mane as she leapt after the woman. "My brother'll not starve so long as I'm drawin' breath."

The woman held out her arm to stave off the attack and met Kiara's intent scowl with her own steely glare. "Stop it, lass. I'm not yar enemy, just a starvin' neighbor hopin' to live another day."

The words sliced through the hazy morning mist and pierced Kiara's heart. The hunger and worry must be driving her barmy. She'd heard of such happenings—men and women unable to deal with the ongoing starvation and suffering of their families going completely mad. Only last week, Mr. MacGowan tied his entire family to himself before jumping off a nearby cliff. All of them had been crushed on the rocks below. Death had finally released them from their agonizing hunger, and the seawater below had washed over their bodies, sanitizing them of the dirt and grime of Ireland.

Kiara stepped back and shook her head as if to release her mind from some powerful stranglehold. "I'll be askin' yar forgiveness, Mrs. Brennan. It's these last weeks of watching me da die and then me ma and now Paddy getting so sick. And then burying them."

"Now, now, child, don't go thinkin' on those last weeks. It ain't healthy."

"I go to sleep at night thinking about me ma and pa laying in that cold ground without so much as a warm blanket around them."

"At least ya protected the boy, and he did na realize the cruel grave they went to," Mrs. Brennan said.

Kiara glanced toward Padraig's emaciated form. "I'm prayin' no one tells him. If he knew the undertaker slid ma's and pa's bodies out o' those coffins into a dark dirt grave, well, he'd likely try to dig them up with 'is fingers."

Mrs. Brennan's head bobbed up and down in agreement. "'Twould be terrible for 'im to find out, but if he does, ya'll just have to explain it's the way of things. Ain't enough wood to build coffins for all them what's dying in these parts. How ya plannin' to make do, Kiara?"

"I'm thinkin' of goin' to Lord Palmerston and askin' him if there might be a bit o' work at his fancy estate. Maybe workin' in the house or even the gardens. And Paddy's good with horses."

Mrs. Brennan gave her a weary smile. "Ya do that, lass, and I'll be prayin' he'll give ya some work. Ya might show him a bit o' your lace. You got a real talent with the thread. He might be willin' to put ya to work makin' lace for his lady friends."

"I do na think he'd hire someone to sit and make lace. Besides, I pinned me last bit o' lace to Ma's dress afore they buried her. 'Twas the least I could do. She deserved so much more than a scrap of fancywork."

The older woman glanced in the door toward Padraig. "Appears the boy's beginnin' to stir."

Kiara turned toward her brother and then looked back at Mrs. Brennan. "Would ya consider lookin' in on him while I'm gone on the morrow?"

"That I will, and may God be with ya, Kiara O'Neill."

"And with yarself, Mrs. Brennan," Kiara whispered as she sat down beside her brother's straw pallet. "Are ya feelin' a mite better, Paddy?"

The boy gave a faint nod of his head. "How are we gonna make do, Kiara?" His voice was no more than a raspy whisper.

"Don't ya be worryin' yar head. I'm gonna take care of ya, Paddy, just you wait and see. I'll be gone for a bit tomorrow, but Mrs. Brennan will stop by to check on ya, and I'll make sure there's a tin o' water nearby. I wish I could promise ya a biscuit or cup o' buttermilk, but I can't."

"I'll be fine."

The day wore on in a slow, monotonous mixture of hunger and fear. As night approached, Padraig slipped into a fitful sleep with Kiara steadfastly holding his hand. Throughout the remainder of the night, the boy wavered between a deep sleep and restlessness that kept Kiara awake and vigilant. When Paddy was quiet, she worried he had quit breathing; when he was restless, she feared his fever was returning. When morning finally arrived, her eyes were heavy and she longed for sleep. But there would be no rest this day, of that she was certain.

"I'm goin' down to the creek and get ya some drinkin' water

and wash me face a bit. Once I bring ya yar drink, I'll be headin' off for a while. I'll be back before nightfall."

"Where are ya goin', Kiara?"

"Never ya mind, but I'm hopin' to be bringin' some good news when I return."

She trekked through the countryside, her body weakened by hunger and threatening to faint on the road. The sight of starving families along the way, their mouths green from the grass and weeds that were now their daily fare, confirmed her decision to seek help from Lord Palmerston. Although she'd never seen the man, she had once passed by his manor with her ma.

It was her ma who had observed Lord Palmerston many years ago when he was riding through the countryside with his companions and their ladies. Her ma had said he was a wee bit more handsome than most Englishmen, but her da had laughed at that remark, saying there wasn't an Englishman alive who could turn the head of an Irish lass. He said Irish women were accustomed to men who would protect them rather than hide in the shadows. Kiara wasn't sure what had caused her da to believe Englishmen such cowards. However, *spineless* was the kindest word she'd ever heard him use when he referred to the men from across the sea. Although her da may have thought Lord Palmerston lily-livered, Kiara was thankful their landlord hadn't begun evicting his tenants like so many of the other propertied Englishmen.

Her strength seemed to swell as the manor house came into sight. She quickened her steps to keep pace with her racing heartbeat and hurried onward, turning when she reached the road leading to the mansion and circling in front of the house. Carriages lined the circular drive, providing an assurance the wealthy visitors were not required to walk far before entering the grand front doors, Kiara decided. She spied a cobblestone path leading to the rear of the huge stone edifice and, keenly aware she would never be permitted entry through the front doors, continued around the manse. The sound of laughter and chattering voices carried toward her on a warm afternoon breeze.

She had barely turned the corner of the house when a man

grasped her arm, then quickly turned her loose. With an air of obvious irritation, he began to rapidly swipe his hand back and forth across his buff-colored breeches. "You are filthy! Where did you come from?"

Kiara jumped back, flattening herself against the outer wall of the cold stone manor house. Her eyes were wide with fear. "I came from across the hills—that way." She pointed to the east, but her focus remained upon the angry man who was questioning her. "I'm in search of Lord Palmerston. Is he close at hand?"

"He may be. Why would the likes of you be asking?"

The sound of merriment filtered across the green expanse, and she guardedly looked toward the guests gathered in the yard. The men were playing some form of game while the women appeared to be cheering them on and laughing.

"Well, girl? Why are you asking for Lord Palmerston?"

"I'm in need of aid. Me and me brother, we're starvin' to death." Her voice trembled in rhythm with her shaking hands.

The man looked at her as though she spoke some foreign tongue. "Benton! You've got a girl here who fancies your attention."

The group of visitors turned toward them and began strolling in their direction. In the front was a tall man in a stylish russet waistcoat and matching trousers, with a woman flanking him on either side like two lovely bookends.

When the tall man finally stood directly in front of Kiara, he extended his walking stick and poked it under her chin. He lifted the cane, forcing her head upward to meet his piercing stare. "Why have you come to my home?" His tone matched the disgust etched upon his face.

Instinctively, Kiara took one step backward, and his walking stick dropped away from her chin. "I'm one of yar tenants, and we're starvin' to death. Surely ya know the famine has claimed the lives of many. Are ya not concerned about the welfare of yar people?"

His appearance quickly changed from disgust to anger, his eyes burning like hot embers as he moved forward and closed the short distance between them. "Don't you speak to me in that tone. Who do you think you are to question my behavior? As for starving tenants, if you'd learn to cultivate your crops in a reasonable fashion instead of insisting upon that ridiculous lazy-bed method you've all adopted, there would be potatoes in your bellies. Head-strong, incompetent people inhabit this country. You refuse to change your ways, so of course you'll all starve to death."

"And ya'll be lendin' us no assistance?"

One of the beautiful bookends tugged at his sleeve. "I think you should find some way to help the girl," she cooed.

The other woman fluttered her lashes and grasped his arm more tightly. "Yes, Benton, let's help her. Devising a plan to help this girl will be much more entertaining than playing bocce. Don't you think so?" She turned toward the other guests and waved enthusiastically, apparently hoping to solicit support from the crowd. Their immediate shouts of agreement caused her lips to curve upward into a charming smile. "Help the girl!" she shouted.

"Help the girl! Help the girl! Help the girl!" The chant grew louder and louder until Lord Palmerston finally brandished his cane aloft.

"Enough! Why do you care what happens to this poor excuse for a human being?"

"We've never done such a thing before—it will be entertaining. Come along, girl. Stand over there, and we'll circle around and decide what's to become of you," Sir Lyndon Wilkie ordered. He prodded Kiara along with his cane until he had her positioned in the center of the grassy lawn, where they'd been playing their game.

Linen- and lace-covered tables lined the edge of the bocce field, and Kiara's attention was riveted upon the servants, who were now arranging food and drink for Lord Palmerston's guests. She watched as visitors ambled by the tables, viewing and discussing the culinary delights before carefully selecting each item. Plates full, they seated themselves on the blankets and small rugs that had been strategically placed on the lawn. She watched the guests feeding pieces of mutton and pork to the dogs wandering the grounds until she could no longer contain her anger.

Pointing to a woman holding a piece of meat over a sleek greyhound, she called out, "There are people dyin' of hunger while ya feed those dogs the finest cuts o' meat."

"Those starving people aren't here, but the dog is," the woman replied. "Perhaps you would like something to eat?" She walked toward Kiara, carrying a hunk of dark bread and a small slab of cheese. "Shall I give you this?"

Had it not been for Paddy, she would have refused the haughty woman. Instead, she grabbed the food, bit off a chunk of the bread, and tucked the remainder into her skirt.

"I've heard tell people can go mad when deprived of food. This girl has a wild look in her eyes."

Lord Palmerston stepped forward. "Sit down, Winifred. The girl is frightened, stupid, and starving, but she's not insane. You were one of those chanting to help her. Have you had a change of heart?"

"No, I suppose not." She turned on her heel and walked back to her blanket.

Lord Palmerston remained beside Kiara. "Now, what would you have me do with the girl? You were all anxious to have her act as your entertainment. What say you?"

"Let's give her a new life. Let's send her to England," one of the women called out.

Another man jumped up from his blanket. "England is already swarming with starving, typhus-infested Irish immigrants. She'd be no better off in Liverpool than she is here. Let's think of some other country we can send her to."

"Yes! In fact, what about sending her to the Colonies? Let her go across the sea and start a completely new life," Mathias Newhouse suggested.

"Don't you have distant relatives who absconded to America, Palmerston? You could send her as an indentured servant to your relatives."

"Hear! Hear! Send the girl to America!" several men shouted as they raised their glasses in a jubilant toast.

Lord Palmerston paced back and forth in front of Kiara several times and then nodded in agreement. "America it is. Now can we get back to our game of bocce?"

Kiara jumped in front of Lord Palmerston. "I can't go to America, sir. I have a young brother, and both me parents have died from the famine. I canna leave Padraig. I *won't* leave 'im."

"What's the problem, Palmerston?" Mathias Newhouse asked. A large number of the guests were striding toward them. "The girl wanting some additional money?"

"She has a brother and simply won't leave without him."

"Well, send him too—that's easy enough. It's not as though you can't afford passage for the two of them. It's the most expedient way of returning to your game of bocce, isn't it?"

Lord Palmerston grunted before looking down at Kiara. "I'll send the two of you, but you'll sign papers for five years of indentured service to my second cousin. Come back tomorrow with your brother, and I'll make the arrangements. You've ruined my afternoon of entertainment with your antics, so you'd best not fail to appear or I'll send my man looking for you, and he'll snip off your ears when he finds you. Do you understand, lass?"

Her lips twisted into a disgusted wrinkle. She'd bite off his fingers before he'd have a chance to snip at her ears! But she and Paddy would appear on the morrow, for if they remained in Ireland, they'd surely starve to death. She had no desire to leave her homeland or the graves of her parents—the very thought weighed heavy on her heart. Yet she knew there was nothing to do but agree. "Yes, sir. And if I might get a bit more food to take with for me neighbors, I'd be grateful."

"Take some food—take all of the food, just be on your way."

One of the women grasped Lord Palmerston's arm. "Now, wasn't that an enjoyable diversion? And look at the good your wealth has accomplished. You've saved two sad souls today. Surely that will buy you a place of honor with God." They all laughed at this.

Kiara took a cloth one of the servants gave her, along with instructions to return it the next day. She circled the table, placing food into the fabric while listening to the group of partygoers, who were congratulating one another on the good they'd done this day. Their words rang in her ears, a mockery of the devastation that abounded throughout the countryside. She longed to confront each one of them and say what selfish dolts she thought them, but she dared not. She took the bundle of food and hurried toward home, anxious to share a small portion of their abundance with Paddy and their neighbors. Anxious, too, to see what joy the small feast would bring this night and yet knowing for some, it would merely prolong life for a few more miserable days.

CHAPTER · 17

LORD PALMERSTON'S servants scrubbed and outfitted Kiara and Padraig for their journey, and when all was in readiness, they were summoned to the front hallway. Lord Palmerston stared down upon them as though they were outlandish creatures that should be banished as quickly as possible.

"This is a letter of reference for my cousin, along with the money for your passage to America and enough for transportation from Boston to Lowell, where my relatives reside. You and your brother will be indentured to my cousin for five years in order to settle up your debt to me. Don't consider any attempt to besmirch these arrangements, or I shall arrange for your brother's demise and force you to watch while he dies a slow and painful death. And don't think I won't find you, girl. I have eyes and ears everywhere, including on the docks and aboard the ship you'll sail on. See that you don't repay my generosity with deceit. My driver will take you to the docks and remain until you board the ship. Do you understand?"

Kiara nodded.

"Speak up, girl. I want to hear more than your brains rattling in your head. Give me a verbal affirmation."

"Aye, I understand. When we arrive in this place called Lowell, will there be someone meetin' us? I do na know how to locate yar relative."

Lord Palmerston looked heavenward and shook his head. "No wonder you people are starving to death. I doubt there's one of you that has the sense of a church mouse."

"We're not starvin' because we're stupid; we're starvin' because our potatoes 'ave the blight. A problem no Englishman has been able to solve, I might add."

"You've a smart mouth on you, girl. Hearken my words, your sassy remarks will cause you nothing but trouble. Now listen carefully—my cousin's name is clearly marked on the outside of the letter I gave you." He snatched the missive away from her and tapped his finger atop the penned words. "You will be indentured to Mr. Bradley Houston, who is a man of importance in Lowell, just as I am in County Kerry. If you asked any of your neighbors how to find Lord Palmerston, could they direct you to this estate?"

She nodded but immediately remembered his earlier admonition and said, "Aye. I'll do as ya've instructed."

"And as for the potato problem, Miss O'Neill, if the Irish had taken the advice of the English years ago and learned to plant properly, their potatoes *wouldn't* be rotting in the ground."

Kiara was certain he was testing her, anxious to see if she'd argue with him. Well, she'd not give him the satisfaction. She knew that from the early days of the blight, the English had argued the lazy-bed method of planting had caused the potato famine. Yet they had no answer why this traditional Irish way of farming had always yielded large, disease-free crops in the past. Arguing would serve no purpose. None of it mattered anymore. Her ma and pa were rotting in the ground, just like the potato crop, and she and Paddy would likely never set foot on Irish soil again.

Lord Palmerston turned to his servant. "Take them to Dingle and wait until they've boarded. In fact, wait until their ship actually sails. Given the opportunity, I'm not certain the girl won't disembark or even jump overboard and swim for shore with my coins in her pocket. I can't trust the likes of her to keep her word."

Once again Kiara remained silent. She wanted to tell him

about the "likes of her"—Irish men, women, and children starving to death while the wealthy English played games on the lawn and wasted food that could be used to save their lives. Yes, indeed, the "likes of her" might just steal his money or food to save a fellow Irishman because the pompous English landlords cared nothing about saving their tenants from certain death.

They'd traveled only a short distance when Paddy snuggled closer and rested his head on Kiara's shoulder. "We'll likely never be settin' foot in such a lovely place as Lord Palmerston's estate again. It was right nice, wasn't it? And all that food. Do ya think the estate in America will be so nice?"

"I don't know, Paddy, but we'll be havin' five long years to find out."

"Ya're sad to be leavin' Ireland, aren't ya?"

Kiara took a deep breath and forced herself to smile. "Leavin' is the right thing to do—the only thing to do. We'll die if we stay in Ireland."

"And our new landlord might be a nice man who will treat us well."

"He's not goin' to be a landlord, Paddy, and we'll not be farmin' our own patch of ground. We'll be servants forced to do whatever work we're assigned."

Paddy gazed up at her, his deep brown eyes wistful. "But we'll not be hungry, will we?"

She pulled him near and ruffled his freshly washed and trimmed black curls. "No, Paddy, we'll not be hungry. There's no potato blight in America. Now take a good long look at the countryside so ya can remember the beauty of yar homeland. One day ya'll have children of yar own, and I want ya to be able to tell them of the beauty of the Emerald Isle."

Paddy rested his chin atop one arm along the edge of the carriage window, doing as his sister bade. He traveled in that position, with his thin body swaying with each pitch of the carriage, until they neared their destination. With an excited bounce, he turned toward his sister. "I love the smell of the ocean. We must be gettin' close."

Kiara clenched her fists, fighting to keep any emotion from her voice. "Aye, that we are."

When the carriage jerked to a stop, the driver jumped down, unloaded their baggage, and opened the carriage door. "Come along. We'll go and pay for your passage and see how soon the ferry will be sailing."

"Do ya think it will sail today?" Paddy asked the driver. "There's more people here than I've seen in all me life. Would they all be sailin' for America? Do ya think they'll all fit on one ship? It'll be mighty crowded if we all try to get on one ship, won't it?"

The coachman gave Paddy a look of exasperation as he hoisted the trunk. "Lord Palmerston said the ship sails today, and since ya can see it anchored out there, I'm sure ya'll soon be taking the ferry. I don't have answers to the rest of yar questions. The two of ya get the rest of yar belongings."

Kiara picked up the satchels and hurried Paddy along. "But what if there's no space available?" Kiara inquired. "Will you stay with us here in Dingle?"

"Don't ya be gettin' any ideas, lassie. If that should happen, I'll return ya to Lord Palmerston and await his biddin'. Now come along with ya."

Kiara and Paddy followed, careful to stay close behind the coachman. With a determined stride, he led them through the multitude of gathered passengers and into one of the shipping company offices.

"I need steerage for two children on the ship that's sailin' for America today," the coachman told the agent.

"Steerage is full. If you wanna pay extra, there's a cabin still available. Ya're late gettin' here. That ship sailed from England, and there's only toppin' off space available. And those two pay full fare, for they're way past the age of being considered children. 'Tis extra for the ferry."

"But there's no other way to get to the ship. Is that not included in their passage?"

"If it was included, would I be tellin' ya it's extra? I told ya, if ya're wantin' to board a ship to America today, the ferry will be leaving in an hour."

The coachman didn't argue. He pulled out a leather pouch, counted out six pounds for each of them, and listened to the instructions the man barked in their direction. They stepped aside, and the man began his speech to the people who had been standing in line behind them.

Kiara tugged on the coachman's sleeve. "Did you hear what he told them? I thought he said we were gettin' the last cabin."

"He sells passage on more than one ship. Come along now. Ya have to go through the medical inspection before ya can board the ferry." He pointed them toward the line outside another building along the wharf. "Just follow along, and I'll be waitin' when ya come out."

The two of them did as instructed, winding through the building and into a wooden cubicle, where they walked by a doctor who asked if they were ill and motioned them on when Kiara replied they were not. A man at the end of the table signed a paper saying they'd passed inspection.

"Ya weren't gone very long," the coachman remarked when they reappeared.

"That doctor did na even check us," Paddy told him. "He jus' asked if we was sick and told us we were fit to sail. He said we should hurry; the ferry leaves in less than an hour."

The coachman bade them farewell as a crewman relieved them of their trunk. Once the passengers were loaded onto the ferry and they had moved away from the shore, the coachman waved, tipped his hat, and strode off toward the carriage. Kiara felt an odd sense of loss watching the man leave. Perhaps because he was their last connection with their homeland.

Once aboard the ship, Kiara waited at the rail until a crewman loaded their trunk. "I'll stow this fer ya, and ya can claim it when we arrive. Ya can take yar smaller baggage with ya." He led them down a dark companionway to a long, gloomy space beneath the main deck. The hold was already teeming with noisy passengers. "Ya get two spaces," he said, pointing to a six-foot wooden square built into the ship's timbers along one side of the hold.

"Wait! We're entitled to a cabin. Our coachman was told the steerage was full. We paid six pounds and we should be havin' a cabin."

The crewman gave a laughing snort. "They tell that same story to ever'one. The only cabin on this ship is the captain's. There's only steerage for passengers. Like I told ya earlier, ya each get a space." He held his hands about a foot and a half apart.

He turned to walk away, but Kiara grasped his muscled arm with her slender fingers. "Wait! Ya mean that's all the space we'll be gettin' to sleep on?"

The sailor gave an affirmative nod. "That space is yar home until we arrive in America. Once we've set sail, ya can come on deck for a bit o' air," he said, then quickly took his leave.

"Psst. You! Come over here."

Kiara looked toward the corner, where an auburn-haired girl was motioning her forward. The girl continued waving her arm in wild circular motions until Kiara and Paddy began walking in her direction. She bobbled her head up and down as though her frantic movements would encourage them onward as they zigzagged through the mass of passengers.

"Do ya have bunk space yet?" the girl asked.

Kiara wagged her head back and forth. "No. We were supposed to 'ave a cabin, but they lied to us. Six pounds apiece they charged for passage."

"They lie to ever'one. Come on, ya can share this space with me. Throw that baggage on the floor over there and join me on this stick o' wood we'll call a bed until we arrive in America. Ya can put your satchels on here. That way no one else will take yar space."

Kiara did as the girl instructed. "I'm Kiara O'Neill, and this is my brother, Paddy."

"Bridgett Farrell. Pleased ta meet ya. Do ya have family in America?"

"No. We have only each other. Our ma and pa died this year—the famine."

The girl looked sympathetic. "Mine too. I got me an aunt, some cousins, and a granna livin' in America. I'm gonna join them and get me a job in the mills. Granna says there's work to be had if I come. Me cousins work for the Corporation, and they saved up the money for me passage. Where do ya plan to make yar home? In Boston?"

"No. We're goin' to a town called Lowell."

Bridgett slapped her leg and smiled. "That's where I'm gonna be livin'. Are ya gonna work in the mills too?"

"I don' know nothin' about no mills. We're gonna be servants on an estate. We indentured ourselves fer five years to pay fer our passage." The complexity of her decision weighed heavily once she had spoken the words to Bridgett. Actually speaking the words of what she had done caused the full force of her decision to crash in upon her. "I think I'll go up and watch as we sail."

Bridgett nodded. "Ya go ahead now. Me and Paddy will stay with the belongin's and save our space."

When the ship finally heaved and swayed out into the Atlantic a short time later, Kiara stood at the rail and watched her beautiful Ireland fade out of sight. All that she held dear was left behind save Paddy. She'd never again see the beauty of her homeland, visit with the friends and neighbors whom she held dear, or put a sprig of heather on her ma's grave. But even if she'd made the wrong decision, there was no turning back now. She shivered against a sudden gust of wind and pulled the warm woolen shawl tightly around her shoulders. "Selfish lass," she murmured into the breeze. "Ya should be thankful the good Lord saw fit to save ya from a certain death instead of feelin' sorry for yarself. If ya hadn't agreed, ya would na even have this shawl to keep yar body warm."

After what seemed an eternity on board the ship, Kiara was more than a little grateful to see the shores of Boston in the distance. So many times she'd been certain they would never make it. Sickness had sent many a stiff, unwashed body overboard to a watery grave, and while it had reduced the number of people on board, it left everyone wondering if they'd be next.

Kiara had entertained Paddy with stories she'd learned as a child—telling him of the fairies and their craftiness, of superstitions that had guided the lives of their people. It had eased the hours of boredom and gave them both a sense of home, which they desperately missed.

"Our people saw that the sun, moon, and stars all went west to die away so that they could be reborn and rise another day," she'd told Paddy at the beginning of their trip. Now, standing at the end of their journey, she wondered if it might be true for people as well. Her journey west had been a small death—an end to the girl she'd once been—a dying to the people she'd loved and known all of her life. Would she be reborn to rise again?

"Just look at it all, Kiara!" Paddy exclaimed. "Fer sure it's a grand city."

"Stay close at hand, Paddy. There's bound to be pushin' and shovin', what with everyone wantin' to get on dry land again. I don't want to lose sight of ya among all the others."

The boy danced from foot to foot. "Isn't it excitin', Kiara? We've finally arrived at our new homeland."

Kiara smiled down at her brother, thankful he hadn't succumbed to the dysentery contracted by so many of the passengers during their voyage. His health had actually improved on the journey, and she had begun to relax as they drew closer to Boston. However, just when she had thought there were no other concerns, medical inspectors boarded the ship, and she watched with increasing trepidation as they denied entry to passengers who showed the slightest sign of illness. What if they were refused entry after the long and dreadful voyage? She pulled Paddy into her embrace and issued up a silent prayer the inspectors would find nothing wrong with them.

There was little control as the crowd carried them forward. Kiara heard Bridgett's voice and strained to see around the hefty woman in front of her. She smiled at the sight of her new friend, who was jumping and waving from among an assemblage of passengers. Bridgett had pushed ahead, and her group had already passed through the medical inspection. "Meet me on the dock," she called out.

"Aye," Kiara hollered back.

"Over here! Hurry along now, and let loose of the boy so I can check him. Hand him over, for you'll not step foot off this ship until he's been examined," the medical inspector commanded as he tugged at her arm.

Begrudgingly, she loosened her grip and continued praying while they both endured the examination. "You'll do," he said, pointing them toward the passengers waiting to disembark.

Kiara flashed the inspector a smile and grasped Paddy's hand. Now that they were in America, where he would have proper nourishment and fresh air, he could flourish and grow into a strong young man. He would be reborn—they both would. "Move into that line," she said. "Once we're on the wharf, we need to be findin' Bridgett and then locate our trunk. It will likely take a while, but perhaps we can find a place to sit."

"Or walk around and explore."

"I'll be wantin' to remain near the ship. The coachman told me we should stay close at hand while they're unloadin'."

"Why?" Paddy asked, his sparkling brown eyes filled with wonderment.

"Because thieves come to the docks, and they steal cargo and trunks that are left unattended. At least that's what he told me. I do na want to take a chance on losin' the belongings Lord Palmerston's servants packed for us. And Ma's teacup is in there too. I would rather die than be losin' Ma's teacup."

"You *would*?"

Kiara tousled her brother's hair and laughed. "I'm supposin' that's an exaggeration, but I would be very sad to lose our only keepsake."

"Then we'll be stayin' close by the docks and watch carefully for our trunk. Look! There's Bridgett, and she's already come across her trunk."

The coachman had been correct. A variety of unseemly-looking men wandered the quay, watching with interest while the cargo was unloaded. Occasionally one of the thieves would skulk forward, hoist a trunk, and scurry off without notice. Once the passengers realized what was happening, they began giving chase, sometimes with success but generally not, leaving tearful families lamenting the loss of all their worldly goods.

"There it is!" Paddy pointed toward their baggage and rushed from her side.

Kiara caught sight of Bridgett, who was now moving in their direction. It appeared as if she'd convinced a young man to carry her trunk. Both Bridgett and Kiara reached Paddy at the same time. He had planted himself atop the hump-backed trunk and his lips were curved in a smile of pure delight. His enthusiasm was contagious, and Kiara leaned over and pulled him into an approving hug.

"Ya've a good eye, Padraig O'Neill," Kiara said.

Bridgett nodded toward a building across from the dock. "There's a lady over there what tol' me where we can buy our tickets to Lowell at the train station. I don't think it's far off."

"If it's not far, perhaps we can just drag the trunks along with us."

"What if the woman gave me improper directions? We could be draggin' those trunks until our arms are so weary we can pull them no further. Do ya not think it would be safe for Paddy to stay with the trunks while we go and make arrangements for the rest of our journey?"

Kiara studied the boy, uncertain whether she should leave him alone.

Paddy's shoulders squared and he raised himself up straight and tall. "You and Bridgett can count on me. I'll protect the trunks with me life."

"I'm more concerned about you than any old trunks," she said, giving him a quick peck on the cheek. She knew his young ego would be crushed if she insisted he go with them, so she cautioned him to be careful and hurried off with Bridgett. The train station was exactly where the woman had promised. The ticket master explained that if the train arrived on schedule, it would be leaving for Lowell in an hour.

The two girls nodded in agreement. They purchased the tickets and then followed the man's directions to find a small shop, where they purchased biscuits and cheese enough to tide them over until their arrival in Lowell. Paddy was still sitting astride the trunk when they returned, with his short legs draped down on either side. The boy looked almost as if he were riding one of Mr. Connelly's horses back in Ireland. Kiara smiled and waved. "I've paid for our train tickets and got us some biscuits and cheese," she announced. "We need to get our trunks to the train station. Jump down and let's get movin'."

"Can I have a biscuit? Me stomach's growlin'."

"Fer sure ya can, but after we get ourselves to the station. We can't go missin' our train to Lowell."

Paddy nodded. He was such a good-spirited little man, Kiara thought. He understood the need to see to the work first and he never complained. Together they pulled the trunk up and dragged it along behind. Kiara thought it unnaturally heavy, but then again, she was unnaturally tired. She had fretted over most every mile across the ocean—worrying that Paddy would take sick, fearing someone might steal him away and harm him, stewing over whether they'd have enough to eat.

Kiara was blessed when the baggageman came forward to take the trunk from them at the station. Bridgett handed her trunk over as well, then tossed the man a penny. Kiara regretted her inability to offer him the same, but she had no choice. She'd not been given money to waste.

Paddy hurried to find a seat and motioned Kiara to a place by the window. He positioned himself nose against the glass, anxious to be started. Kiara smiled and handed him a piece of cheese and a biscuit. "And here's yar lunch, little man."

He immediately devoured it, wolfing down the simple fare as though he hadn't eaten in weeks. It was good to see him with a hearty appetite and feeling well.

"Do ya think there will be someone who can help us find Mr.

Houston's estate when we get to Lowell?" Kiara asked Bridgett. Her stomach had suddenly begun to tighten into a knot, clamping down upon the biscuit and cheese she had eaten in sharp, jabbing pains.

"Don' ya be frettin'. Me granna promised they'd be watchin' for me arrival. They can help ya. Of that I have no doubt."

The train lurched forward, then stopped, then lurched again. The jerky motion caused Kiara to let out a squeal. Her stomach did a funny flip-flop.

"'Tis nothin' amiss," Bridgett told her. "I've been on a train before. It's always like this. Soon we'll sail along as smooth as ya please. Why don't ya have a rest? We'll be there before ya know it."

Bridgett's words helped calm Kiara's fears, and the stabbing pain eased enough for the rocking motion of the train to lull her to sleep. When the train hissed and belched to a stop, Kiara jolted awake with a start.

"We're in Lowell already?" Her fear returned tenfold. She could barely swallow.

Bridgett pressed her nose against the train window and peered out onto the platform, her eyes scanning the crowd gathered there.

"Do ya see your granna?" Paddy asked.

"No, but they'll be here. Come on, we need ta be gettin' off," Bridgett said.

As soon as they were inside the station, Bridgett marched up to the ticket counter and talked to the ticket master. She was there only a few minutes. "He says there should be a wagon outside ya can hire to take you and the luggage wherever ya need to go. He did na know my granna. Says he's not acquainted with the Irish. Kinda insultin', he was. Come on. I'll go outside with ya and see if we can get ya on yar way. Don' ya be fergettin' to come and see me. My granna says most all the Irish live in the Acre. Ya be rememberin' that so ya can come visit."

Kiara agreed as they walked toward the wagon parked in front of the station. "Can ya take us to the estate of a Mr. Bradley Houston?"

The driver looked down from his perch and fixed his gaze on Paddy. "If you got money, I can get you there."

Paddy looked up at the driver with obvious admiration. The man shoved his hat farther back on his head and gave Paddy a grin. "Get on up here, boy," he said. He jumped down from the wagon, and while he loaded their trunk and satchels in back, Kiara bid Bridgett farewell. Kiara turned in her seat, waving at Bridgett until she could no longer see the girl. She barely knew her, yet she felt as though she'd lost yet another member of her family.

The drive to the Houston residence was nearly fifteen minutes by coach, and Kiara was thankful they'd not been forced to walk the distance. The driver tipped his hat, and Kiara walked to the front door while Paddy remained with their luggage. She had barely lifted her hand to knock when the front door flew open and a dour-looking woman pointed them to the rear of the house.

"Not so different from Ireland, is it, Paddy? The likes of us will always be shoved out of sight."

Paddy was busy examining their new home. "It's not such a big house, is it? Not like Lord Palmerston's at all. Do ya think this is the right place?" the boy asked.

"We'll know soon enough," Kiara replied. The same austere woman was waiting for them when they arrived at the rear door. "Good day, ma'am. I'm Kiara O'Neill and this here's me brother, Padraig. We've come from Ireland to work for Mr. Houston. Here's our letter of introduction."

The woman took the letter and motioned them into the kitchen. "Wait here." She stopped short and turned back to face them, her features softening. "Have you eaten? I hear tell there's many a passenger that starves to death on those coffin ships coming from Ireland."

"Aye. We got some biscuits and cheese in Boston," Kiara said.

"But I'm still hungry," Paddy added.

"I'll have the cook bring you some food. Was Mr. Houston expecting you? He didn't say a word."

Kiara shrugged. "Lord Palmerston said he wrote to your master."

Moments later a man with a receding hairline and pale skin walked into the room. Kiara couldn't decide if it was his thin lips or long forehead that gave him an unkind appearance. His gaze settled upon her as he held her letter between his finger and thumb and waved it aloft.

"I must admit that even though I received my cousin's letter, I never expected you to actually arrive in Lowell," he said.

"And why is that? Were ya thinkin' we'd die at sea?"

His laugh was cruel. "No. I was thinking that if you had any sense at all, you'd have remained in Boston and started your life anew. After all, how would I have found you? I had never seen either of you and had no idea what you looked like."

"I gave me word—ya may na think I have good sense, Mr. Houston, but na everybody is a liar. Some of us protect our honor no matter what the cost."

"You'll have five years to prove that to me. I can make good use of you here in the house, but what am I to do with this spindly boy?" Mr. Houston asked while giving Paddy a look of disdain. "He's of little use to me. Perhaps I can sell his papers to someone who could make better use of him."

Kiara lunged forward and, without thinking, grasped the man's arm. "No! Me brother must stay with me."

Bradley's focus moved to his arm, where Kiara's fingers were digging deep into his flesh. "Turn loose of me, girl." He waited until she removed her hold. "Now that I understand how important your brother is to you, I suppose I can find something to keep him busy. What might you recommend?"

Kiara gave him a winsome smile. "Paddy's very good with animals, especially horses. Would ya be ownin' any horses?"

Bradley rubbed his narrow jaw. "As a matter of fact, I do. I suppose he could help muck out the stables and curry the horses. Do you think you could do that satisfactorily, boy?"

Paddy cocked his head and gave Mr. Houston a bright smile. "Aye. I'll work very hard carin' for yar animals, sir."

The man's leering gaze returned to Kiara. "I'm sure you and your sister are going to make me very happy."

CHAPTER · 18

WHEN THE CARRIAGE rounded the driveway, Jasmine was genuinely pleased to be home. Not that she longed to see Bradley—quite the contrary. Although her stomach had settled during the final day on board the ship, she remained pallid and frail, and arriving home was somewhat comforting. Concerned over her continuing infirmity, Nolan had insisted upon escorting the two women on the final leg of their journey from Boston to Lowell. He had been resolute in his decision, stating he would leave for Boston the following day. Alice had argued briefly, but Jasmine hadn't had strength to resist and was exceedingly thankful for the capable care he had provided.

A dark-haired girl was sweeping the gallery when their carriage came to a halt in front of the house. Cupping one hand over her eyes as she stepped down from the coach, Jasmine blinked against the sun until the young woman came into focus. She was certain she'd never before seen her.

"I'll be comin' right down to help ya," the girl called out as she hurried back through the gallery doors.

Before Nolan and the two women had time to enter the front door, the girl came bursting outdoors as though shot from a cannon.

"I'm sorry I was na here waitin' for ya, ma'am," she apologized with a deep curtsy.

Jasmine stared wide-eyed at the young woman. "Who are you?"

"Kiara O'Neill, from the beautiful Emerald Isle. Me and my brother, Paddy, are indentured to ya."

"Indentured? How is that possible?"

Nolan grasped her elbow and urged her forward. "Let's go inside where you can sit. You're much too weak to be standing out here having a lengthy discussion."

"Aye, ya're lookin' mighty pale, missus." Kiara hoisted both satchels and scurried ahead of them. "I'll just be takin' these to yar room, missus, and then I'll be back down to get ya a cup o' tea."

Before Jasmine could assent or object, the girl was running up the stairs with a satchel in each hand, her black mane flying wildly while Alice and Jasmine watched from the hallway.

"I want to get you settled before I leave for home," Alice said.

Kiara looked over the railing at the threesome standing below. "Do na worry yarself about the missus. I'll be givin' her good care, ma'am. I'll be back afore ya can count me out of yar sight."

The remark brought a smile to Jasmine's lips. "Take your time, Kiara. My grandmother will remain with me for a little longer."

Nolan rubbed his hands together and glanced toward the door. "If you two ladies will be all right for a short time, I want to see to the horses. One of them appeared to be developing a limp. I don't want to take him farther if he's injured or has a stone lodged in a hoof."

Sarah, the older pinch-faced maid who had faithfully cared for the house since Jasmine's marriage to Bradley, hurried into the parlor. "Mrs. Houston! How good to have you home. Mr. Houston said you'd be arriving today, but I was out back and didn't realize you'd arrived. Did Kiara or Paddy get your baggage?"

Kiara came bounding down the steps and skidded to a halt in the parlor doorway. "Yes, ma'am, I got their bags, 'ceptin' for the trunk. I'll have Paddy help me take it upstairs when he gets back from exercising the horse. I told the missus I'd get her a cup o' tea, and then I'll be unpackin' 'er bags." The words tumbled out in one rushing breath.

Jasmine took in the black-haired beauty. "Sit down, Kiara, and tell me how you've come to be with us."

Kiara looked toward Sarah. The maid nodded, and Kiara perched on the edge of the straight-backed chair opposite her mistress. "Yar husband owns me and Paddy, missus. We're indentured to him."

"I don't understand. How did all of this occur?"

With a haunting sadness in her eyes, Kiara carefully explained how she had come to Lowell and would be required to spend the next five years indentured to her husband.

Jasmine's mind was reeling with the information. "Bradley agreed to this?"

"Yar husband said I would be workin' as yar personal maid when ya returned from visitin' yar ma and pa. Me brother, Paddy, is workin' in the stable, helpin' with the horses. He's a good boy. I've no doubt ya'll be likin' him fine."

The girl's words sounded genuine, yet doubt was knocking at Jasmine's heart like an unwanted visitor in the night. The entire tale was maudlin. Parents dying and being dumped out of their coffins into the ground without a proper burial, a voyage in a lice- and dysentery-infested ship with only inches of space to sleep, papers of indentureship requiring five years of one's life to pay for the journey. However, the facts might be true, for she knew of the terrible famine in Ireland. Hadn't their ladies' group been collecting funds for relief before she had sailed for New Orleans?

The sound of the front door closing was quickly followed by Nolan's footsteps in the hallway. "The horse is fine. Appears the little Irish fellow knows his way around horseflesh quite well. He removed a small stone from one of the hooves in short order."

Kiara beamed a look of appreciation in Nolan's direction. "He's a hard worker, Paddy is. And he loves animals, especially the horses. Happy he is to be workin' with them."

TRACIE PETERSON / JUDITH MILLER

Jasmine patted the settee cushion beside her. "Come sit down, Nolan."

He made no move toward the couch. "Your grandmother and I should be leaving soon."

"Oh, do sit a moment. I promise not to keep you long. I've something to ask you."

He laughed and moved toward the settee. "Considering our time aboard ship and at The Willows, we've been together for nearly three months. I can't imagine there's anything you haven't asked me."

"Had I known anything about the possibility of English relatives, I would have already inquired. Tell me, Nolan, does your family have relatives in England? Kiara says an Englishman owning vast holdings in Ireland was her family's landlord. She went to him seeking assistance after the death of her parents. It seems that after some urging and perhaps a wager of sorts with his wealthy visitors, this fellow paid for Kiara and her brother to come to America in exchange for five years of servitude. Supposedly, he then assigned the papers to Bradley. Have you ever heard of anything so indecorous?"

"In answer to your first question, we do have some distant relatives in England. My mother's uncle was some sort of nobility, I believe. I'm not certain. Bradley maintained some contact with their children or children's children. They'd be cousins once removed or some such thing, and I must admit I never had much interest in any of them. However, Bradley was rather awestruck upon learning we were related to nobility. He began corresponding and may have visited once when he was in England, but I didn't realize he was still in contact with any of them. I believe their name was Plamerson or Planster. . . ."

"Palmerston. Lord Palmerston," Kiara interjected.

"Yes! That's it. Palmerston," Nolan agreed. "Now, in answer to your second question, Jasmine, owning indentured servants is quite common in England, as it was in this country for many years—still is, to some extent, although it's been replaced in large part by slavery."

"So if Bradley has received papers on this girl and her brother, he could return their papers and let them go on their way?"

"Yes, of course. And I would like to think that's exactly what he'll do."

"Obviously the thought hasn't occurred to him yet, since he immediately put them to work. He refused to allow me to keep Mammy because the Associates look down on slavery. Why in the world would he keep indentured servants? It's akin to the same thing."

"Not in the eyes of society," Nolan replied. "The indentured man or woman can work off their servitude, and generally they've already benefited from their employers. Just as this woman and her brother have no doubt advanced their station in life by receiving free passage across the ocean and a new life in America."

"Aye," Kiara said. "It saved our lives, and while I'll be missin' me homeland, I know we'd be dead by now had we stayed."

Jasmine shook her head. "Still, this surprises me greatly, and I intend to speak to Bradley about dissolving this arrangement."

Nolan tugged at the stiff collar wrapped tightly around his broad neck. "You might suggest the possibility, but I'd wait until he broaches the topic. He's generally more flexible when the discussion is his idea. At least that's been my experience in the past."

"Thank you, Nolan. I'll remember your suggestion."

"And now, Mrs. Wainwright, if you're quite ready, I believe I should escort you home."

"Fine. And I insist you spend the night before beginning your journey to Boston."

Nolan gave her a broad smile. "It's not so far to Boston and there's another train leaving soon, I'm sure. If need be, I can always remain at an inn for the night."

Alice thumped the tip of her parasol on the floor. "I insist! I'll not take no for an answer."

Jasmine giggled at her grandmother's antics, her new servant problem forgotten for the moment. "I believe you've no choice in the matter."

"Indeed. You may tell my brother I'll be spending the night

with your grandmother if he wants to visit with me before I leave for Boston."

"I'll do that. Thank you again for agreeing to escort us on our journey, Nolan. I don't know what we would have done without you. You proved yourself a capable guardian and an excellent instructor. I enjoyed our discussions."

"And just what enthralling topics did you and my brother find to talk about?"

Jasmine startled at the sound of Bradley's voice. She turned, praying that after a three-month absence the sight of him might well stir something inside her. It didn't. His pale skin, intense stare, and tendency to always look as though he were sneering did nothing to endear her. "I didn't hear you come in the house."

"Probably because I came through the back of the house. I wanted to check on the stable boy." His gaze shifted to Kiara. "And what, pray tell, are you doing? Are you sitting in the parlor, playing the part of the lady and expecting tea?"

"There's no need for your derision, Bradley. I invited her to sit and tell me how she came to be living here."

"Well, I'm here now and can answer your questions. Get off to your chores," he commanded.

Kiara jumped out of the chair and fled from the room while Bradley drew close to Jasmine and placed a kiss upon her cheek. "I'm pleased to see your ship returned as scheduled. That means the voyage was uneventful. Always glad to hear my ships have made a safe journey. I trust they also loaded the vessel with cargo for the return?"

"I didn't inquire. However, the captain sent you a parcel," Nolan replied. "I placed it on the desk in your library."

"And Father sent you a letter also," Jasmine added. "It's in my luggage."

"And your mother? Is she upstairs resting?"

"No. She's ill and was unable to make the voyage. Perhaps later in the year."

"Ah, well, that's a shame, isn't it?"

His words rang false, but Jasmine concealed her irritation.

"And this young Irish lass and her brother—I understand you've taken them in as indentured servants."

Nolan aimed a look of warning in her direction and stepped forward before Bradley could reply. "We really must be on our way, but in the event your wife decides she doesn't want to worry you with concerns about herself, you should know that she was quite ill on our return voyage."

"Really? Were the waters rough?"

"Actually the seas were quite calm," Nolan answered.

"That's odd. My Jasmine has always been quite the sailor, haven't you, my dear?"

Jasmine gave him a waxen smile and nodded. "Must have been something I ate. I've been feeling better these last few days."

"And here I thought you must have been quite well. I thought you appeared a bit thicker about the waist when I came in the room."

Alice immediately shot a look at her granddaughter's waistline and then lifted her eyes, meeting Jasmine's gaze. "Could we have a moment alone before I depart?" she inquired. "Perhaps you and Nolan should locate the parcel the captain sent along."

Nolan's brow furrowed momentarily. "I explained it's on the . . . Yes, of course. Let's go into your library, Bradley," Nolan suggested, leading his brother into the other room.

Alice quickly settled herself next to Jasmine and took the girl's hand in her own. "Tell me, dear, have you given any thought to the fact that you may be expecting a child?"

Jasmine hesitated and thought about the probability—one she'd contemplated on the return voyage. Distressing as the concept might be, she knew her grandmother was likely correct. "Yes, it's possible. But Bradley is a poor husband, and he will make an even worse father. I know Bradley Houston." She was aware that verbalizing her fears would not change anything, but her grandmother was now well aware of her opinion.

"A child may be exactly what the two of you need to draw you closer. I'm going to send Dr. Hartzfeld to see you tomorrow."

"If you think that's best, I won't argue." Her tone was dismal as she slumped and rested her back against the settee.

———————

Jasmine was despondent when the doctor departed the next day. He had obtained her consent to tell Alice upon his return to town, for she knew her grandmother would give the poor doctor no peace until he revealed his findings. The old woman would be pleased to hear the news, but Jasmine was in no mood to celebrate.

"I saw Dr. Hartzfeld as he was leaving," Bradley said as he strode into the parlor. "I must say, I was surprised he'd come to call. I thought you were feeling better. However, he says you have some news to share with me."

Jasmine picked up her stitching and briefly contemplated telling her husband she had a terminal illness with only several months to live. The thought was enticing, but she quickly discarded the idea. Bradley would find little humor in her antics when she was finally forced to reveal the truth.

"I'm expecting a child in November," she whispered.

He hurried to her side and knelt down beside her. "Truly?" His voice radiated a joy she'd never before heard and his eyes actually shone with delight.

"Yes, truly."

He jumped up and sat across from her. Leaning forward, he rested his elbows atop his knees and drew near. Grasping her hand, he yelped and then pulled back.

"Did you not see the needle?" she asked. "Here, use this." She pulled a handkerchief from her pocket and dangled it in midair.

He hastily wrapped the cloth around his finger while keeping his gaze affixed on her eyes. "Not even a jab from your sewing needle can diminish the happiness I'm feeling at this moment."

She looked down at her stitching, unwilling to share his excitement, and when Kiara entered the room with a tea tray, she issued a silent prayer of thanks. "You may put it here, Kiara."

"Would you like me to pour, ma'am?"

Jasmine smiled at the lilting sound of the girl's voice. "Yes, that would—"

"No. We'd like to be alone. Go on back to the kitchen," Bradley ordered.

With marked nervousness, the girl skittered off without a backward glance.

"Do you take pleasure in treating others unkindly?" Jasmine asked.

"I didn't treat her unkindly. I told her to leave the room because I didn't want to share this moment with a serving girl."

"Don't you mean with a slave?"

"She's not a slave. I don't own her."

"You own her for five years. She can't leave this place without fear of being sought after by the police. Aside from being five years rather than a lifetime, how is that different from slavery? Your cousin bought five years of that girl's life just as my father buys slaves for a lifetime. And Kiara tells me that in Ireland and England, indentured servants usually are owned for a lifetime because their owners claim costs for their room and board that exceed their ability to pay off the cost of their contract."

"Well, it was kind of the girl to share that information. Perhaps I should begin keeping a tally of costs for her room and board. I may be able to retain the two of them longer than I anticipated."

Jasmine silently berated herself. Why hadn't she listened to Nolan's advice? Instead of picking a fight, she should have used this moment to her advantage. Perhaps she still could. "When Dr. Hartzfeld told me the news, I realized you had been correct in sending Mammy back to The Willows. I didn't notice how much she had aged until we returned to Mississippi. And now, with my confinement, I'm going to need more assistance than usual. I doubt she would have been able to provide the help I'll need."

Bradley's mood lightened at Jasmine's rare and unexpected praise. "You see? I actually do know what is best for you. Kiara is young and energetic. She'll be able to provide all the help you need."

"And if she does well, perhaps we should reward her efforts."

"Of course," he obligingly replied. "Once you've finished your tea, I think you should lie down and rest."

"No need. I'm feeling fine."

"I thought you just agreed that your husband knows what is best for you. I must get back to work, but I'll instruct Kiara to accompany you upstairs for a nap. I don't want anything happening that would adversely affect the baby. You need to take proper care of yourself. When I return home this evening, I don't want to hear that you've failed to follow my advice." Although he was smiling, there was a warning edge to his voice. He expected to be obeyed.

Bradley hastened back to his office with the packet of information from Captain Harmon and the letter from his father-in-law tucked into a leather pouch attached to his saddle. He had planned to ride the chestnut mare today, but the Irish boy was busy currying the animal when Bradley arrived at the stable, so he'd taken the black gelding. Bradley was pleased the boy appeared to have a genuine fondness for the mare. The horse was a beauty and he wanted the animal to receive only the finest care. Bradley had paid much more than he could afford to spend on a horse, but he'd been unable to negotiate a lesser price.

Jasmine's news that he would soon become a father caused Bradley to remain in a state of euphoria throughout most of the afternoon. But as the day wore on, his thoughts returned to the satchel. He decided to examine Malcolm Wainwright's letter and the packet from Captain Harmon before leaving his office. Captain Harmon's information consisted of his usual logs and reports, and after skimming the material, Bradley set it aside to open the other letter.

He carefully read the missive, his euphoria now replaced by an unrelenting irritation. In the letter Malcolm expressed disappointment in his son-in-law. He had gone so far as to set out each payment received, those that had arrived late, and those that remained due. The letter made it abundantly clear that Malcolm had expected to receive a payment when Jasmine visited The Willows.

Bradley paced across his office as he began reading the letter aloud, his irritation growing as he put voice to Malcolm's words.

" 'Not only did you fail to send a payment with Jasmine when she came to visit us, I have yet to receive the three payments due to the Wainwrights. You are aware I did not wish to enter into an arrangement for installment payments, but because you are my son-in-law, I agreed to do so.' "

Bradley's thoughts traveled back to the conversation he'd had with Malcolm. It had taken a great deal of persuasion to convince the older man that such business dealings were a common practice with the Associates. He had carefully explained the Corporation preferred conducting their business on the installment method in order to maintain a greater cash flow. As a businessman himself, Malcolm could understand the difficulty that would be involved if the Associates were required to pay all of the cotton growers simultaneously. Consequently, he had yielded to Bradley's request. However, Malcolm's letter was filled with undeniable disillusionment and anger.

Bradley returned to his desk and pulled out a piece of stationery. No doubt he would need to send funds, but not until he received another payment from the Associates. He quickly penned a letter to Malcolm explaining he would be traveling to Boston for a meeting of the Associates next month and the funds would be forwarded to Mississippi at that time.

CHAPTER · *19*

JASMINE'S ATTENTION waned as Bradley droned on with his list of innumerable instructions she was to follow in his absence. He painstakingly advised he would be traveling to Boston the next day to complete business matters for both the Associates and his shipping enterprise. Jasmine cared little why he was going. However, the length of his stay was of paramount interest. In her estimation, the longer he was gone, the better. Since her return from Mississippi, Bradley's moods had alternated between overbearing attentiveness and brooding irritability, with no apparent logic. Once he finished his tiresome oratory, he advised his wife he would be out of town for a minimum of a week, perhaps longer, depending on the progress of his business matters. Although she dared not reveal her feelings, Jasmine was secretly delighted.

She had noticed the servants, particularly Kiara, gave her husband a wide berth when he was in the house. Obviously, Jasmine wasn't the only recipient of his ill humor. Likely the entire household was going to take pleasure in his departure.

He handed Jasmine the list of duties he'd earlier enumerated, along with a similar list for each of the servants, kissed her farewell, and finally took his leave. As the sound of his carriage grew distant, she leaned against the door and relaxed against the hard, cool wood. She knew she would not miss her husband.

I cannot love him. There is nothing worthy of love. Jasmine sighed and closed her eyes. How very different her life was from the dreams she'd once had, little-girl dreams of living in the South with her own plantation house to run and a loving husband to take pride in her efforts. She touched a hand to her stomach and thought of the child that grew there. She didn't want Bradley's children, but this baby was also her own. She couldn't very well disregard that fact.

I can hardly punish the child because I do not love his or her father.

She put aside her disparaging thoughts and entered the parlor, where Kiara was carefully dusting the furniture she had dusted only the day before.

"Excuse me boldness, but will the master be gone for very long, ma'am?"

"At least a week." Jasmine eyed the busy girl. She couldn't be much older than sixteen—maybe seventeen. "Sit down and let's visit."

"Excuse me? You're wantin' me to sit and visit in the parlor?" The girl looked appalled at the idea.

"I thought we were becoming friends. I visit with you when you're helping me dress or fixing my hair."

"That's different than sittin' in the parlor like I'm company. I don't think Mr. Bradley would be likin' to see such a thing."

"Well, he's gone to Boston so we need not worry. I'm in charge now and I want you to sit and visit."

"Yes, ma'am," she said, perching on the edge of her chair like a bird poised to take flight. "What is it ya're wantin' to hear from me?"

"You remember I told you my mother was ill and couldn't return to Lowell with me?"

"Aye."

"I've been thinking about how much I miss my mother. My longing to be with her has made me realize how difficult life must be for you and Paddy. It's difficult to imagine all you two have suffered."

"We've suffered no more than most of the Irish. And when I'm missin' me mother the most, I try to remember all the good times instead of dwellin' on when the famine struck us down." Kiara stared out the window as though she were in a trance that carried her back to the grassy hills and valleys of her homeland. "We always worked hard, but our house was filled with love and plenty of laughter. Even when food got scarce, we made do for a while with sellin' lace. But when times got really bad, me da fell into a state o' sadness, the likes of which I ain't never seen before—and hope I never see again. He took the few coins me ma had saved back for thread and spent them on ale."

"Your mother made lace to help support you?"

Kiara looked at Jasmine as though she were a stranger. Obviously the Irish girl's thoughts remained focused upon Ireland and memories of a happier time. "Aye, both of us. She taught me how to make the lace. Lots of the women learned so as to help feed their families. The nuns at the convent taught some of the girls in our village, and they taught others. They sold the lace for us—to the wealthy English landowners. Their ladies are very fond of Irish lace."

"I'd like to see some of your handiwork, Kiara. Do you have some of your lace you can show me?"

"No, I had but a wee piece left, and I pinned it on me mother's dress when we buried her. I thought it only fittin' since we could na give her a proper burial."

"What a lovely idea. I'm sure she would have been pleased."

Kiara pointed toward Jasmine's sewing basket. "Do ya know how to make lace, ma'am?"

"No, but I'd be delighted to have you show me. We could go into town and purchase the necessary supplies, if you like. I don't want to place another burden upon you."

"Making even a small piece o' lace takes many hours, ma'am. Some find it tedious to finish only an inch or two after hours and hours of work. But I love keepin' me hands busy with the thread. Watching as a piece of thread turns into a delicate piece o' lace is truly a thing of beauty."

"Then we must get you some thread. I have a meeting tomorrow afternoon, but we could go into town after supper tonight."

"The shops are open for business in the evenin', ma'am?"

"Yes, to accommodate the girls working in the mills. The shop owners know they must remain open if they're going to attract business from the mill workers. Grandmother told me the shopkeepers have maintained evening hours since the very first stores opened in Lowell."

"I never heard o' such a thing, but if you're wantin' to go, I'd be 'appy to go along."

"Good! Then it's agreed."

Kiara cleared her throat and her expression grew tense. Jasmine wondered at the look but had no time to ask before Kiara questioned her. "Ma'am, forgive me bein' so bold, but I'm wonderin' if we could buy a wee bit of material for some aprons. I've only got the one dress and I'm washin' it out every night, but—"

"You've only got one dress?" Jasmine asked in disbelief. "Why didn't you say so sooner?"

"I've never had more than one dress at a time, ma'am. I can make do just fine with it, especially if I have an apron or two. Lord Palmerston's lady servant said she did na have time to sew me or Paddy any clothes afore we left Ireland. She did na pack any material in our trunk either, although she had plenty in her sewin' room—tightfisted, she was. Fact is, she packed us a trunk, but most of the contents were for yar husband . . . not clothes for me and Paddy."

"Well, I cannot allow you to make do with that. We'll buy materials for you and for Paddy. Do you sew?"

"Aye. I can do very fine work, if I do say so meself," Kiara replied.

"Very well. Make a list of what you'll need in order to create two—no, three—work dresses. Better yet, let's buy serviceable material for three work dresses and two gowns of better quality for special occasions."

"Oh, but for sure I couldn't be lettin' ya do that, ma'am. An apron or two will be just fine."

"Nonsense. You're my personal maid—you mustn't look dowdy," Jasmine insisted, trying her best to sound authoritative.

"Oh, I hadn't thought of it that way," Kiara said, touching the top of her frayed collar.

"Don't fret. This will be fun. We'll go and purchase everything you need. Then, tomorrow you'll spend the day sewing instead of worrying about household duties. We'll get materials for Paddy as well, so make a list of what you'll need to make the boy at least three shirts and two pairs of trousers."

"For sure I don't know what to say," Kiara murmured.

Jasmine smiled. "Say nothing at all."

Kiara jumped up from her chair, obviously anxious to hasten back to her duties. But before she could escape, Jasmine grasped the girl's hand. "Are you happy here, Kiara? I know you'd be happier in Ireland if you could have stayed, but are you reasonably comfortable here with us?"

She hesitated briefly. "I'm very fond of you, ma'am, and this is a lovely house. Sure and it's finer than anyplace I ever hoped to live in. And Paddy's happy workin' with the horses."

"And Master Bradley?" Jasmine inquired.

Kiara's eyes grew as cloudy as the fog-layered moors of Ireland. "He can be a bit frightenin' at times, ma'am, but I'll not be sayin' a single bad word about yar husband. I'm just thankful the two of us are alive and together. Now, I best be gettin' back to me chores. Cook will be needin' me soon."

Jasmine nodded. She wouldn't force Kiara to talk about Bradley—she didn't need to. The girl's fears were evident.

———

"They've quite a selection of thread, ma'am. A bit thicker than I like, but we can make do even if it's not quite so fine."

"Let's take a look over here," Jasmine suggested while leading the way through the emporium, which was beginning to hum with activity. Mill girls, anxious to see the new merchandise advertised in the newspaper, swarmed into the store in groups of five and six, their chatter carrying throughout the store, while several were overcome with fits of coughing.

"Mrs. Paxton, did you get your shipment of Dr. Horatio's Spice of Life?" one of the girls inquired.

"Yes, indeed. We received a full shipment this morning, and I've already placed another order. It seems all of you girls are beginning to use Dr. Horatio's rejuvenating spirits. Before long, I won't be able to keep up with the demand."

"You should try it, Mrs. Paxton. It helps my cough and boosts my energy. Ask any of the girls who have used it. Why, it's not only given me more energy, I've found it makes my life more pleasant."

"What she says is true," another girl agreed. "Before I would leave the weaving room feeling completely exhausted, what with the hot, damp rooms and not being able to open the windows for a bit of fresh air. Then I began taking Spice of Life, and within a day or two, I was feeling like a new person—full of energy, not coughing nearly so much, and enjoying myself again."

Jasmine approached the counter where the girls were standing and picked up a bottle of the cathartic. "Forgive me for interrupting, but did I overhear you say you've found remedial success with this product?"

"Absolutely! Why, the medicinal value of Dr. Horatio's spirits is unsurpassed. Those of us working in the mills have found it extremely beneficial. Of course, we're required to work in conditions that you aren't likely to endure. Employment in those mills can drain the very life out of you, but after only a few doses of Dr. Horatio's, I feel wonderful again."

Jasmine held on to the bottle. "Thank you for taking time to explain the benefits of the product. I believe I may purchase a bottle," Jasmine remarked as she watched the girl purchase four bottles of the remedy before leaving the store.

"Are ya feelin' poorly, missus, that ya think ya need that mixture?" Kiara inquired.

"I've just not been able to regain my strength. Perhaps this will help."

Kiara shook her head. "I'm guessin' there's nothin' but a dose of whiskey and water, along with a bit o' flavorin' and perhaps a few herbs in that bottle, missus. Ya're feelin' tired because of yar condition. It's just the growin' babe sappin' yar energy."

"I've talked to other ladies, and they've been able to maintain their normal routine without this constant weariness. I think Dr. Horatio's mixture might be worth a try. Besides, were the contents merely whiskey, I doubt whether these girls would be having such impressive results. The fact that Mrs. Paxton can't keep it in stock is evidence of its benefit."

"Mr. McCorkey could na keep enough ale in the pub on pay-day either, but that did na mean the ale was helpin' them what was drinkin' it." Kiara held the bottle at arm's length and examined the label, which was emblazoned with the picture of a distinguished-looking bearded man. "I'm thinkin' your Dr. Horatio's elixir is no different than Mr. McCorkey's ale."

Jasmine took back the bottle. "And I'm certain Mrs. Paxton wouldn't sell alcoholic spirits. I know for a fact that she's an upstanding member of the Lowell Temperance Union and extremely opposed to the use of intoxicants." Jasmine moved closer to Kiara and lowered her voice. "My grandmother told me that Mrs. Paxton's father was an alcoholic and very mean to her. Furthermore, Mrs. Paxton blames his early death upon his drinking habits. Under the circumstances, I don't think you'd find her willing to sell alcoholic substances."

Kiara handed a bobbin of thread to Jasmine without further comment regarding Dr. Horatio's Spice of Life. "I believe this thread will do nicely."

Jasmine nodded her agreement, ignored Kiara's disapproving look, and added two bottles of elixir to the pile of lace-making supplies. "Now let's go look over the materials for your new dresses." Kiara followed Jasmine across the store.

"Why, Mrs. Brighton," Jasmine exclaimed as she turned a corner. "I've not had a chance to speak with you since returning to Lowell."

Elinor Brighton smiled in greeting, but her eyes remained filled with grief. "Yes, it has been quite some time. How are you?"

"I'm doing well, thank you for asking." Jasmine turned to Kiara. "This is Kiara O'Neill. She's working for us now."

Kiara curtsied. "Pleased to meet ya, ma'am."

"Thank you."

"Kiara makes lace," Jasmine said, anxious for something else to say. "We've come for supplies."

"I learned to tat a bit when I was a girl," Elinor told them. "I'm sure I've forgotten much of what I learned for lack of practice."

"No doubt it would come back to ya, ma'am."

Elinor seemed to consider the statement. "Yes, you are probably right." She sighed and looked once again to Jasmine. "I must be on my way. I do bid you have a good day, Mrs. Houston."

"And you, Mrs. Brighton."

Jasmine waited until Elinor had exited the store before turning to Kiara. "There is a sad soul to be sure. She has lost two husbands in a short span of time, and she has not even one child to offer her comfort in their passing."

"Poor thing. She's quite a beauty, even in her sorrow," Kiara said softly.

"Yes, she is," Jasmine agreed, thinking how tragic that Elinor should so pine for her dead husband while Jasmine could barely endure the sight of Bradley.

"There'll be no comfort for her," Kiara said, shaking her head. "Me ma was that way when Da passed on. He took her broken heart to the grave, same as Mrs. Brighton's husband has done for her."

Jasmine felt strangely sad to know that such a thing would never be her fate with Bradley. Bradley would never break her heart—because she'd never give it to him in the first place.

———

Over the past three days, Bradley had diligently worked on the accounts in his Boston shipping office and was thankful the Associates were assembling for dinner this evening before commencement of the series of meetings scheduled over the next few days.

He was in desperate need of a diversion from the tiresome columns of numbers. Not that his time hadn't been well spent. The accounts of Bradley's oceangoing business now reflected the company's profits and losses over the past six months—at least in the manner in which he desired to have them appear. There remained a number of documents that required his attention, but he would attend to those after his meetings with the Associates had concluded.

He slipped into his waistcoat and checked his appearance in the mirror. Passable, he decided, for a dinner meeting in the hostelry. He walked down the wide staircase of the newly constructed hotel, thankful both the dinner and meeting would be held in the dining room of the facility.

He waved a greeting to Matthew Cheever and James Morgan, who were entering the door as he reached the foyer. "Gentlemen, good to see you. I trust your journey from Lowell was pleasant."

"We looked for you on the train," Matthew said. "You must have come in earlier this morning."

"I arrived several days ago—business with my shipping company that needed attention," he explained. "We might as well go into the dining room and see if any of the others have arrived. Personally, I could use a glass of port."

Bradley gave James a gentle poke in the side as they entered the dining room. "Looks like quite a few of our members were anxious for a glass of port."

"Either that or anxious to solicit one another's votes on impending issues," James said.

"Speaking of concerns, I'm hoping you'll join with me when Robert Woolsey begins pushing for more railroads."

"I didn't realize Robert was going to become a strong proponent for additional rail lines."

"It only stands to reason. He and Tracy Jackson were the strongest proponents of the railroad from the very start. Now, with Tracy's death, he'll likely propose increased railroad usage as some sort of memorial for him. I'm certain he'll think such a concept will garner sympathy votes. Of course, you and I know the only reason he'll be pushing the railroad is because he's so heavily invested."

James peered over the top of his wire-rimmed spectacles. "We're all a bit self-serving, aren't we, Bradley? Besides, with Nathan now partial owner of a shipping line, I'm sure he'll be swaying the members in a direction that will please you."

"Perhaps, but I've grown to believe some of the men have begun to vote in opposition to Nathan for that very reason—they believe his holdings surpass the rest of them, and they've grown jealous of his powerful position."

"You could be correct, although I've not heard such talk. If you'll excuse me, I want to have a word with Leonard."

Bradley watched James walk off and then surveyed the room in an attempt to decide which group of men might be won over to his position. Matthew Cheever was with a small conclave that might possibly shed some light on the evening's agenda. He wended his way through the crowd, stopping to shake hands and exchange civilities with several men along the way. He was only an arm's length away from Matthew when they were summoned to dinner.

Unfortunately, he found himself lodged between two lesser-distinguished Associates. However, instead of becoming disheartened, he used the time advantageously, quickly assessing their views and lobbying their support. By the time the meeting began, he was convinced they would support anything he proposed throughout the meeting. And after several hours of heated argument regarding railroads and seagoing vessels, Bradley was certain he would need their votes.

Bradley's evening of diversion was hastily turning into a nightmare. Feeling he could take no more of the avid support for rail usage, he jumped up from his chair and waved his arm high in the air.

Matthew Cheever gave him a look of exasperation. "I believe we've all heard your opinion on this issue, Bradley. I'd like to move forward and call for a vote."

"Before you do, I believe there are a few matters the members should hear."

"Very well." Matthew motioned for him to come to the front and take the floor.

"As many of you are aware, I have been diligently working to provide our mills with ample cotton to continue production at a steady pace. Much of that cotton comes from the Wainwright plantations; those contracts were implemented with the understanding that the cotton would be shipped on vessels belonging to me or other members of the Boston Associates at a reduced rate. I redirect your attention to this fact because I'm assured that if my wife's family should be required to pay higher prices for shipping their goods, they would consider their contracts invalid and likely return to the English marketplace."

Murmurs of dissension could be heard throughout the room. "Sounds like you're using the family cotton as a bartering tool!" one of the men near the back of the room called out.

Bradley rested his hands upon the table and leaned forward toward the crowd with his jaw tightly clenched. "I'm merely telling you the facts."

Matthew stood and called for silence while motioning the men to be seated. "There's no need to resort to mayhem. We'll resolve nothing by shouting angry accusations. Bradley wanted us to make an informed decision based upon facts that weren't previously known to us. He ought not be the recipient of your anger merely because he's related to the Wainwrights."

"Thank you, Matthew, for your support," Bradley said.

"I didn't mean to imply my support, Bradley. I'm merely offering an explanation."

But apparently his words, along with Nathan's long-winded speech about the cost of additional railroads when ships were already available, had a positive effect upon the men. When the vote was finally taken, the tally was in favor of transporting by ship whenever possible.

Several days later, as Bradley sat in the office of his shipping business, a pleasurable smile crossed his lips. Things had gone very well for him during this journey. He leaned back in his chair thinking of the dark-haired Irish girl at home—thoughts he knew he ought not be having.

"I'll be back later this afternoon," he told the clerk sitting near the door.

He hailed a carriage near the docks and instructed the driver to stop in the business district. After passing several shops, he entered a store specializing in ladies' apparel. When he left the store a short time later, he carried a carefully wrapped blue silk robe under his arm.

"Perhaps she'll be less inclined to move away from me when she sees what I can offer her in return for her affections," Bradley murmured to himself.

CHAPTER · 20

KIARA PULLED Paddy close, her fingers digging into the flesh of his arm. "Ya're hurting me, Kiara." He squirmed, trying to gain his freedom.

"Do ya not realize the consequences of what happened today, Padraig?"

"Aye, but 'twas a mistake, and the horse has only a small cut on his leg. I do na think the master will even notice. Besides, it may be healed before his return."

"Ya best be hopin' that horse is good as the day Master Bradley left this house or that he does na come near the barn. I do na want him gettin' so angry he sells yar papers. I could na bear to have ya taken away from me."

"What else can I say? I did na want the horse to run off and I know I should have made certain the stall was closed. I truly thought it was, Kiara. Ya know I love those horses, and I do na want anything bad to 'appen to them."

"And I do na want anything bad happenin' to *you,* so you best be checkin' those gates two times instead of one," she warned.

"I'll go out and put some more liniment on his leg and make sure he's doing all right. Do na worry so much, Kiara."

She watched her brother run out the door with his flat cap

pulled low over his eyes and his legs flying helter-skelter like a young colt let loose in the pasture. The thought of a future without Paddy was unbearable. Without warning, unbidden tears coursed down her cheeks, and she gave way to the insurmountable sadness that daily filled her. The show of strength she exhibited for her brother's sake crumpled in her solitude, and she wept bitter tears.

"Is it so terrible living here that you are reduced to this level of grief?" Jasmine asked.

Kiara lifted her head and attempted a smile. "I do na mean to seem ungrateful. I'm thankful for yar goodness to me. But I do na know what will happen to Paddy should Master Bradley discover his fancy horse escaped and was running wild for two days—and if that cut does na heal, I fear Master Bradley will sell Paddy's papers of servitude to someone else. I could na live without me brother." The words caused her tears to flow once again.

"You know I would never permit such a thing to happen. If my husband even suggests such a notion, I will vehemently protest his action."

"Thank you, missus. But we both know that if Master Bradley makes up his mind, there's nothing anyone can do that will stop him."

"But I would try," Jasmine vowed. "We'll hope he never finds out about the incident."

Kiara wiped her nose and attempted to cease the hiccuping that had laid claim and was jolting her body with merciless spasms.

"Why don't you and Paddy take some time and go visit your friend Bridgett? I'm sure she'd be delighted to see you, and on a Sunday afternoon she'll not be working. Visiting Bridgett will take your mind off your sorrows."

Kiara brightened at the suggestion. She'd seen Bridgett only once since her arrival, and then it had been for only a short time. Bridgett had managed to find the Houston home and had walked from the Acre to see Kiara and Paddy. That had been only two weeks after they arrived in Lowell. She'd made the visit and told Kiara she'd be starting work at the mills the next day and wouldn't have much time for visiting. Kiara wondered how she liked her new job.

"That would be ever so nice. I'd like to go visitin'."

"Good! We'll take a carriage, and I'll visit with Grandmother while you and Paddy go to the Acre. You can come to Grandmother's when you've finished your visit, and we'll return home. How does that sound?"

Kiara beamed. "That would be grand, ma'am. I'll go out to the barn and fetch Paddy. He'll be needin' to scrub up a wee bit."

"If you'd tell Charles to bring the carriage around once he's hitched the horses, that will save us some time."

"Yes, ma'am," Kiara called over her shoulder as she raced out of the house.

———

Kiara and Paddy jumped down from the carriage when they neared the Acre. "Just follow that street and ask anyone you see if they know your friend," Charles instructed. "All the residents of the Acre know each other."

Kiara took Paddy by the hand and led him through the row of run-down shanties, stopping the first person who looked in her direction. "I'm lookin' for Bridgett Farrell. She lives with her cousin, Rogan Sheehan, and her granna Murphy."

The woman pointed down the street. "Turn right at the end of the street. Third door on the left."

"Thank ya, soul, and God go with ya," Kiara said, hurrying off toward their destination. "Oh, Paddy, I do hope Bridgett's home. We're not likely to soon get this chance again."

Paddy grinned and danced down the street ahead of her, twirling about to face Kiara. "She'll be there. I can feel it in me bones." He turned the corner and ran to the door, knocking several times. Kiara had reached his side when Bridgett opened the door.

"I can na believe me Irish eyes. Kiara O'Neill, get yarself in here and meet me granna Murphy and set a spell. My cousin's gone out to enjoy his Sunday afternoon, but I stayed home with Granna. She has a touch of the gout and needs a bit o' help. I'll put on the kettle, and ya can tell me for sure about life in yar big mansion, and I'll tell ya about life in the Acre and workin' in the mills. Michael O'Donnell lives next door, Paddy. He's about yar age. Get over and meet him. Tell him Bridgett sent ya."

Once Paddy had gone and Bridgett finished brewing a pot of tea, she sat down with Kiara. "Are ya happy and are they treatin' ya well at yar big house?"

"The missus is very kind. She's not much older than me. She lived far away from here on a big farm of some kind until she married the master. She misses her home and family just like I miss Ireland, so we've lots in common."

Granna Murphy appeared to be asleep on the small cot across the room, but Kiara leaned close to Bridgett just in case she might not be sleeping soundly. She didn't want the old woman to hear what she was going to say. "Master Bradley's another kettle o' fish. I do na like the way he looks at me, Bridgett. He frightens me."

Bridgett's eyes widened and filled with concern. "Ya think he might be one who would try and force ya to his bed?"

The sound of Paddy and some other boys playing in the street drifted into the house, causing Kiara to feel even more self-conscious. "That I do. He has evil in his eyes when he looks in my direction. And his wife is a beauty. He has no reason to be lookin' elsewhere. She's gonna give him a wee babe. Ya'd think he'd be content."

"Maybe that's why he's lookin' yar direction. Sometimes when a woman is expectin', she doesn't want her husband a botherin' with 'er."

Kiara shook her head. "I do na think that's it. He's looked at me that way since the first time he laid eyes on me."

"Just keep yar distance whenever ya can, and tell him ya'll tell his wife if he's tryin' to lay a hand on ya," Bridgett whispered.

"I can na tell him that. He'll sell me papers, and then I'd be separated from Paddy."

"It's a bad spot yar in, fer sure, but it was good o' him to let ya come visit me."

"He's gone to Boston. The missus brought us in her carriage

and then went to visit her grandmother across town."

"In her carriage, no less? Well, ain't ya the fancy one?" Bridgett said with a giggle. "I don't believe I've ever had visitors before who came in a carriage."

"What are ya hearin' from Ireland? Is there any relief?" Kiara felt desperate for news. She had no one to write to—no one to give her a word of the homeland.

"The famine is only gettin' worse. Folks dyin' every day from lack of food. It's lucky we are to be here, Kiara. But the Yankee girls in the mills are complainin' about the terrible conditions. They don't know what we've come from, or they'd be thankin' the good Lord for the privilege of the pay they receive every week."

"I heard some of the ladies who come to have tea with the missus talkin' about troubles in the mills. Do they truly keep those windows nailed down so ya can't get a breath of fresh air?"

Bridgett nodded. "Aye. But still 'tis better than starvin' to death in Ireland. They don't quit their jobs 'cause they know there's Irish lasses what would take their place the same day. They don't pay the Irish workers as much as the Yankees, which I do na think is fair, but there's nothin' we can do. If we want to keep our jobs, we keep our mouths shut."

"That hardly seems—" Kiara paused in midsentence.

A blinding shaft of sunlight shone through the door as it opened. Kiara looked toward the entry, where a tall figure stood surrounded by a halo of light. The sun danced across his curly black hair and dappled the mass of locks with streaks of midnight blue.

"Who 'ave we here?" he asked, stepping aside and pushing the door closed behind him.

Kiara took in the man's deep blue eyes and could not help but notice his finely chiseled features and muscular build.

"This is me friend Kiara O'Neill. She's the one what sailed with me from Ireland," Bridgett explained. "And that's her brother, Padraig, outside playing with Michael O'Donnell." Bridgett turned her attention back to Kiara. "This is my cousin, Rogan

Sheehan. He's the one that saved his money to bring me over here." Bridgett's gaze was filled with grateful pride as she gave Rogan a winsome smile.

Rogan motioned her to hush. " 'Twas nothin' special, lass. Quit yer makin' such a fuss. How's Granna doin'?" he asked, looking toward the cot.

"She's been sleeping all afternoon. I let her sleep when she can. At least she's not feelin' the pain when she's having a lie-down."

The three of them visited while the old woman slept, Rogan regaling them with stories of his life since arriving in America, his friendly voice and easy laughter delighting Kiara. He was the kind of man who made her feel very special—although he'd done nothing more than smile and talk.

Kiara glanced toward the window where the sun was beginning a slow descent. "I did na realize it was gettin' so late. I best be on my way so the missus does na worry."

"I wish ya did na have to go," Bridgett said.

"I must na be late, or the missus might na be so generous about lettin' me come again. Besides, it may take me a bit to find the house. I do na know my way about the town."

"In that case, I'll be pleased to take ya and yar brother wherever ya're needin' ta go," Rogan said. "There's no place in Lowell I can na find."

"That's kind of ya, but I do na want to be a bother."

He gave her a jaunty smile and walked to the door. "Ya could na be a bother if ya tried, lass."

Kiara blushed at his flattering remark. Secretly, she was pleased he had offered to spend a little more time in her company.

———

Bradley stormed through the front door with his jaw clenched and his lips set in a tight, thin line. "Where is he?"

Jasmine hurried from the parlor at the sound of her husband's shout. "Bradley! Whatever is wrong? When did you return from Boston?"

"Only a short time ago. Where is Paddy?" His tone remained

strident. He stood before her while slapping his leather riding whip into his palm. "Tell me where he is."

"I thought he was in the barn. I've not seen him."

"Where's his sister? He's likely with her."

"She's in the kitchen helping Sarah and Cook. Supper's nearly ready. I don't think Paddy's in the house."

He strode past her, now slapping the riding whip against his thigh. "Where's the boy?" he barked.

Sarah emerged, her hands quivering at the sight of her employer. "I sent him to town to pick up necessities from the mercantile. He should return shortly. In fact, he's coming now," she said, pointing out the window.

Bradley rushed out the door. His whip came down across Paddy's back full force, scattering the contents of Sarah's basket of goods in all directions. He continued the flogging while screaming and cursing at Padraig until Kiara could take no more. She raced into the yard and attempted to grasp Bradley's arm, but to no avail.

"You can't even properly care for my horse after all I've done for you, you worthless good-for-nothing!" he yelled. "I'm gone for a week and come home to find my prize animal with a gash on his leg. I think I'll sell your papers so you'll find out what it's like to *really* work for a living. I'll send you down south to live on the Wainwright plantation, where you can spend your time in the hot sun picking cotton and hoeing weeds. You'll spend all your time out in those fields wishing you were back caring for my horses. They'll lay the lash to your backside until it's raw, and if you dare try to run away, they'll slice the back of your ankle so you'll never walk right again."

"Ya don't even know what happened and—" Padraig stopped short with his argument. " 'Tis sorry I am. Ya're right. The horse's injury is all me fault. I promise if ya'll just give me one more chance, I'll do better and ya won't have to be worryin' about such a thing ever happenin' again."

The boy's abrupt change of heart surprised Bradley, and he hesitated a moment before replying. "I'll give it some thought and let you know what I decide." Turning abruptly, he caught sight of

Kiara motioning to her brother. She'd obviously signaled the boy to cease his argument. The fear in her eyes reinforced what he already knew: Kiara's greatest fear was separation from her brother.

"Pick up these things and get back in the house and tend to your duties, girl. You've no business out here. And you get back to the barn. There's muck that needs to be shoveled," he snarled at Padraig.

Bradley watched the brother and sister exchange looks before hastening off to do his bidding. He followed Kiara at a distance, enjoying the sway of her hips as she preceded him into the house. There was a degree of satisfaction in knowing the power he possessed over her.

Jasmine was pacing in the hallway when Bradley returned to the parlor. "Come and sit down. I don't want you to tire yourself. How have you fared during my absence? No problems with illness, I trust?"

She seated herself on the brocade-covered sewing rocker and picked up her needlepoint. "I've been well," she replied in a soft voice.

"Good! We don't want any problems with the babe. I want you to continue taking excellent care of yourself. I want a healthy son."

"What about a healthy daughter?"

He frowned at the question. "Is your question an attempt to snuff out the pleasure I derive from anticipating the birth of a *son*?"

She looked up from her stitching. "No, but I do want you to accept the possibility of a daughter. It is my hope that you would not be overly disappointed by the birth of a healthy daughter."

"There's no need to dwell on such a thought. I'll deal with the issue of a daughter only if and when I'm forced to do so. Shall we go in for supper?"

Jasmine remained quiet throughout supper, obviously angered by his earlier remarks. Irked by her behavior, he excused himself after the meal and retreated to his library. He remained there until the house was dark. Once he was certain Jasmine and the others had retired for the night, he removed the package from his satchel, made his way to the back stairway, and climbed to the third-floor attic room. Without knocking, he shoved his way into the room where Kiara lay on the bed. The sight of him caused her to bolt upright. Ripping away the paper, he tossed the silk robe onto her bed.

"It's a gift—for you. Put it on. I want to see how you look in it," he commanded.

Kiara lifted the robe between her finger and thumb as though it were infected with impurity. Her voice trembled. "I . . . do . . . na want your gift. T-take it to yar wife—she's the one ya should be givin' such a thing as this."

Bradley removed his jacket, taking pleasure in the fear that filled her eyes. He yanked at his shirt, pulling it free.

"Do na go any farther. Ya may own my papers, but that does na give ya rights to any more than me labor."

Bradley smirked. "Then you may consider this a part of your labor, because one thing is certain—I'll have my way with you."

"Ya best not be tryin', or I'll scratch yar eyes out."

"Only if you want to bid your brother farewell. I'm sure the lad will find life on a cotton plantation much less to his liking than caring for the horses with his sister close at hand."

Recognition shone in her eyes. "So that's how it's to be."

Bradley continued removing his clothes as she cowered on the bed, pulling the coverlet up around her neck. "Yes, my sweet Kiara. If you want to keep your brother with you, you'll do as I say and keep your mouth shut." He grasped her cheeks, squeezing them between his thumb and fingers as he pulled her forward and forced his lips upon hers. She cringed but did not fight. Her surrender pleased him. Explaining scratches or other evidence of a scuffle to his wife could prove problematic.

A short time later, he left her bed. "I really should thank your brother for his irresponsible behavior. How else could I be assured of a future filled with pleasurable nights?" He smiled down at her form. Her body was curled into a quivering mass, with the covers pulled over her head.

CHAPTER · *21*

A KNOCK SOUNDED at the front door, and Jasmine watched Kiara bound out of the parlor at breakneck speed.

"Good afternoon, my dear," Alice greeted as she entered the parlor a moment later. "I decided if I was ever going to have a nice long chat with you, I'd have to come to your house since you don't seem to find time to come to mine. The only trouble is that I cannot stay long, so our chat will have to be brief."

Jasmine opened her arms to receive her grandmother's embrace. "I promise I'll come see you next Sunday afternoon. Bradley will be in Boston. Perhaps you'd like to come along, Kiara," she said to the girl as she gathered her lace-making supplies. "You could go and visit Bridgett. You could even send a note to let her know your plans."

Kiara brightened. "That would be very nice. I'll be leavin' the two of ya alone for yar visit. I've some chores that need attention."

"I was going to show Grandmother your lace."

"I've not enough done to be showin' to anyone," she said. "But thank ya for the thought," she added before leaving the room.

Jasmine wagged her head back and forth. "I don't know what's come over her. She's become so moody of late. For the life of me,

I can't determine what's amiss. I've asked on numerous occasions, but she merely says there's nothing wrong."

"Strange," Alice remarked. "Perhaps it's just your imagination. Has Bradley mentioned the fact that she's been irritable?"

"I doubt that he'd be any kind of judge of another person's level of irritability. There's been no making him happy of late either. Seems he's constantly finding something that makes him temperamental. Between the two of them, I don't know which is the more changeable. Kiara is sad and withdrawn, while Bradley is angry and explosive."

"Seems strange you'd see such dramatic changes in *both* of them. You do understand that women in your condition become temperamental, don't you? Perhaps it's you that's experiencing changes rather than them."

"I don't think Bradley's shouting vituperations could be considered a change in *my* behavior, Grandmother."

Alice's features knit into a tight frown. "Something must have occurred to cause such radical changes. You can think of nothing?"

"There was an incident a while back when Bradley was in Boston. Paddy had failed to latch one of the stalls and Bradley's prize horse ran off. By the time Bradley returned, the horse was safely back in the stable, but it did have a cut on its leg. Bradley thrashed Paddy with his horsewhip."

"I'm sure Kiara must have been distraught over the whipping."

Jasmine bobbed her head in agreement. "Yes, but I thought she'd gotten over the incident. Paddy's the one who suffered the flogging, and he seems to have forgotten the entire matter."

"It seems improbable Bradley's change in behavior would be connected to that episode. I had hoped to hear you were happier in your marriage."

"I've accepted my station in life, Grandmother. I am pleased I will have a child to love. And, if it's a boy, Bradley will be pleased."

"He'll be every bit as happy should you bear him a daughter. Men always say they want sons, but they love their daughters as well."

"Either way, I think children will make a difference for both of us, and I certainly cannot say I've always felt that way. At first I simply did not want Bradley's children, but then I realized I was being completely selfish. This baby didn't ask to be the son or daughter of such a ruthless man."

"Children are a wonderful gift, Jasmine, but strengthening your relationship with God might prove of greater benefit right now. Drawing closer to God might also help your marriage. Bradley doesn't seem like such a poor husband. He may well be gruff and unreasonable at times, but all men are." She smiled as if she'd shared a great secret. "Why not use this time before the child comes to deepen your beliefs so that when difficult times come, you can lean upon the Lord, knowing He'll see you through? Spending time with the Lord each morning is the best part of my day—and the most beneficial."

"I hope I've already seen my difficult times, Grandmother. Along with marrying a man I do not love, I'm deeply disappointed in my father, I'm constantly worrying over Mother's mental condition, and I've had to give up Mammy. Added to this now it appears as if I've lost Kiara's friendship. I've prayed about all of these matters, Grandmother, but to no avail. I'm beginning to think God has designated me as his female Job."

Alice gave a hearty chuckle. "Oh, my dear, I hardly think your difficulties are any match for Job's, for along with your difficulties, you're also enjoying some wonderful events in your life. Why don't you try what I've suggested for a month and see if it helps?"

"I'll try," Jasmine agreed. "Have you seen Lilly and Violet recently? I had hoped to see them at the tea last week but was ill that afternoon and unable to attend. Bradley was in a complete rage when he discovered I hadn't attended. He feels it's absolutely essential that I be present for every gathering of the wives."

"I'm sure he wants to become more widely accepted here in Lowell and feels you can accomplish much on his behalf, especially among the Associates' wives. Incidentally, Lilly invited me for tea last Wednesday, and we had a nice visit."

"Did she mention anything about the mills or the Associates?

Bradley seems to enjoy hearing any tidbits I glean regarding the business. Perhaps it would cheer him this evening if I could give him a report of some recent occurrences."

Alice closed her eyes and leaned her head against the back of the divan for a moment. Suddenly her eyelids snapped open and her eyes sparkled with excitement. "As a matter of fact, she did mention the mill girls. I think she feels a deep affinity for those working girls, since she once worked in the mills. Apparently many of the girls have been sickly and not keeping a good pace with their work."

"Yes. I heard the same thing when I was shopping last week. Apparently many of the girls were unable to work due to sickness. The supervisors feared they had contracted some unknown ailment and it was being passed among them. The Associates were concerned production was going to decrease if the girls couldn't report for work."

"That's exactly what Lilly told me. It appears the girls have had a recent boost in energy and are back on their regular work schedules with production at an all-time high. Lilly related the girls have begun taking Dr. Horatio's Spice of Life elixir and credit the tonic to their renewed vigor. She said the supervisors even plan to suggest the Associates purchase the tonic and have all of the girls begin taking it on a daily basis."

"I purchased some of that very tonic at Paxton's. I was going to try it, but when we got home from town, Kiara put my purchases away and I've not seen the bottles since. I completely forgot about the tonic. I'll have to look for it. This information should please Bradley."

"I do hope it helps. Now I really must be going home, but don't forget your promise to visit on Sunday. I'll be expecting you."

Jasmine walked alongside her grandmother into the hallway and embraced her. "Thank you for coming, Grandmother. I look forward to seeing you again on Sunday."

Alice patted her cheek. "And don't forget your promise to meet with the Lord each morning before you begin your day."

Jasmine smiled. "I remember."

She stood in the doorway until her grandmother's carriage had pulled away before returning to the parlor. With renewed enthusiasm, she picked up her stitching. She was almost anxious for Bradley's return, pleased she would have news to share with him that might create a renewed sense of unity between them.

———————

As usual, Bradley's mood was sour when he returned home, and although she greeted him with a kiss, he stalked off toward the kitchen. She didn't see him again until supper was served.

"I have some news to share with you," she said.

He gave her a cursory glance. "What news would *you* have?"

She related the information in her most animated voice, hoping to elicit a positive response from him. Instead, he slammed his fork onto the table and locked her expectant gaze in an icy glare.

"You see how much information is to be gained by mingling with these women? We are constantly excluded by the socially elite here in Lowell, while your grandmother receives invitations to so many functions she's unable to attend them all. It's obvious you don't know how to carry on a proper conversation with women who are accustomed to an industrialized city and can intelligently discuss the manufacturing business. If you were a proper wife, you'd know how to converse about something other than the latest English fashions. I want you to begin entertaining these women, become more like them, and listen and learn from them so that my stature will be enhanced with the Associates. Your lack of sophistication is a detriment to my future and the cause of our ostracism from important social functions."

"You forget I capably hosted a tea for you and discussed many issues concerning the mills. If you'll recall, there were many words of praise for your efforts on behalf of the Corporation during that gathering. I related all that information to you, along with talk of the speedup of the looms. Have you forgotten?"

Bradley scowled, and it only served to make his appearance even less appealing to Jasmine. "You believe acting as my hostess on one occasion is what I expect of you? You think gathering information at a single meeting is all that I need from you? If so, you're even more of a detriment than I imagined."

"I thought you would be pleased," she whispered. She folded her hands and lowered her gaze.

"I would be pleased if you would attend these functions yourself rather than relying upon bits and pieces randomly gathered by your grandmother."

Jasmine swallowed hard. She didn't want to cry. "I'll invite the ladies for tea next week. I promise."

Bradley grunted and pushed away from the table. "You look as though you're not taking proper care of yourself. You're pale and appear sickly. Are you attempting to injure my unborn son in an effort to cause me distress?"

Jasmine looked up in disbelief. "How could you think I would do such a thing? I want this child even more than you do."

He didn't answer. Instead, he stomped out of the room without another word. She remained in the parlor all evening until she finally accepted the fact that he was not going to join her.

I don't understand any of this, she thought. *Even when I think I'm doing the proper thing—the pleasing thing—he destroys it before my very eyes. Destroys me.* Jasmine looked at her needlework and realized she'd hopelessly knotted the thread. She tried diligently to free the tangles, murmuring a prayer as she did.

"Father, I don't know what to do. I'm not even sure that my prayers are being heard. Something is very wrong here, and I don't know how to make it right. Please help me."

The threads refused to budge. Exasperated, Jasmine set aside her handiwork. "I might as well go to bed," she muttered, wondering what had become of her husband.

Gathering her skirts, she went upstairs to prepare for bed. As she walked past her dressing table, she caught sight of herself in the mirror. Bradley was right. There were circles under her eyes, and her complexion was pasty. She searched through the drawers in the large dresser until she felt the smooth glass bottles filled with Dr. Horatio's Spice of Life elixir. Kiara had hidden the remedy beneath her undergarments in the bottom drawer. Since Kiara was the one to lay out Jasmine's clothing, she probably presumed that Jasmine would never dig through the drawers for any reason.

Jasmine pulled out one of the bottles and unstopped the cork. Taking a long drink, she started at the taste. She frowned and looked at the bottle. Kiara had suggested it was most likely nothing more than herbs and whiskey. Jasmine had once tasted brandy at Christmas and she had to admit the flavor was somewhat similar. Especially the way it burned her throat.

"I can bear the bitter taste," she told herself, "if it will give me the energy I need." She slipped into her nightgown, climbed into bed, and pulled the covers up to her chin. Unable to sleep, she tossed and turned, waiting to hear Bradley enter the door to his adjoining room. But, as was becoming his habit, it was late into the night before Jasmine heard his door unlatch.

———

When Bradley departed the next morning without bidding her farewell, Jasmine assumed he was still angry. However, she was pleased to find Kiara's mood had improved when she went downstairs later that morning. And by the time Sunday arrived, Kiara actually seemed her old self.

Jasmine pulled on her kid gloves as they neared the front door. "I hope you don't mind leaving early this morning. I'd like to surprise Grandmother and attend church with her since Bradley is in Boston."

"Yar husband will na be unhappy with yar decision to attend the Methodist church?"

"Bradley attends the Episcopal church because that's where he believes it's best to be seen, not because he has deep beliefs in the church—or in God, for that matter. He ought not take issue if I miss one Sunday."

"We should arrive in time for Paddy and me to attend St. Patrick's with Bridgett. At least I'm hopin' we will. It will be good to be goin' to church again."

"You could ride to town with us on Sundays and attend every

week if you like. I had no idea you wanted to attend church, Kiara. I'll speak to Bradley upon his return."

"No. Please do na speak to your husband. Things is fine just as they are."

Jasmine thought she detected fear in the girl's eyes, yet why would her suggestion cause misgivings? "I'll do as you ask, but should you change your mind, please let me know."

"That I will, ma'am, and I'll be thankin' ya for abidin' by me wishes."

Once Kiara and Paddy had been delivered, the carriage driver followed Jasmine's directions to the Methodist church on Suffolk Street. Their timing would be just right.

Hurrying from the carriage, Jasmine climbed the steps to the open door. She stood in the rear of the church and scanned the heads of the worshipers, seeking her grandmother's perfectly coifed cotton-white hair. Her eyes sparkled with delight when she finally located the familiar sight. By the time she reached her grandmother's side, a bright smile was tugging at her lips.

"May I join you?" she whispered.

Alice embraced her before scooting down the pew. "I'm *so* pleased you're here," Alice whispered in return.

Jasmine's fingers clenched around the hard oak wood of the church pew as Reverend Wells announced he would preach from the book of Job. "There is much we can learn from Job's trials and tribulations. Job was a man who had everything men seek: he had good health; a good wife; children, both sons and daughters; an abundance of land and animals. And he was wealthy. Most importantly, Job loved the Lord. Because of his love for God, do you wonder how he managed to maintain that trust? I honestly doubt we can even imagine the depth of Job's suffering," the preacher said.

Jasmine gave her grandmother a sidelong glance before returning her full attention to the preacher. She listened intently, wondering if God had designed this message especially with her in mind.

"When difficulties enter our lives, we are quick to shake a finger toward the heavens and ask why God has permitted something tragic to occur in our lives. We wonder why we should be plagued by suffering or pain when God can prevent such occurrences. Surely these events should be suffered by someone who doesn't love the Lord, instead of us."

"Exactly my thoughts," Jasmine whispered to her grandmother.

Alice placed a gloved finger to her pursed lips and issued a soft shushing sound in Jasmine's direction.

"We must remember that God can and often does prevent misery and disaster from entering our lives. But at those times when God does not intervene and troubles befall us, He will use those circumstances to His glory if we will only trust Him. Just as Job's friends forgot, we also tend to forget that God's character and nature is love. Out of our need we come to Him; we seek His face and unburden our hearts.

"Near the end of Job's suffering, he admits to the Lord that he, Job, spoke of things he did not understand, things too wonderful for him to know. He tells God, 'I have heard of thee by the hearing of the ear: but now mine eye seeth thee.' Just think of the excitement and pleasure Job experienced! Although God had not prevented Satan from causing Job pain and suffering, Job grew even closer to Him. And what can we learn from this?"

Jasmine glanced heavenward. "To enjoy our misery?" she whispered.

The preacher looked out over the congregation. "If we will soften our hearts, there is much to learn. God is waiting, anxious to draw closer."

Alice tapped Jasmine on the arm and tipped her head ever so slightly toward the preacher.

"God can use our trials to allow us to see Him and to know His character. In the midst of difficulties, we often forget the equation of time. We often think of 'poor Job'—but I would submit that Job was blessed. The Scriptures clearly point to the fact that Job was blessed in his early life, but in the latter portion of his life his blessings were *doubled*. Yes, God permitted Job to suffer, but

Job reaped many benefits, the greatest of which was a closer relationship with God. When trials come, my children, remember the blessings that follow as we, too, spend time with our Lord."

————————

They were seated at her grandmother's table beginning their noonday meal when Jasmine commented how much she had been enjoying her time with God each morning. "I must admit the sermon this morning appeared to have been intended specifically for me. For a moment I wondered if you had divulged my difficulties to Reverend Wells," she said with a giggle, then quickly sobered. "I wish I could report that I see evidence of matters easing between Bradley and me."

"It's only been a few days, dear. Why not wait until the end of the month before admitting defeat."

"I know you're right, but it's quite difficult. When I related your information about the mill girls to Bradley, instead of being pleased, he chastised me because I hadn't personally attended the tea. He became very angry and stormed from the room after accusing me of attempting to hurt our unborn child by not properly caring for myself. His temper frightens me at times."

Alice nodded as she forked a piece of chicken onto her plate. "Since our talk the other day, I've given some thought to our discussion. It has occurred to me that Bradley is under a great deal of stress with all of the expectations placed upon him in his new position: the acquisition of new Southern cotton producers and his responsibility for coordinating shipments—and then there's his own shipping business to deal with also. I'm wondering if it has all become too much for him."

"You may be correct. I hadn't given thought to the fact that he's had to deal with many new situations since our marriage."

"I'm thinking that I could write a letter to your father and suggest he have someone else coordinate the cotton shipments and even work toward developing new connections among other growers. Possibly one of your brothers. If your father agrees, Bradley would have more free time to devote to his other duties with the Associates, and he could spend more time at home."

Jasmine could well imagine the workload that awaited Bradley each day. And while she couldn't bring herself to admit love for her husband, she did feel compassion for his needs. "I believe such a plan may very well be what Bradley needs to help him relax and deal with matters in a less agitated state. I've agreed to hostess a tea next week, and I'll do all within my power to attend any of the upcoming events organized by the Associates' wives. Perhaps you could also help me by taking me along to some of your public engagements. That way my introduction into proper Lowell society will be accomplished more quickly."

Alice nodded. "I believe we've developed a workable plan. With prayer and hard work, we may be able to smooth the troubled waters you've experienced these last few months."

Jasmine felt as though a weight had been lifted from her shoulders. "Thank you, Grandmother. I can't tell you how much better I feel. And Kiara seems happier also." She lifted her handbag and removed a small piece of lace. "Look what I've brought along to show you," she said, holding the piece of lace in the palm of her hand. "Kiara fashioned this as an insert for the neckline of my plum silk gown. Have you ever seen such exquisite work?"

Alice carefully examined the intricate pattern, turning it in all directions. "This compares with the finest European laces. Are you certain she made this?"

"Indeed. We went into Lowell and purchased the supplies. During Bradley's absences, she sits with me and works on the lace while I'm doing my needlepoint. It's slow and painstaking to create even this small piece, yet she seems to thoroughly enjoy the task."

"There's every reason to believe she could earn enough to support herself once her servitude has been completed. She should create as much as possible while she's living with you. She can sell it and save her money for the future. The lace will sell itself, and cost will be no object. The affluent women will beg to purchase it. When she has a piece she's prepared to sell, let me show it to some of my friends. I'll have more orders than she can supply."

"I'm certain your news will boost her spirits. I love having both Kiara and Paddy with us, but I know she would be much happier living in the Acre with Bridgett and the other Irish immigrants. She has more in common with them. Not long ago I mentioned Kiara's unhappiness to Bradley and suggested he tear up their papers and give both of them their freedom. That, however, was a terrible mistake." Jasmine shivered. "His angry outburst was dreadful."

"One thing you must learn, my dear," her grandmother said carefully. "No man likes to be dictated to by his wife. You must learn more subtle ways of persuasion. Make him think it's his idea—or someone else of import. The less you try to impose or insist upon your own will, the happier you'll be."

Jasmine now fully recognized the truth of her grandmother's words. Nolan, too, had tried to caution her to do this very thing. Apparently it was advice that merited consideration.

To Jasmine's surprise, her first guest of the day was none other than Elinor Brighton. The young woman stood on the threshold looking much displaced—almost startled to find herself in such a position.

"Good day, Mrs. Brighton. I'm so glad you could come," Jasmine said from the foyer where she stood ready to greet her guests.

"I hadn't thought to come until the last possible moment. I'm sorry that I could send no word."

"Nonsense," Jasmine declared. "We have more than enough food and plenty of room. You are very welcome here." She again thought of the sorrow Mrs. Brighton had been forced to endure. Still, the woman appeared quite capable and strong.

"I haven't yet had a chance to offer my condolences. I am sorry for your loss. I pray God gives you strength to endure your sorrows."

Elinor stiffened and her expression grew almost ugly. "God has long since forgotten my existence—at least I hope He has, lest He suffer any more horrors upon me."

The bitter words so startled Jasmine that she actually took a step backward. "I . . . well, that is . . ."

"Jasmine, don't you look lovely," her grandmother declared as she entered the house.

Jasmine looked to the older woman's smiling face and then back to Elinor, whose countenance had once again taken on a look of serenity. For a moment Jasmine almost wondered if she'd imagined the entire episode, but a remnant of hardness around Elinor's eyes left Jasmine little doubt that the widow had spoken her harsh declaration.

Jasmine's guests began to arrive in groups of two or three, and suddenly there was no more time to consider Elinor Brighton and her feelings toward God. Jasmine did her best to greet each woman with a personal statement.

"Mrs. Harper, I heard that your sister visited last week. I pray you found her in good health."

"Mrs. Donohue, it's so good of you to come. I trust you and Liam have been well?"

Daughtie answered affirmatively and made room for the Cheevers.

"Mrs. Cheever, Violet, I'm so pleased to see you. I was so relieved to hear that little Matthew wasn't injured overmuch when he fell from the tree."

"He suffered no injury from the tree—rather his father's swift deliverance of discipline was perhaps more harsh to his backside than the ground upon which he fell," Lilly Cheever exclaimed.

Violet giggled and added, "Papa has been after Matthew forever to stay out of the trees. Matthew is an absolute reprobate, however. He never listens unless a good spanking accompanies the instruction." Jasmine tried not to cringe at the thought. She could easily recall Bradley's beating of Paddy and wanted no part of the memory. She could only pray that Mr. Cheever had not used a horsewhip in his endeavors to direct his son.

Jasmine sighed with relief as the parlor filled with even more women than had attended her previous tea. Had the turnout been poor, she knew Bradley would fault her.

Fortunately, it wasn't long before Nettie Harper spoke up. "Wilson has developed distressing stomach ailments over the past month. He says there's a new labor movement that has joined both the men and women in an unholy union against the textile industry. Those are *his* words, not mine," she quickly added.

Mary Johnson, one of the supervisors' wives, nodded in agreement. "Michael mentioned the same thing. I'd never tell my husband, but I secretly admire those women who aren't afraid to sign their names to articles being published in *The Voice.*"

"What kind of articles?" Jasmine asked.

"Rather than merely publishing flowery poetry and articles filled with words of praise for their subservient role as they've previously done in *The Offering,* these girls are now stating they believe the female workers should be treated as equals to the men," Nettie explained.

"Well, I for one don't believe that's what the Bible teaches," Wilma Morgan said.

Janet Nash, wife of a supervisor at the locomotive shop, perked to attention. "I've not read in the Bible where it says men and women are to receive dissimilar pay. I believe it says a laborer is worthy of his hire. I interpret that to mean exactly what it says: a laborer should be paid a fair wage. The verse makes no mention of whether the laborer is a man or woman. If the workers are performing identical duties, they should be paid an identical wage. However, I don't believe the girls in the mills should receive the same pay as mechanics and engineers working on the locomotives being built in the Corporation's machine shops. Their work is specialized and requires training."

Mary Johnson fidgeted with her handkerchief, folding it first one direction and then the other. "Have you visited the mills, Janet? Those jobs require training. And there are workers constantly suffering injuries. If it's not a finger being snapped like a twig in one of those monstrous machines, a metal-tipped shuttle is flying across the room with the speed of an arrow and every bit as dangerous, or a girl is scalped when her hair is caught—"

"Do stop this gruesome talk," Rose Montrose interrupted.

"We could argue this issue until next week and still reach no conclusions."

"We're not arguing, Rose. We're exercising our brains by discussing an intellectual issue," Mary asserted. "I've recently read articles by acclaimed doctors who maintain we don't use our minds nearly enough."

Daughtie Donohue walked around one end of the settee and sat down beside Alice Wainwright. "And what of the Irish? They're now working in the mills. None of them, whether man or woman, is paid the equivalent wage of a Yankee mill girl. Are those who are writing articles for *The Voice* making mention of that fact? Are they arguing for the Irish to receive an equal wage, or do they find lesser pay acceptable for those born in Ireland while unacceptable only for themselves?"

Wilma puckered her lips into a bow of tiny creases. "I should have known you'd find reason to sympathize with the Irish, Daughtie. It seems you're determined to address their plight at every turn."

"I'm sorry if you've grown impatient with my pleas, but somebody needs to speak on behalf of the downtrodden, Wilma. I don't limit myself to the Irish. I'd be pleased to address the plight of the Negroes. Even their freedmen aren't permitted the smallest advantage, yet they count themselves blessed because they've broken loose from the shackles of slavery."

"We've taken up collections for those suffering from the famine. The people of Lowell contributed over four hundred dollars for the Irish." Wilma gave a satisfied nod while primly folding her hands and placing them in her lap.

Daughtie tilted her head to one side and smiled. "And I applaud that effort. But what of the Irish living right here in Lowell? And what of the slaves held against their will down South? There is much to be done, Wilma. While that collection of money is admirable, it doesn't begin to address issues that need resolution in the South and right here in Lowell."

"I know we need to do more to help the slaves," Mary chimed in. "I read an article in the Boston newspaper just last week that addressed the issue of Northerners taking a more active role in assisting runaways. While I find the concept frightening, I must admit it is also quite exciting to think of helping someone begin a new life."

"Of course, there may be those among us who don't hold with our views," Rose remarked while turning her attention toward Jasmine. "I believe you and your husband have a slave living right here in your home, don't you?"

Jasmine didn't miss the look of condemnation leveled at her from several directions around the room. She picked at the ivory silk threads embroidered into a spray of meandering flowers that decorated her dress of peach silk. "No, although I will admit she was with us for a time. Mammy was more of a surrogate mother than a slave. I don't say that to lessen the impropriety of owning slaves but rather to explain she was always well cared for. I would have preferred to free her, but *I* do not own her. She is my father's slave. Only *he* has the legal authority to set her free. However, I want all of you to know that I am opposed to slavery. I saw first-hand the poor—no, the outrageous living conditions—in the slave quarters. I had no idea." She shook her head sadly.

"I honestly grew up thinking our slaves were happy," she continued. "I saw no reason to believe otherwise. Mammy was always cheerful and loving. The slaves who worked in the house seemed content, well fed, and always had a smile. I never imagined that they maintained their positive outlooks because it was required of them rather than because of true happiness."

She looked up and met the faces of her accusers. "I saw what my father wanted me to see, and I never questioned whether it was false or true. But now I know the truth—I've seen for myself and I am deeply ashamed to have been a part of such things. I've attended a number of antislavery meetings, as some of you know, and I want to help in any way possible. My grandmother can vouch for the fact that I have embraced the concept of freedom for all men and women."

"Indeed I can," Alice put in. "Jasmine realizes the immorality and impropriety of the issue. Only last week she mentioned the possibility of forming a society to aid runaway slaves, didn't you, dear?"

Jasmine bobbed her head in agreement. "There are enough ladies present right now that we could make a list of those interested in forming such a group."

"Excellent idea! However, I think we should take care, as there are those who would betray confidences. We don't ever want to place a runaway in harm's way," Daughtie said. "Once we have a list of names, we can meet. I may know someone who can assist us with the formation of our group and let us know how we may be of help."

"I agree," Mary remarked. "There are many Northerners, especially those associated with the mills, who speak out against slavery. But in reality, what they're against is the expansion of slavery into additional states. The mills are dependent upon cotton, and cotton can't be grown without slaves."

"I only partially agree with what you've said, Mary," Daughtie replied. "I think cotton *can* be produced without slavery, but there's little doubt it will cut into the profits of the owners of both the plantations and the mills. However, I'm not certain there are many in either group willing to accept a decrease in their own pockets. I believe all of you should be sensitive to your husbands' directives concerning involvement in the antislavery movement. I would only request you prayerfully consider what role you should play in this issue and then follow your heart."

Elinor Brighton got to her feet. "Prayer will do you little good. It has been my experience that a person does better for himself by taking matters into his own hands."

Lilly Cheever came forward. "Elinor, you speak out of your pain. My heart is burdened for you, but I cannot allow you to misguide our sisters. Prayer is a vital tool, ladies. We must each one remember that. There is great power in prayer. I have no doubt in my heart that God has brought us all together in this place for this very purpose and reason.

"Many of you know me and some are less familiar, but when the mills came to this place, I fought hard against them. I was mortified that our beautiful farmlands were being stripped away to make room for horrible brick buildings. It was only through yielding my heart to God that I found any peace at all. Change is not always good, but neither is it always bad. Sometimes we must learn to live in the midst of what we hate with thoughts toward making it better."

"That is well said," Jasmine's grandmother declared. "I can assure you after making my home in the South for more years than I care to remember that working against slavery is a good thing. However, it will come at a price. Whether it be increases in prices for your lovely gowns or reductions in your husbands' salaries—sacrifices will be made. You mustn't rush into this endeavor simply because it sounds noble. This will not be an easy matter. I would admonish each of you to devote yourselves to prayer before we move forward."

Lilly nodded. "I agree."

Jasmine sank back into her chair, wondering if she'd opened Pandora's box without realizing it. Suddenly she felt afraid. What if Bradley learned that she'd instigated an antislavery society? While he may well agree with the premise, she knew he had no problem accepting the institution of slavery when it meant he would make a profit.

When the women had finally departed, Alice sat down to relax for a few moments before taking her leave. "Your social went exceptionally well, Jasmine. The ladies appeared to enjoy themselves, and the conversation was quite stimulating, don't you agree? You'll have much to discuss with Bradley."

"I don't think I'll mention the antislavery issue."

Alice wagged her head back and forth. "I see no need. Except for attending a meeting or donating funds, you'll be unable to assume involvement until after the baby is born."

"I liked Lilly's friend Mrs. Donohue. She isn't afraid to speak her mind, is she?"

Alice laughed. "No. Daughtie cares little what others think. She's a brave woman. Lilly tells me she was reared by the Shakers up in Canterbury and came to Lowell full of courage and conviction—and that has never changed. In fact, she's married to an Irishman. She cared little that many people shunned her because of her choice. Of course, most of them have now accepted her; Lilly Cheever and Bella Manning saw to that. But Lilly tells me there were some rough years."

"I must say that I admire her veracity," Jasmine said.

"As do I. And now I'd best be on my way. I meant to tell you earlier—I did post the letter to your father regarding my concerns about Bradley."

Jasmine gave her grandmother a kiss on the cheek. "Thank you, Grandmother. It's a blessing having you close at hand."

"Tut, tut, dear. That's what grandmothers are for."

C H A P T E R · *22*

KIARA HURRIED off toward town, pleased to be away from the Houston household, if only for a short time. There were no visible locks or bars on the doors, but the home had become her prison just the same. Although Mrs. Houston had readily agreed she could go into town for lace-making supplies, Kiara knew she must be back before suppertime. If Mr. Houston became aware of her treks into Lowell by herself, there was no doubt the mistress would suffer his wrath. Neither of them mentioned the possibility, but they both realized they would be punished for not seeking his permission. They also knew he would not grant his consent if they asked.

She'd sent word to Bridgett she'd be in town, but likely Bridgett would be at work in the mills. However, even a few minutes with her friend would be a pleasure.

Quickening her pace, she hurried into Paxton's and handed the woman the note Mrs. Houston had given her. "I'll be needin' some lace-makin' supplies," Kiara said.

Mrs. Paxton led her to the back of the store, where Kiara had first purchased supplies when she and Jasmine had come to town. "I believe I'll take this thread," she said, pointing toward a bobbin.

"Anything else?"

"No. That's all I'll be needin'."

"You can wait up front. I need to mark my ledger."

Kiara did as she was told, and a short time later, Mrs. Paxton handed over the thread along with another package securely wrapped in brown paper. "Take this to your mistress," she instructed.

"Yes, ma'am, and thank ya for yar help."

She darted out the door and glanced about. Bridgett was nowhere to be seen, but then, it was only five o'clock—too early for the end-of-day bell to be ringing.

"Kiara O'Neill! What are ya doin' in town, lass?"

Rogan Sheehan came alongside her and tipped his cap. "How're ya doin', lass? I asked Bridgett just the other day when we might be seein' ya again."

"I'm doin' as well as can be expected, I suppose. I'd rather be livin' in the Acre with my own people, but me mistress is nice enough. I don't know when I can come visitin' again. The missus lets me come whenever her 'usband is out of town. He's not kindly about grantin' favors to me or Paddy."

Rogan nodded. "Know that ya're welcome whenever ya can come. And bring Paddy with ya. He's a fine lad."

"Thank ya. Tell Bridgett I said 'ello and I'm thinkin' of her."

"That I will, lass."

"I best be hurryin' back before the master gets home."

He tugged at his cap once again and gave her a wide smile. "Ya been a bright spot in me day, lass. Take care o' yarself."

She waved and rushed off, wondering if Rogan Sheehan would think she was such a fine lass if he knew how she was forced to spend her nights. If only she could think of another place where she might hide from Bradley Houston. She'd avoided him for well over a week by hiding each night in the opening beneath the stairs. The space was small and cramped, and she knew it was only a matter of time until he discovered where she was hiding. She knew he was looking; she heard him prowling the house every night after the others were abed. He skulked about like a beast seeking its prey.

"Perhaps I could ask Sarah," she murmured.

The housekeeper had a small corner area off the kitchen with little room for anything more than her narrow bed and a small chest. But Kiara needed only a sliver of space on the floor, and she knew Bradley would never pull aside the curtain and check in the housekeeper's quarters. She wondered if the austere old woman might take pity upon her or instead rush to Bradley and report the Irish girl was making terrible accusations against him. When she delivered the package to the mistress, she would inquire if Mr. Houston would be returning to Boston soon.

Paddy came running around the side of the house as she neared the driveway. "Where ya been, Kiara?"

"Off to take care o' some business fer the missus. I've got no time fer talkin', Paddy. I got to get this package delivered."

"What's wrong with ya, Kiara? Ya're never havin' time fer me anymore. Ya're actin' angry, like I've done somethin' bad. I do na know what's made ya so unhappy with me."

Kiara tousled his black curls and kissed his cheek. "I'm not angry with you, Paddy. There's problems that go on in the house that make life difficult for me. I wish there was some way we could get out o' this place. I wish I could be workin' in the mills and live in the Acre like Bridgett."

"I'm sorry ya're so sad, Kiara. I wish ya liked it here. Except fer missin' Ma and Pa, this is the best place on earth as fer as I'm concerned."

His words tugged at her heart. "I know, Paddy, and I'm thankful fer that. Now get on with ya. I've got to take this to the missus."

He dashed off but then turned around. He hurried back and grabbed her around the waist, giving her a tight squeeze. "I love ya, Kiara."

She held him close for a moment. "And I love ya right back, Paddy O'Neill." He ran off toward the barn, and Kiara hurried into the house with her parcels.

"I've brought ya a package from Mrs. Paxton. She said ya were expectin' it." Kiara handed the parcel to her mistress and hesitated for a moment.

Jasmine held the parcel close but made no move to unwrap it. "Was there something else you needed?"

"I was wonderin' if Mr. Bradley would be goin' to Boston sometime soon?"

Jasmine appeared surprised by the question. "I don't believe he'll be going until sometime next week. Why do you ask?"

"I was thinkin' maybe I could go to visit Bridgett on Sunday if he was goin' ta be in Boston."

"Oh, I see. I think your visit will have to wait until the following Sunday. However, if Bradley should be called out of town before then, I'll be certain to let you go visiting."

"That's fine. Thank ya, ma'am."

She walked out of the room filled with a sense of despair. Spending any more time in that cramped space beneath the stairway would be unbearable. She'd have to take a chance and talk to Sarah.

After helping wash up the supper dishes, Kiara had just begun to make her way down the hallway when a hand clamped around her wrist and pulled her into the parlor and onward into Bradley's library.

He stood with his back against the closed door, his jaw flexing, his teeth clenched in anger. He pulled her against his chest, holding her tight against his body, his arm wrapped around her back. She struggled to free herself, but he grabbed her hair and yanked until her face was turned upward. He forced his mouth on hers, crushing her lips and twisting her arm until she thought it would snap in two. Her scalp ached with pain, and she wondered if he would pull every hair from her head before he was through with her.

"Where have you been hiding? I've been to your room every night, and you've been gone." His grasp on her hair tightened. "Now you listen well, girl. You be in your room when I come to you at night or your brother will be sailing for New Orleans next week to make a new life for himself on a cotton plantation. Do you understand me?"

Fear coursed through her body like a wellspring. "Yes," she whispered.

"You foolish girl. Did you think you could hide from me for the next five years?"

"Bradley? Are you in the library?"

Bradley pushed Kiara away. "I'll join you in a few minutes," he called out, his body still resting against the door. "I'll leave this door slightly ajar when I leave the room. Watch until it's safe for you to exit the other way without being seen. And remember, if anything goes amiss and Jasmine discovers our affection for each other, your brother will be gone and you'll never see him again."

Kiara stared at him in disbelief. "*Our* affection? I detest you."

He chucked her under the chin and gave a husky laugh. "I think Jasmine would believe *me* if I told her you've been attempting to steal my affections. It would be quite easy to convince her you've tried to bargain for your freedom by plying me with your favors."

Kiara remained silent until he departed the room. "Ya're the devil himself," she murmured as she watched him leave the room with his head held high.

Bradley entered the parlor with a sense of jubilation. He had Kiara in his clutches, and there was no way for her to escape. He walked to where his wife was seated, leaned down, and placed a dutiful kiss upon her cheek. "And what did you accomplish today?" he asked.

Jasmine smiled up at him. "You'll be pleased to hear that I went to visit with Lilly Cheever today. She mentioned there's a meeting of the Associates tomorrow."

"Did you think I would not already know there is a meeting, or did you believe me too senile to remember?"

She cowered at his remark. "No, but I was alarmed when she told me there is great concern because many of the mill girls are desperately ill and several have even died. She said the doctors fear there's some sort of epidemic being spread among them."

"Why are you so concerned?" he absently inquired.

"I've seen the horrible results of an epidemic. We fight malaria and suffer dire consequences almost every year in Mississippi."

Bradley glanced over his shoulder in an attempt to see if Kiara had made her way out of the library. There was work that needed his attention and he certainly didn't want to sit in the parlor with his wife for the remainder of the evening. The door remained slightly ajar and he could not make out if she had exited the room.

Following his gaze, Jasmine leaned forward and peered toward the library. "Is something amiss? You keep looking toward the other room."

"Nothing's amiss. You need not concern yourself with my every movement."

She appeared taken aback by his abrupt reply. "I understand the conditions in the mills grow poorer every day," she relayed. "I've been told the windows are nailed shut, and with the steam and humidity in the mills, the fiber-filled air becomes deadly for the girls to breathe. I wonder if the girls are becoming ill because their bodies can no longer tolerate the conditions inside the mills."

Bradley was relieved to note the library door was now open. He wanted nothing more than to escape his wife's company and complete his accounting tasks prior to tomorrow's meeting.

He rubbed the back of his neck and glowered in her direction. "Why are you meddling in matters about which you know nothing? You need to keep out of issues relating to my business."

"What? But I thought you asked me to mingle with the wives and collect information for you. I'm merely doing as you asked. It seems nothing I do can please you."

"I have no time for your childish behavior, Jasmine. I have work to complete." He stormed from the room, knowing she'd not follow after him.

He worked well into the night, transferring and calculating figures, and when he'd finally completed his report for tomorrow's meeting, he was exhausted. He climbed the stairs while giving momentary thought to Kiara. Tomorrow, he decided. He needed his rest if he was to be at his best in the morning. Besides, let her worry when and if he might enter her room.

The little tramp deserves to be sleepless after the way she's led me on a chase.

————————

Bradley arrived at the Cheever home the next morning promptly at nine o'clock. As had been Kirk Boott's custom before him, Matthew Cheever refrained from conducting meetings within the confines of the mills. Too many people could overhear and misinterpret conversations that had never been intended for their ears. Bradley would have preferred they meet in Boston since he had other business that needed his attention in the city. However, Matthew wanted the mill supervisors present at the gathering, and traveling to Boston for a meeting was out of the question for them.

There would be no period of socializing; it was apparent this meeting would be strictly relegated to business. "As most of you know, we've a problem with illness spreading throughout the mills," Matthew began. "Several girls have died, and there's fear of other deaths. The doctors have been unable to find a cause for the epidemic. There appears to be no connection other than the fact that those contracting the illness have been, almost exclusively, girls working in the mills."

"Do the girls who have become ill live in the boarding-houses?" Leonard Montrose inquired.

Matthew shook his head. "Some live in the boardinghouses; some live elsewhere in town; some live in the Acre."

"Any chance it could be the water?" Andrew Smith, one of the supervisors, suggested.

"If it were the water, the rest of us would be ill too. It seems there must be some common thread, but for the life of me, I've been unable to make the connection."

Bradley waved and Matthew nodded for him to speak. "I was hoping we'd have time to discuss expanding several Southern markets."

"Let's stick to the topic at hand," Matthew replied. "We need to focus our attention upon discovering the cause of this illness and hopefully finding a cure."

"Perhaps we should interview the girls and ascertain all of the details related to their illness. We could then compare notes and see if we can discover the common thread Matthew spoke of," Wilson Harper remarked.

"I've located several good prospects in Mississippi as well as in Louisiana who are willing to talk contracts on their cotton," Bradley interjected.

"In light of the fact that we're attempting to solve the mystery of the illnesses and deaths of these mill girls, Bradley, I find your self-serving attitude abrasive," Leonard said.

Bradley scoffed at the remark. "Really? Well, I don't think any of you fine gentlemen were overly concerned about the girls and their illness until production slowed and your profits began to drop. Now that we're experiencing diminished profits, you've donned the cloak of kindness and wave your sword of self-righteousness in my direction. Your behavior emulates my own, whether you care to admit it or not."

"We'll resolve nothing by arguing," Matthew asserted. "Wilson, will you head up a committee to interview the ill workers?"

Wilson nodded his agreement.

"I think we need to be mindful of the fact that some of these girls have little in the way of savings," Matthew continued. "Many, both Yankee and Irish, help support their families with their earnings. Some have no families here in Lowell to help care for them, and certainly few have money to pay for funerals. I think it would behoove us to pay for medical care for the girls and, when necessary, funeral expenses."

A murmur of discontent filtered across the room. "I'm all for trying to find the cause of this illness, but I don't see why you think the Corporation should be saddled with yet another expense when production profits are already down," Leonard objected.

"The better their care, the quicker they'll return to their jobs and the sooner profits will rise," Matthew replied.

"There are more and more Irish arriving every day. All of them are looking for work, and they'll work for lower wages. I say we'd be better off to replace the sick girls with Irish immigrants," Wilson countered.

One of the supervisors stood and asked to be recognized. "No disrespect, gentlemen, but it takes time to train these girls. You can't expect a girl who has never worked in the mills to produce at the level of those who've been working there for months or even years. Production will continue to falter using such a method. I bring this to your attention because I know you'll be looking to the supervisors for answers when you've filled all the positions yet there's no increase in production."

"Exactly my point," Matthew agreed. "Medical care and funeral expenses will be money well spent in goodwill and the return of trained employees."

The men continued their bickering, and it was abundantly obvious to Bradley there would be little time for discussion of his cotton if this matter was not resolved. "I suggest we agree to medical and funeral care but require the girls to sign a covenant agreeing to return to work for a specified period of time or they'll be obligated to repay the costs. The funeral expenses can be a matter of goodwill. We can hope there will be no more deaths, but if so, perhaps you can work out some arrangement with Mr. Morrison at the funeral home, Matthew. Some type of discount for the Corporation if the number of funerals exceeds three or four in the next several months."

"A bit morbid in nature, but I think you've struck upon a good idea," Leonard replied.

In quick order the men reached a consensus. "Now, about my cotton producers," Bradley said, knowing his solution had gained him power for the moment.

———

Kiara heard Bradley's footsteps on the stairs and, like a lamb to the slaughter, knew she must submit to his will. He held her brother's future in his hands, and she could not risk separation from him. Even if she could bear five years apart from him, it would be impossible for Paddy to withstand the rigors of working on a cotton plantation. He would surely die. So she lay quietly, listening for the door to open, awaiting Bradley's arrival like a dreaded curse.

Oh, God, forgive me, she prayed as the door handle turned. *Just keep him from takin' Paddy away. I can bear anything . . . anything but that.*

"I see you have finally taken me seriously," Bradley said, slurring his words badly. No doubt he'd been into his drink this night.

"May God 'ave mercy on yar black soul," Kiara said, scooting up against the wall. "May ya rot in hell for yar sins."

He laughed even as he removed his jacket and began unbuttoning his waistcoat. "I'm already in hell," he replied. "There's nothing more God can do to me. But there's plenty more *I* can do. Especially—" he cast aside his waistcoat, then sat down on the single rickety chair and pulled at his boots—"especially to you." He grinned wickedly, his eyes narrowing.

When he finally left her room, Kiara was buried deep under the covers. Just as she had listened to him make his ascent to her room, she now heard his heavy footsteps descend the staircase. Bitter tears spilled down her cheeks and her body quaked in heaving sobs as she raised a defiant fist from beneath the covers and cried toward heaven: "Why don't ya just kill me if ya care nothin' about what's happenin' in this place? Or must I do that fer meself also? Is that what ya're wantin' from me, God—that I just kill meself and be done with it?" Memories of her mother's admonition that even thinking such thoughts could send her to hell, gave Kiara pause.

Her tears and anger slowly ebbed into the pool of darkness that permeated the room, and for the first time she contemplated death at her own hand. It would be so simple. There were many ways she could attend to the task. Yet when all was said and done, she knew such a feat would prove impossible, for that would leave Paddy alone in the world to fend for himself. And that was a consequence she'd not force him to bear. Nor did she wish to bear further consequences—not in this life or the next.

"My life is over," she whispered into the shroud of blackness. "There's no man who would ever be wantin' the likes of me now—especially a man such as Rogan, with his dreams for a future on a beautiful farm out West."

CHAPTER · 23

KIARA WATCHED in delight from the upstairs window as Bradley handed his satchel to the driver and stepped up into the carriage. Finally he would be gone, and she could go and visit Bridgett on Sunday—and perhaps see Rogan. The thought caused an unexpected smile to tug at her lips. Though she feared there'd be no future for them, Kiara took a moment's pleasure in imagining it just the same. She might as well allow herself to dream—after all, there wasn't anything else she could hope for. As soon as the carriage pulled away from the house, she hurried to Jasmine's room and knocked on the door.

"Are ya ready fer me to fix yar hair, ma'am?"

"Yes, come in."

Kiara carefully brushed and twisted her mistress's hair into the parted and curled fashion Jasmine particularly liked. "I was wonderin' if I could plan on visitin' Bridgett on Sunday."

"Oh, I'm afraid not, Kiara. Bradley will be gone only until Thursday. His plans changed. I'm so sorry. I know I had promised you could go and visit Bridgett."

"I understand. Ya've no control over such things, ma'am."

Jasmine brightened and took Kiara's hand in her own. "I know! You can go tomorrow afternoon."

"Bridgett will be at work, ma'am. I suppose I could visit with Bridgett's granna, though. If I can na see Bridgett, 'twould be nice to see Granna. Yes, I'll go and see her. Thank ya fer yar kindness."

———

After bidding Paddy farewell, Kiara hurried off toward the Acre the next afternoon. She knew the boy longed to come with her, but the horses would need his care, and he dared not leave them unattended.

Jasmine had asked her to stop at Mrs. Paxton's on her way home to pick up a package. She'd even given her coins for more thread since Mrs. Wainwright had already sold a lace-edged handkerchief to one of her socialite friends in Boston, who was now anxious for more. Kiara had carefully tucked away the money and continued diligently working on the lace during her free moments. It was only after seeing the amount of money people were willing to pay for her lace that Kiara began to think of a plan. If she could save her coins, she'd take Paddy and run from this place, servitude papers or not—she'd take her chances with the law. She'd not be able to stay in the Acre, of that she was certain, for the Acre would be the first place Mr. Houston would come looking for her. Living in the Acre with Bridgett and Granna Murphy close at hand was Kiara's desire, but with many Irish immigrants living in Boston, she could surely become acquainted with some of them. Besides, relocating to a larger city would reduce her chances of being discovered.

Kiara arrived in the Acre well before the final bell would toll at the mills. She knocked on the door, expecting to be greeted by Granna Murphy. Instead, Rogan Sheehan welcomed her with a big grin and a hearty greeting. "Come on in, lass. Granna's busy preparin' supper. How is it ya managed to make yar way to the Acre on a weekday?"

Kiara explained Bradley's change in plans. "I knew Bridgett would still be at the mills, but I thought 'twould be nice to visit with Granna, and I'm hopin' I might have a few minutes with Bridgett before I must leave."

Rogan folded his arms across his broad chest, his dark blue eyes alight with an uninhibited cheerfulness. "What a disappointment this has turned out ta be. Here I thought ya were comin' ta see me, and now I find 'tis only the womenfolk ya're wantin' to visit."

She giggled at his response. "I'm happy to see anyone with a bit o' Irish blood."

"Then ya come to the right place," Granna Murphy said while wiping her hands on a worn cotton apron. "Come over here and give me a hug."

Kiara hurried into the old woman's arms, delighting in the warmth of the embrace. "It's good to see you, Granna. I told Rogan I had hoped to come on Sunday, but it appears that won't be happenin'."

"We'll be thankful fer what little time ya get with us. Come on into the kitchen. Ya can be stayin' for supper and visit with Bridgett, and we'll have us a fine time, Sunday or not."

"I do na know if I can stay. I'm supposed to pick up a package for the missus, and I told Paddy I'd spend time with him when I came home. I wanted to leave before his chores were done, so he could na come along."

Rogan sat down on one of the wooden chairs and pushed back until he was balancing the chair on the two back legs. "Once ya think Paddy's had enough time to finish with his chores, we can go back through town and get yar supplies and then go to the house and get him. Do ya think the missus would let ya come back if ya told her I'd walk ya back home?"

Kiara's heart pounded with excitement. "I think she'd agree."

"Then it's settled. After a spell we'll go and get Paddy, and by the time we return, Bridgett will be home and supper will be ready."

"But first sit a spell and visit with me," Granna said, pointing to a chair.

Kiara sat down and pulled a piece of lace from her small tapestry bag. "I hope you do na mind if I work on my lace while we talk."

Granna's eyes danced with mischief. "Ya're an industrious

young lass. Would ya be makin' yarself a weddin' veil?"

"Ah, don' ya be givin' the lass ideas afore I get a chance to win her heart," Rogan teased.

Granna waved her arm as if to shoo him out of the room. "Go on with ya, Rogan. Ya're na lookin' for a wife."

"I'm always lookin' for a lass ta marry me, Granna. I just have na found the right one."

"And likely never will," the old woman replied. "Quit yar teasin' and let me visit with the lass." Granna turned her attention back to Kiara. "That's a pretty pattern ya're making, and fine work ya do." She lifted one edge of the lace and examined it.

Kiara smiled, basking in the compliment of the old Irish woman. "The missus asked me to make lace cuffs for her mum for her birthday. I'm wantin' them to be special. Do ya think she'll like the wild roses I've formed into the lace?"

"Sure and she'll be likin' it, lass. 'Tis a bit of beauty ya're creating. Bridgett used to like to make the lace too, but since she's begun workin' in the mills, there's nothin' much she's wantin' to do when she gets home but sleep. They're workin' long hours, and short of help they are in the mills."

"If I could be spendin' me time workin' in the mills, I'd na be complainin' about anything."

"Ah, lass, ya do na know what ya're saying. Ya have the freedom to move about and go outside when ya're wantin' to; ya can work in a fine house and not a lint-filled room with the windows nailed down—ya should na be thinkin' ya're unhappy in such a fine place."

Kiara could not share the thoughts flashing through her mind—thoughts of the five years she'd have to suffer at the hands of Bradley Houston—so she offered no rebuttal to Granna's argument.

"Aye, and now with all the girls fallin' ill, I worry that our Bridgett will get the sickness. She's worn herself down with all the extra looms she must tend, and she dare na miss a day or there's the devil to pay."

"I heard a bit o' talk about sickness in the mills when some ladies came for tea, but I was helpin' in the kitchen and did na think it was more than a few girls suffering from a stomach ailment or the sniffles. So there's more to the tale?"

"Aye, and I'm wishin' I could be tellin' ya what's causin' the illness, but it seems ta be striking workers in all of the mills. There's been three or four die, all but one of 'em Irish lasses."

Kiara gasped and covered her mouth with her open palm. "That's terrible news, Granna. It's an ill wind that's blowin' over the Irish. Seems we can na escape the cold hand of death."

"Aye, 'tis true. We're a people created fer sufferin' and that's a fact."

Rogan jumped up from his chair and ran his fingers through the thick dark fringe of curls that covered his forehead. "I'll na be listenin' ta such sorrowful talk. 'Tis a fine day, and we should be countin' our blessings instead of sittin' here and mopin' about. I'm gonna go and see if Michael O'Donnell and Timothy Clary will gather up some fiddle players, and we'll have us a time of singin' and dancin' out in the street after supper." He started toward the door and called over his shoulder, "I'll be back to fetch ya in a short time, lass."

"I think the lad's got an eye fer ya," Granna Murphy confided when Rogan had cleared the doorway.

"But ya said he's a lad with a wanderin' eye."

Granna looked up from the pot of stew she was stirring, her lips curving into a sly smile. "Aye, but when the right lass comes along, he'll settle."

"He'll likely find the right lass afore I've completed my five years of servitude, so we best quit our talkin' about 'im."

"Ya might consider visitin' the church more often and gettin' down on yar knees, lass. The Lord knows what's happenin' in yar life, and He's watchin' over ya."

"He was na watchin' over my ma or my pa when they died. And if He cared about me at all, I would na be livin' where I am. I do na think a prayer or two is gonna get the Lord on my side."

"I know ya're unhappy, lass, but do na be blamin' yar troubles on the Lord. It's the devil roamin' around causin' us misery at

TRACIE PETERSON / JUDITH MILLER

every turn. And ya can be sure the devil's likin' it a heap if he can keep ya from prayin'."

Rogan burst through the door, waving a fiddle in the air. "I've taken Timothy Clary's fiddle hostage and told him he'll na get it returned unless he fiddles fer us tonight."

"Ya're a rascal if ever I saw one," Granna scolded.

"Aye, that I am. Are ya ready to fetch yar supplies, lass?"

Kiara nodded and hurried to join him. She kept up with his long-legged stride, taking two steps to his one, and listened to his easy monologue regarding his life in Lowell and the Acre.

"So if it's such a fine job ya have with Liam Donohue, why are ya sittin' about at home today?" she finally asked.

He gave her a lopsided grin and her stomach flip-flopped. "Ya're full of sassy questions, ain't ya, lass? Well, I'll have ya ta know that I been workin' from dawn to late into the night for nigh unto a month now completin' a fine piece o' work, and Liam saw fit to repay me with a few days to enjoy meself. We begin work Monday on another job that will keep me mighty busy too."

"I've heard that name before," she said, thinking for a moment. "I'm thinkin' his wife was at the tea. Would that be possible? Though I do na think she was Irish."

"Aye, she's a Yank—but a fine one fer sure. I been told some of the fine folks do na like her since she married an Irishman. Liam says she has a deep faith and believes what the Bible says. He says she lives her beliefs and does na concern herself with what other people think."

"Good for her." She opened the door of Paxton's and started inside. "Aren't you coming?"

"Most of these shop owners do na like Irish inside. They don't mind when it's a lass who works for a Yank, but they'd rather the rest of us stay away. I'd rather spend my coins in the Acre anyway. Ya go on and make yar purchases, and I'll be waitin' right here when ya come out."

Kiara pulled out the note and handed it to Mrs. Paxton. "I'll go and get my thread while you fill the order," she told the store-keeper.

Mrs. Paxton was wrapping several bottles in heavy brown paper when Kiara returned with the thread. "Is that medicine you're wrapping for the missus?" she asked.

Mrs. Paxton peered over the top of her glasses and down her pointy nose. "If your mistress wanted you to know what was in the package, she would have told you instead of sending me a sealed note."

Ignoring the acerbic remark, Kiara dug into her pocket and placed several coins on the counter. "Here's fer the thread." She took up the parcel and thread and headed for the door. *Just because I'm Irish is no reason to go bein' all uppity.* She would have loved to have spoken the words aloud.

"Let me carry that fer ya," Rogan offered.

The kindness of his gesture delighted her. As she handed him the package, sadness came creeping in without warning, replacing her joy. Determinedly, she pushed it away. At least for this brief time, she would take pleasure in her life. There was no hope that she and Rogan could have a life together. He was a fine God-fearing man, and he would expect a woman of virtue and purity. She could offer him neither. Tears came to her eyes, but she swiped at them quickly and stepped up her pace. There was to be a fine Irish supper and a night of music and dance. She would have the rest of her life to regret Rogan Sheehan, but tonight she would cherish their time together.

CHAPTER · *24*

KIARA LOOKED heavenward at the sound of a loud thud above her head, then raced out of the kitchen, shooting her question at Sarah. "Do ya think the missus has taken a fall?" She took the stairs two at a time and skidded to a halt in front of the closed door. She tapped lightly but didn't wait for an answer before shoving open the door.

"Missus! Oh, Mrs. Houston!" She dropped to her knees beside Jasmine, who lay in a heap alongside the bed. "Speak ta me—are ya all right?"

"Kiara, help me into bed," Jasmine said in a strangled voice.

Sarah came in the door and stopped short at the sight. "What's happened?"

"I do na know. She was on the floor when I came in. Help me get her into bed."

As gently as they could, the two of them lifted Jasmine up into bed. "She feels as though she's taken a fever." Kiara poured water into the basin sitting on the commode and dipped a cloth into the cool water. Gently placing the compress upon Jasmine's forehead, she glanced toward Sarah. "Could ya hand me that bottle on the chest, please?" She covered Jasmine with a thick quilted cover before taking the bottle from Sarah.

"Just as I thought. Dr. Horatio's Spice of Life." The bottle was nearly empty. She took a deep whiff of the contents and ran her finger around the rim of the bottle before taking a taste. "Have ya been drinkin' this?" She held the bottle in Jasmine's view.

Her eyelids fluttered. "It gives me strength," she whispered. The words had barely escaped her lips before she emitted a low guttural groan and drew her body into a tight knot. "I'm having terrible pains. I'm afraid the baby's going to come."

"Don't ya even be thinkin' such a thing. It's only September! It's much too early for the babe to be comin'."

Jasmine wet her dry lips. "It can't live if it's born this soon, can it?"

"I'll na be tellin' ya a lie, missus. There's no way it would live, so you best be stayin' put in that bed. I'm goin' downstairs and try and mix up some herbs that might be o' help. How much of this have ya been drinkin'?"

"I take a couple of spoonfuls every few hours."

"Is this all ya have left?"

"No. There's more in the drawer."

Kiara opened the bottom dresser drawer. It was filled with Spice of Life glass bottles—all empty, except for one. "How did ya get all of . . ." She hesitated a moment, suddenly realizing what she had been carrying home in the paper-wrapped packages. "Is *this* what I've been bringin' to ya every time I went to Paxton's and bought my thread?"

Jasmine nodded. "I knew you disapproved, but without the medicine, I didn't have enough energy to meet Bradley's expectations for a proper wife."

Kiara seethed at the comment. *Bradley!* Self-centered, egotistical Bradley. Mrs. Houston had played the perfect wife, entertaining at weekly teas and attending all the fashionable parties in an attempt to please him. It now seemed that losing his heir might be the price for meeting those demands.

She raced upstairs to the attic room and hurriedly clawed through one of her worn satchels until the feel of slick, cool glass greeted her fingertips. Grasping the tiny bottles in her palm, she flew down the three flights of stairs and hurried into the kitchen. She silently prayed the few herbal compounds she'd brought from Ireland would provide a panacea to counteract the effects of the elixir. Taking great care, she measured and mixed the herbs and was preparing to add warm water to a tonic she hoped would aid her mistress when Bradley caught her around the waist.

"You weren't in your room last night."

"Paddy was na feelin' well, and I went to look in on him."

"You're lying. You were hiding from me. You think I won't keep my word and get rid of the boy. I don't need to wait for a journey to Boston to send him away. I could take him to work in the mills tomorrow. There's not a supervisor who wouldn't take him off my hands and put him to work on one of those monstrous carding machines. Of course, he'd likely end up losing an arm, but since you obviously care little about what happens to him, that wouldn't bother you."

"Get away from me! Your wife is ill and I'm fixin' medicine to help her. Instead of thinkin' of yarself, ya should be worryin' over her."

He drew back his arm in a wide arc. She flinched, expecting to feel the powerful whack of his hand. Unexpectedly, his arm remained extended in the half-moon position. "What's wrong with Jasmine?" He glared down at her as though the announcement of his wife's illness had just registered in his mind.

"I'm fearin' the babe may be comin' before its time. You best be ridin' for the doctor. I do na think I'm equipped to be of much help."

He turned on his heel and ran toward the barn. Kiara prayed Paddy would be quick to saddle the horse, for she knew he'd feel the sting of Bradley's whip should he tarry. Bradley's words of warning had not been forgotten; she dared not hide again tonight. An involuntary shudder raced through her body at the mere thought of Paddy working in the mills. Having her brother spend long days around the carding machines would be fearsome enough, but with the mysterious illness now plaguing the mill workers, she didn't want Paddy anywhere near the factories. She completed mixing the potion, corked the bottles, and hurried back upstairs.

Sarah was hovering over Jasmine, her face creased in a worried frown. "I was beginning to think you were never coming back," Sarah said. She moved around the bed and edged toward the door. "I'm better in the kitchen than the sickroom, Kiara. I'll go down and make some gruel if you think it would help."

"Go ahead with ya, Sarah. I'll look after her. I'm no stranger to a sickbed. You can make the gruel. I doubt she'll eat anything today, but ya never know."

Sarah skittered out the door without a look back. Hiding in the kitchen would have been Kiara's preference too, but she knew Jasmine needed her help. She had grown fond of the young woman who had shown her nothing but kindness since the day she arrived. Why a beautiful young woman with a kind heart would marry the devil incarnate was beyond Kiara's imagination. Yet she knew Jasmine desired this baby with all her heart, so she would do everything in her power to help her.

Cradling Jasmine in one arm, she lifted her upper body. "Drink this, ma'am. It will help stop the crampin'." Jasmine swallowed the potion and sank back against Kiara's arm. "I want ya ta stay layin' on your back, and I'm gonna prop your legs on some pillows until we can get the bed raised up with some bricks. I'll have yar husband help me when he returns. He's gone to fetch the doctor."

Jasmine's eyes were glazed with pain. "Bradley knows?"

"He came into the kitchen when I was mixin' the herbs. I asked 'im to go for the doctor."

"Does he know I've been drinking the elixir?"

"I did na say anything except you were crampin' and the baby might be comin'."

"Promise you won't tell him. If anything happens to the baby, he'll think I've done this intentionally in order to cause him pain. I'll never be able to convince him I was only trying to be a good wife."

The fear in Jasmine's eyes spoke volumes to Kiara. Apparently,

Bradley Houston didn't pick and choose: he meted out his cruelty to all who crossed his path—even his own wife. Jasmine held Kiara's hand, her fingers trembling in a weak grip. "I'll not be tellin' him. Now lay back and rest."

Kiara sat by Jasmine's side, watching as the herbal remedy began to ease the cramping. Within a few hours, Jasmine's restlessness subsided, and she slipped into a deep, peaceful sleep. Kiara pulled the rocking chair close to Jasmine's bed and remained nearby, wondering why Bradley hadn't returned with the doctor hours ago. It should have taken no more than a half hour to saddle his horse and ride into Lowell. She feared the pains would begin anew before the doctor arrived. When she'd nearly given up hope, she heard the sound of approaching horses through the open window.

Dr. Hartzfeld entered the room with the confidence of a man determined to perform the job set before him. "I see she's sleeping," he said, nearing the bed.

"For at least an hour now. What took Mr. Houston so long? I thought you'd be here long before now." Her voice was filled with recrimination.

"I was delivering a baby—breech birth. I couldn't leave one woman's bedside and run to another. There were two lives in danger."

"Aye. And there's two lives in danger here too. The mistress wants nothin' to go amiss with the babe," Kiara said.

Dr. Hartzfeld pulled back the coverlet and began to examine Jasmine.

"Why don't you go downstairs and give Mr. Houston a report. He feared they both might be dead, and he didn't want to come up. Tell him I'm checking his wife and I'll talk to him once I've finished my examination."

Kiara did as requested, distancing herself from Bradley while she relayed the information. Without waiting for possible questions, she ran back upstairs, explaining she was needed to assist the doctor. She hurried into the room, closing the door behind her.

"You've done some fine medical work," Dr. Hartzfeld

complimented. "Do you know if she took a fall or what might have brought on the early labor pains?"

"Do I have yar promise ya'll not breathe a word to Mr. Houston?"

The doctor gave her a sidelong glance. "So long as there's been no foul play."

"Nothin' such so bad as that," she said, motioning the doctor to join her across the room. "Have ya heard tell of Dr. Horatio's Spice of Life?" she asked, retrieving an empty bottle from Jasmine's dresser and handing it to Dr. Hartzfeld.

"These tonics come and go. Many people take them."

"Aye, but I think this one contains somethin' more than the usual whiskey and water. I tasted a bit of it, and I think it contains a poison herb. I used a concoction I knew helped counteract the effects, and it seems to be workin' on the missus."

The doctor's face twisted into a scowl. "And how would *you* know about poison herbs?"

Kiara met his gaze with dogged confidence. "There was them that mixed up evil brews in Ireland, sayin' it would rid ya of the devil. O' course, it did na work because them that took it needed health-givin' herbs, not poison. Mrs. Houston's been takin' this tonic for several months, hopin' it would give her energy. I think the poison has been buildin' up inside her."

The doctor stroked his graying beard. "Possible, possible," he muttered.

Encouraged by his remark, Kiara continued. "While I waited fer ya to get here, I was thinkin' that maybe this tonic is what's makin' the girls in the mills sick. I've heard they take it to give them enough energy to keep up with their work. I even heard talk the Corporation was furnishin' it for them so they'd work faster. 'Course, I do na know if that's true. But I'm thinkin' if the tonic could make me mistress sick enough to take to her bed, it surely could be the cause of them girls getting' sick and dyin'."

Dr. Hartzfeld slapped his hand on his knee. "I believe you just may have happened onto something. I'll go and talk to the mill supervisors and see if they can ascertain how many of the sick girls have been taking the elixir. Possibly the families or friends of the girls who died will know if they were using the tonic. Excellent deductions, girl."

"And what of me mistress?"

"Hard to tell. If I were a gambling man," he speculated, "I'd have to bet against the baby making it, but if she'll remain in bed and take care of herself, there may be a chance. She'll need constant care."

"I can care for her."

"I'll tell Bradley of her need to remain bedfast and mention your willingness to care for Mrs. Houston. You'd be the best choice with your abilities. You've no doubt saved her life today." Dr. Hartzfeld strode to the bedroom window and looked down. "Mrs. Wainwright is here. Bradley stopped to tell her of Jasmine's difficulty as we were leaving town. I'm not surprised to see her. She was distraught when she heard the news. I'd best go downstairs and talk with them."

Kiara remained behind to watch over her mistress, and before long she could hear Dr. Hartzfeld explaining Jasmine's condition. Soon after, the three of them entered the bedroom, and Alice Wainwright rushed to her granddaughter's bedside.

"I've explained your willingness to care for Mrs. Houston," Dr. Hartzfeld said.

"And we are most grateful," Alice added. "I think it would be best if we placed a cot in the room for Kiara. That would permit her to be with Jasmine around the clock. After all, we don't want her alone for a minute, do we?" She looked toward Bradley.

"Jasmine certainly needs care, but I don't know that she needs Kiara sleeping in here at night," he replied. "If she looks in on her several times throughout the night, that should be sufficient."

"Foolishness and stuff, Bradley! That makes no sense. Kiara would get no rest popping up and down throughout the night, and Jasmine might begin cramping at any time. A cot in this room for Kiara is the only way to proceed."

Bradley nodded. "You're right. I'll see to it immediately."

Kiara glanced heavenward. Perhaps God had seen her plight, heard her prayers, and was having mercy after all.

CHAPTER · *25*

SLOWLY, AS THE weeks passed and October gave way to November, Jasmine regained her strength. The combination of removing Bradley's stressful social requirements from her schedule, along with eliminating Dr. Horatio's Spice of Life from her daily regimen, was working wonders. And the time with Jasmine was a blessed relief for Kiara.

The women spent hours talking, with Jasmine stitching her needlepoint while Kiara fashioned her lace into delicate three-dimensional pendants of butterflies, grape clusters, and nodding daffodils that she attached to black velvet ribbons to be worn instead of jewels around the neck. Captivated by the creations, Alice Wainwright had worn one of the designs to the Governor's Ball, which had been held in Boston several weeks previous. She had returned from Boston, delighted to tell Kiara that Sophia Dallas, the vice-president's wife, was in attendance and had been so impressed with her skill she requested five sets of lace cuffs. Kiara had been hard at work on the project, though truth be known, she made more money creating the small pendants. And money was what she needed if she was to accomplish her goal and get out of Bradley Houston's clutches.

There was little doubt that once the babe arrived, she'd be

relegated back to the attic to do his evil bidding. However, by then she hoped to have enough money to take Paddy and run off to Boston. Her greatest blessing was in knowing that she had not conceived by Bradley. It would have been impossible to explain a pregnancy, and no doubt Bradley would have forced her to do something awful to rid herself of the child. She could never imagine thanking God for making her barren, but at this moment that was exactly the praise she offered.

Once I've saved enough money, Paddy and I will head to Boston. No one knows us there and our own people will be more than willing to protect us.

"You're very quiet this morning," Jasmine said, giving her a cheerful smile.

Kiara smiled in return but said nothing. Her thoughts were on the future, but she could not share those ideas with her mistress.

"Bradley was required to make a trip to Boston this morning. He came in to bid me farewell while you were dressing in the other room. He was in an agitated state when he departed, although it seems he's unhappy most of the time. I'm certain much of his unpleasant temperament has to do with my confinement. Likely he'll be fine once the baby comes."

"There's somethin' I've been wantin' to ask ya, ma'am, but if ya do na want to answer, just tell me."

Jasmine grinned at Kiara. They'd become as close as sisters since the doctor had ordered Jasmine to remain abed. "I've told you everything about my life, Kiara. Surely you know there's nothing you can't ask me. We're friends."

"Ya've told me about how ya were forced to marry Mr. Houston, but I'm wonderin' how ya manage to live with a man who is so . . ."

"Sour?"

"That was na exactly the word I was searchin' fer, but it'll do."

Jasmine stabbed her needle into the fabric and met Kiara's gaze. "Even before I married Bradley, I was angry at being forced into a loveless marriage. Then as time passed and I could not please him, I thought God had turned His back on me."

"Sure and I know that feelin'."

"Do you remember the Sunday when Bradley was out of town and I told you I wanted to go early and attend church with Grandmother?"

"Aye. The driver took me and Paddy to St. Patrick's that mornin'."

Jasmine nodded her head. "That morning the preacher's sermon was on several verses from the book of Job. It was as though the sermon had been written just for me. I had become angry with God, blaming Him for my circumstances, but ever since I heard that sermon, I've attempted to apply the principles to my life. I've grown closer to God, even though my marriage has not improved."

"What was it that preacher told ya that made such a difference?" Kiara asked, leaning forward.

"He said our suffering and pain does not come from God because God's character and nature is love. Our woes come from Satan, but God sometimes uses our trials so we will seek Him because He desires a closer relationship with us. He explained that through all of Job's suffering, he continued to trust God. Because of Job's trust and faithfulness, God greatly blessed the remainder of Job's life.

"I'm trusting that God has a plan to bless my life and that I will be happy. Who knows? Perhaps this baby will bring us together and we will find happiness as a family."

Kiara gave her a sidelong look. "Perhaps. And for your sake, I hope that's true. But I do na see why people must suffer so much when God could cause it to come to an end."

"I know. None of us want to go through difficulties, but living with Bradley has made me a stronger person, yet more dependent upon God."

"Ya're stronger, but ya're weaker? That does na make much sense."

"I know my words sound like a contradiction, but being dependent on God is a strength, not a weakness. It's through trusting Him we finally become spiritual warriors, able to withstand the difficulties that come our way."

"I'm na lookin' to be a warrior, ma'am. I'd settle on just lettin' someone else take a few of the arrows that've been directed me way."

Jasmine's lips curved into a sympathetic smile. "Grandmother challenged me to begin reading my Bible every morning and spending time with God before I begin my day. Of course, now that I've been abed so long, it hasn't been difficult. Would you like to read with me in the mornings?"

Kiara looked down at the floor. "I'm na so good at readin'."

"I could read aloud if you like."

"Aye. That would be fine. Ya can read to me about Job, and I can hear firsthand what kind of blessin's he got for all that sufferin'."

"Job it is. We'll begin tomorrow morning. Kiara, I know you're unhappy here, but having you with me during this time has brought me great joy. I want you to know that if I could grant you and Paddy your freedom, I would do so."

"Thank ya fer thinkin' kindly of Paddy and me. 'Twould be a miracle for certain if we could go and live in the Acre."

"After all our talks regarding my desire to help free slaves in the future, you know I don't believe in slavery. And I don't see a great deal of difference between slavery and servitude. I'm going to try to find some way to convince Bradley to release you from your papers. It may take some imagination, but surely I can think of something."

"Don't do nothin' that would cause his wrath. I'd never fergive myself if somethin' happened because ya were arguing for me freedom."

Jasmine angled her gaze at Kiara. "I know Bradley has a foul temper and he's struck Paddy on occasion. Has he ever hit you?"

Kiara shook her head. "Are ya going to keep on with the anti-slavery meetin's after the babe's born?" she asked.

Jasmine's eyes brightened. "Yes. As much as I can, but I can't let Bradley know, and with the baby, it will be more difficult."

Pleased her mistress appeared oblivious to the change in topic,

Kiara picked up a bobbin of thread from her bag. "I'd be proud to help ya if there's any way I can be of assistance. Even if it's just watchin' after the wee babe while ya're busy helpin' with the run-aways."

"Thank you, Kiara. You've become the dearest friend I could ever hope for. Now let me see that new design you're working on."

Kiara held up the piece of lace and wondered what Mrs. Houston would think if she discovered what had happened in the attic room. Would Jasmine believe Bradley had come to her against her will? Or would she believe her husband's lies? Perhaps if Kiara would trust like Job, her mistress would never learn the truth.

Jasmine examined Kiara's workmanship, her fingers tracing the delicate petals of the lace rose. "It's lovely," she said, extending the piece toward Kiara.

Suddenly she leaned forward with a gasp and emitted a shrill cry. "I think the baby is coming! My water has broken." Her eyes reflected the odd combination of fear, pain, and elation that expectant mothers experience when birth is imminent.

"I'll send Paddy fer the doctor and be back before ya have a chance to miss me."

Her sturdy leather shoes barely touched the floor as she raced down the steps and ran outside to the barn. While Paddy saddled the horse, she gave him detailed instructions. "If the doctor is busy, do na wait for him. Tell him of our need and then come back and tell me so I'll na be sittin' here thinkin' somethin' has happened to ya. I'll go ahead and deliver the babe myself if ya can na bring the doctor."

"Aye," the boy replied. He swung himself up into the saddle and was off and down the driveway before Kiara reentered the house.

Sarah met her at the back door, her eyes wide with fear. "The mistress is calling for you. She's begun her labor. I went up there, but you know how I am with sickness."

Kiara nodded as the two of them walked toward the stairway. "I know, Sarah, but this is a babe bein' born, not a sickness. If you can na bear to be upstairs, at least stay where you can hear me should I need to call fer yar help."

Sarah's complexion turned the shade of day-old ashes. "I'll be down here praying—both for the mistress and for you."

Kiara grinned. "Ya might want to add a prayer fer yarself—that I'll not be needin' yar help."

Sarah dropped into a chair in the foyer, her body slumped into an abject heap. "Paddy's gone for the doctor?"

"Yes. He should return soon. And there's yet another prayer fer ya. Pray the doctor is na busy with another patient."

When Kiara returned upstairs, she carried string, scissors, clean sheets, and blankets. By then, Jasmine was writhing in pain. "I think it's close to time."

"It's much too soon. Ya've only just begun yar pains. Can ya roll on yar side, and I'll change the bed and get ya more comfortable. Sure and I'm glad we put that oilcloth on the bed last week," she said in a soothing voice.

Jasmine cooperated with Kiara's ministrations, and by the time the bedding had been changed, Dr. Hartzfeld was entering the room. He carried his black leather medical bag in one hand and his top hat in the other. "I was surprised to see Paddy," he said. "I thought it would be at least another week or two before the baby came. Let's check and see how you're progressing."

Two hours later, Jasmine's baby boy fought his way into the world and, with a lusty cry, announced his arrival. "He's a big, healthy boy," Dr. Hartzfeld announced. "Too bad Bradley isn't here to see his son."

"He should be home within a day or two," Jasmine replied while glancing down at the cherub-cheeked infant. "Hello, Spencer," she cooed while running her fingertips through the baby's downy-soft brown hair.

"Spencer? Is that the name you've chosen?" the doctor inquired.

"Yes. Bradley said the child was to be his father's namesake."

Dr. Hartzfeld chuckled. "Then I'd say it's a good thing you had a boy. Can't imagine a little girl running around with that moniker."

"Nor I," Jasmine agreed, returning his smile.

Kiara listened to the baby's lusty cry and felt awash in sadness. Would she ever know the joy of such a moment? She backed away from the scene, knowing she was imposing and no longer needed.

Bradley walked out of his Boston hotel and hailed a passing carriage. The Associates had called a meeting, one that would be held at the Beacon Hill home Nathan Appleton had recently constructed. Although Nathan had finally succumbed to his wife's request for a home in the posh neighborhood, he'd not given in to an elaborate edifice. In fact, the house was, by Beacon Hill standards, somewhat common. When he'd seen the return address on the envelope, he thought perhaps the Appletons were hosting an open house to celebrate the move into their new home. Instead, the contents had been a rather ominous-sounding notification that all members were expected to be present for the meeting in order to discuss several critical issues.

The message had given him brief concern, but he soon decided there might be talk of further expansion. If so, those favoring such action would want a quorum present in the event the matter could be taken to a vote. Expansion was a fine idea— they'd need more cotton to operate additional mills. He leaned back and rested his head against the supple leather of the carriage seat. Between Jasmine and Kiara, his life had grown increasingly complicated and unsatisfying. He'd been unable to accomplish work of any consequence since the day Kiara had moved into his wife's room to care for her. From his observations, they were becoming much too friendly, and the possibility of Kiara revealing the details of his secret visits to her attic bedroom loomed large in his mind. Instead of concentrating on his work, he obsessed over the prospect—not wanting to admit fear now consumed him.

As a stern-faced servant took Bradley's coat and hat, he noticed that the Appleton residence was brimming with members who were making their way from the dining room into the library. It was obvious he had been intentionally excluded. He hadn't misread the meeting notice; the words had been far too ill-omened. Since there were no other members presently arriving, he wondered if he had been the only member banned from the dinner party. The prospect was disquieting, but he attempted to remain calm.

Intentionally, Bradley wended his way through the gathering and approached Nathan. "Good evening, Nathan. I trust you've had an enjoyable dinner."

"Indeed we have," Nathan replied. "If you'll excuse me, I must speak to Matthew before commencing the meeting." Without explanation, he turned and walked away.

Bradley searched the room for a friendly face. Either his paranoia was taking root, or those in attendance were intentionally avoiding his company. There seemed to be no one interested in making contact with him. He spotted Robert Woolsey near the fireplace and advanced.

"Robert! Good to see you," Bradley said, forcing a smile and clapping him on the shoulder.

"Good evening, Bradley." Robert moved back a step, his discomfort obvious as he inched away. "I was hoping to have a word with Josiah, if you'll excuse me."

"That's fine. I'd like to visit with Josiah also," Bradley said, unwilling to permit his captive's escape. Robert had always been an ally, and right now Bradley needed the support of a comrade. At this point in time he cared little whether the patronage was zealous or reluctant. He would accept any modicum of alliance. "Was the dinner to your liking?"

"Quite enjoyable."

"I must have misread my notice. I didn't recall reading about dinner preceding the meeting."

"That's too bad," Robert said as he drew near to Josiah. "Josiah, I was wondering if I could have a word with you in private."

Josiah gave Bradley a sidelong glance and then turned his

attention to Robert. "Of course. I doubt whether Nathan would mind if we stepped into his office for a few moments. Excuse us, Bradley."

Bradley watched as the two men walked out of the room. There was little doubt they had intentionally escaped his presence. Each time he approached a group of members, they stepped aside. His walk through the room resembled Moses parting the Red Sea.

When the meeting was called to order, Bradley found himself sitting alone. Although he was surrounded by empty chairs, several men stood in the back of the room rather than take a seat beside him. It was abundantly clear that he had committed an offense. When Nathan took charge of the meeting, Bradley knew his behavior would be the topic of this evening's meeting. Matthew never handled matters dealing directly with an individual Associate.

"We need to have some important questions answered this evening—questions that are affecting the business and our profits. I believe you're the person to give us the answers we need, Bradley."

Bradley's muscles tightened into a knot. He gave what he hoped was a nonchalant nod.

"Cotton deliveries have diminished considerably. You've given no explanation for the reduction, though you surely must have realized this decrease would be of grave concern to all of us. I am at a loss as to why you've not brought this matter to someone's attention." Nathan paused for a moment. "Would you care to explain?"

The hairs on the back of Bradley's neck stiffened as the members directed their attention to him. He needed time to formulate an answer. He didn't even realize shipments had decreased. Why hadn't Malcolm notified him if there was a problem? His mind was racing. He thought of the letters that lay unopened on his desk, letters from his father-in-law that he'd pushed aside because his thoughts were centered upon Jasmine and Kiara—not upon business. Jasmine! *She* would be his explanation.

"I don't know if you are aware, but my wife has experienced

great difficulty with her health over the last several months. She's been confined to her bed, and my time has been devoted to her care. Although I've had hired help with her, it's me whom she desires by her bedside. And what husband can turn away from his wife in her time of need? I pray your indulgence, gentlemen. If you had come to me previously, I would have forced myself back to work. I didn't realize the shipments had slowed and will check my latest correspondence for any answer I can find from our Southern growers."

"You can hardly fault a man for taking time to care for his ill wife," Henry Thorne said. "Bradley is correct that none of us spoke to him. We had an obligation to call this matter to his attention before it spiraled into such a severe decline. Communication is the key, gentlemen, and it must go both directions."

Bradley wanted to jump up from his chair and shout his thanks to Henry. Instead, he was the model of restraint and self-deprecation. "Thank you, Henry, but even with the heartrending circumstances that have created a pall of sadness over my household, I should have been alert to my business obligations. What I've done is inexcusable, and I can't expect your forgiveness when my ineffectiveness has adversely impacted the business."

"None of us is immune from such events occurring in our own lives," another member agreed. "I can't fault a man for unbearable worry over his wife and unborn child."

Since the winds were blowing favorably in Bradley's direction, he decided it might bode well for him to add a few morsels of information in order to redirect the conversation away from himself. "I can share that shortly before my wife was forced to take to her bed, my father-in-law had reported many of the plantations were beginning to experience difficulties with their slaves due to the increasing abolition movement. However, he thought the problem would soon be under control."

"We must hold fast to our beliefs, gentlemen," another member admonished. "We can quietly assume a position against the expansion of slavery into other states, but we must be careful not to alienate our Southern suppliers. We need their cotton, and if it takes slave labor to meet our needs, so be it."

The men argued the issues of tariffs, slaves, and strikes within the mills while Bradley's mind skittered back to the unopened letters from Malcolm Wainwright. He wondered if those letters would reveal the answers his fellow Associates were seeking. After several hours had passed, he could abide the suspense no longer.

When a brief pause in the discussion occurred, he stood. "If I could be so bold as to beg your indulgence one more time, gentlemen, I have several matters of business that I wish to complete this evening. If I am able to do so, I will return to Lowell tomorrow morning to be at my wife's bedside."

"Of course, Bradley," Nathan responded. The remainder of the assembled group murmured their assent, while several men offered words of encouragement for his wife's speedy recovery as he was making his way out of the room. He took a deep breath of fresh air, momentarily marveling he'd been able to survive the meeting without receiving threats of an ouster from his position within the prestigious group. No doubt he would have to set matters aright in short order. He hurried back to the hotel. Malcolm's letters were in his satchel of business papers and would likely shed light on the decreased shipments.

"Bradley!"

Scanning the hotel foyer, Bradley saw his brother striding toward him. "Nolan. How are you?" he asked, continuing to move toward the hotel staircase.

"I'm fine. What an unexpected surprise to see you. Come join me for a glass of port."

"I'd like to, but I've several matters needing my immediate attention. Perhaps some other time."

"Is Jasmine faring any better? I'm hoping to visit within the week. From the tone of her last letter, she seemed to be enjoying the little Irish girl's company."

Bradley stopped in his tracks and turned to face his brother. "Jasmine has written you?"

"We correspond on occasion. Why does that surprise you? After all, I spent a great deal of time with Jasmine and

Mrs. Wainwright when we journeyed to Mississippi. Jasmine even sends me an occasional poetic offering for evaluation. At the same time, she usually informs me of what's happening in Lowell and adds a bit of personal information regarding the two of you. Why, if I had to depend upon you, I wouldn't even know of the impending birth of your child."

"You know I've never been one to discuss personal matters."

Nolan laughed and slapped his brother on the shoulder. "I don't think you'd be considered too much the gossipmonger if you revealed to your own brother that he was going to become an uncle. With your consuming desire for an heir, I didn't expect there would be anything that could entice you away from Lowell until after the baby's birth."

Bradley continued edging toward the stairway. "Urgent meeting of the Associates. I have some matters to conclude yet this evening, then I'll be returning to Lowell first thing in the morning—which is exactly why I cannot join you for a glass of port and further conversation."

"Of course. I don't want to detain you. Give my regards to Jasmine and tell her I hope to see her soon."

"Yes, of course," he said, taking the steps two at a time. He slipped his key in the lock, and by the flickering light of an oil lamp, slit open the first of two letters from Malcolm. Thumbing through the pages, he scanned the letter until his gaze settled upon words that sent a chill rippling down his spine. He began to read aloud: "We have received devastating rains in this part of Mississippi, and they could not have come at a worse time. Just as we were preparing to begin our first harvest, the rains came. Consequently we are suffering from boll rot, and our shipments will be reduced throughout the next month. Please advise how we may assist you with this problem. The possibility exists to seek help from other growers in Louisiana and Alabama, as their crops did not suffer from the heavy rains. We anticipate our crop will return to normal for our later shipments, as the remainder of our crop was planted at a later date."

Bradley threw aside the missive and opened the second. His

breath caught in his throat. When he thought the news could be no worse, he read Malcolm's final paragraph: "I will be in Lowell for a visit and hope to lend assistance wherever needed and of whatever nature upon my arrival."

Bradley read the paragraph more slowly and began mentally calculating the length of Malcolm's voyage. His father-in-law would arrive within the week, and it appeared he was planning a somewhat extended visit. This unexpected intrusion was yet another vexing tribulation he must resolve. Not that Bradley feared his ability to handle his father-in-law, but he preferred such matters be on his own terms. However, Malcolm had taken matters into his own hands, and now Bradley had little time to prepare.

He folded the letter and placed it in his satchel. "You may be coming for a visit, Malcolm, but you'll be returning home quickly," he muttered.

CHAPTER · *26*

JASMINE HEARD the heavy footsteps on the stairway and knew Bradley had returned home. His eyes burned with expectation as he searched her face for a clue. She hadn't seen him appear so excited since their vows had been sealed. "Our son has arrived!" Her voice bubbled with delight as she expectantly awaited his reaction.

"A boy!" Bradley exclaimed. "But of course I knew I would have a son."

"Of course. The wee babe would be feared of comin' into the world any other way," Kiara muttered.

"Did you say something, Kiara?" Jasmine inquired.

"Just commentin' on the beauty of the child, ma'am. Lucky he is to be lookin' like you."

Bradley shot a glowering look in Kiara's direction. "Bring my son to me."

Kiara did as she was ordered and lifted the infant from where he slept. Bradley formed his arm into a large semicircle to receive the child. She looked heavenward and shook her head back and forth. "Push yar arm in. The babe will fall to the floor if ya keep yar arm spread open like that." She pushed Bradley's arm closer to his body, forcing it into a cradling position before settling the baby into his arm.

Bradley stared down at the child and then looked back and forth between the two women in the room. "His name is Spencer, and I believe he looks like me." His gaze settled on Kiara. "I'm certain Jasmine no longer needs your continued assistance. I'll have your cot removed from her room later today."

"I don't believe that's a good idea just yet," Alice said as she entered the bedroom. "Jasmine remains quite weak, and it won't hurt to have Kiara close at hand to help with the baby."

"Grandmother Wainwright. I didn't know you had arrived," Bradley said.

"I wouldn't have missed this event for anything. I left home only moments after the doctor arrived to deliver the baby and haven't departed since. I'm sorry you couldn't be here for the birth, Bradley. It would have been comforting to Jasmine had you been home for the birth of your first child."

Bradley handed the infant back to Kiara and turned his attention toward his wife. "The baby was not expected for another two weeks, and Jasmine completely understands the rigors of my business. I hurried home as quickly as I could. You understand, don't you, my dear?" Without waiting for an answer, he continued. "I have a bit of good news to share with both of you, one you will both be pleased to receive. Malcolm will be arriving within the week, and I'm certain he'll be surprised to learn of his grandson's birth."

"Really? How wonderful! When did you learn of Father's arrival? He didn't mention it when he last wrote—of course, that's been some time ago."

"I must admit he wrote some time ago and I mislaid the letter. Thankfully, I found it in my desk at the shipping office while I was in Boston, or his arrival would have taken us all by surprise."

His laugh sounded hollow, and Jasmine thought she had noted a strain in Bradley's voice when he announced her father was arriving. But perhaps it was the excitement of the baby's early arrival. She wanted this to be a time of happiness and healing. A time when they could come together and form a closer union—if not for themselves, then for the baby.

She smiled up at her husband. "Having Father here to see the baby will be joyous. I only wish Mother could make the voyage."

Alice patted Jasmine's arm and smiled. "Be thankful for at least this much, dear. I'm certain Bradley will be anxious to take you and the baby to Mississippi once Spencer is a little older."

Jasmine clapped her hands. "Oh, Bradley, do you think we might do that? The baby might be just the thing to bring Mother out of her sad reverie."

"I think it will take more than seeing a baby to bring your mother back to a state of reality," Bradley absently replied.

"That was uncalled for, Bradley," voiced Alice. "Your wife is recuperating from childbirth, and she needs your encouragement, not a callous rejoinder."

"We'll consider a visit when Spencer is older." He leaned down and brushed a kiss upon Jasmine's cheek. "I must go downstairs and attend to business matters. I'll come back up to see you later in the day."

"Of course. I don't expect you to spend all your time sitting here with us. I understand you must tend to business."

The three women were silent until Bradley's footsteps could be heard crossing the downstairs foyer. Alice closed the bedroom door and sat down beside Jasmine's bed. "It appears your father saw the seriousness of matters and is finally going to make an appearance. I couldn't be more pleased. His visit will be doubly blessed when he sees little Spencer."

Jasmine smiled and squeezed her grandmother's vein-lined hand. "You don't think Father will make mention that you've written and requested he visit?"

"No, I warned him Bradley must not know we've interfered. And your father obviously has concerns of his own. I don't think the plantation owners have been receiving prompt payments for their cotton."

Kiara moved closer to Jasmine's bedside and pointed back and forth between the two women. "Ya wrote to Mr. Wainwright and told 'im to come here to question Mr. Houston?"

Jasmine observed the disbelief—or was it fear?—in Kiara's eyes. "Don't worry. Having Father visit will be a good thing. Bradley has been terribly overworked throughout our marriage, and the stress appears to be taking its toll on him. Grandmother and I thought Father might be able to advise Bradley on how to relieve himself of some of his duties."

"I do na think yar husband will be pleased if he should find out ya've interfered. He's a proud man."

"Don't look so worried, Kiara. Father will be discreet in handling Bradley."

"I hope so, ma'am. I do na want to see anyone suffer should Mr. Houston lose his temper."

Alice gave Kiara an endearing smile. "You worry overly, my dear. I think what you need is some time to relax and enjoy yourself. You've been in this room around the clock for weeks. Why don't you go and visit your friend Bregetta and—"

"Bridgett," Jasmine corrected.

"Oh yes. Why don't you visit your friend Bridgett, and I'll look after Jasmine?"

Kiara checked the time. "She gets off work a little earlier on Saturdays." There was a hesitation in her voice.

"She should be home soon. If you leave now, the two of you could arrive at the Acre around the same time. Do go and have a time of relaxation," Jasmine encouraged. "You've been with me constantly, and you need to get outside. A change of scenery will do you good."

"I do na think Mr. Houston will be pleased should he find out I've gone."

"No need for us to tell him. If he comes to the room, I'll tell him I've sent you on an errand." Alice pulled several coins from her reticule. "Please stop by Paxton's and pick up some additional thread. I don't want you to have any excuse to quit making your lace."

Kiara smiled and took the coins. "Ya're also not wantin' to tell a lie."

Alice returned the smile. "That's true. Now off with you and have a good time."

———————

Kiara peeked over the railing before tiptoeing down the stairs and could see the illumination of light beneath Bradley's library door. She flattened herself against the wall and edged down the side of the hallway where the floorboards didn't creak. Without a sound, she made her way into the kitchen.

Before Sarah could offer a greeting, Kiara placed a finger to her lips and shook her head. She made her way to the table and whispered, "I do na want Mr. Houston to know I'm leavin'. Mrs. Houston and Mrs. Wainwright gave me permission to go into town, but 'tis better if he does na know."

Sarah smiled. "Have a nice time," she whispered back. "What should I tell Paddy if he comes looking for you?"

"Tell him I'll come to the barn later but to say nothin' to Mr. Houston."

Kiara slipped out the door and was thankful for the cover of darkness. She half walked, half ran into town, deciding to stop at Paxton's before going to the Acre. The final bell hadn't rung and Bridgett wouldn't yet be home. Besides, stopping now would save time on her return. She hastened down the aisle, picked up a bobbin, and walked to the counter at the front of the store.

"I hear tell the Houstons have a fine baby boy."

"Aye, that they do," Kiara replied. "Both mother and babe doin' fine." The clanging of the final bell could be heard, announcing the day's end for the mill workers.

Mrs. Paxton greeted two customers as they entered the store, taking time to tell them of the store's latest arrival of bonnets and gloves. Kiara wished she would hurry, for Bridgett would be home any minute.

The customers stopped at a nearby display case, gazing down at an assortment of hatpins and jewelry. "I'm surprised Bradley Houston isn't at home this evening. I thought he'd be spending time with Jasmine and the baby when he finally arrived home."

Kiara listened while keeping her eyes forward. "Mrs. Hartzfeld mentioned he was out of town when the baby was born, but men have their business matters that require attention. You can't fault him for being dedicated to his work."

"I suppose not, but it's not as though he doesn't have servants who could take care of his errands."

"Oh, look at that locket. I believe I may have to purchase it. Mrs. Paxton, could you show me this locket when you finish there?"

"Of course," the store owner replied. She handed Kiara her change and the bobbin of thread.

Kiara clutched the bobbin in her hand, now afraid to leave the store. If what those women said was correct, Bradley Houston was somewhere nearby. What if he saw her?

"Was there something else you needed, Kiara?" Mrs. Paxton inquired.

"What? Oh no. I'm just leavin'. Thank ya." She had no choice but to depart.

Her hand trembled as she opened the door. She longed to silence the jingling bell, which announced to all nearby that some-one was either entering or exiting the business. She prayed Bradley was nowhere in the vicinity, for surely the light from the store would illuminate her as she left the building. She looked down the street and saw only a small boy running with his dog and a number of carriages. Kiara bent her head, pulling her shawl around her face.

Nearing the Acre, she sighed in relief. She'd heard no footsteps and seen no carriage following her. Apparently she'd been over-working her imagination. Bradley had likely returned home. "I will na allow him to ruin my time in the Acre," she murmured before knocking on the door of Granna Murphy's hovel.

"Kiara! Come in. What a lovely surprise it is ta see ya." Bridg-ett's eyes sparkled as she pulled Kiara inside. "How did ya manage to get away from the house?"

By the time she'd explained the latest events of the Houston household, Granna Murphy was standing beside her with a wooden spoon in her hand. "I'm expectin' ya to stay for supper, lass, and I'll na be takin' kindly to the thought of ya walkin' out the door without first sittin' down to the table with us."

Kiara hesitated. "I do na . . ."

Before she could complete her refusal, Rogan burst through the door like the sunshine on a dreary day. "Good evenin' to ya," he said, his gaze circling the room and then resting upon Kiara's face. "What've we here? A lovely visitor from the other side o' town? Pleased we are to be havin' such a fine lady in our midst." He bowed from the waist and swept his cap in front of him in a grand gesture. "I see ya're joinin' us for supper," he said, pointing toward the extra plate Granna Murphy had just placed on the table.

Kiara gave him an embarrassed grin. "Aye. I thought 'twould be good for me to have the taste of cabbage and potatoes on me lips again."

He gave her a hearty laugh. "Sure and we'd be pleased to oblige ya. I'm thinkin' ya must get mighty tired of that fancy food they serve in that fine house where ya're livin'." They all sat down to partake of the meager fare. Rogan issued a quick prayer of thanks and then turned his attention back to Kiara. "And what's this I hear but that it's Kiara O'Neill we have to be thankin' for discoverin' what was makin' the mill workers sick?"

Bridgett nodded in agreement. "Dr. Hartzfeld's been tellin' everyone 'twas you who figured out the elixir was makin' the girls sick. Folks here in the Acre are callin' ya a hero."

"I'm no hero, but glad I am that folks will no longer be takin' that mixture and makin' themselves sick."

Although Kiara attempted to help clear the table and wash dishes, Granna pushed her off to the other room to visit with Bridgett and Rogan. Bridgett excused herself to go and retrieve her mending, and Kiara turned her attention to Rogan. "So what of yar family, Rogan? Are any of them living in this country?"

"My family's all gone to be with the Lord. I'm the only Sheehan to survive the famine. I worked hard, hopin' to supply them with fare for their passage, but 'twas too little, too late. Starvation took them afore I could earn enough money to help. When they went home to be with the Lord, I vowed that so long as there was breath in me body and trust in God, no one I loved would ever go hungry again. I'm thankful God gave me the chance to help Bridgett with her passage, fer it took some of the pain away being able to help her get here."

"So ya *still* trust in God?" Kiara meekly questioned.

"Aye. O' *course* I do. We can na be turnin' our back on God just because an ill wind blows our way."

"But when bad things keep happenin', how do ya trust? God hasn't done much for me and Paddy. Miss Jasmine explained all about Job, and we read the Bible each day. Knowing that a godly man such as Job suffered in his lifetime has helped some, but I'm still wonderin' why things happen the way they do. Ya know . . . why do some of the cruelest people seem to be blessed while good folks are abused? Seems as though God has turned away from those that love 'im."

"Ah, lass, ya can na be thinkin' that way. Just because bad things happen, it does na mean that the Almighty has quit carin'. It's not Him that's caused the grief in this world, but man with his devilish nature. Besides, lass, God has seen fit to give you a great house to live in and food on the table. Ya may be indentured, but ya're not livin' in squalor like most of us here in the Acre. Ya should be on yar knees thankin' God for the safety and security ya have in that big house, while the rest of us face trouble at every turn in this place where we're livin'."

"Safety and security?" she blurted out. "Is that what ya think? I'm hardly safe and secure. What I live is a life of torture and misery. Ya do na have any idea what I'm forced to endure."

His eyes widened at her reply, and she immediately put her hand to her mouth, realizing she'd said too much. Jumping up from the chair, she ran from the house.

"Kiara!" Rogan called.

She could hear his footsteps behind her and then felt his fingers circle her arm. He pulled her to a halt. "Tell me what ya meant back there. Is someone hurtin' ya?"

She looked up into his eyes and realized it would matter little if she told him the truth. She was already defiled. No decent man would ever want her now. It would be easier to tell Rogan the truth than continue living a lie. And so there on the muddy street, feeling as filthy as the trash on the ground around them, she told him of Bradley's visits to her attic room. Never once through the telling did she meet his gaze. When finished with her wretched tale, she turned and walked away, ready to retreat to the home she'd grown to detest.

"Wait, lass," Rogan said, once again at her side. "Do na run off from me. Ya need ta know I understand ya have been forced into a terrible situation. It was harsh of me to assume ya had an easier life than the rest of us. I beg ya to fergive me."

His gentle words of kindness were her undoing. Tears streamed down her cheeks, and he gathered her into his arms. "Do na cry, lass. Life is too short for all these tears. Ya can be certain that what ya have told me has na changed my feelings fer ya, lass."

Kiara leaned against his broad chest. Even if only for a brief moment, she wanted to feel loved and cherished. She leaned back and looked up into his eyes. "I was wonderin' if ya could explain what feelin's ya been havin' fer me."

Rogan gave her a wink and smiled. "I think ya're knowin' exactly what feelin's I'm talkin' about, lass. Come along now. I'll walk ya back to yar house."

The comments she'd overheard in Paxton's Mercantile fleetingly crossed her mind. Surely Bradley would have long since returned home. "I'd be pleased to have yar company," she replied.

CHAPTER · 27

JASMINE WAS delighted when the doctor pronounced her recovery, at least among the genteel women of Lowell, to be one of the swiftest in his career. She'd been anxious to be up and about, and Dr. Hartzfeld had not discouraged her. Of course, he was one of the few doctors supporting short confinements for women after the birthing process, but he had begun advocating such practice after seeing how well the women in the Acre, as well as the Yankee farmwives, seemed to thrive when required to immediately return to the duties of caring for their families after childbirth. Of course, those women had no choice.

"I can't believe you're out of bed," her father exclaimed upon his arrival. "And here I thought I'd already be in Lowell when you gave birth. However, I'm delighted the rigors of childbirth are behind you. You look radiant. Motherhood becomes you, my dear. And your mother will be delighted to hear she has a grandson."

"Do sit down with me in the parlor. I want to hear all about Mother and, of course, my brothers—and Mammy. I've asked Bradley if we can journey to The Willows when Spencer is a little older. I do want Mother to see her new grandson." She looked lovingly at the baby in her arms. "Tell me, how is she faring,

Father? I've had no correspondence for months, and her last letter made little sense to me."

Jasmine's father wagged his head back and forth. "She has little interest in life. I force her out into the garden from time to time, but she much prefers to sit in her darkened bedroom."

"Instruct Mammy to force her outdoors every day," she suggested. "The sunlight will help cheer her spirits. Shortly after Bradley and I were married, I heard a renowned speaker discuss the effects of sunlight upon patients suffering from melancholy. He said sunlight and exercise were of great benefit. Perhaps you could have McKinley take her on a stroll after he's completed his bookwork each morning. I doubt Mammy would be up to any strenuous exercise."

"No harm in trying," he agreed, "although you know your mother can be difficult to persuade. She borders on hysteria when forced to do anything against her will. I fear she's slowly slipping away from me. Dr. Borden thinks your mother has already reached the point of insanity. However, I heartily disagree."

"No! She merely grows sad over the rigors of daily life. She's always suffered from this malady, Father. Don't let Dr. Borden convince you otherwise. Next he'll be suggesting you place Mother in an asylum. Promise me you'll never consent to such a thing! Such a commitment would certainly mean an end to her life."

"You know I'd never send your mother to an asylum, dear. Now quit worrying yourself. It's not good for you. I'll pass your suggestions along to Mammy. She said to send her love and best wishes. She sent along this little white bonnet she crocheted," he said, handing her a small package. "I like the idea of having you visit. Perhaps it would help your mother. I'll urge Bradley to make good on his promise to you."

Jasmine examined the bonnet and smiled. "I'll pen a letter of thanks to Mammy, and you can take it back when you return. Have Mother read it to her. Perhaps it will startle her out of her reverie for a few moments."

"I'll be glad to take your letter. And how have you been faring, dear? The letter from your grandmother concerned me, and I must say that Bradley has somewhat disappointed me with his business acumen. I had thought him quite astute. However, his lack of attention over these past months has me greatly disturbed."

Jasmine studied her father's frowning features. "You know I was sorely disappointed when you chose Bradley as my husband."

Her father's expression took on a look of worry. "Yes, but I hoped that in time you would learn to love him, just as your mother and I learned to love each other and my parents before that. Perhaps I was as wrong about that as I was his competency in business."

"Bradley is a very difficult man to love, Father. He is moody and can be hurtful. I've attempted to make the best of my situation, but I must admit there are times when it has been quite distressing. I'm depending upon the Lord to see me through, and I'm hopeful this child is going to build a bridge in our relationship."

"You've grown up," her father said softly.

Jasmine smiled, realizing the truth of his words. "When I was still at home, I thought there was no better place to be. The Willows was a haven of love and strength to me."

"But not now?"

Jasmine heard the sorrow in his voice. "Papa, so many things have come to my attention, and I am afraid that I am not the naïve little girl who left over a year ago. Even so, The Willows will always remain dear to me. It will always be home in my memories." She sighed. "I cannot say that this place is home. It doesn't feel that way at all. In fact, Grandmother's house feels more like home than this house.

"I also cannot say that I am happy being wed to Bradley, but I am trying, as I said. I know that God is my protector and strength. I have to trust that He will see me through. Spencer will help, no doubt. At least that is my hope."

"I hope so too, my dear. Frankly, my concerns over Bradley's business behavior are disconcerting enough that I've made arrangement for a few private appointments."

"Truly? With whom?" Jasmine inquired.

303

"I'm going to Boston the day after tomorrow for a meeting with the Associates."

"What's this I hear?" Bradley asked as he strode into the room. "I didn't know there was to be a meeting of the Associates this week."

Jasmine turned toward the doorway. Her husband appeared pale and gaunt, and she wondered if he were ill. Even though her father's visit had been secretly arranged, she felt somewhat vindicated when she looked at her husband now. Bradley definitely needed time to relax and refresh himself. Having someone else assist with the cotton shipments would surely provide the relief he desperately needed to restore his physical health and allow him time with his family. Sending the letter had been the proper thing to do.

Jasmine's father turned as Bradley entered the room. "Good to see you, my boy. Thought perhaps you had gone into hibernation," he said with a chuckle.

"You mentioned a meeting of the Associates," Bradley persisted.

"Oh, nothing you need concern yourself with. Before my departure from Mississippi, I requested a private meeting with several of the members. This is not a gathering of the general membership."

"May I be so bold as to inquire what you need to discuss with the Associates that you haven't discussed with me?" Bradley asked. Jasmine startled at her husband's tone. His eyes had narrowed and taken on a menacing glare. He was angry.

"Excuse me, ma'am," Kiara interrupted. "I was goin' to take the wee babe to the nursery unless ya prefer he stay with you."

"Thank you, Kiara. I'd appreciate that," Jasmine replied.

"Incidentally, Malcolm, I've been meaning to discuss the possibility of having you take one of my indentured servants back to The Willows with you."

Jasmine lifted the infant toward Kiara, whose eyes were fastened upon Bradley in an icy stare of loathing and disgust. "He should sleep for at least an hour," Jasmine said.

"The boy's been working in the stables, but he hasn't been meeting my expectations. I really need an older man who has more experience handling horses."

Jasmine's father appeared perplexed but suggested, "We can talk about it when I return from Boston."

"I'll remain in the nursery with him, ma'am," Kiara said as she exited the room.

Jasmine could feel the tension escalate. Bradley was obviously goading Kiara, and Kiara apparently could not hide her hatred for Bradley. They exchanged glares that were charged with conflict. Jasmine knew Kiara would be upset over any suggestion that Paddy leave Lowell, but surely Bradley's offhand remark could not cause such immediate signs of loathing. There was something more at the root of this, and she intended to find out exactly what was going on in her household.

Kiara sat in the nursery watching the baby sleep and contemplating her situation. She had no choice but to get Paddy away from the Houston household before Malcolm Wainwright's return from Boston. She wasn't certain why Bradley was once again threatening to send Paddy away, but he was obviously enjoying the pain and discomfort caused by his latest threats. Had he seen her with Rogan? Surely not! More likely it was that she was sleeping in the nursery with the baby.

There had been little doubt of Bradley's anger over the situation. With Jasmine's quick recovery from her confinement, he had been livid when Alice suggested Kiara move into the nursery with Spencer. "Think of the added comfort and rest you'll be granting your wife," Alice had argued.

Kiara knew he wanted to mount an offensive, but such a move would have met with questioning disapproval. After all, he should want only the best care for the mother of his infant son. And so he had acquiesced. Although she'd been thankful for Alice's plan, Kiara had not been the one who had broached the subject. Surely he could not hold that chain of events against her.

Later that night after Spencer was asleep in his cradle, she pulled out the leather pouch containing her coins. "Pitiful," she murmured. "This isn't enough to rent a room and support us in Boston until I can find work." It was abundantly obvious her lace-making would not yet provide the two of them with a sufficient living. And even if she remained with the Houstons and gave Paddy all of the money she had saved, how would he fend for himself in a city the size of Boston?

She momentarily thought of sending him to the Acre, but Bradley would certainly find him there. Perhaps Rogan would have an idea. She'd have to find a way to slip away. Perhaps Jasmine would give her permission to visit the Acre when Bradley was away from the house.

Placing the coins back in her pouch, she tucked it into the dresser drawer and snuggled under the covers. The sound of Spencer's even, quiet breathing lulled her to sleep without further thought of the Acre.

A hand clasped around her arm, shaking her. She was half awake, not certain what she'd been dreaming, when her eyes fluttered open and she realized Bradley's face was directly above her own. He licked his thin lips, like an animal ready to devour his prey. "Go upstairs," he commanded.

"Nay! I will na go anywhere with ya. I want ya to leave me alone. Ya've done nothin' but threaten and harm me since the day ya laid eyes on me. I've done nothin' to deserve such treatment. I love Jasmine, and I will na permit ya to continue hurtin' her in this way. She's given you a beautiful son, and she's a gracious lady. Better than ya deserve! I'll na be part of this any longer."

"I ought to flog you for your insolent behavior. You'll do as you're told! You need not put on a pretense of virtue; I saw you in the Acre hanging on to the neck of that filthy Irishman. I know you enjoy being with men," he hissed, leaning close to her ear. His utterance spewed at her like venom from a poisonous snake.

Suddenly she understood why his threats had resurfaced. He had followed her the night she'd gone to the Acre, seen her with Rogan, and now planned to punish her by sending Paddy to Mississippi. This was her fault. If only she'd remained at home that evening.

He yanked on her arm. "I said get upstairs."

"I will na go," she shot back. Before she could argue any further, Spencer began to whimper and then burst forth with a lusty cry. "It's time for the babe to eat. If I do na take him to the mistress, she'll come to fetch him."

Bradley stalked to the door and then turned back to face her. His eyes were filled with a mixture of lust and hatred. "Don't think this matter's been concluded," he warned before leaving the room.

Kiara hurried to the door and turned the key before tending to the crying infant. "There, there," she cooed. "Just let me change yar wet nappie and I'll take ya to yar mother." The baby quickly settled, and once he was dry, she wrapped him in a warm blanket. "Thar ya are. Snug as a bug," she whispered. "Now let's go see yar mother."

Jasmine met her in the doorway that joined her bedroom and the nursery. "I'm sorry ya had to get out of yar bed, ma'am. It took me a wee bit longer to change his nappie."

"No need to apologize, Kiara. You've done nothing wrong." She reached for the infant. "Go back to bed. I'll keep Spencer with me after he's finished nursing," she said. "I'm sure you need some sleep. I can rest tomorrow while Father and Bradley are gone to Boston."

"The gentlemen are off on a short trip, are they?"

"Only for the day. Father told me this evening he's going to have Bradley join him, but say nothing, as Bradley doesn't know yet."

Kiara nodded her head. "A surprise, is it? Well, ya can trust me not to be sayin' anything to Mr. Houston." She returned to her room, her heart dancing with delight. She'd try to get word to Rogan tomorrow.

Bradley joined Malcolm at the breakfast table and signaled Sarah to pour his coffee. "I see no reason for you to travel to

Boston, Malcolm. I'm certain I can handle any matters needing attention if you'll merely take me into your confidence."

"I've already made arrangements for the meeting. No need to change them now."

"But it seems a shame to cut into the little time you have with Jasmine in order to conduct business outside of Lowell."

Malcolm forked a piece of sausage onto his plate and helped himself to a steaming bowl of scrambled eggs. "No grits?" he asked, looking in Sarah's direction.

"No, sir. Would you care for some fried potatoes instead?"

"If that's my only choice," he replied, helping himself. "You Northerners should begin serving grits. I'm surprised neither Jasmine nor Alice has begun the practice."

Sarah smiled at Malcolm. "They tell me they're not fond of grits."

"Hurrumph! They never told *me* such a thing."

Bradley found Malcolm's preoccupation annoying. Who really cared what was served for breakfast so long as there was good strong coffee? "Getting back to the topic at hand, Malcolm, wouldn't you prefer to spend your time with Jasmine?"

Malcolm looked up from his plate. "Why don't you come with me? Jasmine doesn't mind in the least that I'm going to be gone to Boston. She learned long ago that men require time to conduct their business if they are going to properly support their families. We'd have time to visit on the train, and you can give me a tour of your shipping business."

Bradley didn't want to show Malcolm his shipping business or anything else for that matter, but if he was going to find out what this meeting was about, he had little alternative. He needed to retain control. Of course, the best way to do that was to keep Malcolm in Lowell, but since that wasn't going to be possible, he'd attend the meeting and hope to bypass a visit to the shipping office. Hopefully Malcolm would decide to make an early departure for Mississippi.

"Thank you, Malcolm. If you insist on attending the meeting, I'd be pleased to accompany you."

Kiara watched from an upstairs window until the carriage pulled away from the house before entering Jasmine's room. "Sarah was needin' some things from town, ma'am. Would ya be mindin' if I took care of that burden fer her?"

"That would be fine. Grandmother's here to help me. Besides, you need to get away from the house more frequently. Be sure you go early in the day so you're home before the men return. I expect them on the last train this evening."

"I'll be goin' this mornin' and will be back afore noon." She dashed down the stairs, retrieved the list from Sarah, and scurried down the road. When she reached the mercantile, she approached Mrs. Paxton. "I have another errand to attend to. Would ya mind if I left my list to be filled and picked it up in a short while?"

"That's fine, Kiara. I'll have it ready when you return."

She ran down the street with her skirt flying in the breeze and her pounding shoes leaving tiny clouds of dust in her wake. She knocked on the door and waited, dancing from foot to foot. "Where is she? Where is she?" she muttered into the morning air. Finally she heard footsteps nearing the door. "Granna Murphy!" she exclaimed when the door opened. "Can I come in?"

The old woman gave her a cordial smile. "You need na ask, lass. Ya're always welcome in our home. What brings ya out at this time o' day? There's no one to visit but your old Granna Murphy."

"I need ya to give Rogan a message."

"Sure, and what would yar message be?" she asked with a crooked grin.

"It's urgent I speak to him. Could ya tell him to come to the Houstons' house and wait at the front of the house near the big tree at eight o'clock? He'll know which one I mean. Tell him to be sure and stay hidden until I call to him. Please do na ferget, Granna. It's important."

"How could I ferget? I'll tell him the moment he walks through that door."

Kiara leaned down and placed a kiss on the weathered old

cheek. "I wish I could stay and visit, but I must be gettin' back to the house. Don't ferget to give him me message."

"Off with ya, lass. I'll na be fergetting, so set yar mind to ease."

———

Bradley forced himself to remain amicable, smiling and nodding at the proper occasions while his level of irritation swelled. Before they departed from Lowell, Malcolm said they would discuss business on the train. However, it now seemed he was more content discussing his sons and their capable management techniques at The Willows. "I'm proud of every one of them. They've taken hold, and all three are excited about remaining in the cotton business."

"Even Samuel? I don't recall him having strong leadership qualities. Has he made some improvement?"

Malcolm bristled at the remark. "There was never anything wrong with Samuel's abilities. You wanted him to whip the slaves into producing more cotton, but he didn't feel that was an appropriate measure—nor did I, for that matter. Our success hasn't depended upon such tactics. In fact, Samuel's duties will be expanding, and David will be taking over his previous duties."

Bradley said no more. He'd once again offended Malcolm Wainwright with his attempts to discredit his eldest son. The remainder of their journey was in silence. Once they arrived in Boston, Bradley hailed a carriage.

"Brackman Hotel on Beacon Street," Malcolm told the driver.

"You're meeting at the Brackman?"

"Yes. Nathan told me he'd arrange for us to use a small meeting room at the hotel since I don't plan to remain overnight."

"You're meeting with Nathan?"

"Nathan, Josiah Baines, Henry Thorne, and several others. I believe Matthew Cheever was going to come in from Lowell. Shame about Tracy Jackson. I didn't realize he'd passed away until Nathan mentioned it in his latest missive."

"Yes. Jackson's passing is a huge loss to the Associates. I didn't realize you and Nathan were on such an intimate basis."

"We've only recently corresponded. I find him an engaging man. Quite knowledgeable and an astute businessman."

Bradley could feel beads of perspiration beginning to form along his upper lip. What was going on? Why had Malcolm begun corresponding with Nathan Appleton? And more importantly, *what* were they corresponding about?

Nathan greeted them in the hotel foyer. "I'm surprised to see you, Bradley. Malcolm didn't tell me you'd be attending the meeting."

Bradley watched the two men exchange glances.

"I thought it might be best if Bradley was present. I find it more difficult hearing things after the fact. Secondhand explanations seem to lose something in the translation."

Nathan nodded. "Whatever makes you most comfortable, Malcolm."

Bradley watched Nathan pat his father-in-law on the back as though they were old friends as they entered the meeting room. Something had gone amiss. He didn't know what, but he was certain he was not going to like the tenor of this meeting.

"Why don't you take over the helm, Malcolm? After all, it was you who suggested this gathering," Nathan said.

"Of course. I'm certain you gentlemen have read my letter and are aware of my growing concerns, both for my cotton shipments as well as my son-in-law's health and well-being."

Bradley stiffened. *My health? My well-being?* What was happening here?

Malcolm continued. "As I told you in my letter, I want to present my proposal for using my son Samuel as the new buyer of cotton from Southern plantation owners. Samuel already has a working relationship with many of the cotton growers that you hope to entice into contracts. I believe you would see positive results from this. Samuel would take over those duties from Bradley, giving him more time for other duties with the Corporation. My hope is that you can assign Bradley to duties in Lowell to allow him to spend more time with his wife and new son."

Bradley barely stifled his rage. He shifted in his chair and reached for Malcolm's elbow. "What are you doing?" he asked between clenched teeth. "I don't want to be released from my duties as buyer for the Corporation," he whispered forcefully.

Malcolm ignored the plea and maintained his focus upon the other men gathered in the room. "With Samuel in Mississippi, I envision his role as a buyer who can travel among the plantations, keep track of inventory, arrange for shipments, and handle any other unforeseen circumstances that may occur with the growers. Additionally, as I stated earlier, with our many contacts in the South, I feel certain Samuel can further expand the number of suppliers as needed. You must realize Southerners are notoriously cautious where Yankees are concerned."

The men chuckled as if completely understanding his point. But Bradley felt like screaming. He was losing control and that was something he didn't brook well.

Malcolm spoke again. "And, of course, should the need arise for someone to accompany a shipment for any reason, I have two other sons who could make themselves available for such an assignment. Overall, I believe this will be a much improved method."

"I couldn't agree more," Nathan replied.

"Nor I," concurred Josiah while the other members murmured their assent. "To be honest, we've been very concerned. I don't know if Nathan informed you, but there have been grave concerns of late regarding the cotton shipments. I, for one, feel much more confident knowing there will be someone in charge who can follow the process and give it his complete devotion. No offense, Bradley, but you've certainly not been yourself recently, and by your own admission you feel the need to be closer to home."

"If I could have a moment alone with you, Malcolm," Bradley urged. If he didn't say something soon, he would explode.

"We can talk during our return to Lowell," Malcolm replied. "Well, gentlemen, if we're all in agreement, I'll have Samuel begin his duties as soon as I return to Mississippi."

The meeting was adjourned before Bradley had time to drink his second glass of port. He walked out of the hotel in stunned silence, and it wasn't until they were settled on the train that he once again voiced his objection to his father-in-law.

"If you had a problem with me, I wish you would have brought it to my attention. I truly do not understand why you think this change is necessary. It's not as though Samuel doesn't have many duties to perform on the plantation already."

"This has nothing to do with the plantation, Bradley. This has to do with the proper handling of the cotton shipments and payments. There needs to be a line of communication between buyers and sellers, an awareness of potential problems or delays. You've not handled matters well, my boy. You didn't even inform your business partners I had written to explain our first harvest would be smaller due to excessive rains and subsequent boll rot.

"After talking with Jasmine and my mother, I'm aware you are suffering under a burden of undue stress. Believe me, you need not feel inadequate. There are few men who could have coped with the magnitude of details and duties you were attempting to handle."

Bradley rubbed his forehead, certain he'd heard incorrectly. "Jasmine and Grandmother Wainwright told you I've been unable to cope with my business interests? They spoke against me?"

"They spoke no ill word against you at all. However, they were gravely concerned about you, my boy. I applaud their efforts on your behalf, and I'm certain that once you've begun your new duties in Lowell, you'll be delighted they took your best interests to heart."

Bradley seethed. How dare those two interfering women go over his head and contact Malcolm? Because of them, he was going to lose all of the income he'd come to depend upon. With Samuel managing the shipments and books, there would be no opportunity for Bradley to underhandedly increase his income. Worse yet, Malcolm was going to find out the percentages were higher than what Bradley had previously divulged. His anger neared a boiling rage, yet he knew he must remain calm.

"When are you planning to return to The Willows?" he inquired.

Malcolm appeared puzzled. "I've booked passage for the end of the week, which means we've much to accomplish prior to my departure."

Bradley arched his eyebrows. "Such as?"

"We'll need at least two to three days to go over the book-work. I'll want to take the ledgers and accounts with me as well as the contracts and any other papers relating to each buyer's position. I want Samuel to have opportunity to review all of the paper work so he'll have a firm footing to begin his new duties. In fact, I gave serious consideration to bringing him with me, but I wasn't positive the Associates would agree to this change."

Bradley grimaced at the thought of Samuel being present for this embarrassment and was thankful Malcolm had thought better of the idea. "Perhaps it would be best if you spent the remainder of your time visiting with Jasmine. I can have the paper work shipped to you."

"I will certainly visit with my daughter, but I want to go over the ledgers with you in order to gain a better understanding of the methods you've utilized so that I can explain them to Samuel. Besides, if I have questions, you can immediately answer them instead of my waiting for weeks to hear from you by mail—and you're not the best correspondent," Malcolm added.

Bradley turned his attention away from Malcolm and stared out the window. A sick feeling churned in the pit of his stomach. In the short time remaining, how could he possibly rework the ledgers before revealing them to Malcolm?

Kiara listened at the top of the stairway as the two men returned home later that night. Bradley stormed into the house and went directly to his library, although Kiara thought Mr. Wainwright appeared to be in a rather pleasant mood. She'd need to keep her distance from Bradley. She wanted nothing to interfere with her meeting this evening.

The baby was fast asleep, and Jasmine and Grandmother Wainwright were busy with their sewing as Kiara entered the room. "I was wonderin' if I might go for a little walk, ma'am. I won't be outside fer long. I'd just like a breath o' fresh air."

"I was thinking about taking a walk myself," Jasmine replied. "Perhaps I'll join you."

Before Kiara could object, Alice came to the rescue. "There's a chill in the air, dear. It could affect your milk. I think it would be best to remain indoors. Midafternoon would be a better time of day for you to take a walk."

"Perhaps you'd join me tomorrow afternoon, Kiara?"

"Certainly, ma'am. I'd be pleased ta go walkin' with ya on the morrow. But ya do na mind if I go tonight, do ya?"

Jasmine gave her blessing, and Kiara made her way down the stairway, careful to avoid Bradley. She didn't know where he might be lurking, but she didn't want to encounter him this evening. The kitchen was dark, and she managed to slip out the door and around the house without being noticed.

"Rogan, are ya here?"

"Aye, I'm here. How could I stay away with such a message as ya left with Granna? It sounds as though it's a matter of life and death."

"That it is," Kiara replied, tears of anger and fear welling in her eyes.

"Ah, it can na be as bad as that, lass," he said, pulling her into an embrace. "Come on now and dry yar eyes and tell me yar problem. We'll get it solved one way or the other."

"Mr. Houston is goin' to send Paddy to Mississippi, where he'll be forced to work on the Wainwrights' cotton plantation. He can na survive such a life, Rogan. And I can na survive without me brother. We're goin' ta be just like those slave families Miss Jasmine told me about. We'll be separated and never see each other again."

"Ya know I'll do whatever I can ta help ya, lass."

"I want ya to take Paddy and hide him. Mr. Houston will come lookin' in the Acre, so ya'll have to hide him in a place where he won't think of lookin'."

"I do na think yar idea is sound. Thar's strict penalties when

315

ya break the servitude laws, Kiara."

Kiara backed away from him. She could not believe what she'd heard. "Ya're more concerned about my indenturin' papers than Paddy being sent off to some cotton plantation that might as well be on the other side of the world away from me?"

"I do na want ya endin' up in more trouble than either of us can handle. What good would ya be doin' Paddy if ya end up in jail, lass? And do na think they wouldn't put ya there. If this Mr. Houston's as mean as ya say, he'll have ya placed on public display before ya're hauled off to jail."

"Do ya not understand what I'm saying, Rogan Sheehan? Mr. Wainwright is leavin' the end of the week, and I've little doubt Paddy will be goin' with him."

"Let me talk to me boss, Liam Donohue. He'll surely be able to give us some sound ideas. He's smart and knows all the right people."

"There isn't time for talkin', Rogan. We need ta be doin' somethin' now."

"If you'll put a little faith in me and a lot of faith in God, we'll somehow find a way to get this whole thing settled. What ya need to do is take yarself inside and get down on yar knees. Pray fer God's intercession to look after Paddy. Will ya do that, lass? Give me but a day. We've got that much time."

"I'll give ya a day, and I'll pray, but I don't believe God cares enough ta do anything. He's given me little hope that He's ever heard one of my prayers."

Rogan gave her a wink and smiled. "You pray, and I'll take care of the believin' for the both of us."

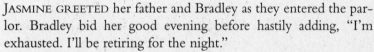

CHAPTER · 28

JASMINE GREETED her father and Bradley as they entered the parlor. Bradley bid her good evening before hastily adding, "I'm exhausted. I'll be retiring for the night."

Jasmine watched from the parlor as her husband made his way up the stairs without so much as a good-night kiss.

"How was your evening, my dear?" her father inquired.

"Quite fine, Papa. Bradley appeared distraught. Was your dinner meeting unproductive?" she ventured.

He nodded. "I'm certain he found our time together extremely disappointing. I thought he planned to discuss the shift of his duties to Samuel, but I was incorrect. In fact, he wanted me to change my decision. He was amicable and repentant when we began dinner, but when he realized I would not be dissuaded, his mood changed dramatically."

Jasmine looked at him in understanding. "I'm not surprised. Bradley isn't accustomed to being refused."

"Well, I'm certain that given time, he'll come to appreciate that this is best for his family. His behavior this evening revealed characteristics I've never observed previously—angry conduct I fear you've been subjected to throughout your marriage, and it grieves me to know I placed you in this situation. I plan to have a long talk with your husband before I depart, but I do wish there were something I could do right now that would help ease your circumstances."

"There is one thing, Papa."

"Anything! You just tell me what you want, and I'll see to it."

"Please don't take Paddy back to The Willows with you. If Paddy leaves here, it will be Kiara's undoing, and she has been a true blessing to me. I don't know how I would have endured my marriage without her support and friendship. Bradley has been angry with Paddy ever since he accidentally forgot to lock one of the stalls and Bradley's favorite horse escaped for a short time. The horse suffered a small cut on his leg, but it healed long ago and no harm was done. The horse was retrieved before Bradley even returned home. It is pure foolishness that he continues to hold a grudge against the child. Paddy is an excellent worker, and everyone speaks highly of his abilities, especially given his tender years."

Her father rubbed his balding head and stared thoughtfully at some distant object. "Bradley seemed insistent. He said the boy is a troublemaker and consistently difficult to manage."

"You should speak with the stable master. Ask what *he* thinks of Paddy. He has told me the boy is a natural with horseflesh and works exceedingly well with the animals. He even mentioned he'd like to hire him on permanently once his servitude ends."

"I don't need to visit with the stable master, Jasmine. I can certainly take the word of my daughter. I'll tell Bradley I won't take the boy with me, but if Bradley feels strongly about this matter, he'll likely try to rid himself of the boy in some other manner, and should that happen, you'll have no control."

Thoughts tumbled through Jasmine's mind as she digested her father's words. He was correct. Bradley would undoubtedly sell Paddy to someone else. *Sell Paddy.* That was the answer.

She clapped her hands together. "I know, Papa. Tell Bradley you want to purchase Paddy's contract—that you wouldn't want to take him into your possession unless you had papers showing you were actually his owner. Then you can sign over his freedom, and he can live with Grandmother and work part time at the stables in town to support himself. He could still see Kiara, yet he'd be out of Bradley's control. What do you think?"

"Sounds like a workable idea, so long as your grandmother agrees."

Jasmine giggled. "She'll agree. Grandmother has developed a penchant for Kiara's lace, and this arrangement will give her ample opportunity to nag the poor girl about her handiwork."

"Sounds like an arrangement your grandmother would relish. She always did enjoy having the upper hand. Now, if you'll excuse me, dear, I think I'll go up to bed. Shouldn't you be doing the same? Spencer will be awake before long, and you'll wish you'd gotten some rest."

She smiled up at her father. "I'll just finish this last row of stitching, and then I'll be up."

Malcolm leaned down and kissed her cheek. "Good night, my dear."

"Good night, Papa. And thank you for your willingness to help Paddy."

He smiled and nodded, his eyes still reflecting some of the sadness she'd noticed earlier in their conversation.

Bradley paced in his bedroom as he waited to hear the sound of footsteps in the hallway. When over an hour had passed, his mild frustration was replaced by acute irritation. Finally he heard someone climbing the stairway. Malcolm must be retiring for the night, as there was no sound in Jasmine's adjoining bedroom. Why had Jasmine remained in the parlor? He had much to accomplish this night, but he dared not return downstairs until everyone was in bed. Had Kiara not been in the nursery, he would have awakened Spencer in order to force his wife upstairs.

Willing to wait no longer, he called her upstairs, feigning he'd heard the baby crying. Jasmine hurried up the stairs and met him in the hallway. "I couldn't enter the nursery," he told her. "Kiara has the door locked, but I'm certain I heard Spencer crying."

"I'm surprised. Kiara is always quick to awaken when he cries.

Go back to bed, Bradley. I know you're exhausted. I'll see you in the morning."

Bradley retreated to his room, glad they were still in separate rooms despite the baby's birth. He leaned against the door, listening. He heard Jasmine speak to Kiara and Kiara deny that the baby was awake. Jasmine then informed the girl she was going to prepare for bed. Bradley hastily made his exit out of the room and downstairs to his study. If he was to present his records and ledgers to Malcolm the following day, he must adjust the accounts tonight.

He had given consideration to taking the books and going into seclusion in Concord or some other small city where Malcolm wouldn't find him. But that would likely send alarm signals to both Malcolm and the Associates. Besides, he needed to meet with his father-in-law regarding Paddy. If he accomplished nothing else, he'd be certain Kiara knew who was in charge of this household and that he was a man of his word.

It would take all night to transfer the figures, but he had little choice. Pulling the books from his desk, Bradley began the tedious task of calculating and reentering figures into a new ledger book that he would present to Malcolm the next day. A ledger that would reflect figures matching those Malcolm believed the Associates were paying for his cotton. It would take little to alter the contract figures. But his thoughts were jumbled, and he'd not yet reconciled how he would explain the higher price he'd negotiated with the Associates. Malcolm, however, had never seen the contract, and Bradley would be safe so long as no one ever mentioned the higher figure. Bradley still maintained hope he might be able to convince the Associates he was to remain the payee on the later contract he'd negotiated for an additional percentage.

The entries were rushed and sloppy, smudged, and hopelessly illegible in places. Although he was exhausted and overwhelmed, Bradley completed the task just before sunrise. He checked his last entries, doubting Malcolm would be able to decipher the final pages of figures.

"He can recalculate for himself," Bradley murmured, looking for a fresh piece of blotting paper.

Finding the last of his blotting paper spent, Bradley spread the open ledger upon his desktop to dry, tucked the old ledgers into a drawer, which he carefully locked, and after turning down the wick of his lamp, shuffled up the stairs. He hoped for at least an hour of sleep before revisiting the ledger books with Malcolm.

———

Jasmine returned the baby to his cradle and heard Bradley's door opening. Then the bed creaked, followed almost instantaneously by her husband's snores.

Something was amiss. She wondered what Bradley could have been doing downstairs at this hour. Returning to her room, Jasmine was overcome by an irresistible curiosity. Candle in hand, she slipped into her robe, crept down the stairs, and entered her husband's study. She touched the lamp's glass globe and found it still warm. So he had been working in his study, she surmised.

She sat down in his large chair and looked at the ledger that lay open on the desk in front of her. This wasn't the ledger Bradley normally used when figuring the accounts. She held the candle closer, looking at the barely legible figures that were so unlike Bradley. Could he possibly be altering the books? Dare he be stealing from her family? She attempted to open the desk drawers. They were locked. If Bradley was stealing, there was no way she could prove her statements without the original ledger. Yet why would he be entering figures from two months ago if he weren't falsifying the books? Her husband was always careful to complete his records and present them to the Associates, for one thing Bradley always expected was immediate payment.

Bradley's sloppy entries left several blotches of ink on the page that had not yet dried. If she closed the books, the pages would smear against one another—proof the entries had all been made at one time. Without a second thought, she closed the book, pressed it tightly together, and left the room.

———

Bradley awakened with a start. A column of sunlight was

streaming through his bedroom window, cutting a wide path across the room. "It must be at least ten o'clock," he muttered while pouring water from a china pitcher into the matching bowl. Thankfully he'd slept in his clothes. He splashed his face with water, quickly finger-combed his hair, and straightened his tie before exiting the room.

It seemed breakfast was long over, although a plate remained on the table at his place. Sarah appeared from the kitchen and offered him coffee. "I'll heat your breakfast," she offered. "It won't take long."

"Just coffee, Sarah. I'm not hungry. Do I hear voices coming from the library?"

"Oh yes, sir. Mr. Cheever and Mr. Wainwright asked if they might take the liberty of using the room for their meeting."

"Matthew Cheever? What meeting? How long has he been here?"

Sarah furrowed her brow. "Forty-five minutes—maybe an hour."

"And no one awakened me?" He pushed aside the cup of coffee and hurried off.

Matthew Cheever was exiting the library as Bradley entered the hallway. "Matthew! I was just coming to join you and Malcolm."

"Good morning, Bradley. No need to hurry. We've already completed our conversation, and I must get back to the mills." Matthew retrieved his hat from the hallway and without further discussion took his leave.

Bradley hurried back to the library, where Malcolm was placing a folded paper in his breast pocket. "Why the early morning meeting with Matthew Cheever?"

"Oh, it was nothing of importance, Bradley. Jasmine informed me you had been up until the wee hours, and I certainly didn't want to disturb your sleep. You obviously needed your rest. Perhaps we should get started on the ledgers."

Bradley breathed a bit easier. Apparently the meeting with Matthew didn't impact him, and the ledgers had been completed last night. Everything would be fine if he kept his wits about him. "The ledger is in my study, Malcolm. I'll just go and retrieve it."

The sound of chatter caused him to look into the hallway, where Jasmine and Paddy were making their way toward the door. "Come in here, Paddy," he ordered. "Jasmine, would you retrieve the ledger from the top of my desk, please? Your father and I need to go over some accounts."

Jasmine nodded and walked away while Paddy entered the room. "This is the boy I mentioned, Malcolm," Bradley began, "the one I want you to take to Mississippi. His name is Padraig O'Neill."

"If I'm to have charge of him," Malcolm said, "I'll want to buy out his indenture contract. I'll not take him with you still holding his papers in your name."

"If you want to buy the papers, I won't object. I was merely offering him to you free of cost, but if such an arrangement makes you uncomfortable, I'm willing to take your money." Bradley flashed a look of self-satisfaction toward Paddy. "I'll get his papers after we've gone over the ledgers."

Paddy's shoulders slumped, and he hunkered down near the door. "Ya can na be doin' this to me, sir. I love takin' care of yar horses. Why are ya sendin' me away?"

"Nooo!" Kiara cried, dashing into the room and clinging to Bradley's arm. "Please. I'm beggin' you, do just this one thing for me. Do na send him away. I'll do anything. I promise I'll make it up to you." She met his hardened gaze with pleading tear-filled eyes.

Just when he thought he could take no more of Kiara's whining, Jasmine entered the library with his ledger tucked under her arm.

"Kiara, what's wrong?" She hurried to the girl and wrapped her in an embrace while handing the ledger to Bradley.

"Malcolm and I are attempting to conduct business. All of you need to leave the library," Bradley ordered.

Kiara ran from the room with Jasmine close on her heels, calling her name. Obviously unable to comprehend the situation,

Paddy remained in place, staring after the two women.

"Get on with you!" Bradley shouted. "Get back to the barn." Startled, Paddy darted from the room like a fox being chased by hounds.

"How much did you want for the boy's contract?" Malcolm inquired.

"I want to be fair," Bradley replied, producing Lord Palmerston's original paper work.

Malcolm examined the papers and said, "I'll give you an extra fifty dollars for the room and board you've provided since his arrival."

"Of course, he did receive excellent training in handling horseflesh," Bradley submitted.

"An additional seventy-five."

"Agreed." Bradley felt a sense of smug satisfaction at the arrangement. Malcolm wasn't such a shrewd businessman. Bradley would have taken nothing for the boy. It appeared matters of business were improving. "Now, then, shall we begin working on the ledgers?"

Jasmine couldn't keep pace with Kiara, and by the time she rounded the house, the girl was nowhere to be seen. Her cries for Kiara went unanswered even though she called out that there was a solution for Paddy's predicament.

Realizing Kiara likely didn't believe her, Jasmine continued searching and calling until her voice became hoarse. Frustrated by her failed attempts, Jasmine finally made her way to the stable, where she found Paddy huddled in a corner. She pulled him into a warm embrace and carefully explained that he would not be sent to The Willows.

"My father has purchased your papers and will send you to live with Grandmother. You'll be able to see Kiara and, if you like, I know Grandmother will permit you to work at the stables in Lowell. I'm certain they'd be delighted to have you."

"And do ya think they'd be payin' me?" he asked with a glimmer in his eyes.

"Of course they would," Jasmine replied.

"Then I'll save up me coins until I can buy Kiara's papers from Mr. Bradley," he vowed.

"As soon as you see Kiara, explain to her there's no need to worry and it's safe to come back to the house. Will you do that?"

"Yes, ma'am, and thank ya fer yar kindness."

For several hours, Bradley and Malcolm were hunched over the ledgers. They had gone over each entry, discussing the accounting procedures and computations.

"I think I'll go upstairs and get a cigar from my room, if you don't mind. I need to stretch my legs after all this sitting," Malcolm said.

"Not at all," Bradley replied. He leaned back in his chair. The explanations had gone well. There was only one final ledger page remaining, and it appeared Malcolm had detected nothing out of the ordinary. Bradley was pleased—especially since he'd already spent the funds he had stolen from his father-in-law.

Considering its unpleasant beginning, this day was now exceeding all expectations. He'd managed to make extra money from the sale of Paddy's contract, and he could now use the leverage with Kiara that if she wanted her brother back, she'd have to grant him favors. The only sour note remaining was the fact that he was going to miss out on the additional funds he'd previously been skimming from Malcolm. He had Jasmine to blame for that loss. If she and her grandmother would have kept their noses out of his business matters, this would have never occurred.

"Interfering women," he muttered contemptuously.

He sat forward and began to turn the final page. It was stuck. Horrified by the discovery, he took his letter opener and carefully pried the corner of the pages. Gently, he loosened the sheets until they finally separated. He stared down at the pages, with his disbelieving gaze focused upon the entries that had been smudged and transferred onto the opposite page. He could hear Malcolm's approaching footsteps and closed the book with a resounding crack.

"I'm ready for dinner. Why don't we take a break from this drudgery for a while? I'm sure working with these numbers is hard on your eyes."

"Nonsense, Bradley. We're nearly done. We can surely wait another half hour to have our dinner."

Bradley pushed away from the desk, his face forming a scowl. "This is my home, Malcolm, and I think I should be the one who decides when we will take our meals. And we are going to eat dinner now."

Malcolm stared at him as though he were a lunatic. "If you're that determined, go right ahead. I'll stay here and complete the ledger work on my own."

"Absolutely not! We'll resume when I say we will." He jumped up from his chair and stormed from the room, the book tucked securely beneath his arm.

CHAPTER · 29

BRADLEY RACED up the steps two at a time and retreated to the sanctuary of his bedroom, uncertain how he would handle this sudden glitch in his plans. Pulling a small case from beneath his bed, he unlocked the clasp and placed the ledger inside before retrieving a piece of stationery from his maple writing desk.

He thought for a moment and then dipped his pen and spoke aloud as he wrote. "'Dear Jasmine, I have been called away' . . . no, that's not good," he muttered, quickly taking out a new sheet of paper. "'Urgent business has developed. I must be away for several days,'" he wrote, nodding his head. That sounded much better. He continued scrawling the note, adding an apology to Malcolm for his hasty departure and giving his regrets that he would not be available to accompany his father-in-law to the docks in Boston. In a hasty postscript, he thanked Malcolm for his willingness to take Paddy to The Willows and wished him well in his endeavor to teach the boy a proper work ethic.

He gave the letter a cursory reading, folded it, and placed it atop his bed. Uncertain of Jasmine's whereabouts, he knew he dare not take the letter to her room and risk the likelihood of facing her. Without time for thoughtful consideration, he quickly packed a few belongings in a satchel and crept down the back stairway and out to the stables.

A dappled gray mare had been saddled in readiness for her daily exercise routine, and Bradley's spirits buoyed at his good fortune. Tying his bag to the back of the saddle, Bradley gave a self-satisfied grunt. His luck had obviously changed for the better. He untied the horse and was lifting his foot toward the stirrup when a hand clasped his arm in a tight grip.

"Mr. Houston, I'm beggin' ya, please do na send Paddy away. You should na be punishin' the boy and takin' yar anger out on him when 'tis *me* ya're angry with."

Lustrous black hair fell around Kiara's face in soft wispy curls, highlighting the beauty of her creamy white complexion. Bradley could not resist. With a rough jerk, he pulled her into his arms. "So now you finally realize the power I hold over you," he snarled, his lips coming down hard and crushing her mouth in a brutal kiss. She struggled against his assault, but her resistance caused him to desire her all the more.

He attempted to capture her lips in another cruel kiss, but she pushed hard against his chest, freeing her mouth. His anger intensified as she bent her head forward and positioned it against his chest in an effort to fend him off.

"Stop! Ya have no right ta hurt me!" she hollered while twisting against his hold.

He heard a rustling sound but didn't have time to turn around before a shocking pain jolted through his skull. His eyes grew wide as the tremor of pain sped throughout his entire body. He stumbled and fell backward.

"Paddy!" Kiara screamed over the neighing of the spooked mare.

Bradley grasped his head, momentarily dazed but quickly regaining his senses. Crawling toward Paddy, he reached for the boy's shirt, missing it, but finally gained enough strength to get on his feet. His arms flailed as dizziness overtook him and he stumbled backward.

"Look out for the mare!" Paddy hollered as Bradley fell beneath the horse.

Kiara screamed and pulled Paddy to her side. "Oh, Paddy, what are we gonna do?" She stared down at Bradley. He lay on the hay-strewn floor with blood pouring from the wound on his face where the horse had kicked him. "He's dead. Of that there is no doubt," she hoarsely whispered.

"We did na do anything wrong, Kiara. He was attackin' ya, and I hit him with the shovel, but 'twas the horse what killed him."

"They'll never believe us, Paddy," she cried. "I fear they'll accuse ya of murder after all the mean things Mr. Houston said about ya. He told Mr. Wainwright what a bad little feller ya are and that ya're hard to manage. No doubt they'll believe the worst."

A rustling caused Kiara to turn toward the stable door, where Jasmine Wainwright stood with a pistol in her hand. "Oh, Miss Jasmine! Please don' kill 'im," she screamed, pushing Paddy behind her skirts.

Jasmine's eyes grew wide and she arched her brows. *"Kill him?"* She lay the weapon down and walked to Kiara and Paddy. "I was outside the stable. I heard and saw everything that went on in here. I know what's been happening, Kiara. I haven't known long, but I know how Bradley has been tormenting you. Since the day I discovered what he was doing, I prayed that God would release you from this misery. I believe this accident is God's way of interceding."

"Why do ya have that gun?" Paddy asked.

"I didn't want Bradley to leave. I wanted him to come in and talk to my father and me. But I thought the only way he'd consent was if I threatened him," she admitted. "Bradley has been making many people miserable with his behavior, and I've prayed God would change him and soften his heart. I did not love him, but I wanted him to become a better man."

"Aye, 'twould have been easier for all of us had he been a better man," Kiara agreed. "I believe there are those what would argue Paddy's blow with the shovel is what caused yar husband's death. I do na think this will be so simple as you think. 'Twould be best for Paddy to run from here."

"No need," Malcolm declared as he walked into the barn. "Nothing but an accident. Pure and simple."

"That's right," Jasmine agreed. "Nothing but an accident."

CHAPTER · 30

FEW TEARS were shed at Bradley Houston's funeral. It was, by Lowell standards, a small gathering. Alice was in attendance, Nolan came from Boston, and Malcolm delayed his return to Mississippi in order to lend his support to Jasmine. A few of the Boston Associates made their appearance, along with a smattering of Lowell residents. Most came to offer Jasmine support rather than to honor Bradley—she knew this well enough. Jasmine cried briefly as the service got underway. For the first time in her life she mourned the fact that someone did not know the Lord and cared nothing for God's truth.

Jasmine had not been exceedingly strong in her faith prior to her marriage, but now it seemed to be the only means of holding her life together. It comforted her to know that God's hand was upon her—that He truly cared for her just as He had cared for Job. She thought of a verse from the thirteenth chapter of Job, remembering it in part. "Though he slay me, yet will I trust in him." *And I will,* Jasmine thought. She would go on trusting the Lord, come what may.

The preacher offered a brief sermon, talking of the resurrection of Jesus and how all those who put their trust in Him would rise again. But Jasmine knew her husband had not come to know

God during his lifetime. Her heart ached with the knowledge that she had failed to guide Bradley into God's saving grace. Bradley had known the truth, but he had chosen to reject God's plan for redemption. And now he would pay the ultimate price—throughout eternity.

————————

Kiara tugged on the sheet and tucked the corner under the thin mattress that lined her cot. Several days had passed since the funeral, and life had returned to a calm ebb and flow. Pleasant—much like the days when Bradley had been gone to Boston on business. From all appearances, Jasmine's words had been true. Nothing was going to happen to Paddy. Bradley was dead and buried, and no one had come forward asking any questions about his death. Mr. Wainwright had returned home to Mississippi, leaving Paddy to continue working in the Houston stables. And although Nolan remained in Lowell, he seemed more concerned about Jasmine and the baby than his brother's death.

Straightening the blanket with her open palm, Kiara gave one final pat to the bed. She owed Jasmine Houston a great deal, yet she'd not offered her mistress so much as a word of thanks.

"It's high time ya got in there," she chided herself. After tapping on Jasmine's bedroom door, she hesitated a moment and then peeked around the corner. "May I come in, ma'am?"

"Of course, Kiara. I'm always pleased to have you visit me. It's been too long since we've had a chat."

"I've come ta offer me thanks for what ya did for me and Paddy. I've never said it, but I hope ya know how much it means ta me that ya didn't hold the boy responsible for yar husband's death."

"Of course I know. There's no doubt you love your brother as much as I love Spencer, and I know how I would feel if someone threatened to take him away from me."

"Thank ya for understandin'. Now can I ask ya how ya happened to be outside the stables that day?"

"Several nights before Bradley's death, I was awakened by the sound of voices in the nursery. I went to the door and heard Bradley threatening you. I listened, not wanting to believe what I was hearing. I finally understood what had been happening right under my nose all these months."

Tears trickled down Kiara's cheeks. "I promise ya, ma'am, I never acted unseemly or encouraged him. I did na want his sinful advances," she sobbed.

Jasmine pulled her into a comforting embrace. "I believe you, Kiara. Please don't cry. I know you were trying to protect Paddy. I heard Bradley making arrangements to sell Paddy to my father and took matters into my own hands. I asked my father to buy Paddy's papers and then turn him over to Grandmother. We were going to have him work at the stables in town and live with Grandmother so you would still be able to visit with him."

Across the room, Spencer whimpered, and Kiara hurried to the cradle and lifted him into her arms. "Is he hungry?"

Jasmine nodded and took the baby, gently putting him to her breast. "You know, Paddy had several people looking out for his welfare. Papa related that Matthew Cheever had approached him, offering to buy Paddy's papers on behalf of a dear friend. At quite a profit, I might add," she said with a smile. "Once my father explained the final arrangements he was making with Grandmother, Mr. Cheever acknowledged the boy would be safe with her and he did not pursue the matter further."

" 'Twas Rogan at the heart of that," Kiara whispered, her love for him doubling as she grasped the depth of his kindness.

"Rogan?"

Kiara's cheeks grew hot with embarrassment. "Rogan Sheehan, Bridgett's cousin from the Acre. He works for Liam Donohue. He knew of my plight and said he would be helpin' find a way to save Paddy. He told me to pray, but I grew angry and told him I did na trust him or God to take care of Paddy. Rogan said Mr. Donohue was a friend of Mr. Cheever and he might help, but I did na think anyone would help. But I was wrong. Look how many people were tryin' to help me and Paddy. It seems God does care about us after all."

Jasmine smiled at her friend. "You know, Kiara, God has always cared about you and Paddy. If you'd only stop being afraid to believe others love you, you might find yourself truly blessed and even happy."

Kiara gave her a lopsided grin. "You're likely right, Missus—maybe that's already true." Kiara gave her a thoughtful glance. "But I still do na understand how ya happened to be in the barn that day."

"Early that morning, I went into Bradley's study, and what I saw made me believe he'd been up late into the night transferring figures. He had a new ledger, not the one I'd seen him use in the past, and the ink was still wet on the last page. That in itself might not have persuaded me, but the entries were for the months prior—all obviously entered that evening. I knew he was to have a meeting with my father to go over the accounts later that morning. I feared he was stealing money from my father and the other cotton producers in Mississippi and Louisiana. But I knew I wouldn't be able to prove what Bradley had done because I didn't have the original ledger book, so I closed the new book, knowing the pages would smudge and stick together."

Kiara looked unconvinced. "He could have told yar father he fergot to blot the pages and that would have been the end of it. I do na understand."

"If the pages were smudged in several places, it showed he had entered the figures all at one time rather than a few entries at a time, as would be normal."

Kiara's eyes sparkled and she nodded her head. "Oh, I see! Ya're quite the clever one, ain't ya?"

"I'm not pleased I had to resort to such tactics, but I knew something must be done to make Bradley come to his senses. I went to my father and explained Bradley was making false entries in the ledger. We agreed it was time for Bradley to admit what he'd been doing. My father was willing to work with him to resolve any misappropriation of money, still wanting to believe Bradley was merely under stress from being overworked. They met as planned, and my father slipped away for a cigar, knowing Bradley would discover the final pages were smeared and stuck together."

"So yar father was off to get a cigar, knowin' Mr. Houston would have to make a decision as to how he was going to handle his lyin' and stealin.'"

"Exactly. However, we thought he would beg Papa's forgiveness and ask to pay back the money he'd stolen. When he stormed from the room without showing my father the final pages, we knew he'd sneak from the house at the first possible opportunity. Papa immediately went to the barn to hide and wait for Bradley."

"And you, ma'am, where did *you* go?"

"I feared Bradley might grow violent when my father confronted him. So I went upstairs to get Bradley's pistol."

"I think I know the rest," Kiara said. "I'm truly sorry for all that's happened. My guilt is deep. Had I never come to this place, yar babe would still have a father and ya'd not be a widow, but I want ya to believe I never wanted nothin' bad to come yar way. I tried to stop him, but I could na. I'm beggin' yar forgiveness, fer ya have been nothin' but good to me."

"Oh, Kiara, you owe me no apology," Jasmine said, pulling the girl into an embrace. "If it will make you feel better to hear me say I forgive you, then know that for any perceived wrong you believe you've done, I give you my forgiveness. However, I know you were an innocent victim, and I believe you would never intentionally hurt me."

Kiara pulled a handkerchief from her pocket and wiped her eyes. Jasmine's forgiveness lifted her burden of guilt, yet she knew that it was God's forgiveness she truly wanted and needed—not for the things Bradley had done to her, for those reprehensible acts were not of her making. The visits he had made to her bed were his sin, not hers, and she knew she'd not face God's retribution for Bradley Houston's ugly deeds.

But she had hardened her heart against God. Even when Jasmine had read Bible verses to her, she'd turned away, not wanting to hear the truth of what God would tell her.

"Please don't cry, Kiara. All is forgiven and you're going to be fine," Jasmine said, obviously confused that Kiara's tears had not yet subsided.

"I'm thinkin' I'd like to be askin' God's forgiveness fer turning away from Him. Would ya be willin' to pray with me?"

Jasmine grasped Kiara's hands firmly in her own. "Nothing would please me more, dear friend."

———

"Kiara, could you come to the parlor? I need some help with Spencer," Jasmine called.

Kiara hurried down the hallway while wiping her hands on the tail of her worn cotton apron, wondering what possible help Jasmine might need with the wee babe. She stopped short when she reached the parlor doorway. Rogan and Paddy were seated side by side on the settee, and Alice Wainwright was settled in the sewing rocker. Jasmine was holding Spencer, while Nolan Houston sat opposite her.

Seeing all of them gathered together caused her to clutch the hem of her apron all the more tightly. "What's all this about?" Her voice warbled unrecognizably in her own ears.

"I sent Paddy to fetch Rogan. I thought he should be here for this gathering," Jasmine replied. "Come sit down and join us." She patted the cushion of a nearby chair.

Kiara's gaze darted from person to person as she made her way to the chair. They all smiled at her, yet she wasn't completely sure she could trust their smiles. There was an ominous feel to such an odd grouping of people. "And why are we all here?" she asked.

Jasmine handed the baby to Alice and retrieved several sheets of paper from the mahogany side table. "This is your contract of servitude," she said, showing it to Kiara.

"Aye. That it is."

"And this is Paddy's, given to me by my father," Jasmine added.

"I see," Kiara said, but in truth she did not.

Jasmine walked to the fireplace and threw the papers into the crackling fire. Kiara watched in awe as the flames licked up around the white pages, charring them as black as night. The fire snapped and ebbed as the burnt paper quickly turned to an ashy residue.

"You're free to go wherever you choose. Nobody owns you; nobody can hold you against your will ever again," Jasmine said. "But I want you to know that it's my hope that you and Paddy will stay here with me for a time. Grandmother has agreed to move in with me, but if you and Paddy are of a mind to make a decent wage, we could certainly use your help."

Kiara stared at Jasmine, unable to say a word. The woman's kindness had rendered her completely speechless.

"Can we stay, Kiara? Can we?" Paddy asked excitedly as he jumped up from the settee and danced about in front of her as though he'd been attacked by a colony of red ants. "Ya know I do na want to leave the horses. Ya do know that, don't ya?"

"I can na even think with you hoppin' from foot to foot in front of me, Padraig. Sit yarself down. I do na know how to thank ya for what ya're doing fer us, ma'am. As fer stayin' and helpin' ya . . ."

Rogan got up and stood before Kiara. "Before ya go makin' any rash decisions, lass, I've got somethin' to say in this matter. Ya know I'm in love with ya, lass, and I'm wantin' ta make ya my wife. Will ya marry me, Kiara O'Neill?"

Tears rolled freely down Kiara's cheeks as she nodded her head vigorously.

Rogan lifted her hand to his lips. "I do na have a ring ta give ya just yet, but I hope ya know my heart is full of love fer ya," he said. "I hope ya're not angry with me, Mrs. Houston."

Jasmine gave him a broad smile. "I had Paddy bring you here because I knew of your feelings for Kiara. I would never deny her the joy of finding true love. I've no doubt you make a fine wage working for Liam Donohue, but it's still my hope that Kiara and Paddy will make their home with me until you wed. I was even thinking that perhaps the three of you might be comfortable in the small caretaker's house until you decide where you might want to eventually settle."

Paddy moved close to Rogan's side. "I told her ya loved Kiara and wanted to buy a big farm out West when ya saved enough money."

Rogan tousled the boy's mop of black curls. "Aye, 'tis true enough."

"If we stayed here, I could help with the housework and the babe while we saved our money to buy a farm," Kiara said. "Do ya think that would work?" She searched Rogan's eyes for any sign of objection.

"I think ya may have a good idea, lass. One that would work well for all of us."

"And I want you to keep making your lace, Kiara," Alice said, holding up a piece of handwork from Kiara's basket. "There are plenty of women who are willing to pay a good price for it."

"I think we've got a plan, but perhaps it should be sealed with a kiss," Rogan said, pulling Kiara to her feet. "If ya will excuse us, I think we'll step outside fer a wee bit."

Paddy hurried to join them, but Alice quickly interceded. "I'm going to take Spencer up to the nursery for his mother. Why don't you come along and help me, Paddy? Do you remember an Irish song you could sing to Spencer while I rock him to sleep?"

"Aye, that I do. Before the famine, me mum and Kiara sang all the time. I'll sing him the lullaby Kiara used to sing to me."

"And I'm certain he'll enjoy every note," Alice said while lifting the baby out of Jasmine's arms. Paddy tagged along at her heels like a duckling following in parade formation.

"Thank ya," Kiara whispered to the older woman.

Alice winked and smiled. "Go on, now, before Rogan decides you're not interested."

The fire burned low. Only Jasmine and Nolan remained in the room. "I understand you've been seeing Velma Buthorne. She's a lovely young lady," Jasmine observed.

"Yes. She enjoys literature, and we have many acquaintances in common. I'm not certain she shares my strong abolition beliefs, but at least she voices a distaste for slavery."

"Her father is a member of the Associates, is he not?"

"I understand he recently invested quite heavily in order to become a member of the group. Prior to that, he owned a small group of mills in New Hampshire, along with a small shipping business. He controlled much of his own operation. I would assume he grew weary of shouldering the entire burden and viewed an investment with the Associates as a way of remaining in a business he knew while increasing his stature and wealth."

"Similar to Bradley," she mused. "Of course, Bradley was primarily enamored with the power he hoped would come his way once he became aligned with the Associates."

Resting his elbow on the arm of the chair, Nolan cupped his chin on one hand and looked at Jasmine. "I'm truly sorry for all the unhappiness you experienced in your marriage to Bradley."

"Yet had it not been for my marriage to Bradley, I wouldn't have Spencer, nor would I have developed a closer relationship to God. And my father and I have also learned some difficult lessons—he about his priorities and I about forgiveness. So, you see, there is good that can come out of even the most difficult situations," she said. "Of course, I must admit that while I was going through my trying circumstances, I didn't see anything but the desperation of my situation. It took God's strength to help me through each day, and now I can say I know I've become a better person because of all that's occurred in my life."

Nolan's eyes shone with admiration. "You're an amazing woman, Jasmine. I'm hoping that once Spencer is a little older and your life has settled, you'll give consideration to joining those of us who are growing bolder in our stand against slavery. I know your ability to work with the movement was thwarted by your marriage to Bradley as well as Spencer's impending birth, but I also know when we visited Mississippi, your heart was heavy when you saw the conditions on your father's plantation. And, as I told you, most plantations are even worse than The Willows."

"I don't know how much I'll be able to help, but you know you can count on my support wherever and however I can be used, Nolan. Grandmother has remained active in the antislavery movement here in Lowell, and now I'll be able to attend meetings with her once again. I've been told there's an even stronger movement here in Lowell than I had thought, and that pleases me."

"True. We've received both financial and verbal support, but it's dedicated workers who are willing to accept the risk and actually help more of our brothers and sisters find their way to freedom that make us truly blessed."

Jasmine nodded. "Placing yourself or others in peril is always a difficult choice. Now that I have a son, I can certainly understand the dilemma. I would give little thought to placing myself in jeopardy, while I would give grave consideration to such a notion should Spencer become endangered."

Nolan pulled his chair closer. "I know this may be an awkward time, but there is another matter on which we must speak."

Jasmine raised a brow. "Pray speak of it, then."

Nolan took a deep breath. "It has come to my attention through our family solicitor that Bradley has left his holdings to me."

Jasmine inhaled sharply. "I . . . what does this mean?" She knew that if she were left penniless her grandmother and father would see to her and Spencer's welfare, but that wasn't the way she wanted it.

"I don't want you to worry," Nolan said, his expression revealing deep concern. "I've already spoken to the solicitor and transferred everything to you, including this property. I do not want Bradley's holdings, neither do I wish to deny his wife and child their rightful inheritance. I have no understanding of why my brother did this. Perhaps he honestly never thought to change his will. Perhaps he did. But it doesn't matter at this point. Quite frankly, I'm surprised he left anything to me at all. The only thing he ever gave me in our adult life was his disapproval. But no matter—I've made it right."

Jasmine felt a deep tenderness for Nolan, for his gesture went beyond expectations. No one would have faulted the man had he maintained the inheritance left to him by his brother. After all, the shipping company had been in their family for many years. "I'm deeply touched you would do this," Jasmine said, lowering her face. She felt tears form in her eyes and willed them not to fall. "You have shown me nothing but honor and kindness throughout my marriage—even before that. Thank you for this."

"You needn't thank me for doing what should never have needed to be done. I do want to add that I have arranged for a man of good repute to handle the business affairs on your behalf. He will send you a monthly report and I myself will review his bookkeeping on a quarterly basis. I have directed him to deposit your funds here in Lowell when he comes to bring you the accounting of your affairs."

"I trust that you know best, Nolan. I have no reason to doubt you have seen to things in the very best of ways." She wiped at her eyes and looked up to meet his smiling face.

"I'm glad we've had opportunity for this chat. As you know, I must be leaving in the morning, but I want you to remember I am at your bidding—you need only send word. I want to be of assistance however I'm needed. Most importantly, I want to spend time with my nephew."

"And that is my desire also. I'm thankful for the time you've been able to spend with us, but I know you have matters needing your attention in Boston."

"What's this I hear?" Alice asked as she fluttered into the room. "You're leaving us?"

"I'm afraid so, but I've told Jasmine I'll be returning soon. I leave her in your capable hands," he said.

Jasmine's grandmother gave him a sly grin. "I think she'd be much better off in your warm embrace than my capable hands."

"Grandmother!" Jasmine felt her cheeks flush. "Nolan is courting Velma Buthorne. He doesn't need you playing the matchmaker. And you need remember I'm in mourning for his brother."

"Oh, pshaw! More likely you and Nolan are mourning the fact that Bradley didn't turn from his malevolent ways before his death. I know society has its code of etiquette and we're expected to hold fast to those rules, but—"

Jasmine held up her hand and silenced her grandmother.

"Enough of this talk. I believe we all need to get some rest. Nolan has an early departure in the morning."

"You will come back for Christmas, won't you, Mr. Houston?" Jasmine looked first to her grandmother and then to Nolan. "Please say you will," she encouraged.

"I would be honored. You are, after all, my only family. I will return with gifts and food and we shall have a festive time, despite Bradley and his passing."

"He was your brother; I do not expect you to forgo mourning his death," Jasmine said softly. She looked to Nolan, hoping he understood that she wanted very much to celebrate the Lord's birth but would put it aside for the sake of Nolan's feelings.

"I will mourn Bradley's passing in my own way," Nolan admitted, "but I will not forsake Christmas in order to do so. What say I come back the Saturday before? We'll go to church together—you too, Mrs. Wainwright. Then we'll have the whole week to make merry and decorate and find a tree. Would you like that?" He looked to Jasmine, his expression hopeful.

Jasmine nodded, knowing in her heart that nothing would please her more, unless it would be having the rest of her family with her for the occasion.

Nolan grinned. "Then it's settled. I'll be here."

CHAPTER · 31

JASMINE FOUND that as Christmas neared, she could hardly wait for Nolan's return. Grandmother said it was because Jasmine's feelings for Nolan were stronger and more important than she gave them credit for, but Jasmine said it was because of the holidays.

She had never looked at Christmas in the way she did this year. Before it had always been a happy celebration of family and friends, gifts and food. This year, however, with the birth of Spencer, she found herself caught up in the Christmas story. How wondrous that God would send His Son to earth as a babe. So tiny and helpless, just like Spencer. Jasmine thought of Mary and how hard it must have been to know the truth of the situation. Her son would also be her Savior. The very thought was marvelous and overwhelming to Jasmine.

When Saturday arrived and Nolan's appearance became reality, Jasmine knew there had been some truth in Grandmother's words. She was happy to see Nolan again; he made her feel safe and content . . . and there was much to be had in those feelings.

"I'm so glad the snow didn't stop you," Jasmine exclaimed as Nolan gave his coat and hat to Sarah.

"I do not think anything could stop those monstrous

343

contraptions of iron," he declared. "The locomotive is truly an amazing beast."

"Smelly and loud, if you ask me," Grandmother said, eyeing Nolan. "Have you eaten lately? You look half starved."

"I will admit that a meal would suit me fine just now."

Jasmine smiled. "Then it is a good thing we are nearly ready to sit to supper. Would you like to wash up?"

"Thank you, I would."

"I've got the bags," Paddy announced proudly as he came struggling through the front door.

"And so I see," Nolan replied as he took the largest of the three. "If you know the way to my room, why don't you lead me on?" He leaned down conspiratorially and added, "I'm supposed to wash up."

Paddy scowled. "The lasses are always makin' us wash up."

Nolan's face grew serious as he nodded. "'Tis the truth of it, my good man. 'Tis the truth."

Jasmine giggled as the men made their way upstairs. She and Grandmother exchanged a humored look and headed into the parlor to wait.

"You seem quite pleased to have him here," her grandmother said with a knowing nod.

"Stop trying to match us," Jasmine protested, but only half-heartedly. Nolan's absence and her reaction to it had given her much to ponder. "He has great virtues, but I'll not shame my family by acting the disrespectful widow."

"Pshaw! You never loved Bradley. You were forced from the start to marry him. If tongues wag because you take up with his brother, then they will have to wag. If you let true love get away from you, you'll always regret it."

Jasmine sobered. "But I don't know that it is true love. I may simply be longing for that which I've never known. I would like to give it time, Grandmother. Please honor my wishes. Nolan is a fine man. I wouldn't want to hurt him."

Grandmother sat by Jasmine and took hold of her hands. "I promise to mind my ways. I just want to see you happy. I feel I had a part in your misery with Bradley, in that I didn't try hard enough to intercede on your behalf. For that I'm truly sorry."

"And you are forgiven," Jasmine said with a grin. "For you have blessed me far more than any harm you perceive done. I thank God for you."

"And I for you, my sweet Jasmine."

Christmas week was delightful for all in the Houston household. Throughout the week they attended parties, and on Thursday, Nolan went deep into the woods and brought back the most perfect of trees.

"I think this is simply the most marvelous of traditions," Jasmine declared. "It makes the entire house smell wonderful. And I love the snow. This is only my second Christmas with snow."

"Come February you'll tire of it quickly enough," Nolan declared. He positioned the tree in the corner of the parlor and stood back to observe. "There. That should serve us quite nicely."

"Grandmother and I have made the decorations," Jasmine announced. "And we have the most marvelous candles to attach to the boughs. It's going to be beautiful."

Nolan smiled, his gaze never leaving her. "I have no doubt."

She smiled in return, knowing in her heart that this time next Christmas, things might be very different between her and Nolan. He'd not even hinted at his feelings, but she could see in his eyes— his expression—that he was feeling much the same as she.

On Christmas morning Jasmine awoke to a wondrous stillness. Spencer was sleeping soundly in the cradle by her bed. She'd had Kiara move him here because she enjoyed tending him herself. Kiara completely understood and because there was no longer anything to fear from Bradley, she relished the idea of going back to her own room.

Rolling to her side, Jasmine watched her son as he slept. From time to time he would suck at the air, his little lips pursing and relaxing in rhythm. It wouldn't be long before he awoke, demanding his breakfast.

Jasmine yawned and threw back the covers. The room was quite warm in spite of the chilly weather outside. Kiara was always good to slip in early and stir up the fire. Jasmine didn't know how the girl managed to do it so quietly, but she never disturbed Jasmine's sleep.

A quick look out the window revealed it was snowing. It seemed rather perfect for the day. Jasmine pulled on her robe and for the strangest reason thought of Bradley. She almost expected him to come bounding into the room demanding his son.

"His son," she mused. "As if I had no part in his existence."

She took up her Bible and, as had become her practice, settled into reading and praying. Still the thoughts of Bradley would not leave her.

"What is it I need to ponder, Lord? Is there something here about Bradley that I yet need to know?" Anger edged her tone, surprising Jasmine. "He's dead. Dead and buried and gone from my life. I need never think of him again."

But she knew that wasn't true. Spencer was proof of that. She would always have some part of Bradley in her life. The thought chilled her. Surprised by her reaction, Jasmine got up and began to pace. Still clinging to the Bible, she tried to sort through her scattered thoughts.

He was a cruel man. He demanded so much of us and nothing of himself. He stole my father's money and my innocence—as well as Kiara's. With each thought, Jasmine felt her anger mount.

He lied and cheated and wounded people just for sport. I'm glad he's dead. I'm glad he's gone. I don't want Spencer to ever know him. I don't want Spencer tainted by his father's blood.

She paused long enough to look down on her child. Bradley's child. He even looked somewhat like his father, only Jasmine comforted herself by believing he looked more like Bradley's mother and Nolan. She drew a ragged breath and suddenly realized she was crying.

"I don't want you to be like him," she whispered. "Please, God, don't let Spencer grow up to be like Bradley."

You must forgive Bradley.

The thought was startling. Jasmine stepped back and shook her head. "I don't want to forgive him. He didn't ask for forgiveness. He didn't believe himself guilty of anything. Why should I forgive him?"

Jasmine tried to steady her breathing and calm her anger. "For-giveness—that's asking an awful lot, Lord."

She went to her rocking chair and sat back down. Shaking her head, Jasmine opened the Bible again, but she couldn't see the words for all of her tears. A knock sounded on the door and before she could acknowledge it, Kiara peeked in.

"Are ya all right?" she asked, then stopped. "No, for sure I can see that ya are na all right." She came into the room unbidden. "Now, what would be causin' ya such grief on the day of the Lord's birth?"

Jasmine lowered her face and shook her head again. "I don't wish to discuss it."

Kiara surprised her by kneeling beside the rocker. "My heart is breakin' for ya. Please let me share yar burden."

"It's Bradley," Jasmine said finally. She looked up and met Kiara's stunned look.

"And how would that man be causin' ya problems today?"

"I don't know. I just started thinking about him and I got so angry. All I wanted to do was shout and scream, and if Spencer hadn't been sleeping right here, I probably would have." Jasmine tried to push down her rage, but it resurfaced. "That man hurt so many people. People I love and care about. He hurt my father and mother—my brothers. He hurt my uncles and their families and you. Oh, I can't even bear to think about the pain he caused you." Jasmine buried her face in her hands, but Kiara reached up and drew them down.

"Miss Jasmine, ya can na go on like this. For sure, Bradley Houston caused a lot of hurt and sufferin', but he's gone. He can na hurt anyone ever again. Ya must forgive 'im and make a new life."

Jasmine gasped. "What did you say?"

Kiara looked confused. "I said ya must forgive 'im and make a new life."

Jasmine closed her eyes and leaned back in the rocker. "That's exactly what God told me. At least the forgiving part. But how can you say that? Can you forgive him for what he did? He stole your innocence. He threatened you. He hurt Paddy and—"

"Stop!" Kiara said, holding up her hand. "There's nothin' to be gained by such talk. Ya'll only hurt yarself—and Spencer."

"I don't understand."

"I know 'tis hard, but forgiveness truly frees the one who does the forgivin' as much as it frees the one forgiven. I will not go on through life holdin' Mr. Bradley a grudge. He's gone and my grudges can only hurt me—not him. For sure he stole what wasn't his to take, but God has restored me. Rogan doesn't care. He knows 'twas not my fault."

"He's a good man."

Kiara smiled. "Aye, he is. And ya're a good woman, and God is callin' ya to forgive yar husband. He can na hurt ya anymore, unless 'tis in this manner. If ya go on like this, then Bradley Houston's wounds will go on as well. Make yar peace, Miss Jasmine. Forgive him for what he's done. If ya don't, ya'll end up holding yar son a grudge because he's the only part of Bradley Houston that's left alive to blame."

Spencer began to fuss and Jasmine looked across the room to her son. Blaming her son for Bradley's mistakes . . . the insight of Kiara's words made her heart ache.

"Why don't I take him to the nursery and change him for ya?" Kiara suggested. "Then ya can nurse him."

"Thank you." She watched Kiara lovingly lift the baby in her arms. She spoke calmly as she crossed the room with the boy. Jasmine looked to the ornately molded ceiling and sighed.

"Oh, Father, I see the truth. I see what you've been trying to show me since Bradley died—maybe even before that. It's hard to forgive him, but I want to, Lord. I'm asking you to help me forgive him. I don't know what caused his heart to be so black, for surely he must have been tender and good at some time in his life."

She thought of Spencer and how Bradley might have been very much like him as an infant. No doubt his parents had been quite proud and joyous over his birth.

"Help me, Father. I want to forgive and forget the past. I want to forgive Bradley for all that he did against me, for I never want any of it to come between Spencer and me."

"Here he is," Kiara called as she returned with the baby. "He's mighty hungry and ready for his Christmas breakfast."

Jasmine laughed and took her son in her arms. "Come, my little one." She nuzzled him to her and smiled down into his open eyes. "My precious little one."

The Christmas revelry did much to lift her spirits. Jasmine was quite pleased to receive a lovely ruby brooch from her grandmother, an heirloom that had once belonged to her great-grandmother on her father's side. She was also deeply touched by a gift of lace from Kiara and a red ribbon for her hair from Paddy.

"Why, Paddy, it's absolutely perfect and it goes very well with my new brooch." The boy beamed.

"I picked it out meself," he said proudly.

"Aye, I can be vouchin' for that," Rogan said. "He took nearly an hour doin' so."

Jasmine laughed. She was so glad that Kiara and Paddy, along with Rogan, had agreed to spend part of their Christmas with them.

"And here's my gift," Nolan said, reaching behind the couch to pull out a large parcel wrapped in cloth. "I hope you like it."

Jasmine tilted her head to one side, trying to ascertain what Nolan had brought her. As she reached to take the package, Nolan waved her off. "I'd best hold it while you untie the string. It's quite heavy."

Jasmine worked to unfasten the bindings. When she'd managed this, she pushed back the cloth and gasped. "Oh!"

"It's my family," Nolan explained. "A family portrait when I was five."

She looked into the faces of the Houston family. Bradley's parents sat regally, while a very young Nolan and a smiling Bradley, fifteen years Nolan's senior, stood on either side.

"I know it might seem a strange painting, but I wanted you to believe and know that Bradley was not always a bad person. When I was young he was a loving and nurturing older brother. All who knew him were impressed with his manners and gentle nature. At times he seemed more like a father than a brother."

Jasmine looked to Kiara and then her grandmother. "What happened to change him?" For the first time she honestly cared to know the truth.

"He would never admit it, but I believe the mantle of responsibility made him old before his time. He was very close to our father, and he longed only to impress him. Little by little it consumed his life—he soon gave up everything that was important to him, even a young woman whom he cared for very much. They had been friends from a young age. They were to be married, but the business distanced Bradley from her and by the time he realized what he had lost, she had married another."

"How very sad," Jasmine said, feeling genuine sorrow for her husband.

"I wanted you to have this portrait of our family because it was made at a time when we were all very close and very happy."

"Thank you, Nolan. This will be a special gift for Spencer. I will prominently display it that he might take pride in his heritage." She met Kiara's gaze across the room. The girl smiled broadly.

The forgiving had begun.

———

That night in her bedroom, Jasmine sat nursing her son. Spencer grew more sleepy by the minute, his eyelids lifting heavily, then closing again. She almost hated for him to fall asleep. With Spencer awake and nursing, Jasmine didn't feel quite so alone.

"Oh, Spencer. You'll never know your father firsthand, and in some ways I think that a better way. Yet you are the best of him.

You are the love that he should have known." The baby finally stopped nursing, closing his eyes in sleep.

Jasmine put him to her shoulder and patted him gently on the back. "He loved you—there's no doubt of that. I think he honestly loved you more than anyone. You actually made him smile."

She thought of her dead husband and the past and knew there was nothing there for her. Nothing but sad memories of a hopeless relationship that could never be put straight. Kiara was right: forgiveness was the better path.

Still, her son was without a father now. She thought of Nolan's kindness and generous spirit and had to admit that those qualities had always attracted her. She had no desire to be untrue to her vows; she was simply sad that she had never seen those qualities in her husband.

But there was hope. With God, there was always hope.

Putting Spencer in his cradle, Jasmine knelt down and smiled. "We are in His hands, Spencer, and there's no other place I'd rather be. We're going to be fine—you'll see. For God has already seen our tomorrows and has smoothed the path before us. He has woven our lives as a tapestry of hope. Hope in His love. Hope for all of our tomorrows."

BESTSELLING
HISTORICAL FICTION
For Every Reader!

The Acadian Saga Continues...

History comes to life in this captivating new story of an American woman in the Court of St. James, formed by the new writing team of T. Davis Bunn and his wife, Isabella.

With the War of 1812 raging, Erica Langston is left to deal with creditors circling her family business. Her only recourse is to travel to England to collect on outstanding debts, but her arrival leads her into the most unexpected predicaments and encounters.

The Solitary Envoy
by T. Davis and Isabella Bunn

Bestselling Author Tracie Peterson's Unforgettable New Saga

From her own Big Sky home, Tracie Peterson paints a one-of-a-kind portrait of 1860s Montana and the strong, spirited men and women who dared to call it home.

Dianne Chadwick is one of those homesteaders, but she has no idea what to expect—or even if she'll make it through the arduous wagon ride west. Protecting her is Cole Selby, a guide who acts as though his heart is as hard as the mountains. Can Dianne prove otherwise?

Land of My Heart by Tracie Peterson

◆BETHANYHOUSE